FRONT ROW

LISA ARMSTRONG

Front Row

Hodder & Stoughton

Copyright © 1998 by Lisa Armstrong

First published in Great Britain in 1998 by Hodder and Stoughton
A division of Hodder Headline PLC

10 9 8 7 6 5 4 3 2 1

British Library Cataloguing in Publication Data
A CIP catalogue record for this title is available from the British Library

ISBN 0 340 75004 9

Typeset by Palimpsest Book Production Limited,
Polmont, Stirlingshire
Printed and bound in Great Britain by
Mackays of Chatham PLC, Chatham, Kent

Hodder and Stoughton
A division of Hodder Headline PLC
338 Euston Road
London NW1 3BH

For Paul, Kitty and Flora

ACKNOWLEDGEMENTS

Front Row began taking shape from the moment I went to a fashion show in a fire station and met a stylist who slept with her shoes. I wouldn't have sat down and done anything about it, however, if it hadn't been for Sally Abbey and Clare Roberts. Or Paul Hadaway, who bought me my computer. Eternal gratitude too, to Carolyn Mays and Harriet Gugenheim. Their enthusiasm and constant handholding has been invaluable. Thank you also to Zoe Souter for her insight into the business side of modelling, to Lucinda Chambers for her insight into the creative side of making pictures and to Fiona Golfar for her insight. To everyone – the designers, the dedicated tailors and the seamstresses, the photographers, the models, the bookers, the agents, the hair and make-up artists, the PRs, the retailers and of course the journalists – who inhabits the fashion world and helps make it so inspiring and provoking, and especially to Matthew Williamson and Antonio Berardi who showed me the agonies and ecstasy of setting up as a young designer. With thanks, too, to Jenny Dyson, Trilbey Gordon, Tamara Yeardye, Vanessa Gillingham and Robin Derrick; to Alexandria Shulman for the trips to Russia, Japan and the lunch dates with Tom Ford, Calvin Klein, Ralph Lauren, John Galliano and Karl Lagerfeld and for some breathing speace; to my mother for not asking too often whether it was finished; to David Robson for two brilliant years on the *Independent* and to everyone at *Vogue* for not being like Alice.

Only those knowing the value of the useless can talk about the useful – Taoist dictum.

Dramatis Personae

FRONT ROW (MAIN CAST)

Janie Pember – wife, mother, fashion journalist

Matthew Pember – husband, father, political journalist, deserter

Seth Weiss – sensitive, brilliant chef with film star looks

Cassie Grange – Janie's workaholic best friend. Runs a very successful model agency called Hot Shots

Zack – Cassie's all-too-laid-back, clairvoyant boyfriend

Sissy Sands – Janie's well-meaning assistant on The *International Gazette*

Gloria Banderas – Matthew and Janie's cleaner

Jo-Jo – Gloria's daughter

Ben Mornay – beautiful, celebrated young Hollywood actor

Anastasia Monticatini – immaculate mystery blonde of indeterminate nationality

Tom Fitzgerald – billionaire New York designer; king of preppie American fashion

BACKSTAGE

Enrico – poncy, celebrated hairdresser

Jean Jacques – Enrico's stressed-out assistant

Dodie Kent – kindly, talented make-up artist

Marcus Lurie – Cassie and Jo-Jo's hairdresser; runs a swish Mayfair salon

Detective Inspector Reece – the bane of Cassie's life

Michael Croft – Cassie's overworked lawyer

DESIGNERS

Madeleine Peterson – rising British designer

Alec Marola – her ex-partner

Aeron Baxter – wildly creative Brit designer talent. Darling of the catwalk

Squidge – Aeron's long-suffering, devoted assistant and muse

Donatella and Giovanna Ecstasia – the two power sisters behind XTC, one of the world's hottest labels

Kristof – ancient pillar of the fashion establishment, purveyor of immensely pompous clothes and absurdly extravagant fashion shows

Boldacci – fifth-time winner of Sissy and Alice's annual personal list of World's Least Talented Designer

Angel Derrida – tortured London-based creator of beautiful footwear

Bella Scarletti – sister of feuding family of designers

Antonio Viro – pretentious designer who makes models sing Kurt Weill songs when they're auditioning to do his fashion shows

Sir Vincent Lambert – dressmaker by appointment to Her Majesty the Queen

Yoko Rakabuto – avant-garde Japanese designer

Paolo Bianco – neurotic Italian king of minimalism

Kevin Krocket – endearing designer-by-appointment to New York's uptown girls

Vittoria & Fratelli – successful Neopolitan duo who are in the process of making a fortune out of blatantly sexy clothes

Gilles de Gaumard – major player in the fashion world through his ownership of a luxury-goods group, maker and breaker of careers, reputations and dreams

HONEST-TO-GOODNESS RAG TRADERS

Nari Sujan – beady entrepreneur behind the immensely successful clothing chain Everything She Wants

Jean Kirkpatrick – Nari's sensible PA

Jasper Goldfarb and **Morton Wemyss** – scions of New York's most glamorous retail dynasties

JOURNALISTS, MAG-HAGS AND THEIR BOSSES

The Proprietor – communications magnate; owns, among many other publications, the *International Gazette*

Dexter F. Ravensburg – chairman of Starlight Publications, which produces, among many others, *Eden* magazine; moves employees around the world like chess pieces

Phyllida Connelly – malevolent deputy/features editor/harridan on the *International Gazette*

Lorna Barrett – Phyllida's much-put-upon secretary

Edward Rushmore – editor of the *Gazette*

Lindsey Craven – *The Python*'s fortysomething fashion editor and victim

Tilly de Montgomery – interiors stylist on *Designers' Digest*

Alice Grey – impoverished underground fashion stylist on *A La Mode* magazine and Sissy's best/worst friend

Caro Luckhurst – neurotic fashion editor on *A La Mode*; Alice's immediate boss

Zoffy Villeneuve – insane fashion editor/muse, given to hysterical outbursts and blackmailing threats

Lee Howard – New York fashion doyenne, about to launch *Eden*, a major new fashion magazine

Hester Carmichael – animal rights activist and fashion editor on the *Washington Chronicle*

Petronella Fishburn – known as the Slasher of Seventh Avenue on account of her cutting reviews

Kiko Umagai – Japanese fashion reporter

Leonie Uttley – Crazee Cable TV reporter

Katie Myers – US beauty editor of *Moi-Même*

Sukie Summers – freelance hack

Heidi Reitvelt – editor of *Prachtvroll*

Magnus Finnegan – fashion editor on the *Daily Clarion*

Gina Martin – editor of the *Gazette*'s City pages

Silas Shoreham – *The Probe*'s patronising religious correspondent

Jacques Villiers – urbane New York art director

MODELS AND THEIR AGENTS

Peace Grant – one of the world's top models; a fragile soul on a mission to self-combust

Grace Capshaw – one of the original supermodels, the jewel in Cassie's crown; latterly having to come to terms with the built in obsolescence of models

Jess Murray – permanently cheery Glaswegian supermodel, also with Hot Shots

Tulah Delaney – one of the new breed; another of Cassie's finds

Kumla – exotic African beauty

Unity Montcreith – ascendant aristocrat

Brigitte – gorgeous amazonian German; irony-free zone

Isabella Suarez – ravishing but unhinged South American

Stacey Mills – timid new girl

Saffron – Cassie acerbic Australian deputy at Hot Shots

Trudy – Cassie and Saffron's secretary

Diego Vincent – president of Allure Inc., a large New York model agency; wolfishly attractive, if you like that sort of thing

Marie-Elise Montperluche – pushy Parisian model agent who runs Roar

Jim and Sergio Zametti – the Brothers Grim, who run Bellissimo, a Milan-based model agency

PHOTOGRAPHERS

Anna Accelli – wedding photographer

Sven Tolssen – currently the world's highest-paid photographer

Nick Squire – louche paparazzo who worked on *Blietzkrieged!!*, and briefly for Janie

Dirk Von Litten – world-famous photographer with bulging portfolio of notoriously sadomasochistic images

Joel Eliot – hip London hotshot

FOODIES

Sebbie McHugh – talented, charismatic, fiery restaurateur

Deirdre Muldoon – charmingly efficient front-of-house at Le Château
Duncan – commis chef at Le Château
Vanessa de Lauret – PR for Seth's restaurant
Damien – the *Gazette*'s lamentable canteen cook, with ideas way, way beyond his capabilities

ACTORS, MEDIA DARLINGS AND VIPs

Todd Woodward – actor boyfriend of Tulah
Nancy O'Kelly – hip singer and lesbian, having an affair with a bald model called Clio Toris
Lorinda Day – Ben Mornay's doting agent
Sid Skidster – louche author and chronicler of the demi-monde
Caleb Bron – increasingly successful TV producer
Martika Jansen – arts presenter on *Late Look*
Barney Frick – Seth and Cassie's architect
Luella Lopez – New York society and fashion groupie; sixty-seven going on twenty-two
Melissa – Seth's actress mother

RIPs (THOSE WHOSE STORY PREDATES THIS ONE)

Louisa Dunne – Janie's reckless, feckless predecessor at the *Gazette*
Dieter Mannheim – dashing racing-car driver
Slobby – Janie and Matthew's Croatian lodger
Finn – Seth's wilful, poetic brother

FRIENDS, FAMILY AND HANGERS-ON

Harry Orsett – Peace's first proper friend
Eleanor – Janie's placard-waving, consciousness-raising mother
Will – Matthew's utterly dependable, stoical accountant brother
Piers – Matthew's charmingly vague marine biologist father
Estelle – manageress of Sigmund's bookshop and a constant source of advice and succour to Cassie

Diana – Sissy's deeply unfashionable flatmate

Jute – drug dealer

Barry – Slobby's cantankerous cat, now living with Janie

Count Nikolai – Diego Vincent's wolfishly attractive Irish setter, with a peerless canine grin, matched only by his master's

PUBLICATIONS

Beau Monde
A La Mode
Blitzkrieged!!
The Probe
International Gazette
Eden

Chapter One

Janie Pember flicked away a piece of plaster that had fallen from the bathroom ceiling on to her left nipple. The state of this house was getting beyond a joke. In fact, viewed from just about any angle, her life showed all the signs of developing into a Jacobean revenge tragedy. The bottom line was that she needed some money – as opposed to the pittance she was getting for putting in the odd hour at Kilburn library. But to look actively for ways of making cash was to concede that Matthew wasn't going to walk through the door any minute, that she really might have become a single mother, and that their three children – she looked down the corridor to where the twins were quietly decapitating a Barbiedoll – were now part of the demon dependency culture. Maybe if she got Nell to write a letter to Tony Blair he'd invite them all for tea and she could put him straight about what single mothers really needed. A job, obviously. But what could a thirty-three-year-old former fashion journalist offer any employer?

That was the tragic bit. The revenge was what, in her sourest moments, she felt like wreaking on Matthew. Of course, it wasn't his fault that his editor had insisted on him attending the global warming summit in Rio so soon before Christmas. He was one of *The Probe*'s chief political commentators, after all. But really, how could he have disappeared there? On sabbatical was how *The Probe*'s subs had put it at the bottom of the next few columns that had appeared under his replacement's byline.

I

But that made him sound like an Oxford don, which, Janie supposed, was what he really should have been, so there was some logic in it. Nevertheless, seeing it day after day made it take on an awful air of permanence in her mind.

Janie let her mind drift back, as it often had lately, ten years to the first time she had met Matthew Pember – anything rather than confront her feelings about him now. He wasn't her type, if she was scrupulously honest. She had been dating a succession of dark, haunted-looking men at the time and Matthew, with his sandy hair and bumbling manner, didn't fit the bill at all. But he had been so convivial about the way she had reversed her car over his bicycle ('it was on its last wheels anyway') that she had been utterly charmed. She had been in a tearing hurry, as usual, on her way to one of Cassie's pre-Christmas dinner parties and had double-parked outside Oddbins. Matthew had been struggling valiantly with the spin-drier in the next-door launderette. The bike was a complete write-off and in the light of the blizzard that was swirling about them, and his mound of washing (how, she wondered had he ever managed to transport it on the bike?), the least she could do was deliver him – and it – whence they had come.

By the time they were approaching his flat in Mount Street, Janie knew that he wrote political sketches for *The Probe*. She remembered having read some of them – they were sharp, funny and memorable enough to be talked about even among the arty fashion friends she had been hanging out with. No mean feat, considering their diminished attention spans. She had also learned that the author of these lucid, disciplined essays was chronically disorganised and hopeless with anything mechanical. Two weeks ago his washing machine had gone on the blink, yesterday his computer had exploded, and today his central heating had ceased to function, though he confided that the last probably had more to do with a bill he vaguely remembered not paying than any electrical fault.

'I don't mean to be a Luddite but at this rate I'll soon be writing with a quill,' he said ruefully. Janie looked into his thoughtful blue eyes and felt her stomach lurch.

'You could always go on a course,' she said helpfully. 'At *Beau Monde* they got in a team of computer experts to talk us through the new technology.' She didn't tell him that two of the 'experts' had run off with £30,000 worth of IBM hardware.

'Tried it,' said Matthew. '*The Probe*'s sent me on all sorts of time-and-motion courses as well. I'm trying this new filing system at the moment. You never throw anything away, just let all the flotsam and junk mail swirl around your desk in the hope that the important bits of information you need all the time will naturally surface to the top. It's based on the natural ecosystem of the sea. My father told me about it.'

'Hmm, in my experience it's only unspeakable things that float to the top of the sea,' said Janie. 'Does your father ever find anything?'

'Occasionally – but somehow, never his way home. He's a marine biologist and a saint. Always on the verge of saving the world, or at the very least some endangered aquatic species. It's terribly time-consuming.'

Janie thought of her own father, always on the verge of saving his own bacon. Matthew's father sounded almost as adorable as he was.

'*Tempus fugit*,' he said. 'I'd better get in and watch this video. I'm researching a piece about government arts funding in Japan.'

Unexpectedly she found herself touched by the thought of this stranger spending a grim winter's evening in a freezing flat in front of a Kurosawa video and eating cold pizza – his oven was playing up, it transpired, and the local takeaway wasn't very reliable. She heard herself inviting him to dinner. Cassie wouldn't mind the numbers swelling, she thought, although she distantly remembered her mentioning something about inviting a film producer she had specifically wanted Janie to meet. Well, it couldn't be helped. The evening could probably do with a maverick interloper anyway. Ever since Cassie's model agency had taken off – there was talk of her being nominated for Young Business Woman of the Year – her life had taken on a somewhat predictable momentum, with friends, cars, clothes and furniture carefully chosen to complement one another and highlight their acquisitor's irredeemably good taste.

The lights were blazing in Cassie's new flat. This, together with the fact that she had just paid a fashionable interior decorator vast sums to empty Oggetti of all its chrome and matt-black fittings and turn her flat into a shrine for eighties aspirations, made it an uncomfortably blinding place to be. The decorator had also had the bright idea of knocking down all of Cassie's walls and installing in the midst of this cavernous space an enormous glass dining table that looked as though it had been smashed to smithereens by half a dozen vandals and reassembled by someone participating unsuccessfully in an anger management course.

Certainly the effect was dramatic. Matthew and Janie agreed later that when they stepped through Cassie's newly distressed iron front door – salvaged from a recent refit of Holloway prison – they both felt as though they had accidentally stumbled on to the stage of the Royal Court. Around the table a dozen floodlit faces stared up at them neutrally, before returning to their sushi.

'There's fashionably late and there's totally bloody unreliable.' Cassie was leaning against the fridge, heaving unsuccessfully on a champagne cork, the shoulder pads of her black leather Alaia suit free-floating somewhere round her ears. 'You'd think by now the finest French brains could have worked out a way to make this stuff with a twist-on, twist-off cap.'

'It wouldn't have the same element of drama,' said Janie, relieving Cassie of the bottle. 'I'm sorry we were so late but we got talking and, well, *tempus fugit.*'

Cassie cocked a sceptical eyebrow. Matthew didn't look like the average Janie inamorato, but since the producer she had been saving for her had turned out to be the most tedious egomaniac she had met all month, she decided to let the matter rest for the moment. 'How do you *do* that?' she asked, as Janie effortlessly uncorked another couple of bottles.

'One of the many useless things I learned at boarding school,' Janie replied. 'The nuns could uncork a bottle of communion wine faster than you can whip out a credit card. By the way, Cassie, Matthew doesn't exactly know I'm a mag hag. He sort of thinks I'm the literary editor at *Beau Monde*.'

'Oh, an intellectual,' said Cassie sagely. She watched Janie saunter towards the others guests with a tray of her new tin goblets, her PVC miniskirt rucking even further up her absurdly perfect thighs. With a view like that, Matthew, if he had any testosterone pulsing through his veins at all, probably wouldn't be too fussed what she did. Four years into their friendship, Cassie was still thunderstruck by Janie's resemblance to the young Jean Shrimpton – except that where Shrimpton's nose was retroussé, Janie's was a definite, dainty snub. That was it: the sum total of her physical imperfections. And even that gave her face a disarmingly humorous look, as if she were permanently savouring a joke. Straight, thick hazelnut-brown hair, greenish eyes, heavily fringed with dark lashes, a mouth that looked as though it had been collagened but hadn't. She had a ridiculously serendipitous share of the gene pool. And bless her, she was oblivious to it all.

Cassie gazed admiringly at Janie's disappearing back. Since she had started working on *Beau Monde* a year ago, Janie had been looking sensational – it must be all the discounts, although God knew, the magazine paid pathetically. Cassie was constantly pleading with Janie to come into business with her at Hot Shots – and not simply because she felt *Beau Monde* undervalued her. Janie had a shrewd brain. Cassie knew that Janie felt she had sold out. Running a model agency wasn't what they had planned for one another at Oxford. When Cassie told Janie that she loved being involved in the celebration of female beauty, Janie had primly told her that, although she would never allow it to cloud their friendship, she considered Cassie's work to be morally reprehensible, since it encouraged women in their relentless pursuit of perfection. Shortly afterwards, she had taken a job as a fashion assistant. Admittedly it was a form of journalism, but when they were students, Janie had lead Cassie to believe that she wanted to follow in the footsteps of Brian Hanrahan rather than mince along behind the editors of *Vogue*. Oh youth,

youth, mused Cassie, what happens to your illusions? She was twenty-six.

Over what remained of the sushi, Janie became painfully aware of the superficiality of the conversation. Why couldn't they at least make a passing reference to the miners or Afghanistan, something like that. As she wasn't quite sure of the ins and outs of Soviet Foreign policy, she opted for a less risky route that would still show Matthew she was connected to the Body Politic. Waiting until she was sure he could hear her, she asked the producer next to her whether he thought the Tory government's philistine approach to the arts was killing off the British film industry.

'Basically, Jenny,' he slurped, 'as long as Maggie doesn't raise taxes on Porsches and cocaine, anything she does by me is absolutely cool, sweetheart.'

Appalled, Janie took a large bite of wasabi and turned the same shade as the raw tuna. What must Matthew be thinking? But as the producer launched himself into another rant against the BBC and its measly drama budgets, she stole a sideways glance at Matthew and was heartened to see him chuckling over one of Cassie's self-deprecating stories.

On the way home that night, Janie caught sight in her mirror of Matthew's clothes, still sodden on the back seat. 'I tell you what,' she said, suddenly anxious to delay the moment when they would reach his flat and she would have to go through the motions of double-parking and keeping the engine ticking while she waited for an invitation that might not materialise, 'why don't you come back to my place and use the tumble-drier there?'

As romantic overtures went, it lacked a certain glamour. But it worked. He never did move back to Mount Street.

That's all very well, thought Janie, snapping out of her reverie and cajoling some more hot water out of the tap with her toe. But that was then and this was now, and still nothing ever seemed to work properly in any of the places where Matthew lived. Back then, Aurora Snow, *The Python*'s clairvoyant, whom Janie reluctantly found herself reading every day, had said that rogue electrical forces were about to turn her life upside down. In a manner of speaking, she'd been right. In nine years of marriage, they had worked their way through six videos, three dishwashers and two spin-driers. Computers turned to pulp under Matthew's influence. As a joke Janie had bought him an ancient typewriter in a car boot sale for seventy-five pence – but he actually seemed to prefer working on it. She sifted through her store of hazy recollections – which was all she could muster from around the period just before Matthew had left. Relations between them hadn't been exactly cordial – that much she was clear about. She was tired – always tired – and increasingly worried about money, and Matthew was being exasperating. Well, actually, he was being Matthew – gentle, distracted and on a certain practical level hopeless. It wasn't that he was feckless. But the practicalities of life eluded him. For one thing, he actively seemed to dislike dealing with money on any level, except to give chunks of it away to good causes. The last cheque he had written before leaving for Rio had been to his friend Mungo, who was setting up an orphanage in Guatemala.

He was also hopelessly disorganised, which meant that Janie bore the brunt of looking after the children while Matthew scrambled to finish an article in the office at midnight. From time to time Janie would read something in the *Daily Mail*'s personal finance section about Tracker funds or Peps and resolve to make provision for the children. She never did, of course – but Matthew didn't even get as far as reading the articles. He'd rather spend his precious spare time on his watercolours than going through bank statements. He was probably the least worldly person she had ever met. And Janie loved him for it. In fact for a long time – probably before they were married, she mused – she had found this trait very sexy. But there were times when it could be provoking. Cassie said it was because, as she got older, she was reverting to mercenary type.

'Face it, at heart you're as bourgeois as they come. It's in your blood, sweetheart, no matter how many refugees you have ransacking the house.'

Janie had been genuinely affronted. Early in their marriage, she and Matthew had decided to open up their home to political asylum seekers. Cassie said it was just to appease their guilt at buying such a whopping big house. Be that as it may, the experiences, apart from a few unfortunate exceptions, had been richly rewarding, spiritually speaking. It was deeply offensive of Cassie to keep harking back to the one or two guests who'd abused their hospitality.

Janie also hated any reference to her father, particularly, Cassie noticed, just after she'd had a baby, when the spectre of bringing a clone of him into the world loomed extra large. Cassie had never met Janie's father – though she'd taken quite a shine to the tall, distinguished figure in the one photograph she'd ever seen. He was a barrister and workaholic whom Janie hadn't seen for years – ever since he had left her mother for a younger (by twenty-five years) version. Normally even-tempered, she was unfailingly riled by any suggestion that she resembled him.

They hadn't broached the subject again. But it had set Janie brooding. What if she and Matthew were fundamentally incompatible? The day after Cassie had challenged her with being bourgeois, Janie and Matthew, who had been arguing with increasing frequency since the twins' arrival, had quarrelled bitterly. *The Probe* wanted to send him to California for three weeks to cover the gubernatorial election there – with a view, Matthew strongly suspected, of posting him to Washington.

'I can't believe you're even suggesting it,' she shouted indignantly, over the fluffy heads of the twins, who were each hanging off a breast.

'We've been through this before,' Matthew had replied wearily. 'Hugh says if all goes well in California I'm a dead cert for the Washington job.'

Janie knew how much this meant to Matthew. Washington was the plum posting for any political writer – a prelude frequently to the editorship of a paper. 'I don't even know if I want to live in Washington,' she said querulously. 'I'm not sure it's a good idea for the children. What about their schools and their friends?'

'Janie, the twins are only three months old,' said Matthew patiently.

'Well, what about Nell, then?'

'Five-year-olds are remarkably adaptable.'

'She's almost six, in case you hadn't noticed.'

This was a dig at the amount of time Matthew had been spending at work – and an unfair one at that. He adored the children, and he'd only been taking on mounds of extra freelance to help pay the mortgage on the house in Michaelmas Road which she, especially, had been so keen on buying. The ensuing row was spectacular. Janie, who was postnatal and fed up with having to sleep on a plastic sheet, with a towel wrapped in clingfilm under each armpit to stop leaking milk ruining the mattress, felt entirely justified in abandoning all rational thought, accused Matthew of gross dereliction of paternal duty. He told her she was petty and selfish. It was the first time they had ever resorted to character assassination, and although they ostensibly made up – Matthew hadn't gone to California – the bruises never quite seemed to heal.

Perhaps Cassie was right, thought Janie, reaching for some shampoo. Perhaps she really was the prisoner of her father's materialistic ideals. Now she came to consider it, as far back as their honeymoon she had been disturbed by Matthew's lack of foresight. Well, not disturbed exactly, but certainly aware. She remembered the day they had reached Udaipur, and the Lake Palace Hotel, dusty and exhilarated from the long journey from Agra, and longing to spend the next four days swimming, sleeping and mooching round the markets. She had been eyeing a little seed-pearl bracelet when Matthew had dragged her away, casually mentioning that he had to get back to the hotel to finish a piece on Norman Tebbit that he'd meant to hand in just before the wedding. In the end he spent two days on it, shuttered away in the hotel library, and they'd had their first major row. Janie had locked him out of their room and eaten two meals in the restaurant in solitary confinement while Matthew wandered disconsolately around the dusty streets of Udaipur. She hated Norman Tebbit.

It had all come right in the end once Matthew finally managed to explain his elaborate plan of reconciliation to one of the barmen. As Janie drank the dregs of her gin and tonic she nearly choked on the enormous chunk of ice at the bottom of the glass. Scooping the melting fragments out of her mouth she came across the seed-pearl bracelet that Matthew had got the bar-tender to plant in the cube. It was the most romantic thing that had ever happened to her, she thought at the time. (And typical of Matthew, thought Cassie when Janie told her the story, that the one piece of jewellery he'd ever bought Janie had almost ended up wrapped round her appendix). But that was Matthew, maddening, beguiling and ultimately, Janie had always thought, irresistible.

The trouble was, in the past few months, the maddening bits of Matthew had eclipsed the other parts. By the time he had set off for Rio (and it was typical of Matthew to let the news desk bully him into going early in order to get some extra local stories in before the conference started) Janie had barely been able to contain her exasperation at almost everything he did. They'd even talked about a trial separation.

They decided – or at least Janie had, she couldn't remember now whether it had been unilateral or not – that the month-long Rio conference should be used as serious reflection time.

In the second week of December, just before the end of the conference, Matthew met up with Mungo, who had flown down to Rio for a few days' break from the orphanage. Matthew telephoned Janie – another distorted, echoing line that only served to exaggerate the cavernous silences between them – his voice ringing with enthusiasm. 'Mungo's project sounds extraordinary and he says Guatemala is fantastic . . .'

He paused, waiting for her response, and gave up. 'Janie, he's invited us to see it. I think it would be the trip of a lifetime. I think you'd love it. I think—'

'And what about Christmas?' she enquired tersely.

'We could spend it here.'

'Oh, for God's sake, Matthew, grow up. Daisy has chronic heat rash as it is. And your father – in case you've forgotten – is planning to come back from the irrigation project in the Philippines especially so that he can spend Christmas with us all for the first time in God knows how long.' She hated how shrill her voice sounded, loathed what it was saying.

She could no longer recollect how it arrived there, but the conversation ended with her telling Matthew to use up the six weeks' sabbatical he'd saved up at *The Probe* working with Mungo in Guatemala.

Absence should have made them fonder, but for some reason things had steadily deteriorated between them. The longer Matthew was away, the more inured to his charms she felt. Each passing week disclosed more of his foibles. The urgent letters to the bank he had undertaken to write but, she now discovered, never finished, materialised in recipe books. Final demands arrived for things which they should never have bought. She heard about impulsive offers of help to friends in trouble when he barely had time to see his own family. Exasperated and stifled, she longed to be self-sufficient.

His passionate accounts of the orphanage ought to have moved her, but somehow she couldn't relate to them. The undoubtedly noble work Mungo was doing sounded like moral luxury; struggling as she was to get through the days with three children in relatively affluent Britain. And the thought made her ashamed. She found herself not wanting him to call.

Well, she hadn't heard from him for seven weeks now. Her own fault, she knew. One day Matthew had rung to say that *The Probe* had asked him if he would consider standing in for their South American correspondent, who was on maternity leave. Hardly promotion. She could tell he wanted her to protest about his absence. To ask him to come back on the next flight. But she couldn't, so he didn't, and instead she heard herself instructing him to confine future communications to letters.

★   ★   ★

At least Jake and Daisy were easy. Janie gazed tenderly at the
twins as she laid them down for a nap. She hoped Jo-Jo would
remember to buy a newspaper when she brought Nell back
from the park. She scooped up the letters by the front door,
made herself a pint of coffee – the single luxury she had clung
on to in her last round of self-imposed cutbacks – and settled
down at the kitchen table. Typically Matthew had omitted to
tell Hugh St Clair, his editor, that he wasn't taking his family
to live in South America and *The Probe*'s accounts department
had conveniently slashed Matthew's salary on the grounds that
life there was cheap. Every month the quetzals poured into the
Willesden branch of Lloyds – thousands of them. Looking at
the zeros on her statements, before they were converted into
pounds, was the only time Janie ever felt rich. At this rate she'd
have to give up her voluntary work at the Cambodian women's
collective in Camberwell on the grounds of not being able to
afford the petrol. She decided she would only allow this to
happen *in extremis* – she was damned if she was going to let
Mungo have the moral upper hand as easily as that.

The mail made dismal reading: two final reminders and a
note from Catherine at Kilburn library saying she didn't need
Janie that week:

> *Tried to call you but the answer machine seems not to be
> working. Could you fit in three hours next Thursday?*

Three hours in ten days was hardly going to support the four
of them, Janie thought with a grimace. Of course, Catherine
hadn't been able to reach her. She had spent most of the previous
week with bank managers and Pep brokers. In utter despair she
had called Matthew's brother. Will, incongruously, given the
rest of the family's allergy to money, was quietly becoming an
immensely successful accountant with a large house in Islington
that only required a wife and about seven children to fill it,
and normally Janie would have cut off her legs rather than go
whining to him. But she was starting to feel ill about their
financial situation. The other night she'd woken in a sweat

after a nightmare in which Harriet Harman, Aurora Snow and her mother had loomed at her out of the swirling mists on the Edgware Road like a Greek chorus to mouth depressing statistics about single-parent families. This had been followed the next night by a dream in which her bank manager had morphed into Pol Pot and tried to evict her and the children from the house.

'Things aren't quite that bad,' Will had smiled at her gently. 'But perhaps you should think about turning the house into more of an asset. It is rather large, Janie . . . maybe you could think about taking in some lodgers – ones who pay, I mean.'

This was as close to criticism as Will ever came. But the reference to Slobodan was unmistakable. Matthew had come across Slobodan Kirowic, a charismatic young Croatian student (of what, Cassie and Will had never quite discovered), in Biddy Mulligan's, a local Irish pub, when he was researching a piece on the government's proposed changes to the immigration laws. Garrulous and opinionated, Slobby turned out to be all the colour Matthew needed to make the story come alive. As a thank-you, Matthew had invited him to supper at Michaelmas Road. Slobby had turned up with three bottles of Croatian wine which he then proceeded to consume with frightening speed. He had gazed soulfully at Cassie through his floppy blond fringe and recited acres of patriotic poetry at her before weeping uncontrollably for the motherland all over her new velvet trouser suit. Recovering heroically, he produced his mouth organ and launched into a rollicking version of 'Born In The USA', whereupon Matthew had sat down at the piano and Cassie and Janie did their Three Degrees impersonation. By the morning, Slobby had moved in. Nell adored him because he was the only adult she had ever met whose imagination outstripped hers. The only problem was Slobby's fondness for alcohol and inverse ability to hold it.

Dear Slobby, thought Janie fondly. Life certainly hadn't been dull, what with the regular visits from the police and everything. It was a shame about the brawling and the unfortunate occasion when he'd tried to sell Ecstasy to the midwife next door because in every other way he would have made a brilliant father. Sometimes between 'lectures', at the LSE he'd put in an hour at Janie's collective. The women there were all mad about him. Unfortunately Slobby had recently had to vacate Michaelmas Road in a bit of a hurry, leaving behind a tear-splashed, highly ungrammatical and remorseful letter, a stack of unpaid bills and his malevolent brindle cat Barry, who was turning into the bane of Janie's life.

'They all desert in the end, darling, it's in their genes,' said her mother, who, in view of her experiences at the hands of Janie's father, took a dim view of men. 'Men leap. Women weep.'

Janie winced. She knew Eleanor's intention was to show solidarity but tact had never been her strong point. And where in God's name did she keep digging up these terrible homilies?

'Matthew hasn't deserted, Mother. We're just taking some time apart to work out how we feel.'

'Well, that's precisely the sort of nonsense your father spouted at me when he ran off with Her. We're better off without them, believe me. If I hadn't been educated to be such a ninny I would have realised that decades ago and been much happier. Just make sure the house is in your name. Should have stuck a machete in your father years ago, of course. Had the chance when we were living in Kenya, but I was too damn timid.'

Janie was amused despite herself by the results of her mother's belated forays into the local women's consciousness-raising groups in Oxfordshire. 'The house is held jointly, Mother, and I can assure you, it won't come to that anyway. Dad was, if nothing else, unique in his shittiness. I can't imagine Matthew trying to sell my home without my knowledge. He wouldn't know how to for a start. And in any case, we're not divorcing, just breathing.'

'Sounds like desertion to me,' replied her mother, almost – Janie could have sworn – cheerfully.

*   *   *

The final blow came last week when, summoning the energy to do something about the damp patch above the bathroom cupboard, she had discovered Nell's collage box stuffed with uncashed cheques for Matthew's various freelancing assignments. Some of them were four years old and utterly useless. All that overtime for nothing.

There was a muffled banging at the front door. Nell had stuck a red nose through the letterbox and was calling to her. Jo-Jo bundled her into the kitchen, tipped a bucket of twigs on to the table and passed Janie the papers. 'We're going to make animals,' she announced. 'I saw how on tots TV. Just as well – it distracted Nell while those little fuckers hogged the swings.'

Janie decided to overlook the profanity and busied herself with Jo-Jo's newspapers. Jo-Jo's methodology was somewhat unorthodox but, at seventeen, there was no doubt that she adored children – or Janie's children at least. And any daughter of Gloria's had to be trustworthy. She had started by doing the odd night baby-sitting for Nell three years ago, when Gloria had first come to lend a hand with the housework. And over the past few weeks she had begun helping out during the day, cramming the odd few hours in between shifts in the local café and college, where she was resitting some of her GCSEs. She didn't even ask for money.

'You can pay me when Matthew gets back and stops earning quetzals,' she had said firmly. They had been in the park. Nell had fallen over, the twins had been ravenous, and their combined vocal output was attracting vitriolic looks from passersby. 'I need the experience – I want to be a child facilitator, see. You look knackered. It's mutually beneficial.'

From time to time Janie guiltily asked her whether she shouldn't be putting in more hours at college. 'I get more sense from your kids than all the teachers put together,' Jo-Jo told her.

Janie dragged herself from Aurora Snow, who was predicting a period of intense travel – fat chance – and scanned the To Let section of the broadsheets. Her spirits rose when she saw how high rents were these days. On the other hand, she wasn't sure that the spare rooms in her house would prove to be very commercial, not now that Barry had deconstructed the wallpaper in Slobby's old room, and certainly not with the rafters still clearly visible in another, and the damp patch in the bathroom showing extremely invasive tendencies. 'I think what we have here is Industrial without the chic,' Cassie had ventured the last time Janie had dared show them to her. And that was months ago. They had declined pitifully since. At this rate the council would be dragging the children into care, thought Janie glumly.

She flicked to the Appointments pages and the media columns for anything remotely suitable. They made dismal reading. Her eyes wandered towards the garden where the viburnum was busy putting on a spectacular display of white starbursts, and found herself planning an elaborate grave for herself there. From time to time magazine editors had approached Janie with job offers – out of desperation, Janie always felt, and less as the years passed. But even in the darkest days of Slobby's rent arrears, she had never been remotely tempted. Even now she felt herself blushing whenever one of Matthew's colleagues from *The Probe* asked her what she used to do before having children. She felt light-years mentally from the task of writing about frocks. On the other hand journalism was the only career she'd ever had any experience in. Still, judging from the paucity of jobs on offer, it wasn't going to be a breeze. She wasn't sure if she could still pass as a Hard-nosed and Happening Rock Hack, for instance, which was what the *NME* was advertising for. Then again, perhaps in the present economic climate (hers if not the country's, which seemed to be doing irritatingly well), she would have to be more flexible in her expectations. Will had told her to think positively, so she made a list of things about which she had become knowledgeable in the past eight years:

Children
Gardening
Electrical Wiring

As an afterthought she added Eastern European wines. There was potential there somewhere, she thought brightly. She just couldn't quite see it at the moment. She turned back to the media section and desultorily ring-fenced a couple of possibilities.

The offices of *Cycle Monthly* were in a stone-clad terraced house in Lewisham. It had taken Janie an hour and a half to get there and cost £4.30 on the Tube because she had got on the wrong line. And the editor was telling her that in the light of her limited experience in the field (she had prepared an anecdote about her first meeting with Matthew and then thought better of it) he couldn't offer her a huge salary.

'Still, you would get commission.'

'Commission?'

'Didn't I say? The job entails selling advertising space as well.' One of the telephones on his desk began emitting a mournful bleep and he picked it up. 'Lift-Off Publishing here.'

Janie gazed morosely at the medallions thwacking against the bilious lime-green track suit and wondered distractedly if he ever wore anything that didn't glow in the dark. The basic salary would barely cover her Tube fares. Another of the phones began ringing. 'Get that, would you, love?'

Janie stepped gingerly across the swirly carpet – she had noticed a rogue nail paring lurking in its thickets earlier – to the battalion of telephones on his desk.

'Hello,' said a reedy voice, 'is that Seditious Sue . . . ?'

'So what d'you think?' the editor of *Cycle Monthly* and proprietor of Lift-Off Publishing was asking her cheerily. 'It's definitely a job with potential. We're going places.' The girl didn't know a hell of a lot about bikes, he suspected, but she looked great and he could do with a bit of class about the place. Yup, he thought complacently, she could be just the ticket for the ever-expanding portfolio of magazines at Lift-Off Publishing.

'Er, I'll have to think about it,' Janie procrastinated meekly.

'Well, lovie, I'll need to know soon. Lots of keen applicants and all that. Who was that on the other phone, by the way?'

'Wrong number,' said Janie. 'I believe they wanted someone by the name of Seditious Sue.'

The editor frowned momentarily and then forced a laugh. 'That's not a wrong number, love. Susan is this month's pet on *Gentleman's Relish*. Didn't I tell you that's one of ours as well? 'Course, Seditious Sue doesn't really exist. Whichever one of us answers the phone does the patter. Thirty-nine pence a minute. Nice little earner. Actually I was thinking of changing the name to *GR*. Initials seem to be all the rage. What d'you think?'

Janie mumbled something non-committal while backing politely out of the room.

'Anyway, as I said, I'm seeing a lot of people.' He clamped her hand against his medallion. 'Let me know ASAP.'

'God, Janie, why didn't you tell me things were that desperate?' Cassie nuzzled the mobile into her neck. The traffic was horren-dous. She wondered whether moving offices to Hammersmith had been such a great idea after all. But she did adore the Richard Rogers design – and he'd done her a great deal. She tried to place Lewisham on her mental map of London and gave up.

She knew better these days than to suggest Janie come into the business. Besides, if she were honest, she would rather keep their friendship – precious as it was – separate from the piranha-infested world she so successfully inhabited at work. Janie had always refused Cassie's offers of financial assistance, but Cassie suddenly saw a way she could help. She'd heard on the grapevine that the *International Gazette* was looking for a fashion editor/director, or whatever they called the journo who churned out the stuff about hem lengths and Isabella Suarez's latest hairdo. The last one had done a bunk with the season's photographic budget and an Hermès Kelly bag, or so rumour had it.

The *International Gazette*. That was more like it, thought
Cassie, pleased with her brainwave. Smart new offices in
Victoria and the money would be good too. Of course, Janie
hadn't actually written about fashion for eight or nine years,
and she had made a bit of a thing about leaving to do more
worthwhile things – not a good move, all things considered,
thought Cassie. But what am I saying? She was one of the
stars of her day. She's literate – always a bonus in journalism
these days – laconic, and the eight-year gap will have given her
a distance and an objectivity that would be of immense value
to such a high-minded organ as the *Gazette*. Cassie felt herself
effortlessly rolling over the engine of her peerless sales talk.
Besides, Phyllida Connelly, the *Gazette*'s deputy editor, owed
her a favour after Cassie had given her an exclusive interview
with Grace Capshaw.

'Janie,' she announced triumphantly as the lights turned red
for the fourth time, 'I think I've just found you your job.'

Up on the tenth floor of the *Gazette* building, Phyllida Connelly
was wiping mascara off her sunglasses while she waited for
Lorna, her secretary, to show Janie Pember up. She worshipped
her glass cube of an office, had fought despicably dirtily to secure
it in the face of brutal competition from the sports editor – but
it was hell on a sunny day. She also had a faint suspicion that the
glare wasn't entirely flattering. Lorna looked bloody awful in it,
and once Phyllida had caught her staring at her with something
close to disgusted fascination etched on her pasty features (Lorna
had in fact been contemplating whether to break the news to
Phyllida that the blazing sun was busy melting her foundation,
which was in turn suffocating her clammy open pores). 'It was
like watching a David Attenborough film on killer fungi in slow
mo,' Lorna had told her boyfriend that night. But since Phyllida
had snarled at her to get a life when she had complained about
bad period pains that day, she was damned if she was going to
tell her. Let her look like Gloria Swanson.

Still, mused Phyllida, the office never failed to impress

visitors. From the photograph Cassie had shown her, Janie certainly looked the part. But so had Louisa Dunne.

Phyllida cleared her throat nervously. She couldn't afford to make another disastrous appointment. Not after the débâcle with Louisa. Bad enough that the silly cow had absconded to Australia with the *Gazette*'s catwalk photographer – a damn good one as well – without leaving behind a heap of potentially explosive unfinished business. For all her hard-won worldliness, Phyllida still couldn't get over how much a set of Hermès luggage cost. Nor could she understand why, given Louisa's departure, all these designers persisted in addressing their invoices for her wardrobe to the *Gazette*'s accounts department. Worse still, it had come to her notice that Louisa had spent the best part of her budget for the next six months of fashion pages indulging a costly vodka habit.

So far, Phyllida had chosen not to share this information with the editor and most of the outside world. She hoped the new fashion director, whoever they were, was good with money. They would have a lot of making up to do.

Janie sank into the ivory leather chair opposite Phyllida and felt the safety pin holding in her trousers perform a mini-Caesarean just below her navel. In the end she had plumped for the navy Calvin Klein suit from Cassie's Thin Period which, although it was still one size too large, seemed to fit the bill in every other way.

The view from Phyllida's wraparound windows was distractingly spectacular. Janie tried to remember something pertinent from the skyscraper of newspaper cuttings that Cassie had collected for her. Reading them had turned out to be unexpectedly reassuring. For all its shock tactics, the fashion world was touchingly conservative. In the eight years she had been away nothing, fundamentally, had changed. There had been several major hem-length revolutions, of course – at least one every season, according to the cuttings – and a dizzying number of designers launching new lines, closing them, going bankrupt, starting up again and going bankrupt. Grunge had been. And gone. Chiffon, boot-cut trousers, something called Geek Chic, something else called Heroin Chic. They had all promised to change the way women dressed. For ever. Even the disasters were predictable; every winter the fashion editors had foretold the death of black. Then last year they'd tried a new tack and announced that the new black was . . . black – at which point in her revision Janie had sunk into a deep depression. Had the fashion world been this stupid when she'd been at *Beau Monde*? At least the names were all familiar, although Versace, whom Janie had always rather liked, was no longer there, and one or two others – Aeron Baxter, for instance – seemed to have got amazingly grand. Not that it stopped him holding his shows in the same old schlock-horror venues he'd always favoured. What was it about bombed-out carparks and abattoirs that he found so irresistable?

Realising with a jolt that she remembered his first-ever show, she grew momentarily nostalgic for the days when she would happily spend three weeks' salary on a pair of snakeskin hot pants.

He'd had a flair for publicity even then. While his fellow graduates had been content to use the temporary catwalk in the college gym, pathetically grateful if a couple of journalists turned up to watch, Aeron had lobbied the fashion press for weeks with a series of cryptic messages which, when decoded (God, the hours they'd spent in the fashion cupboard poring over them), turned out to be directions to a desolate patch of Wormwood Scrubs. He'd even persuaded Grace Capshaw to appear. That had been quite a coup.

Well, he did have prodigious talent, thought Janie, although as far as she could tell, not for making clothes anyone could wear.

'So what do you think of, er, Aeron Baxter? He seems to be the name on everyone's lips at the moment.' Phyllida was running through her list of questions. And this was a trick one, since in her view the only design house worth anything was Escada, which Louisa had categorically failed to feature on a single one of her pages. Probably on account of the fact that their stuff looked like clothes, as opposed to sex aids. Phyllida loathed interviewing fashion writers. She could never follow their jargon. All their talk about *witty* this, *directional* that and sodding Fashion Moments made her feel murderous. At least you knew where you were with news reporters – they either got cautioned by the Press Complaints Commission or they didn't. Still, Janie seemed okay, nothing outlandish. Phyllida hated what she called ponce fashion – clothes designed by gay men to make women look foolish. In fact she was convinced the whole thing was a conspiracy, like the masons, and Aeron Baxter was the new godfather – now that would be a story. She liked the navy trouser suit . . . And of course there was that favour she owed Cassie. She tuned back into what Janie was saying.

'. . . the point is, it's not always fashion that's stupid, but the way it's reported. I think it's time to make it seem much more relevant again. It shouldn't just be for fashion victims. It's relevant to all of us; we all have to get dressed in the mornings. And if you consider the way women in former Eastern bloc countries are embracing fashion as a life enhancer, you see how fundamental it is in all our lives. I know a lot of fashion editors are self-referential and indulgent and like to write about bargains that cost two thousand pounds. But that doesn't excuse other writers on the paper for treating fashion like a moronic, embarrassing relative. I've noticed how other sections sneer at fashion while totally failing to understand its nuances and subtleties. And why is it okay to send someone who knows nothing about clothes to write up the shows? Would you send someone who knew nothing about sport to cover the Olympics? Designers are arguably as relevant to popular culture as artists and writers. The British are amongst the most fashion-literate people in the world and it's time to stop writing down to them.' Janie paused for breath, amazed that she had so much to say. It would be ironic if after eight more or less blissful years in the real world she turned out to hanker for a taste of one that she had written off as trivial, self-obsessed and morally indefensible.

'Above all, a fashion editor should be able to put the fashion world in perspective for her readers and yet still hold on to a capacity for being amazed and delighted. Treat it intelligently and it will become an intelligent subject.'

Phyllida snatched off her sunglasses and stared intently at Janie. She didn't have a clue what she was talking about but she recognised someone with the gift of the gab. Here, finally, was a route back into the editor's good books. 'Are you good with budgets?' she demanded.

'My brother-in-law's an accountant,' replied Janie tentatively. 'He's – er – been teaching me a lot lately.'

'Right, then,' said Phyllida briskly, 'the job's yours.' She ran her finger down the schedule in front of her. 'Be in Milan by next Tuesday, will you? It's the start of the autumn collections.'

Chapter Two

Seated at Janie's battered kitchen table, Cassie looked up from her goddaughter's nails which she had been inveigled into painting with her new Chanel nail varnish, a delicious metallic chestnut she'd brought back from New York. She'd had a foul day. After weeks of ignoring Zack, she'd finally taken his advice and made an early-morning appointment to see his rolfer friend, who had stuck his fingers up her nose in an attempt to source her stress. Then she'd spent the afternoon staring at endless photographs of models slumped over lavatory bowls in preparation for a symposium that *A La Mode* was chairing entitled 'Fashion and Morality'. A bit late, thought Cassie grumpily, given that their publication had been the chief instigator of fashion and immorality. She could murder Bill Clinton. Every time he made another dreary speech about Heroin Chic, magazines fell over themselves to shove fat models all over their pages in an attempt to prove how responsible they were.

Anyway, she thought indignantly, she never had liked the trend for photographing models on toilets with their arms akimbo, as if they were ready to jack up. She couldn't recall any of Hot Shots' models posing for such explicit pictures, although Peace had gone through a period of looking unhealthily thin.

Janie drifted into the kitchen in one of the six trouser suits Cassie had brought round for her to try on. 'Well – what do you think?' she asked, flushed with the unexpected pleasure of dressing up after so long in what Cassie called her drudge's uniform.

'Stanley thinks it's gross,' said Nell, wrinkling her nose. Cassie sighed. Nell's invisible friends were multiplying like rabbits since Matthew's departure. Stanley appeared to be based on Slobby – at any rate, he had equally forthright opinions.

'You look terrific. Camel really suits you – just as well it suits someone, I suppose, otherwise Calvin Klein would be sunk. God only knows if he's old hat among the fashion hags. You know how peculiarly they always dress. But in my humble opinion you can't go wrong with a well-cut trouser suit. Come to think of it, you could make that your first column. I see they fit.'

In fact Janie had cinched in the trousers with a large Indian silver belt she had bought on her honeymoon and bunched them up at the back. But she saw no reason to disclose this information. Cassie had been on a diet since she was nine and Janie was committed to curing her – before she passed her obsession on to Nell. 'It's all flooding back – unfortunately,' she said, flopping into a sagging Lloyd Loom chair. She'd watched *The South Bank Show* documentary the night before on Yves Saint Laurent. The Freak Show would have been a more accurate description. Most of the participants seemed demented. Zoffy Villeneuve, a legendary sixtysomething fashion editor who for some reason kept addressing Melvin Bragg as Moby, had hogged the screen endlessly, shamelessly claiming to be one of Saint Laurent's first muses.

'Ee as been vairy eel most of ees life, but what a genius. Ee ees the Peecasso of fashion,' she announced, the yellow starburst of feathers that shot out of the top of her purple satin toque waggling emphatically in agreement. Watching her, Janie groaned. Was Zoffy's skin-tight velvet dress with sheer panels that partially revealed a Wonderbra and g-string any way to convince the public to place their trust in fashion editors?

She had called Cassie in a blind panic. 'I can't do it. It was horrible. Zoffy brought it all back – everyone sitting at the shows like bored *tricoteuses* waiting for the next designer or model to fall flat on their faces. The weird clothes that no one in the real world ever wears but fashion editors spend their lives in hock for, the monumental obsession with black . . .' she wailed.

Cassie made soothing noises about Richard Tyler trouser suits and Jil Sander dresses until Janie calmed down.

'You'll love it once you get there,' she soothed. 'You always did.'

'I'm not in it for the enjoyment,' replied Janie primly. 'I'm working to rescue my children and what's left of my house, not to build up my wardrobe.'

Cassie considered taking Janie to task about her sancti-moniousness but thought better of it. Janie's redoubtable sense of humour would return soon. Give her five days in a swanky hotel, plump pillows, a clean bathroom – Janie was obsessed with white towels, though God knows they eluded her in her own house – and unbroken nights and she'd be her old self.

As Janie flitted upstairs again to try on the Richard Tyler, Cassie ventured gingerly into the bathroom for some nail varnish remover. Janie's bathrooms had always been famous for their petri-dish qualities. Ever since Cassie had known her she'd had bottles of rainforesty-looking ingredients fizzing away on her shelves. From the time of her involvement with the Cambodian refuge these had multiplied dangerously until the whole place looked like a mad experiment, though judging by the gangrenous colour of some of the bottles, the contents dated back to the field trip she'd gone on to Pakistan when she'd been at university. Cassie gave up trying to find anything useful and walked back out on to the landing. The front door began to rattle violently while a torrent of expletives scudded round the front garden. Someone had lost their keys and was attempting to pick the lock. It must be the new nanny/au pair person. Janie had told Cassie about Jo-Jo's colourful language. She opened the front door, and Jo-Jo, crouched over her bag with a bent hairslide, almost toppled on to Cassie's feet. 'Fuck,' she said.

'I'm Cassie. Enchanted to meet you,' said Cassie icily.

'Shite,' said Jo-Jo, flicking the gravel off her tracksuit bottoms crossly. 'The fucking lining of my bag ripped.' Really – Matthew and Janie were too irresponsible. If Matthew had had his way, reflected Cassie, the entire house would have been bulging with convicted felons. As it was, one of the asylum seekers they'd given a room to in return for a little light dusting had been done for a little light shoplifting. And Slobby's undeniable cuteness didn't excuse his appalling behaviour either. Now they'd got a psychopath looking after their children.

Cassie didn't know much – anything, if she was honest – about child-rearing, but she had a vague notion that nannies ought to be dressed in some kind of uniform and not say 'fuck' all the time.

Jo-Jo had retrieved her rucksack – and her composure. She held out a hand to Cassie. 'Jo-Jo. Pleased to meet you. Gloria's daughter,' she added.

If the last piece of information was meant to reassure Cassie, it failed. She knew that Matthew and Janie doted on Gloria and that unlike any of their other 'employees' she had arrived with a string of impeccable references. But ever since Gloria had sent a beautifully antiqued Voyage dress that Cassie had lent to Janie to the Sue Ryder shop, relations between the two women had been strained. She might be a brilliant cleaner, but Cassie thought she was unbearably bossy. And Gloria thought Cassie ridiculously frivolous.

'That dress cost nine hundred pounds,' she had informed Gloria coldly.

'I sorry for you,' retorted Gloria unrepentantly. 'Sue Ryder send it back.'

Jo-Jo beamed down at Cassie, unfazed by her frosty tone. 'Sorry. I haven't got used to keys yet. Where I used to live with Mum the door got kicked down so often we decided it was cheaper to let them walk on in.' She stood up – five feet ten and a half, possibly eleven, Cassie calculated, and from what she could detect through the fuzzy polar layers, fine-boned and long-limbed. She had to hand it to Janie. This petty criminal did at least have aesthetic potential.

Daisy flung her arms round Jo–Jo's knees and Nell sauntered up, evidently pleased to see her. 'Look, look at my nails. Cassie says it's the *dernier cri*. What do you think – cat excrement or what?' Cassie was amazed her goddaughter hadn't said 'shit', or something even worse. Perhaps Jo–Jo kept her swearing under control in front of the children. She swept Daisy up and swung her round on to her back. 'I think it's very chic. Nell's nails look like those magic coffee beans we were reading about yesterday, don't they, Daisy?'

Cassie softened at the cosy scene this conjured up. At least the girl could read. Or maybe Nell had narrated. The point was, now that Cassie could see her in the kitchen light, Jo–Jo looked ravishing.

Once she had tugged her flap–eared hat off and a waist-length dark rope of hair had uncoiled down her back, Jo–Jo did indeed look extraordinary, with her pale caramel skin, glowing from the recent cold, slanting hazel eyes and chiselled bones. In fact she was amazing. Her ancestors must be a right old mixed bunch, reflected Cassie. She could see a bit of Hispanic wildness there in the hair, a trace of orientalism in the eyes. The cheekbones looked El Salvadorean, and if she wasn't mistaken the mouth had a touch of the Irish about it. It was Grace Capshaw all over again, but reconfigured into an innocent, fresh, utterly modern package. Cassie had discovered future stars in all sorts of places – her doctor's surgery, outside a phone booth. She'd never expected to stumble over one at Janie's.

Epiphanies went off in her head like a twenty-one-gun salute and her heart started to pound. Oh, she did love a melting-pot – especially when it was tall and slim. It was rare to feel so sure about a girl so quickly, but Jo–Jo was a classic and, besides, Cassie's sixth sense told her that the mania for inbred aristocratic English girls was about to implode. She had to sign Jo–Jo up. Tonight if possible. Either that or ensure she never made it to the West End where the other agents had their offices.

And then she would have to find Janie another nanny.

Janie wasn't sure about the bead-encrusted Gucci tunic. It

looked wonderful – the bits of it she could see through the editions of Nell's prodigious artwork that were Blutacked on to the tarnished gilt-framed cheval mirror in her bedroom. But it weighed a ton and seemed a little ostentatious. If she could sell it it would probably pay off half the mortgage, she thought mordantly. Janie's usual going-out attire consisted of an ancient grey cashmere polo neck and a worn 1930s black velvet skirt she'd found in Portobello market the same day she and Matthew had bought the mirror. This also happened to be the day she had discovered she was pregnant with Nell. It was riddled with woodworm and the frame was starting to look like the inside of a Crunchie, which just made her love it more. Sod it. Why did everything in the house have to have such poignant associations? she wondered. She descended the staircase majestically to seek Cassie's appraisal.

As she approached the foot of her stairs she heard Cassie's voice, low and compelling, deep in earnest conversation, floating out of the kitchen. She wouldn't dare, thought Janie. Cassie could not seriously be trying her patter out on Jo-Jo. Was Jo-Jo model material? Janie realised with a pang that the past few months she had been in such an emotional fug she could barely remember what her own face looked like, let alone Jo-Jo's. If she conjured up the elements of Jo-Jo in front of her – the thick wavy hair, the slender limbs, the wonderful, ingenuous wide smile – she supposed they did amount to loveliness. But Jo-Jo was becoming indispensable. Christ, she sounded like the worst kind of Victorian owner-employer, but she still couldn't resist hovering at the foot of the staircase.

In more neutral circumstances, Cassie's sales pitch would have fascinated Janie. It was so perfectly calibrated to incite maximum excitement in its object – as indeed it should have been. Cassie was, quite simply, brilliant at her job. It was in her blood. She had started off temping as a secretary in an agency during the university holidays. She'd become so popular with models and clients that when she left to go back for her final year, they had begged her to set up on her own.

Ever the pragmatist, she had decided not to finish her

degree in German and Italian. 'The model world is trivial, amoral and fun,' she had said by way of explanation to her tutor, who was heartbroken at her defection. He had earmarked her for a first. Starting from a tiny flat in Earl's Court, Cassie had gradually turned Hot Shots into the most prestigious agency in the country, with a reputation for integrity as well as ground-breaking ideas. She had been the first to intuit the trend for waifs, and later for aristocrats and for curvy girls; the first to set up a subsidiary business devoted to placing sports personalities in a growing number of lucrative sponsorship deals; the first to send out monthly press releases stating clearly and honestly what her key clients were up to – as a result of which she had always basked in excellent relations with the press.

She had also been the first to grasp that although the press constantly predicted the death of supermodels, the public would always be ineluctably drawn to glamour and beauty. She knew that the idea of spoilt teenagers earning thousands of pounds for scowling at a camera no longer went down very well, and that the public resented the way that these girls had become personalities everywhere from Hull to Honolulu, even as they still bought into the whole package. No one who wasn't part of the business would ever really understand why a scrap of a girl like Peace Grant should get paid half a million pounds for a TV ad that showed her gorgeous little face peeping out of a Jeep – and why that image would then help Chrysler sell another forty million pounds' worth of car. And Cassie was wise enough not to try to explain. Instead she successfully explored other ways of diffusing the hostility. She urged her models to act responsibly and famously refused to tolerate tantrums. All the girls were sent on business seminars and Cassie kept a raft of lawyers, under the watchful eye of her own solicitor, Michael Croft, on retainer to help the girls out with anything from buying their first house to negotiating big contracts.

Hot Shots was practically a household name, and Cassie had become something of a media personality, invited to premières and 11 Downing Street when the Prime Minister wanted glamorous guests; her opinions were constantly sought by the features pages. She had even appeared on *Call My Bluff* (she hoped her old tutor was watching) and starred in an ad for Olympus cameras which had paid for her silver convertible Mercedes. The big trick, she confided to Janie, was to take on fewer models than other agencies. That way you could be truly selective and really devote the necessary time to each girl's career. It also made you seem even more exclusive. Since the early days of supermodeldom, the business had become more rapacious, the constant turnover of new faces more frenetic than it had ever been. Cassie, however, prided herself on the longevity of her models' careers and what she called her 'aftercare' – the way she guided them on afterwards to film work and other interesting careers. Whatever reservations Janie had about the modelling business, she could only admire the way Cassie had steered a moral path through it. But she was damned if she was going to take Jo-Jo with her.

'I wouldn't mess you around, for heaven's sake,' Cassie was saying. 'Have you ever heard of Hot Shots?' There was a sullen silence. Jo-Jo, wounded by Cassie's initial disdain, thought she was winding her up. Cassie continued regardless. 'Well, it's an agency I set up fourteen years ago and it's pretty successful. I've seen hundreds, probably thousands, of young women in that time. I do have some idea what it takes. All I'm saying is I'm pretty sure that you have it.'

That was bad, thought Janie. It sounded so sincere.

'So who've you "discovered", then?'

That was good. Jo-Jo sounded bolshy.

'I could recite lists, but it's so crass. I deal in people, not names. Why don't you come to my office and get a feel for the way I work? Or,' she added, feeling it could hardly be necessary (Jo-Jo must have read about Hot Shots in one of the teen magazines), 'ask some models about my reputation.'

That was good. It made Cassie sound pompous.

'So, no Grace Capshaw on your books, or Peace Grant?' Jo-Jo retorted, desperate not to be impressed.

That was bad, thought Janie. Very bad.

'As a matter of fact, yes, I discovered both of them. And

twelve years later Grace is still with me, which, believe me, is the real test. So of course is Peace, Jess Murray, Tulah Delaney, Unity Montcreith and Greta Krafzyk.' Janie whimpered quietly. It was a roll-call of some of the most successful models in the world. Cassie meanwhile was exasperated with herself for falling into the trap of tossing these household names into the conversation so early. It wasn't the approach she approved of. She preferred to plant the ambition to be a model subtly in girls' minds and then let it take root gradually. She found it a far more effective tactic than a hard sales pitch in the long run. She also preferred to let people discover her blue-chip credentials gradually by word of mouth. It was what distinguished her from some of her cruder peers, she believed. But she wasn't used to girls reacting as coolly to her approaches as Jo-Jo.

Believing distraction was the order of the day, Janie burst in, arms fluttering in a mock balletic pose. 'Ta-dum. Well, what do you think – belle of the ball or sad old bag?'

'You look heavenly. The gold looks wonderful against your skin,' Cassie said, genuinely touched by this vision of Janie dressed up and enjoying herself. She hadn't seen her look what she, Cassie, called glamorous since – well, since she married Matthew, if the truth be told.

'Those other fashion editors won't be able to hold a candle to you,' said Jo-Jo. 'Well, not for looks anyway. We've yet to see your writing talents.'

'Thanks for the vote of confidence. Jo-Jo, would you mind just popping Nell in some relatively clean water? I've run the bath, though what I thought was Postman Pat bubble bath turned out to be filled with green poster paint. Jerk chicken, anyone?'

'Janie, I thought your culinary talents began and ended with cheese on toast,' Cassie remarked distractedly as she regretfully watched Jo-Jo march Nell towards the bathroom.

'They do. But Jo-Jo's mum is a whiz in the kitchen. Since she arrived we've been feasting like kings.'

'What exactly do you mean by arrived?' Cassie sounded querulous. 'I thought she only worked two hours a week, which just about gives her time to blast her way through the industrial-strength gunk on three bottles of Ecuadorean conditioner.'

'Oh, come on, Cassie. You didn't think I was going to leave the three of them – four if you count Stanley, who's becoming quite a handful, I can tell you – for a whole month with Jo-Jo. I mean, she's terrific and all that, but she's only seventeen, and anyway, she has to go to college two days a week. She's set her heart on a career with children,' she added pointedly.

Perfect age, thought Cassie. 'Isn't it time you had Stanley assassinated?' she asked crossly. 'It isn't cute any more, Janie. It's displacement therapy for Matthew.'

'So anyway, I was agonising about what I was going to do with the children now I've got to trek to all these silly fashion shows, when Jo-Jo mentioned that Gloria was having a vile time with her landlord. Poor thing. She hasn't had proper heating for six months. And before you say it, yes, I am getting the boiler seen to here. And you know how brilliant she is with children . . .'

Janie was off on one of her Gloria eulogies. Cassie had heard it all before – how Gloria used to work in a crèche when Jo-Jo was a baby; how she'd got the twins into a routine after only two days. Cassie knew all the lurid details of Gloria's miserable life. How she'd come over from Cuba when she was fourteen. How she'd been married at seventeen. If she'd only kept her figure she'd have been the perfect subject for a miniseries, Cassie thought spitefully. Gloria's first husband died. Cassie never quite found out why. Bossed to death probably. Then Gloria had met Jo-Jo's father, who was Irish. They married, but it didn't seem to work out. He was from Donegal, a poetic soul but not reliable, and Gloria had brought Jo-Jo up on her own in a succession of cramped, run-down flats. There'd been a third husband who'd tried to beat her up – big mistake, thought Cassie. In between times Gloria had had about thirty-nine jobs simultaneously, become the best cleaner in the world – with a waiting list, for heaven's sake – and somehow managed to find time to reorganise Matthew's study. And now she appeared to have moved in.

'Incredible, isn't it,' Janie was saying thoughtfully, 'how someone like that could be bullied? It just shows that it could happen to anyone. All that rubbish about certain women being marked out as victims . . .'

'Yes, yes,' said Cassie impatiently. Normally she was more than happy to debate women's issues with Janie, and not simply because, as a successful single woman, she considered herself singularly well qualified to lecture endlessly on any female-related subject, but because she couldn't help feeling, in her heart of hearts, that Janie had rather let things slide when it came to female emancipation. 'Are you sure it's good for Jake to be surrounded by so many bossy women? I know you went on that Gay Pride march, but is that really what you want for Jake?' she said.

Janie ignored her. She knew Cassie didn't mean half the more cynical things she uttered. 'Gloria gets home most days around five – this is one of her late nights. But she should be back before you go. She must be at the Scotts'.' For some unfathomable reason, the Scotts loved Gloria so much that when they moved from Belgravia to Suffolk they had begged Gloria to go with them as their housekeeper. They had even reserved an entire floor for her and Jo-Jo. Gloria had declined on the grounds that Jo-Jo was at a sensitive juncture in her education (on the crest of failing most of her GCSEs, as Cassie dimly recalled) and because Lord Cooper had threatened to hang himself if Gloria was no longer able to go in and do for him three times a week. The upshot was that the Scotts paid for her to go for one whole day to Suffolk every week. Once or twice they'd even helicoptered her down, but mostly she went by train. 'First-class ticket and the chauffeur collects her . . . amazing, isn't it? But she is a treasure. I never really knew her when Matthew was here. Two hours a week was all we could afford. But you know I already really feel I can trust her. I mean, this weekly trek to Suffolk must knacker her, but she's up the next morning bright as a button. Her energy's amazing.

And you know what, I think she might be getting the Stanley situation under control. To be honest, I wouldn't mind if she moved in for ever.'

'Fascinating,' said Cassie. Janie sounded dangerously like those boring housewives who witter endlessly about their staff problems and their Jacuzzis. Cassie knew the type well, having spent the longest weekend of her life in Surrey last year with her sister and her banker husband. She castigated herself for this uncharitable thought. Janie was nothing like Yvette, and if she was anxious about who was going to take care of the children while she was away earning a crust, well, who could blame her? She put her mood down to her inconclusive conversation with Jo-Jo. New talent always put her on edge.

'Far be it from me to question Gloria's extensive knowledge of the child's psyche, but for someone who talks so much she seems to say very little that's actually comprehensible.'

'That's because you never listen,' said Janie defensively. 'What's got into you anyway?'

'Apart from an alien pair of fingers, you mean? Well, if you must know, your proprietorial attitude to your nanny.'

'She is not a nanny,' hissed Janie. 'She's a child facilitator.'

There was a silence.

'I tell you what,' said Cassie, removing a spatula from Janie's hand, 'why don't you go upstairs and change? Then you can finish reading Nell that article in *Cosmo* while I heat up the chicken.'

Halfway up the stairs, Janie realised that she had cleared the way for Cassie to have another tête-à-tête with Jo-Jo – and then felt wretched for being so selfish. She helped Jo-Jo scoop Nell out of the bath, parcelled her up in a towel, deposited her on her bed, and told Jo-Jo she'd see to the rest. *Che sera sera*, she thought – and was horrified to find two huge wet greenish patches where Nell had placed her feet while hanging upside down from Janie's waist forming concentric circles on Cassie's tunic.

Nell wanted the Guatemalan story again – the one in which Matthew rescued hundreds of orphans from marauding soldiers (the crosser Janie got with Matthew the more she compensated by turning him into an archangel for his children). *Cosmo* – hah! Cassie was just jealous because Nell was already au fait with current affairs and knew her way around *The Spectator*. By the time Janie had finished, they were both plunged in gloom at the perfidy of the world's totalitarian governments. 'It's terrible what happens in some countries,' said Janie earnestly. 'That's why we have to be very grateful for what we have and try and do what we can to help.'

'I know,' said Nell, taking Janie's hand, 'but don't get too depressed, Mum. Shit happens.'

Outside the front door, the rustling process had begun all over again. But on this occasion, keys were produced and by the time Cassie had reached the hall, Gloria had let herself in and was unhooking and untying the various overstuffed carrier bags that were tethered about her small frame.

'Mum, you've got to stop schlepping all this junk around,' admonished Jo-Jo, helping Gloria with some of the knots. 'You'll do your back in.'

'Is nothing,' said Gloria jauntily. 'Now I don't 'ave to climb all those stairs any more I can schlep much more bargains. Is no problem.' Noticing Cassie, she nodded stiffly in her direction. Jo-Jo began burrowing in the bags. Cassie was always fascinated to observe exchanges between her models and their parents. She stirred the chicken enthusiastically.

'What have we got here?' mumbled Jo-Jo rhetorically from the depths of a bag. 'Unidentified herbs, chilli powder – probably explosive – coconut milk' – examining the label – 'three years past its sell-by date. Purple wool – not for me. Please don't knit this for me. Halal meat . . .'

'Is special offer,' said Gloria defensively.

'Jelly beans, more second-hand books – is this for Nell, Mum?' She brandished a child's plastic iron and ironing board in her mother's face. 'Janie's mum won't approve of that. She thinks all household implements are symbols of female oppression.'

'Is because she uses them to oppress her cleaners.'

'Mum, *what* are you doing with manure in here?'

'Is for Janie's camellias. The man on the stall said ees got blood in it. He say ees fantastic for growing, but people don't like the idea of blood spattered all over their gardens. So, another bargain.' Gloria's hands alighted on her hips in a triumphant flourish. 'And I know that Janie has worried very much about her camellias. You want to eat jerk charcoal? Here, let me.'

This was to Cassie, who, observing intently the exchange between mother and daughter, had taken her eye off the pan which was spitting at her cashmere jacket. Gloria removed a tea towel, now flambéing nicely, out of the flames. 'Ees safe now, I sort it.' She held out a small hand still indented by marks from the carrier bags. Cassie sighed. Gloria's bustling capability really bugged her. 'Stop rummaging. Ees so rude,' said Gloria sharply.

Jo-Jo immediately stopped fishing among Gloria's bargains and looked mildly contrite. The chastisement had struck home. Gloria was clearly someone worth wooing.

'You're looking amazingly well, Gloria,' said Cassie silkily. 'The Sussex air clearly agrees with you. Janie tells me the Scotts can't do without you. How old are their children now?'

'Suffolk. You look peaky. Too much parties,' retorted Gloria. 'Or maybe the colour,' she added tauntingly.

Cassie was drenched in beige – or honey as she preferred to call it. Her trouser suit, her Manolos, her carefully streaked hair and manicured nails, all toned beautifully. When she wanted fashion advice from a polyester junkie she'd ask for it. Or shoot herself.

'You been to that shop again?' said Gloria, stabbing some chillies. This was a reference to the pale gold ethnic-looking velvet coat hanging in the hallway and to Voyage, the Fulham Road shop, a favourite with Cassie which only allowed in membership-card carrying customers. For some time Gloria had been following the antics of its sales staff apoplectically, via the pages of the *Evening Standard*.

'It's Dries actually.'

'Dross? Ees funny name for a designer. But honest.' She loved tormenting Cassie, though she didn't quite know why.

In theory Cassie was precisely the kind of person Gloria might idolise – a successful businesswoman who had made it on her own, without any help from men. The world she operated in was shallow and corrupt, but Cassie had done her best to change it. But there was something in the way Cassie behaved whenever Gloria had seen her with Matthew, a look in her eyes that betrayed a certain lack of respect, which turned Gloria's stomach. She adored Matthew. He had found her when she was at a low point – weeping on the pavement outside her flat when the bully had locked her out. Gloria had watched, her hands clenched in helpless fury, as bits of smashed furniture had rained out of the upstairs window. Thank God Jo-Jo had been at school. A dozen people had walked by, refusing to catch her eye, a couple even crossing the road to avoid the scene. But Matthew had stopped, asked if there was anything he could do and taken her for a cup of tea to steady her nerves. One thing had led to another – Matthew had put her in touch with the citizens advice bureau, lent her the deposit so she could move into a new flat (never had Matthew had a loan repaid so promptly) and encouraged her to get a better job. When Gloria had insisted on sticking to what she knew, Matthew had recommended her expertise on the domestic front to everyone he knew. Gloria was germ phobic but she would have swum through sewage for Matthew.

The only time she ever got dispirited was when she felt she was failing to raise her daughter with higher expectations than she'd had. Jo-Jo was turning out a sad disappointment on the academic front. Not because she was unintelligent – Gloria knew the opposite was true – but because she had been bored and under-stimulated at school. And the same appeared to be happening at college.

For the thousandth time, Gloria felt a pang of regret at not moving her daughter away from the den of iniquity that she considered London to be.

'The kitchen's looking clean,' Cassie said, trying again.

Gloria sniffed, but took the bait. 'Well, I been finding all sorts of things that been missing a long time. The house was

39

a beeg mess. I never had enough time before to sort out the catastrophe.' She emitted a whistling sound to indicate the extent of the chaos she had found. 'Orderliness is not Meess Janie's strong point. Jo-Jo, pass me those chillies, please.'

Personally, Cassie thought Janie's sense of order was just fine. It was Matthew who created havoc. But now was not the time to go into all that with Gloria, though she had a feeling that there might be many opportunities in the future to do so. Still, it did seem that Janie had landed on her feet with Jo-Jo and Gloria after all. The latter was obviously a borderline national treasure. And judging by the way she was salvaging the chicken, perhaps Janie was right, and she was a deft cook to boot.

Having finally settled the twins, Janie had changed back into some black jeans and bare feet – Jake seemed to have glued some conkers into her slippers – and though she meant to finish trying on Cassie's outfits, the aroma of Gloria's chicken had enticed her back downstairs.

'Late night tonight, Gloria?'

'She's been to the Scotts,' explained Jo-Jo. 'Mum must be the only cleaning lady in England on air miles. Worst luck. It wears her out.'

'They need me,' said Gloria heroically. 'They told me, "No one in East England cleans like you, Gloria." So every week I go.'

'It takes two hours each way – when the trains are running,' said Jo-Jo crossly, 'but it's the children. She adores them. Says no one else would know where their toys go.'

'In that case,' said Cassie, seizing her chance, 'sit down, put your feet up, Gloria, and I'll make you some tea and finish supper.'

Janie found this concern highly diverting. Cassie hadn't boiled a kettle for five years, let alone cooked a meal. Her immaculate flat was kept pristine by a rota of anonymous house-keepers from a Knightsbridge agency. She ordered everything in. Well, thought Janie, she's going to have to wangle her way into Gloria's affections all by herself. If Cassie was going to persuade Jo-Jo to set her sights on loftier planes than the local sandpit – and Janie had acknowledged while she was reading to Nell that Cassie would ultimately succeed in her mission – then she, Janie, might as well get some enjoyment from watching her scramble through hoops to get there.

She sat down at the table between Jo-Jo and Gloria, chatting expansively, sipping tea and later – when Gloria had extracted a murky-looking bottle from one of her bags – rum and Coke. Cassie meanwhile flustered around the kitchen, every so often looking beseechingly in her direction – to no avail.

'Oh, Meess Janie,' began Gloria. Cassie looked at her friend tauntingly, *Meess* Janie. But Janie assiduously ignored her. 'I nearly forgot. Some terrible men came for your piano – at six o'clock this morning while you were asleep. I give them piece of my mind.'

I bet you did, thought Cassie.

'I say how dare you come at thees uncivilised hour. But they say ees best time to catch people. Well, I know how to deal with those parasites, I tell you, Meess Janie. If nothing else my second landlord teach me that. Anyway, I theenk they say they are from Fag and Sons. Well, I tell them they can faget it,' said Gloria, savouring her pun.

'Ferguson's,' Janie corrected her softly. For her birthday last summer Matthew had surprised her with a Bechstein upright maple piano. Early Victorian, they had thought, in good condition with two delicate gilt candle sconces attached to the front. It was a little beauty. They had gone to Ferguson's auction house to buy a kitchen table, but Janie had fallen in love with the piano and she knew Matthew missed not being able to play one. 'Imagine the children learning on this,' she had said lightly, before wandering off in the direction of scrubbed oak tables.

'Surprise,' announced Matthew on the morning of her birthday as he led her eyes blindfolded, downstairs. It certainly had been. Janie was tone deaf – a defect she had never seen the necessity of revealing to Matthew, who had been a promising choirboy. Anyway, Nell was showing great promise on the recorder so maybe she'd be a gifted pianist.

Except, as she now realised, Matthew's cheque must have bounced.

'Supper's ready,' Cassie announced tactfully. She served up the salad as if it were an eight-course banquet she'd spent three days slaving over, with divine intervention from Marco Pierre White and casually drew up a chair to the place she had laid for herself between Jo-Jo and Gloria, both of whom seemed to be eyeing her with an unwarranted degree of scepticism.

'The other bad news I get before I leave this morning,' continued Gloria, enjoying her new position as fulcrum of the household, 'was a letter from your maths teacher who says you haven't been to his classes all term, Jo-Jo. Explain, please.'

'Waste of time,' replied Jo-Jo monosyllabically. Then, seeing the stern expression on her mother's face, she felt instantly remorseful and became more communicative. Gloria regarded academic knowledge as a sacred pursuit and had done everything in her limited power to promote her daughter's chances of gaining a decent education. Considering her own curtailed time in academia, her limited grasp of English and the desperately under-resourced schools to which Jo-Jo had been assigned, this had been a Herculean task. At one time she had even been on the verge of taking a job as housekeeper at a large girls' boarding school in Hertfordshire so that Jo-Jo could get a free place there. But Jo-Jo, brimming with evidence of the sadistic and racist bent of such establishments (most of it hearsay from envious classmates), had begged her not to go and Gloria had bitterly regretted her moment of soft-headedness ever since.

'The thing is, Mum, I've been thinking that maybe there's not a lot of point in going on at college. I'm mathematically challenged – it's Dad's genes. You know he could only ever count when he was inside a betting shop. And even if I do get a couple of GCSEs, there's no guarantee that it'll be any easier to get a job. It's like I'm part of a lost generation,' she said, hitting her stride. 'I thought maybe I should just concentrate on getting a career going now without wasting any more time.' She broke off. It had taken a lot of effort to get through such an emotionally charged speech without lapsing into a torrent of expletives. Gloria deplored swearing – she regarded it as a failure on her part as a parent the one time she had heard Jo-Jo do it and had washed her mouth out with cut-price kosher washing-up liquid – and Jo-Jo saw no reason to cause her further pain in this regard.

'And what kind of career would that be?' enquired Gloria sarcastically. 'Because without exams you end up a cleaner. You think I work thees 'ard so my daughter can do the same. Without exams, you not even fit for Tesco's.'

'If you must know, there are all kinds of things I could do.' Jo-Jo cast around desperately for some examples and cursed herself for not having explored any. Her mother respected a well-researched argument.

Gloria looked at her daughter expectantly. 'Cassie says I could be a model.' Shit. This was the last thing she had wanted to drag in.

For that matter, Cassie, silently ruminating on a radish, wasn't sure she was ready to be hauled into the conversation at this juncture. She looked up from her plate to find three pairs of eyes surveying her with varying degrees of hostility.

'Your daughter's very striking-looking,' she began gently. She found eye contact invaluable at moments like these, but Gloria was now ferreting around in one of her bags for some discounted mangoes.

'But of course, as I always tell the thousands of hopefuls who write to me . . .' Make them feel the full weight of fate's bountifulness, thought Cassie, as she paused for a fraction of a second. '. . . looks on their own aren't enough. The most beautiful girl in the history of the world could walk into this kitchen now and I wouldn't necessarily recommend that she become a model. It's a question of temperament as much as anything. Some of the most successful models aren't classically beautiful. They have an attitude, a certain something, a toughness . . .'

'Are you saying that Jo-Jo has thees certain something or not?' interrupted Gloria. 'Because as it 'appens, modelling isn't something I had in mind for her.'

It was all Cassie could do not to choke on a coriander leaf.

'I thought you said all models nowadays either had to be oiks or toffs,' said Janie coldly. 'In fact I expressly recall you saying you were having a recruitment drive on titles.'

Cassie glowered at her.

'You say she's striking. Hah! You must be very clever to see it through those very scruffy clothes of 'ers.' Gloria was a staunch believer in not praising children within their earshot. But it was hard not to detect pride in her affected nonchalance. 'Anyway, it's only the 'ight that makes her look good. 'Er father was big man – physically I mean. The brain – that was something else. Still, 'e got something right, I suppose. For all the good it will do 'er. I've 'eard about these models. Drugs. Spoilt. Ees not good for them. All thees fuss in newspapers. Ees ridiculous. And far too thin. I 'ate to see bones.'

'With all due respect, Mum, it's not particularly relevant what you had in mind for me,' interjected Jo-Jo sulkily. 'I mean, we live in a democracy and all that. Not that I am bowled over by the idea myself.' She looked at Cassie reprovingly. 'Supermodels are dead. And anyway, it's always seemed a very boring, not to mention naff, way of passing time to me. But at least hear her out. It's only polite,' she said in her most reasonable tone, knowing the plea of politeness would secure Cassie a few minutes' free speech.

Here goes, thought Cassie. Normally, she exercised enormous restraint in these matters, but it required every fibre of her self-control not to hurl a lasso round Jo-Jo. 'You're quite right, Jo-Jo. It can be mind-blowingly tedious. It's also pretty hard work. Not just the travelling – all over the world and to exotic places – but learning how to make clothes work, how to make the blo . . . blindingly awful dress look like a work of art that millions of women will want to buy. That's a real skill, you know. It's not just a question of putting something on and gawking around till the photographer's used up a roll of film on you. It's knowing which light works best, what angle, sussing out how to move on camera, how to sell a product. Then there's learning how to strategise a career – which jobs to take, which not to, which people bring out the best in you and vice versa. There's thinking about where you want to end up, educating yourself about money, making it work for you, planning for the future, when you can do something really interesting.

'There's learning how to take rejection and how to give rejection to the many dubious characters who will cross your path. How to get on with people, how to get to the bottom of a person's motives in double quick time – it's a crash course in United Nations diplomacy, frankly. The ones who really make it big are anything but dumb. All this stuff about the death of the supermodel is rubbish too – pure envy. People will always be willing to pay for a certain look and they'll always be fascinated by beauty, and a few girls will always be very famous, purely because of their looks. But the backlash is a very good example of the kind of negative thing that models have to deal with. They may not have formal educations—'

'They're eel-educated, spoiled 'oydens,' said Gloria witheringly.

'—but they're smart and they grow up very fast,' persisted Cassie. 'Too fast, you could say, though personally I think that depends on whether the individual can handle it. Looks-wise, there's no doubt in my mind that you could be very successful – and I mean *very*, although of course we'd have to take some test shots. But Jo-Jo, it's not just about having the right look. It's about being tough enough to handle the success as well as the failure, and about losing your naïveté at an age when some older people might consider you were better off hanging on to it. And as a successful young woman you would inevitably meet some of the dregs of humanity who will stick around like an unwanted tattoo. And understandably, Jo-Jo, you may find that a rather daunting prospect.'

It was this last comment – crudely disguised challenge that it was – which, as Cassie knew it would, turned things around in Jo-Jo's mind. The lure of foreign travel had left her cold – must remember to scrap that bit, it's becoming a rather crass cliché, thought Cassie, and anyway, most of these girls have backpacked their way halfway round the world by the time they're fourteen.

But the part about not being naïve, the hint that this would irritate a few adults, and the prospect of encountering a slew of creeps, never failed to appeal to the average teenager.

Jo-Jo assumed her most unimpressed expression, which entailed curling her lower lip and sniffing a lot. 'Big deal. Mum and I have had to do that stuff all our lives ... Do you really think I've got the looks?'

Janie could hardly bear to listen to Jo-Jo's ensuing capitulation. She stared disconsolately out of the French door, across the sodden lawn to her peach trees. She had coaxed them to their present robust health from two scrappy little stumps Matthew had rescued years ago from a derelict fruit farm in Sussex, together with miles of Russian vine, when he had been covering the Tory party conference in Brighton. Normally the sight of them lifted her spirits. But not tonight. Oh, even the sodding weeds have got Matthew memories, she thought aggrievedly. And her Himalayan rose was looking spindly.

She wondered whether Gloria's talents extended to gardening. She cursed herself for not giving her a crash course. Now that Jo-Jo was going to be a cover girl, who would water the tubs of lavender, make sure the hydrangea didn't get waterlogged and mulch the wisteria? Come to think of it, who would see that the children were all right – *really* all right, not just clothed, fed and cleaned? Janie trusted Gloria and Jo-Jo with her life, otherwise she would never have countenanced leaving the children with them. But with all Gloria's commitments and Jo-Jo's soaraway new career, would there be time for cuddles and bedtime stories? The twins were a handful and Nell could be truculent. She must be mad, she thought ruefully.

For the first time it occurred to Janie to be nervous about her new role on the *International Gazette*. Until now, she had been so preoccupied with the mechanics of becoming a working mother that she hadn't had a moment to think about the job itself – and whether she was up to it. Never mind a model's hard life, she thought dolefully, the awfulness of life as a fashion journalist was flooding back to her – the exhausting schedules, the desperate casting around for non-stories, the consuming nature of fashion trivia. Matthew had once told her that he thought *The Probe*'s style director had a much tougher time than the political writers. She had to make stories out of nothing half the time, whereas often the reverse was true for them. At the time Janie was astonished that Matthew had even noticed what the fashion editor was doing. And later, she realised, she had also been vaguely disgruntled that he expressed admiration for her work. But it was only much, much later that she understood that this was because one of the main reasons – never expressed, never acknowledged, even to herself – why she had renounced her career was because she somehow felt that working in fashion was not a fit occupation for someone married to Matthew.

She dragged herself wearily back to the present in time to hear Cassie's exposition on anorexia nervosa. 'I'm going to bed,' she announced. No one heard. Gloria had extracted a bottle of sherry from one of the bags and was pouring two glasses. To Jo-Jo she handed a carton of Ribena. As Janie stepped out of the tunic and flopped into bed, she heard Cassie at the door handing out her card to Jo-Jo and Gloria. 'Think about it, and call me, if you like. But remember what I said. Not everyone can handle it.'

Shit, thought Janie. And turned out the light.

Cassie poured herself a celebratory turnip and papaya shake. It was disgusting, and given that she'd already badly dropped off the food-combining wagon tonight by demolishing most of Gloria's extra-sweet sherry, she might as well have had what she really wanted, which was a tumbler full of icy champagne, just as she liked it, which was pretty much straight from the freezer, and to hell with her intestinal tract. Only unfortunately, in a flamboyantly abstemious gesture, she had given the lot away last week to Zack's mother.

Ah, sweet, sexy, dyslexic Zack – cute as a koala, and almost as bright. All her friends adored him, of course, but that was because they enjoyed having their astrological charts read by him and didn't have to put up with his pathological untidiness.

She gazed across the expanse of scrubbed slate floor where, for the fourth night running, a trail of his possessions marked the route from the Aga to her bedroom. The sight of the red polka-dot handkerchief Zack wore over his head, pirate-style, the bottle-green velvet jacket and a pair of biker boots, sent her spirits plummeting. The cuckoo had clearly taken it into his head to move in, a state of affairs which, if Cassie could possibly help it, was not going to be a permanent feature in *her* astrological chart.

The bloody Aga was going to have to go as well. It had taken four workmen two days to heave it up to her floor – it was far too large to fit in the lift, and after only eight months there were distressing signs that it was causing subsidence on one side of the kitchen. Good excuse, thought Cassie. Extravagant as she was, some long-dormant frugal gene from her father, who'd spent his life tracking figures in the bought ledger department of a printing company in Weston-super-Mare, gave her moral twinges every so often. She knew instinctively that profligacy was a bad thing, but she did love to redo her flat completely every two years. She'd had it with Shabby Chic – she realised now that it looked ridiculous in a flat with fifteen-foot-high ceilings that stretched across two white stuccoed Georgian buildings in Little Venice. Minimalism was more in keeping with the era and the area and with her new simplified existence – and at least she'd be able to get the microwave out of the cupboard and use it openly.

How extraordinary that Janie had such a glorious creature as Jo-Jo under her nose all this time and never noticed the potential. In her *Beau Monde* days, Janie was as susceptible to a ravishing object as Marie Antoinette. How curious, thought Cassie, not for the first time, that Janie had so whole-heartedly taken it upon herself to cultivate a life of dilapidated penury, while she, Cassie, has spent her life trying to eradicate all memory of it. She flicked through a *Designers' Digest* and jotted down the number of Barney Frick, architect to the *chicerati* and the author of a building site next to her offices which looked as though it might turn out to be pretty bloody spectacular.

★   ★   ★

Janie looked at the alarm clock. It was 5.30 a.m. It had been a fairly sleepless night. In a fit of self-pity, and already missing the children, she had carried Nell's slumbering form from the child's bedroom and plopped her into her bed on Matthew's side. Pathetic – and against all Penelope Leach's instincts. Still, she'd got her just deserts. Sleeping with Nell was a bit like being in bed with a windmill – six hours of low-level disturbance. Nell looked serene enough, but Janie was in turmoil – the job, Matthew, child care, the bills, Harriet bloody Harman. In the frosty blackness that had seeped in from outside they all looked like insurmountable problems.

The taxi wasn't due for hours. Unable to get back to sleep, she slipped out of bed and automatically thrust her feet into the ancient leather slippers that Matthew adored but had typically forgotten to pack. The air was quiet and chilly, but she thought she detected the first stirrings of spring. The trees, which had been swaying about in gales for weeks like arthritic ballerinas, were just starting to come into bud. She looked for her dressing gown and saw that Gloria had washed it – it was drying in the laundry room – so she grabbed her Barbour instead and made herself some coffee. Hugging the mug inside her coat for warmth, she stepped into the garden.

It was one of her favourite times of day. A ghostly mist hovered a few inches above the grass, revealing a smattering of daffodils and crocuses pushing up through the grass beneath the lilac tree – a sight that never failed to move her. She looped back a frond of evergreen honeysuckle that was dangling wantonly from the rackety veranda and breathed in the slightly sweet, damp air. She loved this garden. It was disproportionately large. In the 1950s the owners of the house had bought a patchwork of allotments that backed on to the existing garden and built a tennis court and planted a small orchard there. (The council had been delighted to facilitate what it saw as the gentrification of the area.)

As the owners grew elderly, the garden had become increasingly overgrown and chaotic. By the time Janie and Matthew had bought the house, it had been reclaimed by the wild. The tennis court, swamped beneath a mass of bindweed and moss, was beyond repair. But its rambling south-west aspect had proved remarkably hospitable. Whatever she planted, from tiny cuttings and seeds to plum stones, flourished and, restoring a sense of verdant wellbeing to its long-neglected borders, gave her enormous satisfaction. Last summer Matthew had built Nell a tree-house – a magical Swiss Family Robinson affair (more Heath Robinson, Cassie had observed), painted pale blue and almost finished. They had all camped out in it one night until Barry's caterwauling had driven them back into the house. Janie suspected that deep down Matthew would probably have liked to set his office up there. The first year they had moved in, she had discovered some pre-war gardening tools in the shed. She loved the old patched fruit cages and the worn handles on the hedge clippers. Even her anxieties – and the white camellias at the front were not thriving as they should – seemed manageable ones here. She trudged into the shed for some bonemeal and spotted Gloria's fertiliser. Bless her. It was good stuff too.

By the time Janie returned to the kitchen, she was feeling positively perky. Even the vignette before her, of Jo-Jo hunched furtively over the telephone, evidently talking to Cassie, was no longer so alarming. 'So see you Tuesday, then,' Jo-Jo mumbled sheepishly. Child facilitators come and go, Janie thought. I'm going to make a success of this job. I'm going to turn a hopeless situation around. I'm . . .

The doorbell rang. It was her taxi. 'The flight's been changed,' the driver explained sympathetically, eyeing her nightie. 'Apparently your new ticket is at the desk. Didn't that dozy girl that works for you tell you?'

Fifteen minutes later Janie was in the back of the taxi, having shoved everything she could find into the Louis Vuitton case Cassie had lent her. There had been no time to shower, and they'd all decided it was better not to wake the children, so she had crept around the house searching for the coat Cassie said she was going to leave for her. She'd been wrong about spring too; it was starting to blizzard. As the taxi pulled away, Janie turned back for a final look and saw Daisy howling against the upstairs window. Barry was spraying her camellias with unfailing accuracy. It was not an encouraging scene.

It was a pretty safe bet that Janie was in the right queue. The women in front of her were in various states of undress. See-through petticoats fluttered under fur-trimmed coats and, despite the swirling blizzard, they were all bare-legged. She glanced down at her ticket and passport again, and got out the photo of Nell holding both twins in a half nelson. This morning's resolve was evaporating fast. She wished she had managed to track down Cassie's Dries Van Noten coat – and then castigated herself for being sucked into the fashion victim's cycle only thirty-four minutes into the job. She glanced idly at the news-stands, but all the front pages seemed preoccupied with the fashion shows. What was the world coming to when acres of newsprint were devoted to Givenchy's dayglo knickers?

'Janie, Janie, over here.' Sissy Sands clattered towards her in a pair of Perspex stiletto boots, pale marmalade hair flying out at right angles. 'Sorry I'm late. Angel promised me these boots would be ready to pick up yesterday, but then he went out and got stoned so he had to stay up all night to get them finished this morning. He wasn't going to bother. Said he had food poisoning or something. But I told him we'd never use so much as a bootlace of his again if he didn't get them done by seven a.m. So I got my driver to stop off on the way to the airport. Actually he was still stitching them at twenty past. I had to make the car wait forty minutes and Angel's fingers were bleeding from pushing the needle through the luminous bits, poor love. He's not used to working with Perspex. They'll probably be agony to wear. Well, to be honest, they *are* agony and I've only had them on five minutes.'

Janie looked at Sissy's rig-out aghast and hoped the rest of the queue didn't think they were together. She shuffled her trolley forward slightly.

'You won't believe it but it took the whole journey to

get them on. I bet he made them too tight on purpose. He's got my measurements for Pete's sake. But they are fantastically calf-hugging, which at the end of the day is what matters. You can't believe the fuss he made – he's obsessed with his nails. I'm sure it's kinky. "Well," I said, "does you good to go back to your roots once in a while, Angel." All that rubbish about every shoe being personally moulded by him. I bet he hasn't sullied his hands for ten years.' Her indigo eyes sparkled indignantly.

'The taxi driver had to go the fastest he's ever done. Or so he said; probably trots that out to Americans all the time. I gave him a massive tip all the same because he looked all sort of sweaty and harassed at the end and I thought it would be cheaper than being sued for bringing on a heart attack. I've upgraded us, by the way, so we don't need to be in this queue – it'll really bug the other editors, not to mention Phyllida. But I thought your stock was high enough at the *Gazette* at the moment to get away with it. Gosh,' she exclaimed, eyeing Janie's Barbour curiously, 'is that Japanese?'

She nudged her trolley, buckling under the weight of half a dozen or so black nylon cylindrical bags and a couple of trunks, into a wedge-shaped gap in the next queue, in front of two pin-striped City types who studied her Perspex boots and furry maxiskirt thoughtfully.

Janie followed gingerly and wondered how she might best channel Sissy's irrepressible energy. The fundamental problem was clearly going to be finding a pause in Sissy's stream-of-consciousness commentary in which to lodge a word, let alone teach her a few basic principles about real working life. Not that she knew anything about real working life. I must be stark, raving mad, she thought, tidal waves of panic washing over her. The only reason she had ever thought she might be able to pull this job off was because she had blithely assumed – encouraged in the mirage as she had been by Cassie – that she would have an ace assistant, someone cool, intelligent and detached who would be able to lead her through the illogical and murky workings of the fashion mind, until she could fathom it out on her own. But Sissy didn't look – or sound – like someone who could begin to understand that kind of role. Janie was, at heart, an optimist, but as Sissy babbled on, she felt gloom envelop her like a thick velvet blanket.

She looked again at the fashion editors at the front of the next queue. They must work for the glossies. If her memory served her correctly, the effect of working alongside so many middle-aged men made newspaper fashion editors dress more soberly than mag-hags. This bunch must work somewhere really avant-garde, *A La Mode* at the very least. It was incredible they hadn't been arrested for soliciting or gross indecency. She'd say one thing for fashion – with its label snobbery and inflated prices it had completely upturned thousands of years of preconceptions about what was common and tarty. 'Which magazines do they work for?' she asked Sissy.

'Oh God, *they* don't work in fashion, Janie.' Sissy could barely suppress her merriment at the notion. 'No one's worn lace slips for eons. Stockbrokers the lot of them, probably. That's the *A La Mode* and *Vogue* lot over there.'

She nodded towards the City types. Janie gave up. No doubt she'd worn some pretty silly rig-outs in her day at *Beau Monde* and enjoyed it hugely, as had Matthew. The difference, she couldn't help observing, was that she had been ten years younger. She was too old to be worrying about fashion must-haves. She scanned the fashion editors' faces for signs of kindred emotions. A transvestite was screeching at one of the check-in staff for not giving her an upgrade.

'That's Lindsey Craven from *The Python*,' said Sissy, distastefully. *The Python* was a scurrilous gossip sheet that had had the dubious distinction of being cautioned three times in the past year by the Press Complaints Commission. 'She's poison. And she really, really wanted your job.' Janie felt another surge of homesickness for Nell and the twins – an inauspicious start, she thought grimly, considering she hadn't even made it to the departures lounge.

★　　★　　★

Sissy was right about one thing, thought Janie, absent-mindedly flicking through the in-flight magazine. The other fashion editors had looked most put out to see her and Sissy in business class. Sissy had insisted they board early, in order, Janie now realised, that everyone should have to pass them on their way to Economy. 'You meet a better class of marriage material when you're at the front of an aircraft. I mean you don't get Liam and Patsy travelling coach. And in any case, it gives you an unsurpassed opportunity to gather good copy. If only Phyllida would realise that and stop obsessing about her piddling false economies . . .' Janie didn't suppose this was a good moment to tackle Sissy about budgets.

'It's Peace Grant,' whispered Sissy, grasping Janie's arm in excitement. 'She skipped last season because she was suffering from Nervous Exhaustion.' Sissy's eye popped conspiratorially. 'And we all know what *that* means – a–n–o–r–e–x–i–a,' she mouthed. Janie peered across the aisle at a frail-looking girl with long wispy hair and a ravishing if weary little face, and tried to square what she saw with the half-dressed, radiant siren she had seen staring haughtily out of billboards all over London. 'What a scoop,' exclaimed Sissy excitedly, fishing a tape recorder out of her vanity case. 'This interview alone justifies the extra money on the flight, not to mention the snazzy hotel I've booked us.'

Sissy clambered over Janie and perched on the armrest next to Peace, who was lying back with her earphones on and an eye mask clamped to her head. Sissy reached for Janie's glass of water and chucked its contents over Peace. 'Oh God, I'm *so* sorry. Here, let me.' She negotiated with the passenger next to Peace to swap seats. Janie closed her eyes and repeated the mantra Cassie had taught her to try to help her memorise the salient features of the big Italian designers. *Armani's beige army drives some people barmy; and Prada's gone Dada. But Jil cuts a cute suit and Dolce . . .*

Peace didn't return to her seat until ten minutes before they were supposed to land. 'Incredible, isn't it? Peace earns at least a million a year, and her accessories are crap. Still, I never realised she was so chatty. Didn't stop talking nineteen to the dozen. We could serialise it.'

They were delayed on the tarmac at Linate airport for half an hour because of heavy traffic. 'That just means the baggage handlers have been for an extra cappuccino break,' said Sissy sagely. By the time they disembarked there were no trolleys left and the other fashion editors were scrabbling amongst a chaotic jumble of bags from the previous delayed flights. Janie had never seen such tense expressions.

'It's very stressful,' explained Sissy, sprinting for a solitary empty trolley. 'A missing suitcase can blow your whole schedule. Still, you can always stick in a claim for five grand – you know, adding a bit on for the traumatic effects of having to do your job with inadequate cocktail wear. That's what Louisa did anyway; got enough in the end to put a down payment on her flat. The trouble was, she was usually so sloshed when she got off a plane she forgot to pick up any of her luggage. Aeroflot were completely heartless about it, I must say. Didn't give her a beanskie in compensation. Louisa said she wouldn't mind but she knew whichever Russian had pinched it wouldn't appreciate all her Helmut Lang. She never forgave Phyllida for making us fly Eastern bloc. That's why I always book British Airways now – at least you know they can afford to cough up if the worst does happen. Are you sure you've brought enough clothes?'

She darted through the exit doors and lunged towards a young Robert de Niro look-alike carrying a placard bearing the legend 'Signorina Sissy and Companion'. He was wearing a navy Barbour, almost identical to Janie's.

'*Buon giorno*, cutie,' giggled Sissy, giving him a kiss. 'Janie, this is Massimo, our brilliant driver . . . I know what you're thinking,' she trilled, as Janie gazed at the other editors languishing in the taxi queue. 'False economy, believe me. They'll probably miss the first two shows. And think of the wear and tear on the nerves. And if you book the same one for the whole week you get a discount. I think. Anyway, the price they quoted didn't sound too bad, but I'm never sure whether you divide lire by five or by seven.'

Sissy beamed up at Massimo, who manfully took the helm of her overladen trolley. 'English not too hot,' Sissy whispered to Janie, 'but a demon behind the wheel . . .' She trailed off as Massimo unsuccessfully tried to navigate her trolley round the taxi queue. Janie turned for a last look back through the glass doors and caught Silas Shoreham, *The Probe*'s supercilious part-time religious affairs correspondent, furtively combing his oily cowpat of a toupee. Every so often Silas, whose main claim to fame was that he had never once split an infinitive in print, bullied the fashion desk into sending him to the fashion shows so that he could show off his superior knowledge on every subject under the sun and make cruel jokes at the other fashion editors' expense. That put the kibosh on any hope Janie had ever had of going incognito. Silas would relay her every gaffe to all Matthew's colleagues back at *The Probe*, not to mention half a million readers. There was a sickening lurch as a lorry juddered into their back bumper. Massimo let out a steady stream of unmistakable expletives and raised his middle finger as his car rolled inexorably into Lindsey Craven's taxi.

Chapter Three

Only vaguely aware of where she was, Peace Grant fumbled for her eye mask. Slap-dash when it came to removing her make-up, hopeless at exercise, refusing point blank to tweezer her stray pubic hairs the way other models did between waxes (despite Cassie's good-natured admonishments), Peace was nevertheless meticulous about applying her eye masks. Karl Lagerfeld had even designed a quilted one especially for her. She was a poor sleeper, a state of affairs that had not been enhanced by the numerous time zones she crashed through weekly. Although she had come increasingly to rely on pills, munching her way through vast quantities of Prozac, Temazapam and aspirin, she only ever achieved fitful slumber, and had become so neurotic about the smallest chink of light encroaching into her consciousness that she'd bribed one of the chambermaids at the Grand to stick black bin-liners all over the original eighteenth-century windows. She'd also pulled out her phone socket, leaving a chunk of plaster the size of Sissy's new XTC vanity case on the floor by the bed next to an overflowing ashtray. Consequently she didn't hear the mobile at the bottom of her suitcase for several minutes. By the time she located it, whoever was calling had rung off, and Peace buried herself back under the blankets.

It had been Cassie calling from London to make sure Peace got up in time to get to the Kristof show before it was over. Finally Cassie called the hotel manager and insisted he went up to Peace's room himself to make sure she was out of bed. Cassie liked to think that she wouldn't normally nanny a girl as experienced as Peace. It wasn't true – Cassie's maternal instincts frequently got the better of her and she spent half her free time sorting out her girls' contraception, listening to boyfriend problems and sending round food parcels from Harvey Nichols' Fifth Floor and Planet Organic. In any case, Peace was easily capable of screwing up the simplest arrangement, and since this particular one involved a million dollars (she had just been appointed the face of Kristof, an open secret that was finally being officially confirmed today), the mother-hen phone calls were a legitimate business exercise.

Amando Cracci, the Grand's manager-in-chief, had pulled himself up by his bootstraps, as he liked to tell his staff, from kitchen porter to his current lofty position, and had done every job in the hotel along the way. Delivering early morning calls was not part of his mandate, but curiosity had got the better of him. She might be scrawny, badly dressed and English, but according to this mornings *La Reppublica*, she was also a modern cultural icon.

Opening the door of Peace's room – she had forgotten to lock it – he stepped into a miasma of stale cigarette smoke undercut with a sweet-sour odour he couldn't quite identify. He walked over to the bed and gingerly pulled back the covers from the swampy heap they had formed above Peace's head, and debated whether to shake the sleeping girl awake or call for an ambulance. An experienced witness of debauched hotel scenes, even he had never seen anyone emerge from such a coma-like sleep and go on to lead a normal life. 'Signorina, it's seven o'clock. I've taken the liberty of ordering your car for seven fifteen . . . you were meant to be there twenty minutes ago. The kitchen is making you a sandweech to eat on the way.' Peace jerked awake and yanked off the mask, swatting him away as if he were some kind of gargoyle that had plopped off the Duomo, and reached for her cigarettes.

Dimly recalling that she was in Milan and meant to be on her way to something important, she stumbled towards the bathroom. Dishevelled as she was – somehow she'd never quite got round to getting undressed and there was still a bit of antler in her hair from doing Paolo Bianco's show – Peace was a compelling vision. Even the mound of plaster crumbs on the carpet by the phone socket couldn't destroy the beauteous image for Amando. A mass of tangled hair, jutting cheekbones, doe-like eyes and long, spindly legs, she was undeniably a beauty. Despite the fetid bundles of clothes and overflowing ashtrays that littered his prized suite, Amando couldn't help but marvel at her fragile elegance. Suppressing a desire to skim a vacuum cleaner round the rooms then and there, he turned to the door and headed to the lift where the sounds of Peace retching over the basin reverberated quadraphonically round his freshly renovated marble hallway.

After the third time Jake had asked her whether she was still on the aeroplane, Janie resolved to bring the telephone conversation to a close. But then Gloria commandeered the line instead and gave her a twenty-minute discourse on the three different manures she had tried out on the climbing roses. Janie was grateful for the loving care the garden was receiving and extremely impressed with the speed at which Gloria's horticultural knowledge was increasing, but it made getting out early in the morning hellish.

She changed suits twice and almost regretted not bringing any of Cassie's Hungarian folk skirts with her. She had packed the more elegant classic pieces from Cassie's extensive wardrobe, in the belief that they would lend her some gravitas. But none of them made her look what Sissy would call modern, though she still couldn't decide whether this was a good or a bad thing. The main point, she was realising, was that being modern – in the fashion world's terms – meant looking rather odd. Sissy told her it was because any old person could look chic – it was far more challenging to look strange. Two years ago the stylist Isabella Blow had gone to the shows with an oily bicycle chain wrapped round her, to represent the burden women must carry through life, and as yet no one had bettered this style statement. Janie found herself wishing she'd been to art school so she could look modern, and wondered whether she ought to get her Cambodians to rustle Sissy up some manacles. No, she needed all hands on deck, or at least on Apple Mac. Doug Channing, the *Gazette*'s news editor, had already been on the line panting for copy.

'Only 'cos he's desperate to get a picture of Jess's breasts on page two. It's the same every season,' said Sissy philosophically. 'Even if you studiously avoid all mention of the B word, they edit into your copy. Might as well just give them what they want in the first place.'

'We'll see about that,' Janie snorted, resolving to revolutionise the *Gazette*'s news coverage of fashion as a matter of acute priority. She glanced at the clock, cursed, poured her untouched cappuccino into a stray plastic cup, absent-mindedly grabbed her Barbour and ran down to meet Sissy.

Sissy was nowhere to be seen, but Massimo was, prowling the lobby with one eye on his watch and the other coolly appraising every female under seventy. Taking in Janie's navy cashmere crew neck, he explained in his best American – a strangled gruffness which he mistakenly believed made him sound like Mickey Rourke – that Sissy had gone on ahead to do a backstage story.

Sissy's insatiable thirst for a story was starting to make Janie feel inadequate. Also, she couldn't understand anything Massimo was saying. He seemed to have acquired a speech impediment since yesterday. 'She gut scoop,' announced Massimo reverently for the third time, as if he personally had inculcated Sissy with the tenets of journalism. Janie wondered sourly what exactly a fashion scoop comprised. GATT talks stall over hemline disagreement? Scientists discover cure for bad taste? What would Matthew say if he knew that after all her protestations she was back trailing taffeta? That thought set her mind racing in reverse. Bugger Matthew. It was all his fault anyway. She followed Massimo to the car just in time to see it being towed away.

*   *   *

Sissy was having mixed feelings about the massive furry micro-phone she had purloined from her friend Violet, who worked at the BBC. The mike made her look very important but it was so intrusive that everyone dried up the moment she approached them. Still, she needed all the presence she could muster. There were at least twenty other journalists backstage. It was all very well Kristof's PR faxing her at seven this morning to say she could have a special backstage pass, but it wasn't much use to her if every other two-bit publication was there too. She had already had a run-in with a video crew from Caracas who had tried to film her trying to interview Grace Capshaw. And now Alice Grey was hogging Grace.

Secretly Sissy was hugely relieved not to have secured time alone with Grace, whose rampant desire for academic learning was running Sissy ragged. Ever since Sissy had made the mistake of confiding to Grace that she had read English at Cambridge, Grace had been using her as a kind of one-woman Open University course, asking her for reading lists, devouring them, demanding more, and latterly, posting her essays, great rambling tracts on a succession of Victorian depressives. The last one had been entitled 'Baudelaire's Sickness' and it had taken Sissy six entire evenings to get through it. Confiding in Grace about her Cambridge degree had been a complete fiasco. For one thing, Sissy disapproved of journalists who babbled on about themselves – unless, of course, what they were saying was a pack of lies designed to draw out the interviewee. For another, throughout her career in fashion, Sissy had gone to considerable lengths to leave people with the impression that *she* had gone to St Martin's.

She looked across to where Grace was evidently giving Alice a hard time – not for nothing was she known as Grace and Disfavour. Alice, to give her her due, appeared to be holding her own. Ever since she'd decided to reinvent herself as an underground stylist in the hope of becoming a muse to someone like Alexander McQueen, she'd successfully acquired all the characteristics of a semi-literate yob who was always sounding off about how naff all the other fashion hags looked in their labels. Grace yawned and eyed Alice's mottled legs and torn hot pants distastefully – Alice had made them herself out of a freebie Hermès rain hat and was particularly proud of them. Alice had also shaved her eyebrows and got Angel drunk and then forced him to cut her hair round a tea cosy and dye it with the leftovers of some ancient henna, which had resulted in a hideously uneven black Karen Elson Botched Bob which she had taken to back combing manically à la Monica Lewinsky. Even though no one got the ironic gesture, Sissy had to concede that going down this route had been effective: Alice had started to get pictures of herself into lots of style magazines. She watched fascinated as Alice obligingly stuck out her tongue and tilted her Nazi helmet for Kiko Umagai, a photojournalist from Japanese *Elle*, who slaved night and day during the collections to bring her readers an outfit-by-outfit account of the most eye-catching members of the fashion pack. It wasn't just Alice's strident new wardrobe that Sissy found a bit trying. Her glottal stops bruised the air around her with the fury of a prize-fighter who finds himself being mugged on the way back from the cashpoint. It was a bit rich given that Alice had taken the fifth-form prize for Girl Who Tries Hardest at Roedean. But Alice was a brilliant source of magazine gossip and her flat was almost as disgusting as Sissy's, so a love–hate relationship persisted between them. Besides, Sissy could see why Alice was transforming herself. She had to get herself noticed. She couldn't stay on work experience at *A La Mode* for ever: fifty pounds a week hardly met the down payments on her handbags, let alone her bed-sit.

The money was one reason why Sissy stuck it out on newspapers. Whenever Phyllida's open pores and the combined psychedelia of the newsroom's novelty knitwear got too much for her, she simply repeated the mantra 'thirty thousand pounds a year' over and over to herself. In an ideal world she would have loved to swan around on *Vogue* or one of the other glossies. But a girl had to live, and she was always broke as it was. She caught Grace trying to catch her eye and sighed. She'd have to tackle her sooner or later. A few days earlier Grace had been 'released' from a four-year contract with Vittorio e Fratelli, the successful Neapolitan duo whose business had skyrocketed recently. It was a big story that begged all kinds of questions. Grace was pushing thirty, and although she was arguably the biggest name in the business, she couldn't go on for ever.

Sissy stuffed the microphone into the XTC raffia basket she had bought yesterday, and gazed upon it lovingly. For the past two years, the two Ecstasia sisters, Giovanna and Donatella, had managed to produce the season's key accessory – the one object that united all fashion editors; the first season it had been a wooden wedge; the next an enamel choker. Last season's python boots had propelled the once-small family business on to the stock exchange. The new baskets hadn't even gone properly into production yet, but they had all the hallmarks of a cult. Massimo, whose sister worked in the XTC warehouse on the bleak outskirts of town, had bought ten of them and was selling them on to favoured clients at a minimum mark-up of two hundred per cent. Unfortunately the baskets weren't waterproof, and Janie couldn't understand why Sissy didn't wait until the weather got warmer to use hers, even though she kept trying to explain that being ahead of the fashion pack meant not just having the key accessory, but having it in the wrong season before anybody else. By summer Sissy would have moved on to the winter collections.

'Isn't your body permanently at the wrong temperature, or do fashion people all live in their own microclimate?' Janie had asked, eyeing Sissy's halter neck suspiciously. Sissy looked at her mystified. It was going to be an uphill process educating Janie. What with Grace as well, she ought to join the NUT.

'Pathetic, isn't it?' sneered Alice, mooching up to Sissy. 'No one's done ponytails for yonks. How's a woman s'posed to look modern when her follicles are slowly being asphyxiated? Enrico's only doing them because he wants to plug his crappy new Stay "n" Hold gel.'

They both looked at Grace, who was simultaneously blowing smoke and wisps of her chiffon collar out of her mouth and scowling in the mirror while her dark glossy mane was wrenched back into a ponytail. Beneath the famous circumflex-shaped eyebrows, one eyelid was daubed with a deep slick of orange gunk. Why, when all the other models were wearing the same exotic-warrior make-up, did Grace manage to look far and away the most terrifying? Sissy, who was acutely aware of the hierarchy that operated backstage, knew that Grace would be fuming that Enrico wasn't doing her hair. Ever since he had flown out to Los Angeles to sculpt Nicole Kidman's hair for the Oscars, Enrico had been unbearable, refusing to sully his hands on all but the most up-and-coming scalps. Poor Grace was more been-and-going.

She scanned the room to check who Enrico, in his new mission to be seen as happening and avant-garde, was oiling up to. Sure enough, he was flexing his hairdryer over Tulah Delaney's paprika-coloured wisps. The more fabulous your career, the more you were only allowed to be surrounded by other people on a similar trajectory. He saw Sissy and waved. He was desperate to get a story about his new oil-free conditioners into the *Gazette* and had been on a charm offensive for months. Sissy's bathroom cabinet was overflowing with samples.

'He doth bestride the centre parting like a colossus and we petty men walk under his huge Cuban heels,' giggled Alice.

'I know what you mean. It almost makes you feel sorry for Grace,' said Sissy, softening. 'She used to be the superest of them all. And at least she believes in making a dress look as fabulous as possible and not slouching around as if she had osteoporosis.'

'Don't make me hurl,' said Alice, grinding her cigarette into a pot of Enrico's Whoosh 'n' Blow. 'How you can pity Her Fabulousness after the way she harassed you over *The Mayor of Casterbridge* I don't know. Look, if she cared so much about her precious status she wouldn't keep doing all those cheesy high-street campaigns. Ooh, fabulous – there's trouble at mills.'

Stacey Mills, a myopic-looking fifteen-year-old newcomer with wire-coat-hanger shoulders, had wandered up to Isabella Suarez, an unhinged Brazilian with concave breasts, and asked her nervously if she could borrow her eye-shadow brush. 'Only the make-up people are running late and I think I've got the hang of what they've been doing . . .'

'Oh, great idea,' said Isabella neutrally. Stacey brightened in the first glimmer of warmth she had experienced in weeks. 'Then we can all get conjunctivitis. Tell you what, why don't you pass it round the whole room?' Her voice rose. 'Then when you've finished you can stick it up Kristof's chihuahua's backside.' She picked up the pot with the remains of Alice's cigarette in it and dropped it daintily at the girl's feet. 'Here, this should suit your standards of hygiene.'

Grace shuddered. Whatever happened she didn't want to end up like Isabella, whose career had been through more highs and lows than a cardiogram. Isabella couldn't think of life after modelling, and became increasingly manic in her bid to remain at the top. Her latest comeback was almost entirely sustained by a prune juice diet and a radical realignment of her cheekbones. She picked up her copy of Bertrand Russell's *History of Western Philosophy* and tried to suppress her fury and humiliation. She was devastated that Enrico had so far studiously ignored her. Supermodels got supersnippers – particularly when there were camera crews around.

Christ, when she thought of the times she'd helped him out. All those years ago (ten, or was it twelve? – she'd lied so often about her age she sometimes had to ask Cassie what it really was) when she was the most talked-about discovery of the year and she'd found him sweeping up split ends in Vidal Sassoon's . . . Grace had just been discovered and all the magazines were scrabbling to get her on their cover. She had gone to Sassoon's for a lark; it was the first West End salon she'd ever been into. She'd struck up an instant rapport with the slim-hipped, suntanned junior. He'd been head to toe in black, quite a novelty at the time, with a gold hoop through his ear that made him look like George Michael. The star stylist couldn't fit her in – she wasn't famous yet – and Enrico, seeing her desperation, has shyly offered to pop round to her place and do it that evening.

He had been a great cutter, she'd give him that. She'd raved about him to the fashion editors at *Vogue* and *Beau Monde* until they'd booked him for his first-ever magazine shoot. They'd had a ball that first session in Antigua. He had a real gift for flattery — he was, as he never tired of telling everyone, from Seville, though Grace happened to know his parents had settled in Cardiff in 1961 and Enrico had visited Spain twice in his entire life; the paella got him down. Ultimately she decided against having an affair with him, although she had very nearly succumbed to his macho patter during a shoot in Patagonia. They'd do much better, Grace told him, to remain best friends. And she'd been right; they had been a more or less inseparable team. Rising inexorably to the top, like the bubbles in Kristof's anti-wrinkle water spritzer, they floated through charmed lives in a froth of mutual loyalty. Year after year they topped the magazines' lists of power couples. The *Independent on Sunday* had even run a How We First Met feature on them. Glamorous apart, they were substantial together.

But recently they hadn't seen much of each other. She had put this down to the fact that Enrico had been busy working on his new range and collaborating with Katie Myers, the respected New York beauty writer, on a glossy coffee-table tome about his genius. But perhaps he had been avoiding her. Grace was too shrewd not to have realised that latterly her career had shifted into a different gear. She was still making more than enough to keep her accountants happy, but she was less and less frequently booked to do cutting-edge editorial. Sven Tolssen hadn't shown any interest in photographing her for sixteen months or more, and the last time she'd bumped into him at some awards dinner, she could have sworn he'd looked bored. Perhaps it was time for a full and frank discussion with Cassie.

She drifted back to the very early days, when Cassie had discovered her. It had been a classic scenario, real rags-to-riches stuff — or rather Brixton, where Grace lived with her father, to Belgravia, which is where Cassie's tiny offices had just moved to. Grace would be forever grateful to Le Fou, which had, at the time, been Chelsea's most fashionable restaurant, for double-booking Cassie's table. Instead Cassie had gone next door to the Dome, where Grace was working as a waitress. 'I'm an agent,' Cassie had told her in her deep, attractive, trust-me voice, 'and I think you could be a very big star.' She had left her card on the little silver plate, along with a tip, and Grace, summoning up all the worldliness she possessed, had shrugged, and merely lifted what she hoped was a sardonic eyebrow when the other waitresses quizzed her.

Cassie had managed her career extremely shrewdly. Within six months she had her first *Beau Monde* cover. Then the *Vogues* began using her. At Cassie's suggestion she did *The Face*, naked except for a pair of trainers – for street credibility, Cassie had explained – and after that she had become ubiquitous in all the most stylish magazines. At twenty she had been round the world three times and received thousands of letters from ethnic girls who told her how inspiring they found her (not that her Middle Eastern looks were very defined. Her father was half Algerian, which meant that while Grace was gorgeously exotic, she was easily Western enough not to deter magazine editors from putting her on their covers).

She snapped out of her reverie to see Enrico's sorrowful eyes lock with hers in the mirror in a hollow attempt at intimacy. Behind him cowered Jean-Jacques, his chief assistant. Funny how most of her conversations over the past decade had taken place with people's reflections. Everyone she knew always looked beautiful, whether they were angry, frightened or subsumed with grief. No face-contorting grimaces for them – they'd all scrutinised themselves in the mirror far too often for that.

'Hi, Graceful.' Enrico's oleaginous South London lilt shouted to make itself heard above the roar of hairdryers. Grace's expression hardened momentarily before settling into an inscru-table blank – always a bad sign in Enrico's experience. Any moment now, he thought, she would lower her eyelids halfway, suck in her cheeks and fix him with the haunted look she had used to such memorable effect in her billboards for Cal Boyd's jeanswear. On cue, Grace narrowed her marmoset eyes and projected her voluptuous, famous lower lip as far as she could without disturbing the equilibrium of her startling contours.

To the neutral observer, this in itself was a dazzling work of art. To Enrico it was another reminder of why, three months from her thirtieth birthday, Grace really ought to consider retiring from the catwalk. She had, as he knew, scores of facial expressions which she had rehearsed thousands of times in front of cameras and mirrors, each in its own way a gorgeous construct. And that was the problem. The industry had moved on from the rehearsed and the perfect.

'C'm'on, Gracie,' he wheedled. 'You know I wouldn't ask just anyone. But I thought you'd be fabulous at showing Jean-Jacques the ropes. He's a total genius, but a bit nervous and some of the girls just aren't up to it.'

'Why don't you ask the Honourable Unity Montcreith, then? She simply *oozes* confidence.' Grace jabbed her blusher brush through a gathering nimbus of hairspray and *abyss!*, Kristof's latest scent, in the direction of Unity's traumatised hair, which was starting to look like an artistic arrangement of burnt-out filaments.

What was it with Grace? Enrico fumed inwardly. Couldn't she see that he was in the middle of doing Unity's *and* Tulah's hair, a stressful and complicated procedure, since Unity had dyed her carrot crop so many different colours in the last three months that it was in imminent danger of coming away in somebody's hands. And Enrico didn't want them to be his. She was also a model whose time was now, unlike Grace, who should have the dignity to get out and get on with the business of making exercise videos. He levitated his hands in a beseeching gesture, the way Warren had in *Shampoo*. 'I'll get to you as soon as I can.'

'Oh, please,' said Grace coldly, 'don't let me distract you from the landed gentry. I gather forelock-tugging is next season's big look.'

Grace was going to have to get over this prima donna act, thought Enrico huffily – it really dated her. In the next mirror, Isabella was having a mini-tantrum over the sleeveless toga Kristof had designed for her first entrance.

'She's been in a foul mood all week,' confided Jean-Jacques

to Grace. 'Jasper Goldfarb just cancelled her for his international lingerie campaign. He threw a fit when he saw the swastika on her bicep.'

'Why in God's name did she get it done?' asked Grace, who was always appalled whenever any model deliberately vandalised her God-given beauty.

'The tattooist told her it was the CND symbol.'

It would be amusing, thought Grace, if only she didn't have to work with these people.

Janie got to the entrance twenty minutes after the show was supposed to start. The combination of nerves and her Barbour had made her perspire profusely. Her cheeks were vermilion, and to make matters worse a Japanese girl had insisted on taking half a roll of pictures of her, which made her even later. Eyeing the half-dozen bouncers in their Ray-Bans and shiny mafiosi suits, she was appalled to find herself shaking. Christ, she was stressed out, and she'd only seen two shows – well, one and one-fifth. They'd missed most of the first one yesterday because Sissy had got Massimo to run them past the Gucci store on the way from the airport so that she could pick up a pair of sharkskin flip-flops before all the others got there.

'*Scusa, mi scusa. Stampa. Sono molto* – er, late.' Janie brandished an invitation in front of the Ray-Bans.

''S okay' said one, nodding her through. 'Chill out. It no start for one more hour.'

Janie squeezed past. It was dark inside the auditorium, apart from some Mount Olympus-style torches which were lining the walls and fizzing ominously. The room was packed – standing room only. A low-level disgruntled buzz had settled over the place. She stumbled over a dozen pairs of bony knees to get to her seat, only to discover it was already occupied.

'Er, *scusa*. My seat,' she said politely. Sissy had told her to be really authoritative. 'My seat. Look, here's my invitation,' said Janie firmly. 'Pees off,' came the reply. Janie retreated back across the scrawny knee-caps – it was like wading through the killing fields. A slow handclap was gathering momentum, and for a moment, thinking it was something to do with her, Janie blushed furiously. She eventually found perching room on some steps, a few feet along from a phalanx of photographers. She sat down with a thud. From the recesses of her bag she heard a tinkling that sounded like glass shattering.

'Oh, typical. Bloody typical,' hissed a woman who was being forcibly lifted from her seat two rows from Janie by two immense bodyguards. In the half-light Janie could just make out Lindsey Craven's curtain of straight red hair and purple moue of a mouth. 'Oh, *très chic*,' came the unmistakable patrician purr of Silas Shoreham sucking on a Fox's Glacier mint. '*The Python*'s esteemed fashion editor is being evicted before the show even starts.'

'Up to her usual tricks, I see,' said a dapper voice behind Janie. 'Lindsey never sits in the seat actually allocated to her. Usually because it's in the twelfth row and she considers it beneath her station. *The Python* sells three point five million and some – and it's Europe's fastest-growing newspaper.' He had assumed Lindsey's affronted, nasal twang. 'Allow me to introduce myself. Magnus Finnegan, the *Daily Clarion*.' He held out a gloved hand. 'Now let me see, you must be the new gel on the *International Gazette*. What do you think of it all so far? Pretty motley crew, aren't we?'

Through the murk Janie just made out two coruscating blue eyes, behind a pair of lorgnettes. 'I say,' he exclaimed, as Lindsey Craven's fishnet legs stomped past, 'do you think she's concurrently working on an undercover story on Milanese prostitutes? You were saying, my dear?'

'I was wondering how long the shows normally take to get started. When I used to cover them years ago they were only an hour late.'

'Oh, we count ourselves lucky nowadays if they start the same day. If you get bored just amuse yourself by reading the murdered syntax in this press release. Whoever translated it should be done for grievous bodily harm to the English language.'

Janie cast her eyes over the eulogy Kristof's PR department had cooked up: 'Kristof's new collection is a disturbance of art, removed from its value of isolated fruition, for the modern woman who instinctively understands the purity and puritanism of Plato, and yet at the same time, simultaneously as it were, worships at the shrine of religious modernity . . .'

'Now, where was I?' continued Magnus. 'Ah yes, that woman centre-front at the end of the catwalk with the sausage-roll hairdo is Suzy Menkes of the *Herald Tribune* and the one next to her in the sunglasses is Anna Wintour, the editor of American *Vogue*, and the one next to Anna, with the cloak and unfortunate squint, is Suzy's American counterpart, Petronella Fishburn, the Slasher of Seventh Avenue, so called because of her cutting reviews. They're just about the most powerful triumvirate in the business. That odiferous little twerp behind us' – he lowered his voice – 'is Silas Shoreham, The SS for short. Thinks he's so intellectual . . . happen to know he cheated in his finals.' He paused while Silas leant forward to rummage in his briefcase for another sweet. 'He was sitting behind me then. The rustling was unbelievable. Nothing's changed . . .'

Janie stared across the catwalk; the first two rows, masqued by sunglasses, looked like a wall of shiny black sequins. 'Good Lord, who's that?' she asked, as a tall, thin woman with exquisite posture and an immaculate melon-coloured bob was ushered to the seat freshly vacated by Lindsey Craven. Against the backdrop of long nails and dark sweaters, her lilac shift dress made her look like an exotic hothouse flower.

For once Magnus was stumped. The slow handclap was now accompanied by foot-stomping. Heidi Reitvelt, the languidly elegant editor of *Prachtvoll* magazine, had fallen out with Kristof last season over the number of advertising pages the designer had taken and was threatening to lead a walk-out in the German section of the audience. 'Watch that space,' advised Magnus. 'I think we're about to witness bloodshed.'

There was a fresh flurry at the end of the catwalk as Nancy O'Kelly, the diminutive folk singer with a buzz-cut and an album that had been at the top of the US charts for twenty-three weeks, arrived with a retinue of bodyguards, press attachés and Clio Toris, the bald model with whom she was conducting a tumultuous affair.

'Heavens, Kristof really is pushing the boat out this season,' Magnus exclaimed. 'He must have paid Nancy O'Kelly a king's ransom to come to the show. She certainly won't have come out of love for his clothes. She only wears Jean-Paul Gaultier's menswear.'

Janie adored Nancy O'Kelly's music and fished in her bag for her spectacles so that she could gaze on the purveyor of all those sensitive lyrics, only to discover the source of the earlier crunching. All that remained of her glasses was one shattered lens. The other had ground itself into a thousand discarded chewing gum wrappers. Great, she thought miserably. No bloody seat, and no bloody vision.

Sissy's attention had momentarily been diverted from Grace by a slender, olive-skinned boy who would have been rather good-looking if it weren't for his goatee beard. She'd noticed him backstage before, but he never hung around for long and didn't seem to have any identifiable job. If he was hoping to become a model groupie, he had his work cut out. It was standing room only backstage, what with all the unkempt rock stars and actors and their attendant paparazzi littering the place. Jason Buzzard, the attractively dishevelled lead singer with Stench, was ogling Tulah's every pout. It was always the same, thought Sissy – whenever a celebrity had a new film or record to plug they suddenly discovered an all-consuming interest in bias-cut dresses and herringbone tweed.

The floors and counters were strewn with fashion detritus – bleeping mobile telephones, packets of cigarettes, bottles of Evian and state-of-the-art vanity cases. Some of the models had already been harnessed into their saffron leather togas with chiffon trim and were fanning themselves manically. Enrico's chirpiness seemed to have switched to low voltage as he watched his hairdos wilt in the heat like mounds of dying maggots. Dodie

Kent, a normally cheery-looking brunette, leant over a vast palette of eyeshadows and attempted, for the umpteenth time, to tone down the orange. She was flushed to the boundaries of her extensive cleavage and wished desperately that she had finally had the nerve to tell Kristof what to do with his Aphrodite-meets-Demi Moore concept. But that was Kristof: too many girls to do in too short a time – and too much money to say no. Out of the corner of her eye Dodie saw Isabella Suarez frantically beckoning to her. 'Here, take this,' Dodie said soothingly, handing a baby wipe to Stacey, who had been dabbing at her smudged lipstick so long she was about to make her mouth bleed. 'I'll be with you as soon as I've finished Isabella.' She could sense Enrico looking at her scornfully. He disapproved of senior artistes wasting time on rookies. 'It'll only take a tick,' she mouthed helplessly.

Enrico looked at Dodie scornfully. Momentarily deflated, he headed off towards Grace for some banter, and then decided against it for fear of being bullied into doing her hair. Pity her career was on the slide – he would miss her sardonic comments. Relatively deep in thought, he almost collided with Sissy.

'Sis,' he exclaimed, carefully navigating past the microphone. 'What have you been doing with yourself? – you look genius.'

'Thanks. I might ask the same of you, you naughty boy. This hair is pretty genius too,' said Sissy, gesturing towards Brigitte. 'For the benefit of my esteemed readers, can you tell me: what exactly *was* the concept here?'

From the recesses of Grace's Hermès bag her mobile rang. It was Cassie. 'Tell me it's not true,' Cassie's voice crackled cheerfully. 'Tell me Dodie hasn't put you all in orange lipstick.'

'Worse,' said Grace flatly, 'she's only put half of us in it. The audience is baying for blood. And those scrawny airheads Peace and Bethany haven't even shown up yet. Tell me, Cassie, was I as bloody arrogant as those silly, emaciated bitches when I started out?'

'Far worse,' replied Cassie breezily. 'Don't you remember telling Gianni Versace that you wouldn't be in his show until he pulled himself together and started designing clothes that didn't insult women?'

'But that was because I cared about him wasting his talent, poor darling. Not because I couldn't be bothered to get out of bed,' retorted Grace. 'And look at me now, pounding up and down the catwalk like the worst kind of whore for any has-been with enough money.'

'Talking of cheque books,' began Cassie smoothly, 'I wondered whether you'd like to fly back to London tomorrow for the première of the new Bond. They want to up the glamour quotient and they've agreed to pay you an obscene amount.'

'But I've got the shows – and you know I hate being part of rent-a-crowd.'

There was a pause. 'Actually the bookings have been a teeny bit slow this season, Grace. The last ones were confirmed today . . .' Cassie reeled off half a dozen lucrative but lacklustre names. None of the more prestigious, cutting-edge designers had requested Grace.

'But what about Aeron?'

'Oh, darling, his clothes are getting more and more absurd. Do you really want to put yourself through all that and all for the sake of being paid in Boob-Buggers?'

Grace knew that this was Cassie's diplomatic way of telling her she could no longer carry off Aeron's esoteric flights of fantasy. She had to admit that last season's Boob-Bugger, a metal device that Aeron had inserted into all his clothes to squeeze the breasts together until they looked like ripe pairs of buttocks, had been a disaster for all concerned. He'd practically given them away at the sample sale.

Yet even though he could only afford to pay them in clothes, Aeron's show was a benchmark of any model's career. Girls not booked for it made sure they were out of town that night, ostensibly on lucrative advertising contracts, although as everyone knew, no fashion house would schedule any business involving a half-decent model on the same night as Aeron's shows. Last season Isabella had faked her own mother's death so she would have an excuse not to be in town.

Fortunately for Grace, she and Aeron went way back. He didn't mind that her career had recently taken a mass-market turn ('It's totally genius,' he had said warmly of her swimwear calendar). There was no way she would miss his show; it was her best chance of proving to Sven Tolssen she could still be cutting-edge.

A minor scuffle broke out by the door and a score of flash-bulbs detonated as Kristof entered, his customary solid-silver walking cane dangling over the crook of one arm, and Peace Grant nestling in the other. His eyes, as tiny as the diamond studs glinting in Peace's ears and equally sharp, darted round the room suspiciously. 'Stand back, stand back PUH – LEASE,' beseeched Kristof's exhausted PR. Waiting with Kristof for Peace to show up had proved the longest two hours of his life. 'Signor Kristof is about to make an important announcement front of stage about the new face of Kristof.'

'Is it true it's Peace?' piped up Leonie Uttley. 'And what about Beatrice Le Clerk,' she continued, referring to Kristof's erstwhile muse. 'Are you two really not talking?' Kristof extracted one of his four hundred antique Irish linen handkerchiefs from his left breast pocket and mopped the black hair dye trickling down his hairline.

'Frankly, if Beatrice stopped speaking to one, would one notice?' Leonie tittered sycophantically. 'I would never speak ill of Beatrice,' Kristof boomed, 'but for her to declare that she is retiring from modelling is a bit like an amputee saying they have had enough of the decathlon – redundant.' He lumbered round to face the cameras. 'Yes, as I am shortly to announce, Peace *is* the new face of Kristof . . . Peace in our time . . .' he guffawed. 'And I know that the thousands of women who buy Kristof will take her to their hearts.' He launched into a drone about how modern and youthful Peace was while his arms tightened proprietorially around her drooping shoulders.

In the absence of Grace, Enrico rolled his eyes conspiratorially at Bethany, who had finally arrived from another show where, to Enrico's fury, her hair had been caked in red clay. Stefano, the hairdresser responsible, had only done it out of spite, because he knew it would hold Enrico's team up even more. Enrico grabbed Bethany's head and thrust it under a hand shower. Bethany winced and motioned for him to light a cigarette. For someone who had kept a thousand people waiting for nearly two hours, albeit unwittingly, she looked remarkably serene, thought Enrico.

Twenty minutes later, he had resigned himself to the fact that his vision wasn't to be entirely realised. He'd given up on the Stay 'n' Hold and was gluing Bethany's more stubborn coils on to her scalp instead, hoping she wouldn't notice. 'Chill out,' he said when Dodie pointed frantically at her watch. 'It's only fashion.' Bethany, who had never thought she'd hear Enrico, of all people, utter such a heresy, stared at him in amazement while a dollop of Superglue dribbled down her cheek.

On the other side of the catwalk, Magnus Finnegan had finished dissecting the journalists for Janie's benefit and had moved on to the socialites. He was interrupted by Nick Squire, the *Gazette*'s new catwalk photographer, who sauntered up to Janie, his Minolta zoom lens cannoning into a dozen heads along the way.

'Watch it, moron,' screeched Lindsey Craven as he knocked her tiara flying. Ignoring her, Nick launched into Magnus's punch line. 'Just thought I'd let you know I'm off to wire the piccies. Catch you at one of the other shows?'

'But this one hasn't even started,' remonstrated Janie.

'Yeah, well, I used all me film up on Nancy O'Kelly. She had 'er tongue in Clio Toris's ear for a good eight minutes. Tried to catch your attention to see if you was of like mind, but you was too busy gassing.' Phyllida had drafted Nick in at the last minute from *Blitzkrieged!!*, a scurrilous underground gossip magazine which normally paid him to doorstep royals. Something told Magnus it had been a big mistake.

'Don't worry,' Nick breezed, catching Janie's horrified expression, 'the news desk'll love it . . . at least the news desk at *Blitzkrieged!!* would have done,' he muttered as he trotted off. You could never tell with these posh papers. Still, nothing ventured, nothing gained. And on second thoughts, maybe he did have just one film left.

Cocooned in her orange Kristof towelling robe and trying not to dislodge the cotton wool wedged between her tangerine-tipped toes, Grace padded over to the rail where her six outfits were hanging in order of hideousness, complete with matching orange tights and shoes. Seeing them reminded her of the débâcle at the fitting the night before, when Kristof had accused her of putting on weight. He was just saying this to taunt Grace. He had hired Sophie Dahl to promote his knitwear range, and had been sweatily excited by the first Polaroids showing the gaudily patterned tank dresses stretched across her ample curves. But it had plunged Grace into a depression all the same.

'Bet yours aren't as gross as mine,' a throaty Scottish drawl burbled behind her.

'Jess,' exclaimed Grace, throwing her arms around the sun-scorched Glaswegian. 'I seem to recall that as of last season you weren't ever – and I quote – going to haul your ass down the runway for a bunch of demented, sad tossers again.'

'I wasn't, but the movie's been postponed. Judd Ragley's had a tragic dye job. They spent twenty thousand dollars flying Stefano in to get his hair back to its natural colour, but it still showed up blue in the rushes. So we're all on sabbatical till it grows out.' She waggled her little finger for Grace's benefit so that she could see the enormous diamond ring on it. 'A present from Judd for being such a pain. Anyway, Milan here I am – ready to indulge in a little shopping, a little partying and *lots* of money-making. I have to subsidise my artistic pursuits, you know. Okay,' she said, eyeing Grace's sardonic expression, 'I admit it. The script of *Stoned Again* lacks a certain depth . . .' She broke off, giggling. 'Anyhow, where have *you* been? I tried calling the Grand but they said you'd checked out.'

'They double-booked my room,' said Grace gruffly. It was a sore point. 'Peace bloody Grant got it.'

'Oh well, move in with me. I've got Enrico's suite at the

Four Seasons. First come, first served, as they say. You look great, by the way.'

'I feel like shit,' said Grace flatly. 'And more to the point, Kristof practically told me I look like it.'

'Oh, I wouldn't take any notice of someone with quite such a marked predilection for pubescent boys. No, you look younger. Let me guess – Dr K upped the botulism injections?'

'Suffice to say I've almost lost the entire use of my upper face. No more frown lines or crows' feet for me. Of course I can't actually close my eyes properly and if they cut me open there's enough germ warfare slugging away under my forehead to wipe out the world's population . . . What are we doing to ourselves?'

'Best not to think about it,' said Jess cheerfully. She began humming the tune of 'Rebel Rebel'. 'We'll die young but we'll look divine . . . Now where's that little shit Enrico? Enrico.' She popped a finger and thumb into her mouth and whistled. 'Get your gorgeous little backside over here and finish our hair . . . Jeeze, is that really how Kristof wants us to look?' She shuddered delicately at the streaked orange eyeshadow Dodie and her team were smearing on in mounting frenzy.

'Oh well, once more unto the peach, dear friends.'

Sissy had been riveted by the little scene she had just witnessed in a corner of the room. The Goatee Beard had sidled up to Peace, handed her a tiny package and then sidled off again. Nervous exhaustion indeed. God, the sheer brazen cheek of it. In no doubt as to what was in the package, Sissy scurried over to Peace. Even though Dodie was mid-smear, Sissy flung her arms around Peace's hunched body and warmly asked how she was doing. It was a ploy she frequently used on strangers and it never failed. Either they were too shocked to tell her to get lost, or they assumed they must know her from somewhere and felt guilty for having forgotten who she was. Anyway, after their conversation on the plane, she felt she and Peace were practically sisters.

'How are you doing? You look wonderful,' gushed Sissy. 'Oh.' She knocked her heel against Peace's crocheted bag, nudging out the little packet, and stooped to scoop it up. Miraculously energised, Peace ducked down and snatched it from her. 'Headache pills to take the pain of Kristof's colour clashes?' asked Sissy jovially. 'Or diet pills? Whoops, forgot. *You* don't need those, do you . . . ?' Before Peace could retort, Dodie, who always took the side of any model where a journalist was concerned, hastily rammed her mascara wand into Peace's open mouth on the pretext that it would help her draw a more accurate apricot outline.

'Christ!' exclaimed Alice, watching Grace and Jess zip each other into their togas. 'Which of your mentors said that the only bad taste is no taste?'

'Diana Vreeland,' said Sissy instantly.

'Well, she was wrong.'

A row was reaching crisis point by the stairs to the catwalk. Isabella Suarez was squawking at the girl in headphones. 'There's been a mistake. I'm going out first. It's in my agreement with Kristof. I open and I close this show.'

'No,' persisted the headphones valiantly, 'Peace does.' She ran a finger down her list. 'You are third, twelfth, thirty-third. And in the finale,' she added brightly. Isabella let out a raucous, half-strangled scream. In the harsh light, her elongated features, flattened by the orange panstick, looked almost freakish, as if they had been stretched out on CineScope. 'Are you crazy? Peace is a leetle runt from Nowheresville.' She began waving her fists and yelling for Kristof.

Kristof lumbered up, beads of sweat glistening in the undergrowth of his black sideburns. 'Isabella,' he wheezed menacingly, 'if I were you I'd be thankful to be anywhere in this line-up.'

A techno version of 'Zorba the Greek' started up. Peace extracted a cigarette from her exquisite little mouth and stubbed it out with Brigitte's beaded handbag. She threw a pitying glance at Isabella, took a deep breath in the darkness and began to glide down the catwalk towards the phalanx of spotlights and blinding flashbulbs at the end.

★   ★   ★

Jess and Grace caught up on each other's gossip over a pot of hot water in Luigi's. Grace thought Jess looked wonderful – less thoroughbred these days perhaps, but much sexier. Jess thought Grace looked – not tense exactly, that went without saying – but weary, sad even. It was as if she were wearing a mask. The features were just as striking, just as harmoniously aligned, but the animation that made Grace so arresting had vanished.

'So how is LA?' Grace asked.

'Shallow, callow and disgustingly vulgar. I'm loving it. How 'bout you?'

A waitress in a black dress and frilly apron approached their table with a jug of steaming coffee. Regretfully they declined and asked for more lemon instead. Caffeine was a major taboo on Dr Keller's Beautiful For Life programme. It was one of the unhappier discoveries in their lives, that as they approached thirty their stupendous natural assets were becoming a little more artificial.

Grace wondered whether Jess knew that her relationship with Enrico was on the skids, her contract with Jolie Cosmetics up for renewal and her editorial bookings not as scintillating as they might be. She flirted briefly with the idea of confessing all, but decided to save her depression for Cassie. A year or so ago she had fantasised about carrying on into her fifties, of becoming a British Carmel dell' Orefice. But it was becoming increasingly hard to deal with the rejections.

'So tell me about the film.'

'Well, I get gang-banged in the first scene. Murdered in the fifth and then it turns into a comedy. It's quite a challenge, as you can imagine,' said Jess merrily. 'Talking of losing the plot, I hear *Beau Monde* Publications has offered Sven Tolssen five million pounds to work exclusively for them,' she went on.

'First I've heard. Does Dr K deliver gossip intravenously?' asked Grace, amazed at her friend's antennae. 'Did Cassie tell you?' she added jealously. Why wasn't Cassie keeping her abreast of news? Perhaps she thought it wasn't worth it.

'No, it was Zack actually. *Beau Monde*'s editor asked Zack

to look into his crystal ball and see if it would be a good move to hire Sven. Anyway, after due consultation with the stars, Zack told her it wasn't. She went ahead anyway so now Zack doesn't know if she simply ignored him or whether she misheard. Don't worry about Enrico, by the way – jumped-up little prick. I never thought he was as good as Sam McKnight.'

The discussion turned to monstrous egos, which led seamlessly to Aeron Baxter, about whom they could afford to be irreverent, safe in the knowledge that they were sufficiently part of his inner sanctum to tease him. A tortured genius whose collections were notoriously abstruse: complex puzzles of strangely beautiful, but baffling, deconstructed clothes, and only the cream of the fashion press were invited because Aeron was worried that the message behind his collections would float over most people's heads. Not that it really mattered. Hardly anyone actually bought his clothes. The chairman of Nathan Wemyss, the chain of exclusive North American department stores, had dryly remarked last year that all he'd ever managed to sell in five years of stocking Aeron Baxter's avant-garde designs were two sleeves and a hem.

But he was acknowledged to be a towering influence in world fashion, and of all the designers he was the one to whom Grace felt most loyal. Her mobile rang again. 'Grace, it's Aeron.' He sounded shaken, slightly breathless.

'Hi, honey, how's it going? Save the most slimming dress for me,' she joked.

'Isabella's been on to me again. She threatened to destroy the entire collection this time.'

'What d'you mean?' Grace asked. 'I thought you weren't taking her calls.'

'She pretended to be my mother,' said Aeron, outraged. He worshipped his mother. 'I was well peeved. Then she got a bit hysterical so I told her she was looking wicked at the moment but there was no way I could fit her into the show. She went berserk. At one stage she actually accused me of wrecking her career. Said didn't I realise she had a mother and four sisters to support.'

'Mummy's been reincarnated again, then. She has a point, though. Doing your show will get her tons more work. You do hold all our careers in your twitchy little fingers, you know,' said Grace lightly.

'I think it's serious this time. When I got back to the atelier this afternoon one of the dresses was ripped to shreds. There were jagged bits of glass all over the place and blood that looked as though it had been spray-gunned on to the appliqué. She could have confined it to the unembroidered bit. Anyway, it was her blood, I guess. A really genius colour actually – I got Squidge to Polaroid it for future reference – and a note threatening more damage.'

To the clothes or to herself, wondered Grace, and which would distress Aeron most? She banished the uncharitable thought. 'She'd signed it and stamped it with a swastika,' Aeron continued, truly appalled since his brother, unbeknown to anyone but Squidge, was a rabbi. 'Grace, I think she's just gagging to do something really bad. She's been totally mental since this latest comeback.'

Grace had gone quiet. She could tell Aeron was steeling himself to ask her something. He laughed nervously. 'Grace, I don't know how to say this, but you're the only one I can turn to.'

'Let me guess. You'd like me to pour peroxide in Isabella's champagne.'

'No.' She could hear him fiddling with a Rizla. 'I want you to give the show a miss this once and let her do it instead . . .'

'Aren't you overreacting?' she broke in. 'Or if you're so worried, why don't you just run something up for her.'

'You know I can't have an odd number in my shows.' He sounded wounded.

'But I've always done your show.' Infuriatingly she could feel her eyes beginning to smart. That was twice in twenty-four hours. 'Aeron, really, it's not a good time to ask me this . . .'

'Well then, I'm not asking,' he retorted petulantly. 'Grace, there isn't an outfit for you. Not this time . . . Grace, are you there?'

The phone clattered on to her plate. From her lap Aeron's muffled voice garbled on, first peevishly, then placating. 'Jess,' she heard herself saying in a surprisingly calm voice, 'do you mind if I give our shopping spree a miss? I'll catch you later.'

Clutching her jacket, she marched towards the front of the restaurant, sending a gaggle of bemused-looking Japanese teenagers in head-to-toe Vivienne Westwood careening into a patisserie trolley. *En route* for the door she caught sight of Sissy Sands, who was talking animatedly to a rosy-cheeked woman in a waxed coat who looked remarkably like Cassie's best friend Janie. Although the two had rarely met, Grace knew all about the tragic turn of events that had reduced Janie to grubbing around for a living as a fashion hack. Well, she might as well start her solidarity-for-hard-done-by women campaign straight away.

'Have I got a story for both of you,' she said, pulling up a chair at their table and moving aside a giant tureen of minestrone so that she could look directly at Janie. Sissy's eyes, normally vague behind her drifting violet contact lenses, suddenly became greedily focused and she passed Janie her laptop. 'Just type while I dictate,' instructed Grace.

'Today, world-famous supermodel Grace Capshaw trod the catwalk for the last time. The twenty-five, no, the twenty-*nine*-year-old face of Jolie Cosmetics, blah, blah, blah, you can fill in that bit, turned her back on the fickle, destructive world of fashion and will be studying Nineteenth-Century French Literature and Existentialism: the Missing Link at the Sorbonne. Asked why she was leaving when she was still in such demand, the highly articulate supermodel declared that she had always promised herself two things – that she would get out while her IQ was still greater than her waist measurement and while her breasts were still her own.'

When she was sure Janie had it all down, Grace strode magnificently to the door. 'My God, Janie,' gulped Sissy, wiping the condensation from the minestrone off the screen of their laptop, 'I think that's what you call a scoop *du jour*.'

Chapter Four

Jo-Jo's test shots were extraordinary, better than Cassie had dared hope. The camera had embraced her bone structure, hugged her chiselled jawline and all but self-detonated over her attenuated limbs, as Cassie had known it would. The huge mouth with the slightly asymmetrical lips (the upper one was fuller than the lower one) looked phenomenal as a sensuous pout, but even better, Cassie thought, curved into an endearingly gaping grin. As she spread the black-and-white prints and colour transparencies of Jo-Jo over her light-box, she marvelled at the mysterious process that converted some lovely faces into unforgettable ones on film.

That was part of what she loved about this business – the indefinable magic you found in one girl in every thousand – and the fact that you could never entirely predict where it would crop up. She had seen beautiful girls who looked ordinary in pictures and others with far from perfect features who radiated charisma in front of the camera. The public perception was that the model business was a meat market in human flesh, and Cassie understood that view. But on another level, *her* level, it went far beyond signing up a set of fashionable statistics. For Cassie it was about pinning down an elusive spirit, someone with strength of character and enough of a quirk in their personality to turn them into a role model for a new generation of women. A special girl, as Cassie knew, might not only become the inspiration for designers, influencing the way they thought about clothes, she could also help define the way women the world over would want to look.

And that's where Jo-Jo was a triumph. There was nothing difficult to understand or perverse about Jo-Jo's looks. She was a classic beauty. There was a languid gracefulness in the way she moved in front of the lens. She had terrific posture – a real rarity these days, and due any moment for a comeback on the catwalk. It was probably the result of Gloria's nagging, thought Cassie gratefully. There was a softness about her facial contours and a wistfulness in her eyes which gave her face a haunting quality. The cheeks hadn't lost all of their babyish fullness, which lent a heart-melting vulnerability to the slightly imperious way she held her head. Yet, for all her photogenic fragility, there was also a hint of some inner strength, stubbornness even. Other agents would have been tempted to dispatch Jo-Jo straight off to the collections, to cash in on her novelty value. God knew she was a quick study. But Cassie wanted to make sure Jo-Jo was mentally prepared. The shows were like a psychological assault course even for experienced models. It wasn't just the physical demands: seven shows a day, starting at five or six in the morning, and the fittings that went on past midnight. It was the constant pressure of having a thousand pairs of eyes scrutinising you for the faintest signs of sagging or cellulite. She wanted Jo-Jo to have time to learn that the very ordinariness of her upbringing and outlook, offset by her extraordinary beauty, could be one of her great strengths. And anyway, there were little physical details to sort out. The waist-length hair would have to go – it was thick, wavy and Jo-Jo was drowning in it. They'd take a few inches off, up to her shoulder blades, just enough to bring out Jo-Jo's fine-boned features and so that there would be plenty left to make more dramatic statements with later on. Once she was established they could give her a crop – Cassie, drunk with adrenalin, could almost calculate the column inches now.

Jo-Jo also needed some guidance with her style, especially now that all the magazines were as obsessed with what models wore off duty as with what they did on the catwalk. She must have been buying her baggy track suits at least four sizes too big, thought Cassie, and she would have to introduce Jo-Jo to a pair of tweezers. Then she'd like to get her together with Sven Tolssen and Dirk Von Litten, who, she had a hunch, was about to pull off a huge comeback. All in all, she hadn't seen such promising first pictures since . . . well, since Grace.

This was not a salutary train of thought. Cassie couldn't help feeling betrayed by Grace's latest defection. At least when she'd retired in the past she had always consulted her agent. This time she'd heard the news on her answer machine, via Janie – or an incomplete, garbled version of it. Unbeknownst to her, Zack had invited some friends round for a séance that night and unplugged the telephone halfway through Janie's message. By the time Cassie had retrieved the tape she'd pieced most of the story together from the *Gazette*'s report. To be fair, Grace had called Cassie before she called anyone else, and certainly before she told any of her family, which wasn't actually saying much, but still Cassie felt hurt. Anyway, by now, mused Cassie, glancing at the date on her organiser, Grace would be in Majorca, where she was retracing George Sand's footsteps. She had to admire Grace's determination to get an education, even if personally she doubted the merits of a university one. On the face of things, Cassie's disdain for formal education was a puzzle – it wasn't as if going to university was an everyday occurrence in her family: she had been the first. It had been brave – bloody headstrong, her father said – to give it all up. But even if she hadn't been sure, the fact that on hearing the news that she was chucking it all in her mother had gone to bed with a migraine for two months would have been enough to convince Cassie she had done the right thing.

'Want to go out for supper?' she heard herself saying to Zack on the telephone. This was one nettle she had so far failed to grasp, but tonight she would set to it with secateurs. She had to before it put down permanent roots in her home. For someone so spiritually motivated, Zack possessed an amazing number of consumer durables, all of which seemed to be rapidly finding their way into Cassie's flat. First it had been his astrological charts cluttering up the walls next to her Damien Hirst dot painting, then an exercise bike and the entire range of Clinique for men, followed by his portable wardrobe and a cabinet full of seaweed and vitamin and mineral supplements. Then there was what he laughingly called his Library, which comprised a copy of Deepak Chopra's *How to Raise Your Wealth Consciousness through Spiritual Means*, an illustrated introduction to psychic healing and a signed copy of a Jeffrey Archer. Some time in the past fortnight two hundred of his favourite CDs had turned up, although all he ever played was 'I Will Always Love You' which, Cassie had a horrible feeling, she was meant to take as deeply significant. Yesterday morning he had mumbled something about needing his trampoline and his Nordic Track ski machine.

Cassie categorically didn't want any more gym equipment littering the flat. Her own unused exercise bike, next to the state-of-the-art bathroom scales, was a constant mute reproach to her. She didn't want any more people littering the flat either – at least not Zack. He was sweet and guileless and staggeringly good-natured, but they simply weren't compatible. For one thing Zack was pathologically untidy. For another, he was completely untainted by the work ethic. He would unblushingly tell her he was knackered when Cassie knew the most taxing thing he'd done all day was turn the volume up on Whitney. Also, Zack's idea of an art-house movie was anything that didn't star Arnold Schwarzenegger.

The problem was that Cassie had simply never got to grips with ending love affairs. Despite going all the way to California last year to attend a week-long seminar on emotional closure, her track record was dismal. If anything, it had got worse since the seminar. At least in the past she'd had a vague sense of control at the start of her relationships, even if this always petered out by the end. But with Zack she didn't remember there even *being* a start. One minute they'd been having a one-night stand (literally) under the aromatherapy power shower in their gym, during which she had managed to stress – and she distinctly remembered hearing herself say this – that she wanted a strictly no-strings sex-fest. And seemingly the next nanosecond he had asked her to sign his application for a parking permit for Blomfield Road. Estelle, the manageress of Sigmund's, the self-help bookshop in Hammersmith where Cassie had whiled away many a miserable lunch-hour, said it was because Cassie subconsciously enjoyed the element of chaos this brought to her love life.

'You're such a control freak in all other areas, Cassie, that if you didn't let your romances run completely amok, your emotional life would be as lo-cal as your salad dressing.'

Cassie had been deeply stung by Estelle's comments. Was her love life so completely amok? It was true that the last person she had been remotely seriously involved with was Jim Zametti, the American-Italian head of the Bellissimo model agency in Milan, and that relationship had turned dangerously toxic after she'd discovered that he'd been repeatedly unfaithful with a succession of his models. Was her professional life sterile? More to the point, was she a control freak? Granted, the last time she was in New York she had caught herself not just buckling herself into the back seat, but jerking herself forward every five minutes to check that the fraying belt still worked and giving the Iranian driver the number of a garage she'd seen advertised in Queens that could fix new ones in two hours. But did that count as freakiness or just road safety?

'Am I a control freak?' she had casually asked Saffron, her deputy at Hot Shots.

'Is Zack thick?' was all Saffron had said, in her blunt antipodean way.

'He might not be academic,' said Cassie, who had been rereading *Emotional Intelligence* that weekend, 'but he has a certain instinctive—'

'Thickness,' said Saffron.

Cassie looked at Saffron, a wisecracking firebrand who reminded her of herself ten years ago, and solemnly resolved to delegate more and not to override anyone's decisions in the office. It had taken a great deal of soul-searching before she had handed over the men's division to Saffron, and she knew that she ought to devolve more power to some of the other bookers. It was just that every time she walked through the bookers' room and heard Karen, one of the trainees, agreeing to let Tulah model for *The Globe* or one of the other Sunday papers, she found herself snatching her headset.

'No, no, not newspapers. A girl at Tulah's level *never* does newspapers.'

'But it's for the magazine section . . . what about *Miss Behave*? Their booker's desperate. Said they've got a really amazing concept.'

'No,' hissed Cassie. '*Miss Behave* hasn't had a decent fashion editor for two years. And they can't get a good photographer to go near them.'

It had been the same thing when she'd heard Jackie negotiating fees for Brigitte to star in an East Seventeen comeback video.

'But they were paying fifty thousand a day,' protested Jackie.

'It's not the right image. When the Verve or Stench call, then we'll think about it.'

Nuances, nuances. It was so hard to teach new bookers when it was all right for girls to do lingerie (when it was Calvin Klein, Guccis, Prada or Dolce e Gabbana) and when it wasn't. When it was okay to do blatantly commercial work and when it backfired. When a cover on *The Face* could triple a girl's credibility and when it just looked foolish. When to blitz a girl's image all over the world and when to hold back. Saffron understood all of this, but she'd been at Hot Shots for eight years and back then there'd only been four of them at the agency. Now there were twenty, an annual turnover of eleven million – and Cassie simply couldn't superintend them all.

'You'll just have to learn to trust our instincts,' said Saffron, 'and that means accepting that sometimes our decisions will be different from yours. But that's okay, Cassie,' continued Saffron gently. She knew how much Hot Shots and everyone who worked there meant to her, from Grace to Millicent, the cleaner. 'You've made Hot Shots a fantastically successful midsize company. Now it can only grow from here by being diverse.'

Cassie sighed. She knew Saffron was right. But it was going to be tough. Maybe if she concentrated on her private life for a bit she would relax her grasp on Hot Shots – which brought her back to Zack. She decided to tell him her whole building was suffering from acute subsidence, was about to topple into the canal and that regrettably they would both have to move out. She made a reservation at Pharmacy, one of Zack's favourite restaurants, and spent a cheery hour leafing through back issues of *Designers' Digest*, *Elle Decoration* and *The World of Interiors* in anticipation of a new house style. It was an expensive way to get rid of somebody, but she had never been averse to redecorating Casa Cassie.

'Hi, sweetie-plops. Has Barry still got diarrhoea?' She knew how Nell enjoyed a decent scatological interlude.

But it wasn't Nell, it was a researcher from Radio 4 calling her up fearsomely early to ask if she would speak on the *Today* show about the sociological implications of Grace's retirement. Janie heard herself say no – she had heard James Naughtie and John Humphrys spray-gun the studio with the bloodied remains of too many interviewees – and also heard the researcher blithely overriding her response. 'Don't worry, we'll give you Sue MacGregor,' he said matter-of-factly. 'Speak to you tomorrow at six forty.'

'That's what you get for coming up with the scoop of the season,' chirped Sissy on the way to the Bella Scarletti show. Janie scanned Sissy's pale, freckled face for signs of envy and was impressed to find none – only a cheerful sort of camaraderie. 'Tell you what, why don't I pretend to grill you?'

She preceded to lob some harrowing questions about the fashion world at Janie while Massimo snaked around the cobbled allies of Milan looking for Bella's venue. She had been forced to switch her show to her studio at the last minute after the torches at Kristof's show had scorched one of the walls and blown the electrics.

'I don't think the questions will be that gruelling,' said

Janie testily, after Sissy had harangued her about under-age models. 'The researcher said they specifically wanted to talk about Grace. I thought I'd take the line that she was letting down older women and—'

'Let's face it, Janie,' said Sissy, 'when all's said and done it's not a very ethical world, is it? Bet they ask you about Kristof's Turkish harem. Don't s'pose they'll give you Sue MacGregor either. Still, just so long as it's not John Humphrys.'

Bella Scarletti's show was a revelation for Janie. Until now she'd only seen bits of what might have been quite promising collections or sat through interminably gruesome ones, and she had become increasingly dejected. There had been the sickening gaudiness of Vittorio Chacha's show where unspeakable things had been done to animal skins, and the mind-boggling silliness of Boldacci's Lolita revival.

But for sheer pretentiousness Antonio Viro's Eastern Bloc Redux collection, which as far as Janie could tell comprised slimy synthetic fabrics dip-dyed the colour of overboiled vegetables, took the biscuit. And the music, great gashing swoops of screeching electric guitar, followed by what sounded like veins being slashed and agonising stretches of jagged silence, had nearly driven Janie mad and sent the rest of the British contingent into uncontrollable fits of giggles. Bored almost beyond endurance, Magnus Finnegan had whispered that the reason Lindsey Craven had been directing such poisonous looks at Janie was that she was jealous of Janie's scoop. 'It means that the *Gazette* will keep you on for at least a bit – not that they'd ever give it to her anyway. Far too common.' He was silenced by another vein.

Alice thought Antonio's show was brilliant. 'He's trying to push the boundaries,' she said to Sissy. But for once Sissy found herself agreeing with Janie, and said that she thought Antonio had almost certainly hurled them over the edge. The models, according to Alice, who got it directly from Caro Luckhurst, the fashion director at *A La Mode*, had all been given strict instructions to read Karl Marx and to look as miserable as if they'd been standing in a bread queue for fifty years. 'I don't know why he didn't just make them watch the show like the rest of us,' said Sissy tartly. The models, who hated it when other designers told them to smile and do twirls, loved being in Antonio's show. It gave them a chance to method-model and they hammed it up shamelessly.

Seventy-two hours into Milan, Janie was wondering how she had ever endured this whole business last time round. The heat, in all of the shows, was suffocating, the lights scorchingly bright – and she was missing the children desperately: thrown as she was out of her normal routine, she was somehow more acutely aware than ever of the Matthew situation. She had even asked Gloria outright that morning whether there was any kind of message from him. There wasn't.

Bella's presentation was slick and upbeat: the music consisted of all Janie's favourite tracks and the models not only looked healthy, but actually seemed to be enjoying themselves. Even Peace threatened momentarily to snap out of her apathy and, by the end of the show, had almost whipped up enough energy to crack a smile, at which point she looked ravishing. The clothes were pretty good too – beautifully cut, simple shapes in sumptuous cashmeres and burnished silks. There were immaculately cut slim trousers and wraparound coats of a wool so soft and luxurious that they almost shone under the lights. The evening wear consisted of a dozen exquisite lace dresses edged with tiny bands of velvet roses. The audience, still reeling from Kristof's show and numerous other unwearable depravities, were gratefully appreciative.

'Total bloody rip-off of Comme des Garçons four seasons ago,' carped Alice afterwards. 'And did you see those velvet trims? Top Shop was doing those last summer.'

'It's definitely all about shoes this season,' explained Sissy to Janie as they trooped into the hotel bar for double *lattes*. 'And I have a theory on that. Basically, the worse your legs the more hideous the shoe should be to act as decoy. Clumpy leg equals clumpy shoe, get it? It's a sort of holistic approach—'

As they debated whether or not to move on to margaritas, the woman who had sat in Lindsey Craven's seat at Kristof's

93

show brushed past them, a pashmina shawl the size of a small Balkan state carelessly thrown round her shoulders.

'Good God, who's that?' demanded Sissy.

It was Magnus's socialite, sweeping past in another immaculate shift dress, on her way to the lifts.

'Wasn't she at Bella's show with her minder friend?' asked Sissy.

'She's been at a few,' said Janie, polishing off the last of the pistachios. 'She always creeps in just as the lights are dimming. Magnus is convinced she's an arms dealer at the very least. I'm starving. Shall we eat here before the next show or get something later?'

'No time for *food*, Janie,' said Sissy, sliding off her stool and making a beeline for the lift before its doors closed on the socialite.

There wasn't enough time to lie down before the next show so Janie went to the hotel kiosk and bought the British newspapers to read while Sissy was upstairs. She hadn't dared look at her first report – the one about Grace – because Sissy had warned her that the *Gazette*'s copy-takers always pretended to be deaf so they could stitch up reporters for a laugh. 'It's a power thing. Don't take it personally. But just be prepared for the fact that sometimes your own copy will seem like something in code,' Sissy said. But apart from spelling Cassie's name wrong, the Grace story had been error-free. Sissy must have been exaggerating or perhaps the subs had a vendetta against her.

Between them, she and Sissy were commanding a lot of column inches. Doug Channing, the paper's news editor, was thrilled. The more fashion he packed into the front few pages, the more pictures of Helena Christensen he could squeeze in. Even when she wasn't in a show Doug's imagination found ingenious excuses for running pictures of her. Today Sissy had something on page three about backstage neurosis, which also contained some pretty heavy innuendo about backstage narcotics. 'God knows what he'll do when Helena retires,' said Sissy. 'Check himself into a rest home for traumatised old hacks probably. Still, better Doug than Phyllida. At least he likes fashion.'

Sissy was very good, Janie had to acknowledge, at taking a tabloid subject and couching it in broadsheet language. Janie, on the other hand, only seemed able to achieve the opposite. Every time she tried to write an important, probing piece it just came out trashy and glib. Yesterday she'd offered to write a serious piece about the powerful women who were taking over Italy's famous fashion institutions, but while she was trying to explain it to Doug, on the hotel phone in the lobby, a cracking row between Tulah and her actor boyfriend Todd Woodward escalated into fisticuffs. When Janie explained what the racket was to Doug, he promptly asked her to write it up.

'You could call it "The Curse of Celebrity Relationships",' he suggested helpfully.

'But what about the powerful women piece?' she asked, trying hard to suppress her distaste.

'We'll run it tomorrow, promise. Now get eight hundred words to me on the bonk-bust syndrome by lunch-time, there's a lamb.'

It was unfortunate that her sentence about Todd Woodward making a career out of portraying a series of laconic wits had made its way into print as a line about him being a moronic shit. And Sissy didn't think Helena Christensen would be happy about the five-year-old picture showing her and Paula Yates in the back of a limo. But Janie had poured a lot of her hitherto unresolved feelings about her own marriage into the article and all in all, said Sissy, it almost read as a useful piece of analytical journalism.

Thanks to her conversation with Peace on the plane to Milan, Sissy had managed to get the story about Kristof's deal with her and its record fees into the *Gazette* before any of the other papers printed it. She had also been in the XTC shop when a Japanese tourist, despairing of being allowed to buy any of the stock, had offered one of the terrifying sales assistants eighty thousand lire for the curtain in the changing room. Even Phyllida had liked that story because it perfectly illustrated the imbecility of the fashion world. So all in all, the *Gazette*'s fashion team were enjoying a record run. Their only failure, as predicted, was the eleven rolls of film that Nick Squire had squandered on Nancy O'Kelly flicking her tongue in and out of Clio Toris's various orifices, since even Doug Channing's ingenuity had failed to put a respectable spin on them and he'd had to drop them. 'Unless you could run me up five hundred words on "The Sapphic Influence on Fashion"?' he asked Janie hopefully. She demurred, on the grounds that she was due at a show.

'What about if we just run a straight catwalk picture of Kristof's show?' said Doug, trying one last time to find an excuse to mention Kristof's harem of under-age boys.

'I'm afraid we haven't got one,' said Janie apologetically. 'Nick used up all his film before the show started.'

'How come there's one in *The Python* with his byline on, then?' asked Doug slyly. 'I'll let it pass this time, Janie, but if Phyllida sees it, she'll probably have to be put under a restraining order.'

Janie didn't need telling. Inexperienced as she was, she knew it was a grave breach of professional conduct for a photographer who was being paid by one newspaper to sell his work to another. She couldn't believe that Nick had been so idiotic as to moonlight using his real name.

Overcome by the stresses of the day, exasperated by the constant shuffling and queuing and waiting and feeling lacerated by the whispering campaign that she knew Lindsey Craven had been conducting behind her back, Janie suddenly saw red. She would show Nick Squire and all the others who thought she had got the *Gazette* job through some kind of nepotism. She marched up to the reception desk to leave him a curt note. His key wasn't there, so she went straight to his room, ignoring the Do Not Disturb sign, and rang the bell authoritatively.

He opened the door in a damp towel. There were torrents of sweat running down his temples. His hair, bleached white from his last assignment (doorstepping Todd Woodward in South Beach, Miami) and unkempt at the best of times, resembled a patch of shagpile that had had something nasty spilt on it.

'Hello, darlin',' he chirped, blocking the doorway. 'Just doin' a spot of developing.' From the bathroom, Janie could hear rustling and the shattering of glass. 'My assistant,' said Nick ingratiatingly. 'We've set up a darkroom in there. Thought it would save you some money.'

'Kindly explain this.' Janie thrust a copy of *The Python* against the moist thickets of his chest. He glanced at the photograph of Peace and Kristof standing at the end of the catwalk surrounded by cyber-nymphs. At first he couldn't understand why Janie was so worked up – a stream of sweat was misting up his eyes.

'One, you told me you didn't have any more film. Two, it's completely unethical to sell pictures I'm paying for to other papers.'

'But it's not mine, darlin' . . .' he began.

'Then why does it have your name next to it?'

He blinked and turned the page sideways to check. 'Oh, you stupid cow,' he barked over his shoulder, forgetting all discretion and squelching towards the bathroom. Janie followed. A woman in a leather g-string and a Boob-Bugger was on all fours picking up shards of glass, and doing a remarkably good impression, Janie couldn't help thinking, of an Allen Jones mannequin. The reek of Eau Savage was so strong it was bouncing off the tiles.

'Hello, Lindsey,' said Janie coldly. 'Perhaps you could explain. Or possibly you'd like to contribute two thousand pounds towards Nick's hotel bill.' She glanced pointedly at the champagne bottles cooling in the bidet. 'He's proving rather expensive to run . . .'

'I thought you promised to use my *nom de plume*,' Nick yelled, all attempts at bonhomie appearing to have evaporated with the Eau Savage.

'The picture desk thought that Avedon Penn sounded too ridiculous for words,' snapped Lindsey, mustering all her dignity as she tried to saunter casually past Janie towards a bathrobe on the floor by the television. 'Oh, all right, I forgot. It's not the end of the world. I mean, you're not exactly cut out for life on the *bored* sheets, are you? The *National Enquirer*'s about as intellectual as it gets with you.'

He shot her a venomous look. 'You should know. How many begging letters is it you've sent in for jobs on one now? Oh, sorry, I forgot. You don't bother with *formal* applications, do you?' he added nastily. 'It's strictly informal with you. One on one. Or is it one under one? Well, a word of advice, Lindsey. After this afternoon's performance, I'd stick with the conventional CV approach.'

Lindsey lunged towards a purple stiletto and appeared to be preparing to aim it at Nick's chest. He grabbed it roughly from her. 'Sorry about this, Janie, sweetheart. Er, it won't happen again . . . any of it. See you in a jot.'

'Actually it's no to both those observations,' said Janie. 'You're fired.'

She stalked out of the room leaving two ovoid mouths gaping in disbelief behind her.

Sissy said a silent prayer for her great-aunt Cora's charm bracelet. She didn't often wear it – during the great reign of minimalism she'd seriously considered pawning it. But she and Alice had decided a charm bracelet revival might be in the offing so for once she had packed it. And very handy the bracelet had proved too. It had taken most of the lift journey to disentangle it from the socialite's pashmina shawl.

'Sissy Sands,' she said, holding out her hand the minute it was free.

'Anastasia Monticatini.' The woman opposite her smiled radiantly and took Sissy's nail-bitten hand in her slender, creamy white ones.

By the time they reached the penthouse floor, Sissy had expressed such a deep abiding interest in shawls that Anastasia invited her into her suite to show her her collection of antique embroidered ones.

'The nuns taught me,' said Anastasia dreamily, picking her way carefully through sentences in an unidentifiable Middle

European accent. 'I learned to hand-smock and to ruche too. For a while I thought I would make my living as a seamstress. Which museum did you say your fashion department was in?'

'Er, it's not exactly a museum. Though we are terribly interested in the history of fashion, naturally. It's just that Phyllida, the *Gazette*'s deputy editor, likes things to be available on the high street.'

'Hmm, the *International Gazette*,' purred Anastasia. 'At least it's not a tabloid. I love the British broadsheets. I'm such an Anglophile, you know. My first governess – she came from Yorkshire. Like your Jane Eyre.' Her laughter tinkled prettily. Sissy thought she was enchanting, especially after Anastasia had shown her the Chinese rug, the small but exquisite Stubbs and the collection of Manolo Blahnik shoes that she always travelled with.

'There must be a hundred pairs,' she exclaimed admiringly.

'I'm very indecisive,' trilled Anastasia, 'but there are many more at home. I love shoes,' she said helplessly. 'My second husband said I was keeping the Italian leather industry alive all by myself. But I suppose I was making up for my childhood. I was brought up very modestly – my great-grandparents had to flee the Russian Revolution – and we lived very humbly in Italy for two generations. Humbly, but always, I think, with an appreciation for the higher things in life. Then, of course, when my parents died and I went to live in the convent—'

'She's absolutely amazing,' Sissy told Janie later. 'She's obviously been married about a hundred times and absolutely loaded – and do you know, although she knew all about Manolo, Jimmy Choo and Christian Louboutin, the really weird thing is that she'd never heard of Angel? I'm going to introduce them the minute she gets back to London. He could do with another backer. Oh, and she's invited us to dinner in her suite tomorrow night.'

Janie groaned. She was worn out and she had to be up early tomorrow to prepare for her *Today* interview.

Sissy looked at her aghast. 'You can't possibly think of not going. I've seen the guest list – it's very select. Just Suzy

Menkes, Anna Wintour, Petronella Fishburn, Bella Scarletti, Stefano Palacci, Antonio Viro, Valentino and us. You know, I think she might just agree to do an interview. It could be rather poignant. She's yearning to go back to Russia but she's worried she'll find it too vulgar. A modern dilemma: what happens when White Russian breeding meets new Russian money. Very topical, Phyllida will love it. Maybe we should get Nick to take her picture at one of the shows just in case.'

'I've had to fire Nick Squire,' said Janie flatly.

'He hasn't dropped his lens cap down your blouse already? . . . God, Janie, good for you. No one's ever stood up to him before. Never mind, I expect we can find another one in the yellow pages. I won't tell Doug if you don't.'

Beau Monde had just called Saffron to confirm that they were expecting Jo-Jo and her portfolio at three that afternoon.

'I've decided that Jo-Jo shouldn't do any go-sees. She doesn't need to. And they're ghastly ordeals,' said Cassie when Saffron told her.

'I must admit I've never understood how the models can bear to hang around while some bored fashion editor snootily flicks through their book. It was you who always insisted that it was good for them to start at the bottom and take a few knocks.'

'Well, I've changed my mind,' said Cassie, remembering what Jo-Jo had said about living in a flat where the door was always being kicked in. 'I think Jo's already taken enough of those. Anyway, the more I see of this business, the more I realise that it's not success that screws the girls up, but failure.'

Saffron looked at her quizzically.

'I just don't feel right about it, that's all,' said Cassie.

'And that's your idea of being more open to other people's ideas, is it?' said Saffron. '*You* don't feel right.' She began to giggle. 'I give up. I can't argue because I can't help agreeing. You know the real trouble with you is that you're always bloody right.'

Word of Nick Squire's dismissal spread through the British journalists like quick fire. Janie had no problems recruiting a new photographer. At Sissy's suggestion she rang up Anna Accelli, the first name they came across in the phone book. Doug would have committed hara-kiri if he ever discovered his desk was running pictures that had been taken by a local wedding photographer – the catwalk posse was supposed to have graduated through the ranks: local paper, war zone and finally, when their nerves were tough enough, fashion shows. But Janie and Sissy decided that if Anna could cope with endless stroppy wedding guests, a few models wouldn't pose much of a problem.

Janie liked the idea of hiring a woman. Somehow it made the meat market seem a little less like Smithfield's, and a bit more like Fortnum and Mason. By the second show that evening, she was aware of a new respectfulness among her colleagues. Some of them actually congratulated her on her stand against Nick Squire, and Suzy Menkes, the doyenne of the *Herald Tribune*, smiled at her across the catwalk. Even Lindsey Craven's toxic looks seemed to be slightly less noxious. Or perhaps Janie was just getting used to them.

Janie didn't get Sue MacGregor. And although John Humphrys left her jugular relatively intact, she nevertheless felt humiliated. She had tried so hard to steer the discussion away from the supermodel question, which she found a vexed one, and on to the Cambodian refuge which had just started pioneering morale-boosting visits to local hairdressers and style advisers. But instead she had found herself justifying supermodels' fees.

'They might be paid absurd amounts,' she heard her voice echoing down the line, 'but they generate even greater sums for the companies that hire them. It's a question of market forces,' she was horrified to hear herself say. 'You could argue that Grace Capshaw and Peace Grant are among our most valuable export commodities. And in any case, the high price our society places on female beauty is merely a reiteration of social values that date back to Ancient Greece. I'm afraid the current backlash is probably rooted in old-fashioned envy.'

'You were a bloody triumph,' said Cassie from Hammersmith roundabout.

'I sounded like William Hague,' wailed Janie. 'Thank God Matthew wasn't around to hear it.'

Cassie nearly said that Matthew wasn't actually around for a lot of things these days, but refrained. 'No word still? Well, I expect he's doing a lot of thinking . . . by the way, Grace called from Deia. She loved the piece. That's a first. Said she thought it was exceptionally cogent and literate.'

'Not surprising, really – she practically wrote it.'

There was a message at reception for Janie from *Newsnight* inviting her to debate by satellite link-up the issue of 'Female Beauty – Exalted or Exploited?' opposite Germaine Greer.

The morning was rapidly degenerating into some kind of horrific psychological blood-bath. She decided to ignore the fax.

'I hear congratulations are in order,' trilled Sissy in the car. 'I just spoke to Doug Channing and he says you were great. They all had it on in the office. Even Phyllida conceded a few grudging words of praise. We can relax now and enjoy Anastasia's dinner.'

Anastasia was having a mild panic attack and driving all the staff at the Four Seasons mad into the bargain. She had already sent Gunter, her chauffeur-cum-minder, to the airport to wait for her monogrammed napkins, which at the last minute, she had decided to have sent out from London along with her Meissen china. She'd also hired Tilly de Montgomery, a stylist from *Designers' Digest*, to jazz up her suite and make it seem less like a hotel. Tilly was a great talent who'd made a mint during the recession helping half of London's hostesses spruce up their shabby dining rooms with bits of borrowed props she'd called in for the magazine. And now, according to her brother Freddie, who'd helped Anastasia on a few points of etiquette, she had her sights set on higher things – Hollywood set design, for instance.

Anastasia wished Tilly would hurry up and arrive. Now that Gunter wasn't there to give her a massage, her neck had gone into spasm and she was twitching like an angry wasp. She was desperate for tonight's dinner to be a success. If they liked her, Petronella, Anna and Suzy could launch her on to a world stage – she well remembered how American *Vogue* had once featured Ivana Trump on its cover. And the Janie woman would be a useful entrée into British society – the *Gazette* was pretty classy as papers went. She picked up a copy of *The Mill on the Floss* and turned to a well-thumbed page.

The happiest women, like the happiest nations, have no history.

How true. She flitted restlessly over to the dining table which was smothered in linen and crystal and tanker-sized vases of white lilies and whipped out her silver tape measure. 'Fiammetta,' she screeched. A brow-beaten-looking maid in a black dress and frilly apron shuffled sulkily towards her.

'The plates are not aligned,' said Anastasia sharply before retiring to her bedroom to calm her nerves with some needle-point. It was no good, she still couldn't concentrate and she ended up pricking her finger and bleeding all over one of her embroidered pale pink roses. And she hadn't decided what to wear tonight: the dove grey shift with the petersham collar, or the eau de Nil? The breathing exercises her elocution teacher had shown her weren't helping either – if Gunter didn't arrive soon she'd die of hyperventilation. She was just summoning up the energy to try the dresses on again when there was a thud in the next room followed by an outburst of Italian curses. Fiammetta had dropped one of the bowls of lilies all over the

Chinese rug and was on her knees wailing, while blood gushed out of her wrist. Anastasia's first impulse was to rescue the rug; her next was to throttle her useless maid.

Fortunately the door burst open and Gunter staggered in under a mountain of antlers, candelabra and heavy gilt frames. Tilly had raided the grand country seat of one of Freddie's more absent-minded friends and stripped the ballroom of its showiest pieces, promising on her mother's life to have it all back after the weekend.

'God, Anastasia', she drawled, peering over her sunglasses at Anastasia's carpet, and puffing heavily on a cigarette she had filched from a passing bell-boy, 'I see what you mean about the decor. This Chinese rug's an abortion. Never fear, Tilly's here. We'll have this looking spiffy in next to no time. I can't tell you the hell we had squidging forty metres of tartan into the overhead locker, though.'

Tilly was as good as her word, even if her vision had become a little grandiose lately. By seven o'clock, the Four Seasons' penthouse suite had been transformed into a mini-Scottish baronial castle. Tilly had swathed the windows in heavy Prussian blue velvet curtains, tossed huge antique tapestries over the beige sofas and put away the best part of two bottles of Anastasia's Moët. 'A genius, though I say it myself,' she said, collapsing on a tartanned armchair.

Anastasia was speechless with admiration. 'Now remember, Anastasia, darling, napkins on the service plates and—'

Anastasia threw Tilly a poisonous look.

'Just teasing,' Tilly giggled. 'Freddie says you passed his etiquette classes *summa cum laude*.'

'Ugh. Never again,' exclaimed Sissy, hurling herself on to Janie's bed.

'Delicious food, though. That was the best caviar I've ever had.'

'I don't know that it was such a good idea eating Petronella's,' said Sissy.

'I couldn't let it go to waste and she hadn't touched it. Anyway, I thought it might break the ice.'

'A nuclear bomb wouldn't have broken that ice.'

'Mmm, things were a bit quiet. Why was that?'

'Well,' began Sissy, 'Petronella massacred Antonio in her last review; Stefano's suing Bella Scarletti for plagiarism; Suzy Menkes fainted in Valentino's last couture show and he took it personally, and Louisa was always so rude about Antonio's shows that in the end he banned her for life. He probably thinks you're her.'

'Poor Anastasia. What a disaster,' said Janie.

'Oh, I dunno. As fashion parties go that was pretty friendly, and at least you managed to have a chat with her.'

'She's obsessed with the whole industry,' said Janie disapprovingly. 'Couldn't get enough model gossip – can you believe a grown woman would be so interested? – and when she found out I knew Cassie, there was just no stopping her.'

'Yes,' said Sissy, still thinking about the pashminas that had been casually draped over some of Tilly's tartan throws, 'and earlier today I saw her being whisked off into a café after one of the shows by Vladimir Miscov, that sleazoid at Bellissimo. *Very* friendly, they were. Now how on earth do you think she'd know a creep like that?'

Anastasia sat in the lotus position on one of Tilly's bearskins ruefully examining the outbreak of hives on her pale hands. It had been the most nerve-racking evening of her life. She wasn't quite sure how it went – Freddie hadn't covered How to Tell if Your Guests Had a Good Time. She certainly hadn't, but she had been nervous, and in her experience society events weren't really meant to be enjoyed. That was one of life's great dichotomies. But Anastasia had made up her mind – she'd had enough of living among nobodies. She wanted to join society, even if it meant dying of boredom and coming out in a hideous rash.

Chapter Five

Peace had flown back to London a day before the Milan shows ended. What with her Kristof contract, Cassie felt she should be careful about overexposing herself. Cassie had also been fussing about her health again. Well, it wasn't Peace's fault if all those hags in the audience bitched about her all the time. She trotted outside to the street where her dark green Jeep squatted by the pavement like a sleek, self-satisfied toad. She felt so hot that she decided to get inside, just for a few minutes, and luxuriate in the air-conditioning.

Even Peace acknowledged that the Jeep was a ludicrous car for her to own. She didn't care. She checked to see if the package she'd left in the glove compartment last time was still there. Her stuff was always going missing these days. Clothes, bags, money just seemed to dissolve into the ether. No one ever saw it happen. Sometimes she wondered whether she'd ever owned the things in the first place. But she definitely remembered putting the stuff in the car. She began to giggle. If it had gone then whoever had taken it would have been hallucinating solidly for the past three weeks. As she spied a white wodge glistening in its plastic skin at the back of the compartment, like a grotesquely obese glow-worm, a wave of relief flooded through her. She got it out. It wasn't as big as she'd remembered. Maybe someone had been at it after all. Shit. Despite her Bohemian veneer, Peace had a healthy horror of the law.

She twiddled some of the buttons. She still didn't know how to operate half the gadgets. After the ad had been such a hit, Chrysler had given her the Jeep. And although she would rather pluck every hair on her body than admit it, she was besotted with it, despite the fact that it had room for six, a steering wheel she could barely see over the top of and an odour of smugness about it that Grace, who hadn't been given one, said was repugnant. Peace didn't care. Sometimes she would creep out at night and just sit in it, smoking and listening to CDs and imagining she had five children in the back and a banker husband waiting at home in Surrey.

Maybe she should just whiz it down the road. Zack said it wasn't good for cars to sit by the kerb day after day. Shepherd's Bush would be about the right distance. While she was there, she'd just look in on Jute to check he was okay. Her eyes misted over as a picture of Jute hunched over his red kitchen table deftly cutting up lines of coke shimmered tantalisingly above the gear-stick. Gone chopping, he'd coo into her answer machine, a message that always worked on Peace like a clarion call. To be fair to herself, though, she reflected, Jute had become more than her extremely resourceful dealer. He was her friend. She had a sneaking suspicion he might even have become her lover. But, her memory being what it was these days, she wouldn't swear to it.

She caressed the accelerator with her foot. Her toes were killing her, and had been ever since Isabella Suarez had shown her how to insert a needle between them to avoid track marks on her arms. Last month, when she had been in the Maldives on a shoot for *Beau Monde*, the make-up artist had given her some eyedrops to counteract her constantly dilated pupils.

'You gotta get those pupils down to normal size, Peace. One day an art director's gonna forget to get them airbrushed and then every hack in the business will be on to you.'

Despite the dark, damp early March evening, she switched on the air-conditioning full blast. Was it her imagination or was it unseasonably warm? Then she remembered she always felt she was about to melt when she was high. The faintly gritty rubber on the pedal felt mercifully cool, erotic even as the Jeep broncoed away from the kerb. The driving test she'd taken at Cassie's insistence had taken place in Nevada in a haze of desert. The star-struck instructor had been very complimentary about the way she used her wing mirror, but as Cassie had remarked during a white-knuckle ride Peace had given her into town one lunch-time, sand-dunes were no preparation for roundabouts.

She turned the volume to max. Nancy O'Kelly's haunting voice engulfed her. *I spent my life on a losing streak. But I'm leavin' that indulgence behind. I won't be weak. I'm movin' on to Paradise . . .* and I'm moving on to Shepherd's Bush, decided Peace, ignoring the image of Cassie's reproachful eyes that hologrammed up from the dashboard.

Jute was about as close as she got to a great mate these days, she thought forlornly. There just wasn't time for any others. She would have liked more, and she was forever buying lavish little gifts for people, then realising they were embarrassingly extravagant given the extent of her acquaintance. So she gave them anyway and then, feeling awkward, retreated further into her loneliness. She wasn't shy. At least not on first meeting. But that was because first meetings weren't a big deal. When you'd never met someone before it didn't matter if they liked you. It was only as the acquaintance deepened that the stakes became higher and Peace got frightened and backed off. God, Nancy O'Kelly must be getting to her.

The journey from Notting Hill to Jute's flat in minimal traffic normally took eight minutes. But Peace's sense of direction was hopeless at the best of times, and it took her a quarter of an hour to find the right end of Ladbroke Square.

I won't weep any more. What doesn't break ya makes ya strong and carries you to Paradise, or so my good friend Nietzsche always sighed . . . the plaintive chorus swooped around inside the car like a trapped canary. The drizzle turned to sleet and Peace had all the hazard lights going before she located the wipers. Shepherd's Bush loomed up ahead, a crown of car lights dancing round it. Nervously she lit another cigarette. She hated roundabouts. Her stepfather had always told her that attack was the best means of defence. A retired brigadier who, against the better judgment of everyone who knew him, had married Peace's hippie mother when Peace was four, he had spent the next fifteen years barking military aphorisms at them and doing his utmost to turn them into respectable county Sloanes.

Desperate to please him and get some attention from her mother, who had indeed become a model officer's wife, Peace had always been baffled by the attack–defence issue, at a loss as to how she might apply it to real life. At boarding school, or Parkhurst, as the pupils had called it, taking up more or less permanent residence in the loos had been the best form of defence. But now, approaching the roundabout, she felt her stepfather's advice could finally come into its own. She snaked into an inside lane, in the splashstream of a lorry carrying what looked like a concrete mixer, waited for it to pull out, closed her eyes and pressed the accelerator. It worked. She was out there, part of the crown. She circled a few more times until she'd worked up enough confidence to pull over to an exit lane that would take her back towards Shepherd's Bush.

Euphoric, she fished in the glove compartment for a more upbeat CD and whammed a Motown compilation into the player. She felt chirpier than she had for months. At the traffic lights she waved to a little girl who was picking up her teddy bear from a scrubby municipal flowerbed. She watched the child place it carefully in her pushchair and pulled over to an off-licence to get some beers and a boxload of Doritos for Jute. By the time she reached Jute's turning, Peace was tapping her toes and ululating to 'Baby Love' with such gusto that she almost missed it.

She peered through the misted-up window, squinting for the street sign, and saw an enormous rat perching on the Jeep's bonnet. It was gloating at her. Peace was phobic about rats ever since she'd been locked in the dorm with a nest of baby ones by a group of sixth-formers at Parkhurst. She became hysterical. She rammed the steering wheel as far round to the left as it would go and accidentally flicked the wipers off. The car almost spun on its left wheels and emitted an impressive squealing noise. Peace giggled. A teddy bear flew over the bonnet. Someone else, far off, from the sound of things, let out a scream. Then she felt a thud and the steering wheel made contact with her bony chest about the same time as the lorry juddered into the Jeep's back bumper and the front bumper made contact with three-year-old Shareen's pushchair as it made its way home after a long day at the childminder's.

Sissy had also flown back to London a day early so that she could drop by the office and check that they both had all their invitations to the British shows which officially started at the weekend. Janie stayed on to see Paolo Bianco's show – everyone should see one, as a standard-bearer of abominableness, Sissy had said. Also, Bella Scarletti, who had unexpectedly taken a shine to Janie after the dinner with Anastasia, had called to offer Janie an exclusive interview. Sissy seemed to think it was a major coup. So Janie reluctantly changed her reservation to the last flight of the day.

It had been an exhausting encounter. Ever since a well-publicised row with her brother, Giuseppe, in the eighties had riven the family company in two and culminated with both setting up rival houses, Bella had kept her distance from the press. Even when the rumours had reached a crescendo and everyone had been saying that Giuseppe had Aids and even, at one stage, that he and his sister had been lovers, Bella had refused to talk publicly.

'You absolutely must ask her about the blood changes,' Sissy said casually. Janie looked dumbstruck.

'She and Giuseppe are supposed to have their bloodstream cleared out every month or so – as a protection against Aids. No wonder they're always moaning about feeling drained. Still, gives a new meaning to Nervous Exhaustion. Loads of them do it. Bit hard to slip into the conversation, I know. Try flattery first, then move in for the kill.'

Bella's collections were going from strength to strength and she could afford to be magnanimous even if Giuseppe couldn't.

She poured her heart out to Janie, telling her how they had been unnaturally close as children. Giuseppe, who was six years older than she was, had paid for her to go to art school. But although he'd been very proud of her to begin with and they'd flourished together, he'd grown jealous of her, Bella told Janie sadly. And when she married, he'd hit the roof.

'Giuseppe say my husband not good enough for me,' said Bella, tears welling in her eyes, 'he say Giorgio only want my money. But I know Giuseppe don't want me to marry anyone. He selfish, selfish boy.' She had agreed to sit for a portrait by Anna Accelli, which took for ever because Bella's mascara kept smudging and then she insisted on Janie staying for tea to meet her children. Janie only just made the flight back to London. It took all her self-control not to storm the cockpit when the captain announced that one of the passengers was still missing in the terminal.

'It's an absolute pest, isn't it?' said a deep, sympathetic-sounding voice next to her. 'It seems to happen every time I come to Milan. It must be God's way of telling me not to freelance.'

Janie looked up and saw an attractive, delicate face with vivacious eyes and a glossy mane of auburn hair that she recognised as belonging to the up-and-coming British designer Madeleine Peterson. Her spirits dipped; she was so tired she couldn't face having to make conversation, especially not about fashion. 'Fashion editor, right?' Madeleine remarked, nodding towards a wedge of press releases sitting on top of Janie's laptop. 'In which case the last thing you probably want is me asking you what you thought of the shows. How about a drink instead?' Madeleine closed the scrapbook in front of her and beckoned a stewardess, who was unceremoniously pushed aside by a sheepish-looking Anastasia, who had just boarded.

It was another two hours before the plane was allocated a new take-off slot, during which time Janie and Madeleine downed nine packets of peanuts and two bottles of Pinot Grigio. Madeleine's easy, open manner acted like a laxative on Janie, who found herself pouring out confidences; telling

Madeleine all about Matthew, details that she hadn't even run past Cassie. Madeleine responded sympathetically but neutrally, something Cassie, loyal as she was to Janie, could never do. In return, Madeleine told Janie all about her work problems.

'You tell me all about your husband and all I can bang on about is my business,' she acknowledged ruefully. 'I don't even have any cats. Away too much. It does feel as though I'm married to that bloody business most of the time. And at this particular moment I'd quite like a divorce.'

She had been in Milan doing some consultancy work for an Italian knitwear company. 'Dreary stuff and absolutely hideous by the time it reaches the shops. But the cheques are gorgeous even if the clothes aren't, and I once saw this wonderful huge dilapidated castle in Andalucia. It's always haunted me and I've got this crazy dream that if I can just keep going, one day I might even be able to buy it and spend the rest of my days weaving textiles – which is what I always set out to do. And frankly five days' work in Milan pays what I earn in three months in London.'

At thirty, Madeleine Peterson seemed to have achieved as much as any young British designer could hope for. A hot favourite to win the coveted British Designer of the Year award this year, her collections were wearable but quirky enough to have achieved credibility with the press. Last season the editors of every single major international magazine, who generally found British fashion a little too avant-garde for their tastes and who spent most of their time in London going to see *Cats* or raiding Portobello market, had flown in early from Milan especially to see her collection. Not only were the clothes strong enough to be featured regularly in lavish editorials in the likes of *A La Mode* and Italian *Vogue*, but they were commercial too: the Madeleine Peterson label was prominently displayed in Harvey Nichols and Joseph. On one of her rare trips into Knightsbridge, Janie had fallen in love with a pair of paisley trousers, fastened with tiny mother-of-pearl buttons up one side, which had haunted her for so many months that she vowed never to go window-shopping again.

Madeleine's quizzical, bark-coloured eyes frequently gazed out of glossy Sunday supplements: Madeleine Peterson at work in her Soho studio; Madeleine Peterson in her cool, elegant Islington home. She used a lot of antique-finish buttons and trims on her clothes, and when she wore them herself, she mixed them with strikingly modern accessories. Janie had often been struck by how self-possessed Madeleine appeared, her shiny hair casually twisted up the back of her head like an exclamation mark. Yet, lighting one cigarette after another, Madeleine sketched a hellish picture of glamorous foreign department stores that put in huge orders and then never paid for them; of factories that mysteriously closed down overnight after they'd taken stock of a designer's precious fabrics but before they'd actually made up any of the clothes; of the unassuming-looking figures who sat quietly in the audience sketching furiously for the rip-off merchants who sent them there and, most hurtful of all, of shattered partnerships. Madeleine Peterson had formerly been one-half romantically as well as creatively of Marola/Peterson. Janie vaguely remembered the furore in the press when they'd split up and the business had collapsed.

'Least said about that the better,' said Madeleine, unwrapping her duty-free cigarettes. 'The terrible thing is that you feel a tremendous responsibility to your team. It's the bleakest feeling when you have to let everyone go. I never want to go through that again. Especially now that I've got together a really fantastic staff. They're a really talented bunch. Some of them have families. And they all depend on me.'

For all the scintillating coverage Madeleine got in the press, Janie got the distinct impression that her business was teetering on a knife-edge. Without the frequent trips to Milan she would have had to have closed the business months ago. As the plane hovered over the lush, shadowy gardens at Kew, Madeleine pulled her brocaded shawl round her shoulders (Janie had bought her mother the same one for her sixtieth birthday) and put her cigarettes away as if to signify a new paragraph.

'Oh, don't take any notice of me,' she said brightly. 'The past months have been a nightmarish blur but I'm just tired and nervous. The show's only two days away and there's still masses to do.'

'I'm looking forward to it,' said Janie genuinely. 'I'm dying to see what you've done.'

'So am I,' came the wry response.

It was 9 p.m. before Cassie heard about Peace. She had been in the Groucho Club with Barney Frick, who, to her delight, had agreed to cram a complete redesign of her flat into his busy schedule. Cassie had felt so guilty about what she was on the verge of doing to Zack that she had switched off her mobile for the evening. She walked into her hallway to see him signalling to her from his Nordic Track.

'It's Jute,' he panted, passing her his earphones. 'He sounds pretty bad.'

The name was familiar. Jute . . . Alarm bells exploded in Cassie's head. Jute was a walking department store of drugs. Cassie had even sat outside his flat a couple of years earlier while Jim Zametti had paid a flying visit *en route* to their tryst at a country hotel. Gingerly she took the phone from Zack.

It was some time before Cassie could make any sense of Jute's gabbling, especially as every so often he had to put her on hold while he attempted to calm the wailing twosome next to him. The gist, she reprised, shakily pouring herself one of Zack's Rescue shakes, was that Peace had somehow upsided her Jeep into a wall in Shepherd's Bush, narrowly missing a mother and child. Thank God, thought Cassie. The mother and little girl were currently installed in Jute's front room where the dope fumes, Cassie hoped, would be doing them a power of good. Peace, however, was nowhere to be found.

Cassie was hardly an innocent when it came to drugs. In her early twenties she had never knowingly been caught without a bag of hash. She had served her apprenticeship as a model agent in the early eighties when modelling shoots had been notoriously drawn-out, self-indulgent affairs in which all the participants were, to varying degrees, tripping to places not strictly on the map. Things had got so bad that there had been talk of forming a regulatory body after the fashion team from *Miss Behave* had returned from a £38,000 bikini shoot in Acapulco without any pictures. Once, half curious, half dreading what she might hear, Cassie had asked Grace whether it was true that the snow so prettily frosting the model's cheeks on the December cover of *Eve* had really been cocaine. 'You don't want to know,' Grace replied.

But Cassie did. She considered it her responsibility to her girls and to the clients who were starting to pay vast sums for the privilege of using the better-known faces in their campaigns.

She never felt as though she'd quite got to the bottom of the drugs issue. And as fees rocketed and everyone began to realise how much was at stake, the modelling business cleaned up its act. Cassie had been amazed at how circumspectly the most successful models lived their lives in the late Eighties. By the time the tide turned and drugs became much more openly passed round again, Cassie was not as aware of it as she might have been. In the early days of Hot Shots she'd spent a lot of time going to photographers' parties and hanging out with the models backstage. But as she got older and busier she spent more time at work, or in places like the Groucho. When Peace had checked into the Fountain nursing home for exhaustion last season, Cassie had given her a stern lecture on the perils of marijuana and casual drug usage, but it had never occurred to her that the problem might be more serious.

She gleaned as much as she could from Jute, sleepwalked into the kitchen and sat down heavily at the table, suddenly sick with remorse. Christ, how could she have been so complacent? Peace had even casually introduced her to Jute one night when Cassie had dropped into her flat in Notting Hill with a contract for Peace to sign. But she had never connected the Jute helping himself to some of Peace's Diet Coke with the Jute whose flat she'd sat outside. Oh, why hadn't Peace felt able to confide in her? And why hadn't she interrogated Peace more effectively when she'd gone to the Fountain? Or at least actively confiscated the bloody car? If she, Cassie, had a shred of integrity in her genes, she would have long ago set up a kind of boarding school for the younger, more naïve models, so that she could act as a moral guardian the way Katie Ford did in New York. The headlines were going to be sensational. Why, oh why didn't I keep a closer eye on Peace? she wailed inwardly.

'You're not her mother.' She looked up blearily and saw Zack's trim, tanned frame leaning in the doorway.

He came over and wrapped his arms round her shoulders as she began to sob uncontrollably. 'Peace has been on a one-way mission to destroy herself since she was about eight, from what I gather,' he said gently. 'You mustn't blame yourself. I take it that Jute hasn't exactly been racing to get the police involved?'

Cassie nodded mutely.

'And since the mother and child are okay, thank God, there's no legal need for them to be brought in. Peace must be all right otherwise she'd be lying under the car. She's probably in shock. Our priority has to be to find her.'

By the time they got to Jute's, Shareen and her mother had calmed down sufficiently to be watching a rerun of *Through the Keyhole*, while Jute ran backwards and forwards from the kitchen with chipped mugs of tea, beakers of Ribena and baked bean sandwiches.

'They're all right,' he snuffled, exhausted from all his domestic efforts. 'Shareen got a bit of glass in her forehead, but it missed her eyes and we've got it out. Jute Nightingale or what? Anyway, Carmen's not the vindictive sort. More the grateful, praise-be-the-Lord alleluia sort. Says all those Sunday Masses have been worthwhile. I knew it was Peace's car – 'cos of the, er, music,' he added.

Carmen and Shareen lived next door, which meant that Jute, who had even been known to keep an ear out for Shareen when Carmen had to nip round the corner to get something for supper, hadn't found it too difficult to convince Carmen that police involvement was unnecessary. He'd even got Carmen feeling almost sorry for Peace. Bloody good little salesman, thought Cassie later. If the merchandise had been missiles instead of smack he'd probably be on his way to a knighthood.

Fridays were when Carmen had to work her late shift at KwikNosh, which was why she and Shareen were still making their way back from the childminder's at seven – that and the fact that lately Shareen had insisted on walking and using the pushchair for her teddy bear, which made the journey very slow. 'Thank the Lord Almighty,' exclaimed Carmen fervently. 'Normally I'm cursin' at her slowness by the time we reach the top of the road, God forgive me. But I never will again, as you all be my witnesses . . . We screamed so loudly,' she continued with satisfaction, 'we must have disturbed the whole of Shepherd's Bush. That poor girl,' she added magnanimously, 'probably thinks she killed us.'

Between Carmen's fervent thanks-be-to-Gods and Jute's non sequiturs, the story that emerged was less terrible than Cassie had first envisioned. But no less chastening. As well as the teddy bear, the pushchair had been stacked up with vegetables and Carmen's Friday night bottle of Bailey's. It was too heavy for Shareen, although she insisted on trying to push, and she and Carmen had locked horns in a battle of wills, the upshot of which was that the buggy had bumped off the kerb in front of Peace.

Cradled awkwardly on a sagging leatherette sofa between Carmen and a restless, wiry Jute, Cassie looked at Shareen wriggling over an orange bean bag and felt a weight rise from her shoulders. Temporarily. She contemplated the menacing crimson and black spirals on Jute's walls, wondered whether she was experiencing a stress hallucination, and decided it was one of his paint effects. One moment they seemed to be zooming in, the next they receded. Trust Jute to have walls that loitered with intent. Still, you had to admire the technique. Peace had mentioned that he'd graduated with a first from the Royal College of Art. His tutors would be thrilled to know it wasn't entirely wasted, thought Cassie distractedly. God, Peace had been lucky. But it didn't make the situation any less grave. She felt her terror being sluiced down with anger, irritation and frustration.

'She can't have got far,' Zack said briskly as they strolled back to Cassie's car. 'Are you up to looking for her?'

They must have patrolled every street in W6 and W12, peered over every wall, rustled in every bush. At midnight Cassie went home to call the designers whose shows Peace had been due to appear in the following day. She hated letting them down, particularly as the London ones didn't have the budgets to call in other big names and regarded Peace as their patron because she did their shows for nothing. Zack stayed behind to continue the search.

'She might even have made it back to her flat,' he said, in a heroic attempt at optimism. 'You never know.'

You never do, thought Cassie, gazing after him wonderingly.

Madeleine Peterson sat cross-legged on the floor of her studio, compulsively cutting up ever tinier swatches of lilac, mauve and rose-pink silk and watching the candle flame limbo across the gnarled floorboards. 'You've lived through worse. You've lived through worse,' she repeated doggedly as the tears streamed down her cheeks.

Cassie's phone call, not such cataclysmic news in the grand scheme of things, had been the last straw in a hideous month. The bitterest pill was that until recently everything had been going brilliantly. She had been poised on the brink of real success. The clothes were selling, her profile was high. There were the contracts – tedious but lucrative – in Milan and talk of launching a scent with Jolie Cosmetics that would set her up for life. Hollyhocks, the swish uptown department store in Manhattan, had even given her her own shop on the first floor, alongside Calvin Klein and Antonio Viro.

But a month earlier Hollyhocks had filed for Chapter 11, owing her £200,000. Then the studio had been broken into and thousands of pounds of fabrics and samples had been stolen. She had been gazumped on the shop space she had been hoping to rent at Brompton Cross. And without the shop, Jolie Cosmetics had informed her, the scent launch was in jeopardy. To cap it all, she had been receiving lawyers' letters signed, very formally, she noted sadly, on behalf of Alec Marola, threatening to sue her for copyright infringement.

Alec had never got over her leaving him, especially as he had been the dominant partner for so long in their relationship. The press had adored him too – everyone did: he was flamboyant, good-looking and romantically unpredictable. But his manic depressive moods had rapidly sapped the limited creative talent he had and then turned on her. She spent three of their five years together feeling frightened, confused and belittled. Finally, one day she had been mooching round the fabric shops in Berwick Street when she discovered twenty metres of pale blue Chantilly lace for sale on a stall. The only people who'd had access to that lace had been Madeleine and Alec when they'd found it at an antiques fair in Nice. It was perfect for their next collection and even though it had been horrendously expensive, Madeleine had paid for it out of her own account. Alec must have sold some of it behind her back – stolen technically – and pocketed the money. The day after she discovered the lace she left him. By the sound of things, he hadn't forgiven her.

Every time she thought things couldn't get worse they did. Tonight, when she got back from the airport, there were three messages on her answerphone, one from Sally, her chief pattern cutter, informing her she was leaving to work for Chanel. Another from Lindsey Craven apologising for having lost the devore evening gown she had borrowed from the new collection to preview in the *Python on Sunday*. The third was from her sister to say that their father had been rushed to hospital. She trudged over to the fridge where a note was pinned to the door.

Borrowed the last bottle of wine. Pay you back Monday.
Sally.

'So to recap,' Edward Rushmore, editor of the *International Gazette*, was saying portentously, 'you think the judiciary in this country needs to be brought to account and that a campaign waged in this paper is long overdue?'

'We've got the evidence, chapter and verse, to prove it, Edward,' said Doug Channing, eyes shining in his pasty, rumpled face. 'We've been collating it for the past six months. The Massing fraud trial threw open a can of worms, as you know. What went on behind the scenes was almost more interesting than the public story, and God knows that was a scandal. Of course, we'll have to handle it carefully, it's dynamite stuff. But done right I think it could rock the Establishment to its core.'

There were admiring clucks and whistles of approval around the room. 'We don't just run stories on boob-tubes,' said Doug pompously. And then in a stab at self-deprecation he added, 'Much as we'd like to.'

Janie cringed inwardly. It had been Phyllida's idea that she attend morning conference. It was a privilege, she had said. 'It's not just any old hack who gets to come, Janie,' she had lectured huffily. 'Some of those anoraks on the news beat never see the inside of the conference room in thirty years. I'm inviting you because I think it's important that *they* recognise how crucial women's issues are to the lifeblood of this publication.'

By *they*, Janie supposed Phyllida meant the 207 male journalists working on the *Gazette*. She was all for female complicity, but she couldn't help wishing that she had someone more trustworthy on the paper to be complicit with. As she stared at a flag bearing a Japanese ensign which was slapping about in the breeze on a building opposite and sprouting out of the top of Edward Rushmore's head, she wondered whether Phyllida hadn't set the whole thing up to humiliate her. What had they had so far? A leaked White Paper from the Department of Education, an explosive investigation into the Vatican, and the City team's undercover story on an American consortium's attempt to destabilise the Tokyo stock market. After that, whatever convoluted terms she couched it in, Janie couldn't see an article about stilettos making much of a mark.

'And now to lighter things,' said Edward Rushmore sonorously, as Phyllida began beating a nervous tattoo with her Biro. 'What have you got for us, Phyllida?'

Furious at his patronising tone, Phyllida rattled off the features on her list, dressing each successive idea up in increasingly sensationalist terms.

'Splendid, splendid,' said Rushmore absent-mindedly. 'That should keep the girls happy. And now for fashion. Interesting addition to our meeting,' he said genially to the room. 'Er, what have you for us, er . . .'

'Janie,' prompted Phyllida tersely.

'Yes. Thought you were terrific on *Newsnight*, by the way.'

'Kitten heels,' said Janie, praying for an earthquake.

'Ah, yes,' said Rushmore. 'I hear that chap Angel Derrida did masses of them. And Manolo Blahnik, of course. My daughters tell me they're hoping Bertie's will come up with some affordable ones. Wouldn't think something so flimsy could cost so much, would you?' Phyllida's Biro snapped in half. 'Think that their revival has anything to do with the political climate?' he continued.

'Could be,' said Janie, forgetting her nerves. 'The most obvious corollary between fashion and politics is hem lengths, of course − short when things are buoyant, long when the economy's flat. But there are lots of other examples. Did you know, for instance, that women's clothes always tend to get extremely ornate and feminine at times of maximum social upheaval?'

'Fascinating,' exclaimed Rushmore, 'but then I've always thought that, correctly analysed, fashion gives a brilliant and useful snapshot of society. We've just never had the right person to do it.' He looked pointedly at Phyllida. 'Well, I look forward to reading it. It's about time we had some authoritative coverage of fashion. I enjoyed the Milan reports, by the way. I still think Bella Scarletti's overrated, though'.

As the last of Madeleine's little celadon and lavender broderie anglaise cocktail dresses with their embroidered roses and daisies, each one hand-sewn by Madeleine's loyal little team of seamstresses, floated across the rose-petal-strewn catwalk to meet the oyster-and-ivory-coloured organza evening gowns, Janie witnessed her first fashion standing ovation.

'You're experiencing what's known as a Fashion Moment,' yawned Magnus. Isabella and Jess, who had flown in from Milan to do the show in return for a couple of coats each (or in Isabella's case, as much of the collection as she could walk off in under her coats), led Madeleine to the end of the catwalk to rapturous applause, and Zoffy Villeneuve was so overcome that she fainted.

'That'll crease her Galliano,' remarked Alice to Sissy as they passed two Red Cross orderlies telling a nauseous-looking Zoffy to put her head between her knees. 'First time she's sat down in years. Puking's a new twist, I must say. I suppose she thinks it's edgy.'

There was an undignified scramble on to the catwalk as a mob of fashion editors swarmed to congratulate Madeleine. Janie would have liked to have seen Madeleine, but she couldn't face the orgy of slipped lipstick and smudged foundation. She would leave a message on her work number. Back at the *Gazette* she switched on her light-box. The pictures from Madeleine's collection looked fantastic. She had already decided to use her report on the show to write a serious think-piece about the business side of fashion. The gist of the article would be that Madeleine's sophisticated, luxurious ideas could, if properly backed, form the apex of a profitable market pyramid that could set a new precedent in British fashion. Perfume, tights, sheets, shiny large white crockery . . . she could see it now. Doug told her he would run it across half a page.

'I'd prefer stark raving bonkers fashion, of course,' he said good-naturedly. 'Always gets the readers going in the shires. But in the absence of that, something pretty will do.'

Just before she was leaving, Janie called Madeleine's studio. To her surprise, Madeleine picked up the phone. Janie had assumed she would be out celebrating.

'Made an offer on that castle yet?'

'I've gone bankrupt,' said Madeleine, her voice echoing round the spartan studio.

'What do you mean?' asked Janie incredulously.

'The bank foreclosed yesterday. Couldn't bear to throw any more of their loyal customers' money away.'

'But the reviews are going to be amazing. Even Petronella Fishburn was clapping.'

'Too late,' interrupted Madeleine lightly. 'Story of my life.'

Cassie was nearly out of her mind with worry about Peace. Forty-eight hours after the crash there was still no sign of her. As diplomatically as she could, she ascertained from Peace's parents that she hadn't turned up in Gloucestershire. The more she attempted to trace Peace the more desperate she became.

Clearly, Peace had a serious drugs problem. Cassie would never forgive herself for not recognising it earlier, even though, as Zack reasoned, Peace had been away working so much the past year that Cassie had hardly seen her. The press, she knew, thought that Peace had anorexia, but Cassie had seen her pack away huge amounts of food and knew enough about eating disorders to be certain she wasn't bulimic. Now she understood why the girl was so thin and tired.

The irony was that, externally, things couldn't be better. Her accountant had just called to say that this year's figures were the best ever, up by thirty per cent. After months of flirtatious talk on the phone about rising stock and equity shares, Diego Vincent, president of Allure Inc., New York's premier model agency, was flying in to have breakfast with her next week to talk about merging their companies into the world's most powerful agency. *A La Mode* had already got hold of some of Jo-Jo's test shots and had booked her for three shoots and a potential cover. At a cocktail party for the fashion industry at 11 Downing Street the night before, Cassie had judiciously let slip to selected guests that Grace was writing a book and by ten the next morning seven publishers had faxed her with their bids. Zack had turned out to be a revelation; dependable, resourceful and sensitive. 'He's obviously one of those people who needs a crisis to bring out the best in him,' said Janie from the office, where she seemed to be spending her life at the moment. And Barney Frick's builders had called to say they could start work on the flat in a fortnight.

All in all she felt utterly wretched.

'Who'd have thought Eddie-babes would have turned out to have a pash for fash?' said Sissy, pouring Janie a restorative cup of camomile tea. Furious at the way Edward Rushmore had fawned on Janie in the meeting, Phyllida had bawled her out afterwards, and sent her a copy of a letter from a colonel in Woking who had written in to complain about the ludicrous clothes featured on the paper's fashion pages.

'Take no notice. Phyllida's tragic,' clucked Sissy. 'Have you noticed how even her slang's always out of date?' They were in the fashion cupboard, ostensibly going through the rails of clothes Sissy had called in for a shoot. Located to the west side of the news floor, it was an oasis away from the Styrofoam coffee cups and computer-generated heat of the rest of the paper, and Sissy zealously kept it off limits to the other reporters, firmly telling any would-be intruders that its contents were far too valuable not to be kept under lock and key. She called it a cupboard to avoid making the other journalists jealous. And since no one but the fashion team had ever been invited in, they could hardly dispute her claim. In fact it was quite a sizeable room with evening sun and a coffee filter that Louisa Dunne had used for batching up her freebase, before she cleaned up and moved on to vodka. Sissy had found empty bottles for months after she left, and in despair called in Rentokil one night to fumigate the place. Then she painted the walls Kinky Pink, cajoled Angel Derrida into giving her an old purple velvet chaise-longue left over from his last shop refit, and tacked up a few yellow and orange swags made from old velvet Georgina Von Etzdorf scarves. The effect was striking, if not exactly soothing.

'What d'you think of inglenook fireplaces?' Sissy asked, handing Janie an organic flapjack. 'Only Angel's new boyfriend Pedro makes faux logs and stuff. He made one for Nancy O'Kelly's log cabin in Montana. They're so realistic her cleaning lady chucked them out. Nancy was furious – apparently they cost a bomb. But Angel owes us a favour and he said he'd get Pedro to install one for next to nothing. It would make this room very cosy in winter.'

'I think we've got to stop this flow of "favours",' said Janie sanctimoniously, remembering the colonel's letter Phyllida had shown her. 'I don't think we should accept freebies either. And I think we should stop featuring French products after all that nuclear testing they did in the Pacific.'

Sissy looked baffled. 'The advertising department will hit the roof.'

But Janie wasn't listening. If Matthew could go all holy, so could she.

Cassie felt betrayed on every front. She'd raced over to Janie's for a quiet supper only to discover that Janie had just called Gloria to say she wouldn't be able to get home from work until ten. Hugging one of Gloria's hot toddies, she gazed forlornly across the garden to the bay trees, feeling like one of Matthew's refugees. She had spent the previous evening packing up her belongings ready for the builders to move in at the end of the week. It had been a weird, existential sort of experience. Unable to decide which of her most valued treasures she wanted to take with her, she had allowed Zack to persuade her to leave them all behind, apart from a favourite photograph of Nell. 'I've got a feeling that this will probably prove to be the single most liberating act you ever do,' he said, boxing up his Nordic Track. 'You may never want your stuff back.'

The whole point of minimalism, as far as Cassie was concerned, wasn't that you actually got rid of things, but that you had lots of cupboards built so it just looked as though you had. She wasn't even sure she wanted to live in an empty space, yet she was about to spend thousands of pounds stripping her flat naked, and all on the pretext of getting rid of Zack, who had somehow managed to move into her suite at The Hempel with her anyway. She watched Nell polish the French doors in the kitchen, using a chamois leather the way Gloria had shown her. At this rate, she thought crossly, Gloria would be done for child labour.

Fifty-one hours after the crash, there was still no sign of Peace.

Regretfully, Cassie headed back to The Hempel, but found herself circling Blomfield Road like a homing pigeon. She decided to take one last peek at the flat just to convince herself that she really didn't need her scales.

The flat was eerily still. Emptied of its furniture, it had already assumed an air of vacant possession. The sisal matting was discoloured by the sun even in the early evening murkiness and she could see where the sofa had been, could even make out the imprint of Zack's exercise bike. It all looked depressingly impermanent and unappetising.

Dispirited, she took the lift down to the communal gardens. It was an unseasonably mild evening and she had an uncharacteristic yearning to smell the earth. Tracing the shadows of the neat, clipped hedges, she felt a semblance of tranquillity descend, or perhaps it was just exhaustion. She stood under the ancient, stately oak tree in the centre of the lawn, watching the moon slip through the clouds. As a rule, Cassie wasn't much moved by nature, but she loved the strict formality of these communal gardens and the clear proof they offered of man's ability to impose order on anarchy. She sat on the bench and listened to the schizophrenic chatter of the blackbirds, trying to marshal her chaotic thoughts into something resembling their old meticulous logic.

She must have been there for a good half-hour when she heard a groaning and Peace crawled out of the shadows behind her. Cassie was shocked out of her trance. Barefoot, in a torn chiffon dress and an old tweed coat, Peace looked shrunken and filthy. Her hair had been twisted into tiny plaits and matted with heaven knew what. Her legs were caked in rancid-looking mud and smattered with bruises, and her face . . . dear God, her face was lacerated and swollen. One eye was half closed and she was sucking her thumb. She looked half crazed. She dragged herself over to Cassie, who did her utmost not to recoil, laid her head in the older woman's lap and began to whimper like an injured cat.

It was an hour before Cassie could do anything with Peace. The girl sat huddled at her feet, every so often lurching into incoherent exclamations while Cassie stroked her hair and attempted to calm herself down. She didn't even know where to take Peace. The heating and hot water had been turned off in her flat and she didn't want to go back to Janie's. It would frighten Nell and would be the end of Jo-Jo's modelling career as far as Gloria was concerned. The paparazzi, who permanently loitered outside The Hempel in the hope of snapping Jack Nicholson or Tom Cruise, meant the hotel was out of the question.

In the end she coaxed Peace into her car and drove to the office. At least there was a shower, a sofa and somewhere warm to think.

As she fumbled with the keys, she felt herself being pierced by the glare of a powerful torch.

'What the fuck's going on?' growled a voice. It was her new neighbour, Seth Weiss, the ridiculously good-looking Irish chef who'd made quite a name for himself at Le Chateau, a grand, but until recently, fading restaurant whose lustre had been growing steadily brighter since his arrival there three years earlier. He was now in the process of buying a large converted warehouse next door to Cassie on the river, where he planned to set up on his own. Cassie turned, inwardly cursing, and nearly had her eyes prodded out by the probing beam of his searchlight.

'Only me, Cassie Grange. Your neighbour,' she said, trying not to sound flustered.

'Can I help at all?' he enquired more gently. 'Sorry about the aggression. It's just that we've had a couple of looters and pillagers recently. And now I've finally signed the lease, I can't leave the place alone. I set off for home every night and find myself doing a spot of breaking and entering.' The stark features softened into a disarming smile and then turned quizzical as he caught sight of Peace.

Cassie never could satisfactorily explain afterwards, least of all to herself, why she chose to confide everything, and she meant everything – Peace, the accident, Zack, her doubts about minimalism – to Seth that night. It could have been his initial gruffness – she liked the fact that he was singularly lacking in smarminess. It could have been instinct – she prided herself on her ability to read people's characters rapidly and accurately (all except potential life partners that is, she thought glumly). Or maybe it was his intensely honest, intensely . . . well, intense brown eyes. Cassie was a sucker for brown eyes.

Whatever the reason, it was one of her better decisions. Seth took over, driving them to his flat in Old Street, which amounted to one big kitchen with a small bedroom off it. It had an industrial style about it – not a bad idea, Cassie couldn't help reflecting, and she liked the cerulean splash of colour behind the double steel sinks. She cajoled Peace into a hot bath, put her into Seth's bed, where she lay curled in the foetal position, eyes staring blankly into the pitch black; she had made them blot out every last chink of light from the streetlamps below.

Immensely relieved to have found Peace, even if there was clearly a traumatic psychological journey to be embarked on, Cassie spent the rest of the night drinking delicious Irish *lattes* (Seth's own brew: plenty of whisky in them) and listening to Seth tell her unemotionally but movingly, about the experience he'd been through with Finn, his older brother who had died three years before from an overdose. He was still coming to terms with it — perhaps, he said, he never would. 'But one thing I have learnt is that self-reproach is utterly futile. It'll devour you.' He looked directly at Cassie, who seemed to be shrinking back into the sofa and hoped his warning wasn't already too late.

Chapter Six

Janie looked up from Silas Shoreham's eviscerating fashion exposé in *The Probe* and studied the audience. They were in Paris, but they could have been in any of the fashion capitals – the seating plan, which Janie was beginning to think was deliberately divisive, was always the same: Suzy and Petronella at the end of the catwalk; the other glossy magazine editors seated at the front down the sides, and all the other journalists, buyers and their entourages arranged behind them according to their status. It was the most public caste system in the world. And Silas had just massacred the lot of them, writing that 'the world's fashion press exhibit the combined intelligence of a brick, the sensitivity of Adolf Hitler and the dress sense of a group of blind day-trippers from eastern Europe'. Janie didn't know whether to be relieved that Silas hadn't mentioned anyone by name, or frustrated, since it meant he would live to write another tale.

Janie supposed it was John Galliano who had set the trend for elaborate tableaux. At any rate, all the new, avant-garde designers went in for them now. It was stiflingly hot in the labour exchange that Aeron had chosen as the backdrop to his winter collection, and the audience fanned itself in unison with the flimsy invitations Aeron had sent out – the French equivalent of a P45. Aeron's last few shows had got such rave reviews that there was talk that Gilles de Gaumard, the president of Tigre-Luxe, the giant luxury goods conglomerate, was about to give him a top job at one of his fashion houses. Not that Aeron was remotely interested in working for the Establishment – as he kept telling every journalist who interviewed him, while casually flexing the new skull and crossbone tattoo he'd just got done during a drunken weekend bender in Amsterdam. But all the same the tension was giving everyone a headache, compounded by the champagne that was being served to the audience by a bunch of scowling male models dressed up as eighteenth-century jailers, all courtesy of Mystere Champagne, Aeron's latest sponsors. Luella Lopez, a sixty-seven-going-on-twenty-nine-year-old Southern belle frockaholic who rarely missed a single show, had had to skip the Milan collections this season to host an engagement ball for one of her granddaughters. Determined to make amends, she had flown in specially to lend Aeron moral support and was seated next to Petronella, beneath a light sprinkling of diamonds and a flapping poster declaring war on poverty.

'Amazing, isn't it?' drawled Magnus, glancing up from his crossword. 'Luella can make it from New York with twenty minutes to spare and every strand of her shellacked hair standing to attention – why the UN didn't post the woman's hair out to Bosnia as a standing human shield I'll never know. Aeron, on the other hand, only has to move ten feet and he's still two hours late.' It would be after eleven when the show finished, and there'd be a stampede to reach the limos that were waiting outside for the lucky ones. The rest would have to hang around for taxis or risk the walk to the nearest Métro which was miles away, and the photographers would be so whacked out there'd probably be a brawl. Janie gazed mistily around the Exchange at the crowd. The champagne was clearly starting to ease the pain of the day's frustrations. Pity the photographers hadn't been offered any. She still couldn't get used to the way so many fashion editors wore what were essentially cocktail outfits throughout the day. And none of them ever seemed to feel the cold, skipping from show to show with bare legs, strappy high-heeled sandals and flimsy beaded dresses. Sissy said it was limo-life dressing and the ultimate form of one-upmanship on all the plebs who had to rely on the Métro. Janie had to admit the crowd at Aeron's was amazingly good-natured, given the time and unsavoury location. Silas wouldn't write about that, of course. What was his problem? He was clearly chippy about something. She tried to remember what Matthew had said about Silas – and found herself thinking about the postcard that had arrived for Nell from Guatemala that day. Nell had read it over the phone to her, between sobs.

Darling Nell, this is the most beautiful country. I hope one day I can show it to you all. There is so much to tell you but in the meantime, study the rainforest in the picture and look for the tallest tree. That's the one Mungo and I have been camping under. Look after Mummy. Big kisses to you all.
  Love, Dad.

How dare Matthew go upsetting Nell like that, fumed Janie. He couldn't just keep dropping in and out of their lives. She'd have to get Will to write to his brother and explain how unsettling it was for all of them. Just thinking about Matthew made her so apoplectic that she didn't notice a slight figure slip into the seat next to her. Lee Howard shifted slightly on the fluorescent-yellow plastic bench, glanced at her Cartier Tank watch and introduced herself to Janie in a clipped East Coast American accent. 'I've been reading your pieces in the *Gazette*,' she smiled. 'They're very perceptive.' Janie smiled back, flattered. Lee was an intelligent, forceful fashion director who was always championing the real working woman. She had worked on every major publication in New York and was highly respected – and feared – for her integrity, and was said to be on the verge of launching her own magazine.

Backstage, Aeron was a sodden mulch of nerves. He was desperate for 'Modern Match Girls' to be a hit, and secretly for de Gaumard to sweep him off his feet and offer him an obscenely large salary and an atelier in Paris. In his more confident moments he knew the clothes were some of his best ever – ethereally beautiful and, with only a few adjustments, potentially quite commercial. There was no doubt – he was a genius. *Women's Wear Daily* was already desperate to interview him. *Beau Monde* would have to slug it out with *A La Mode* to see who managed to get hold of the whole collection first.

'Of course, it's not a proper scoop.' Lindsey Craven brandished the article Janie had written about Bella Scarletti in front of the accessories editor of *Beau Monde*, who was sitting in front of her. 'I expect Bella just wanted to plug her new underwear range.'

'You've got to admit, though, that it's a pretty wicked piece, especially that bit about Giuseppe threatening Bella with a knife if she got married,' said the accessories editor. 'No one else had a whiff of that one.'

Crestfallen, Lindsey had to concede to herself that wicked was exactly what it was.

Cassie had done an enormous amount of soul-searching at Seth's. Her first inclination had been to hush the whole affair up, to get Peace's lamentably naïve mother to take some responsibility for her daughter and cover track marks as quickly as possible. Perhaps Peace could take the summer off and spend it in the bosom of her family in Gloucestershire – the country air and all those hunters her stepfather bred were bound to do her the world of good.

But Seth persuaded her that the situation was too far gone to be solved by a couple of weeks' mucking out. 'Peace is seriously ill,' he said gravely. 'This isn't a new thing.' He recalled the last few minutes of an interview he'd caught between Peace and Clive James months earlier – even filtered through a television screen her manic chatter and distracted eyes had struck him as suspicious.

Cassie winced with shame at what, despite Zack's best attempts, she still perceived to be her own benign neglect.

As a pallid-looking sun made a brief appearance through the grey London haze, Cassie left Peace slumbering fitfully in Seth's bed and made her way back to the soothing creamy stripes and fluttering muslin curtains of The Hempel to shower and change.

Zack was sleeping blissfully. She let him sleep on. She needed to think. By ten she had filled Saffron in and was back at Seth's.

Peace was awake and curled up on the sofa, a thick white plate lodged between her knees and stomach, a cigarette in one hand, a honey-scented croissant which she nervously broke into thousands of tiny crumbs in the other. Seth silently beckoned Cassie out on to his terrace where, in less tense times, even Cassie would have been delighted by the array of herbs and vegetables growing.

'She's still babbling, but it's starting to piece together,' he began.

'Where on earth has she been?' asked Cassie, sick with anticipation.

'I think she's genuinely blanked the last few days, but from what she says it sounds as though she's been with some pretty unsavoury characters and has probably spent at least one night on the streets,' he said quietly.

Cassie flinched. 'God knows how no one recognised her and brought her in,' she said.

'She's not exactly looking her best,' replied Seth gently. 'She was half crazed with fear. She thought she'd killed that poor kid and seems to have spent the last three days ricocheting between wanting to turn herself into the police and wanting to run away for ever. I think she's been delirious.'

By half past eleven Cassie's own doctor had managed to drop by and give Peace a sedative. Seth had made discreet enquiries about the rehabilitation clinic his brother had been to. 'It doesn't work for everyone. It didn't for Finn in the end,' he said softly, 'but it's the best there is. But before we get her in, she has to admit she needs to be there.'

At lunch-time Seth had to meet his architect, Barney Frick, to go over plans for the restaurant. Cassie sat by Peace's bed and made intermittent calls on her mobile, including a sobering one to Jute, which she hadn't had the strength to do while Peace was still missing. During the course of Jute's rambling monologue (one that would haunt Cassie for the rest of her life), Cassie established that Peace had been experimenting dangerously for over a year and had developed what could only be described as an impressively catholic taste in Class A drugs.

'To be honest she's one of my best customers,' mumbled Jute. And as he ran through Peace's shopping list, Cassie felt herself plummeting into a cosmic gloom. 'Mountains of dope, and I mean Himalayas, not the poxy Alps; twenty grams of coke, speed, Es, an awesome amount of smack. Y'know, if the government only made it legit I could have had it all done by direct debit which would have been a hell of a lot easier all round. I don't like to think of nicely brought-up girls like Peace wandering round with such big wads of dosh. It's an unscrupulous world out there . . .' He trailed off as an icy chill of disapproval blasted along the telephone line. 'Anyway, she only came to me – she said she didn't trust anyone else – so at least you know she was injecting quality,' he continued blithely. 'And of course I never gave her any crack, though she was up for it. But for a waif and everything, she sure could put it away.'

When Peace woke up at eight p.m., she was strangely calm and coherent. Seth was still out, but Zack, faintly piqued at being left out of the drama, tracked Cassie down. It was just as well. Peace seemed to feel a special bond with Zack which surprised even Cassie, newly converted to his charms though she was. Listening to him convince Peace that Shareen was indeed alive and toddling, and later – much later – hearing him delicately broach the subject of Peace's relationship with drugs, she could only be thankful that she'd never quite got round to offloading him that night at the Pharmacy. When Seth finally got back from lunch with Barney she introduced them, painfully aware that she and Zack must seem a seedy, ineffectual couple. What a way to get to know the neighbours.

The three of them took turns to watch over Peace throughout the next night. By eight the next morning, Peace, still showing no signs of falling into a natural sleep, had agreed to allow Zack to book her into a clinic. Cassie called an emergency summit meeting with Saffron which lasted all day. Eventually they decided that the best tactic would be to come clean in the press. It was a miracle that no one had recognised Peace in the past three days. But they couldn't rely on the same thing happening at the clinic. She would issue a formal statement and give the first interview to Janie. If anyone was going to benefit from this nightmare, it might as well be her. She dialled Janie's mobile in Paris and got straight through to her at Aeron's show.

'Switch on that laptop and I'll call you back in ten minutes. I want you to be *compos mentis* for this one.'

'The thing is, I think Aeron's about to start.'

'Sod Aeron. This is hold-the-front-page stuff, Janie. It's also complicated and so sensitive that the only reason I'm entrusting a journalist with it is because she's my best and oldest friend.'

Much to the consternation of everyone sitting around her, Janie pushed her way to the back of the room and out through the swing doors, past the hopeful fashion hordes milling outside the labour exchange. Eventually she found a street bench and, perching between the empty wine bottles and hamburger wrappers, waited for Cassie to call back.

To her astonishment, Cassie found herself tearing up halfway through the story. She handed the phone over to Seth, who explained to Janie in calm, unemotional tones the full extent of Peace's addiction.

'Perhaps you can say that by being so open she hopes to help others with the same problem,' he said. 'She hasn't actually said that but in a few weeks she probably will.'

It wasn't until she'd filed the story and actually heard Doug Channing whistle admiringly down the phone that Janie was able to digest the enormity of it all. The poor girl. Poor Cassie. She'd sounded terrible. He'd sounded rather nice, though. Sympathetic, capable, unemotional and yet somehow very moving. Lethal combination in her experience. Not that she was very up to date on that score. Still, she couldn't help but wonder, now she came to think about it, who on earth he was.

★   ★   ★

Aeron finished massaging Jess's neck, handed her two rolls of loo paper to stuff under her armpits so that the sweat didn't stain her dress, and above her head solemnly made the sun, moon and stars sign that he'd learned from a Tibetan monk he'd met at a polo match underwritten by his last but one sponsors. This had become as much of a ritual with him as the naming of each of his outfits. Every season, as the collection was nearing completion, Aeron and Squidge would get plastered on Guinness, try on all the clothes and christen them. Jess looked up from the handwritten scroll he'd sent her and grinned. It was always the same. Only the name of the dress changed. This year her petticoat was called Sabotage. She liked that. She looked at the scroll again and giggled.

> *No twirling. No old-fashioned poncy modelling. No cheesy tits out for the paparazzi.*
> *Loveya, Aeron*
> *PS: You are wearing the star dress and you look genius.*

The PS was Squidge's idea. They'd written it on all the scrolls, which Aeron thought was a bit deceitful, but Squidge had convinced him the girls needed all the emotional support they could get at times like these. His headphones crackled. It was almost time to start. Just one more girl to do.

'I can't go on,' Stacey intoned noiselessly, her voice a weak signal over the surging hairdryers. A fat tear rolled down her thin face and began to coagulate with the white powder on her cheek. Seeing two hours' worth of Kabuki make-up about to bite the dust, Aeron decided to skip the sun, moon and stars and hugged her instead.

'I cannot go out in a dress called Harlot,' she wailed, scrumpling the scroll. 'My father will kill me. He's already made my agent promise I'll never do swimwear.'

'Well, it's a reformed prostitute,' said Aeron, hastily extemporising. 'It becomes a nun when it grows up – doesn't the scroll say?'

'No,' said Stacey shakily. She stood up and began unfastening the hooks. 'I am a great admirer of your work, Aeron, but I have my principles.'

Aeron looked over the mirror and saw Squidge gesticulating frantically. A voice crackled over his headphones from front of stage. Gwyneth Paltrow, whom Aeron had set his heart on dressing for the Oscars, was about to leave. He made a snap decision and grabbed Jess's scroll from the counter where she was studying it and swapped it with Stacey's. It nearly broke his heart: the vibes would be all wrong for the dresses now and Jess would be livid – she had been perfecting Sabotage expressions for days. But he couldn't afford to lose Gwyneth and his sponsors in one evening. Ignoring Jess's expostulations, he signalled for Squidge to tell the DJ to begin.

As the lights dimmed, Lee put her newspaper away and silently dared Aeron Baxter to astonish and amaze her. He did. His modern matchgirls wore beautifully fitted wool challis Empire-line gowns, as delicate as whispers. Their deep, inky colours were partnered with bizarrely beautiful cobwebby tights and etiolated box-leather mules. In their notebooks and sketch pads the spellbound audience hastily scribbled out the fashion spreads they had planned in Milan and began plotting fresh ones based round Aeron's New Silhouette. For night-time, there were fronded featherweight organza and tweed dresses which lapped round the models' bodies like petals round a calyx. The models, strangely ethereal-looking, their hair tautly swept back into latticework chignons, weaved gracefully between the benches, which were threaded with fairy lights. Dodie Kent had spent sleepless weeks designing extraordinary half-pixie, half-kabuki inspired make-up especially for Aeron's show. Only Jess looked anachronistic. Normally she was painstakingly accurate in her method modelling. But furious with Aeron for changing her dress's name at the last minute, she wiggled her hips as vampily as any transvestite on the rue St Denis, twirling camply every ten feet and thrusting her bosoms so brazenly at the cameras that one of them popped out of the gauzy bodice right in front of Gwyneth Paltrow. She'd give

Aeron Sabotage. 'Jess's C Cup Runneth Over,' cackled Lindsey Craven into her Dictaphone, thrilled that a headline had come so easily. The standing ovation lasted ten minutes, during which time Isabella Suarez made a particular point of personally leading an emotional-looking Aeron out to take his bows.

Luella Lopez, friskier than ever, was the first to congratulate Aeron backstage. 'Darling, what a clever, clever boy. Those beggar culottes – divine! Ooh, love that tattoo. So macabre. By the way, my husband says the last dress I bought from you was the sexiest vision he'd ever seen. And he just loves those boob-buggers.'

'Er, fanks,' mumbled Aeron, aghast at the idea of someone as ancient as Luella in his clothes. 'Pleased to oblaadge.'

'Oh, you *amusant* boy. I can't understand a word you're saying – talk about divided by a common tongue!'

'Common being the operative word,' said Jess sulkily.

'Christ,' exclaimed Aeron to Squidge as Luella trotted off, 'she looks as though someone's been practising cryogenics on her.'

Sissy and Alice clattered down the steps to the labour exchange clutching one another and blinking back rapturous tears. 'It was like a symphony,' Sissy burst out when she found Janie. 'Everyone working in harmony – the models, Dodie, Enrico . . . those tiaras made from hair were incredible. The beading mixed with the wool and satin, the music. That's what fashion history is about. You could see that and die happy.' She stopped, finally noticing the tears streaking down Janie's cheeks. Could it be that Janie was finally starting to understand it all? Fashion really did move in mysterious ways.

Cassie could barely get into her office the day after Janie's article about Peace broke in the *Gazette*. The other newspapers had all opted for lead pictures of Jess's left breast and were consequently incandescent with envy about her scoop. Cassie's fax machine had been spewing out requests for interviews about Peace which had come in from as far afield as Paraguay and Kyoto. The office was one giant, slippery snowdrift.

'The absurd thing is,' said Saffron, 'you couldn't have planned this better. The tone of the coverage so far is universally sympathetic. You're seen as some kind of beacon in a foul, amoral sewer. Bloody ironic, isn't it?'

Cassie didn't see why it was that ironic. She *did* keep a vigilant eye on all her models, as far as possible. But she knew what Saffron meant: they had both known that Peace used drugs socially and neither had been as firm with her as they should have been. As Cassie spent the next few days carefully picking her way through selected interviews, the picture that emerged of herself in the press was of a woman who had taken a courageous stand in finally bringing the issue of drug abuse in the glamorous world of modelling out into the open, even at the risk of losing business and face.

The reality, thought Cassie wearily, was far more complicated. It was true that by coming clean about Peace's drug abuse she might have jeopardised Peace's name, but she was far more likely to have imprinted it even more strongly on the world's subconscious. It had been plastered over the news for days now. True, some of the multinational beauty companies might balk at using her for a bit – the first whiff of scandal always had them ruthlessly junking million-dollar contracts and running to their lawyers. Cassie understood why: no one wanted to risk having their billboards defaced with the slogan 'Skincare by heroin'. But fashion designers were a different issue. Some of them would positively relish the notoriety of being linked with Peace. A good many others would turn a blind eye. And then of course, if Peace made it through rehab, there would be masses of mileage out of her relaunch, followed by the anticipation of a slide back into her old ways, articles about how fantastic she looked on it all – or how terrible. Either way, if she had the stomach for it, Peace could capitalise on her mishap to the tune of millions. Diego Vincent was delighted and called Cassie to invite her to a fashion gala at the end of the month in New York.

'Great exposure for you, baby. They're all talking about you.

Listen, maybe you could get that new girl of yours to present an award. The new face presents the newcomer gong. Great idea or what? Tell you what, I'll fix it. I gotta tell ya, sugar, I'm very impressed by the way you handled things back there,' he drawled. 'Coulda been shaky, but you took the waves like a real pro.'

'Don't mind about Peace, sugar,' growled Cassie after she put the phone down. 'She nearly died back there, but I gotta tell ya, babe, it was a great career move.'

'Oh, don't worry about Peace,' said Saffron. 'I know it doesn't seem entirely appropriate to say so just now, but deep down that one's tougher than the Praetorian Guard.'

Janie had thought that things would ease off once they got back from Paris, but this was the third night in a row that she had found herself working until nine o'clock. She hadn't spent a whole day with the children since she'd gone to Milan, and she felt stiff with guilt. She rang home to speak to Nell. Since Janie had been going away they'd established a pattern of bedtime stories over the phone.

'She's in bed,' said Gloria. 'She was sleeping by 'alf past seven. Worn out, poor lamb, she was. Just as well. Stanley left.' She could barely keep the triumph out of her voice. 'Nell make the deecision. She say Stanley was getting on hair nerves.'

Janie watched Sissy stonily as she wafted out of the fashion cupboard, swathed in a floor-length shaggy yellow coat and balancing two cups of applemint tea. Of course she was pleased that Nell no longer needed Stanley. She knew that she should be grateful that Gloria had been able to find a temporary replacement for the Scotts so that she could spend all week at Janie's, but she couldn't help wishing that she had been around to solve the Stanley situation.

'Do you really hate it so much?' Sissy asked her, catching her mutinous expression. 'I suppose it can be a bit . . . well, intense, what with Phyllida and everything. And sometimes it seems like a lot of work for something quite trivial.' She put her arms round

Janie's stooped shoulders. 'Just go with the flow. That's the way
to survive. At least you've had a run of scoops. When Louisa was
here they farmed out anything interesting to the news desk.'

To cheer Janie up, Sissy suggested they investigate a Lebanese
restaurant that had recently opened on a particularly bleak stretch
of Brick Lane. 'It's really cosy and off the beaten track,' she told
Janie. She didn't mention that it was also becoming a Mecca
for the fashion pack.

Chez Ramoush's higgledy-piggledy interior unfolded, maze-
like, behind a battered exterior. The walls, crudely painted a
dark red, were festooned with tasselled swags and fringed rugs.
The tables, tiny and overcrowded and far too numerous to satisfy
fire regulations, were hemmed in by towering banquettes in
various not quite matching offcuts of spice-coloured velveteen
that Ramoush had got cheaply from a friend who supplied John
Lewis. Plates of fragrant steaming food were piled on enormous
circular pewter trays which floated above the waiters' heads like
ethnic UFOs. The place was a ramshackle, noisy, atmospheric
mess, and when the first influx of fashion pioneers had started
coming regularly, Ramoush, a lugubrious soul who wore frilled
shirts and piped tuxedos, had been in turns perplexed and
rhapsodic. He didn't want his restaurant becoming known as
a hangout for freaks and the kind of men who went in for what
Ramoush and his brothers referred to as That Perversion. But
as he had become more familiar with their magazines (he now
received eight on complimentary subscription) he had got into
the swing of things, and the constant ringing of the till.

'Good God, Angel, what are you doing here?' Sissy's voice
twanged with stagy astonishment. 'I thought I was the only
person who knew this little secret.'

Angel looked at her archly and shifted uneasily, trying
to take up more room on the cinnamon-coloured velour
banquette. He was two-timing Pedro and didn't want Sissy
plonking herself down and asking his companion awkward
questions.

'Hi, Sissy,' he said coolly. 'Oh look, there's Aeron.' He
waved across the room to Aeron's overpopulated table, which

until Sissy walked in he'd spent the past hour studiously ignoring.

'Janie, what are you doing here?' Jo-Jo bounded up, eyes sparkling. She was wearing a new soft black leather jacket, a skimpy white t-shirt and an antique fuchsia silk skirt. She looked sensational. In less than six weeks, Cassie had transformed her. She must be slipping, thought Janie.

'This is Joel Eliot.' Jo-Jo introduced a lanky giant slouching behind her. Joel was an up-and-coming photographer whose radically out-of-focus technique had taken the fashion world by storm. Sissy was desperate to work with him on the *Gazette*, but secretly acknowledged this was unlikely to happen since Joel, whom she nicknamed Swampy, preferred artistic territory that was strictly underground. 'He's been doing some pictures of me for *A La Mode*,' said Jo-Jo. 'Had me hanging off a motorbike. It's been a bit of a laugh, actually. I'd love to stay and chat but we're just going to do a reccie for tomorrow's shoot.' She pirouetted round to face Joel and accidentally sent a glass of smoking green tea flying into the nearest lap. 'Whoops,' she giggled. A morose-looking middle-aged moon face half obscured by impenetrably dark glasses and a Peruvian bobble hat peered round from the banquette and stared at her.

'Gawd, I'm sorry. Is it really hot? Can I buy you another?'

The face made no response, but stared at her so intently that the little cluster around Jo-Jo began to grow uneasy. From behind, Joel nudged her and tried to whisper something, but Jo-Jo ignored him.

'Oh, go fuck yourself. I said I'm sorry,' exploded Jo-Jo, and then corrected herself. 'Er, sure I can't do anything?'

The face remained mute.

Jo-Jo turned back to the others and shrugged helplessly. 'There's no point apologising to some people.'

'It's Sven Tolssen,' Sissy mouthed theatrically.

'Oh, right,' said Jo-Jo blankly.

'He hasn't been to London for five years,' whispered Sissy as a waiter dabbed at Sven's crotch. Jo-Jo and Joel made their exit and Ramoush steered Janie and Sissy to a table at the back.

Alice was on the next banquette, squirming up to the style director of *Shag*, a new avant-garde fashion magazine that had become mandatory reading. Sissy frowned. 'This place is a bit fashioned out. Sorry, I had no idea.'

Tightening her arms around Joel's waist as his Vespa skimmed along the Embankment, Jo-Jo had to admit that so far modelling wasn't too bad. She would not be telling that to Cassie, however. Let her sweat. The moment they had got enough first-rate test pictures to put on her card, Cassie had sent it out to a handful of glossy magazines. Jo-Jo didn't approve of the vital statistics being included, of course – that was just bloody demeaning. She and Cassie had had a bit of a row about it, but Jo-Jo's heart wasn't really in it. She decided to put her feminist principles on hold until she'd had a bit more of a chance to read up about them. She could probably do that on all the plane trips. And she couldn't help getting a kick out of seeing how . . . professional, yes there was no other word for it, she looked in front of the camera.

The outfit had been Cassie's idea. She'd taken Jo-Jo shopping at Brompton Cross and introduced her to Joseph and Voyage. She'd told her how to push her bottom out so that the gap between the tops of her thighs was accentuated, and on a more general level instructed her to be friendly but not gushing, firm about not doing things she felt uncomfortable with (but never stroppy) and not to take it personally or lose her rag when photographers were rude to her or kept her waiting. But so far no one had. Even Cassie had been surprised by the rapture that had greeted Jo-Jo's card.

'Don't get too excited,' she said waspishly. 'It could all be a flash in the pan – idle curiosity, boredom or both. We'll wait to see how many of these reservations actually get confirmed. Then we'll work out a schedule. In the meantime please destroy your old wardrobe and set aside a day in the next week to go to my hairdresser for a grooming session.'

Jo-Jo thought Cassie was a complete bitch, which rather

relieved her. Everyone else had been so nice that she needed a hate figure.

For her part, Cassie also thought she was being a bitch. *Vogue* had already confirmed a first option on Jo-Jo for a cover try, which was almost unheard of. There was no need to give Jo-Jo such a hard time but she couldn't help it. She felt guilty about Peace and was taking it out on Jo-Jo. In return it seemed to Cassie that Jo-Jo was deliberately out to rile her. Whatever she suggested, Jo-Jo pretended to ignore. But there was more to Cassie's exasperation than that. She'd dealt with stroppy, naïve teenagers a thousand times before, and won, transforming them into shrewd, smart and sophisticated-for-their-years operators. The problem was, Cassie wasn't sure she wanted to turn Jo-Jo into an operator. A month ago she'd seemed so deliciously belligerent and unpredictably bolshie. Why was she proving such a pushover?

Marcus Lurie, Cassie's hairdresser, a former foster child and now the proud possessor of a black Porsche, a 1967 bronze Mercedes 280 SL and a waiting list at his Mayfair salon that was at least three months long, had the good sense to make only minimal changes to Jo-Jo. In fact, watching Marcus painstakingly nip at her waist-length hair with what looked like nail scissors, Jo-Jo felt like asking for her money back. Except that she wasn't paying. Cassie was. It was only after she had spent another four hours having her legs and bikini line waxed, her eyebrows subtly reshaped, a pedicure, a manicure, a facial and ordering every fruit shake on Marcus's menu, that Jo-Jo began to notice something different when she examined her reflection. She looked sleeker and radiant, as if she'd been on holiday somewhere glamorous. Her eyes looked extraordinarily feral. Her skin shone as if it had been polished with Gloria's Brasso. The contours of her face were even more chiselled.

As the new improved Jo-Jo emerged from her pupa, the sulky attitude she had marched into Marcus's salon with began to evaporate. By the time Marcus was explaining that next season they'd add a few streaks to the front of her hair, she was ready to kiss him. Instead she promised to teach him to rollerblade. She had barely left the salon before Marcus was on the phone.

'Cassie, she is *amaaazing*. I take it you're sending her to do the shows in New York?'

'I don't know about that,' said Cassie airily. 'It'll be months before that one's ready for the catwalks. Too immature and walks like a stevedore.'

Marcus was nonplussed. Jo-Jo was one of the most naturally graceful creatures he'd seen in years. 'You know best. But you better guard her like the crown jewels. Otherwise someone else will snap her up. It's getting more and more cut-throat out there, you know.'

Cassie did know. But she didn't want Jo-Jo drifting on to the catwalks halfway through the season, when everyone would be too jaded to take notice – and she wouldn't be able to chaperone her. Diego was right. The annual design awards that were due to take place at the Plaza Hotel in eight days' time, at the end of New York Fashion Week, were the perfect place to introduce Jo-Jo globally – and Cassie would be able to keep an eye on her. The world's leading designers would be there, along with half of Hollywood. She'd call Diego and get him to fix it. A brief appearance at the fashion world's most glamorous charity event of the year would be good practice for Jo-Jo, as well as stamping her indelibly as Cassie's property.

Sissy couldn't seem to get Janie to snap out of her oddly distracted mood. Even when she told her about falling over Nick Squire in Chez Ramoush's loo, she failed to raise a smile.

'He was on his back photographing that crocheted loo-roll holder for Kristof. His next collection is going to be Middle Eastern and he's got every photographer on the beat looking for inspiration.'

'The thing is,' said Janie, not really listening, 'do you think after New York there might be time to take a few days to go down to Guatemala?'

For three days an impenetrable fog tucked itself over the

bedrock of Manhattan. Unable to detach itself from the water around the island, it gave the city a ghostly appearance and a ghastly, sulphurous smell, trapping in all the noxious pollutants until the place simmered like a pressure cooker waiting to explode.

Janie felt lousy. It was a quarter to three in the afternoon, which gave her fifteen minutes to cross town in the drizzle, so that she could call Nell from the hotel for her bedtime story. If she was any later Gloria would make disapproving noises about children needing routines. She was turning into a bit of a Tartar, thought Janie woozily. She'd have to do something about it when she got home. She was homesick and exhausted and in a semi-permanent state of panic about the hotel bills. Sissy had booked them into the Westbury, where breakfast cost thirty dollars. Doug Channing had taken to calling her at four in the morning New York time for a news conference, and what with that and having to race back to the hotel at three to read Nell her story every day, she was worn out. By mid-week she had laryngitis. Sissy did her best, scurrying round to her favourite drug-stores for gargles and lozenges and gallons of orange juice, but Janie couldn't seem to shake it off. Enrico, who was still hoping for an article on his hair products, produced a brown paper bag bulging with homoeopathic pills which Sissy passed on to Janie. 'He swears by them and he's an absolute hypochondriac, so they must be brilliant. Apparently you have to shove copious amounts of them in your mouth. The more the merrier.'

In the name of scientific research, Sissy also dragged a practically delirious Janie to Bergdorf Goodman's to see if shopping really could cure minor ailments, and persuaded her to buy an excruciatingly expensive navy Calvin Klein gown to wear to the fashion gala. By the time the sales assistant had added on city and state taxes and converted it all into sterling, Janie was sweating profusely.

'You look amazing in it. You'll wear it for ever, so it's an absolute bargain. Just divide it by a thousand and you'll see,' suggested Sissy helpfully. 'Oh, and hang it at the end of your bed so it's the first thing you see when you wake up. Honoured fashion editor tip. I guarantee you'll feel a hundred per cent better in the morning. And the dress will seem like a snip.'

Janie felt sick with self-loathing when she woke the next morning, and the dress seemed like a financial catastrophe. How could she have spent nearly a month's mortgage on one flimsy, totally unembellished length of jersey? She could always take it back, she supposed. But then she'd have nothing to wear to the gala, since she'd forgotten to put the case of clothes Cassie had packed for her into the taxi. Perhaps she could skip the gala. But she had been personally invited by Lee Howard. It was a great honour, Sissy said. More to the point, everyone knew that Lee was on the verge of launching a new magazine. If Janie played her cards right, there could be new jobs all round.

Ben Mornay stepped off the private jet that had been put at his disposal by Tom Fitzgerald, on whose table he was sitting at the awards ceremony, and breathed in the damp New York stench. God, it was good to be back.

At twenty-eight, Ben Mornay was so dedicated to the craft of acting that he'd had little time to cultivate the sort of demonic reputation that Hollywood expected from its leading men. So Lorinda Day, his extremely diligent agent, had assiduously cultivated one for him.

Lorinda, who was besotted with her client, worshipped his dedication and fantasised about trampling through his baby blond hair or high-diving off his cheekbones. To this end she had done all sorts of things for him way beyond the call of duty – if he would only realise it – including taking his wardrobe in hand. The latter had been pretty easy. From the moment he had arrived in Hollywood three years earlier, discovered by a talent scout when he was playing Lysander in the most acclaimed Central Park production of *A Midsummer Night's Dream* for years, every store on Rodeo Drive had bombarded him with presents, invitations to cruise on various designers' yachts and free clothes. Tom Fitzgerald's gifts had been the classiest, and also, as Lorinda informed Ben, his suits were the best. She had almost made up her mind that Ben would wear a Tom Fitzgerald tuxedo to the Oscars next month, so when Ben was invited to New York to present Tom with an award for his outstanding contribution to American fashion, she naturally accepted.

'Why? If it's not too impertinent a question,' Ben had asked, as she arrived at his house laden with suit bags. He was beginning to find her omniscience spooky. She had taken control of his life to such an extent that she sometimes forgot to inform him of the decisions she was making on his behalf. And while half of him appreciated the freedom this gave him to plunge ever more deeply into his roles, the other half realised it was an unhealthy situation that was getting out of hand. 'And an award! Lorinda, I don't even know the first thing about fashion.'

'But you love New York. You're always saying you wish you got there more often. This way you get to spend three whole days there, plus it's totally legit and studio-approved because in the next few weeks before Oscar night you have to get your gorgeous little face in front of the cameras as often as possible. That way all those geriatric Academy members can't possibly have the excuse of saying they don't know who you are. And the best of it is that I've got three days' holiday owing to me so I can accompany you.' She was owed about two hundred days' holiday in fact, but something told her Ben wouldn't find her inability to take time off endearing. What mattered was that at last they would finally have some downtime together. She could hardly wait.

Unfortunately for Lorinda, she got a call on the way to LAX airport from her other star client who was threatening suicide following a botched liposuction on her knees. Lorinda had wept the entire journey back into town. Ben, meanwhile, spent the flight to New York brooding over the time he was about to waste. He'd just been sent a fascinating script set in Northern Ireland and he wanted to take a trip to Belfast to get a feel for the place. But as the familiar jagged Manhattan skyline came into view, and his uniformed driver sped towards the Pierre, he felt a rush of elation – and a guilty sense of relief that for once there was No Lorinda.

Seth volunteered to take Peace to Ashwood and Cassie was too relieved to demur. She had a gothic imagination that was running away with her; every time she tried to picture Peace in rehab, images of bedlam swirled in front of her. And after being initially relieved that Peace was safe, she was starting to find just being with her so unnerving that she was itching to find an excuse to go to New York early. It would do Jo-Jo good, she decided, to spend several days acclimatising to New York before being let loose at the gala, so two days before Peace was due to check in at Ashwood, Cassie and Jo-Jo left for JFK.

Seth was brilliant with Peace – supportive, gentle, but clearly not prepared to put up with any nonsense. Since her own mother was clearly incapable of offering Peace any support, Seth took a few days off work, made sure Peace had plenty of marijuana and took her on a whirlwind tour of London's more recherché sights – haunted pubs, famous old plague grounds and disused lidos – until they were both exhausted. In the evening he taught her simple recipes because she said she wanted to learn to cook in her new life. From being almost mute the first few days after her return, Peace chattered non-stop. She had blanked a lot of what had happened in her three-day absence – she told Seth that she thought she had probably blacked out for much of it. She didn't remember getting out of the Jeep, but she dimly recalled getting into a taxi and asking the driver to take her to Paddington. 'I kept thinking I've got to get home, I've got to get home. But needless to say I didn't have any money on me. I couldn't even pay the cab.' She shivered, and Seth put his arms round her. He'd treated her to lunch at Le Manoir aux Quatre Saisons and afterwards they had gone for a walk along the river near Henley.

Once Zack had sewn the seeds of rehabilitation in Peace's mind, she began to fixate on the idea and on all the constructive things she was going to devote her energies to while she was at

Ashwood. She made Seth take her to Foyle's, where she bought two boxes of Linguaphone tapes so that she could learn French and Spanish. By the time admission day came round, she was hooked on Lorca and determined to come out of the clinic being able to read him in the original.

She was unusually quiet on the journey down. She had repacked her case eight times, editing out anything that was too fashionable or what she called modelly. In the end she had taken only APC jeans, a stack of TSE cashmere jumpers, her favourite CDs (the selection of which had caused further agonising) and the Linguaphone tapes. Seth tried to distract her with a rundown of his top twenty cooking ingredients. By the time they reached the twisting Surrey lanes he was feeling nervous too. The last time he had seen Ashwood it had been to collect some of Finn's belongings after he died. He wasn't sure how he would feel sweeping through the gates with yet another troubled passenger at his side.

Ashwood was a pleasant surprise. An early Victorian manor house of honey-coloured brick, with gothic details that were further softened by a thick curtain of ivy and wisteria, it stood in twelve rolling acres overlooking an ornamental lake. Dr Bridgwater, who admitted Peace, was charming enough, and her room, though spartan, overlooked the gardens. Even so, Seth couldn't help feeling anxious as he left: Peace looked so small as she waved to him from the arched doorway; her pointy little face so determined to maintain a brave expression. It hadn't helped that a well-meaning nurse had bustled straight in and removed all Peace's books and CDs from where she had just carefully placed them on the chest of drawers – it was the clinic's policy, she said, and besides, the patients at Ashwood were kept so busy she wouldn't miss them. As he checked her fragile figure in his wing mirror, memories of his brother Finn flooded back, and it was all he could do not to cry.

Theoretically Jo-Jo knew she ought to be furious with herself. She was meant to be giving Cassie a hard time, but New York was so incredible, the Pierre was so incredible, the Givenchy sheath dress she and Cassie had chosen for her to wear to the gala was so incredible that, as she told Gloria over the phone, she just felt, well, incredible.

'I see America 'as worked wonders for your vocabulairee already,' said Gloria tartly. 'Now excuse me while I put the twins to bed. Their routine must not be interrupted.'

Diego Vincent trotted into the dining room at the Pierre trailing a jetstream of Chanel's Egoïste and Count Nikolai, his Irish setter.

'Darling Cassie, you look *deevine*.' He flashed her his most wolfish grin and managed to smother her hand with kisses while allowing his eyes to slither over her curves. 'Such a charming idea. English breakfast at my favourite hotel.'

Count Nikolai placed his elegant noble head in Cassie's lap, stretched his moist lips into a lascivious smile that almost matched his master's for brilliance, and sent her napkin fluttering to the floor. Like his master, he managed to look appealingly dissolute. In an instant Diego had returned the napkin, carefully tucking it into Cassie's groin. She felt herself blush. If she didn't know better, she might just have been convinced by his flirtatiousness. As it was, nothing would ever persuade her to get romantically involved with another agent after the débâcle with Jim Zametti.

'I thought you might like to talk me through the flotation plans,' she stuttered.

It worked like magic. Fastening the top button on the waistcoat of his Savile Row suit, Diego instantly switched modes and began talking Cassie through his strategy. Once the two agencies had merged, making them equal partners, Diego thought they should open up branches in Paris, Sydney and Buenos Aires, and predicted that ultimately they should have no problems turning over about eighty million dollars a year. After that, he proposed making an initial public offering, which would raise about two hundred million dollars.

'We could raise twice that if the underwriters exercise an over-allotment option. And,' he said with a flourish, 'I think I can confidently predict that they will.' He snickered. 'It's funny, modelling isn't the biggest business in the world but somehow those big swinging dicks on Wall Street all want to get involved. You don't think it's because they all imagine themselves ending up with Tulah on their arms, by any chance?'

Cassie was speechless. Diego had clearly done his homework. If he was anything like as convincing with the underwriters as he was with her, they'd be richer than Croesus. The man must have a calculator instead of emotions. He was so brazenly excited about money that it was almost endearing. Every morning, since arriving in New York, she'd had to fight her way through the jungle of exotic flowers that Diego kept sending to her room. Each thicket arrived with a message extracted from a song. So far, she'd had 'Money, money, money . . .'; 'Who wants to be a millionaire? (we do)'; 'Material girl'; and 'Talkin' about money, money.' Subtle it wasn't. Crass, vulgar and distasteful perhaps. But Cassie had to admit that the thought of being hugely, crassly, oodles-in-the-bank-triple-stretch-limo rich quite excited her too.

Generally speaking, Sissy believed whole-heartedly in the fashion mantra that *il faut souffrir pour être belle*. In slack moments, she even doodled it in different scripts on her notepads to see what it might look like on her tombstone. But Angel's new vermicelli sandals were the last straw. They were the first pair he'd designed to incorporate his logo, an enormous silver Art Deco A that doubled up as a buckle, and he'd given Sissy a pair to try out. Loyally she'd worn them day and night in New York, even though it had snowed one afternoon. And now the A had gone and tattooed itself indelibly into her left foot. She wouldn't have minded if any of the four names she'd been christened with began with A, but as it was it just looked silly, and now she was doomed to wear the same sandals for the rest of her life.

To cap it all, Janie appeared to be semi-catatonic when she

had spoken to her twenty minutes earlier, and now Doug kept ringing Sissy to find out if it was true that Grace was boycotting the gala that they were due to be at in half an hour.

'It's just pathetic that a serious newspaper like the *Gazette* should have become so obsessed with trivial gossip stories,' she said to Cassie as they waited downstairs in the bar for Janie. 'I blame it on Lindsey Craven.'

'I blame it on Grace,' said Cassie dourly. Cassie had half expected this to happen. It was probably her subconscious that had prompted her to bring Jo-Jo out to New York for the ceremony in the first place. It was just as well that Jo-Jo had a chink in her schedule and had been able to come. Now all Cassie had to do was get on the phone to the organisers to say that as well as presenting the newcomer award, Jo-Jo would be delighted to do the honours for Grace by standing in for her on the podium alongside Aeron. They were bound to agree – with fifty-five minutes to go before kick off they'd be desperate. In fact, it could all work out brilliantly, what with the double exposure for Jo-Jo in front of the most important people in the fashion world. Still, she wouldn't let Grace know that. They'd had a blazing row an hour ago when Grace had rung to say what a great time she was having in Majorca, sipping sangrias by the pool bar and learning to write poetry, and by the way, could Cassie pass on her apologies to the International Fashion Committee, but she was afraid, after all, that she couldn't be there tonight to present Aeron with his Most Talented Foreigner award.

'Tell them I'll be there in spirit, blah, blah, blah. Or rather spirits,' giggled Grace, downing her third sangria in one.

'Oh, for God's sake, Grace!' snapped Cassie, pretending to be furious. 'Have you any idea how badly this reflects on your reputation? And mine. And what about how crappy this is going to look for Aeron?'

'Precisely,' said Grace. '*Adiós, amigo.*' Cassie heard a splash as Grace dived into the pool, followed by a cascade of raucous laughter.

★　　★　　★

155

By the time Janie floated into the bar on a flying cocktail of Tylenol and Enrico's homoeopathic pills, they were running a bit late. Cassie bundled them into the waiting car and told Jo-Jo not to sit down, otherwise she'd crush her dress. Secretly she was elated with Jo-Jo, whose crimson strapless gown made her look like a Sargent painting made Caribbean flesh. Her dark hair was wound in a simple twist at the back of her neck and she was wearing the merest slick of make-up. Oh, the nonchalance of great beauty, thought Cassie contentedly: she never got tired of looking at lovely things. Sissy didn't manage to sit down properly either: her beige Aeron dress was so tight that from only a short distance, she looked as though she wasn't wearing anything. Angel had lent her a Masai necklace – his warrior beads, he called them – and its dark brown strands flecked her chest like a virulent outburst of malignant moles. Despite having to half crouch, half strap-hang, Jo-Jo thought that even the journey to the gala was glamorous: Fifth Avenue had been clogged with nose-to-tail stretch limousines. Then she, Cassie, Sissy and Janie had to walk along a red carpet, under a marquee, while crowds of people ogled them and flashbulbs exploded all around them. The annual fashion awards were clearly a big deal, and for the first time in their history were being relayed live on national television.

Janie felt wobblier by the minute. Clutching a glass of champagne, she followed the others on to the gallery overlooking the grand ballroom, which was heaving with Hollywood starlets in sequinned dresses that shimmered in front of her like a desert haze. It was several moments before she'd noticed that Leonie Uttley had plonked a microphone under her nose and was asking her how important British designers thought these awards were. Cassie and Jo-Jo were too elated to notice anything amiss and Sissy had evaporated into the crowd. Janie found the seating plan and stood in front of it, swaying, until the hieroglyphics stopped cartwheeling. She prayed that she could just get through the next few hours without falling into the industrial-sized flower arrangements that flanked every entrance and exit to the room. Somehow she teetered over to her table, where Sissy was frantically ingratiating herself with Lee, who looked elegant and serene in oyster satin Donna Karan.

'Oh, hi there.' Sissy looked up at Janie with a guilty start. 'I was just telling Lee how great you are to work with – what a good *team* we make. Are you all right?'

Cassie escorted Jo-Jo over to one of the top tables, gratified by the attention she was attracting. She was having a whale of a time, despite professing to despise awards ceremonies. It was fun catching up on old colleagues, and she was touched by the number of people who congratulated her on the way she'd handled the Peace affair. Enviously eyeing Jo-Jo's fellow diners – the lucky child was seated next to Sean O' Riley, the famous poet who'd been roped in to present Antonio Viro's prize. Brad Pitt and Tom Cruise were on the opposite side of the table . . . reluctantly Cassie made her way towards Diego, who must have spent the entire afternoon taking calls on his sunbed because the whites of his eyes now stood out from his chestnut permatan like a pair of lighthouses on rocky headland, and could be seen flashing at all and sundry from the other end of the ballroom.

For a moment Jo-Jo tottered on the brink of a sense of humour failure. Of all the people in the room, she had to be seated next to a geriatric poet. The chair on her other side was still empty. Then she discovered Nick Squire crawling under the table, trying to get a shot of her thighs. 'Fuck off, creep,' she hissed, scowling at Cassie's departing back. She was so affronted she didn't notice that the chair on her other side was now occupied by a tall, athletic figure. He stretched a tanned hand with the lightest dusting of blond hairs across to her glass. 'Ben Mornay. You look like a first-timer like me. What say we get blasted?'

The dinner went on for ever and a few of the speeches were interminable. No wonder some of the audience looked glazed. Jo-Jo was transfixed, watching Ben Mornay chase baby cherry tomatoes so tiny they were almost foetal around his plate for twenty minutes, and finally dissolving into silent guffaws when one ricocheted over to the next table and splattered onto Luella Lopez's scraggy decolletage. Lee Howard, faintly disconcerted by Janie's blurred voice and the way she stared glassily at the Chinese dragons on the carpet, wondered whether Janie was hallucinating. Perhaps the poor thing was ill. Or maybe it was a regional British accent – she wrote too well not to be given the benefit of the doubt. She would have to set up another meeting.

Halfway through dinner Ben led Jo-Jo out to the fountain in front of the Plaza so that they could practise their bows. Then, when they were waiting backstage to present their awards, he asked her what part of London she came from. When she explained that she was temporarily lodging with Janie in Michaelmas Road he said, 'No, really?' And shyly explained that he was thinking of playing the part of a West London lawyer who gets mixed up with the IRA in his next film. He asked for her number in case he needed some dialogue coaching. She was so excited she forgot to be nervous, and almost brought the house down when she said that back home where she came from, people didn't know whether to wear Aeron's clothes or lag the boiler with them, but that they were proud of him all the same.

Cassie couldn't believe it. Who would have thought Jo-Jo would handle the occasion with quite such aplomb? Already about thirty people had come up to her to ask who Jo-Jo was. Diego was practically shovelling share options into her lap. She was going to have to play this very carefully indeed. It looked as though Jo-Jo might well be bigger than Grace and Peace combined.

'I cannot *belieeeve* it, Cassie darling,' shrieked Kevin Krocket, purveyor of phenomenally expensive sportswear, darling of the uptown set and Luella Lopez's walker for the evening. 'Where d'you find her? I mean I was giving up hope that there might be a girl left on the planet who looked healthy, clean, drug-free and promising the distinct possibility of *booosoms*. Although God knows, after all this androgyny I don't know whether I can handle a pair of breasts any more – metaphorically speaking, *naturellement.* Still, we could always photograph her back to front. And photograph her we shall. I want the entire autumn campaign shot on her. She is *soooo* right for my collection. Waiter, get me my bank manager.'

Sissy couldn't believe it. How could Enrico accidentally have given her his diet pills instead of the homoeopathic prescription?

'I don't know why you're so upset,' he said peevishly over the char-grilled langoustines. 'Most people would be thrilled to get hold of those. They cost a fortune. One pop and you're speeding for months – hyperactive thyroids don't come into it. *I'm* the one who should be devastated. Sven Tolssen said he'd shoot me for the new Gap campaign, if I lost twenty pounds by the thirtieth.'

Sissy didn't quite know how to break the news to Janie about the pills. But by the time Janie passed out in the car back to the hotel she was so worried that she confided the truth in Cassie.

'Typical Janie,' laughed Cassie, 'I've been trying to get hold of some of those for ages.'

There was a stony silence. God, thought Cassie, even Sissy thinks I'm shallow. What was coming over her? She was obsessed with losing weight, dreaming about liposuction, hankering after Slimfast. She considered blaming it all on Zack. His cult of the body was having a bad influence on her. But she knew deep down that it wasn't his fault. He was always nagging her about healthy eating and inner body beauty. Perhaps she was drunk. She was certainly on a high from this evening's triumph with Jo-Jo and Diego, and from alcohol. On top of all that, she was dreading going back to London where she would have to go and see Peace.

They carried Janie up to her room and called a doctor, who suggested that a stomach pump wasn't necessary but that plenty of water was. Cassie sat with Janie all night, forcing sips of Evian through her lips. When Janie sat bolt upright at 7 a.m. to call Gloria to tell her to put green fly-killer on the wisteria, Cassie knew God had forgiven her. After four rounds of waffles, three bagels and a plate of hash browns, the atmosphere in Janie's room was so cheerful, Cassie even considered asking Janie if she could take the diet pills, but she decided against it. Best not to raise the issue until Sissy had confessed all.

Relieved to be distanced from the problems back home, Cassie stayed on another week, visiting friends in the Hamptons, and when Diego heard of this he insisted she also spend a couple of days at his place there. But sooner or later, she knew she had to go back and face Peace. The thought of visiting the rehab terrified her. Cassie had never been able to cope with hospitals of any kind. But she was anything but a coward, and besides, she couldn't stay on Long Island for ever, pleasant though it was. Sitting on the deck of Diego's beach house overlooking Georgica Pond, she decided there was no time like the present. She rang Trudy, her secretary in London, and got her to arrange an appointment as soon as Dr Bridgwater deemed it appropriate.

Chapter Seven

Janie felt better just being on the plane. She couldn't wait to soar over the three and a half thousand mostly water-logged miles that sloshed fathomlessly between her and the children. She loved New York's effervescence, even though it sometimes overwhelmed her. Since the gala she hadn't slept at all – she seemed to have gone into an energy over-drive. The other night she had been to a late-night viewing of Conquistador Art at the Metropolitan Museum of Art, watched *Hiroshima mon amour* twice on the video *and* written a two-thousand-word piece for the features section on the war between Morton Wemyss and Jasper Goldfarb, the two scions of Manhattan's most glamorous retail dynasties. It had been a work-intensive assignment, entailing about fifteen interviews which she had had to slot in around the usual relentless cycle of shows – and emotionally draining, not least because her two leading men seemed to throb with hatred for one another.

'Oh God, they *loathe* one another, it's a war zone in the buyers' enclosure,' said Madeleine when Janie called her for some background information. 'Don't be fooled by those gracious smiles. It's their equivalent of gunboat diplomacy. Morton always wants the designers Jasper's just signed up and vice versa. Their hatred for each other is rivalled only by their contempt for the poor bloody customer when she refuses to buy some bilge-coloured dress they've each bought six hundred of.

You are going to get this feature checked over by the lawyers, aren't you?'

Madeleine had sounded a little less suicidal and was even talking about setting up business again. The Store Wars piece was a huge hit too, so Janie ought to have been in a good mood. But then Phyllida faxed the Westbury demanding a sequel. Janie faxed back to say this was out of the question as they had already checked out and there were no vacant rooms to be found anywhere in New York that night.

'Good on you, Janie,' exclaimed Sissy, impressed. 'It's about time you stood up for yourself or Phyllida will have you writing the entire features section.'

As the plane glided off the tarmac at JFK, Janie drifted into a deep sleep, her first in a week, and dreamed that Matthew was invited by the Queen to an investiture at Buckingham Palace for services to humanity. Just as Her Majesty's sword was coming down on his shoulders he had stood up and announced that knighthoods were a corrupting carbuncle on the sole of society. He had then pointed an accusing finger at Janie's Calvin Klein dress and recited the whole of Dante's *Inferno* on the balcony of Buck House. She only surfaced from it six hours later when they were circling Heathrow. She felt even more dreadful by the time they'd loaded their bags off the carousel and she realised that she'd forgotten to pack the Klein dress. According to Sissy's price-per-wear equation, that meant it had cost her approximately £400 an hour, enough to keep one of Matthew's Guatemalan families in maize for the rest of their lives.

'Bloody brilliant bargain that turned out to be,' she snapped as Sissy sprinted off to the W.H. Smith kiosk to load up with newspapers.

'Gosh – sorry. Didn't I tell you? I knew it was causing you ructions and, fearful for your mental state, I took it back. I've got the money in my vanity case. I haven't changed it into pounds yet, but we can do that tomorrow. In fact,' she continued, scanning the currency rates at the bureau de change, 'you may even have made a slight profit on it.'

'But I'd already worn it,' exclaimed Janie.

'Not really,' said Sissy reasonably. 'You passed out in it, which isn't the same thing at all. Crikey, look, Cassie's made it into the *Financial Times*.'

Cassie and the rather pastoral view of the Thames that she enjoyed from her office had indeed made it on to page three of the FT, accompanied by an article about her merger with Allure Inc. and the subsequent plans to float the company on the New York Stock Exchange.

'The best of it,' said Cassie later that day to Saffron, 'is that I've had two other agencies on the phone begging to do a deal with me.' Bellissimo, Jim and Sergio Zametti's Milan-based agency had even accused Cassie and Diego of creating an illegal monopoly and were making furious noises about taking her to court.

'Not that they would. I don't suppose they'd like the police crawling all over their books again. Still, it's rather flattering to be threatened.'

Saffron looked at her disapprovingly. 'Speed freak.'

'Why is it,' sneered Phyllida, looking at the catwalk pictures from New York, 'that there is no longer a single designer capable of producing anything life-enhancing?' In the past she had always relied on the Americans to do nice, easy-to-understand clothes. Now they'd gone all avant-garde on her. 'I wish the lot of them would bloody well get real.'

'I think they feel they have a mission to educate,' said Sissy helpfully. She was determined to stop flinching every time Phyllida dredged up some out-of-date slang.

'More like a mission to keep you in work. If they just got on with making proper clothes, you'd have nothing to write about.'

'Would you like some applemint tea?' Sissy asked politely.

'Oh, get a life,' snarled Phyllida.

★   ★   ★

'Any news from Matthew?' asked Cassie.

'None,' said Janie morosely. She conveniently omitted to tell Cassie that Will, on her instructions, had told Matthew to stop writing to them for a bit. 'Just a message from the computer department at *The Probe* saying they were coming to collect Matthew's fax machine as he obviously doesn't need it at the moment.'

Cassie didn't know what to say. Poor Janie. Even Matthew's byline seemed to be appearing less and less frequently. It was tough, Cassie knew, for journalists in South America to get stories into their newspapers. At this rate he'd slip off the face of the earth altogether and no one would notice.

Changing the subject, she told Janie how brilliantly she'd written the article on Peace. 'It could have been really maudlin or fatuous, but you hit just the right note. You're very good, you know.'

'Who was the Angel Gabriel, by the way?' asked Janie, suddenly remembering the mysterious man who had sounded so sympathetic the night that Cassie had called her at Aeron's show.

Cassie pretended to ransack her memory data. She wasn't sure she wanted to share Seth just yet, especially now that Janie appeared to be hurtling towards singledom.

'Seth Weiss, you mean? Oh, just some chef who's bought a warehouse next to the office.'

'The Michelin-starred one with the beautiful eyes?'

'Possibly. I hadn't noticed,' lied Cassie. 'Mad as a snake, though. Definite touch of the Mrs Rochesters about him.'

'He didn't sound mad.'

'That's what makes it so creepy.'

A day after getting back from New York, Janie was still flying. She decided to work out some of her aggressive energy by relocating the compost heap. Digging always calmed her down. Without really noticing, she extended her kitchen garden by two feet all round and began making a trench for some box trees. She had always fancied the structure of a formal garden – laying the foundations for one would make her feel she had at least imposed some order on one area of her life. When Gloria got back with Nell they found Janie at the bottom of the garden chopping up bits of wood to make a gazebo.

'I don't know what it is about New York,' she panted, 'but it's given me a hell of an energy boost.'

Gloria looked her up and down suspiciously. 'Well, if you don't mind me saying, Meess Janie, you look a bit peaky. You lost weight? 'Cos if so me and Nell is going to rustle you up the best curry you ever tasted. We've perfected this recipe together. This daughter of yours is one enthusiastic cook.'

By the time Janie had had a hot bath and gazed upon the clean towels piled on the shelves, she felt much better. It was good to be back, she reflected, gazing contentedly across the garden as the shadows lengthened into nocturnal gloom. Gloria had worked wonders on the house. With the lightest of hands, she had tactfully spruced it up, finding permanent, sensible homes for the endless clutter and polishing the wooden floors until they shone. The whole house was faintly scented with beeswax and the delicious poppy-seed bread Gloria baked twice a week. She had dusted furniture so that it looked cherished and cared for, ironed and starched linen until it was inviting and luxurious, and tactfully disposed of Janie's more heinous-looking unguents. Under her husbandry, towels had become soft, snowy white and deep-piled, the way they always looked in magazines, instead of loofah-textured and scurf-coloured, which, in Janie's experience, was how they invariably looked in life. Light bulbs worked. The Aga sparkled and emitted aromatic spicy smells. Fires warmed the rooms instead of making them uninhabitable with smoke. Even the inexorable march of the damp upstairs seemed to have been temporarily routed. Gloria had brought out the potential that Janie always knew lurked somewhere in Michaelmas Road. To Janie's gratification, even Cassie was impressed. Never mind *The Probe*'s obsessive stinginess. Forget about Matthew's psychopathic incompetence. She and Gloria and the children were doing just fine.

★　　★　　★

Stepping out into the Via Borgonuova, Vladimir Miscov breathed in deeply the polluted Milanese air. Delicious – his first real inhalation since leaving that stinking police cell. After yet another two day session of solid questioning the police had reluctantly released him and Jim Zametti, but Vladimir had a nasty inkling that it was only a temporary reprieve. It was obvious the police were convinced of their guilt and it was just a matter of time, he reflected grimly, before they unearthed the necessary evidence. Unless, of course, he could kick up enough dirt to obscure their traces. The best way would be to implicate as many agencies around the world as he could. He reached into the breast pocket of his impeccable five button jacket and pulled out his mobile. It barely rang before a silky purr answered it.

'Anastasia,' he said hoarsely, 'who do you hate most in the world?'

'Apart from you, you mean?'

'Very funny. Don't let's mess around. We both know who I mean. So about that "favour" I owe you. I think I've found a lovely way for you to extract your revenge.'

Cassie had never thought much of Surrey, ever since her sister Yvette had moved there – but she had to hand it to the county, you came across a nice class of clinic there. Seth had shown her the low-key brochure for Ashwood Hall, a Gothic manor house set in acres of pristine viridian velvet lawns behind a high mature brick wall.

'It looks poncy but the staff are incredibly dedicated and Dr Bridgwater, the consultant there, is one of the world's leading authorities on substance abuse,' said Seth. 'For a while it even looked as though they had a handle on Finn. And they're very discreet, considering the place is crawling with more celebrities than the Groucho.'

It was a miraculous April afternoon. The torrential rains of the last week had wiped the sky clean and it now glittered like neon. Everywhere Cassie looked there were drifts of acid-yellow daffodils and clumps of bluebells. The grassy banks were an almost bilious shade of chartreuse. Tiny emerald buds were beginning to unfurl. Nature was a most adventurous colourist. She must remember that the next time she redecorated. God, please let Barney do something nice to her flat. No, this was a bad line of thought. She tried other distractions but it was no use. As the car whooshed through the narrow lanes, twigs snapping against the wing mirrors, she was appalled to discover how nervous she felt.

For the first ten days of her stay, Peace hadn't even been allowed to receive any external phone calls – a state of affairs Cassie found almost too terrifying to contemplate. Apart from Seth, she was Peace's first visitor, although Nick Squire had squealed up the driveway on his motorbike the first week she was there pretending to be her brother. Zack had offered to come with her, but although she was grateful, Cassie knew this was something she had to do on her own. Peace's mother had told Cassie that she wanted to go and see her, of course, only it was the Easter holidays, the boys were home from school and it was all very difficult at the moment. She would go and see Peace the minute term started.

The wrought-iron gates swished open and Cassie's Mercedes scrunched up the gravel drive. At least there appeared to be no lurking photographers. A secretary ushered her down its cheerful pale yellow corridors to Dr Stevens. The trustees of Ashwood had gone to some pains to decorate the house in a style dripping with appropriate gravitas. They had called in Tilly de Montgomery, who had agonised for weeks over whether to put plush carpet everywhere, which she found vaguely creepy in a padded-cell sort of way, or stripped polished boards, which she thought people of a sensitive disposition might find institutional. In the end she compromised with sea grass. The furniture, a mixture of what were meant to look like family heirlooms and one-offs from Heals, was a fitting metaphor, Tilly thought, for the adventurous, open-minded and above all successful approach of the clinic. Dr Stevens's office was a large, elegant room, with panelled walls that had recently been painted the colour of parchment and full-length windows that opened on to a vast York stone terrace. In the grate, neat hunks of cedar crackled comfortingly. The room reeked of discretion and money (it was always best to let relatives and friends know what kind of bills they were in for, Tilly felt). All in all, she considered it one of her outstanding triumphs.

Dr Stevens bustled forward and seized her hand, pumping it vehemently. Unlike his superior, he hadn't yet become thoroughly inured to the glamour of celebrity. Clever, well-meaning and practically frothing with integrity, he was nevertheless a tiny bit star-struck.

When Cassie managed to extract her arm from his grip, she saw that he was extraordinarily youthful-looking – early thirties at most – with the open, freckled features and wilful tufty hair of a boy, which made her even more depressed.

'I'm acting *in loco parentis* – as indeed you are,' he said, cheerfully. 'Dr Bridgwater is giving a lecture tour in Korea, via an interpreter, of course. God, can you imagine the scope for misunderstanding? Now, let me see.' He walked over to a reproduction Biedermeier escritoire and scanned his notes.

'Ah, yes. Peace has been with us, what is it, four and a half weeks. Well, she is making tremendous progress. It's early days, of course, but all the signs suggest that she really doesn't want to be in her predicament any more. It's not always the case, as I'm sure you're aware. A lot of addicts are in love with their addiction just as much as with the substances they take. But Peace is very keen to channel her energies in more productive ways. And of course, while many addicts are highly intelligent and conversant with the kind of things they think they ought to say, Peace seems one hundred per cent genuine. The biggest problem is going to be dealing with her guilt over the accident. She's really intent on beating herself up over that. But the therapist seems to think they'll make progress there. She appears not to have gone in for a huge amount of self-analysis in the past, which is unusual with addicts. Still, in the end, it makes our task easier – fewer preconceptions, you see. A lot of them come in and think they know it all – more than we do, in any case. In some cases, they're probably right. Hmm. Er, cheerful soul, isn't she?'

Cassie wondered whether he'd strayed on to someone else's notes but gave him the benefit of the doubt. His boyish enthusiasm was so engagingly straightforward. Peace's favourite part of the day, Dr Stevens told Cassie, was the group psychotherapy sessions. 'She's very good, you know, very articulate. She's made a couple of friends too.' Cassie's heart sank. She wanted Peace to make a completely fresh start. The last thing Peace needed was to come out of Ashwood with a bunch of sad hangers-on.

'So now I expect you'd like to see Peace,' said Dr Stevens breezily.

Oh God, oh God, thought Cassie, she absolutely wouldn't. Rationally, she knew perfectly well that Peace wouldn't be wearing a straitjacket or weaving baskets, but she couldn't quite dislodge the image from her imagination. She considered asking Dr Stevens for a tour of the kitchen garden but thought better of it. Better get straight to the point.

Peace was doing laps alone in the indoor pool. There was an eerie silence, punctuated only by the occasional echoing splash and the sound of Peace calling out numbers every time she completed a length. She had reached eighty when Dr Stevens called her gently. Peace pushed her goggles back on to her swimming cap, looked at Cassie blankly and then broke into a shaky smile. Dan, the counsellor who took Peace through her weekly psycho-drama sessions, had warned her not to become too obsessive about the swimming, but Peace couldn't help it. After the first ten laps her mind went into a trance-like free fall and she felt powerful enough to tackle all the painful thoughts she had always tried to suppress. During this morning's swim, she had been thinking about her mother, calmly and without any distress. She pulled herself out of the pool – she seemed very thin, Cassie noticed – and reached for a pale blue bathrobe. She looked about ten years old. She shook out her hair and threw her arms round Cassie. Dr Stevens tactfully withdrew.

'It's so lovely to see you,' she enthused, her beautiful hazel eyes softening. 'I haven't had many visitors. Mummy really wanted to come but what with running the boys backwards and forwards to all their holiday club things she just hasn't had a moment. Not that I haven't met some fantastic people . . . How's Shareen?'

Cassie stayed for two hours. She was amazed at how lucid and calm Peace seemed – she hoped they hadn't put her on Prozac. No, Dr Stevens had assured her that Peace's bloodstream was so devoid of chemicals they could probably bottle it and sell it to Volvic.

'She needs another couple of months probably,' he said, walking Cassie to her car. 'The chemical addiction is relatively straightforward to deal with but she's taken a bit of a battering emotionally over the past few years. Any chance of a bit more contact with the family?'

Cassie looked doubtful.

'Well, it's just a thought. She does seem rather isolated somehow . . . Oh, by the way,' he said, bringing his head level with her window, 'I hope you don't mind my asking, but is there any chance of a signed photograph of Grace Capshaw? Not for me, of course, but for my son . . . ?'

'It's a triumph,' declared Sissy, stroking the viridian silk throw that was casually draped over an ochre-coloured sofa. 'The whole place is a masterstroke.' She had zipped round to Angel's in her lunch-hour, ostensibly to talk to him about Anastasia but also because she was dying to see his flat again. Angel's three-room garret in Southwark was a constant source of inspiration to the fashion world and had been on the cover of *Designers' Digest* twice. Tilly thought he was the most talented homemaker of all the fashion designers she'd ever interviewed. 'And that's saying a lot,' she told one of her wealthy Arab clients. 'Designers all have simply brilliant houses. It's being gay, you know. Their homes are like surrogate babies.'

Angel's baby was a runt in terms of size but it was a riot of colour and popping with ideas – not to mention knick-knacks which he picked up in flea markets for next to nothing and endless framed photographs of the Queen Mother and Wallis Simpson. Sometimes he expended so much time and energy on his flat that he hardly had time to get dressed. He was still pottering around in his kimono and clearly hadn't got round to having a shower. It was his purple bathroom with its Victorian duck-egg-blue bath that Sissy liked best at the moment. If she played her cards right, Angel might even give her the tasselled cushion that he'd made out of an old Schiaparelli scarf. He often passed on little bits and bobs to his friends, as he was constantly falling in love with new pieces and kept running out of room. They never looked quite the same in Sissy's flat, though.

'So, all we've got to do is arrange a meeting,' said Sissy. 'Invite Anastasia over for tea when the new collection's ready and your financial problems will all be solved. She's itching to get involved in fashion, I can just tell.'

'How many pairs of Jimmy Choo shoes did you say she had?' said Angel, sitting down at the eau de Nil dressing table in his bathroom and picking up an antique tortoiseshell comb.

'Who cares?' said Sissy, taking the comb and pushing it through his wispy hair. 'She just bought her last pair.'

Sissy's flat in Baron's Court, on the other hand, was a catastrophe. She kept meaning to do something about it, like move, but she never seemed to have enough time or money. Last year she'd made a half-hearted attempt to cheer the place up by painting the hall, but the bright pink had only made the bumps on the Anaglypta wallpaper stand out like boils, and she had given up halfway. Then her flatmate, Diana the optometrist, had complained that the fuchsia was doing her head in and had taken it upon herself to paint the hall mocha instead, which, combined with the liver-coloured carpet, made Sissy feel as though she was trapped inside someone's intestines.

Increasingly Sissy sought solace in her bedroom, which she had turned into a bird-of-paradise sanctuary, festooned with items of clothing and underwear – anything to disguise the drab paintwork and hideous furniture. Since the trip to

Ramoush, the room had taken on a Lebanese air. Rose-scented candles sputtered from every surface. Geranium and aquamarine tumblers trailed across the IKEA dressing table next to two framed photographs of Coco Chanel and Vionnet, and her favourite Angel shoes dangled on coloured ribbons from the ceiling. She had managed to cover the carpet with dhurries and kelims and – now that she'd worn it a few times and the stain was proving indelible after all – she was considering cutting the shaggy yellow coat up into a rug.

But it never really came together. Diana was becoming a bit of a downer as well. It wasn't only the mocha hallway. They just had nothing in common any more. Diana's friends – doctors and biologists mostly – only ever seemed to want to hold beer-drinking competitions in the flat which, unfortunately, seemed to be the most convenient rendezvous for all of them. Honestly, thought Sissy contemptuously, what kind of people considered Baron's Court central? And after the night they had all got very drunk and smoked the hemp mini dress that Aeron had given her, she'd found it very hard to forgive them. But the worst of it was that Diana reminded her of a time that was simply no longer relevant to her life. Sissy was a consummate reinventor of the past and had put a lot of effort into erasing from her official history the three years she had spent in the Army Cadet Force. Diana, on the other hand, made it her life's mission to remind her. She thought Sissy's systematic denial of the past was sick, especially as Sissy had shown all the makings of a first-rate soldier. She had outstanding leadership qualities, her kit was always immaculate, and she could strip a MIG faster than all of them put together.

At least Diana and the lager louts appeared to be out tonight – probably trashing some hooray pub somewhere in the suburbs, Sissy thought glumly. She ran the shower, but Diana had used up all the hot water, so while she waited for the immersion heater to kick in she slavered herself in Dead Sea mud, realising too late that this meant she wouldn't be able to sit down for twenty minutes. There was nothing for it but to hover by the phone listening to her messages.

Normally Sissy avoided doing this, knowing that the tape
was bound to be hogged by her mother, her bank manager and
some designer demanding payment. Sure enough, there was a
message from Mr Dean suggesting she make an appointment for
a little chat; a diatribe from her mother, who muttered darkly
that if Sissy didn't pay the family a visit soon they would never
get The Situation sorted out; and a plea from Angel to call and
tell him what size shoe Anastasia took. There followed various
routine messages from friends and about seven calls from Lorna,
Phyllida's grumpy secretary. Sissy was about to get into the
shower when a mellifluous male voice, with the faintest trace
of an Indian accent, confirmed that he had received her note
and agreed to her request for an interview. It was Nari Sujan,
the owner of Everything She Wants, a phenomenally successful
chain of discount fashion shops aimed at teenagers (and people
with no taste, thought Sissy, although she had refrained from
mentioning this in her letter).

If it hadn't been for Phyllida's constant nagging, Sissy would
have severed all contact with the mass end of the market. Taxis
to the centre of town cost her a fortune because the sight of
Oxford Street made her ill and she always ended up taking
a massive detour. But a tiny paragraph in one of the trade
papers had caught her attention a year ago and she had been
following Nari's progress closely ever since. He had started his
business from the back of a Transit van and in just five years had
acquired thirty-five branches in the north of England and had
now set his sights firmly on the rest of the country. He'd already
shifted some of his operation from Halifax to the East End and,
according to Sissy's research, had recently bought a large house
in Knightsbridge. Sissy thought he'd be perfect for a profile on
the business pages – a domain that had barely impinged on her
consciousness until now. She suggested the idea to Gina Martin,
the editor of the City section. 'He's a real pile it high, flog it
cheap merchant. If he carries on expanding at the same rate, it's
bound to put a squeeze on the other chains,' said Sissy.

Gina looked gratifyingly impressed and, once she'd got over
her astonishment, commissioned Sissy to write a lead story. This,

Sissy knew, was her big chance to prove she wasn't a complete flake. She was pretty sure Nari Sujan's business practices were sharp, borderline crooked. If she played her cards right this could even turn into a major exposé. She left a message at his office agreeing to the appointment, and then ransacked Diana's room for her brochure on evening classes. If she was going to have to go undercover, then Hindi might come in very handy.

Anastasia contemplated her tumescent breasts in the mirror above her bed admiringly. She had to admit, they were magnificent – as indeed they should be. They had cost a fortune. Since she wasn't the kind of woman who attracted hordes of female friends (no one was prepared to play stooge to quite the extent she required) she had become her own most loyal fan. She buttoned up her silvery lace negligee, lay back on the mound of freshly plumped pillows and reached for her phone, which was precariously perched on top of a pile of brochures cataloguing the English Season. Nine in the morning was always a good time to get the staff in her Moscow office before they all slunk off for one of their infernal long lunches. Anastasia was paranoid that Irina and Nadjia were skiving in her absence and bombarded them at least six times a day with unnecessary phone calls. It was either that, she reasoned, or go back and live in the god-forsaken dump – and she had long ago resolved never to do that. Secretly she acknowledged that Nadjia and Irina did a very effective job without her. The franchises were breeding faster than rabbits on fertility drugs. Business was booming.

Irina's voice came on the line.

'How many times do I have to tell you? It's good morning, how may I help you. Forget all that have a nice day rubbish,' snapped Anastasia.

'How may I help you, Anastasia?' said Irina insolently.

'You can tell me how things are going in St Petersburg.'

'Well, in the eight hours since we last spoke, I think I can honestly say that things are moving steadily along there. Oh, and we've had some enquiries from Georgia.'

'Peasants!' hissed Anastasia. 'I hardly think they're ready for our way of doing business.'

'You could be right, but things are changing here every day. Mustn't get left behind. I must go, Andrei's on the other line. *Ciao.*'

Andrei Nimsky handled all of Anastasia's business in eastern Russia and she was frequently tempted to sell out to him. Then she could put all that lovely money into something glamorous and respectable – and in her heart of hearts Anastasia knew that her business interests in Mother Russia could never be remotely described as either. She flicked through the newspapers on her breakfast tray, which put her in a foul mood. More on that Cassie woman and her piffling little business. Janie Pember had done an absolute rave on her in the *Gazette.* Well, since they were apparently such great friends, she would. At least it showed loyalty. Besides, reflected Anastasia, calming down, there was nothing wrong with a little slavish flattery now and then. She could certainly use some, particularly if she was to launch herself successfully as a mover and shaker in the fashion world. She reached for the telephone again, dialled the *Gazette* and asked to be put through to Janie.

Janie was deeply flattered by Anastasia's invitation to tea at her house in Mount Street. An informal prelude to an interview, Anastasia had called it. Since she had politely rebuffed all requests from the press to profile her at her lovely home until now, even Phyllida would see this was quite a coup. Janie still thought there was something fishy about Anastasia which would only make her seem more enticing to the features department.

But Phyllida had other plans. She stormed over to the fashion department, angrily circumnavigating the curtain of flowers shielding Sissy's and Janie's desks – a present from Cassie for the supportive pieces.

'Never mind useless old socialites. I've arranged for one of you to interview Seth Weiss this afternoon. He of the smouldering griddle or whatever it is trendy chefs cook on these days. I told him it's a business piece about his new restaurant, it's the only way he'd agree to do it, but actually I thought he could model Boldacci's new men's line for us – he's threatened to pull his ads from the supplement if we don't start photographing his poxy stuff. A couple of suits should do it. Oh, and don't forget to ask him about the actress girlfriend he dumped – and please, don't get sidetracked by dreary stories about start-up loans. Now, which one of you will it be?'

Sissy, wading through a stash of blank receipts, glanced at Phyllida shiftily. She'd arranged to go and edit Angel's new collection in the afternoon.

'Don't worry, I'll do it,' said Janie super-casually. 'I can easily rearrange Anastasia.'

Seth fidgeted nervously while Janie tried to get her Biro to work. He hated being interviewed. He wasn't quick enough with pat answers, not like Sebbie, the erstwhile master chef at Le Château. But then Sebbie was always well oiled by the time he got to any appointment, and within twenty minutes of arriving he made sure everyone else was too. Seth wished he'd brought along something to drink – it might have calmed them both down. Janie shook the Biro violently and its innards drenched her and Seth in navy blotches.

'Shit,' she exclaimed, looking at his white shirt in horror.

'Never mind,' said Seth, finally relaxing, 'at least you've got a valid excuse now to get me into those horrific suits you've been hiding.'

Janie blushed. It was all going hideously wrong. Seth wasn't mad at all. He was, however, the most fatally attractive man she'd met in years, with hair the colour of chocolate cake and an expression in his brown eyes that seemed to hover precariously between humour and sadness. No wonder Cassie hadn't wanted to bring him round for supper.

She couldn't possibly quiz him about the actress, so instead she asked him whether he had any tips for making beans on toast more interesting. Seth laughed. 'Is that a personal request?'

'I am the world's joint worst cook, I'm afraid – along with Cassie,' she added pointedly. 'D'you know, the first time Zack made himself a cup of tea at her flat he almost poisoned himself? Her last-but-one cleaner had left limescale descaler in the kettle and strict instructions for her to remove it twelve hours later but . . . that's Cassie for you. Not very domesticated.' Seth looked blank; Cassie hadn't gone into details about her friendship with Janie.

'We go way back,' said Janie, 'though she's a couple of years older than me, of course.' Seth suggested Parmesan, and a dash of Tabasco and Worcestershire sauce for the beans and Janie told him about her herb garden and a nursery she'd discovered in Cornwall that grew the most aromatic rosemary. By the time the photographer turned up she'd unilaterally decided that Seth shouldn't have to degrade himself by dressing up in the Boldacci suits, although by then he would have modelled Vivienne Westwood's collection of codpieces if she had asked. They kept the shirt on because Janie said navy suited him, and photographed him from the neck up.

Janie almost panicked when the photographer left. Something about Seth made her feel strangely vulnerable and unpredictable. She heard him asking her out to dinner and – equally faint – heard herself accepting. She didn't dare look at him so she kept her head clamped over her notebook and wrote everything he said down twice until her hand was stiff with cramp.

Chapter Eight

'So how was it?' demanded Cassie. 'I want to know everything. Where did he take you? What did you eat? How did you play it? How did *he* play it? Did he give all the dishes marks out of ten?'

'I thought you said he was barking,' said Janie with the flattened cadence of someone in deep shock.

'Did I?' said Cassie, sounding vague. 'I think I meant obsessive. Dedicated to his skillet. Anyway, don't change the subject. What happened?'

'We kissed,' said Janie. 'Don't ask me how it happened. He must have put something in my Evian. Either that or he didn't drink the three bottles of Chablis that were left on the table entirely on his own.'

There was a throbbing silence.

'Janie, there isn't anything else, is there? Exchange of bodily fluids? Post–coital cigarette?'

'He doesn't smoke,' replied Janie. 'And by the way, I'd say he was definitely more Mr than Mrs Rochester.'

Cassie was profoundly shaken by Janie's news. Janie's marriage to Matthew, creaky though Cassie considered it to be, and positively sagging as it presently was under the dead weight of his stupid absence, was one of the great constants in her life. If it ever did collapse it would have the same effect on Cassie as seeing her parents' marriage crumble. Except that Cassie's parents' empty carapace of a marriage, cracked and squeaking though it was, had never had the good grace to actually collapse. Oh God! Oh God! And just at a time when Cassie needed all the emotional stability she could muster, what with the merger, Peace and all the other things that were contriving to hound her into an early mid-life crisis. It was one thing for Matthew – bloody Matthew – to swan off, but they all knew he'd be back. Janie couldn't have an affair. Poor Nell and Daisy and Jake.

Poor Matthew.

No, that was going too far.

During a quick mercy dash into Sigmund's bookshop, Estelle, the manageress, bossily told Cassie she mustn't on any account interfere. And she definitely shouldn't ring Seth, even if Cassie was worried that Janie, sucked along on the rapids of lust, might have omitted to tell him she was married with three children. Feeling only marginally appeased, Cassie left Sigmund's clutching a copy of *Coping with Your Best Friend's Love Affairs* and went straight back to the office to call Seth.

Seth's alarm clock, ancient but normally reliable, let him down badly – not surprisingly, as he'd forgotten to set it. It was a quarter to nine when he woke up, which gave him ten minutes to get from Old Street to Hammersmith, where he was meant to be having a meeting with Barney Frick to go over the lighting. His loft – really one huge, airy white room that floated high above the traffic of EC1 – was dominated by a deceptively spartan-looking stainless-steel kitchen and a series of glass doors that opened on to an enormous roof terrace. This Bauhausian space had been precisely designed by Seth to make his life as ruthlessly efficient as possible. The only thing about his modus vivendi that wasn't streamlined, he mused wryly, was that his home was a long way from Le Château and on the opposite side of town from his new restaurant. But he was too fond of both areas to consider forsaking either. He loved the anonymous, vaguely menacing atmosphere of Old Street, where the ghosts of London's more unsavoury gangsters seemed to lurk on every corner. Besides, the journey to work gave him time to think. He loved the drive back too, in the middle of the night, when he turned the music up and felt the adrenal rush of Le Château slowly ebb away.

Usually he made time for a leisurely cooked breakfast – bacon, poached eggs, spinach, *boudin*. It was his favourite meal of the day, the only one he ever had a chance to sit down and enjoy. There wouldn't be any fry-ups this morning, he thought regretfully, and then, remembering why, broke into a broad grin.

Last night had been extraordinarily enjoyable and relaxing, all things considered. Seth hadn't meant to ask Janie to dinner. In fact, he'd been astonished to hear the words tumbling out of his mouth. For two years he hadn't asked anyone anywhere – not since Martha had stormed out for good. As usual, they'd been arguing about the amount of time he spent working – or rather she had been arguing, he'd been thinking about new recipes and the lavish *Modern Fusion Cookbook* he was meant to be contributing to. Martha had accused him of being a workaholic – and if he wasn't then, he reflected ruefully, he had become one after she left him. In the past few months his social life had reached an all-time low – and until now he hadn't even noticed. What with raising capital for the restaurant, sorting out the plans, finding staff, working round the clock at Le Château to make amends to Sebbie, the owner, for having the temerity, finally, to leave and set up on his own, his hands had been pretty full.

Sebbie McHugh, unfortunately, still hadn't come to terms with the departure of his star chef, even though Seth had gently nudged Steven, Le Château's chronically introverted sous-chef, to spectacular new heights. Seth had also given Sebbie his word that he wouldn't poach any of Le Château's staff. Despite this Sebbie, a charismatic and talented restaurateur who had always said that he would die a happy man if his restaurant ever achieved three Michelin stars – which, thanks to Seth, it had – had threatened to kill Seth if he came within five miles of Le Château once his new restaurant opened. But as the time for

Seth to leave drew closer, Sebbie had adopted a different tack and was now threatening to kill himself and most of the kitchen staff with his beloved Purdey in what promised to be a rather dry blood-bath as he was an appallingly bad shot.

To say that things had become tense in Le Château's kitchen was a massive understatement. Seth, whose own temperament could hardly be described as placid, had so much pent-up aggression that he had hacked his way through four chopping boards in one week, and Steven, normally so taciturn that he could go for days without saying anything, was moved to tell Seth to calm down.

'Don't let the Irish bastard get you down.'

Since this was the longest speech Steven had ever made, Seth, half Irish himself, overlooked the racist aspect of this unsolicited solidarity and was instead profoundly moved.

He discovered that if he focused on Janie, his murderous feelings for Sebbie melted away like black pudding in a scorching frying pan. It had been a wonderful evening, all the more so for being unexpected. The last thing he'd anticipated when he agreed to Phyllida's interview was that he'd enjoy it. But Janie had been so warm and sympathetic, so uncalculating – bloody slow writer though, perhaps he should buy her a tape recorder – that the invitation to dinner had just tumbled out of his mouth. He'd forgotten that not all women were ball-breakers. He didn't know whether it had been a good idea to kiss her – he still couldn't work out how that had happened, only that it had felt wonderful. She must have felt a bit the same because she had invited him round for supper – to show him her herb garden, she said – and now he found himself counting the hours until Wednesday.

It didn't even worry him that Janie was married with three children. There wasn't a lot of slack in his life right now for a major relationship. But he could do with a good friend – especially one who was self-deprecating, bright and, now that he came to think of it, beautiful. Seth got so lost in contemplating Janie's long, soft brown hair, slightly sardonic expression and endless legs that the next time Sebbie marched in, waving an

enormous Sabatier knife above his head like some demented
pirate, he didn't even notice.

Jo-Jo was so excited she thought she was going to explode.
Sven Tolssen – *Sven Tolssen* – had got his assistant to call Cassie
personally to book her for a twenty-page extravaganza he was
shooting in Russia for the September issue of *A La Mode*. Cassie
couldn't help being amused. Five months ago Jo-Jo hadn't heard
of Sven Tolssen and now it was Sven Tolssen this, Karl Lagerfeld
that. She had even suggested to Cassie that it would be nice to
do a Frida Kahlo shoot. Cassie had quickly dispensed with that
idea, which could only have come from Joel Eliot.
    'Frida Kahlo's been done to death,' she snapped. She had
always considered Kahlo, who had inspired so many fashion
shoots, to be overrated, and there was no way she was going
to allow Jo-Jo to get rigged up in a unibrow and bulky ethnic
clothes. Even the idea of Jo-Jo working with Sven unsettled
her. Saffron thought Cassie had gone mad. Sven was one of
the most brilliant fashion photographers in the world with a
phenomenally successful record for spotting future icons. There
was alchemy in the way he looked at the composite features
of a model – in geometric, almost architectural terms – and
exaggerated them with his lens so that a lovely girl became
extraordinary and unforgettable. Not for nothing was he known
in the business as Sven Gali. But he was despotic. His shoots
were elaborate, high-concept affairs in which the concept was
usually Sven's ego. Damn him for spotting Jo-Jo so early – she
was too raw to be moulded by Sven, especially when Cassie
didn't feel *she* had finished moulding Jo-Jo.
    'Don't get too excited,' she said to Jo-Jo acidly. 'His first
choice was Brigitte but she dropped out after she discovered it
was in Moscow. Sven has some rather unorthodox techniques,
I should warn you. And apparently Cartier-Bresson is his
latest hero.'
    Jo-Jo looked blank and shrugged.
    'One of the world's greatest photographers,' began Cassie

impatiently, 'and renowned for his intelligence and honesty – so you'd think that alone would put Sven off – and his fascination for India. Apparently Sven's livid that they wouldn't switch the shoot to Rajasthan. He's discovered religion, by the way, so watch your language please. He's also extremely sensitive, a manic depressive and completely brilliant, so if he asks you to pose on a bed of manure, just do it. Work like a dog and don't put on any airs and graces – everyone else will have more than enough.'

She paused, wishing that she could chaperone Jo-Jo – the potential for disaster on a Tolssen shoot was terrifying and the trauma with Peace had made Cassie more protective of her models than ever. But with Diego panting down the phone every five minutes she couldn't afford to leave the office. In any case, Sven had a Greta Garbo complex and insisted on a closed set – apart from his own extensive entourage, no one was allowed near. She looked at Jo-Jo's guileless grin and felt a pang – she was still such a baby, it seemed a shame to let Sven and the rest of them loose on her just yet. Perhaps, Saffron could go out with Jo-Jo, maybe not onto the set, but just to keep an eye on her in the evenings. 'Jo-Jo,' she said more softly, as Jo-Jo untangled her legs from Cassie's armchair and bounded irrepressibly towards the door, 'don't let him tape you up *too* tightly.'

The flight to Moscow was uneventful, except that Jo-Jo was deeply impressed by the vastness of Russia. She'd had no idea it was so monumentally huge. It was a bit creepy to think that you could fly for hours and hours and still be hovering over the same country. She also felt strange being all alone at the back of the plane. Sven, Sven's assistant, Sven's masseur and Sven's masseur's boyfriend were in first class. Saffron had gone down with flu at the last minute and the agency was snowed under with work, so Jo-Jo was on her own. Caro Luckhurst, *A La Mode*'s highly strung senior fashion editor, and Alice, whom she had dragged along as her assistant, had missed the plane and were currently stuck on the M25 between Heathrow and

Gatwick in a frantic bid to get another flight before the editor of *A La Mode* discovered what had happened. Dodie and Enrico, who had been booked to do hair and make-up, were flying in from another job in St Bart's.

Even though it was early June, a chilly gust lashed at Jo-Jo's cheeks as she sauntered out of the airport with her rucksack towards the dusty Skodas and Ladas that were lined up outside the gloomily lit airport. After twenty minutes the others still hadn't appeared, so she went back inside. The place was deserted, eerily silent apart from two soldiers who shuffled backwards and forwards, and the occasional clack as their rifles knocked into one another. Eventually, after two hours – which, it transpired, was how long it had taken the Russian authorities to unpack and search their twenty-three pieces of luggage, pack them up again, then repeat the entire exercise – Sven and his entourage emerged from a door in the far corner. Max, the masseur, jostled Jo-Jo out of the way and ushered Sven into the most ostentatious stretch limousine she had ever seen.

At least the delay had given Dodie and Enrico time to catch them up. 'Hello, gorgeous. Have I been hearing stacks about you,' gushed Enrico to Jo-Jo, greasy charm to the fore. 'Look at that skin, Dodie. And the hair . . . *we* should be paying them to do this job.'

They bundled into the front two rows while Max laid a towel over the back seat and got out his unguents so that he could cleanse Sven's aura. Jo-Jo, deprived of any company for the best part of the day, kept up an incessant stream of questions about the other models until Max barked at her to keep schtum. Sven was in deep shock after the luggage incident, he said, although Sven had said so little on both occasions Jo-Jo had met him that she was at a loss to know how Max could tell.

Max's oils were extremely pungent, and by the time they got to the Metropol they were all on cloud nine – which was just as well because the hotel lobby, a huge marble forecourt overhung with hideous giant chandeliers that looked like mushroom clouds, reeked of cigars, stale sweat and boiled cabbage. To dampen their mood further, *A La Mode*'s accountant, who had been to the same school of manic cost-cutting as Phyllida, had secretly changed Caro's booking to three rooms instead of seven rooms and a suite.

'Welcome to Moscow,' snarled the receptionist.

It was midnight before Sven's assistant, in a fit of pique, got the reservation changed again, this time to ten suites (one extra for the cameras, and one extra extra just in case). Jo-Jo was desperately tired and had promised Cassie she'd get to bed early as Sven had a thing about dark circles under the eyes, but she was far too excited to sleep. She had also sworn on her life to call Gloria the minute she arrived. Knowing whom she feared most, she sighed and resigned herself to an hour's haranguing from her mother.

The first two days weren't too bad. Sven was on an up and didn't stop telling Swedish jokes all day, which lightened the atmosphere a little, although Jo-Jo couldn't really get the hang of his punch lines and spent most of the first day mystified. Sven made her hold complicated positions for hours – until he got the lighting right or she got pins and needles. It seemed odd to Jo-Jo that *A La Mode* should be haemorrhaging all this money so that they could come all the way to Russia and spend the whole time in the studio, but no one else seemed to notice anything unusual. Dodie had told her that Moscow was now officially the world's most expensive city and dinner for the seven of them last night, which no one had been able to eat because it was so disgusting, had come to £700. But because Cassie had made it clear to Jo-Jo before she left that she was to be on her best behaviour, she didn't say a word. To compensate for the atrocious meal, Sven organised them into two teams to play charades, but since he insisted on miming the titles of all Ingmar Bergman's films, he was the only one to win any points, which put him in an even better mood. 'It's going brilliantly,' whispered Dodie, squeezing Jo-Jo's knee halfway through *The Seventh Seal*.

Caro and Alice had been diverted to Frankfurt along with all the clothes they were meant to be photographing on Jo-Jo, and then German air traffic control had gone on strike, which Max, who'd grown up in Tel Aviv on a diet of wry jokes about

Teutonic efficiency, found hilarious. Normally in this kind of situation Sven would have gone and sat in the sauna for two days, but because he was fascinated by the proportions of Jo-Jo's face he decided to spend the time until Caro showed up taking head shots of her for the beauty pages.

When Sven's imagination was engaged, he worked like a demon – and made sure everyone else did too. He was a technical wizard, his lighting second to none, so each shot took hours to set up amidst a babble of increasingly surreal jokes that wafted out from behind the tripod and then hung around polluting the atmosphere like discarded satellites. Enrico combed Jo-Jo's hair onto giant rollers, set it, brushed it out and piled it on top of her head in shiny, fat brown curls that looked like a litter of sleeping puppies. It was certainly imposing – it made her about six feet tall – but it meant she couldn't move her head in case she dislodged it, and by the time Sven was ready her neck had lost all feeling. In the afternoon Sven made Enrico unpin it all and then stood her naked in front of an icy wind machine, with her hair tumbling over her shoulders like Botticelli's Venus. Jo-Jo had no idea modelling could be so uncomfortable, and she began to miss Joel, whose approach was altogether more casual. Two hours later, when they were all freezing, Sven miraculously found the warm switch on the fan and Jo-Jo began to suspect that he'd only blasted her with cold air to make her nipples erect. But after she had thawed out and the hot air began to caress her bare arms and shoulders, a curl of excitement wrapped its way round her stomach. Everyone was focusing intently on her now; even Sven told her she looked great. When everything was going well, being a camera's object of desire came pretty close to good sex.

On the second day Sven positioned her naked again on a freezing white marble slab with a little heap of coral salmon eggs on each naked breast and a triangular sliver of smoked salmon arranged over her pubic hair as a way of livening up a beauty feature on the healthy properties of Russian food. She was chilled to the core – but, with a glint in his eye, Sven had ruled out the fan heaters because, he said, they made the smoked salmon curl at the corners.

'What did your last model die of – rheumatism?' she asked in an attempt at levity after the first pose had given her cramp. Sven ignored her and in the afternoon announced that he was going to play with her features, at which point Cassie's comment about the tape, which Jo-Jo had assumed to be a joke, took on a horrible reality. Sven's assistant appeared with a roll of masking tape and proceeded to stick bits of it behind her ears and beneath the hairline on her temples. When Jo-Jo was finally permitted to look in the mirror, her face had been transmogrified into an elf's – her almond eyes yanked up into two dramatic slits and her skin stretched to translucency over her cheekbones.

And yes, she snapped to Dodie, the good behaviour and bad food of the past two days proving too much, it fucking did hurt.

Anastasia swept through the lobby of the Metropol like a pastel squall and contemptuously surveyed her compatriots slobbering into their cups of tea and mobile phones while they conducted ostentatious deals on the grimy leatherette sofas. They thought they were the bee's knees, of course, dressed head to toe in Versace and Kristof, fingers growing arthritic beneath the weight of their diamond and ruby barnacles, and chucking their money around as if it were confetti. But if she knew her confrères there were probably several shots of vodka in each of those teapots. A spotty youth behind the reception desk snatched her passport from her.

'My usual, please,' said Anastasia.

'It's taken. We've got a fashion team from London staying with us for the next week,' said the spotty youth, trying to sound dismissive.

'Well, take it back,' hissed Anastasia.

The youth ignored her and pounded the bell on the counter for a porter.

For once Anastasia was too exhausted to argue. 'How delightful to be back,' she said sarcastically. The youth scowled. Comparing her pale blue cashmere pullover and immaculate grey silk trousers with the gaudy orange-and-purple Boldacci suits polluting the lobby, Anastasia wondered, for the millionth time, how it could possibly be that she was part of the same race as these oafs.

The decor of the Metropol hadn't improved at all, she grimaced, as a surly porter dumped her monogrammed cases on top of the bruise-coloured bedspread. They'd do better to flatten the place and put up a parking lot. She wondered if Irina had already thought of that. She flicked on the TV – still the same old diabolically lit porn and over-made-up news announcers – and flicked it off.

The bile-green tiles in the bathroom were cracked and the room smelled sour – clearly democracy had done nothing to improve Russian hygiene, so what was the point of it? wondered Anastasia mordantly. Every time she came back, she found more things to appal her, not least the smell – two parts stale sweat and unwashed wool, two parts cabbage and sour grapes that had been left to simmer for eighty years – which pervaded everywhere. It was strange to think that she had never noticed it all those years she lived here. But a lot of things had seemed perfectly normal while she was growing up. The poky, damp flat on Ploshchad Vosstania that had teemed with a father, a stepmother, three sisters and two half-brothers; the endless petty, pointless shortages; the greyness; the bleak winters that seemed to go on for ever; the resigned, sullen expressions on people's faces; the dirt – and the sheer, grinding banality of everyday existence.

She had always known there must be a better life, somewhere beyond the vastness of the Soviet Union. As a precocious, exquisitely pretty child, she had knuckled down to her studies at a school that was romantically located in what used to be the Count Kuchatsky's townhouse. Its location was all that was romantic about it, but at least the rigours made her aware that beauty alone might not get her very far. Then, one day, when she and two other girls at the school had stayed after hours on cleaning duty, she had gone to fetch some more dusting rags from the boiler room in the basement. Her cardigan, a too-large hand-me-down, had caught on a loose, chipped wall tile and she got tangled up. Tugging on the cardigan, the tile had come away, bringing some of the crumbling brickwork with it. In the hollow she glimpsed what looked like a lock. Curiosity, always a driving force in Anastasia, gave her a physical strength that belied her size. She scrabbled away at some more bricks until she had cleared a large enough space in the wall to see the casket in its entirety. Her classmates helped her lift it out and, dutifully, they took it to the school head.

The casket turned out to contain hundreds of thousands of roubles' worth of Countess Kuchatsky's Cartier baubles. And for their pains, the three diligent students were each presented with a coin bearing President Brezhnev's lumpy profile. This outstanding meanness finally confirmed what Anastasia had always subconsciously felt, but never articulated; namely that her country was only good for one thing: escaping. The cultural exchange programme to East Berlin seemed to answer her yearnings. She had swotted up German literature for months and, although at fifteen she was officially a year too young to be accepted on to the course, the examiners felt it would be a shame if her heroic efforts went unrewarded. East Berlin had been a huge, sickening disappointment to Anastasia – no better than Moscow. But then, shortly before the programme ended, she had met Dieter Mannheim, a good-looking, thirty-two-year-old, moderately successful racing car driver who had swept her off her feet in a nightclub. Dieter had only crossed the border for a bet and had low expectations of finding anything to entertain him in the East. But instead he found Anastasia and fell head over heels in love with her icy beauty. Anastasia was equally smitten – by Dieter's West German passport. They married after three weeks. She didn't tell him her real age. He didn't tell her that, when it came to sex, two was a crowd. He preferred her to watch him perform solitary stunts, usually with a silk rope round his neck, which she was supposed to tighten gradually in time to the *Messiah*. She'd never been able to listen to Handel since.

In the beginning, Anastasia – or Olga, as she still was then – felt that ropes and the *Messiah* were a small price to pay for life in the West, but when Dieter began demanding that she bring along her best friend to watch, and then anyone she knew, she began to wonder whether her teachers in Moscow hadn't been right about capitalism addling the brain. But on the whole, it was a relatively harmonious marriage. She loved playing house in Dieter's flat in Monaco, and when Dieter's accountant had to do a spell in a French prison following some irregularities in his professional conduct, Olga turned out to have an exceptionally shrewd business brain. Dieter was so grateful for the way she managed his affairs that he drenched her in jewels and furs and even promised to buy her her own little floating gin palace.

Life was good. Flitting through the world's flashier cities and staying in a succession of luxurious hotels more than compensated for what she called her rope tricks. She happily fell in with the nomadic Formula One set and studied them carefully for etiquette tips. And while the other wives went through agonies every time their husbands competed, barely able to watch the race, Olga sat serenely sipping champagne and working out what, if the worst came to the best, she would do with the fruits of Dieter's various life assurance policies.

Of course, when the inevitable happened and Dieter finally wrapped his car round the wheels of an articulated lorry on the way back from a party in Nice one night, it was typical that Olga should have been on a rare mercy mission to visit her father in Moscow, where he was slowly and painfully dying of emphysema. It was even more par for the course that Dieter should have turned out not exactly to have finalised his divorce from his first wife and, worse still, that because of her deep mistrust of all Russians, she had left her jewellery in Monaco. So there she was, aged twenty, passport-less, broke and back in the USSR – and even more ravenous for life outside.

On the plus side – and Olga always forced herself to see one – she now had a veneer of sophistication and a solid grasp of business practices which she was determined to exploit to the hilt. Her homesickness for the West only intensified her ambition, while her contempt for everything Soviet made her ruthless. There had been a desultory attempt at modelling – but there wasn't much of a market in those days and Vladimir, the photographer who'd promised so much, had fled to the West the moment he found a route out. So she opened a tiny beauty salon in Petrovsky Passazh which Russian women, always struggling to make the best of themselves and desperate to share a little of her cosmopolitan glamour, flocked to. By the age of twenty-six she had made a small fortune by Muscovite standards. When glasnost came a year or two later, her first inclination was to get a one-way Aeroflot ticket out – but her entrepreneurial instincts got the better of her.

Under the new regime it became blindingly clear to her that the resulting anarchy could be of huge advantage to those with the nerve to swashbuckle their way through the chaos. While ninety-eight per cent of the population struggled to make ends meet, two per cent of the New Russians were making vast fortunes, and Olga desperately wanted to be part of the mood. Business was cut-throat, unorthodox – half the time laws simply didn't exist to deal with the new markets – and utterly exhilarating. She branched out into property deals, renting or selling vast, rambling apartments that had previously belonged to party members to the influx of Western bankers. She even bought a couple of old state factories. Moscow, an unsophisticated provincial city at heart, began to throb with a brashness born of desperation. Everywhere Olga's business dealings took her, the air jangled with the sound of billion-dollar fortunes being made. Decadent nightclubs were launched. Western designers opened boutiques and tripled the prices of the goods they sold there. It was the Mafia, roaring into the city in their ludicrously vulgar cars, double-breasted Italian suits and glittering handfuls of jewellery, who first made her realise that the beauty salons hadn't realised their full potential. Their molls had started coming to the salons first, then the men, vain, preening creatures, who demanded facials and manicures and, after a short while, a list of her 'other services'. At first Olga had resisted. She was doing nicely as it was. But greed had got the better of her. Why not take advantage of Russian's entrepreneurial spirit? And the oldest profession was nothing if not entrepreneurial.

The more money she made, the more exasperating she found

Russia, but everyone kept telling her to be patient and that things would get better and the climate less philistine. So she enrolled on to every art and literature course in the city. One entire room of her apartment on Manezhnaya Ploshchad was filled with copies of *Designers' Digest*, *The World of Interiors* and the house magazine of the Royal Academy, of which Olga had become a Friend. She took piano lessons and found an old KGB agent to teach her English. Irina told her she was becoming a real culture vulture. But Olga felt that, alas, the same wasn't true of anyone else.

She began to travel abroad, especially to Italy, which she found an excellent source of stylish recruits to her 'beauty salons'. It was there that she met Guido Monticatini. Intoxicated by the delicious wine and the sixteenth-century frescoes that vaulted over her head, she was overwhelmed by this charming, erudite, aristocratic-looking art teacher. Unfortunately for Anastasia, as she now was, aristocratic-*looking* was all Guido was. His father was a taxi driver in Rome, but by the time she discovered this it was too late. She was deeply in lust with Guido, who represented the apex of a three-thousand-year-old civilisation, and proposed to him a month later on her next trip to Florence.

Guido taught her an enormous amount about art and culture, but the marriage was doomed to failure. Guido simply had different aspirations from Anastasia's. A voluptuous, molten sunset was all he needed to make him happy. It wasn't that he had rejected the pursuit of material success, simply that it had never occurred to him as an option. Anastasia tried to find spiritual enrichment in Guido's nature walks and trips to the Uffizi but it was futile. After two years the pair amicably agreed to go their separate ways. Guido kept their eight-bedroomed Tuscan farmhouse, which Anastasia had never got round to renovating properly. In return, he told her she would always be a welcome guest, and had kissed her so passionately when the taxi came to take her to the airport that she almost regretted leaving him.

At least the Florentine diversion had shown her that, spiritual though she wasn't, the philistine new élite at home meant Moscow was out of the question as a permanent base. And so it was that, entranced by her Royal Academy magazines and the first edition of *Our Mutual Friend* that Guido had given her, Anastasia finally pitched up in London, which was utterly and completely to her taste.

The sooner she severed all connections with this god-forsaken dump the better, she thought, gazing pityingly at the waiter slamming a tea tray on the revolting fake walnut console by the bed. She couldn't wait to get back to London. After the small dinner she had hosted in Milan she was finally starting to feel she was ready to launch herself properly in English society. But as she began to go through the accounts that Irina and Nadjia had left in reception for her, she realised, as she always did on these trips back home, that she was simply making far too much money in Russia ever to break with the place completely.

On the fourth day, Caro and Alice finally arrived in Moscow and Caro immediately got Alice ironing the mountains of clothes that had been crushed on the terrible journey. They now had three days to shoot eighteen pages, but Caro was so distressed by her ordeal that she sent Alice to deal with everything. The sun had put in an appearance and Sven, via Max, announced that they would be shooting outside from now on. 'At least those gaudy onions will help fill a few double-page spreads,' said Alice, as they trudged across Red Square. Jo-Jo was so relieved to be out of the studio that she began to cartwheel across the cobbles.

'We're not shooting a tampon ad,' said Max disdainfully. The light was falling in the wrong direction to photograph the vivid colours of St Basil's Cathedral, so Sven's assistant set up a white canvas backdrop and told everyone to come back in half an hour. Alice skulked off to cadge some cigarettes from the spotty youth at the Metropol, while Jo-Jo cantered off down an alley before anyone could join her, ignoring the bundled-up figures that swivelled to look at her admiringly as she sprinted gracefully past, and headed towards a little coffee shop she had noticed earlier, to shelter from the Siberian wind that felt as though it had blown straight off the tundra.

Anastasia followed Jo-Jo into the coffee shop. She couldn't resist it. The girl was exquisite, clearly not Russian. She was tall with amazingly fine bones. Her skin looked as though it had been lit by the national grid – though in Russia's case, of course, that didn't amount to much. Most of all she looked hungry for all the good things that life might throw her way, as if she didn't quite know what they would be, but would run with them anyway. Anastasia recognised that expression – it was the one she'd started out with. She put on her sunglasses, knotted her Hermès silk scarf at the back of her head, *à la* Grace Kelly, and casually asked Jo-Jo if she could join her. Jo-Jo had just settled into American *Vogue*. The café wasn't full, but Jo-Jo didn't mind, even when the woman began to chat her up in flowing, flawless English. She'd met the type loads of times before. They were usually harmless – probably the bored wife of some wealthy industrialist. Loaded, by the looks of her, and out to spice up her sex life.

Anastasia launched into her patter. She told Jo-Jo that she could find her plenty of work. That she could make a wonderful life for herself, call her own shots, earn more money than she'd ever dreamed of, maybe even see the world. She danced round the subject so prettily that Jo-Jo couldn't fathom out whether she was offering to make her a Russian supermodel or a hooker. A broad smile tugged at her stupendous lips. She couldn't wait to tell Saffron. She had just tucked Anastasia's business card into her rucksack when Sven's assistant appeared.

'You better put your running shoes on,' he said breathlessly. 'I've been looking for you everywhere. The light's right but Sven thinks it might only last the next ten minutes Come on.' He tossed some dollars on to the table, in front of Anastasia, and dragged Jo-Jo out through the door.

Anastasia knew enough about the fashion world to guess exactly who Sven must be. It all made sense. They must be the fashion bunch staying at the Metropol, and Jo-Jo was obviously the model. Mortified, Anastasia uttered some profanities in Italian – they sounded so much prettier. Then, because that didn't help, she repeated them all in Russian.

★ ★ ★

'And the same to you, creep!' Saffron slammed down the phone indignantly. That was the fifth journalist she'd spoken to that morning, all making invidious enquiries about the health of Hot Shots' finances – as well as half a dozen or so of its most successful models. It was three months since Cassie had first spoken out about Peace and nearly a year since the entire management of the Bellissimo agency had first been called in by the police for questioning about tax evasion. But *Blitzkrieged!!* had just published a long article, implying that Bellissimo was somehow linked to the Mafia, using its models' bank accounts to launder money. In the two days since the *Blitzkrieged!!* article had appeared, the dailies had all picked up on the story and were in a frenzy to find more evidence against the modelling world.

'Fuckwits,' she said to Cassie. 'It's in *Blitzkrieged!!* so it must be true – as if.'

'It is a vile rag,' agreed Cassie, 'but amazingly it has a very good track record on its exposés. I wouldn't be surprised if they're right about Bellissimo.'

In the first few years, Cassie had dealt with Bellissimo on an almost daily basis. It was quite normal for agencies that didn't have global businesses to work in partnership with other agencies around the world. When Cassie signed up with a model in London, Hot Shots became what was known as her mother agent, processing all requests that came through the London office. But once Cassie felt a model was ready to work abroad, she would arrange for agencies in the relevant cities to take her on. In New York she had tended to work with Diego Vincent's agency, Allure. In Paris she had a good relationship with Rave. And for a time, she had worked with Jim and Sergio Zametti at Bellissimo in Milan. That had gone well too, until her affair with Jim Zametti had fallen apart and she began, coincidentally, to have misgivings about the way he and Sergio were running things. There was nothing concrete; but she had strongly suspected that, at the very least, it had an unsavoury approach to its clients and that it didn't nurture its models. It was certainly ruthless, working its models relentlessly, treating them impersonally and, in Cassie's opinion, putting immense pressure on the younger ones to reach their potential far too quickly. Many of Hot Shots' home-grown models had complained about Bellissimo's methods. She had even dubbed Sergio and Jim 'The Brothers Grim', and when Grace had mentioned casually a few years ago that Sergio Zametti had made an aggressive pass at her, she had severed all links. But judging from the phone calls she and Saffron had been getting, the press still thought she was somehow involved with them.

'I don't understand it,' wailed Saffron. 'The newspapers were all so sympathetic when we first broke the story about Peace. I thought by coming clean we'd actually trumped them at their own game. But now they seem to want to dig up any dirt they can find on us. It's getting really nasty.'

'I wouldn't worry,' said Cassie breezily, looking up from a fax from Diego Vincent demanding to know what the hell was going on. 'They'll get bored and go and hound somebody else in a few days.' She didn't feel as blithely confident as she sounded; she was still rattled from having to push her way past a couple of unappetising reporters from *The Python* who had been lurking outside The Hempel for the past few days.

'How is Peace, by the way?' asked Saffron.

'Dr Stevens seems to be happy with her progress. Her mother finally pitched up, but could only stay for quarter of an hour because those bloody boys of hers had left their entire sports kits in the boot and she was driving a hundred-and-sixty-mile round trip to drop them off. Anyway, you know how it is. Once an addictive personality, always an addictive personality. Even after they release her in a few weeks, she'll have to go back for regular visits. The sick thing is, all this notoriety has sent her rates soaring. She's never been more in demand. I just don't know if she shouldn't run away and marry some nice man in the country. It's not that I mistrust her willpower. I don't want to put it to the test, that's all.'

With one day of the shoot left, Sven Tolssen was on a downer again. He had found a cockroach in his bed and promptly developed an incapacitating rash on his back. Caro Luckhurst was still indisposed and even Alice was so twitchy about the lack of progress that she made Jo-Jo and Sven's assistant sneak out with her to Gorky Park so that they could get some more pictures. By the evening Sven had made a miraculous recovery and imprisoned them all in the studio until six in the morning while he machinegunned everyone with another fusillade of jokes and snapped Jo-Jo in six more outfits.

Nevertheless, Jo-Jo felt strangely dispirited. The shoot was a débâcle. She hadn't eaten a square meal since leaving Gloria. She was tired of being prodded and pulled as if she were an inanimate object, and she felt lonely. On her rare excursions on to the streets she would pass clusters of animated students making their way somewhere lively and was frustrated to think that out there somewhere was an exciting, pulsating city that was passing her by. She couldn't decide what was worse, Sven's spiralling depressions or charades. At this rate, slitting her wrists would constitute an entertaining diversion. To cap it all she had run up such a huge phone bill moaning to Gloria that she was going to have to do a midnight flit. Just as she was contemplating how to tie the grubby velour bedspread to the window ledge, the phone rang again. She considered not answering, but hell, she was hardly inundated with options.

'Hi, Jo-Jo? This is Ben Mornay. Saffron in your office gave me your number. I just, um, called to let you know that I won't be doing the IRA movie after all. My agent didn't think it was a good idea. I'm gonna do *Sons and Lovers* instead. So I'll be in England anyway. Next week, as a matter of fact. I don't suppose you do Northern accents too? Anyway, I was wondering whether maybe we could meet up – Tuesday week? That's if you're around?'

Jo-Jo heard herself saying she could probably rearrange her dates to fit him in, which was pretty cool considering she didn't have any.

★   ★   ★

The encounter with Jo-Jo had really rattled Anastasia. She had never misjudged an approach so badly before. If the girl blabbed, Anastasia might just as well sell up and leave London for good – and she would kill rather than do that. In her more optimistic moments, she wondered whether Jo-Jo had perhaps not fully understood what had been proposed. She couldn't figure out how explicit she had been. Then she remembered Jo-Jo's smirk and was plunged into despondency. She had understood all right, so it came down to one simple geographical fact: the town wasn't big enough for both of them.

Once the editor of *A La Mode* got used to the idea that most of the Russian pictures had been shot against plain white backgrounds, she had to admit that Sven was a genius. The photographs were astonishing. The head shots and the nudes were particularly beautiful. Jo-Jo was so fragile-looking and so streetwise at the same time that the pictures almost looked like social documentary. In contrast to the quirky, slightly odd-looking models who had been in fashion for the past couple of years, Jo-Jo was physically perfect, a heart-stopping, classic beauty. What with Dodie and Enrico's slightly tribal hair and make-up, she practically burnt up the page. Her eyes looked like those of a caged puma, and in some of the pictures (the ones in which Sven had taped her) she looked as exotic and fierce as a Masai warrior. They'd use the head-and-shoulders as a cover and to hell with the advertisers. They'd just have to use twice as many clothes in the next issue.

Back in London, Anastasia made some discreet enquiries and discovered that Jo-Jo worked for Cassie Grange, Janie's friend who had been getting so much publicity lately. She was also Peace Grant's agent, if Anastasia wasn't mistaken. Nothing if not thorough, she immediately got in touch with a cuttings agency so that she could look up every article that had been published on Cassie in the last fifteen years. Then, determined that her little brush with Jo-Jo was not going to affect her enjoyment of the London season, she went upstairs to select an outfit for her midsummer dinner with other trustees of the Royal Academy the following evening. It was there in the tented courtyard where Anastasia, shimmering in lavender duchess satin, found herself seated next to the urbane and distinguished-looking proprietor of the *International Gazette*.

'Your friend Cassie's taking a bit of a battering,' said Gina Martin to Janie over lunch in the *Gazette*'s canteen. Sissy had slipped off to check out a private Hindi teacher.

'All I can say is it must be a slow week on the news desk. Peace is practically ready to come out of the clinic.'

'Not Peace,' said Gina, surprised, polishing off her second bag of Cheesy Wotsits, 'I mean all those rumours about Cassie Grange's involvement with that dodgy Milanese agency. Apparently they had a reciprocal arrangement whereby Bellissimo kept an eye on Hot Shots' models when they did the shows in Milan. The word is that Cassie and the people at Bellissimo had girls trundling backwards and forwards delivering drugs at each end.' Gina chuckled. 'You never told me that you had friends who were international dealers, Janie.'

Janie looked aghast. 'Cassie would never, never get involved in something like that. Apart from anything else, financially she has no need.'

'Sounded far-fetched to me too,' said Gina, helping herself to Janie's untouched sandwich, 'but now that the Milanese agents are under arrest several of the papers have got their investigative teams checking all the British agencies out. In fact Rushmore's asked me to put a journalist on to it. Look, she's okay for the moment, there's nothing conclusive, so far as I can gather. All the same, if I were you, Janie, I'd go back to my desk and call my friend. Right now.'

Chapter Nine

Lately, Seth had felt strangely peaceful when he visited Finn's grave. He supposed the grief would always be with him, but it was no longer searingly painful. For a long time he had felt so angered and betrayed by his brother's suicidal trajectory that he could barely bring himself to go and sit by his final resting place. He still couldn't understand why Finn, so gifted, so charismatic and doted on by a wide circle of admiring friends, had been so intent on bringing his life to an early finale. It wasn't even as if, in his last few years, he had had a lot of fun doing it.

As children Seth and Finn had been uncannily close. There were barely thirteen months between them. Melissa and Fergus, their parents, were an unconventional couple, not the types to go in for cautious, planned gaps between their offspring. By the time Seth was two and a half, he also had a six-month-old sister, Sarah. There would have been others, but Melissa miscarried her fourth baby and after that Fergus finally got his big break – as Dr O'Connor in an American daytime soap. At first he'd commuted between Beverly Hills and Merrion Square, where he bought his family a dilapidated but imposing Georgian house, but after a while he began to find the travelling wearisome. The arrival on the soap of Nurse Wittington turned his life upside down. He bought another house, this time with a kidney-shaped swimming pool, in Pacific Palisades, moved in with her and pursued a gratifyingly lucrative career doing voice-overs and made-for-TV movies. So it was that Melissa Weiss, formerly a pampered Jewish princess and promising ingenue at the Royal Shakespeare Company, found herself bringing up three children on her own in Dublin, where her beloved Fergus had swept her on a wave of promises about setting up their own theatre company.

To her credit, Melissa never did go running back to her parents' comfortable house in Hampstead, although Fergus, sweet-talking himself into believing he had ultimately acted in everybody's best interests, persisted for thirty years in believing she would. Instead, she set up the theatre company herself and persuaded the local authorities to pay her and her actors to perform at festivals, schools, hospitals and prisons.

What with the troupe and the drama workshops she held every summer in their rambling, dun-coloured Georgian house in Merrion Square, it wasn't a bad life. The children would have liked to have seen a little more of their mother, but as they grew older they appreciated the ever-changing cast of motley thespians who periodically took up residence in their home. They were fiercely proud of Melissa's achievements and her broad-minded attitudes. When Seth, aged twelve, proposed that they adopt her name instead of Fergus's, the other two supported him unanimously.

Ever since he had become aware that Finn had a dangerous addiction to drugs, Seth had frequently raked over the foundations of their childhood, torturing himself with unanswerable questions. Would Finn have turned out the same if Melissa had been less Bohemian? If Fergus had never gone off to Hollywood? If he, Seth, had been less introverted? If they had all been less indulgent when Finn swapped from chemistry to medicine, then to architecture before finally dropping out to be a poet? Of course, he knew that Finn had been born with a compulsive personality, but with a little foresight couldn't it have been channelled in a more positive direction?

It had seemed perfectly natural to go and see Peace at Ashwood. And with every visit it became increasingly painfully obvious that he and Cassie were her only regular contact with the outside world.

'I've just never acquired a facility for making friends,' Peace told him one day. She who had been so inarticulate was becoming more candid and perceptive by the day. 'I don't think people actively dislike me. They just don't *consider* me. I'm not on the horizon as "friend". I'm just a celluloid image made flesh.'

'You're being a little hard on yourself. You have Cassie and me, for starters.'

'Exactly. I didn't meet you until I overdosed. And Cassie – well, let's just say she has a vested interest in me.'

They were sitting on the terrace in the dying rays of a glorious late June afternoon and Seth had gently broached the issue of her leaving Ashwood.

'Perhaps you need to meet more down-to-earth people,' suggested Seth. 'I imagine modelling can make everyone seem a bit artificial from time to time.'

'Yeah. That's what's been great about being here. People from all walks of life. I've been practising making friends and, you know, I think I really might get the hang of it one day.' She looked across the lawns to the lake where a figure in a long black riding coat was waving to her from a rowing boat. 'I know I've got to come out in a few weeks and, to be honest, I think the best thing would be to do some more modelling for a bit. Otherwise it will always be a demon that haunts me, something that conquered me, rather than the other way round.'

Before Seth left, Peace took him over to the living quarters of Ashwood.

'I want you to meet someone who's been teaching me about friendship,' she said.

The door opened on a tall, cadaverously thin figure with a prominent, hawkish nose, mournful features that hung limply on his bony face like a cloak that was several sizes too big, and light brown hair that looked as though it had been imprisoned on his scalp far too long and had decided to do a runner in wild, random directions. His large, slightly bulging eyes glistened with delight on seeing Peace. Seth instantly recognised him from the tabloids littering the staffroom at Le Château.

'Seth, I'd like you to meet my friend Harry.'

Harry's lugubrious expression broke into a sweet, open smile and he shook Seth's hand vigorously. On the way back to London, Seth couldn't help being amused that Peace's first down-to-earth friend should turn out to be the sixth Viscount Orsett.

When Anastasia launched one of her charm offensives she was irresistible. She knew enough about a lot of subjects to make her sparkling company. She was a marvellous listener, asked pertinent questions, and when she swivelled the full beam of her attention on someone they felt as though they were the only person who mattered to her. Meeting The Proprietor at the Royal Academy had sent her confidence skyrocketing. He had clearly been so taken with her, was so encouraging about her plans to launch herself into the fashion business, that it had seemed only natural afterwards to call up a journalist on his flagship newspaper and resurrect the interview that should have happened weeks ago.

Seth found himself thinking about Janie constantly. Every time he went out on to his roof garden to pick a herb he was reminded of her; just passing a newspaper stall instantly conjured up a picture of her face as he remembered it from their first dinner, laughing, but tinged with a slight sadness. It was like having a schoolboy crush. He had gone to supper at Michaelmas Road, even though it meant having to rearrange his shifts and risking Sebbie's explosive ire. He'd found her up to her elbows in congealed pasta, and they'd ended up eating fish and chips. 'My favourite,' Seth had assured her, uncertain whether it was the right moment to risk another kiss. As the summer deepened they had snatched time from their impossibly incompatible schedules; quiet drinks in pubs by the river, walks in the park. She gave him tiny pots of herbs for his terrace which she had grown from seed, and he started cooking her steak and kidney pie and blinis with caviar, her two favourite dishes.

Seeing their acquaintance taking on a momentum of its own, with or without her blessing, Cassie tried another approach. 'So glad you've become good mates,' she said one day as Seth escorted her round the building site that was finally starting to look like the beginnings of a restaurant. 'Janie really needs a good friend – she misses Matthew so much.'

Seth knew when to take a hint. It was fine, he kept telling himself. What with the new restaurant there just wasn't room in his life for any other distractions. If only he could stop thinking about her.

'So Janie, finally I thought why not face the inevitable and go with the most intelligent journalist?' cooed Anastasia. 'Your pages have become compulsive reading – all my friends agree. No mean achievement when you consider the way fashion is treated on most newspapers. Not that I understand this attitude. As I was saying the other evening to my fellow trustees at the Royal Academy, fashion is a subject as worthy of academic study as art or architecture. After all, what are clothes if not architecture of the body? But so few people in this country seem to see it this way. You're quite a ground-breaker, you know. More tea?'

Janie's attention, which had been diverted by the Fragonard and The Gainsborough that adorned the wall opposite her, tried to focus on what Anastasia had been saying.

Anastasia beckoned to Janie to follow her, her charm bracelet tinkling as she pushed open the French doors that opened on to a small, lush courtyard. The air, heady with the combined scent of lilies and the Diorissimo that Anastasia drenched herself in, was motionless. It was turning into an earth-warpingly hot, dry summer. She fanned herself delicately. Janie, who'd served a stint in the beauty department at *A La Mode*, suspected she'd had plastic surgery, but whoever had done it had every reason to feel pleased with themselves – she really was sensational-looking. The pale primrose-coloured hair had been expertly cut into a gleaming chin-length, fringeless bob to frame the Slavic-looking cheekbones. Her skin, which was strikingly pale, had the extravagant dewy lustre of an arum lily. Janie wondered whether she chose her foundation to match her decor, like Wallis Simpson. With her blond, delicately arched eyebrows and light brown lashes, she looked like a delicious lemon sherbet. She was a paint-by-numbers picture of good taste and impossible to date. She could have been a sophisticated thirty-eight or a wonderfully preserved forty-eight.

What Anastasia didn't want, she explained to Janie, was to become one of those tiresome creatures who took up permanent residence on the social pages.

'That's why I thought it would be so wonderful to be interviewed by you. It would give the article some intellectual credibility.' She flashed an entrancing smile at Janie. 'And then perhaps all those other journalists will leave me alone.'

A maid laid tea for them outside and they moved from Anastasia's pretty, sun-dappled Colefax and Fowlered drawing room – a symphony of pale yellow and cream – into the garden, where they nibbled on delicious, translucent almond wafers. Or rather Anastasia played with hers and Janie devoured several platefuls.

'I suppose it has been rather a romantic life,' Anastasia was saying in the carefully modulated tones of someone who has been to elocution lessons. 'My grandparents fled Russia in the revolution, first to Paris and eventually settling in Florence.' Her father had been a respected but impoverished Russian émigré poet, her mother a shy, naïve girl who had had to run up dresses for the local Italian aristocracy to make ends meet and died, shortly after her husband, tragically young.

'I was brought up by Carmelite nuns who taught me to hand-smock. For a while that's how I made my living. It was an austere life,' she sighed, 'but a spiritually rewarding one – and one which also gave me a great appreciation of beautiful things. To this day I have an ascetic approach to life, which I think is traceable to Sisters Ignacia and Monica.'

There was more, much more, along these lines. Years of practice had made Anastasia a slick raconteur, even if her inventions were overly inspired by Hans Christian Andersen.

'You don't take many notes,' she remarked beadily.

'Oh, I can't write very fast. But I'm lucky. I've got an extraordinarily good memory. I can jot down key words and remember entire paragraphs.'

Appeased, Anastasia explained to Janie that after her husband died, she had spent an uneventful time in Tuscany, eking out his dwindling fortune by opening a small made-to-measure shop in Florence until a long-lost cousin from Moscow had tracked her down to tell her that if she returned to Russia she would be entitled to some of the vast lands and fortune her family had been forced to flee seventy years earlier.

'I didn't think the Russian government had paid out compensation like that,' said Janie dubiously.

'So it turned out,' replied Anastasia smoothly. 'It was just another of the rumours swirling about the place at the time. But we managed to locate, shall we say, substantial amounts of jewels and silver that had been hidden in the Ukraine. Really, it was a most incredible twist of fate — rather like a fairy story. My family's winter residence had been turned into a school and the treasure was discovered by three of the pupils in the cellar.' The grey eyes grew damp.

Janie tried not to sound incredulous. Phyllida would go berserk if she wrote up all this Mills and Boon stuff. 'Perhaps we could photograph you in some of your favourite outfits?'

Anastasia pretended to consider. 'Well, I don't know. I don't want to seem vulgar or shallow . . . but, oh well, I trust you implicitly, Janie. Would you like to see my dressing room?'

She led Janie up to the next floor and across a vast expanse of sand-coloured carpet, past a cherry-wood *bateau lit* to a wall of maple cupboards. Everything in the bedroom, which along with its limestone and maple-wood bathroom occupied the entire floor, was blond, including the pale camel cashmere wrap dress and pale beige slingbacks Anastasia was wearing. It was like being in an enormous honeycomb. Janie, dressed in a black sarong and faded blue shirt, felt like one of the sansculottes storming Versailles.

'This is where I keep my nightgowns, negligees, bathrobes and lingerie,' said Anastasia, gliding over to the banks of built-in drawers and shelves, 'and this,' she continued, stepping right into what looked like another deep cupboard but turned out to be a door leading into the next building, 'is where I keep everything else.'

She beckoned Janie to follow. 'I had to buy this,' said Anastasia casually, as if buying an entire penthouse flat to hang clothes in was the most normal thing in the world. 'These buildings are so narrow, there's simply no storage space. So here in this room is the knitwear, winter this side, lighter-weight over there. Through there are the suits. That room has dresses. This one' – she pointed at what must once have been the hallway, now lined with mirrors – 'is for checking details, so important I always think, don't you? And this one' – nodding at a space with ballroom proportions – 'is for evening wear.'

The entire flat was thermostatically controlled, a cool micro-climate against the torpid summer weather outside. It hummed like a jumbo jet. As they crossed the beige carpet, Anastasia explained that the crème caramel colour scheme was a tribute to Madame Chanel, on whose salon in the rue Cambon in Paris it was based. The carpet had come from the same factory that had made Chanel's. Light filtered in through thick cream silk blinds at the windows, and a column of switches in the ballroom controlled the tungsten spotlights throughout the flat. Thick wooden poles were suspended from the ceilings on silk ropes and hung with clothes wrapped in transparent bags. On one was a sequence of blue suits, ranging from washed-out aqua to deep Prussian blue; on another were the pinks, from dusty rose to cyclamen. There were roughly six inches between each bag. It was like watching hundreds of highly trained headless soldiers troop the pastels, mused Janie. A faint trace of cedar scented the air – the hangers. In the corner of the room an Apple Mac thrummed quietly on a large Hepplewhite writing table. Unselfconsciously, Anastasia switched it on and called up some files to show Janie, revealing herself to be a surprisingly deft typist. There were numerous documents – shoes, bags, jackets, coats, shirts, cocktail dresses as well as a combinations file – and some colour programmes she had commissioned from a company that specialised in supplying architectural software which gave her three-dimensional diagrams of all her outfits.

By the time Janie left, she had arranged for Anastasia to be photographed later that week, in the wardrobe-flat, wearing a selection of her favourite clothes. It was too delicious for words.

'I don't want to seem ostentatious,' said Anastasia, doubt beginning to cloud her enjoyment.

'Don't worry, we'll just photograph the one room,' said Janie mischievously. At least fifty per cent of Anastasia's story couldn't possibly be true, but she had seen the wardrobe with her own eyes. 'Flat-Packed Wardrobe with a Difference' – she could see the title now. Phyllida would be ecstatic.

She couldn't help thinking, however, that a proper journalist would get to the bottom of Anastasia's real story. She felt certain that would be even more riveting than her wardrobe.

At the end of July, Peace put the Notting Hill flat on the market and gave back the Jeep. She started looking for a place around Clerkenwell.

'I want something really urban,' she explained to Cassie, 'because at weekends Harry's letting me use a cottage on his estate.'

Cassie was cautiously impressed by the new Peace, even if late summer was a rotten time to try to sell property. It was extraordinary, she mused after one meeting in which they had both reviewed all Peace's contracts and current options and decided on a course of rationalisation, that Peace had previously managed so thoroughly to disguise her intelligence.

'Oh, and one other thing,' said Peace, calling her later that evening from Harry's cottage in Dorset, 'I'm going to need quite a bit of flexibility over the next few months because I'm setting up a charity to help teenagers and children with drug problems. Actually I'd love you to be on the honorary board, what with all your contacts and shrewdness.'

Flatterer, thought Cassie cynically, even as she succumbed.

'I thought we could start by getting all the designers to design a Fashion Says No to Drugs t-shirt which all the models could be photographed in – I've got Jess, Tulah, Unity and Brigitte to agree already. Even Isabella said she'd wear one. Sven wants to do some of the pictures – and Steven Meisel and Peter Lindbergh. Mario Testino's getting back to me . . .'

My God, she'll be convening meetings with Hillary Clinton next, thought Cassie, and banished the image instantly because it had a horrible plausibility. Well, if the industry was going to clean up its act, she was all for it.

Why was it, thought Seth, doing his utmost to stop himself from sighing adoringly every time he looked at Janie, that having kissed her on the first date, he now found it impossible so much as to hold her hand?

Over the past few weeks she had somehow constructed an invisible Maginot Line around herself which he didn't dare cross. In the middle of July, she had had to go to Paris for three days to cover the couture shows, and when she got back their relationship seemed to have become even more constrained. Perhaps Cassie had been right when she'd told him that Janie took her marriage vows more seriously than anyone else she knew.

Seth's terrace was a miracle of urban tenacity. Paved with bricks, it was edged with tallish bay trees in large terracotta tubs, which sheltered it from the worst of the winds. She had rearranged the beds of rosemary, thyme, parsley, oregano, purple and black basil, adding valerian, feverfew, marjoram and fenugreek in a formal, Elizabethanesque pattern to complement the strictness of his flat. Sometimes on hot days, the scent of the plants reminded her of the spice markets she and Matthew had visited in India.

He gazed across to where she was kneeling by the rosemary. It was one of the hottest days yet, relieved by a faint breeze; the tangled fronds of vine leaves that grew round the French windows kept fluttering through the open doors into the living-room area.

Feeling his eyes burning a hole in her neck, she stood up and smiled at him. 'What you need for this lemon tree is some crushed lupins. And you'll have to bring it indoors in the autumn. Fancy some camomile tea?' She walked past him to the kitchen, her hands frothing over with sweet-smelling white flowers.

While she waited for the kettle to boil, Janie stole furtive glances at Seth. Everything about this man said Soul Mate: his intensity, his passion for his work, his self-containment, even his melancholy. He had told her all about Finn – even read her some of his poems, which were extraordinarily good. He told her about Melissa and his sister Sarah, who had become a children's book illustrator in New York, and had just landed a contract with Disney; made her laugh about Fergus, whom he heard from intermittently and saw even more rarely, and shyly suggested that she might like to visit Dublin with him the next time he went to see Melissa. And yet they still seemed compelled to observe some mysterious form of etiquette that forced them to dance in fragile circles around one another.

She had decided that he wasn't Mr or Mrs Rochester, but strictly Laurentian, given to brooding introspection which she found incredibly sexy. So why, she wondered miserably, did she behave like a prim fourth-former when she was with him, engineering situations so that physical contact was awkward at best and more often impossible? The answer, as she knew, was Matthew. Matthew whom she hadn't spoken to for nearly six months. Matthew who she'd prevented from writing to the children. Matthew who, she knew, got all his news about them from Will. Was this marriage really so worth preserving that she should pass up all opportunities for alternative happiness?

Seth, almost irresistible in his faded fisherman's jumper, wandered in from the terrace. 'It's so good to let someone else loose in this kitchen,' he smiled, 'even if it is only to make tea. I know I can be a little obsessive about it.' He moved a little closer to her, but before he could do anything more demonstrative, she thrust a mug of camomile tea in his hands.

Cassie examined the bone-coloured ceiling of her bathroom in The Hempel and wondered if Anouska would mind her asking what it was called; it might be just the thing for the flat. Thank God, Barney was making good headway with the plans. Zack, having exfoliated her with home-made lemon zinger – whatever that was – and massaged her with peanut oil, appeared now to be eating her. He was most imaginative, she had to give him that much – and it was utterly wasted, because his voracious appetite had put her off sex for life.

'You okay?' she enquired politely when Zack surfaced for air.

'Not really, I must admit. I can't concentrate. I've been hearing terrible rumours about your business. One of the women whose charts I've been doing has a friend who works on *The Python* and, well, today we got talking and . . . Why didn't you tell me things were so bad, Cassie?'

Cassie sat bolt upright. Janie had told her about the warning she'd had from Gina Martin. And now, from the sound of things, *The Python* was about to crucify her on its front page. Determined to get to the bottom of the Bellissimo business, she got straight on the line to Jess, who was lying in her hot tub in Santa Monica trying to learn lines for her new part.

'What is it?' burbled Jess. 'You sound terrible.'

'Jess, I need to know – did anything horrible ever happen to you with Bellissimo?'

Jess laughed. 'When didn't it? There were so many teenage girls doing bunks in the middle of the night I'm surprised they didn't name the agency St Trinian's. They were creeps, especially Sergio and his little photographer pal Vladimir. Vlad the Inhaler, we called him, he snorted so much coke. Anyway, once, when I'd been out there a couple of weeks doing some catalogues, Sergio invited me, Vlad and this other model,

Zandra, I think her name was, round to his flat. He told us he was going to take extra-special care of us, talked about our careers for hours and what a difference having a good booker made and how important it was that models listened to their bookers' advice. Because it just so happened that Sergio thought we should do some pictures with Vlad, who was really going places. And then he asked us to perform oral sex on one another in front of them so that Vlad could film it for his "home movie" collection.'

'You mean Vladimir Miscov, the photographer who hung up his lens to become a partner in the agency? Why didn't you tell me at the time?' asked Cassie, outraged.

'Oh, you know,' said Jess, shrugging her shoulders, 'I was sixteen − I just thought it was part of the deal. And I was so desperate to succeed. No-job-too-small Jess, they called me. You didn't think I knew. I remember you trying to tell me tactfully that the best I could hope for was a career in lingerie catalogues. You thought I'd be upset, but I was thrilled. And then the fashion for curves came along and I was in . . . Anyway, we didn't do it, the "home movie", I mean. We spiked his water so it was all he could do to hold his Canon Sureshot straight, let alone a video camera. Bad things happen out there. It's no big deal. You can stop us being ripped off financially, Cassie, but you can't be our guardian angel, you really can't.'

Jess was right. The lucky ones, like Jo-Jo, could rise to the top seamlessly without being contaminated by any of the flotsam. It was the ones who hovered for too long around the bottom of the food chain, doing the grotty little jobs in the sewage slipstream, who really got damaged. And although she could gently advise them to think about other careers, there was nothing Cassie or anybody else could really do to make them give up on all their dreams. All the same, she was appalled that Jess thought she had known and simply turned a blind eye.

'Was Jim ever involved in anything bad?' she stammered.

'Jim? Oh, Jim was a bad boy, all right. One of the baddest.' Jess laughed mirthlessly. 'Not so much on the sexual harassment front, but he liked it if we could carry little parcels around with us. No pressure, of course. But put it this way; if you didn't co-operate, the jobs dried up pretty fast. Hey, Cassie, don't beat yourself up over it. You were in love. You weren't to know. Besides, he looked like an angel compared with Vlad.'

Still shaken, Cassie got straight on the phone to her solicitor, Michael Croft, whose wife sounded less than thrilled at being disturbed at nine o'clock in the evening.

'Calm down.' Michael's voice was reassuringly even. 'It's the silly season. They've nothing else to occupy them. They won't run it. Even *The Python* wouldn't print a completely unfounded story.'

'But Zack says they're planning to put something in this Sunday,' said Cassie, sounding frazzled.

'Right, well, that gives us time to put an injunction on them. I'll get on to it. That is if you're absolutely sure there's nothing in it. That none of your girls has somehow got mixed up in this and unwittingly implicated you.'

'On my mother's life,' said Cassie, flinching. God knew if *The Python*'s reporters had talked to any of her babies.

'Well, leave it with me, then. Oh, and Cassie, try to stay calm.'

'Oh, don't worry about me, I'll be fine,' said Cassie, feeling anything but.

Anastasia was livid. Through assiduously studying *The Tatler*, she had drawn up an action-plan chart that resembled a social chessboard on which a front-row seat at the haute couture shows in Paris was writ large. She had decided that it would be her little reward to herself for not being able to shake off her business interests in Russia, and had applied for invitations to the major houses months ago. But two days before she was due to fly to Paris, she got a call from Moscow. Nadjia, who was standing in for Irina, had had a minor run-in with an organised crime cabal and was clearly out of her depth. There was nothing for it but to postpone Paris and go to Moscow instead. Nadjia, who had staunchly resisted handing any money over to an unfamiliar branch of the Mafia, was clearly shaken.

'Just pay them their dues in future,' said Anastasia ungratefully the moment she arrived. 'It's as straightforward as paying rent or rates. More so, since the Mafia's the one thing that works efficiently in this god-forsaken country.'

She had flounced out of the bare new offices on to the dusty pavement of Ulitsa Kuznetsky Most, one of the city's foremost avenues. Cutting past the wedding-cake Bolshoi Theatre, sherbet-pink pashmina shawl flying behind her, she was oblivious to the stares of passers-by. Out on Teatralnaya Ploshchad, she looked past the babushkas hawking cigarettes and magazines and stared despairingly up at Karl Marx's statue. She blamed him for a lot of her native country's attitude problems. It was because of his lofty ideals that respectable professionals – teachers, doctors who had dedicated their lives to others – were now having to sell off all their possessions, one by one, spending their Saturdays huddled over flimsy makeshift stalls on street corners to supplement their pathetically low salaries. What was the use of her trying to upgrade her company's image if none of the local importers could get her any of the bloody furniture she'd ordered? What was the point of trying to bring a little Mediterranean flair into the lives of her employees when all any of them wanted was a guaranteed job for life and annual holidays by the Black Sea?

How lucky – and how spoiled – the West had been, she reflected sourly, her mind wandering seamlessly to Cassie. The way that woman was lauded as a great self-made business success riled her beyond belief. It was pathetic. Cassie wouldn't have lasted a lunch hour in Moscow. Anastasia yearned to teach her a lesson. She punched Gunter's number in London into her mobile. She had been calling him daily, ostensibly so that he could keep her abreast of events on the arts pages of the British newspapers.

'Yes, yes,' she broke in impatiently as he laboriously mangled his way through a piece on the Royal Opera's latest saga. 'And the business pages – any news of that Grange woman, by the way? I gather she might be about to merge and float – could be an amusing investment.'

Gunter, extracting himself from the tentacles of an ebullient hitchhiker from Auckland whom he'd ended up on the previous night giving a lift as far as Anastasia's deliciously pristine gold and cream suite in Mount Street, battled his way through the newspapers. *The Python* carried a large picture of Grace at Nice airport, accompanied by one short paragraph lamely hinting that she might be just the first of many to leave Hot Shots. Barely bothering to say goodbye to Gunter, Anastasia called Vladimir in Milan.

'It's hardly what you'd describe as public assassination, is it?' she said icily.

'Give it time,' said Vladimir testily. 'You of all people should know, Anastasia, that one has to be a little subtle about these things in England. Anyway, I have it on good authority from a little colleague of mine at the Rave agency in Paris, who just happens to be best friends with the number three booker at Hot Shots, that the police have been paying quite a few visits there lately. Play your cards right,' he continued silkily, 'and I might even get hold of a time-table.'

For a few moments Anastasia felt elated. Then the reality of what Vladimir had said sunk in. He was right, she thought as she caught her reflection in the Versace shop window, it was going to take ages.

The sight of two beggars squabbling over the dregs of a bottle of vodka depressed her so much that she left the next day for Cap Ferrat and stayed there for two weeks. As soon as she got back to London she called Janie, anxious to pick up with the interview where they had left off.

'I'm sure you'll do it absolutely brilliantly,' she purred over lunch at Fortnum and Mason. 'How was couture? I was so sorry not to go.'

'Oh, terribly clever,' said Janie, 'and half of it completely hideous. It's amazing how much unattractive detailing a hundred thousand pounds buys you. Chanel was beautiful, though.'

'You appear to have had a busy time while I've been away,'

remarked Anastasia silkily. 'Considering August is normally the silly season, you've been quite rushed off your feet.'

'What do you mean?' asked Janie, only half listening as she silently debated whether to pop into Hatchards on the way back to the office for a copy of *Container Gardening Made Easy* for Seth. He'd appreciate it, she knew, but might it look too domesticated, too pushy, too four-wheel drive and 2.4 children?

Anastasia babbled on. 'I thought you would be busy researching lots of stories about that agency – Cassie Grange's – and all its nefarious involvements with the drug world.' She broke off, taking in Janie's puzzled expression. 'Those were the rumours in the South of France, anyway. They're probably completely groundless. You know how people gossip when they're bored.'

'Why on earth would she say all that stuff about "nefarious involvements with the drug world"?' Janie asked Cassie over the phone ten minutes later. 'How does she even know about it? There hasn't been even a whisper about any of it in the papers.'

'I haven't a clue,' said Cassie bleakly. 'All I know is that this morning Saffron and I had the pleasure of being Spanish-Inquisitioned by two Rottweilers from Scotland Yard. Oh, my mother will be pleased. All my chickens well and truly coming home to roast.'

Jo-Jo floated back from Nottingham in a daze. It had been the most incredible, wonderful, fantastic weekend she'd ever had. Not that that was saying much, she reminded herself. Life was so amazing at the moment that she had promised Gloria she would endeavour to have one down-to-earth thought every day. Okay, here it comes: eight months ago I lived in Kilburn and couldn't name a single photographer.

There, that was two. But it was getting harder. Everyone was being so nice. American *Vogue* wanted to shoot three stories on her in Zanzibar, wherever that was. Italian *Vogue* were flying her to Vietnam. Coming back from Rome the week before, where she'd been working for Bella Scarletti, she'd seen her face on the cover of six magazines, and yesterday Cassie had phoned to say she was putting her day rate up to £25,000. And then there was Ben. Gorgeous, funny, laid-back and interesting Ben. For the first twenty-four hours they had just talked and talked. Then they'd spent the next thirty-six hours in bed. Then Ben had had to get up at 4 a.m. to shoot a pit scene.

'It takes 'em two hours to arrange the coal dust on set,' he said. 'Be here when I get back? *Please?*'

'I can't,' said Jo-Jo. 'I have to be in Madrid this afternoon to shoot something for *A La Mode*.'

Christ, jet-set or what? I can't believe this is happening, she kept chanting as she threw her clothes into a rucksack and Ben's driver whisked her to the train station. Tempted to hurl herself into first class, she forced herself to sit it out in second, and just for good measure swayed her way to the buffet for some stewed tea. There, Mum, that's two more down-to-earth experiences – in case I forget to have any tomorrow.

Cassie was at her wits' ends. The article in *The Python* had never materialised. Michael Croft had been right when he'd said they evidently couldn't make anything stick. *The Python*'s gruesome twosome, who had been shadowing her on and off for weeks, disappeared – probably trying to get topless pictures of Princess Stephanie. But somehow, after that, nothing seemed to go right. Cassie sensed that someone had whipped up a whispering campaign against her – even though no sound had yet reached her. Then Janie called to say that Gina Martin had, reluctantly, assigned Bill Gardner, a cub reporter with a haunted, wet-nosed puppy-dog look, to investigate the story. But he was not getting very far – most of Hot Shots' models and staff were on holiday.

Cassie was pretty sure all her models were above board, but of course you could never be entirely certain about these things, though she didn't tell that to Michael Croft. All agencies had had problem girls over the years, but why had the press focused so intensely on hers? She cursed herself for doing all that publicity when the news about her deal with Allure Inc. first broke. She could hear her mother's mincing voice mocking her: 'Pride comes before a fall.' *The Python* would have been some fall. Still, she'd learned her lesson.

Too nervous to think about relaxing, she cancelled a holiday in Sardinia – she couldn't face two weeks on a forty-foot yacht alone with Zack anyway. No one was around. Seth was working night and day with Barney on the restaurant, and on extra shifts at Le Château as a sop to Sebbie, and Janie had taken the children to Eleanor's for a fortnight. Cassie threw herself into work. August, normally a dead month in the fashion industry, was turning out to be action-packed and Cassie put on quite a performance, striving to keep an inchoate sense of panic from swallowing her alive. When she spoke to Grace's publishers, who called to say how thrilled they were with the deal they had struck with Cassie for Grace's first novel, she told them, with Oscar-winning sincerity that things were great. When Calvin Klein rang in person to tell her that Sven Tolssen had just shown him a preview of *A La Mode*'s September cover and that he was *very interested indeed* to meet Jo-Jo with a view to offering an exclusive contract for her to launch his new fragrance, she assured him that things couldn't be better. When Genevieve Fairfax cosmetics called to ask if it was true that Jo-Jo and Ben Mornay were an item, because if it was they were keen to talk to her about becoming their new Face, Cassie even managed to sound jubilant. By the time Diego called, in a foul mood, ostensibly because his lawyers had taken the month off and were delaying the deal with Cassie but in reality because he was getting the jitters about all the rumours, she was able to laugh him out of his temper.

'It's a wind-up. They've heard that Peace is planning to set up a charity to help drug addicts and they're looking for dirt, that's all. You know how hysterical the British press is. We're as clean as the bone china that divine hound of yours eats off.'

It was only after Zack called to say that, given her current tribulations, he couldn't let her move back into the flat by herself, that she finally burst into tears.

Nari Sujan turned out to be a pleasant surprise. Sissy had expected him to have a fat belly, a turban and a gold-plated Rolls-Royce. Instead he wore a beautifully cut black suit with a blue open-necked shirt, drove a convertible navy blue 1972 Aston Martin, and was slim and toned, with fine chiselled features and mischievous dark eyes.

At the end of August, he took her to lunch at Claridge's.

'I loathe all those trendy fashion restaurants, don't you?' he said, lightly brushing her hand as he poured some Chardonnay into her glass.

'Mmm, absolutely,' averred Sissy.

'So, you want to do a business piece – I take it the clothes in Everything She Wants don't quite merit a style feature?'

Something in the tone of his voice – sardonic? intelligent? – prompted Sissy to be honest.

'To tell the truth, this is my big bid to be taken seriously on the *Gazette*. I know they think I'm a moron. And the scary thing is, I've spent so long pretending I am, I think I might have become one. Anyway, I know nothing about business, so I'd appreciate it if you confined yourself to words of two syllables or less.'

Nari, who had been at the receiving end of some blistering journalistic techniques in his time, told himself on no account to be taken in by her. They joked and small-talked and she found herself admitting that she hadn't after all been to St Martin's.

'But that's enough about me. I don't normally ever tell the truth about myself in interviews. I've always found it far more productive to lie. Some of my best scoops came after I admitted to being a kleptomaniac and a manic depressive . . . but something about you has brought out my nobler instincts. It's all rather worrying.'

By the end of lunch, he was utterly disarmed and ready to open up – in his fashion.

She rootled around in her shoulder bag for her tape recorder. 'I do love India,' she said conversationally, wishing she had been there.

'Personally I think it's rather overrated,' said Nari. 'I don't go very often.'

'Oh, right,' said Sissy nervously, switching on the recorder. His mood seemed to have darkened. 'Now, shoot. From the beginning, how did you start Everything She Wants?'

'By accident, really,' said Nari, smiling at the memory. 'I was completely broke and so in the holidays I got a job helping out on a market stall. I think it was the third day that I realised they could double their profits by halving the number of lines they stocked – a businessman was born. So I set up my own stall, then a shop, then I got a factory and moved to the north of England because overheads were much lower. When I was twenty-six I had thirteen shops, but then I nearly lost everything by over-expanding. Then the recession came. I rationalised the business, concentrated on the basics and . . . well, it seems to be working. I'm ready to take on the South.'

Sissy would have liked a little more of the human-interest side, but since this was for Gina she supposed a straightforward business piece would do. In any case, she detected a marked reluctance in Nari to discuss his personal life. But she couldn't resist asking what his parents thought of it all. She imagined them to be a simple couple who'd fled the poverty of Bombay, been overwhelmed by the hostility of the new country and finally, in their twilight days, found themselves blinking in the dazzling success of their son. Poor things. They weren't to know the merchandise in Everything She Wants was a style avatar's nightmare.

'Let's just say they've come round,' said Nari dryly. His family, he told her matter-of-factly, were originally from Bombay, had settled in England in the 1950s, after Partition. Nari had been educated here, although at some stage his parents had decided to go back to India. Somehow he'd managed to stay. It must have been a terrible struggle, Sissy concluded, because he seemed reluctant to talk about it.

'Look, if you like I could show you some of the factories. No other journalist has seen them. It would give the story tremendous authenticity.'

To her astonishment, Sissy heard herself agreeing to drive up with him the following week. She felt quite crushed when he called a few days later to say he'd suddenly been called to Manila.

'Jess, you won't say anything about Jim or his little packages to anyone, will you?' Cassie's voice down the line sounded faint.

'It's already the stuff of legend amongst those who were close to Bellissimo,' said Jess merrily. 'We all assumed that's why you fell out with the Zamettis.'

'Well, yes,' said Cassie hesitantly, not wanting to sound naïve or callous. 'I just meant if the police asked.'

'Oh, honey, what do you take me for? My word is my bond – or rather my James Bond if all goes well at the next audition. Fingers crossed.'

'And toes and legs,' said Cassie automatically, feeling, for reasons she couldn't satisfactorily explain to herself, irredeemably soiled.

August was normally a quiet month: magazines, advertisers and agencies ran on skeletal staffs and the models went on holiday for several weeks which for some of them simply meant exchanging one set of photographers' attentions (the fashion brigade) for another (the paparazzi, who swarmed around the honeypot resorts of the Caribbean and the Mediterranean. Cassie inevitably spent the first few weeks of September consoling the more naïve models over the stream of topless pictures of themselves that kept tabloid and readers happy through the silly season and persuading them, on the whole, not to sue the editors, who could turn very nasty if provoked). Sven had been rhapsodising about his new find and a few of the most important workaholic designers had demanded to see Jo-Jo. Throughout July and much of August, she had been criss-crossing the Atlantic so often that she felt she was permanently locked in the foetal position. Bruce Weber had spotted Ben cramming *tagliatelle carbonara* into her mouth one night in a small trattoria in Little Italy and whisked her away the next day to photograph her on Long Island for American *Vogue*. Hearing that American *Vogue* wanted Jo-Jo for another three stories, Italian *Vogue* immediately block-booked her for five. Saffron was elated. Italian *Vogue* had a tiny circulation but yielded more power and influence in the fashion world than almost any other publication. Gloria, who had been out of sorts for weeks, finally confided to Janie in the children's shoe department in John Lewis that she was desperately worried Jo-Jo was going to fall to earth with a crash.

'Look, if anybody can control a career in modelling, it's Cassie,' said Janie, steering Nell away from some pink elasticised slip-ons with lace trim towards a pair of dark brown Start-Rites. 'Besides, Jo-Jo is incredibly down-to-earth still.'

'How would I know?' said Gloria indignantly. 'I 'aven't seen 'er for weeks. I say to 'er, don't tell me they don't 'ave phones in all these foreign places you're goin', 'cos I know different . . . she's too young. She 'ave no experience.'

'That seems to be the way it is in modelling,' said Janie sympathetically. 'If you're going to make it you make it incredibly fast. And I know this much, Jo-Jo's an amazingly quick study. Cassie can't believe how sophisticated she looks.'

'*Looks*, maybe.'

'She'll be fine. When all's said and done, Cassie *is* a very good agent, you know.'

Gloria grunted. 'I 'ate life when it's this good. I just don't trust it.'

As the restaurant neared completion, Seth began to suffer from sleepless nights again. He had put his life's savings into it, plus some of Melissa's and Sarah's money and, he winced just thinking about it, even more of the bank's. On good days he was pleasingly confident in his talents, but every time he glanced at a newspaper or magazine he got scared: the media had become obsessed with new restaurants and celebrity chefs and were creating a climate of hysteria. It was getting to the point where flawless, delicious food wasn't enough; customers now wanted their warm sashimi of lobster with sesame to get up off the plate and perform a tap-dance before it consented to be eaten.

The place looked wonderful anyway – at least that's what Cassie and Janie had said when he took them round it. He couldn't tell any more. Like his flat, it was airy and white, with a wall of glass doors that opened on to the river. Barney had devised a marvellously light, serene space that he had divided with a glass wall, so that when customers arrived they could have drinks at the bar or be served on tan leather sofas that flanked the French doors. The restaurant itself was flooded with so much light – a glass ceiling that had been fitted with blinds for use in hot weather ran the length of both rooms – that it felt like being on an old-fashioned cruise liner. The daffodil-and-emerald-coloured tub chairs were being delivered next week. And Janie, having seen the bedraggled patch in front of the restaurant straggling forlornly down to the river, had just taken a week off work to oversee the installation of a gravel terrace and a kitchen garden. It was cheating, really, to plant such large shrubs, instead of growing everything from cuttings and seed, but the place had to look welcoming for when Seth opened in three weeks' time.

He still hadn't thought of a name. The bank believed he should capitalise on his growing reputation and call it Chez Seth's, but he couldn't bear the idea of seeing his own name daubed everywhere. He didn't want to call it something specifically French or Italian since the food would be a mix, predominantly British and Irish. In the end it was Peace who suggested the solution.

'Why not Finn's?' she said.

Finn's it was.

★   ★   ★

Jo-Jo's test shots with Sven Tolssen for Genevieve Fairfax cosmetics were brilliant. If they weren't such a maddeningly cautious company – they were waiting to see how the market research on the pictures showed up in the Midwest before finally signing the contract – Cassie would have cracked open the champagne. As it was, she was still playing down Jo-Jo's success as much as possible, although this was getting more and more difficult, now that Sven Tolssen seemed to have decided to work his Svengali treatment on her. Already she had cut her hair again, had her eyebrows reshaped and, in the newest pictures she had done with him, was starting to gaze into his lens with a studied but arresting candour. This was the cleverest trick of all: Jo-Jo apparently stripped bare of any artifice was, along with Sven, in the process of constructing a perfect mask for herself in front of the camera.

Cassie had never seen such a fast learner. Even Grace had taken a couple of years to learn what Jo-Jo had picked up in seven months. She seemed to know instinctively what a story demanded – grandeur, camp glamour, gritty realism. It was almost uncanny. The September issue of *A La Mode* finally hit the news-stands midway through August with Sven's picture of Jo-Jo with her hair rippling sexily round her face on their cover. At the same time the billboards of Jo-Jo wearing nothing but a heavily anaesthetised cobra and Antonio Viro's first new fragrance in eight years went up in Times Square, sparking a mini-furore about the snake's pornographic significance. Suddenly every designer requested her for their upcoming shows. *Sons and Lovers* had moved from Nottinghamshire to London for ten days' shooting and Ben had promised to stay on for a few more weeks when he wrapped, which meant he could help Jo-Jo look for a flat.

And, Cassie had to hand it to her, she hadn't as yet become objectionable – no whining about hotel rooms not being up to scratch, no demands for Concorde tickets. She had announced, rather touchingly, that she wanted to be normal. Hoping to keep her unspoiled a little longer, Cassie had ruthlessly rejected all requests for interviews, including one from Janie.

'Cassie says it might just be the thing that tips her over into obnoxiousness,' Janie duly reported back to Phyllida, who was desperate for an exclusive.

'Christ, Janie, surely you don't have to go through the official channels. She lives in your sodding house, for God's sake.'

'Not really,' explained Janie patiently. 'She seems to live mostly on aeroplanes. I haven't seen her for weeks.'

'The weird thing,' said Cassie to Janie during a trip with Nell to London Zoo (they were standing next to the snake terrarium, which presented them with a vista that seemed poignantly apt to Cassie in her present mood), 'is that if Jo-Jo gets this Fairfax contract it'll make her a millionaire.' She was frightened by the speed with which events were turning around for Jo-Jo.

'Well, maybe the sooner she's a huge success, the sooner she can get out of modelling and do something useful. She does look amazing – even I can see that. That sixties story she did for *Beau Monde* was terrific. I loved the one of her writhing on the floor with the two boys – very *Blow-Up*.'

'If I were really brave, I'd turn that Fairfax deal down here and now on her behalf,' said Cassie thoughtfully. 'She's just not ready . . . it's happening too fast. In the old days at least the girls grafted in obscurity for a couple of years. Now, everyone's so obsessed with finding someone new that there's no time for the girls to develop. It's a whole new ball-game, Janie, and I'm not sure I'm fit enough.'

'Oh, rubbish,' said Janie. 'You're just depressed. Jo-Jo's having a whale of a time. And she seems to be falling head over heels in love as well, lucky thing.'

Janie didn't know why she seemed suddenly to have become a cheerleader for the modelling industry, but Jo-Jo's metamorphosis fascinated her. Every time she saw her – or pictures of her – she marvelled at the emerging woman she saw there. Besides, there was clearly something troubling Cassie, and she couldn't get to the bottom of it. Whenever Janie broached the subject of Cassie's alleged connection with Bellissimo she either turned prickly or made a joke out of it. In all the years they had known one another, Janie realised, Cassie had never really told her when events – at least the ones that really mattered to her – were going badly. It was as if she couldn't even acknowledge the possibility of failure to herself. Janie didn't imagine Cassie was confiding much in Zack either – at this rate she would implode. On the way home from the zoo, Janie tried again.

'Any news on the Bellissimo case? Gina says it might actually go to trial. That'd be a first for the Italian police.'

'Inconclusive. Bellissimo won't go down lightly.'

'What d'you mean?'

'If they can't bribe their way out of the charges, they'll make everyone else look so black, the police will be relieved to drop the whole thing.'

'How ghastly for the rest of you.'

'It's not Bellissimo I'm worried about,' said Cassie, trying to sound blasé. 'It's Gloria. When she's fretting about whether I'm doing right by Jo-Jo, frankly she scares the hell out of me.'

Chapter Ten

Janie stood collecting her thoughts in the lengthening shadows of Finn's kitchen garden, breathing in the mingled aromas from the restaurant and the clumps of thyme that were growing along the embankment wall. She found she desperately wanted the place to be a success.

It was a beautiful September evening, balmy and fresh after two days of torrential rain. The sky was indigo and pierced with stars. The Thames, almost full, scudded past briskly. Someone had threaded fairy lights through the trees on the opposite bank. Behind her, Finn's, blazing with light, looked like a modernist's vision of a greenhouse. Inside, she could see Seth's team of waiters, sleek and calm in their white t-shirts, navy trousers and stripy butcher's aprons, darting between the emerald-and-yellow chairs with armfuls of plates and cutlery. She hadn't seen Seth for hours. For four days he seemed to have been suffering from what Zack diagnosed as chronic nervous tension. Occasionally, aware that Janie was eyeing him anxiously, he broke into a halfhearted smile, but he hadn't fooled anyone. The vein in his forehead, always visible when he was exhausted, had developed a throbbing twitch, and was now so prominent it seemed to be in danger of setting up as a separate, volcanic free state. Sissy had suggested he take Valium, which she said was more chic than Prozac and less ubiquitous. Cassie had dropped by with some homoeopathic pills. Zack had offered a massage. All suggestions had been rebutted.

'Sorry. I'm beyond help. Just ignore me for a week,' he had said apologetically to Janie in one of his rare forays into speech.

Cassie had taken it upon herself to find Finn's a PR by interviewing everyone in London, finally plumping for Vanessa de Lauret, a twenty-seven-year-old, terrifyingly dynamic Quebecois who was, Cassie remarked acidly to Zack, hip in the way only ex-colonials were – comprehensively and humourlessly. When Cassie had interviewed her she had been wearing a mannish Ann Demeulmeester trouser suit, but when she turned up subsequently in a transparent Aeron Baxter mini-shift, revealing legs that were as thin as angel-hair pasta and bosoms the size of large-to-huge pumpkins, the dynamics of their relationship were sealed. Cassie loathed her and set about – in the most constructive way – making Vanessa's life a misery by overseeing the plans for the opening at every stage and questioning each decision, down to the size of the reply cards that went out with the invitations. Having toyed with the idea of a soft opening, they had eventually gone all out for an extravaganza. Janie was worried that it was simply intensifying Seth's stress, but was powerless to do anything. At least the diversion was giving Cassie something else to think about while the Bellissimo enquiries rumbled on ominously and Barney's joiners redid her kitchen cabinets for the third time.

Poor Cassie. In between tearing around hollow-eyed, she could go for hours at a time looking heroically stoical and calm, while working like a maniac. At five o'clock on the day of Seth's party she had managed to close a deal with the *Mail on Sunday*, which had agreed to pay Grace £100,000 for first serialisation rights to her book. Ironically, Cassie's star performers had never done better. Several of her new girls were starting to take off in a most encouraging way and Jo-Jo looked set to become one of the most talked-about models of her generation.

Nevertheless, Janie knew that Cassie was only too aware of the increasingly wild rumours that were proliferating about the agency. *Shag* had printed a spiteful glossary of revised cockney rhyming slang based on Cassie's life. Consequently everyone in the business now referred to a Jess when they meant mess; a Grant (as in Peace) when they were talking about plant (as in weed, dope, hash, etc.). Zack had become industry shorthand for smack and crack. Giving good Jeep was the latest expression for a hit-and-run accident (as in driving over a heap), and only yesterday Janie had heard some wit on the *Gazette*'s style pages refer to a dodgy business set-up as a Cassandra (as in Grange, rhyming with short change). Gina's cub reporter, Bill Gardner, had even written a joky snippet on slag's glossary for the *Gazette*'s diary page, until Janie caught it on the computer just in time.

In as much as they provided Cassie with a diversion, Vanessa de Lauret's melodramas were a blessing in disguise. The restaurant nearly hadn't opened at all. Three weeks earlier Vanessa had woken in the middle of the night with what she called an epiphany; Finn's had to have a covetable ashtray that everyone would want to steal. Barney, grappling with an awkward gradient on the glass roof and a consignment of slate that had gone missing in Cumbria, nearly had a nervous breakdown.

Somewhere along the way, it had been decided that instead of hosting a sit-down dinner which might be stuffy and formal, they would hold a full-blown party and invite the world – which left Seth with the nightmare of organising thousands of delicious and original canapés.

At least he had gathered together a brilliant team – without poaching from Le Château. This hadn't been easy, however, as one by one Sebbie's long-suffering staff had furtively approached Seth for a job.

'You know I can't,' Seth said wistfully to Deirdre Muldoon, an elegant, rangy Scot who ran the floor at Le Château with all the charm and diplomacy of a Lord Carrington.

'I respect that,' said Deirdre sadly, 'and you know I wouldn't be so treacherous normally. But Sebbie's gone way over the top. Last night he marched in firing his Purdey at the kitchen ceiling. They were blanks, thank God, but it's not good for our nerves. The week before he was cracking his whip – literally. Duncan, the new commis chef, got so pissed off that he crapped on the pastry chef's favourite tray and served it up to Sebbie as chocolate soufflé. The place isn't the same without you, Seth.'

'Christ, he didn't eat it?' asked Seth, smiling for the first time in weeks.

'No, he passed out and Duncan's been suspended. We'd all come running west if you so much as clicked your fingers . . .'

'I'm touched . . . but no,' said Seth firmly.

'Just remember we're there,' she said, swinging gracefully towards the door.

Ben scrabbled around in his pockets for some pound coins to pay off the taxi driver. He and Jo-Jo had forgotten to change any money at Heathrow and just about scraped up the £37.50 between them, which didn't leave much for a tip. The cabby scowled at the derisory amount of coins Ben gave him and screeched off, leaving their bags in the middle of Michaelmas Road.

'Same to you, fuckface,' said Jo-Jo equably.

'Oh, very Chaucerian,' said Ben, mock-chidingly. 'How I love your quaint turns of phrase. Are you sure she won't mind us staying?' he added, surveying the row of large, mellow brick houses. 'I mean, we coulda checked into Blakes.'

'Nah,' said Jo-Jo, heaving two of the bags up the path and brushing aside a frond of Virginia creeper that dropped across the front door, 'my mum would go berserk if she thought I was staying in a hotel in London and not with her. She's already furious that I'm buying a flat – says Janie needs the rent. Anyway, it'll be much cosier and far more private here.'

The place was eerily peaceful. The children had gone to stay with Eleanor for a few days and Gloria had just that afternoon left to visit the Scotts. Truth to tell, Jo-Jo wouldn't have come if she hadn't know that. She didn't much feel like being lectured by Gloria these days.

Gloria and Janie had decided to take the bull by the horns. The sagging ceilings had been shored up, the worst of the damp miraculously mopped up and the house painted from top to bottom. No longer peeling, with moist swirls of discoloration, the walls were painted a soft bone. Someone had finally finished scraping and sanding the staircase until it had reached the same high gloss as the rest of the floor. A huge glass vase of lavender stood on an oval rosewood 1920s table – a present to Janie from Seth for doing the kitchen garden. As redress, Janie had hung a colourful abstract painting Matthew had done at university. She had always liked it, but he had buried it in the attic, along with the others, claiming it was too derivative of Howard Hodgkin. It looked very pretty in the hall.

'It's great,' exclaimed Ben. 'So British. You are clever.'

'Thought you'd like it,' said Jo-Jo, mildly surprised herself at the transformation. Someone had even been baking bread.

She felt Ben nuzzle up behind her.

'So where's ye olde bedchamber? I've been two inches from you for the past fifteen hours and unable to do anything about it. I don't think I can wait much longer.'

'Ben, we have to be at Seth's opening at eight thirty.'

'Then what's the problem? That gives us one whole hour – two if you switch to Greenwich Mean Time.'

Sissy glanced nervously at the clock on Nari's dashboard. Half past six and they were still way up north in Birmingham or somewhere. At this rate she wouldn't even have time to go home and change. She'd have to get Nari to press an ejector button at the Hammersmith roundabout. Cassie would kill her if she was late for Seth's, particularly as Sissy was practically a co-host, having made a strong case for inviting fashion people who were, she argued, if nothing else glamorous. She particularly needed to be there at the start as she had ended up sending out two hundred invitations instead of the fifty they'd all agreed on and, as everyone seemed to be going, she suspected there might be a few scuffles.

God, she was factoried out. She'd read up on *North and South* before the trip but nothing prepared her for the industrial bleakness. She sank back into the beige leather seats and closed her eyes as Nari swooped round Spaghetti Junction. No one could say she wasn't researching this piece thoroughly. They had been to the knitwear factory in Bradford, the shoe factory in Leeds and a monolithic monstrosity somewhere near Halifax that was Sissy's idea of Hades – bland, boring, and all the women forced to scrape their hair back in unsightly mob-caps. That was the factory that produced coats which Nari unblushingly said he sold in Everything She Wants for £59.99. Sissy was appalled – most of her underwear cost more than that. He had probably taken her to other factories but she had blanked the rest of them from her mind.

'Of course, lots of stuff gets made in China, the Philippines, India . . . I'm assuming your budget won't run to sending you to the Far East?' He continued before she could answer. 'Pity, because I'm proud of my set-ups there.'

Sissy was silent. She was busy working out how she could get Gina to bankroll a trip to Manila. If she could find four-year-olds sweating over Nari's casual-wear that really would be a good angle.

He took her to see some of his shops.

'In four months there'll be three in the South-East. By the end of next year we should have twenty,' he said proudly. Sissy could barely suppress a shudder at the thought of all Nari's cheap merchandise and garish signage flooding south. Yet factories apart, it had been a surprisingly pleasant day. He had taken her for lunch at a converted Georgian mill house in a picturesque cobbled square somewhere in the south Yorkshire Dales where she'd discovered that he had a very dry sense of humour, and he'd driven her through countryside so luscious the valleys seemed like cleavages. There were still some wild roses flowering in the tangled hedgerows, and the late spurt of sunshine had coaxed a stunningly voluptuous performance from the blackberries. The contrast between the industrial urban areas and the rural spots was staggering.

Nari certainly seemed to be admired by his staff. He had introduced Sissy to his foremen and left her alone to wander around the factory floor. There were lots of Bengali women seated at the machines, as well as English women. She strained her ears to see if she could pick up any words in Hindi – perhaps they were complaining about Nari's perfidious slave-driving. It took her a quarter of an hour to realise they were actually discussing, in broad Yorkshire dialects, last night's TV debate about ethical art on *Late Look*.

As they reached Oxford, she stole a furtive sideways glance at Nari. He was pretty good-looking now she came to study him – firm chin, bit of a dimple, strong, straight nose, high forehead. His hair was receding a bit, but she even liked that. And ravishing eyes. Eyes you could never take advantage of but would happily be exploited by. What if he was kinky? It would be just her luck. What if *she* was? It was so long since she'd had a relationship with a man who didn't like wearing high heels more than she did that she couldn't actually remember what her sexual preferences were. Or whether she even had any. The realisation made her unexpectedly morose. She heard herself asking Nari if he'd like to come to Seth's opening. He would. She hoped his eyelashes were real.

Janie wandered back into the restaurant and began nervously rearranging the black anemones on the tables for the umpteenth time. The mauve calla lilies, black baccarole roses and burgundy cotinus had seemed such a good idea at the time – resonant and modern, yet classic. But now she wondered whether she shouldn't have gone for the splashier, more colourful bunches of scarlet acers and orange and candy pink gerberas that she'd originally envisioned and then dismissed as too faddy. Then she remembered passing a garden in one of the neighbouring streets with a hypericum bush – the bright berries would be perfect. She headed towards the kitchen for a pair of scissors, saw the intense concentration on the faces in there and made her way instead towards her handbag, where she fished out a pair of nail scissors. Then she scooted out into the night.

★　　★　　★

If Zack didn't remove his cute little rear from her bathroom in the next five minutes – three hundred seconds, if her powers of rational thought hadn't entirely forsaken her – Cassie was going to stab him with her Tweezer-Man. What was the point of paying Anouska Hempel two thousand pounds a week for a Zen oasis when she had to share it with a New Age goon who was driving her to the brink of insanity? Weeks ago she had made a pact with herself not to lose her temper with Zack – she found the mental exertion of curbing her irritation strangely therapeutic. She could just about concede that it wasn't his fault if Inspector Reece had taken it into his head to summon her to a 'little chat' in her office at 7.45 that evening. But something about the blithe pertness of Zack's physique and his unshakable niceness made her want to blame him anyway. Stressed beyond measure, she blew out his celery-and-ginger aromatherapy candles and raked her fingers through her hair for the twentieth time since she'd emerged from Sean's salon an hour ago.

She wasn't feeling her best, and surveying her sagging layers in the bedroom mirror made her despair. It was too bad that at the precise moment you found a look that suited you, fashion could, without fail, be guaranteed to move on. Every cocktail dress Cassie had bought in the last year was either on the bed in a rumpled mound or cascading over the sides like silken lava. And somehow it all looked even worse in the haughtily pared-down aesthetic of her suite. She could really grow to hate minimalism, she thought petulantly, which was unfortunate as she had just spent eighty sodding thousand pounds turning More into Less.

Why did the way she and her surroundings looked matter so much to her? she wondered. It wasn't even as if this evening was about her – it was Seth's night and, by association, Janie's, who was probably, if Cassie knew anything at all about her, halfway up a tree chasing catkins or whatever it was that grew on trees this time of year. She decided to blame her insecurity on her mother, who'd always dressed her in the nastiest clothes the seventies could produce. Cassie was sure she'd gone out of her way to find unattractive dresses to humiliate her. As a teenager she'd become convinced that her mother placed ads in the *Weston-super-Mare Echo*: 'Vile garments wanted. Reasonable prices paid.' Reasonable! Hah! That was a joke. Her mother was never reasonable about anything. The querulous, would-be genteel voice floated back to her . . . three hundred seconds must be up. Cassie pulled herself back to the present.

She promptly wished she hadn't. The telephone rang. It was Reece, laconic and maddeningly casual as ever, changing their appointment to a quarter past seven, in *his* office. Cassie tried to maintain a polite, professional veneer. She would now be late for Seth, which would leave him entirely at the mercy of his PR's uniquely charmless hospitality. The lists of proposed guests – which Cassie had wilfully and endlessly revised – spun in front of her eyes. Vanessa's speciality, as she had explained to Cassie in her initial interview, lay in what she called Social Homogenising. In plain English this boiled down to a thumpingly good address book – Vanessa was on dinner party terms with every newsworthy face from Liam Gallagher's to the Prime Minister's, and the events she organised were always a media-fest of names from every walk of life, which of course made them extra tempting to the press, as there was always the chance of catching a bishop *à-deuxing* with Lindy St Clair. She had even hinted that she could persuade Jude O'Kelly, the sado-masochistic performance artist, who was having a rampant affair with a senior Liberal Democrat, to come *avec* boyfriend. Seth, who only managed to surface from menus and Barney's increasingly complex redesigns every few days, had no say in the matter.

At first Vanessa's dizzyingly eclectic guest lists had seemed like a brilliant, right-on millennial idea to Cassie. But what Vanessa's game plan really meant, she now realised with sobering clarity, was that Finn's would be jumping with liggerati and that their pockets would be bulging with fin-shaped ashtrays. Why hadn't they kept it small and select? *Le tout* London had been invited, and because Vanessa was so damn good at her job, doubtless *le tout* would turn up – everyone from Kate Winslet and Peter Mandelson – who, as Cassie knew of old, was partial to any new restaurant – to the Lord Chief Justice. She might just as well invite DI Reece along after their 'little chat'. You could spin-doctor all you liked – it still had the makings of the evening from hell. Groaning inwardly, she plumped for her Depression Dress, an ancient black, asymmetric, floor-length Yoko Rakabuto shift that Zack called The Marquee.

'Don't take this the wrong way, Cass,' began Zack convivially a few minutes later, brushing up close to her and in the process releasing millions of CK One droplets from his glistening follicles, 'I mean, wow, you look great, of course, and Yoko is, or *was*, a wicked designer, but it's not very happening, is it? Hey, babe.' He gently raised her chin level with his own and began to press his thumb and forefinger into her temples. 'Chill out. You look destroyed. You can't let those fascists fuck your mind, man. How about the bumsters Alexander McQueen gave you that time you fixed for Peace to be in his show? They'd look frigging *genius* on a curvy piece of booty like yo's.'

Cassie eyed him glacially. Since dealing with Sissy and Vanessa over the party (Zack had appointed himself as aromatherapy consultant, until Seth had finally blown a fuse at the thought of his lamb cutlets being overpowered by the smell of a thousand candles reeking of frangipani), Zack's slang, faddy at the best of times, had become completely incoherent. Count to fifty. To sixty. To a thousand. To two point five million, went the mantra in her head. She ignored it. It was Zack who had pointed out, waving a copy of *Arena* under her nose, that the bloody Japanese were having a revival.

'Zack, I know that because of your chronic attention deficiency syndrome – which, those less forbearing than myself might say, borders on the psychotic – your acquaintance with the English language has always been, at best, casual. But might it not be possible, in future, when trying to communicate at least something of your thoughts, such as they are, that you could confine yourself to words and phrases which are intelligible outside the pages of *Yo Motherfucker Monthly*? Don't look so worried, I'm not looking for anything as highfaluting

as articulacy, just something the average three-year-old could
manage . . . Do you think we could try?'

In the Cassie canon of insults, it was pretty tame, although
delivered with the chilling thud of an avalanche. But because
their affair had long ago assumed the dynamics of a relationship
between a patient pedagogue and a slightly backward child,
it was doubly wounding. The crimson shadow of pain that
flickered across Zack's face – like a baby, he was so easy to read
– made Cassie wince inwardly. And the wince made her guilty,
which only made her more recalcitrant. He was so vulnerable,
so in need of protection, so . . . violent in his wilful massacre of
the English language. She hardened her heart and slipped on the
frump pumps that went with The Marquee. She couldn't bring
herself to tell Zack about the meeting with Reece, so she might
as well leave on non-speakers whilst the going was still bad.

'Look, it's gone seven,' she said curtly. 'They're going
to need me there. I'm ready, you're not, so I'll see you
there, okay?'

Zack slumped down heavily on the bed as Cassie floated
out, The Marquee in full sail. He was too distracted to tell her
that the dry-cleaning tag was still attached to one of the hems.
The paparazzi hanging outside the hotel waiting for Tulah and
her ski-bum boyfriend would no doubt point this out. He
slipped on his new chartreuse silk XTC shirt, borrowed a glob
of Cassie's Aveda hair pomade – last time: he knew it infuriated
her; tomorrow he'd get his own – and sauntered perkily down
to the bar.

Janie longed to creep up behind Seth and hurl her arms around
him. She'd been on the verge of doing just that at one point, but
had stopped short, ten paces from him – he looked so absorbed
in the chaud-froid of chicken oysters he was preparing that she
turned on her heels and went up to Cassie's office instead to
shower and change. Madeleine had sweetly lent her a beautiful
lilac silk crêpe cowl-neck dress from her last – in all senses –
collection.

239

'You must be the only living fashion editor who doesn't expect to be permanently lent everything,' exclaimed Madeleine when Janie had initially demurred. 'I'd love you to wear the lilac. It would really set off your hair. Don't look like that – you have lovely hair. I may even have the shoes the models wore with it on the catwalk – Angel did them and I have to say they're divine. Keep the outfit, otherwise the receivers will only get their grubby mitts on it. It will be a pleasure to see you in it, honestly.'

Janie fastened the silver ankle strap of the sandals and surveyed herself in the mirror. The shoes brought her up to about five eleven. The lilac silk made her skin look radiant – she was still faintly tanned and freckled from the summer – and the low back and spindly straps showed off her fine shoulders and arms which, now that she had finally put back on a little weight, were nicely slender and toned from digging out Finn's garden. She smudged a little brown shadow over her eyelids, peered into the mirror and sighed. She looked tired and her hair badly needed a trim. She wondered if Matthew would notice that she had aged when he finally got back, and realised with a jolt that this was the first time in days that she had given any thought to his return. Realistically, of course, she might have aged forty years by the time he finally got around to showing up. The prospect didn't flood her with panic the way it might have done six months ago. Is this how all separation ends, she wondered mournfully – the sharp, gut-churning pain, the dull ache of adjustment and, finally, nothing more than a neglected store of congealed emotions?

By way of distraction she borrowed some Touche Éclat that was on Cassie's desk and began jabbing it on over the great bruised circles shoring up her eyes. The agency smelt of a heady concatenation of scents – mainly Body Shop Dewberry, which, Cassie had told her, the new girls always wore (it made them smell wholesome and vulnerable, she thought), but which they rapidly dumped on getting their first job in favour of something strong, sexy and altogether more overbearing.

Janie squirted on some of Cassie's Mitsouko and glanced

in the mirror again. Now all she could see was the desperate ungroomed state of her eyebrows which had accumulated more stragglers than a sponsored charity fashion walk. Impatiently she twisted her hair into a French pleat and secured it with a giant bulldog clip. The saving grace of working in fashion, she had weeks ago decided, was that you could wear the silliest things and people would assume they were a trend.

Now that she was ready she felt at a bit of a loose end. She would have liked to have dragged Seth away from his marinating squid for a bath up here, but their relationship simply didn't lend itself to that kind of intimacy. When he was tense, Janie had learned, he became withdrawn and taciturn. She had never seen him lose his temper but she could sense him wrestling to control his impatience when people made mistakes. She felt it would be intrusive to get too close to him at the moment.

Although she'd never confronted Cassie, Janie knew that her best friend thought Matthew was a liability – and it hurt deeply. Weeks ago, when she had intimated to Cassie that she and Seth had slept together, she had done so in the hope that Cassie would have protested *in loco Matus*. She wanted Cassie to balk at her infidelity and say something about Matthew being a wonderful person deep down. Then Janie would reveal that she'd only been teasing. Cassie's notable lack of remonstration had put the kibosh on all that. And as it seemed rather puerile to admit she'd just been testing her, Janie was now cast irredeemably in the role of scarlet woman. This was doubly galling given that she and Seth *hadn't* slept together – although she couldn't quite work out why. He seemed to feel as intensely drawn to her as she was to him. She glanced at her watch. Twenty minutes to go. She wished Madeleine had been able to get over to change with her. But even business-less, Madeleine was still frantic. Not only was there her work for the Italian companies, but she was also getting a portfolio together to send off to a couple of big designers in Paris. But she'd promised Janie she'd get over to the opening at some stage.

Janie padded idly over to the bathroom. Maybe she should have another shower – at least it would keep her occupied. A

series of glottal clicks in the corner of the room made her jump.
A fax was coming in. Janie took it from the machine, meaning
to place it on Cassie's desk so that she wouldn't miss it in the
morning. She didn't mean to read it, but, marked urgent and
confidential, its one terse sentence leapt out at her.

Get rid of the evidence

Janie pressed her head against the cool window. Her mind
went into overdrive. The message was so hammy it had to
be a wind-up. Surely not Zack? With police wandering in and
out of Cassie's office, even Zack wouldn't miscalculate a joke so
badly. No, whoever had sent it was clearly no friend of Cassie's.
But who disliked her enough to contemplate something so
malicious? Stupid question – you didn't get to be as successful
in the modelling world as Cassie was without making enemies.
There was no doubt in her mind that the fax was a set-up.
She looked at the fax number at the top of the page. It was
definitely a Milanese exchange. Her heart thudding, she looked
up all the Milanese numbers in Trudy's Rolodex. There was
nothing there that corresponded with the number on the fax.
Handling the paper as if it were a piece of contaminated waste,
she tore it into tiny pieces. Then she rootled in one of Cassie's
drawers for her reserve cigarettes and, while she smoked one,
thought how much she longed to confide in Seth.

Eight cool, gardenia-scented fingers spread themselves over
Seth's eyes as he patiently rescued a vat of oysters from one
of the kitchen hands who'd been about to wash them.

'Lost in mucus, I see,' soothed a husky voice behind him.
The veins in his forehead visibly contracted. He'd know that
scent anywhere.

'Mum.' He turned around and engulfed the small, dark
figure behind him in a bear hug. 'What kept you?' he said,
beaming – the first time he had looked relaxed in days.

'Ophelia. She's had a nervous breakdown.' She pressed a

slim hand, weighted with heavy silver rings against her forehead in a mock melodramatic gesture. 'Darling, I'm sorry, I know I was due weeks ago — at least it feels as though I'm weeks late. It's all Helen's fault. When are you going to come and meet her, by the way? You haven't been home in eons. Have I really failed to intrigue you about her? Well, maybe it's for the best. She's so highly strung she makes Ophelia look like a tower of emotional strength. I've told her that nervous breakdowns are Hamlet's prerogative but she won't have any of it. It's the first time she's played Ophelia — first time she's played Shakespeare, if you ask me — and the poor child simply can't cope. It's not just the verse. The psychodrama we did at the start dug up all her suppressed childhood anxieties and . . . well, how was I to know she had a thing about her father? Anyway, did I mention that she's exquisite? She looks divine on the posters. But if she doesn't get her act together soon we're going to have to recast and that's not a pleasing thought so close to panto season. But enough of me. Seth, this place is heavenly, darling. Are you sure London deserves it?'

Seth made a wry grimace and, casting his eye round the kitchen to reassure himself that no disasters were in the making, led his mother to a quiet corner of the restaurant, grabbing a bottle of Cardhu *en route*.

Melissa whistled stagily. 'It's huge, extraordinary. I love all the glass and the lighting. It's so . . . shiny and glamorous. Great ashtrays — I'm almost tempted to take up smoking again. I didn't know you were so stylish. Nothing personal, darling, but I always had you down as Barbour Man. You sly thing. I can't believe it's all yours and, possibly, a teensy bit mine and Sarah's.'

'Mainly NatWest's, if you want to be really technical,' said Seth, pouring his mother and himself two generous fingers of the whisky each. 'I feel like escaping. Perhaps I could open a pub in Dublin. Jesus — when I started this, the idea *was* to make it somewhere you could go without dressing up — you know, small, intimate, unpretentious with deli- cious food — but you know me and architects. Never could read the plans properly. Just as well I decided to become a cook.'

'Only the best there is. Even the sodding critics think so, so I'm not just being a Jewish mother. The point is,' said Melissa, splashing some more of the Cardhu in their glasses, 'you've got this far without once resorting to cooking kangaroo and all that disgusting Pacific Rim stuff. That alone deserves a medal. Anyway, you can't come home at the moment, Seth. They're so proud of you in Merrion Square that you'd probably get mugged.'

Seth was touched. Melissa didn't bestow praise indiscriminately. Often, as children, he, Finn and Sarah had accused her of not taking any interest in them, only to be shamed by her suddenly revealing some tiny insight into their innermost thoughts.

'Sarah is furious that Disney wouldn't let her even have two days to come over for this, but I suppose they have given her a huge project. You children . . .' She broke off poignantly. 'How did I end up with such overachievers? . . . all of you.'

Seth reached over and took her hand. 'I still miss him too, the sod. I suppose we always will?'

'Now, darling, go and change,' said Melissa, briskly switching subjects. 'Even you need to make an effort occasionally – you must be the least fashionably dressed person invited. And by the way, where's the famous Janie?'

The flattering white glow of Finn's halogen lamps lit the swirl of animated faces below as if for a glamorous Hollywood film. By the time Cassie had escaped Inspector Reece, the party was in full flow. Seth couldn't lose, she noted wryly – even if the kitchen burnt down, people would still come for the age-defying lighting. Both Sir Norman Foster and Sir Richard Rogers, by Cassie's special request, had dropped by and were congratulating Barney Frick. Daniel Day-Lewis was ensconced in one corner with Nicholas Hytner; in another, Liam Gallagher was chatting animatedly to Edmund Connor, the *nouvelle* Scottish *vague* film *auteur*. There was a scrum of sports personalities over there, a clique of models in the other direction, even in this glamorous setting their perfection setting them slightly apart from the other guests; John Mortimer, Harold Pinter and the latest literary establishment scourge Sid Skidster at the far end; a nest of luvvies at the other end; a perfect binding of glossy magazine editors exiting from the cloakrooms; an ebullience of designers towards the middle; two Macs – Stella McCartney deep in conversation with Euan MacGregor. What a scoop to get a picture of Peter Mandelson talking to Isabella Saurez – spin doctor meets swivel queen.

Cassie was bitterly regretting The Marquee. Zack's misgivings about it had been perfectly justified. She no longer felt the dress made her look like an intellectual refusenik – it hadn't made her feel like one in at least ten years – but rather like a one-woman Greenham Common convention – worthy, sexless and fat. It could be worse, she thought morosely; she could be experiencing death by compression in the tube dress that Peace had wanted her to wear, in support of her new charity work, on which was emblazoned the legend Say No to Blow. The sick thing was it looked divine on Peace, who arrived with Harry Orsett, both of them as thin as a wraith of opium. On Cassie the dress would have looked like a badly printed balloon, the letters stretched beyond legibility. She was starting to wish Zack were here; at least he could shadow her to make sure no one caught her rear view. She was attracting intrigued glances all round. Trevor Nunn, mid-sentence to Martika Jansen, the blonde arts presenter of *Late Look*, looked quite nonplussed and, if she wasn't mistaken, rather fascinated. Taking a deep breath, Cassie marched purposefully towards him.

Melissa, looking like Delilah in an exotic hand-embroidered, ruby-coloured velvet Madeleine Peterson evening dress that Seth had bought her for her birthday, had accosted David Mellor. She vaguely recollected that he was no longer the Minister for Fun or whatever his official title of state had been, but since she couldn't for the life of her remember who had succeeded to the post, she took him to task anyway over the government's funding of the arts. Having read him the Riot Act she was regaling him with lewd stories of her Shakespeare tours around the west coast. By the time she got to her anecdote about the time she'd slept in a Morris Minor estate with Sean O'Riley, the night he heard he'd won the Nobel prize for poetry, and they'd woken up the next morning to find themselves up to the axles in peat bog, an experience which had duly prompted O'Riley's immortal 'On Sitting in a Peat Bog' sonnet, he looked utterly captivated.

'So you see,' Sir Vincent Lambert, OBE, was telling Angel Derrida, 'I don't mind the fact that there are all these Johnny-come-latelys doing peculiar things with rubber, but I do object to the fact that they know buggery-boo about accommodating a catheter into an evening gown if needs be. Until you've had to drape a train round a tube, you know nothing about dressmaking, believe me.'

'Told you you'd look great,' said Madeleine, sidling up to Janie. 'I should have had you wearing my clothes years ago.'

'Nothing to do with me. It's a beautiful dress – not that Seth would notice,' said Janie a trifle unsteadily. She'd had two salty dogs and a neat whisky already and was starting not to give a damn if her baccarole roses were drooping. 'Did I ever tell you about my crush on a man who's pretty oblivious to my existence most of the time?'

'No,' said Madeleine soothingly, 'you told me about the husband you adore.'

'Yes, well, that was before he forgot he was married. Where is he now? Where are any of them now?' asked Janie, waving her glass around. 'If I ever do an autobiography, that's what I'll call it: *What Went Wrong? The Lives and Whines of Janie Pember*. Be a bit repetitive, though.' She snatched another drink from a passing tray.

Phyllida stood in the middle of the restaurant radiating fury. John Mortimer had failed to recognise her even though she'd taken him to an unforgettably expensive lunch at the Oxo Tower a year ago in an attempt, unfulfilled, to persuade him to write a short story for the *Gazette*, and Buster Lloyd, one of the senior commissioning editors at the BBC with whom Phyllida assiduously cultivated good relations in the hope that he would one day recognise her potential to be the next Sue Lawley, had been very cool. Worse still, she felt uncomfortable. She had finally shaken off the stigmata of power dressing and chucked out all her suits, only to discover it had apparently made a comeback. When? How? Why hadn't anyone told her and how long did a sodding trend last these days anyway? The vermilion silk shirt-dress she was wearing, unbuttoned way too low and coupled with her thunderous expression and a leather-and-gold pendant the size of a sputnik, made her look terrifying. She scowled at Martika Jansen in her black leather jacket and subtly see-through sprigged dress and felt suddenly and irrevocably middle-aged.

'Hello, Phyllida. What brings you here? I thought party politicals and boot camps were more your thing.' Lindsey Craven's smoky Bristolian twang emerged, as if from the depths of a gravel pit, from somewhere beneath her large, freckly breasts, which had been vacuum-packed into a low-cut lime-green t-shirt with 'Babe Power' emblazoned on it. Phyllida's heart sank further. Lindsey tried to maintain a similar relationship with Phyllida to the one Phyllida had been attempting to establish with Buster Lloyd.

'Looks like *le tout* London is here,' rasped Lindsey with what she hoped was appropriately *Gazettish* world-weariness. A leg of spatchcock chicken dangled between her thumb and forefinger, brushing precariously close to the satin revers on Phyllida's iridescent dress. The cigarette in her other hand was dangerously close to setting light to her nicotine-stained hair. 'Apparently Melvyn Bragg's thinking of doing a *South Bank* on "The British Chef," focusing on Seth Weiss. Mad, isn't it? Still, he is pretty photogenic. Food's not bad, either.' Slightly the worse for wear, she was swaying gently and nursing a goblet of vodka on to which was tattooed a cyclamen-coloured silhouette of her lips. Buster Lloyd, deep in conversation with Martika Jansen and stationed tantalisingly close to Phyllida, drifted away.

Phyllida felt trapped, and her mood took a malevolent turn. 'Who's that?' she snapped, determined to make some use of Lindsey's shallow but wide-ranging general knowledge.

Lindsey gazed over at a radiantly good-looking couple sweeping through the double-height glass doors that led from the bar into the restaurant.

'Oh, that's Tulah Delaney and Todd Woodward. *People* magazine voted them Last Year's Sexiest Couple in the World, shortly to be superseded no doubt by Ben Mornay and Jo-Jo. They're really the hottest thing right now. It's amazing how Jo-Jo's blossomed in the past few months. They say it's being constantly told you're beautiful that does it. Apparently it makes a girl more confident and that releases endorphins or something. I thought she was pretty good to start with, but now . . .'

Realising that she'd barely scuffed the surface of Lindsey's vast repository of trivia, Phyllida gave her mind permission to vacate her body and for the next ten minutes tuned in only intermittently to Lindsey's flow. Buster Lloyd was now on the other side of the room. Lindsey wittered on. It was almost fascinating how long fashion people could discuss a single inane subject. Now she came to think of it, Phyllida remembered timing Sissy and some girl dressed in a tea cosy in the *Gazette*'s canteen while they discussed the merits of the interlocking Gs on a new Gucci belt. After twenty-seven minutes Phyllida had had to go back to her desk but Sissy, Alice and the Gs were still going strong.

'Apparently Sukie Summer's doing a killer feature on Ben and Jo-Jo for *Vanity Fair*. He's given her a bracelet with diamonds on the inside. Very romantic, don't you think?' Phyllida looked appalled at the senseless waste of this gesture. Lindsey blathered on. 'The rushes on *Sons and Lovers* are fabulous, apparently – Oscar-winning stuff – and Sukie even got some quotes from Ben's agent . . . Nothing from Jo-Jo, though. That stuck-up bitch Cassie said she's not doing any interviews. Still, her comeuppance can't be far off.'

Phyllida suddenly perked up. She was livid. She had once fired Sukie Summers, ostensibly for fiddling her expenses on a press trip to Singapore, which, it transpired, Sukie had never gone on (instead she had filed her copy after accessing the Reuters reports on the computer in her flat in South Kensington where she was holed up with some MP). In fact the whole affair had been a pretext – everyone fiddled their expenses at the *Gazette*, some so expertly that they were thinking of publishing an anonymous book on the art. Phyllida had been dying to get rid of Sukie, who though useless had extraordinary legs which had earned her the undying admiration of Edward Rushmore. If that imbecile could slap together a profile of Ben and Jo-Jo for *Vanity Fair*, surely her bloody fashion editor, who lived with the girl, could do the same for the *Gazette*? She would bloody well make her do an exposé on Cassie.

'Where's Janie?' she snarled at Nick Squire.

'Couldn't tell you darlin',' he minced. 'We parted company months ago. More trouble than she's worth,' he mouthed, making a beeline for Patsy Kensit.

'Look this way, girls.' Richard Young, the high priest of paparazzi beckoned to Jess and Grace, who had arrived together. Grace, in a short sky-blue chiffon-and-lace Empire-line John Galliano dress and pointy kitten-heeled rose-embroidered Manolos, looked radiant and relaxed after a triumphant summer off which had culminated in an audience with the Dalai Lama. Her hair had been left in its natural, crinkly state, cupping her shoulder blades. The tendrils round her temples had been bleached by her summer at Berkeley. Jess, gleaming hair waved over one eye like Veronica Lake, lips painted a deep, glossy claret and wearing a canary-yellow Chloe slip and contrasting ivory La Perla underwear, looked as unbelievably voluptuous as a food stylist's meringue.

'So what've you been up to, Grace? You look terrific,' purred Richard Young appreciatively.

Grace was about to tell him about her half-finished book, the rights to which had been snapped up by Vickers and Snood for £250,000, when Jess mischievously linked her arm through Grace's and nibbled on her left ear. The winking cameras – Young had been joined by a dozen other photographers – exploded in a blizzard of popping flashes.

'Say no more, girls,' said Nick Squire, winking conspiratorially, as Grace and Jess waltzed majestically past him and into the crowd.

Seth was back in the kitchen garnishing a plate of lobster salsa. He knew he should be out at the front of house being gregarious, if only to please Vanessa, but he was fast coming to the conclusion that he just wasn't that kind of chef. It was all right for Sebbie – acting mine host was the only way of life he knew. Sebbie had given up cooking years ago, even though he was one of the most gifted chefs of his generation. But Sebbie had burnt out – thanks to a particularly violent attack of kitchen fright which struck whenever the restaurant was more than a quarter full. Seth suspected drink had had something to do with it. But now, tonight, with what felt like a helicopter whirring away in his stomach, he was beginning to understand what Sebbie had meant about having panic attacks. How had it all got so out of hand? This was turning out to be the biggest restaurant opening of the year – and it was his. It was all too absurd not to be a bad joke. He had only ever wanted a simple little place – but one thing had led to another and now he was the proprietor of the sort of restaurant he wouldn't have dared set foot in ten years earlier – wouldn't have wanted to, either. This thought might have prompted a moment's self-congratulation in some people, but it caused Seth only distaste. He couldn't help hearing his dead brother's wry overview. Never mind Finn's, he thought despairingly, they should have called the place Hubris.

'Where are you going?' asked Sissy nervously as Nari spun left off the Finchley Road. The evening was shaping up for catastrophe. Late for the opening of the season, and out with a mad rapist.

'Well, it's obvious we don't have time to go home and change, and that it's all my fault for keeping you out so long – and at a bunch of dull factories, to boot – so the least I can do is buy you a new outfit,' said Nari smoothly, pulling up outside Joseph on St John's Wood High Street.

Normally Sissy would have made a small stab at demurring. She'd had plenty of practice with all the designers who felt obliged to lend her clothes. But time was paramount. She flew out of the car and through the shop door just as one of the assistants was about to lock it.

Fifteen minutes later, having modelled half a dozen outfits or so on the pavement for Nari's approval (pleading an allergy to shopping, he had refused to get out of the car), she emerged triumphantly in an XTC buttermilk strapless suede tube dress that set off her marmalade hair, matching coat and XTC dark brown knee boots. At that moment, Sissy wanted the outfit more than she had wanted anything else in the world. Her heart began to pound with a familiar urgency, so violently she feared it might rupture her ribcage and ruin the dress. The outfit came to £2,300. Nari signed for it in the car. Somewhere in her euphoria she was dimly aware of having abused his generosity, but she couldn't help herself. She looked amazing. As Nari nudged the Aston Martin into the traffic, she sank back into the faintly musky-smelling upholstery and luxuriated in the sensation of having money. It was the first time she had ever bought anything at full price.

It was twenty to nine. Ben dragged himself towards the shower. He had been lying on the bed for ages, stroking Jo-Jo's back and staring out of the windows across Janie's emerald lawn. He had grown to love the way the grey English light thickened at dusk into denser grey light. It was all so gentle.

'C'm'on, hon, we gotta go,' he called softly to Jo-Jo, pausing at the door to give her one last lingering look.

Jo-Jo stretched out a long silky leg and looked at her toenails, still sparkling with the gold leaf that Dodie had used for the *Harper's Bazaar* shoot. Ben groaned softly. Of all her many physical attributes, it was Jo-Jo's toes that drove him wild. Maybe he should see someone about it, he thought gleefully. In the meantime, as a surprise he had commissioned Solange Azagury to make her ten diamond toe rings. He popped the first one in his mouth. 'Come and get it,' he mumbled to her, and she sprinted off the bed after him, laughing that deep, unrestrained laugh of hers.

It was even later when he finally made it, reluctantly, into the shower, reflecting, as he switched it on full, on Jo-Jo's heady success with both the public and normally heavyweight commentators. Endearingly, for the most part, the adulation seemed to be wafting over her beautiful head. Last week an art critic who'd seen her in a SoHo gallery had written in the *New York Times* that she possessed a tentative, fawn-like grace, going on to remark that: '. . . with her eclectic, spontaneous way of dressing, this gloriously fragile yet tough young woman is the epitome of cool: a new role model to a whole new generation.'

Still sprawled on the bed, Jo-Jo caught her reflection in the mirror on the chest of drawers and giggled shyly. She was learning to perform like a diva for the camera, but she still felt uncomfortable being scrutinised in person. The funny thing was that before she started modelling no one had ever seemed to take much notice of the way she looked. Certainly whether or not she was beautiful hadn't been an issue. She hadn't even given it much thought herself, beyond feeling gratified that she never had to diet like some of her friends. And now, because she was being held up as a beauty, suddenly everyone just seemed to accept that was what she was. It was as if there were certain ways of seeing people – as a beauty, as fat – and once you were perceived that way, that was that. People stopped really looking at you after a while – they just accepted your reputation. And that reputation got you everywhere. So in a way, beauty was one of the most powerful currencies in the world. She trotted off to join Ben in the shower.

'I'm getting quite deep in my old age,' she said, sliding her arms around him. 'Must be what *Vogue* called your "profoundly philosophical approach to every role you take on". It's turning me into quite an intellectual.'

★   ★   ★

Aeron and Angel had come to the party together and got caught
in the crush surrounding Jess and Grace. Ever since Grace had
stood him up at the New York awards Aeron bridled whenever
she was mentioned, particularly now that the press had got wind
of a rift between them and kept asking him whether he had
another muse. Grace hadn't even been his bloody muse. He
didn't need a muse. He was his muse. But even Squidge had
reproached him the other day over the way he had handled the
whole affair.

'You shouldn't have been so mean to Grace. Especially
not now she's writing that kiss "n" tell book,' Squidge had
ventured.

This was news to Aeron. He knew that he wouldn't emerge
from it honourably. He'd have to get back in with Grace. But
it wouldn't be easy.

'What goes around comes around, Aeron,' Squidge said
prophetically.

Fair enough, thought Aeron, who considered himself to be
as spiritual as the next designer. When he saw her tonight he'd
mention the possibility of her being in his next show. She was
bound to be gagging for it.

'Hi, Grace. You look genius.' He practically genuflected
before her. His expressions had the kind of mobility that made
his features look as though they were chasing one another
around his face and were in danger of a major pile-up.

'Oh, Aeron, I thought you were the scrubber,' she said,
barely slowing down on her way to Melvyn Bragg, who greeted
her as if she were the reincarnation of Michelangelo. Aeron felt
crushed. He knew his Fuck The Establishment t-shirt and ripped
jeans looked very tired – especially as he didn't feel up to fucking
the Establishment these days. He'd rather make their ballgowns
and cash their cheques.

Seth had finally taken off his apron and ventured into
the fray. He couldn't believe the scene beyond the kitchen.
Everyone Vanessa and Cassie had hoped would be there was,
all of them beaming, animated, apparently having a good
time – and he couldn't see anyone he knew well enough

to talk to. Ten minutes later, Melissa found him clearing some glasses.

'Leave that to your highly efficient staff, darling, and come and meet Johnny Mortimer. You'll love him.'

Seth looked at her morosely.

'A hit, a palpable hit. Seth, darling, you've done it. Now if you don't want to say hello to John, at least introduce me to Janie.'

'I don't know where she is.' He scowled and disappeared back into the kitchen.

Janie had been cornered by Lindsey Craven, whose sudden oily bonhomie was about as convincing as Isabella Suarez's new collagen-enhanced lips.

'You look nice,' smarmed Lindsey, fingering Janie's dress, 'and so does Cassie, *all things considered*.'

'What do you mean?' Janie enquired icily.

'Oh, come on,' snapped Lindsey, 'everyone knows she's as bent as a mini-crini. And the authorities are finally on to her. Still, it's nothing we haven't all known for years. How else did she manage to feed her own heroin habit?'

Janie looked at Lindsey as if the latter were stark raving mad.

'Oh, and by the way,' said Lindsey, becoming shrilly defiant, 'thought you'd like to know – your boss wants you to write the story.' Janie felt sick, faint – and useless. She was utterly incapable of helping Cassie, and worse still, didn't know anyone else to ask. Even Seth had gone underground. She drooped against a wall.

'Genius dress, Janie.' Sissy clattered over and waited for Janie to compliment her. Now that she had got over the exhilaration of everyone – even Angel, who always got petulant when Sissy wasn't wearing shoes that he'd designed – telling her how gorgeous she looked, she was starting to feel vaguely uncomfortable about the way she'd acquired her new stash of clothes. Nari was perfectly polite to her, but she sensed that he'd rather be talking to someone else. She led him over to Janie, who looked rather embarrassed to be caught pressing a handful of ice cubes down the front of her dress, and having formally introduced them, went in chase of Anastasia Monticatini, who had just waltzed in wearing a ravishing pale pink silk embroidered Dior cheongsam that showed off her spectacular figure to perfection. Janie turned away quickly. Phyllida had taken a violent stand against socialites and Janie still hadn't been able to run the piece on Anastasia.

'Would you like to take a walk outside?' asked Nari solicitously, offering Janie his arm. 'The courtyard looks so beautiful.' Sissy had told him of Janie's connection with Finn's.

Wobbling slightly, Janie leant against him, nearly tripping over her sandals.

'Whoops–a–daisy,' she giggled. 'I suppose that's what they mean by head over heels in love.'

Nari fetched some water.

'Sissy tells me you're the best boss she's had.'

Janie was touched. She gulped the glass of water and felt herself begin to sober up.

'That's kind of her. I don't know what I'm doing half the time, but it pays the mortgage – I think,' she went on.

'I know what you mean,' said Nari wryly. 'It's given me a very nice life, and provided a living for the people who work for me.'

By the time Ben and Jo-Jo arrived – she in an adorable 1930s chiffon tea-dress which she had bought in a thrift shop on Melrose Avenue in LA – Nari and Janie were deep in conversation and neither couple noticed the other. Janie made him roar with laughter about the fashion shows, which he had always wanted to see, and now he was telling her all about his side of things. Janie was fascinated by the mechanics of selling vast amounts of clothes to millions of customers – how did Nari know what they wanted? – and charmed by his business acumen which was at once clear-sighted and humane. He knew an enormous amount about all aspects of the business, from the cost of retail space in Leeds to Paolo Bianco's latest muse.

She found herself leading the conversation slyly on to Cassie, although she didn't mention any names. They were so engrossed that Janie didn't notice Anastasia gliding towards her.

'Janie, how nice to see you, and you, Mr, er—'

'Sujan,' said Janie, introducing them.

'What a wonderful place,' cooed Anastasia. 'I do so love the mix you find at London parties,' she added pointedly, as Cassie billowed past. 'It was so stuffy in Florence. The merest whiff of scandal and people were forced into purdah. Jo-Jo's here too, I see.'

Nari swivelled round to look.

'There she is,' said Anastasia obligingly, pointing across the room. 'Heavenly-looking, isn't she? Though anything but an angel. I know I shouldn't gossip, but dear Patrick Lichfield was taking my portrait for *Country Life* last week, and his assistants were buzzing with it, so it must be common knowledge. Apparently Jo-Jo was quite a naughty girl in the past. Not that you can blame her. A girl has to supplement her studies somehow.'

Cassie's skin tingled as if it had been poked with a cattle prod. She recognised the sensation. She'd felt the same way when she came bottom in physics in the third year – the only subject she'd ever failed in. No one had said anything unpleasant to her face at Seth's, but she could see the distaste in their eyes. One whiff of failure and a model agency – so dependent on image – was on the road to ruination. And she reeked of impending doom. She wondered whether she should try to sell the business to Saffron tomorrow, get out while they all had a chance of retrieving something. If she went quickly Saffron might even manage to push through the deal with Diego.

'It's funny, really,' Sissy was explaining to Anastasia, several tequila slammers down the line, 'how incredibly broke my entire family are, having been once so fantastically grand.' She didn't know why she was telling Anastasia all this. But Nari had cleared off, and Anastasia seemed so interested and sympathetic. And she was beautifully dressed. Sissy couldn't understand why Janie was so wary of her.

'So,' began Anastasia casually, 'did you say that your family had a title?'

'Oh, loads of them,' said Sissy airily. She was far more interested in studying Anastasia's breasts, which seemed desperate to launch themselves from her chest like an over-energetic pair of heat-seeking missiles. 'Contessa this, Marquesa that. Dad was a Duca of something or other. But they're Italian titles, so basically utterly useless. My real name's Francesca. It seemed a bit pointless calling myself Contessa Francesca di Pomerosa-Santorini at Seldon Grammar. And by the time I got to Cambridge I figured that the only thing a mouthful like that would get me was ten minutes behind everyone else at exam time. Honestly, for a couple of hundred I'd sell the lot.'

Anastasia stared at her so intently that Sissy almost blushed.

'Well, perhaps a hundred and fifty . . .'

'Hi, Cassie,' said Zack, his voice warm with sympathy.

'Hi, Zack,' said Cassie bashfully, remembering how vile she'd been.

'I owe you an apology—' they both began, and laughed.

'My career's up the spout,' said Cassie.

'So's mine,' said Zack. 'I didn't tell you this but I was supposed to give a tarot reading this week to a new and potentially very important client – and I forgot.'

Cassie winced sympathetically. 'I was supposed to be running a responsible model agency. Only I forgot that too.' She reached for another two glasses of champagne.

'I know what you mean,' said Zack, sounding uncharacteristically serious. He took her elbow and edged her out towards the terrace.

'Look,' he said, pulling a crumpled fax out of his pocket. 'I found this in your office just now.' He'd been up there to check out his new tangerine velvet jacket in her full-length mirror.

It was admirably brief, she had to concede that much.

You owe us. She read the words again and allowed Zack to lead her into a cab back to The Hempel.

★   ★   ★

It was almost midnight when Janie looked at her watch. As she sobered up, she began to feel nauseous, wondering if she'd been incredibly stupid to tear up the fax. She said goodbye to Nari and went in search of Seth. She longed to be on her own with him. The crowd had begun to thin – a little. In their place, a hard core of revellers had settled down for the night. Deirdre had slipped out of Le Château a little before closing time and arrived at Finn's with her fiddle. Seth, cares apparently tossed to the winds, was dancing a jig with a mesmerising dark-haired woman in claret-coloured velvet and flashing bracelets. He never looked that carefree with her, she thought despairingly. Well, God knew, she was hardly a catch. In fact most men with half Seth's appeal would run a marathon to get away from a jilted wife with three children. It was some minutes before he noticed her and, when he did, she pointed theatrically to her watch, blew him a kiss and made a beeline for the door.

On her way she was accosted by a tall brunette with eyelashes that were so long they threatened to get tangled up in her fringe and a husky voice that men presumably found sexy, but which Janie, in her current mood, thought very common.

'Oh, hi, Janie, it's Sukie Summers. You don't know me, but I'm writing a huge feature on Jo-Jo and Ben Mornay for *Vanity Fair*. I gather you've known Jo-Jo since she was a kid.' Her voice became even huskier and stared soulfully into Janie's eyes. 'Tell me, journalist to journalist, is it true she's thinking of leaving Hot Shots, along with half a dozen or so of the other star girls there? I think your writing's terrific, by the way.'

Janie gave her a withering look. 'Is it the lilies giving you asthma?' she asked icily before marching off.

'Well,' husked Sukie, staring after Janie's back. 'La-di-fucking-da.'

'What I don't understand,' said Zack, puzzled, 'is what happened to the first fax. The machine recorded two since seven p.m.'

They were back at The Hempel, finishing an almost-defrosted bottle of champagne. Cassie had confided in Zack about her emergency summit with Reece and that it had been changed at the last minute from the office to Scotland Yard.

'What I don't understand,' she said, her voice sounding painfully small in the empty space of the bar, 'is what exactly it means.'

'It means, my darling,' began Zack carefully, remembering Cassie's plain English campaign, 'that someone wants to get you into trouble. Somehow, someone knew that you were meeting Reece at the office tonight. Otherwise why bother to send a fax into your private office where only you would see it?'

'But how?' asked Cassie helplessly. 'And more to the point, who?'

'I don't know,' said Zack. 'But whoever it is is clearly trying to scare the hell out of you and—' He stopped. By the look of her, they'd succeeded.

Chapter Eleven

'Are you getting divorced?'

Janie looked at her eldest daughter with a guilty start. She had been thinking about Cassie's fax, which she had tried to retrieve from the wastepaper basket the day after Seth's party. But Millicent, the office cleaner, had got there first.

'Oh, I shouldn't think so, darling,' she replied, more breezily than she felt. 'Whatever makes you ask?'

'Henry and Sophie's dad has gone to live with his accountant, so they're moving to a smaller place and Sophie and Henry are getting bunk beds.'

Nell's voice grew tentative.

'Could I have some bunk beds too – even if you don't divorce?'

Not for the first time Janie marvelled at her eldest daughter's ability to digest seemingly complex situations and extrapolate from them the really important issues. Divorce – did things between her and Matthew really look so terrible?

'Possibly, darling. Oh, look, there's a Barbie with hair down to her feet.'

They were on their way back from a Saturday matinée at the Tricycle and were sauntering down Kilburn High Road, a thoroughfare that never failed to delight Nell with its imaginative display of low life. Janie and Nell's weekly mid-morning rendezvous had become a regular fixture. It had been Gloria's idea. She had got back to Michaelmas Road one Sunday night after a weekend in Suffolk to find Janie frazzled and close to tears because Nell had refused to talk to her all day. Trying to coax her out of it, Janie finally hit on the idea of baking a chocolate cake, Nell's favourite. But they'd squabbled when Janie had tried to stop Nell sticking her fingers in the Magimix. A clump of Janie's hair had ended up getting caught – and removed by – the blades, and Nell spent the rest of the afternoon noisily counting the minutes until Gloria got back.

The three or four hours Nell and Janie spent on their own every Saturday worked wonders. Gloria took the twins – and somehow got them to nap and eat their lunch by 1.30, which meant Janie and Nell had time to nip into Pizza Express as well. On the rare occasions when Gloria went away, she had arranged for her friend Ivy to stand in. It occasionally occurred to Janie that Jake was surrounded by far too many women, but since the men in his life (and here she unfairly lumped in Seth, who had only ever seen Jake twice, both of which times he had been asleep) had proved to be useless role models, maybe this wasn't such a disadvantage.

A weather-beaten drunk with a complexion like bolognese sauce was threatening to do a moony at them, so Janie diverted Nell into Woolworths.

As Nell gazed rapturously at the line-up of Barbies, Janie's attention flicked back to Seth for the thousandth time since she had last seen him. She couldn't believe that after weeks of fobbing her off with sob stories about work and stress, she should find him practically cheek to cheek with another woman. Given her own unresolved relationship with Matthew, she had tried all summer not to feel territorial about Seth, but it was difficult when she felt so recklessly attracted to him. It was as if they were soul mates – or had been. She blinked back angry tears and steered Nell to the till. Thirty-six hours and not a peep. It was disgraceful that men felt they could still give women the runaround in this day and age. It wasn't as if she and Seth were teenagers, after all.

'Better off without 'im, believe me,' Gloria announced breezily on seeing Janie's expression when she and Nell got back. Since the party at Finn's, Janie had taken to confiding in Gloria, even though her prejudices about men made for some uncomfortable counsel. It just didn't seem fair to bother Cassie with her problems right now.

Janie helped Nell devise seven different hairstyles for her new Barbie. It really was better this way – no emotion-sapping diversion to distract her from the children. God knew she saw little enough of them now that she was working full time. In future there would be no room for extra-curricular activities in Janie's life. She would devote herself exclusively to the welfare of her children and to keeping her job, which now that Phyllida was fuming about Sukie Summers's forthcoming scoop on Jo-Jo was going to be no mean feat. Henceforth, whenever Seth's dark, sensitive features metamorphosed in front of her, she would banish them back into the ether.

The house seemed very quiet now that Ben and Jo-Jo had migrated back to their respective locations. So by four o'clock the remaining residents of Michaelmas Road decamped to the park's sandpit. Gloria got out her knitting. Janie, congratulating herself on her resolve, began to wade through the weekend newspapers. Trying to avoid all reminders of Finn's, she turned to Aurora Snow's horoscope and was devastated to discover that she had passed to the other side. It seemed a poignant footnote to Janie's own life somehow. A certain person's tender gaze and throbbing vein seemed to assail her from all the other pages. Why was it, she wondered, that in tabloid-speak parties were always glittering? She switched to the serious papers. The reviews of Finn's were unanimously ecstatic. In *The Times*, Jonathan Meades declared it the jewel in London's culinary crown and predicted that this time next year Seth would have three Michelin stars to his name. Even Silas Shoreham managed to get a full-page rave about how restaurants – spearheaded by Finn's – were the new religion. Sukie Summers had been busy; as well as her much-heralded exclusive on Jo-Jo and Ben, she had scribbled a profile on Seth for *The Clarion*, in which she declared that a new English superstar had been born. When had she managed to squeeze an interview with Seth into her hectic schedule? Janie wondered peevishly. Sukie's syntax was abominable. And during the course of 1,800 torrid words, she referred to Seth as Britain's pre-eminent God of Food no fewer than four times. Nor, Janie noted scornfully, could Sukie resist declaring him the Mr Darcy of the kitchen, adding, in the final paragraph, that his sizzling dishes had nothing on his smouldering looks.

Janie fumed. Didn't Sukie check anything? Seth was Irish, for God's sake.

Cassie placed both hands on the cool glass of her Philippe Starck desk. Coming into her office when no one else was there used to give her such a thrill. She had spent more weekends than she cared to remember luxuriating in that small confirmation of her power, revelling in the stillness – and the chance it gave her to reflect on the week's achievements in calm solitude.

It had taken her fifteen years to build up Hot Shots. Fifteen years and God knew how many sacrifices. Of course, it had been fun, stimulating, exhilarating – but it had also been all-consuming, draining and a convenient diversion from the lame way in which she had chosen to conduct her personal affairs. She had broken up with Jim Zametti, whom she supposedly loved, because he'd cheated on her with a succession of models; but in her more morose moments Cassie sometimes doubted whether the personal hurt she'd sustained had been as painful as her fear that Jim's behaviour would jeopardise her own professional reputation. Janie might have committed to the wrong man with Matthew, thought Cassie grimly, but at least she had committed – and had three wonderful children to show for it. Whereas she had nothing. Still, all that might be about to change. If she sold out to Saffron, she too could devote all her time to her non-existent family. Fifteen years to build and a matter of weeks to unravel. And there didn't appear to be a thing she could do about it.

It was the unfamiliar feeling of impotence which most troubled Cassie. Melodramatic as it seemed, Zack's conspiracy theory had an authentic ring about it. Ever since Diego had made his initial overtures to her eighteen months earlier, there had been acrimonious rumblings from other agents who felt threatened by the alliance. One or two had taken the opportunity to try to poach her most successful models. Marie-Elise Montperluche, a pushy French agent, had even sent a letter to every model on Cassie's and Diego's books, offering them contracts with her agency, promising them *personal*, friendly service – as if Cassie gave them hostile, impersonal service. Fortunately, none of her models had taken the offer up. One or two had tried to use it as leverage to cut Cassie's percentage of their earnings, but when Cassie pointed out that if everyone joined Marie-Elise's agency it would no longer be quite so small and intimate, they had backed down. There had also been a few snide quotes in the press from the odd less-than-sparkling designer, chafing against the power wielded by certain 'megalomaniac' model agents. But all this Cassie regarded as par for the course.

The putative merger between Hot Shots and Allure had put a lot of noses out of joint. The deal would have placed her and Diego firmly at the helm of the largest, most prestigious and powerful modelling agency in the world, and would, if all went well, have multiplied their worth twentyfold. She and Diego had also privately mulled over the possibility of offering a handful of their most successful clients share options to ensure loyalty. Inevitably this idea had leaked out – nothing in the fashion world ever remained secret for more than half an hour – and caused a minor furore both inside and outside their respective agencies, with everyone speculating wildly about who the chosen few might be, and rival agents fretting that they might have to follow suit.

Despite all this, Cassie couldn't seriously conceive of any of her professional rivals resorting to blackmail or any other kind of time-wasting chicanery. On the other hand you never knew. The fax the other night was clearly meant to intimidate her. Zack was right; the best thing was to destroy it and hope that whoever had sent it got tired of tormenting her before Reece got wind of it. It might make things tense for a while:

he and his doppelgänger had been back sniffing around the office yesterday, but as Saffron had pointed out, they couldn't possibly be unearthing anything genuinely incriminating.

'We would have known if there was anything concrete linking any of the girls with the drug-smuggling at Bellissimo,' she said reasonably. 'Everyone knows Hot Shots is one of the cleanest agencies in the business.' But Cassie wasn't convinced. Since she hadn't even realised one of her star models was a junkie, how could she possibly trust her instincts anymore?

When had things first begun to go awry? She racked her memory. When Peace crashed outside Jute's, obviously. Except that publicity-wise, that hadn't turned out to be the disaster she had feared. No, Scotland Yard hadn't started paying calls until a few weeks before the opening of Finn's – the discreetest, most polite of enquiries to begin with; just sounding her out in the spirit of European co-operation, along with all the other agencies, Reece had said, almost lethargically – to find out what she knew about Bellissimo. *You owe us.* The words from the fax came back to her again. For the umpteenth time she wondered who could have sent it. A morally indignant bystander or someone more proactive? The terse hamminess of it suggested someone with no sense of irony, or a poor grasp of English. In her current mood, Cassie felt that ruled out only herself and Janie. Who disliked her? A roomful of ex-boyfriends, rejected would-be models and clients who had paid what they perhaps considered over-generous fees swarmed in front of her eyes. Not good enough. She edited. Who hated her? She drew up a list of suspects.

1. Bellissimo – in serious trouble. Several bosses, including Jim and Sergio Zametti, about to be indicted for fraud and drug-laundering. Motive: smokescreen and revenge on her for doing so well. Suspect rating: low. Jim, whatever his other faults, wasn't malicious and was probably otherwise occupied. Was hardly likely to have access to fax machines in police custody.

2. Isabella Suarez – scalding grudge ever since Hot Shots very publicly ceased to represent her after she stole four Vuitton cases from A La Mode *shoot. Motive: restoration of tattered reputation. Suspect rating: low owing to incipient insanity.*

3. Marie-Elise Montperluche. Motive: jealousy. Suspect rating: mid-range; would be higher but too busy writing letters to all Cassie's models.

4. Every other agency in the world. Motive: see above. Suspect rating: high, if they all ganged up together . . .

This was hopeless. Cassie tossed the list in her bin. On the other hand, perhaps it would work as some kind of therapy. At any rate, it was helping her get things straight in her own mind. She retrieved the list and continued.

5. My mother. Motive: utter despondency that her elder daughter didn't turn out to be the failure she predicted. Suspect rating: fair to good.

She could hear her old German poetry tutor chiding her for being flippant. But, thought Cassie, many a true word spoken in facetiousness. And one way or another, thoughts of her mother always galvanised her. *You owe us,* repeated Cassie. We'll see about that.

Gloria had gone to one of her Saturday night whist drives with her friend Ivy. Janie, reluctantly emerging from a steaming, rose-scented bath, answered the door in her bathrobe and a pair of Gloria's hand-knitted slippers – part of her new stay-at-home, go-to-bed-early-with-the-children regime – to find an enormous bunch of lavender, thyme and peonies.

'Just to show you that something from Finn's is thriving, even if I'm not.' Seth's voice floated out from somewhere behind a clump of mauve flowers. 'It occurred to me,' he continued, following her into the hall, 'that it's possible that when you shot me that parting glower the other night, you might have got the wrong end of the stick?'

'Which was?' She had taken the bouquet from him and was rummaging in one of the kitchen cupboards for a vase.

'Janie, is there anything – anything at all – between us?'

She continued rummaging.

'I need to know.' He prised her gently away from a pair of pliers. 'Look, I know things have been very difficult for you since Matthew left and that part of you still waits for him to ring every day . . .'

Janie was about to refute this, but Seth was on a roll.

'I can see that you're still in love with him – that's why I've tried to do the right thing and leave you alone. I even thought I might really be able to survive by having you as a friend. All summer when I wanted to . . . well, anyway, I came tonight to tell you that if things don't work out with Matthew, I'll be here for you, even if it means not seeing you while you both work things out. The thing is, Janie, as far as I'm concerned, there's something very important between us. I don't think I realised quite how important until this morning when Vanessa rang me to tell me about the reviews, and I realised that if I couldn't see you they didn't actually mean very much.'

He snatched a lock of dark hair out of his eyes, clearly agitated by his display of emotion. Janie was touched to her core by his honesty, although she couldn't help wishing, right at that moment, that he didn't respect her quite so much. She hadn't felt like this since . . . well, since those early nights with Matthew. She heard herself sounding exceptionally restrained.

'I think there's something important between us too,' she said softly, 'though God knows, all those steamy nights during the summer when you barely came near me, I began to think it was all one-sided.' She took both his hands and stood gazing directly at him. Her skin was still glistening from the heat of the bath and there were beads of perspiration on her forehead. Her wet hair coiled round her long neck and disappeared into the V of her robe. Seth could just see the tip of it curling round her nipple.

'Look, I can't pretend that Matthew isn't a complication but
. . . perhaps not quite in the way you think.' She hesitated,
not wanting to be disloyal to her husband. 'There are things
Matthew and I have needed to sort out for ages – since for ever.
They're so fundamental they're not even an issue between you
and me. You're not a part of whatever's gone wrong between
us, you're something separate. The problem is, he's not here to
work out those problems with me, so I've had to make a start
by myself, only I'm tired of wasting energy on someone who's
not around. I don't want to keep my life on hold indefinitely so
I . . . What I'm trying to say is that if you feel like being around
– and God knows I'll understand if you don't – then, well, I can't
think of anything I'd want more.'

Seth pulled her towards him and held her so tightly she
thought they would both implode. 'She was my mother, you
know – the dark woman I was dancing with.'

'Oh, darling, you didn't think I was so petty as to be worried
about that,' laughed Janie unconvincingly. She kissed Seth until
they both had to surface for air. Then he made the only thing a
man who finds himself alone with his beloved and three small
sleeping children can make. Spanish omelette.

Sissy was in a delirious daze. Even her failure to get a taxi
and the Monday morning odour on the Tube – weekend
hangovers and people who'd got dressed in too much of a
hurry to shower – couldn't puncture her happiness. She had
had the most incredible, extraordinary weekend. It had begun
on Saturday morning when she had received a hand-delivered
note from Anastasia suggesting they meet for tea at the Ritz
on Sunday to continue their conversation pertaining to a *certain
matter*. Sissy couldn't think for the life of her what the matter
might be but curiosity, as ever, had her firmly in its grip.

Delicately sipping lapsang to the strains of a stringed quartet,
Anastasia hadn't messed about. 'You said a couple of hundred for
the titles, so I did a little research and I have to say I think you
were a little on the high side.'

Titles? It was a few moments before Sissy realised she was talking about her noble lineage – the throwaway conversation she had had with Anastasia at the opening of Finn's was starting to come back. Crikey. Anastasia had obviously taken Sissy seriously and was actually trying to buy them. Sissy knew that title-broking was big business these days. The *Gazette* had run a feature on it recently – and Sissy sodding well wasn't going to let Anastasia have them for less than two hundred pounds.

'Or perhaps you meant US dollars,' Anastasia continued silkily. 'After all, that does seem to be the international currency for these things. How does a hundred and fifty thousand pounds sound for the contessa bit, two hundred thousand if you throw in the lot?'

Sissy nearly choked.

In the end, she had decided, for the sake of her mother, not to divest herself of all the titles and merely parted with the contessa bit, which Anastasia seemed touchingly eager for and which Sissy never used. With any luck her mother need never know.

'I'll get my lawyers to sort out the details,' said Anastasia, looking supremely satisfied. She had overpaid, she knew, but this was a title with real class. Better still, it hadn't been used for decades.

Good job it's Sunday, thought Sissy, floating up Bond Street, or I'd blow the lot in DKNY. She considered this last *pensée* dubiously. Surely, now that she was practically a millionaire – or at least solvent – she wasn't going to turn into Scrooge?

Still euphoric, she marched out of the *Gazette*'s lift at 9.17 the next morning feeling that neither Monday, Phyllida nor the noxious smell of thrice-fried chips that was wafting out of the *Gazette*'s new cook's supposedly hermetically sealed canteen on the ninth floor could wither her or stale her infinite variety.

'My, my, who had uproarious weekends, then?' enquired Gina Martin. 'You can feel the endorphins positively somersaulting in the fashion department this morning.' She eyed Janie's beatific smile suspiciously.

'Sissy, I was wondering when we could have the Nari Sujan

profile, only the bird's-eye view of Selfridges has toppled off its perch again and your piece would fit in Friday's page perfectly.'

Nari. Sissy felt herself blushing. The further she got from Thursday night's shopping spree in Joseph, the worse it looked. She had hoped somehow to avoid seeing him for a few weeks, until either he or she had forgotten about it. Now she was going to have to call him today to tie up the loose ends for the piece. Or write it without tying up the loose ends. Either way, after Friday she would have no reason ever to see him again.

'Actually, Gina, I wanted to talk to you about that. It's going very well. Brilliantly, in fact. There's loads of inside stuff – I went to various factories in Yorkshire and, er, other northern counties. And I'm afraid to say the conditions were pretty astonishing and . . . Well, what do you think about me going to Manila or Hong Kong and really blowing the lid off child labour? Could be explosive.'

'Not a lot,' said Gina breezily. 'We did child labour six months ago. Anyway, I thought Nari Sujan was scrupulous on that score. In fact my friend Tiggs, who was with him at Eton, says he's one of the most principled men he knows. Feels very strongly about not exploiting the Third World. A sort of Anita Roddick for the rag trade. I must say, I rather expected that to be your angle.'

'Eton?' repeated Sissy guardedly, images of Nari's impoverished past and hovel-bound parents disintegrating before her eyes.

'Head boy or whatever they call it there. Still, you know all that. Funny that he refuses ever to go to India. Why do you think he's so set against the culture? Is it really true that he refused to learn a single word of the language? Tiggs thinks it was something to do with some terrific rift with his parents when they decided to return to India. He didn't want to leave Britain. According to Tiggs, they weren't too thrilled either when he started that market stall. Did they ever patch things up? I assume you've got quotes from them. Tiggs says they're frightfully pukka and still living the life of Riley in some old maharaja's palace near Bombay. Should be a really good read.'

Sissy felt dizzy. A shimmering mirage of irregular Hindi verbs swam before her eyes, the painstaking results of four weeks of intensive lessons.

'Monday week, you said?'

'Friday. Don't let us down. At the moment we've got eighteen very blank inches.' Gina trotted off.

Janie raised an uncharacteristically manicured eyebrow. Sissy had been experimenting with a number of well-worn displacement activities, including spring-cleaning the fashion cupboard and reorganising the filing system, since Gina had first assigned her to the piece. Janie sympathised. She still hadn't written up the Anastasia article; the two of them would have to knuckle down sooner or later.

'I don't know why you're looking so jaunty,' sniffed Sissy as she flicked desultorily through the scratch 'n' sniff Kristof calendar on her desk. 'Fashion, as you know, is nothing if not cyclical, so if it's September the sixth, then it's time to write our annual, futile letter requesting an interview with Tom Fitzgerald.'

'But Tom Fitzgerald never gives interviews,' said Janie.

'Precisely. But it flatters him to be asked, which keeps his PR department happy, which keeps our mob in advertising happy, which keeps us in jobs. Joy all round.'

Janie spent a blissful morning composing a letter to Tom Fitzgerald's people, in between permitting herself the rare luxury of endless daydreams in which she and Seth had the starring roles, which meant composition on the Fitzgerald letter was slow to non-existent. In many ways it was fortuitous that Seth had had to leave early on Saturday night to be at Finn's in time for the main courses, otherwise she might have ravaged him. What was it Jane Austen had written about Emma's visit from her sister? – perfect, in being much too short.

Of course, it was frustrating that there didn't seem to be any way they could consummate their relationship at the moment. But Janie couldn't help admiring their resolve not to do so in her and Matthew's house with the children around. At the same time she hoped they would find a way round the problem – and fast. She tried to remember 'Ecstasy', her favourite John Donne poem. She got as far as

> *Where, like a pillow on a bed,*
> *A pregnant bank swelled up, to rest*
> *The violet's reclining head,*
> *Sat we two, one another's best.*

And hoped that Seth liked the metaphysical poets as much as he liked Wilfred Owen and Siegfried Sassoon, whom she considered to be a touch morbid. At midday, she was interrupted, deliciously, when he called her. His voice, deep and lilting, bounced down the line as if it were coming from the moon.

'I'm on the roof terrace, standing by the acres of lavender you planted,' he echoed. 'Tell me, what do you think about planting some mandragora up here? Don't know what it looks like but I love the name. On second thoughts, that's not why I rang. I miss you. Or did I already tell you that?'

'Mmm, but three hours ago.'

'Can I see you tonight? Same place, same time. Monday's much quieter so I might even be able to stay till nine thirty.'

Perfect. She could probably find a distraction for Gloria that would keep her out of the house until then.

By lunch-time she decided she had squandered enough energy on the Fitzgerald missive, printed it out, along with the John Donne poem, which she wanted to fax to Seth, and popped it into the mail tray on her way to see Phyllida, who had summoned her to a crisis management meeting that she had entitled 'Missed Opportunities'.

The rupture, when it came, was delivered with surprising finesse.

'Cassie? Diego Vincent here.' Normally it was 'Honey, Latin lover on the line'.

'Listen, you and I both realise this drugs case is bullshit, but you know New York lawyers . . . they're not quite as robust about these things as we are. And frankly their jitters have got me going. So listen, baby, let's just cool things on the deal for a little. Try again this time next year. No hard feelings?'

'Here's to next year,' said Cassie. Her voice sounded very small.

Jo-Jo followed the trajectory of the flight from New York back to London on the screen on the seat in front of her. That was a nice touch. But as for the rest – well, Concorde was surprisingly cramped. Still, it felt pretty good gliding through FastTrack on to one. Even better that Dominic Fairfax, grandson of Genevieve Fairfax and CEO of Genevieve Fairfax Inc., had been so keen to meet her in person that he was picking up the bill for her entire trip. Perhaps that was the whole point of prestige products; their intrinsic worth didn't match their actual worth. It was the price tag that made them seem special. She wondered if her £35,000 daily tariff made her seem special to Dominic Fairfax. If so, he'd been fairly grudging in his praise. Throughout their meeting he had continually remarked that he had never seen a model rise so quickly, and more than once asked her, rather indelicately, Jo-Jo thought, about her relationship with Ben.

'We need to satisfy ourselves that you're an established medium,' he told her. 'Genevieve Fairfax is a credible brand of luxury products and, according to our in-depth market research, our customers respond to faces they know and trust. With due respect, yours is a little untested in both those areas as yet.'

Why the fuck are you bothering to see me, then, you stupid git? thought Jo-Jo. She flashed him what Ben called her Oscar-night smile.

'Don't worry,' said Dominic Fairfax's secretary, walking Jo-Jo to the elevators, 'the company's marketing strategy is conservative bordering on comatose. But the PR department love you and that's half the battle. They think you're really hot. Edgy's the word I think they used.'

Edgy. As her plane approached Heathrow, Jo-Jo mulled over the word. It was one she had been hearing a lot of recently. Calvin Klein had also used it when she'd gone to meet him after seeing Dominic. Except he seemed to mean it unambiguously as a compliment. Jo-Jo had the feeling that as far as some fashion and beauty people were concerned, edgy carried with it an undercurrent of undesirable adjectives – troublesome and druggy amongst them.

'Sven tells me he hasn't been this excited about a model since he first laid eyes on Christy and Kate,' Calvin had drawled in the serene oasis of his white office high above the din of Seventh Avenue.

Jo-Jo was astonished that Sven had been so complimentary. Perhaps Calvin was ad-libbing. Either way she was charmed. Especially when he told her she would be perfect to front his new scent campaign.

'Crikey, Janie, you're not going to believe this, but Tom Fitzgerald's said yes.' Sissy dangled a fax in front of Janie's nose. 'What on earth did you do to persuade him – offer your body? No, now I come to think of it, Louisa tried that one two years ago to no avail.'

Janie couldn't think for the life of her what she had put in the letter. All week she had thought only about Seth. In the forty-eight hours since Monday, he had cooked two meals for her (pumpkin risotto and linguine with mussels and white wine) and exchanged dozens of ardent kisses, several of which had tested Janie's willpower to the utmost. They couldn't go on like this. Fortunately Jo-Jo had only touched down at Michaelmas Road for one night before flying out to Peru to shoot with Mario Testino. But she was running out of excuses for keeping Gloria out of the house. And her sense of propriety was only so strong.

She stood up and read the elegant, aubergine-coloured handwriting over Sissy's shoulder.

Dear Janie,
   Was I touched by your letter! I'm thinking intelligent,

sensitive, kind . . . please don't disillusion me by turning out to be like Petronella Fishburn. Ouch. Is that indiscreet? Who cares. I feel we're soul mates already. I too am a great fan of John Donne, though frankly I prefer 'The Good Morrow'. Still, we can discuss that when you come over. I take it you'd like to get some pictures of Firefly, my place on Long Island? It's quite new – no one's covered it anywhere else. It's not as big as the house in Maine, but I'm immensely fond of it and it pretty well sums up this particular time in my life. Of course, you'll have the worldwide exclusive. Well, let's be honest, I may just do one interview in America. Then again, I might not. Hah. Drives my press people crazy. The 11th and 12th look good. Make a week of it, if you want. There's a guest house – and a great library.
    Yours in anticipation,
    Tom Fitzgerald
    PS: I know you won't betray me. Don't disappoint.

A PR from the New York office had typed an addendum.

Because of the dynamic nature of the company and the constant changes being implemented, Tom Fitzgerald would like the piece to be as topical as possible and in agreeing to be interviewed, makes it a condition that it run by 4 October latest.

'But the eleventh's only two days away, and if we run the Fitzgerald piece before the fourth, we won't be able to squeeze the Anastasia in and I can't postpone it much longer,' muttered Janie half-heartedly.
    'You'll have to. This is a S-C-O-O-P, Janie.'
    Janie looked unimpressed. Sissy began flicking through a copy of *Women's Wear Daily* that had just landed on her desk.
    'The crafty old fox!' she exclaimed. 'Never mind John Donne, he's got a new perfume to plug. It says here it's due out some time next spring. Probably because that's when Calvin's is coming out. And Ralph's. I told Angel to do one

and call it Heaven Scent. Get it? But of course he's got no cash. And has he pursued Anastasia? Honestly, you'd think the Brits could produce one decent pong between them. Well, no wonder Tom's agreed to an interview. Still, it should be great copy, provided you don't get bogged down in top notes and floral undertones. You do realise he hasn't spoken to any of the press for nearly a decade. Ever since Petronella Fishburn accused him of ripping off Armani back in the early eighties. It'll be like disinterring Howard Hughes. At one stage he became so reclusive that everyone thought he was going to stop doing shows altogether. But *Women's Wear Daily* ran a front-page story saying it would wipe out his business. He's famously monosyllabic, so you'll have your work cut out. At least his houses are incredible. But the main thing is, this should give Phyllida something to think about. Missed opportunities indeed.'

On the flight to JFK, Janie waded through a seascape of press clippings that Sissy had called up from the *Gazette*'s library. Tom Fitzgerald might not have granted many private audiences to the press, but he had snagged acres of print all the same. She examined the studiously choreographed photographs: Fitzgerald on an exquisite palomino; Fitzgerald windsurfing in Tobago; Fitzgerald in his seaplane. Judging by his trim, wiry frame and bountiful, pale gold hair, he was a well-preserved fifty – the dates in the cuttings varied.

His story was a familiar New York garment district one: poor boy from New Orleans makes staggeringly good. He had started out as an artist. His early paintings – mostly outsize, splashy abstracts – had done surprisingly well at an auction at Christie's a year earlier. To pay his way through art school he had freelanced as an illustrator for various designers on Seventh Avenue, before spending two years in Paris working for Emanuel Ungaro. The rest was fashion history. He was now designer royalty, a founder member of America's big four – along with Donna Karan, Calvin Klein and Ralph Lauren. Billion-dollar empire, homes around the world, marriage to Belinda Wessingham, the requisite sleek, toned blonde to whom he'd been married sixteen years. As a genuinely creative force, he hardly ranked alongside the likes of Chanel, Dior, Balenciaga or even Aeron Baxter. But his clothes and his homeware were luxurious and wildly coveted in most circles.

But Tom Fitzgerald's real talent lay – curiously for someone who seemed to spend most of his time out at sea or up in the air – in tapping into the world's next zeitgeist. His perfumes, like those of Calvin Klein, his great rival, had been launched sparingly every half-decade or so, and had unfailingly captured the mood of the times. In the eighties there had been Desire and Rapture, both instant bestsellers; in the early nineties he had launched Spirit, a light, ozonic scent promoted, with unprecedented success, by Peace. Appealing to Generation X as well as the more conventional perfume consumer, in the five years since its launch it had racked up £400 million in sales. And now he was about to try to do the same again. None of the articles captured any of the flavour of his personality, and yet, if his letter was anything to go by, he did have one.

She called Seth from the Westbury – another blow-out bill was in store, but Sissy had persuaded her that since it was a world exclusive they should splash out. It was midnight, East Coast time. Seth was in the kitchen at Finn's. She could almost hear him grinning.

'I can't stop smiling. Everyone here thinks I've developed a tic. What's the soonest you can hurry back?'

'The day after tomorrow. If all goes well, I may even catch the flight tomorrow night. If I can just get away with spending a couple of hours there, which must be enough time to get the low-down on any perfume – even out of a mute – I should make it.'

By 8 a.m. it was already seventy degrees in Manhattan. The trees on Madison Avenue looked dusty and defeated. A silver

Lincoln, complete with liveried chauffeur, was waiting outside the Westbury for Janie, courtesy of Tom Fitzgerald.

As they rocked gently over the city's potholes, the driver turned the air-conditioning on full and Janie shivered gently, luxuriating in the cool, while flustered-looking pedestrians outside wilted in the heat. Since waking at six she'd had a disturbing two hours. Firstly there had been an inscrutable but insistent letter delivered up to her room from the office of Dexter F. Ravensburg requesting her presence at a small cocktail party he was hosting at his home in Gramercy Park on Thursday evening. Then there was the matter of the small item tucked away at the bottom of page three of the *New York Times* about a series of explosions in remote Guatemalan villages that were thought to be caused by land-mines.

Janie rang *The Probe* and demanded to be put through to the editor's office.

'I'm sorry, but he's gone to lunch at Downing Street,' came the insouciant response.

'Well, could you please ask him to call Janie Pember the moment he gets back,' said Janie lamely. It was about time that blasted paper did something useful. And about time Matthew stopped giving her grief.

Then she rang Sissy.

'I don't even know Dexter F. Ravensburg from Adam.'

Sissy giggled. 'How appropriate because he owns *Eden*, the first issue of which is about to appear any nanosecond. You really are an innocent abroad. He's only the owner of Starlight Publications, arguably the most powerful glossy magazine corporation in the world. Don't tell me you hadn't twigged? Obviously you'll have to go and see him. It's my bet that Lee Howard wants to take you on the staff and Dexter's going to check you out. The pay'll be phenomenal, and I have to tell you the expression on Phyllida's face when she saw the reservation for the Westbury was not a pretty one. Listen, try and stay for the launch party. It'll be genius. Whoops, got to run, Gina Martin's on the prowl.'

Firefly, just two and a half hours from East 69th Street, was a miracle of geography and architecture. Sighted on a narrow sandy spit, it nestled in twenty verdant acres between ocean and lake, offering guests the choice of salt- or clear-water swimming. That is, if they could tear themselves from the aromatic indoor pool or the outdoor Olympic-sized one, which was located at the end of the vast balustraded terrace and seemingly fell away into the Atlantic Ocean. There were four tennis courts, two squash courts, stabling for half a dozen horses and a jetty for the seaplane that was Tom Fitzgerald's habitual mode of transport into work. The house itself was school of Lutyens — one of the few examples of his style on the island — a truncated E of mellow gold stone that was almost entirely obscured under a thick veil of wisteria, hibiscus and Virginia creeper.

He was waiting for her on the terrace, wearing a faded turquoise shirt with a discreet Fitzgerald crest on the breast pocket, much-patched jeans and a pair of cowboy boots. He was taller and more impressively built than the photographs had suggested. Janie was surprised at how good-looking he was.

'How're you doing?' He beamed broadly and led her across the terrace to a mound of cream chenille cushions under which, somewhere, lurked a brace of enormous wicker sofas. A white-coated attendant stepped silently through the French doors to take her drinks order.

'So you're Janie Pember.' His clear turquoise eyes appraised her coolly. 'I've been reading a lot of you lately.'

When she had gulped her drink, he led her on a tour of the house. It was enchanting. She had been expecting a series of contrived room sets, crammed with ostentatious showpieces and paint-by-numbers good taste, all artfully arranged for the glossies' photographers. Instead the interiors were clearly a highly personal mix of fine antiques and glorious flea-market finds. The rooms were handsomely proportioned, each opening out on to a terrace or a balcony, all with views of water. While respecting the original layout, Fitzgerald had injected the necessary American modern luxury of *en suite* bathrooms awash with stupendously plush towelling.

The double-height hall with its worn chequered flagstones and wide, carved staircase opened on to a light-filled drawing room that ran almost the length of the front of the house and was decorated with slightly faded damson-coloured stripes and peony-patterned cushions. A pair of chandeliers twinkled in the sun like old rose-cut diamonds. This was shabby chic *par excellence*. Cassie would love it, it was far more her style than minimalism thought Janie with a pang, suddenly remembering how miserable Cassie had sounded the last time they had spoken. Upstairs the bedrooms, with their wide, dark oak floors, were unexpectedly simple – outsize beds with oceans of crisp white linen, huge bedside tables with vases of pink and white roses and piles of books, a couple of large cream armchairs in one, a Victorian sofa in another, a thirties chaise-longue in a third. And he was right. Firefly's library, on the west side of the house and with books perched on every surface, was a delight.

'I hope your journey wasn't too unpleasant. The traffic can be hell if you catch it the wrong way.' His voice was clipped, very toney East Coast. Perhaps the rumours about elocution lessons were true. 'I wanted to fetch you in the seaplane but Belinda nabbed it early to do a little shopping in town. She always likes to be the first to buy the new collections. All of them.' He laughed lightly.

The house had taken four years to renovate and had generated dozens of apocryphal stories. It was said that the Fitzgeralds had demolished two buildings in Charleston and transported the interiors; that they'd bought a farmhouse in Tuscany because Belinda wanted the tiles for her kitchen; two nurseries in Cornwall specialising in hardy shrubs and hydrangeas had had to close for the summer after the Fitzgerald orders cleaned them out of stock.

Tom looked amused as Janie recited them to him. 'Yes, we did do a little landscaping. In fact, it was a good job the US military wasn't planning a war someplace because we had all the Semtex here. That was bad enough. Then Belinda fired the second lot of landscape gardeners and hired Son of Capability Brown, who planted two thousand trees. I said, "Cape, we're not shooting *Hansel and Gretel* here. You have to leave something for Canada." And see this terrace – looks ancient as the hills, doesn't it? Well, it's twelve months old. Cape had thirty assistants rubbing Genevieve Fairfax age-defying exfoliator into it to distress it, though why Tom Fitzgerald exfoliator wouldn't do I know not. Then those poor guys spent a week arranging fronds of camomile and moss between all the cracks because the seeds they planted first time round got blown away. Hell of a gale down here some days, which Cape would have known if he'd done any research. Still, the upshot was that what with the noise and stuff, none of the other residents spoke to me for months, so every cloud . . .'

Janie smiled and told him how charming the house was.

'You really like it?' he said, sounding pleased. 'Did it myself. Down to every last soap dish. The first lot of interior designers made the place look like some kind of shop set. So I thought, Come on, Tom Fitzgerald, you're the guru of American style – you do it. Can you believe it? Somehow I'd found time to write four books about interior design – but I'd never actually had time to do my own house . . . Now that you've seen it, I'm not sure where to go from here. It's so long since I've done an interview. Is it time for another drink yet?'

They settled under the parasols and Janie got out her notebook. Tom was an engaging mixture of rugged American matter-of-factness and garment district hyperbole, although less camp than his letter had led her to believe. Once he'd coloured in his biography for her, he was temporarily at a loss for words.

'I feel I ought to tell a joke – I know, did you hear the one about Zoffy Villeneuve gluing her PVC trousers to the front of her legs to keep the seams straight? They had to be amputated in Tangiers General Hospital – the trousers, obviously. She was working for Lee Howard at the time and Lee had to have her helicoptered off the side of some Atlas mountain – it's true, Lee told me herself . . .'

He was a mine of anecdotes and recent fashion history. When Janie mentioned casually how odd it was that Petronella Fishburn always gave Boldacci such glowing reviews in the teeth of everyone else's opprobrium, he looked genuinely surprised. 'Don't tell me you don't know about the Warhol sketches he sends her every year for Christmas? And I thought journalists were all such cynics.'

He didn't seem in the least bitter. 'When you put yourself slightly outside the world, you get to hear a lot more about it, and in the end you realise the only way to survive it is to adopt an easily amused sense of humour,' he said. By the time he'd done a very credible imitation of Leonie Uttley, using a giant peony as an improvised microphone, Janie was weak with laughter.

Before lunch, he suggested a swim. It had grown humid; the morning's breeze had dropped completely. He led her to a spare bedroom with a closet full of Tom Fitzgerald swimwear.

At four, a seaplane pierced the blue sky and gracefully settled by the jetty like a flying fish. Belinda emerged from the plane, head wrapped in a vivid silk scarf, accompanied by a vast configuration of bronzed, over developed muscles which went by the name of Travis. Travis, it seemed, was Belinda's trainer-cum-seaplane chauffeur-cum-bodyguard. Over a some-what stilted tea, Janie found herself agreeing to return the following morning to choreograph the photographs.

'It would make me feel so much better to know someone with a good eye was here to oversee things and tell me if I'm making a monkey of myself. Please stay the night if you like,' said Tom.

'Yes, please do, I'm sure we can squeeze you in,' Belinda managed, with exquisite condescension.

But Janie wanted to check if there were any messages at the hotel about or even from Matthew. And also, if she were scrupulously honest with herself, she wanted to spend at least two hours on the phone to Seth, even if it meant leaving the Westbury at six the following morning to be back at Firefly in time for the shoot.

They didn't make as early a start the next day as she had hoped, thanks to Belinda. But when Belinda emerged, Janie had to concede, she looked amazingly fresh and outdoorsy for someone who had just spent two and a half hours having her hair and make-up done – and redone.

'Nightmare,' mouthed the make-up artist over Belinda's shoulder.

Shortly before they broke for lunch, Belinda and Travis scampered off to the gym.

'She gets a little touchy if she doesn't fit in two work-outs every day,' said Tom apologetically. 'You have to hand it to her. It pays off.'

He had already told her his life story – the truly harrowing childhood, the averagely profligate youth. He moved on to the new scent, the name of which, he said, he was under pain of death not to reveal. But it would be something that reflected the late nineties preoccupation for traditional values.

Janie couldn't quite get the measure of Tom Fitzgerald. She had never come across anyone so apparently frank and indiscreet in an interview – his conversation was awash with scandalous anecdotes. He was either utterly guileless, which couldn't possibly be so, given his phenomenal success in business, or the greatest media manipulator of all time, in which case, why had he been so wary of the press for so long? She remembered what Sissy had said about his rift with Petronella, but she never found the right moment to broach it with Tom. Instead, much to her own disgust – she liked to keep a personal distance in interviews – she found herself showing him pictures of the children.

'That's Jake under the lilac, and there's Daisy dismembering a camellia. That's the top of Nell's head.' Janie wasn't the best photographer. Tom studied the photographs with polite concentration. Then he looked at his watch and said it was time she was going, if she was going to be at Dexter F. Ravensburg's by eight.

'How did you know about that?' she asked.

'Oh, Dexter and I are old friends.' Tom's eyes sparkled mischievously. 'I happened to mention to him that you were coming out to interview me and he was most interested to meet you.'

'Aren't you going to the party?'

'Oh, you know me – or should do after listening to my life's history,' he said wryly. 'I've too many family commitments to go gadding about. Enjoy the view.'

The view, as Tom Fitzgerald's seaplane skimmed the sunset, was indeed beautiful. When Manhattan's spiky outline erupted from the horizon, the pilot, seeing Janie's face pressed against the window, kindly circled the island. It was a marvellous golden evening. The woods at the north of the island sprawled for miles beneath. Ahead was Central Park, splayed out for her inspection like a green heart, and below, the twinkling arteries of Park, Madison and Fifth Avenues. They flew so close to the glamorous Art Deco silhouette of the Chrysler Building, Janie felt she could reach out and touch it.

The nineteenth-century red-brick mansions flanking Gramercy Park were amongst the most beautiful townhouses in the world. Dexter F. Ravensburg owned three of them, which he used partly to showcase what was reputed to be one of the most extensive collections of modern art in private ownership. He was a small, fit-looking man in his early fifties, with startlingly gold cuff links and a stern expression. Standing in front of two vast abstracts by Cy Twombly and Mark Rothko, he extended a stiff handshake to Janie before leading her through a room full of guests to Lee Howard.

'I believe you two know each other,' he said awkwardly before withdrawing.

Lee smiled warmly at Janie. 'Don't let his exuberance put you off. He's bowled over that you managed to get an interview with Tom Fitzgerald. I think you might be hearing rather a lot from him over the next few months. Dexter's most persistent — and he invariably gets what he wants. And I know he'd love you to come to our launch party — it's at the Guggenheim on the fifteenth. In the meantime, how would you like to see the finest paintings Jackson Pollock ever did?'

Clutching a bellini, Janie followed Lee in a daze, past a series of Jasper Johns and Rauschenbergs into a large room brimming with animated people. Life, she conceded, could be most exhilarating.

Back at the Westbury, there was an urgent message to call David Carter on his mobile. David, an old colleague of

Matthew's from *The Probe*, was a kindly, dedicated correspondent whom Janie considered to be a dire warning of what too much diligent foreign reporting could do to a marriage. A year earlier, when David had been covering events in East Timor, his wife, whom he had always believed to be as happy with their long-distance marriage as he was, had left him, taking their four children with her.

A bleary voice answered the phone. She realised sheepishly that it was three in the morning in London.

David Carter, it turned out, had just got back from a trip to Guatemala where he'd briefly made contact with Matthew via some of his colleagues at the orphanage. Once he realised who she was, David was lucid and to the point.

'Matthew was involved in the explosions – he and Mungo were together in the Guatemala highlands, but neither of them are seriously hurt. I've spoken to Matthew myself. They took him to hospital in Momostenango, just to check his arm.'

She was rustling around for her book of flight schedules.

'Janie, don't do anything. Just come home.'

'But he is my husband.'

'Janie . . .' He sounded awkward. 'Matthew expressly said he wanted to be left on his own. Listen, I'm being posted to Moscow for a few months – I'll call you when I get back—'

But she had hung up.

Chapter Twelve

Sissy's interview with Nari appeared in the *Gazette* while Janie was in New York and plunged Sissy into a Slough of Despond. She didn't feel she'd given it her best shot after all. She had rung Nari for his parents' telephone number outside Bombay but he was in Manila and a tart-sounding Scot on the other end of the line who went by the name of Jean had refused to give it out. Even Gina, who nearly always put a positive spin on everything, said she thought the profile could do with a bit of bite.

'It's terribly flattering. I mean, I know he's a marvellous businessman and everything, but it's a tad, how can I put this—'

'Sycophantic, unctuous, utterly nauseating,' said Sissy morosely.

'That's the word – the last one, I mean. How about having one more try at uncovering a bit of dirt? I mean, no one's *that* perfect,' said Gina, scampering off to the canteen.

Sissy rang Jean again. 'When will he be back?' she asked, trying to sound frail and desperate and not like a creepy news hack.

'Due middle of next week,' Jean said briskly, 'but really, there's no knowing. He may decide to take a detour.'

Bloody genius, thought Sissy miserably. Her most flattering profile ever was about to appear and wreck her reputation as a mordant commentator, and its subject wouldn't even be around to wallow in it.

Cassie decided she would host a party in her flat. If Peace could manage to pull off a charity fashion show at the Saatchi Gallery – and it looked as though every famous ex-junkie would be flying into London to support it – surely she could get together seventy or so friends to celebrate the unveiling – at last – of Blomfield Road mark four.

The first night of London Fashion Week at the start of October would be a sensible gesture. The crowd from Peace's gala would still be in town and it would certainly provide a welcome distraction for the poor senior fashion editors, who normally had to spend that evening sipping warm wine with some dreary minister or other from the Department of Trade and Industry. It would also send out a positive message to the fashion world. She might even lure Grace over from Paris, where she had just embarked on her course at the Sorbonne. She asked Finn's to do the catering and got Zack to sort out the music. And while she was at it, she would go and inspect the flat – the past few weeks she hadn't had the heart to look.

Pushing through the brushed steel door, she held her breath. She hardly dared open her eyes. She was pleasantly relieved when she did. Given that her extended stay with Zack and his debris at the Hempel had considerably cooled her ardour for minimalism, she was surprised to find how pleasing the newly opened-up rooms were. The sun poured through the renovated shutters. Barney had done a terrific job. It was empty without being . . . bare. Symbolic, she thought, of her new life, which would henceforth be uncomplicated, straightforward – and devoid of Zack. She seized the moment and dialled his mobile.

From the panting and whirring in the background, she surmised he was in the gym.

'You'll never guess what!' he gasped.

'You've just completed three hours on the Stair Master?'

'Better than that. I've got a job. That's job as in regular S-A-L-A—.'

He was slowing down, so Cassie broke in with her sincerest congratulations.

'Remember that tarot reading I forgot to do for that new client the day of Seth's party? Well, on Monday I did it – and she only turns out to be wimmins editor on *The Python* and it only turns out they want someone new to do their horoscopes now that Aurora Snow's snuffed it. And it only turns out that they want that someone to be yours truly.'

It was an enormous honour. Aurora Snow had been a national institution and *The Python* had spent several months since her illness had first been diagnosed surreptitiously trying to find the right replacement. So thrilled was Zack at the prospect of earning a proper salary again that he insisted on treating Cassie to lunch at the Connaught, even if he did have to ask her for a sub to pay for it. By the time their syllabubs arrived, he was burbling about possibly being invited to host the lottery, and was even talking about taking out a mortgage on the flat next to hers in Blomfield Road – as an investment in the future. It was no good. She was going to have to tell him.

The afternoon had turned spitefully cold. The autumn sun had given up working for a living and retreated into early retirement, as it so often did these days.

Cassie pulled the collar of her coat up and succumbed to a wave of despondency. Zack had been a good sport about it, she had to admit. Now that she had finally ended their affair, she had expected to be flooded with relief. But so far, so numb. There had certainly been *longueurs* in their relationship – but at least Zack had been someone to go home to. She kicked her way wistfully through a scattering of fallen leaves and wondered what would become of him. He had looked at her so sadly with his chocolately eyes – rather beautiful ones, she had noted with a slight pang – that she began to worry that he might really love her as much as he said he did. Then he had taken her hand in both of his, kissed it and told her that he understood, respected her wishes and would be there for her.

'Some psychic I turned out to be,' he said, hugging her on

the pavement outside the Connaught. 'I never saw it coming. Still, better not tell that to *The Python*.'

The phone conversation with David Carter had devastated Janie. Her own husband didn't want to see her in his hour of need.

'It's because he doesn't want to panic you, Janie,' Will told her. He dropped in at the *Gazette* a day later to see her. His large, angular frame seemed to swamp the department. Janie wished there weren't so many ostentatious bouquets spilling over the desks – they made everything look so decadent and trivial. She tried to hide the fax that had just come in from the Environmental Protection Agency lecturing her for using a shatoosh shawl on last Thursday's page. And Sissy had sworn on her Aunt Cora's life that shatooshes weren't cruel.

'I've spoken to someone at the orphanage who heard from a pretty reliable source that Matthew's all right. He and Mungo were camping a few hundred yards or so from the worst explosion – he's bruised and a bit winded, but that's all. Oh, and a broken arm. That really is it. Apparently the army didn't mean the damn things to go off – they were just testing. The whole thing sounds anarchic.'

He looked at Janie's horrified expression.

'Janie, I'm sorry – I'm sure Matthew will be fine. He's always had a sixth sense when it comes to survival, although you might not think it sometimes.' He stretched out a big, square hand to comfort her, accidentally knocking over a bottle of Kristof scent. 'So this is where you work,' he said brightly. 'Nice views.'

'Why is he so set against seeing me?' asked Janie quietly.

'As I recall, you were the one who wanted to make a complete break—' Will began gently.

'I didn't think he'd take it quite so literally,' she said petulantly. 'Isn't he interested in his own children?'

Will looked away, embarrassed. 'I didn't think you'd mind if I sent him a regular update, photographs and so on. Nell did a few paintings. I . . . I would have asked but I didn't want to upset you.'

Janie was riven with remorse. Matthew was having to communicate secretly with his children because she was acting like a member of the Stasi; her brother-in-law, a highly successful professional who advised captains of industry and sat on at least one progressive think-tank, was too scared to approach her on any emotional matter. What was happening to her?

On the other hand, perhaps what this all amounted to was the sign she had been waiting for: a green light for her relationship with Seth.

'I'm flying out there on Monday,' she heard Will saying super-casually. 'I've always wanted to see the country—'

Everyone seems to be heading down to Guatemala apart from me, she thought bitterly. She pretended to look at a slide on the light-box so that Will wouldn't see how distressed she was.

'Perhaps I could take a message for you – or a letter?' he said hopefully.

'A message? Will, we're talking about a nine-year marriage and three children.' She was crying, dammit.

He took her in his arms while she sobbed. His gentle concern reminded her so much of Matthew she didn't dare look at him. They sat for a while, with her head buried into his scratchy tweed jacket, until Lorna, who had been tactfully hovering with a summons from Phyllida for as long as she dared, finally interrupted them. Will gave Janie's shoulder another squeeze. 'We'll get to the bottom of this, Janie, you'll see.'

Anastasia had been as good as her word. Three days after the Nari profile appeared, Sissy became the proud investor of £144,000 and fifty-seven pence, which she lodged in a high-interest building society account (she had left her overdraft with Mr Dean, who, she felt, richly deserved it). Sorely tempted though she had been by the italic typeface on the Coutts cheque books, their rates simply didn't compete with the Bradford and Bingley Young Savers' Scheme, and she had resolved to be sensible. The remaining £6,000 were earmarked for a special and ultimately, she hoped, fruitful holiday, which began to take on the utmost urgency with every hour that passed without her receiving a vast floral tribute from Nari in grateful thanks for the piece.

Janie tried to scrawl a note to Matthew but she couldn't come up with anything that didn't sound like a rebuke. She told Will to give him a hug and threw herself into her Tom Fitzgerald profile. Two days after beginning it, she was quietly pleased with the results. She felt it was fair, but funny, and that she had managed to gain some insights into one of the fashion world's biggest players. Suitably inspired, she steeled herself to finish the interview with Anastasia, who had left several messages at the office while Janie had been in New York. If she could manage to inject some humour into the piece, Phyllida might overcome her antipathy to socialites and run it.

She still couldn't put her finger on what it was about Anastasia that repelled her. The woman was politeness incarnate, and yet beneath the tinkly laugh and studied interest in people, there was no warmth. She reminded Janie of the beautiful pastel sorbets that were her least-favourite dish at Finn's — decorative, but cold and ultimately unsatisfying. But a scoop, as Sissy would say, was a scoop — or a sorbet scoop. She would see if Anastasia could meet up tomorrow.

She got through to Anastasia's secretary, who after consulting lengthily with a diary, assured Janie that the Contessa could indeed make the following day.

Contessa. Janie smiled to herself. Wait until she told Sissy about that one.

'But you love London Fashion Week,' whined Angel Derrida, when Sissy broke the news that she wouldn't be able to help with the catwalk show he was planning in conjunction with two other accessory designers.

'A woman has to do what a woman has to do,' said Sissy earnestly. 'I'm sure Alice will help you out. Promise I'll look for some ancient buckles.' The timing of her holiday wasn't brilliant, even she admitted. She hated missing the shows – but she hadn't had a proper holiday in three years, and if she didn't go now there would never be a right time, and before she knew it she would have squandered all her money on python boots. It was now or never. Alice's transmogrification from Sloane to seditionary (and the concurrent boom in her freelance schedule) had made a deep impression on Sissy. The fact was that like Coco Chanel and Diana Vreeland before her, Alice had, in her own peculiar way, alighted on her own trademark style, however schizophrenic. It was becoming increasingly clear to Sissy that if she was ever to make it as a respected fashion maven, she had to take some time out and focus on her Personal Signature.

Anastasia's dulcet laughter reverberated around the raspberry-coloured walls of her winter drawing room. The charms on her bracelets, which were the size of petits fours, tinkled against the teacups as she poured the milk.

'It's just a silly title that I came into during the summer when my great-aunt died. I was her only living descendant. So officially my full title is the Contessa Anastasia Montecatini di Pomorosa-Santerini. I'm rather embarrassed to use it in these egalitarian times of ours, but you know what staff are like – such sticklers for etiquette.'

'I thought you said all your family were Russian,' said Janie casually.

'Really?' More melodious laughter. 'You must be mistaken. You didn't take that many notes, if I remember.' The voice was coolly emphatic. 'Perhaps you would call me when you come to write the piece, Janie – just to double-check your facts?'

'No can do love, British Airways is chocka.' The girl at the *Gazette*'s travel agent sounded sympathetic. 'Dunno why but there's a real run on flights to Buenos Aires. Must be a press junket down there, or some film festival.' It was the same story at Virgin, KLM, Lufthansa . . . in the end even Sissy's optimism ran out and she settled for a flight that left two days later than she'd planned. She was definitely going to miss out on the London shows at this rate. Better not tell Janie just yet – except that these days Janie's moods were weirdly unpredictable. She had seemed close to tears the first few days she got back from New York. Then writing the Tom profile had cheered her up. The Anastasia rendezvous had depressed her . . . Sissy couldn't keep up. And there hadn't been a squeak out of Nari, either. Sissy didn't expect bouquets every time she wrote an article on someone, but a note would have been polite. She considered ringing Jean to find out whether she had faxed Nari the piece in Manila, but remembering the frosty tones the last time, restrained herself. Roll on Buenos Aires.

Cassie decided not to move back into Blomfield Road until after the party. That way, if its new layout proved to be unworkable, at least she wouldn't be forced to put a brave face on things in front of a hundred or so people – the number kept rising. Peace's efforts on her fund-raiser were turning out to be phenomenally effective. People couldn't say no to her. For someone who had so few close friends, she had enormous social cachet. She faxed Cassie endless revised guest lists with asterisks by the names she thought Cassie should invite to her own party the next night. And Cassie threw herself into organising both events. Time had taken the sting out of Peace's past problems and Cassie had begun putting her own culpability into perspective. As Janie, Saffron, Zack, Seth and Michael Croft, to name but five, had repeatedly pointed out, she was a paragon as agents went; not just on the subject of illicit substances, but on all the moral issues agents had to deal with. Eleven- and twelve-year-olds who sent her photographs of themselves accompanied by letters in which they begged her to take them on their books and lied about their age received polite but firm rebuttals, a signed picture of Grace or Jess, and were told to come back after their GCSEs – which was more than Cassie could say for some agents.

'I know it's supposed to be friends only,' said Peace, running through Cassie's guest list one night, 'but in your present parlous position you should make a really defiant stance and invite everyone who's anyone in the business.'

Cassie appreciated the sentiment, even if the situation that prompted it sent her into a spiral of misery. Like the British Empire, she was beginning to feel like a study in decline. To make matters worse, she had had her first serious row with Saffron. It had started because the *Mail on Sunday*, who had bought Grace Capshaw's extracts sight unseen, on the basis of a synopsis that Cassie had knocked off over one weekend, were making noises about wanting to see some proper samples. The problem was that the kiss-and-tell that Cassie had promised the *Daily Mail* turned out to be not quite the kind of book that Grace had in mind. In fact, Grace insisted that the only kind of book she was interested in writing was a feminist perspective on Victorian fashion as described in George Eliot, Dickens and Henry James.

'It's your own fault,' exploded Saffron. 'You shouldn't have been so dishonest. You knew Grace was serious about that pseudo-intellectual crap of hers.'

'How was I to know she'd still be serious eight months later?' pleaded Cassie.

'You know what this smacks of to me?' snapped Saffron. 'Desperation!'

Cassie stared at her retreating back with mounting despair. Maybe Saffron was right.

Finn's was booked up until Christmas. Seth decided to ignore Vanessa, who had advised him to hold back a couple of tables every night in case a celebrity called for a last-minute reservation. He loathed everything that sort of practice stood for. Which only added to the restaurant's reputation.

He couldn't remember feeling so contented for years. It was true he wasn't managing to see very much of Janie, and the collections were coming up any minute. But perhaps it was best to take things slowly. She needed time to absorb the ramifications of her marital conflagration. Besides, his early evening visits to Janie *en route* for Finn's had fallen into a reassuringly regular pattern. He had even been introduced to Gloria and Nell and had finally seen the twins awake. After a cautious, stilted summer, there was, at last, a pleasing easiness about the way he and Janie acted with one another — as if they'd known each other for years. After his previous tortured relationships, and the way he had felt betrayed by Martha, this new happiness felt like a revelation. When Janie got back from seeing all the shows in November, he would whisk her away somewhere for a week so that they could properly be alone. And then he would concentrate on getting to know the children.

Janie was just the tiniest bit chuffed. She felt Tom Fitzgerald had come alive in her interview. He'd given her some scintillating quotes and sounded bright, generous and nicely self-deprecating. She didn't fancy her chances of a friendly reception next time she bumped into Belinda, however, but too bad. Edward Rushmore had telephoned her personally to congratulate her on the piece, which he said was very entertaining. It had sparked three days of correspondence on the *Gazette*'s normally highbrow letters page from readers who debated the decline of a world in which someone as frivolous as a designer could make as much money as Croesus. Four Sunday newspapers had used Tom's comment about Belinda's shopping habits in their Quotes of the Week sections. *Newsnight* wanted her to go to the studio to discuss why America's hold on luxury products was eclipsing France's traditional role. And Phyllida had stopped pretending to look at other fashion editors' CVs. That didn't prevent her from snarling at Janie, though.

'I'm surprised you haven't heard from Tom Fitzgerald. You made a complete pillock of him.'

Janie had heard, as it happened. A brief communication on gold-crested Fitzgerald paper had arrived by Federal Express.

Dear Ms Pember,
I'm told that the British think we Americans have no sense

of irony, hence the tone of your piece. I suppose you thought you could send me up and I wouldn't understand.

Well, my lawyers will be in touch shortly. I hope you're insured.

Yours, etc.

PS: How's that for irony? Pretty bad, I guess. You'll have to give me lessons. Seriously, thanks. I haven't sounded human for a couple of decades at least. Call me when you get to New York.

Tom

Encouraged, she dashed off a couple of thousand words on Anastasia, resolving to do a really thorough investigative job when she got back from the shows. She typed in various suppositions in bold so that when she had more time she could follow them up, and underlined the facts she hadn't checked. It would have to be cut and, on rereading it a day later, she realised it would end up a pretty tough piece. That was no bad thing, she reflected; she'd had enough of peddling soft journalism.

Zack's house-warming present to Cassie – to show there were no hard feelings – was to send his friend Wu Li from the Eastern Mysticism Centre round to Feng Shui her flat.

'Don't worry,' he told Seth, who looked aghast, 'I've given him strict instructions to report back to me first, so that if it's bad news I can work out how to break it to her.'

It was terrible news. Cassie's kitchen was in the wrong place entirely. It needed to be where the second bedroom was, otherwise Cassie was doomed to a life of intense stress. However, Wu Li thought the situation might be salvaged by transposing it with a bathroom. Someone was going to have to break the news to Barney Frick. Zack approached Janie.

Janie was livid. So much so she paid a visit to Wu Li's herb shop, which was round the corner from the *Gazette*.

'I'll tell you what's stressful. Stressful is having to fork out thirty thousand pounds on a load of mumbo-jumbo.'

Wu Li took one look at her expression and jettisoned his principles. On second thoughts, he said, perhaps a drastic reconstruction of Cassie's flat wouldn't be necessary. In fact, now he thought about it, he had a very special crystal that might just do the trick. He trotted upstairs and resurfaced a few minutes later with an enormous and stupendously expensive lilac rock. Janie took it and put it on Matthew's credit card. If nothing else, the colour, one of Cassie's favourites, would prove uplifting.

'Here, let me help you with that,' offered Sissy, bumping into Janie in the lift. 'Crikey, don't tell me you've gone Buddhist?'

'Don't ask. God knows how I'll get it to Cassie's.'

Sissy had her car and offered to drop it off on the way home. Janie had to stay late for another of Phyllida's interminable features department pep talks. Normally Sissy didn't drive to work – the Panda was too frail for daily outings – but this was her last day in the office before going on holiday and she wanted to borrow a couple of Globetrotter suitcases from the fashion cupboard, and a few bikinis and pareos.

Janie found an enormous basket of blue hyacinths waiting on her desk – and a note that said 'I'm still chuckling. Tom'.

And I don't get so much as a telephone call from Nari's secretary, thought Sissy wistfully. Perhaps they didn't have fax machines in Manila.

With the two Globetrotter trunks protruding out of the back door, Sissy's ancient Fiat Panda was a sorry sight. One of the speakers had been stolen and the seat belts only worked if you had a 32A bust. She'd have to do something about it. Get rid of it, for instance. It wasn't as if she was even emotionally attached to it. It had been the scene of a traumatic break-up with her last serious boyfriend five years ago, and its annual MOT had become something of an ordeal for Sissy and the local mechanic who had taken pity on her.

As she and the suitcases juddered round Hyde Park Corner, she wondered whether she was smarting about Nari's thundering silence because she was genuinely attracted to him or because she was lonely. It was an uncomfortable notion. Sissy didn't normally indulge in much introspection. In recent years she hadn't given much thought at all to her emotional status. She had been too busy going to parties with Angel and his crowd, as well as putting in appearances at the endless perfume and sunglasses launches that were part of her job. She knew so many people in the fashion world that she had long ago lost track of where her professional duties ended and her personal life began. For the first time since leaving Cambridge, it occurred to her that she might not have one.

Just past the twirly outline of the Queen Mother's gates, an Aston Martin pulled out in front of her. She glanced at the registration idly. NS 400. It was Nari's. He was back. A shoal of tangled emotions and rapidly forming schemes swam through her head. A year or so ago, one of Diana's drearier solicitor friends had spent an evening going over the finer points of the Highway Code with her. The gist, if Sissy's memory served, was that everything was always the driver behind's fault. It was make-your-mind-up time. She only had third-party insurance, but in any case the Panda was worth £350 tops. Nari was probably doing about thirty miles an hour, which couldn't possibly cause serious damage to her – nothing, anyway, that a fortnight by a pool wouldn't cure. She took a deep breath, put her foot flat down on the accelerator and began to overtake him. It took what seemed for ever but eventually, in a final valiant display of braggadocio, the Panda edged level with the Aston Martin and, perhaps sensing its impending apocalypse, finally inched ahead. She slammed the steering wheel left and braced herself for the impact.

It was pretty dramatic. The sickening sound of collapsing metal, glass everywhere, a Globetrotter in the back of her neck – and Nari's voice coming anxiously through her smashed side window.

'Are you all right? . . . Oh, it's *you*.'

His tone was a little hard to gauge, but Sissy had long ago mastered the outer vestiges of Silent Agony. She smiled bravely and pointed to her leg. Nari lifted her out of the Panda and drove her to Casualty where, Sissy was gratified to note, he sat with her for two hours until a harassed young doctor found time to attend to her.

The *Independent* had asked her if she would review the British collections for them, but Madeleine wasn't sure if she could face London Fashion Week now that she wasn't actively taking part in it.

She had sold her flat in Islington and moved to a studio in Belsize Park. It was cramped but it was the only way she could pay off her debts. Then she had swallowed her pride and written polite letters to Marks and Spencer and just about every other high-street chain. A gratifying number had taken up the offer of her services. She was working flat out, earning more than she had most years when she had been self-employed, although she saw precious little for it – it was all going to the bank. She was busy enough with her work, but it wasn't the same as having her own personal creative outlet.

The truth was she wasn't good working for other people, particularly those less talented than herself. She had had a blazing row the other day with Geoffrey Pugh, a small designer she had been helping out in London. When she asked him what coats he was planning for the next season, he had replied, in an appallingly mixed-up metaphor, that coats were old hat.

'Not doing them. Global warming, sweetie. No need.'

'Geoffrey, it reached four below zero this February. What are you talking about?'

He had looked at her pityingly. 'Darling, I think when it comes to commercial matters, you're hardly in a position to lecture.'

The loss of her label, it was only just beginning to dawn on her, was starting to feel like a bereavement.

Janie began to suspect that Madeleine was working *too* hard. There had been too many evenings lately when she had been in some studio or other until midnight, only to return to her empty bedsit and leave it the next day again at eight. Madeleine saw very few of her old friends, her social life had dwindled to the occasional trip to see a film at the Screen on the Hill, and the odd *à trois* supper party. With three weeks to go before London Fashion Week, Janie suspected that Madeleine was feeling the loss of her company more strongly than ever. Madeleine assured her that she was happy with things the way they were, but there seemed to be something almost sacrificial about the spartan life Madeleine was now leading. Madeleine denied this vehemently when Janie broached the subject. Her life was far less stressful, she insisted, with no responsibilities, no fashion editors making impossible demands, no factories letting her down on deliveries two days before a show, no unpaid bills from department stores.

She had taken a stall in Portobello market and sold off most of her furniture. It was a surprisingly satisfying day, she told Janie: she was a good saleswoman, and with every departing knick-knack her future seemed more streamlined. She decided she liked clean slates.

'You and me both,' said Cassie. They were eating baked monkfish round at Janie's, courtesy of Seth. Cassie felt it was the first time she had seen Janie properly in weeks. She had changed, blossomed almost, except that it seemed a very strange thing to do after being deserted by your husband. But she was certainly calmer and more confident than Cassie had seen her look for years. The missing clump of hair had grown back completely after the Magimix incident, and if Cassie wasn't mistaken Janie had even been to a professional salon instead of getting one of her Cambodians to hack it. Her tousles had a hairdressy sleekness about them. She wondered how it was that Janie always managed to look wholesome and at the same time as if she had just that minute finished having amazing sex. She was real wife material. Cassie was certain that even Seth, brooding sex god of the tabloids that he was, would eventually ask her to marry him; serious intentions oozed from those soulful Irish eyes of his. Then, not for the first time, she speculated about what it was about herself that made her a homing post for flakes.

'You're looking morbid again,' slurred Madeleine, pouring Cassie another glass of wine.

'I feel fine,' said Cassie dully. 'Never better. I've even got my very own stalker, in the shape of my friend DCI Reece – what could be more chic? Now, let's see if we can sort *you* out.'

They talked into the small hours, working their way through Zack's Zodiac in *The Python*, as well as the case of wine Boldacci had sent to all the fashion editors as a sweetener in the run-up to his forthcoming show. Their only salvation, they decided, lay in getting out of the fashion business.

'Who needs it?' said Madeleine morosely. 'Did I ever tell you about the time The Witch called me at midnight?'

'Who's The Witch?' they chorused.

'She shall remain nameless. Oh, all right, it was Zoffy Villeneuve, and she'd just finished shooting twenty pages for *Le Télégraphe* on Ayer's Rock. They got stuck there for six days because no one in the office had bothered to book a helicopter to pick them up. Anyway, I think the experience had finally sent her over the edge because she was ringing from Sydney on her way back to Paris when she threatened to set fire to my entire collection – she'd borrowed it for a shoot – unless I could lend her one of my satin ballgowns to wear to the gala she was going to the next day. "But Zoffy," I said, "I don't make ballgowns." And do you know what she said? "Don't get fucking smart with me. I'm lighting the match right now."'

'What did you do?' asked Janie.

'I did what a designer has to do in these situations – stayed up all night with Sally making a satin ballgown, of course. Actually it wasn't really satin – we had to take down some curtains from Sally's flat to do it. Then Sally flew out with it the next day to meet Zoffy at Charles de Gaulle . . . Those were the days. The sick thing is I miss it.'

'I think I'd miss Hot Shots too,' said Cassie wistfully. 'There's something wonderful about being surrounded by so much hopeful beauty.'

'How can you say that?' said Janie, outraged. 'It's so destructive and all it does is focus everyone's attention on the superficial all the time. Anyway, I wouldn't miss journalism one bit.'

'Crap!' exclaimed Cassie and Madeleine in unison.

By 2 a.m. Janie had remembered who had a wry sense of humour similar to Madeleine's: Tom Fitzgerald.

'How about New York?' she suggested brightly.

Cassie stared at her in amazement.

'Well,' said Janie, swaying slightly, 'it's an exciting city. The pay's good and there are plenty of hugely successful designers in search of British assistants.'

'That's right,' chipped in Cassie. 'You want to leave this sodding country and all its negative attitudes way behind you.'

'Why?' asked Madeleine archly. 'You haven't.'

Cassie ignored her. 'This time next year you could be sketching in a hammock in St Bart's. That's where all New York designers seem to go to recharge their batteries.' They found Gloria's shopping-list pad and jotted down the big four New York designers in order of wealth.

'Might as well start at the top,' said Janie briskly. 'Try Tom Fitzgerald.'

Ever since *People* magazine had reported that Ben Mornay was disillusioned by LA, he had been hounded by New York realtors until he felt it might almost be worth buying an apartment there just to get rid of them. At first the endless trips across town had been fun – he liked peeking into other people's kitchens, appraising their aspirations, which were always nakedly on show, and trying to guess what they did for a living. A gifted observer, he was invariably right. Apartment-hunting, he decided, was really just sanctioned voyeurism. He wondered whether it was too soon to ask Jo-Jo to move in with him.

'I've been thinking it might be kinda fun to get a place together.' He had tracked her down on the telephone to a lagoon in Nepal.

How long had she known him – five months? Romantic or what? Visions of Gloria flashed in front of her.

'Er, that would be great, Ben, but it's not as if I sleep anywhere but the back of a 747 at the moment.' This was all too true. With the exception of Calvin Klein, everyone expected her to emerge from fourteen hours in Economy and radiate loveliness.

'I know it's quite soon but . . . just tell me, do you at least like the idea in theory?'

'In theory I love it. As long as you tell my mum.'

'Sure. We'll explain it's for your career. Every model ends up living in New York.'

Later that day, as she lay pinioned to a raft, while Dodie glazed her with olive oil to make her skin shine for Dirk Von Litten's camera which was firmly positioned half a mile away on the shore, she wondered whether Ben might not be right.

'Very Talita Getty,' Dodie whispered encouragingly.

'I'm seeing too much of ze foot. Get rid of eet,' bellowed Zoffy Villeneuve through a loudhailer from the beach. The scratchy sequined trench coat Jo-Jo was half wearing, and the pain of having most of her eyebrows plucked out, made it hard to concentrate. The sun was beating down so hard she thought she was going to black out. It was true that all the models who had entered the gates of superdom had served time in New York. Only the previous night, over a candlelit salad, Zoffy had asked her when she was moving there. Never, had been Jo-Jo's off-hand response – she was determined to remain normal and play the game by her own rules. Zoffy disdainfully arched her trademark unibrow.

'I just thought you'd like to make ze clean break,' she said.

'Oh, Jo-Jo's very loyal,' Dodie jumped in tactfully. 'After all, Hot Shots has been very good – for her.'

Dirk looked at them contemptuously.

Zoffy stubbed her cigar out in his butter. 'My God, don't tell me you're 'aving a main course too, Jo-Jo.'

As she tossed restlessly under the ceiling fan that night, suffering from acute sunburn, Jo-Jo couldn't help harbouring treacherous thoughts towards Hot Shots. A year ago she wouldn't have been able to identify one school of photography from another, let alone rank model agencies in order of prestige. But the past few months, especially since meeting Ben, things had changed. The very fact that she was even having a relationship with someone like Ben Mornay was symptomatic of a life that would have been unthinkable to her not long ago. Her career, embarked on so haphazardly and opening so many unforeseen doors, had become increasingly important to her. It wasn't just the narcissism and money which appealed to her: she enjoyed the camaraderie that came from working with a small team. There was nothing like the pressure of having to produce beautiful pictures halfway up a mountain for fostering friendships. She was even starting to see the point of women like Zoffy, even though her sadistic demands on Jo-Jo made Sven look like a social worker.

Increasingly, when she wasn't posing herself, she was studying pictures of models she admired – everyone from Grace to Lisa Fonssagrives, the exquisite forties mannequin – and experimenting with her own look. She had learned that the way to look skinniest was to put her weight on the foot that was furthest from the camera. She had worked out that if she leaned forward, her breasts – the feature she liked least about herself – looked more voluptuous.

Intuitively, she seemed to know how to manipulate the hyper-reality of a famous, or semi-famous, existence. Even when she and Ben slipped out to a local bistro, they quickly became a magnet for other people's attention. So Jo-Jo had begun investing in good clothes – and discovered that the process wasn't entirely unpleasant. Gloria had always taken a puritanical view of fashion, which she considered dangerously akin to vanity, and therefore a deadly sin. Even if she hadn't been broke, thought Jo-Jo, she probably wouldn't have treated herself to decent clothes. But ever since the gala in New York, Jo-Jo had been entranced by the glamorous people she had seen there. She was fascinated by the care with which they dressed: the orchid-coloured lipstick that so perfectly highlighted the luminous pallor of Tulah's skin; the expensive precision of Jess's rampant hair streaming down her back in casual abandon; the way everyone's clothes fitted so beautifully. People simply didn't look like that where she came from, and she found being even tangential to that world intoxicating.

Sven had given her a book on Irving Penn's work in preparation for a retro forties story that he was planning to shoot for *Beau Monde*, and she spent hours in front of the mirror trying to replicate the steely elegance of the period.

'Terrific,' he had muttered almost inaudibly.

She was elated.

Partly because it had all fallen into her lap so easily, Jo-Jo had dismissed modelling as a self-conscious joke, until it seemed that she might be very good at it. And now, it appeared that her top-of-the-range agent might not be quite so tip-top after all. Zoffy wasn't the first to hint that she might be planning a defection. Of course, Jo-Jo wasn't. Cassie irritated her, but loyalty had to count for something, didn't it?

It was all very well for Harry to tease her over what he called her budding Gestapo tendencies, thought Peace, but ultimately he wasn't the one whose photograph, complete with the caption 'Chairperson', was fronting the gala programme. She was well aware that her image at large was that of an airhead – and that was on a good day. So she moved from the cottage in Dorset into Harry's house in Onslow Gardens and happily worked eighteen-hour shifts to ensure that the fashion show was an operational success. No detail was too petty for her attention. For someone who'd seemed such a dolt, Peace was proving to have an amazing grasp of business strategy. Cassie began to wonder if she was some kind of idiot savant.

After the No To Blow logo had been lampooned mercilessly in the press, Peace couldn't help feeling that her own salvation depended on the success of the evening as much as the future of the charity did. Having obtained details on how to register the charity officially, her immediate priority was to sort out a name for it. Cassie had put her in touch with Sir Tim Bell, and after a summit one evening with Harry, Seth, Janie and Cassie, the six of them had decided on HOPE – Help People Emerge from Opiates.

'You've got the Peace and the HOPE,' said Cassie. 'Let's keep our fingers crossed for a little Charity.'

A week before the gala, posters of a dozen models and photographers including Grace, Jess, Jo-Jo, Tulah and Brigitte went up all over London with the HOPE tag line on them. She spent the next three days phoning her way through her address book, pinning down everyone who had promised their services for the show. When Harry gave her one of his looks, she shrugged her shoulders.

'Look, I have to remind them. I know how bloody unreliable some models are.'

Confined to a hospital bed for twenty-four hours' surveillance, Sissy found that her conscience throbbed more than her head. Nari had been very kind; waiting by her side in Casualty until they X-rayed her, arranging for her to be given her own room and even staying to see that she was comfortably settled. Torn between the impulse to ask him if he'd had a chance to read her profile yet, and a desperate desire not to seem too *compos mentis*, she kept telling him how much she had enjoyed the day in Yorkshire.

'I liked it too,' he said thoughtfully. 'I haven't had so much fun in a long time.' He patted the skinny freckled arm that hung limply over the side of the bed. 'It made me realise that I ought to get out more.'

'And the outfit – you must let me know how much I owe you,' she said tentatively, wondering how numerate someone with delirium would sound.

'I told you – it was a present for keeping you out so long.'

'No,' said Sissy firmly. 'I went a bit mad in there. You really must let me pay.'

'Please say no more about it.'

She closed her eyes, leaving a small slit through which she could just see Nari gazing at her with what Sissy, freeze-framing the moment repeatedly later on, could only describe as acute concern. Emitting a small whimper, as if the bright bedside light were too strong for her, she hurriedly turned her head, before he could see the radiant smile snaking across her face.

She was so touched by Janie's get-well present – an enormous flacon of her all-time favourite Chanel No. 5 which Sissy particularly appreciated in view of the fact that Janie was still supposed to be boycotting French goods in protest against the nuclear testing activities in the South Pacific – that she briefly contemplated postponing the trip to Argentina. But for once her luck was in: the hospital diagnosed mild whiplash and ordered her to take things easy for a while. 'I'm so very, very sorry, Janie,' said Sissy, propped up on a mound of cushions in her bedroom souk. 'I can hardly bear to think of you doing the shows in London without me, but the doctors said the sun was the quickest way of curing the agony.'

Janie didn't see how going on a dig constituted taking things easy, but Sissy assured her that she was now only going as an observer. 'I may do a bit of cataloguing, but that's absolutely it,' she promised. Two days later she hopped on a plane to South America, scattering vague promises about bringing Janie back a souvenir from the Draguita Indians and guarantees that she would join her in Milan.

Janie couldn't allow herself to contemplate life at the collections without Sissy around to help her satisfy the *Gazette*'s insatiable appetite for fashion news. If she hadn't still been in turmoil about Matthew and Seth, she might have found a way to prevent Sissy from going, even if it did mean that she would miss out on taking part in the last really important archaeological dig of the century.

Chapter Thirteen

It was an odd sensation being in a country where your reputation didn't count for anything. Madeleine wasn't exactly mobbed on the streets in England, but mention of her name always seemed to secure her good tables in restaurants. She was used to solicitous service in shops and to being rung up for her opinions when journalists needed to fill pages. If the surly reaction from the immigration desk at JFK was anything to go by, all that was a thing of the past.

It was even odder to feel the air getting crisper, the leaves turning red – and not to have to go through the stomach-churning, ulcer-frazzling, nerve-fizzing ordeal of gearing up for a show. Odd – and not entirely enjoyable. Still, she'd wished for a blank white page and here it was.

She lugged her Hermès cases off the carousel – they had been a present to herself after the reviews of her first show five years ago. A fierce-looking policeman with a sniffer dog eyed her sternly. She must cut a very bourgeois figure, she decided, with her pristine luggage and gleaming cashmere camel coat. If only they knew. She had about £300 left in her account.

It had all happened so fast. The day after her dinner with Janie and Cassie, she had written to Tom and he had been amazingly prompt in replying to her letter. He was delighted to hear from her, he said when he rang her, because he was on his way to London for some creative inspiration and yes, of course he was familiar with her work. They'd had a relaxed dinner at Claridge's – Madeleine adored the Art Deco restaurant there.

'Tell me,' he said expansively over coffee, 'what's the general attitude to fashion designers in this country?'

'Pretty benign, I'd say. I mean, the British public thinks we're all mad but our antics seem to amuse.'

'The fashion press, for instance, gives you guys a pretty rough ride.'

On the whole, Madeleine felt the British press had always gone out of their way to support her. 'They've been quite kind mostly.'

'Yes, sure. And then they go off and massacre you in their reviews. Or tell you that they would have loved to have featured your clothes this season, but the photographs were too fuzzy.'

Madeleine wondered what he was driving at; commercially and creatively, he was too important a designer not to have his clothes used by the major magazines. It occurred to her that he might be referring obliquely to the interview Janie had written.

'I suppose it's better than being lapdogs like the French journalists,' she said. 'Probably healthier all round in the long run. And sometimes, once you get over the sting, their comments can be quite helpful.' She brought herself up short, remembering his notorious run-in with Petronella Fishburn.

'I wouldn't know,' he said, signalling for the bill.

If Tom had a score to settle with Janie, thought Madeleine, it was just as well she had gone to Eleanor's for the weekend. She offered to take him round Portobello market at the weekend.

'The north end is by far the most interesting now, and most tourists still don't get up that far.'

Afterwards they went on a tour of vintage clothes shops, ending up in Hugo Speck's three-storeyed emporium on the Fulham Road, where to Madeleine's amazement he spent £17,000 on a couple of dozen exquisite couture gowns by Vionnet, Schiaparelli and Chanel, two marcasite evening watches dating from the 1930s and a trunk full of stoles, capes and beaded evening bags.

'Don't look so stunned,' said Hugo, catching her expression as Tom disappeared to look at the specials in the back room. 'They've all been in here this year – Boldacci, Baxter, Paolo Bianco, Derrida, Vittorio Chacha, Bella . . . I could write an A to Z of fashion designers. They call it research. Shan't complain. You get the best prices from people buying on expenses.'

Within two weeks of her lunch with Tom, all the straggly bits of her everyday existence – work permits, moving – had been tidied away with the painless efficiency that the very rich regard as a fact of life. And now, here she was, working her way into Manhattan on her own set of expenses. She got in line for the taxis. Her official title was Senior Design Director, which meant, as far as she could gather, that she was a glorified sounding-board. She knew that there were at least three other Senior Design Directors in the company. Tom Fitzgerald had a twenty-five strong design team working on his three main clothing lines – Tom Fitzgerald, TF and Fitz. There were separate teams for the furnishings, homeware and sports collections. The jeans, bed-linens, cosmetics, sunglasses, hosiery, shoe and handbag lines were licensed out to various manufacturers, although one of the purposes of Tom's visit to London was to investigate the possibilities of persuading a talented English accessories designer to sign up and bring the shoes and handbags in-house.

Madeleine's chief responsibility, Tom explained, was to inject some youthfulness into Tom Fitzgerald, his top-of-the-range collection which had become overly influenced by the rather staid, uptown taste of Belinda and her cronies. She began to wish she had met the other Design Directors before taking the job. If fashion the world over was shark-infested, in New York the sharks each came with their own nuclear capability. But Tom had wanted to get her on board quickly, so that she might make an impact by the time he launched the new perfume in the spring. And the salary he had offered her − $350,000 a year − had been irresistible. At that rate she'd be able to pay off the rest of her debts in eighteen months or less.

She already knew at least half a dozen acquaintances who'd moved out to New York in the past year. It seemed the Americans couldn't get enough of the Brits at the moment, and the exodus from London looked likely to continue. Now that Dexter F. Ravensburg, a renowned Anglophile, had finally launched *Eden* magazine, with Lee Howard, another Anglophile, as editor-in-chief, to universal acclaim, another recruitment drive was bound to be afoot.

The taxi queue shuffled along ineffectually and it began to hail. Eventually an empty cab rattled up alongside her and the driver watched impassively while she heaved her cases into the boot.

'The Carlyle, please.' Madeleine tried to buckle herself in but the seat belt was broken. An empty packet of condoms jiggled on the floor. Her head felt as though it were cracking open − she could never sleep on planes − and her hormones were in collision with one another. Fifty per cent of them were excited and exhilarated by this new rush of freedom. The other fifty wanted to get back on the plane.

'You vish stink?' the driver snarled at her.

After several goes Madeleine ascertained that he was enquiring whether she was visiting.

'No. Moving.'

He grunted.

'You single?'

Madeleine nodded.

'Vursht city in the world for beink single,' he gargled. 'You got more chance of beink raped than beink dated.'

Madeleine gazed out of the window at Shea Stadium.

'You got a gun?'

He didn't wait for a reply

'Get one. Vursht city for violence. Me, I'm here two veeks before I get held up in my cab by this scumbag who puts gun to my head and says "Give me your dough motherfucker" −

three times this happens to me in my first year. So then I get a gun and . . .'

There was a mile–long tailback out of the tunnel. It was an endless drive into Manhattan.

As far as Janie was concerned, the London shows seemed flat without Madeleine. Not that anyone else seemed particularly bothered, she noticed glumly. Attendance figures for foreign journalists and buyers were at an all–time high. Kiko Umagai had done a quarter-page photo-story on Janie's 'English Country Look', and devoted a whole page to Alice, who had permed and dyed her hair auburn and was now modelling herself on Bianca Jagger. The person Kiko was most avidly following, however, was Jo–Jo, who wore clothes with an easy elegance and nonchalance that made whatever she had on seem instantly desirable, even the simplest white t–shirt. She had natural good taste and, pointed in the right direction by Cassie, and freed from the poverty that had obliged her to adopt baggy track suits as her 'political uniform', she was rapidly developing a strong personal style.

Cassie's party in her remodelled flat was a master–class of kept–up appearances. Mustered together, Hot Shots' models, who had racked up thousands of magazine covers between them in the past few years, were a sparkling constellation, twinkling prettily on Cassie's behalf. *A La Mode* had sent a photographer to cover it and all the right people had gone – Helmut Newton and Bruce Weber had flown in from Paris. Janie couldn't help feeling many of the guests had gone out of a ghoulish curiosity rather than solidarity, but Cassie had looked gratified. Presumably right now she was thankful for small mercies, although to her dismay Janie couldn't be entirely sure if this was really the case. Cassie was keeping her own counsel these days. Throughout the summer she'd spent an afternoon a week with Nell, partly to relieve Gloria and partly, she said, to teach her about the finer things in life. They'd been for tea at the Ritz, the ballet, the Aveda spa at Harvey Nichols and, at Zack's suggestion, the Planetarium. But latterly Nell seemed to be learning more about fielding hostile phone calls from the office where Cassie, unable to get away, had ended up trying to entertain her. Janie didn't like it, but she couldn't face hurting Cassie's feelings.

The days passed in a lonely blur. She got a letter from David Carter in Moscow, telling her to be patient with Matthew and not to worry about him – neither of which instructions proved practicable. Lindsey was openly hostile; Magnus had decided he couldn't cope with any more edgy music and had gone down with gastric flu. He had called Janie at the *Gazette*. 'Don't worry. I think I can guarantee that I will have a miraculous recovery by Milan. I can never resist the *osso buco* in Bice.'

Desperate for sympathetic company, Janie found herself giving some of Sissy's tickets to Lorna, whose pasty features broke into a smile so radiant that Janie felt dreadful for never having offered her anything before. Halfway through the week they were joined by Alice, who had found, much to her chagrin, that she was bereft without Sissy. She had devised a complex equation for working out how many people she could afford not to be on speaking terms with at any one time before being in a room became impossible, but it had gone horribly wrong when she'd caught most of the third row snickering at her fake beauty spot, and now she was forced to hang out with Janie and Lorna.

It was impossible to get within half a mile of the shows without being besieged by camera crews demanding instant soundbites on each designer. They were desperate for glamour and for signs of zany or even not-so-zany British street style. At least there had been saturation coverage for Peace's fashion gala. The evening raised £300,000, and during the following weeks opened the floodgates for a Niagara of faxes from companies wanting to co-sponsor events. A serene, confident-looking Peace had even made it on to NBC's news and entertainment slot, which had run a seven-minute segment showing Peace organising the event from her makeshift office in Harry's house in Onslow Gardens, as well as footage from the show and subsequent party, thereby securing forty-five million American viewers for Jo-Jo's debut catwalk appearance.

Jo-Jo, whom Cassie had only allowed to do four London shows so that she would still be fresh for the big payers in Milan, was a natural on the catwalk: graceful and sexy with a rapturous smile that hovered permanently round her lips and lifted the spirits of the audience. She loved watching the designers tweak each outfit before the models went out and felt privileged that they were entrusting her to bring their clothes to life.

'Good Lord, you are keen,' said Unity Montcreith, watching Jo-Jo trying to balance in a pair of Angel's Attila the Hun bondage boots. 'Me, I just take 'em off the minute I'm out of the designer's eye-line and go barefoot down the catwalk. It's a sort of Sandie Shaw approach.'

'I don't think I'm established enough yet to get away with that sort of thing,' said Jo-Jo shyly. 'God, it's quite a challenge trying to balance on these.'

'The only balance I worry about is the one at the bank. As for being established, you'll have to be the judge of that. Everyone in this business will take you at your own word. Blowing your own trumpet, that's the name of the game.'

Jo-Jo, instinctively mistrusting most of the people she came across these days, inspected Unity's little whey face for signs of hostility. There were none. 'I'm a bit nervous, to tell the truth. It's only my third show.'

Unity scuttled away and returned with a magnum of Moët which she handed to Jo-Jo. 'Get pissed. Does wonders for the balance.'

After the show Unity had taken Jo-Jo and the remains of another magnum shopping in Voyage, although for a moment they weren't allowed in because Unity kept brandishing her London Fashion Week pass instead of her Voyage membership card. Uma Thurman was already in there, flitting in and out of the changing room in the most beautiful russet silk dress Jo-Jo had ever seen. Intoxicated by champagne, Unity and the constellation of events that had led to her being in the same shop as Uma, one where you needed a membership card before you were allowed the privilege of blowing thousands of pounds, in short, a shop that her mother deeply disapproved of, Jo-Jo had a trying-on frenzy. Between them, she and Unity racked up a bill for six thousand pounds in less than half an hour, and afterwards Jo-Jo felt her knees buckle. That was almost the down payment on the flat she was supposed to be buying for Gloria.

'Trouble with you is you look gorgeous in everything you try on. Me, I'm quirky. No, no, don't deny it. Daddy says if I wasn't titled, I'd have to muck out the pigs. I quite like pigs, as it happens. I'm going to rear rare breeds when this is all over . . .'

The shop was winding down. It was gone five. Uma had gone and the doorbell, which had been ringing incessantly with people begging to be let in, had finally fallen silent. Over by the counter, a couple of fresh-faced girls festooned with Harvey Nichols and Conran Shop carrier bags and skunk-striped hair looked slyly in her direction. Despite their curvy Dolce Vita dresses, they were clearly in their early teens and bore all the hallmarks of having done a bunk from school. After nudging one another a little obviously, they made their way to Jo-Jo, now in a velvet-trimmed lime cardigan with fuchsia silk marigolds on it, and politely asked her for her autograph. If this was fame, Jo-Jo liked it.

'You don't mean you paid full price?' Peace asked her aghast later that evening. Revelling in her new, self-appointed role as elder stateswoman of the modelling sisterhood, Peace had decided to become a fairy godmother figure to Jo-Jo, who had looked so adorable at the charity show, and invited her for Japanese takeaway at Harry's.

'You do realise that by the time you've done one season's worth of shows, you'll have been given enough free clothes to see you through to your nineties?'

'But how do they know what you like? I mean, surely sometimes it's nice to buy your own things? Woman can't live by freebies alone.'

Looking at Peace's hairy clogs, Jo-Jo realised she had probably said the wrong thing. They looked like two guinea pigs engaged in some macabre mating game with her feet. After those, the stripy socks and cerise beaded shirt that Peace was wearing somehow seemed inevitable.

'Oh, Peace couldn't give a toss about clothes,' Harry said fondly, moving his arm from around her shoulder to examine the label inside her shift.

'I mean, this says Kristof Couture, for instance, but it might as well be Oxfam for all she cares.'

'That's not quite true, Harry. As a matter of fact I was thinking of organising a charity auction of famous people's clothes,' said Peace, accidentally smearing some wasabi paste into her denim skirt. 'It's just that I don't feel I have to write a dissertation on them as well.'

'Yes, but how can you help sell them if you don't have any interest in them?' asked Jo-Jo, baffled. She wanted job satisfaction and that came from throwing yourself into the task whole-heartedly. She was beginning to worry that Peace might not have much to teach her. There was so much to learn and so little time. She would be off to Italy any minute, and everyone said the Milanese took the business of selling clothes very seriously indeed. She contemplated asking Cassie for some advice, but she seemed hopelessly distracted these days. Jo-Jo was really starting to wonder if she had lost her grip. If she got through the shows in one piece, it would be no thanks to her frigging agent.

Seth, when he wasn't thinking about Finn's or Janie, was growing concerned about Cassie. She looked strained and somehow smaller than when he'd first met her. The police were still paying visits – once or twice she had brought them down for morning coffee into the bar at Finn's in order, Seth imagined, not to have them hanging around the Hot Shots office unsettling her staff. 'You don't suppose there *is* anything in these allegations?' he asked Janie one evening.

'No.' She looked shocked. 'None at all. For all her world-liness, Cassie's as straight as they come – and in some ways she's even quite a naïf. That cynicism is a front. I just hope she isn't winding the police up.'

She made Seth promise that he would try to eavesdrop the next time Cassie and Reece came in. In all other respects he was absurdly happy. He was really starting to believe Janie when she said that her marriage to Matthew was over. He knew he couldn't rush things, but that suited him. He decided he should definitely whisk her off somewhere exotic – perhaps when she got back from New York, around the middle of November – so that they could be alone together. He'd have to plan it in secrecy otherwise she might object to leaving the children, and he'd have to sound out Gloria to see if she would mind looking after them while Janie was away. Gloria. There was a stumbling block. Janie swore that she was a treasure, but Seth found her prickly and entirely resistant to his charms. But as images of sun-swept coves and romantic hotels increasingly distracted him from the weekly figures at Finn's, he resolved that even Gloria wouldn't stand in his way. He was just browsing in the travel section of his favourite bookshop when he noticed a copy of a second-hand book on topiary that had been put back in the wrong place.

'That's a rare one, that is,' said the assistant helpfully. 'Been out of print for ages.' Seth added it to his pile of books on Africa, India and the South Pacific. He would send it to Janie's hotel in Milan so that it was waiting for her when she got there. He knew how much she was dreading going, and couldn't help hoping that he might have a little to do with her regret at leaving London.

To add to Janie's impending sense of catastrophe, Edward Rushmore was on a big PR drive, and over lunch at Kensington Place with Janie and a scowling Phyllida had told them he wanted them to accept every television interview that came their way.

'No daytime TV chat show too humble, girls. Our market research people assure me that every time a *Gazette* journalist appears on television or radio our circulation increases by two to three per cent. Incredible, I know, until you consider all those undecided, floating readers hovering at the news kiosk every morning. And if it's a question of a Janie Pember appearance, I'd say that figure increases by ten per cent at least,' he continued teasingly, blissfully unaware of Phyllida's savage expression. 'After your performance on *Newsnight* I'd say you were a natural. We'll have to bear that in mind if we ever manage to get our cable channel off the ground.'

She also felt that every statistical blip in the newspapers identifying a new malaise amongst children whose mothers worked full time was aimed directly at her. Gloria was increasingly tense as well. To soften the blow of her departure, she had agreed to carry on doing the ironing for some of the families she used to clean for, and parts of the house were starting to look like a Chinese laundry. As Departure for Milan day loomed, Janie was by turns tearful, resentful and, most confusingly, excited.

'Welcome to Guilt-Ridden Mothers Anonymous,' Gina Martin, looking more harassed than usual, commiserated with her in the *Gazette*'s canteen the Friday before Janie was due to leave. Damien, the new cook, had installed some stripy parasols in a baleful attempt to make it look continental.

'You can't win, Janie,' said Gina, sounding resigned, 'because whatever you do it's an awful, messy, frustrating compromise. And husbands don't make much difference as far as I can see. I'm still the one who always gets the kids to school. The worst thing is you know the alternatives aren't any better. Look at me. I've been promising I'd go part time ever since my eldest was six months old and now he's thirteen. I felt vile about it for years' – she stabbed a soggy chip— 'and angry as hell with the male conspiracy that made things so tough for me. Then I realised I was quite enjoying it all.' She trotted back to the counter and returned with some apple pie that looked as though it predated Damien's redesign by several decades.

Janie wondered what kept Gina so buoyant. 'The trouble

is,' she began tentatively, pushing some lurid coleslaw round her plate, 'that there really aren't any role models on the *Gazette* who inspire me with any confidence. I'm starting to think that newspapers and children just don't mix. I mean, out of three hundred and forty full-time journalists, probably only a tenth are mothers with more than one child, and – no offence, Gina – they're all either superwomen or maniacs.'

'None taken. I'll assume I fall into the former category. Only of course I don't – no one does. We all get by on a wing and a prayer. I suppose it was that report in the paper yesterday about the children of career mothers being more prone to depression and petty crime that's set all this off? God, that survey comes out every year. I wouldn't be surprised if Phyllida commissions it to give the rest of us really low self-esteem. What all that research never takes into account is how proud children are of their parents' achievements – how they enjoy boasting about their mum's high-powered job to all their little school chums. Okay, maybe keeping pace with Phyllida and getting home in time for bedtime stories does make us a bit manic – but have you ever spent more than a week with the lot who don't work but drive themselves and their offspring mad competing to see whose child can cram in the most after-school Suzuki violin lessons?'

The strange thing was that Janie couldn't very clearly remember much about her existence before Matthew left. She had been back at work less than twelve months, but frighteningly, her time at the *Gazette* seemed more vivid than the years she had spent at home. She supposed she must have frittered them, whereas now she was engaged in the important pursuit of interviewing fashion designers and socialites . . . She wondered if she would feel better about being separated from her children if she were working on a cure for cancer or a car that didn't foul up the environment or even a shampoo that hadn't, in any of its constituent parts, ever been near a rabbit's eyes and didn't start fizzing after a fortnight.

'None of it would be quite so bad if what I was writing about wasn't so futile and embarrassing,' she said dolefully.

'Hmm,' said Gina thoughtfully, 'I see your point.'

And then there was Seth. Thoughtful, wonderful Seth, whom she'd seen for about ten hours in the past fortnight. And just when it looked as though he might actually get the odd day off from the restaurant to spend with her, she had to go to Milan, Paris and New York. Half of her wondered if she could do the whole season by satellite link-up. The other half found itself drawing up lists of the outfits she would wear while she was away.

In her first fortnight in Manhattan, Madeleine's realtor had shown her thirty-three apartments. Staving off the inevitable hour when she would have to close the door on her hotel room and settle down to another TV dinner, she had seen an average of three rentals a night – from downtown lofts in the meat packers' district, to chunks of converted brownstones in the village, to small suites of rooms on the Upper West Side, to even smaller suites of rooms on the Upper East Side.

'It would help,' her indefatigably cheery realtor began, sounding distinctly peeved, 'if you could decide which bit of Manhattan you wanted to live in.'

'The thing is,' Madeleine explained for the umpteenth time, 'I don't really care about the district. It's the apartment itself that matters.'

'So what was wrong with the three you saw last night?' The voice was being patient and the strain was becoming audible.

'The first one only had two windows. The second one looked out on to a morgue and had no central heating, no air-conditioning and no elevator past the ninth floor. The third, on the corner of Sixty-ninth and Madison, was smaller than my trunk.'

There was a wounded pause. 'Getting picky, are we?'

Things were a little better at work. Since her arrival, she had been shadowing Tom, for whose natural good humour she would be eternally grateful, particularly as some of the

other design directors had predictably looked as thrilled to
see her as if they'd just been asked to design an outsize
range for K-Mart. Her own team, the one that worked on
the mainline Tom Fitzgerald collection, were a little more
polite, but nervous, especially some of the older ones who
had heard rumours that Madeleine had been brought in to
modernise the range and lived in fear for their jobs. There
was a pervading neurosis that Madeleine found exhausting, and
there was none of the after-hours casual socialising that she used
to enjoy so much in London. But there were compensations.
There was certainly plenty to keep her busy, and Tom was
packing her off on a state-by-state tour just as soon as the
show was over so that she could get a real sense of who she
was designing for.

She loved the back-up that came with a big organisation;
being able to order up samples in six different colour ways, have
Tom's accessory designers submit three different proposals for
the next collection. Also, her department was on the fifteenth
floor of a solidly built pre-war building, and the view up Seventh
Avenue was exhilarating. The Fitzgerald empire occupied five
floors altogether, and part of a building round the corner. Kevin
Krocket also had a floor of the Seventh Avenue building, as did
Oscar de la Renta, Carolina Herrera and Bill Blass. Madeleine
couldn't get used to bumping into them sometimes in the
elevator. The New York fashion world, for all its global
aspirations, operated like a village.

The best thing about her move was that, to her immense relief,
she genuinely liked the simple and refreshingly casual clothes that
were the basis of Tom Fitzgerald's design philosophy. Looking
back through some of the archives, she realised that when he was
on form Tom had produced some of the best American sportswear
around. Even though the collections had been under par during the
last few years, and there had been too much focus on fussy fads in
a misguided attempt to be cutting-edge, Madeleine was confident
she could help steer the company back to its much-admired origins.
The more time she spent researching in the library, where Tom
kept all the files of editorial coverage over the years as well as

the seminal outfits and accessories from each collection, the more she became convinced that the road to salvation lay in redefining and updating some of the old products. The Fitzgerald hacking jacket that had been such a massive hit in the seventies was a great shape. She was sure that if they reintroduced it in a slightly longer version, this time with a tie-belt and manufactured it in ponyskin, dark denim and suede as well as the tweed it had been made up in first time round, they could have another cult smash.

'They're kinda neat.'

Madeleine looked up from her sketches, startled, and came face to suntanned face with a crooked smile and floppy fringe that she recognised as belonging to Leonardo Lamotta, design director for Fitzgerald menswear and only recently returned from a store-opening in Stockholm.

'Neat?'

'Isn't that what British people expect all Americans to say? Neat. It's meant to sum up our general inadequacy in the face of the English language.'

Sensing that he may have set off on the wrong foot, he smiled at her again, a little sheepishly this time.

'Actually, I mean it. Those jackets you've drawn really do look neat – as in sleek and trim and somehow tidy. A nice change from those dumb power shoulders. I think you might be on to something. I've been feeling for a time that it's the moment to get back to neatness and clothes that look, you know, sort of well bred. The fashion world's crying out for an end to idiotic gimmicks. Everyone's waiting for a kind of modern Jackie O look.' He fished out a restaurant card from his pocket and doodled something on the back. He pushed it over to her: it was an exquisitely precise sketch of a knee-length, slightly flared wrap skirt, a pair of wide-legged trousers that stopped just above the ankle, and a flat circular bag that would look perfect with her jacket. There was another silence while she watched his long, fine fingers slotting Madeleine's jacket over the skirt he had drawn.

The silence unnerved him.

'Look, sorry if I sounded a little defensive earlier—'
But Madeleine wasn't sulking. She was in awe.

Well, bugger me slowly, thought Squidge as he looked up from
the six-page Channel 4 crested document that he had absent-
mindedly arranged into a fan shape on Aeron's Maurice Dufrene
desk. Even Aeron, who was becoming difficult to please lately,
had to admit that it was quite a coup to have Martika Jansen
begging to profile him on *Arts Nouveaux*, her *Late Look* spin-off
series. For in a fit of artistic consciousness-raising or, as its
more cynical critics suggested, a craven attempt to divert the
television watchdog commission from its forthcoming season of
Chinese pornography, Channel 4 had given Martika a weekly
hour-long profile slot that was scheduled to go out opposite
The South Bank Show on Sunday nights. Squidge thought it
sounded drearily pretentious, but it would certainly increase
Aeron's credibility. He resolved to send a video of it to Gilles
de Gaumard at Tigre-Luxe.

Half an hour later Aeron sauntered upstairs to the studio
with Unity and Jo-Jo, who had dropped in together for their
fittings on their way to the airport. Even though London
was considered hip, Squidge and Aeron, in their bid for The
Holy de Gaumard, had decided to continue showing in Paris,
but were having fittings in both places to accommodate the
models' schedules. Chewing on a Rizla, Aeron slipped an
embryonic absinthe silken slip dress over Jo-Jo's head with
the beginnings of velvet appliqué traced across the train which
lapped like a puddle around her bare feet. He began working
the cloth with his hands, delicately bunching little folds of it
here and there with his left, while his right alternately pinned
and chalked.

'Okay, so give us the low-down, Aeron. What's the story
this time?' twittered Unity, reaching for her nicotine patches.

Aeron took a deep breath.

'It's . . . nothing. You know, *le grand néant* – Sartre and
all that lot. It's kind of minimalism meets existentialism meets

nihilism, y'know? There is no story. No gimmicks. No distractions. I may not even have any bleedin' music. Look, the point is, it's just beautiful clothes, right?'

Squidge was about to shoot him a poisonous look when his eyes locked with Jo-Jo's in the speckled mirror precariously wedged on a window sill. Like Squidge, she was inspecting herself in the dress for the first time. Aeron had somehow curved it into the small of her back and over the valley of her stomach so that it clung to her like perspiration. The outline of her breasts and hips was gracefully accentuated, although the dress had no padding or interfacing. It was amazingly erotic. Aeron twisted Jo-Jo's hair into the nape of her neck.

'It's gonna be really simple, sort of thirties Modigliani. Dodie's designed the make-up so it looks really mournful, and there'll be very little jewellery. You know that thing Vreeland said about elegance being refusal? Yeah, well, that's what this is, refusal.'

Jo-Jo wrapped her elbow round the crown of her head in a languid pose that was straight out of a Horst photograph. Surrounded by the detritus of Aeron's studio, she looked breathtaking. The dress, even in its unfinished state, was exquisite. Not for the first time, Squidge was rendered speechless by his partner's prodigious talent.

Janie pulled Seth's arms further round her and edged her head further up his chest. They were lying on her sofa feeding each other king prawns in a Last Supper scenario. They had spent the morning with Nell and the twins in Richmond Park, which had seemed like the most natural thing in the world. Nell had slipped her hand into Seth's and told him that she had overheard her teacher saying that her social skills were above average because she had such a varied cast of people in her life.

'Would you say your daughter was a teensy bit precocious?' he asked Janie, grinning.

'Only when she's flirting.' It was true. Nell had developed a crush on Seth, perhaps because he was teaching her to cook, unlike Gloria, who after an initial burst of enthusiasm on the culinary front, had directed Nell's energies towards household cleaning. Seth's encouragement had an air of permanence about it. It had been a wonderful day. Janie had barely given Matthew a thought except to wonder whether she should send a card to Guatemala for his birthday.

Later Seth had asked her if she'd like to come away with him for a few days when the shows were all over.

'I thought maybe somewhere warm, peaceful – where there's no option but for you to be with me the whole time – where I can get intimate with your psyche, discover your darkest secrets – have a stab at getting you into bed . . .'

Janie's mouth twitched.

By mid-evening the mood had turned slightly melancholy. She was flying to Milan the next morning and had begun recounting the low points of her last trip to the collections. But to her chagrin, Seth was laughing.

'The trouble with you is that you secretly enjoy it all.'

'I do not,' retorted Janie indignantly, retrieving a piece of shell from her tongue.

'Okay, what's the single worst thing?'

'Impossible to narrow it down.'

'See.'

'Okay, okay. The single worst thing – apart from the people, the clothes, the designers, the shows . . . oh, and having to wear sunglasses indoors at night, you mean? Well, it has to be missing the children – and missing you.'

There, she had said it. And instantly regretted it. Seth would have to respond in kind, if only out of politeness, and she wasn't ready for any protestations of love, or even friendship, right now. She went to fetch another bottle of wine from the fridge, then pretended she had heard Jake crying and spent the next ten minutes hovering by his cot, willing him to wake up and trying to figure out why she was being so stupid.

Chapter Fourteen

It was Tulah's phone call from the police station, almost comical in its childish defiance, which caused Cassie's carefully nurtured stoicism to crumble.

'Hi,' she said in a sad little attempt at perky rebelliousness. 'Er, I've been busted. Me and Dodie and Enrico.' As if there were defence in numbers. 'For possession of cannabis.' Attempt at outrage. 'We were relaxing after a hard day's grind with Dirk, you know, just chilling out in Dodie's room and the pigs jackbooted in.'

Tulah, of course, was too wrapped up in her own martyrdom to have devoted much thought to what the consequences of her predicament might be for anyone else.

'So, Cassie, how soon d'you think you can get your lawyer, Michael thingummy, up to me? This cell, now I look at it in the clear light of day, is grossaroo. I wouldn't be surprised if it turned out that I could sue the police for abusing my human rights.'

'Except that to do that you'd have to show evidence that you were human,' Cassie snapped. There was an ominous silence, then the unmistakable sound of muffled tears. Cassie felt wretched. Tulah wasn't a bad girl, and it wasn't her fault that she had only managed to acquire the most rudimentary education. She meekly told Tulah that she would get on to him right away. In fact Michael had already called her at ten past seven that morning, just as soon as he'd heard Tulah's news on Radio 4, but Cassie didn't feel it was the right moment to tell

Tulah that her private tussle with the police was now an issue for national debate.

She dragged herself into work, expecting the cool, dry hand of Inspector Reece to be placed on her shoulder at any moment. But the office – or her direct line, at any rate – was ominously calm. Cassie couldn't help feeling that the entire Hot Shots enterprise radiated defeat. In the past, the phones would have been ringing non-stop around the clock from across the globe. In fact, they still were, but most of the calls for Cassie were from tabloid reporters, and Trudy valiantly shielded her from them.

She wished Saffron were there, but Saffron had brought her holiday forward so that she could be her best friend's birthing partner in Melbourne, and she and Cassie hadn't had time to patch up their quarrel. It was just as well she'd gone, thought Cassie glumly. Any minute now Inspector Reece would probably confiscate their passports. At 9.30 Trudy finally put a call through to her. It was Seth.

'I just wanted to say you're not to panic. I don't know much about the law but I'd be amazed if they could pin Tulah's little indiscretion on you.'

Cassie was touched and pretended to be comforted, but nothing could quell her mounting alarm. She had half a mind to hand herself into Inspector Reece now – the suspense was unbearable. The phone rang again. It was Zack.

'Listen, I know it's probably the last thing on your mind, but I've just taken up Boxercising and it's brilliant for stress. I could get a trainer over to you this afternoon.'

At a quarter past ten, Janie called her from Milan airport. But before she could do much more than ask Cassie how she was feeling, she ran out of tokens and the pips went.

As she put down the receiver in frustration, Janie heard someone behind her mangling the words to David Bowie's 'Fashion'. She turned round, her frown dissolving mid-rotation. She hadn't realised until this moment quite how much she had missed Sissy.

'Listen, I need a tights conversation and pronto. Here I am, having slaved for three weeks to get my legs glossy and brown – no mean feat, let me tell you, when they're prone to suffering from acute sun allergy. And what do I see at the carousel? Only that we're having a black trouser-suit moment. I wouldn't mind, but that bunch of crows from *Beau Monde* and *A La Mode* expressly tell their readers in this month's issues that white and pussy pelmets rule this winter.'

Sissy's legs were gleaming and naked, as was quite a lot of the rest of her. Janie stepped back and looked at her admiringly. Her carrot mop had softened in the sun to a strawberry blond. The freckles on her lightly tanned face intensified the effect of the violet contact lenses. Dressed head to toe in cream, where normally she was a field of khaki, black or some other sludgy colour that was uniquely unbecoming to her, she looked scrubbed, youthful and glamorous – and something else, which Janie couldn't quite pinpoint. She hugged her.

'Oh, Sissy, it's always a black moment. I wouldn't worry. Revivals are coming round so fast now, they'll be back in the pelmets by the end of the week. I never thought I'd say this, but I am so glad to see you. It's been deathly without you.'

'Not what I gather. Did Tom Fitzgerald sue, by the way?'

'It wasn't that bad,' said Janie indignantly. They were standing in the taxi queue. In Sissy's absence, Janie had quailed at Phyllida's ranting and taken some cost-cutting measures. There would be no Massimo this season. Sissy appeared not to notice. Janie had never seen her look so relaxed, or so normal.

'I can't get over it,' she blurted, when they had decanted their luggage into the boot of a taxi. 'You look so un-fashion. No funny tics, no odd accessories . . . you look terrific.'

'Oh, I'm over tics,' said Sissy blithely. 'I've been thinking long and hard about my life and career while I've been away. Do you know that this is the first real holiday I've had in five years? Anyway, I decided that too much fashion is bad for your sex life. I thought it might make a good piece, actually. I don't want to look cutting-edge any more, I want to look like Sharon Stone. Isn't it amazing how cream reflects light on to the skin, by the way? Now I know why clever old Anastasia never wears black during the day.'

She shrugged off her single-breasted cream Prada coat and adjusted the straps beneath her silk shirt. As she wriggled around, Janie glimpsed Sissy's newly rounded contours. Either she had eaten very well in Argentina, or she had discovered a miracle bra. Before she could engineer the conversation delicately on to the subject, Sissy was asking her about Seth.

'It's wonderful – except that we never seem to have enough time together. But we're going to try and sneak off for a weekend in the country after the shows, which will be wonderful. Nell seems to have really taken to him, and even Cassie, who's never liked my boyfriends, thinks he's—'

'Wonderful,' chimed in Sissy. 'He's done wonders for your objectivity, at any rate.'

They made a small detour via the XTC and Gucci stores, where Sissy negotiated large discounts on two investment pur-chases and Janie amazed them both by buying two pairs of sunglasses, one of which was a present for Lorna, who had given her vital moral support through the London shows and had even got her byline into the paper for the first time, with a small review of the Fabio Piras show. The second pair she put straight on to shield her from Lindsey Craven's increasingly vitriolic gaze.

Sissy's purchases were symbolic of her new departure into result wear: the first was a slinky knee-length dress in a dull gold knit which, they both agreed, worked fabulously under the cream coat. The other a pair of strappy high heels. As she tried the dress and sandals on together in the XTC shop, Janie realised what was different about Sissy. She looked sexy. And from the way the dress clung to her nipples, Janie was intrigued to see that it clearly had nothing to do with lingerie technology.

'You cannot be serious,' exclaimed Sissy as they dragged their luggage across the chipped tutti-frutti-effect lino of Il Splendido's lobby.

'It is a bit bleak,' conceded Janie, tufts of the antique raffia-trimmed lampshade she had bought in a shop opposite

XTC catching on her lip-gloss. 'Phyllida said it was standard *Gazette* accommodation.'

'Standard when exactly? I don't suppose a single journalist from the *Gazette* has been to Milan since Mussolini.'

Janie looked depressed.

'Look, here's what we do. We tell Phyllida that Il Splendido is overbooked – they're always doing that in Milan – and that the only rooms in town were at the Grand di Milan.'

Months later, when Janie came to appraise her life in fashion journalism objectively, she realised that it was at this precise moment that she must have reached some kind of moral turning point, because she didn't have the slightest inclination to argue with Sissy.

'Of course, you know why that lot always look so sleek,' said Sissy, looking up from a copy of the *Financial Times*. They were waiting for Vittorio Chacha's show to start.

'Which lot?' asked Janie sleepily.

'The American magazine posse? It's because they get up at five every morning to have their make-up and hair professionally done. Isabella told me that one of Dodie's assistants goes to Lee Howard's suite morning and evening during the collections. Slaps it on her expenses as part of her PR budget.'

'Don't even think about it. Phyllida would never sanction it,' said Janie nervously.

'Still, it makes a change from tattoos and piercing. Isabella's got so many studs in her navel she'll start to leak soon . . . this agro-chic look's going a bit far, don't you think? I mean, what will fashion victims do next to shock – go in for a bit of amputation?'

'Nice to see you're finally taking an objective stance on victimhood. I didn't know how to tell you this, but it got pretty exhausting sometimes trying to work out when something had gone badly wrong with your outfits and when it was a deliberate style statement . . . When did you see Isabella, by the way?'

'Oh, you know, just around. And Petronella sleeps with her

Manolos, by the way. How kinky is that? Any feedback about the Nari profile?'

'Mm, lots. Very positive,' lied Janie. She had been desperately trying to drum up support for Sissy's piece amongst the editorial heads at the *Gazette*. 'I've been thinking; we should work a lot more in collaboration with the City pages. Try and get out of this rut of sensationalist profiles and petty dissection of what people are wearing.'

Fortunately, before Sissy could respond, the lights went down and Bethany and Isabella stomped down the catwalk in matching feathered Maori cloaks.

At last, Detective Inspector Reece felt he had more than legitimate reason to cross-examine every one of the models on Cassie's books. This time he would accept no excuses about the sacred nature of uncancellable assignments. And if any of them got stroppy, he'd haul the lot of them in for mandatory drug testing.

'You could always share mine.'

'Thanks, but I don't do frothy milk.'

'I wasn't talking about the *latte*. I meant my apartment.'

They were sitting in the window of Lucky Strike in Sotto, basking in the autumnal sunshine.

'Leonardo, that's terribly sweet but—' Madeleine had glimpsed his apartment briefly one night when she had called to collect him on their way to the cinema. It was big and airy, and if you leaned a long way out of its large windows you could just glimpse little green patches of park.

'Listen, I'm not hitting on you. It's just that one, I happen to live in this great, spacious apartment on the Upper West Side, two blocks from Central Park. Two, the guy who's been sharing it with me has just been posted to Shanghai. Three, I can't afford to keep it on my own. I should be able to on my salary I know, but well, I'm helping my family out a little at the moment. And

I know you've had a few financial difficulties of your own—'
startled – he had never broached the subject of her business
collapse before, nor even hinted that he knew anything about
it, she looked at him suspiciously. Tactfully he didn't pursue that
line. 'So you would be doing me as much a favour as I would you,
because if you don't move in I don't think I can face interviewing
fifty responses to an ad. And if I don't find someone to share, I'll
have to move out on my own, which would make two of us
looking for squalid, overpriced rat cages. Which doesn't make
economic sense at all. As you well know.'

Madeleine tried desperately not to sound too eager.

'How do you know I'm not a single white female?'

'You *are* a single white female, but if you move in with me
you'll be a semi-detached one.'

'Economically and even ergonomically you're right, but . . .
Oh, I don't know, Leonardo. Living *and* working together – is
that wise?'

'Well, it's not as if we're on top of one another at the
office. Half the time we're in separate buildings. And frankly,
Ms Peterson, being my room-mate might give you some much-
needed credibility about the place. You have to admit that right
now you could use all the public displays of friendship you can
muster.'

He was right, thought Madeleine ruefully. She wasn't exactly
Miss Popular over at Planet Fitzgerald. Leonardo said it was
because she had too many good ideas and because Tom was
obviously mad about her, which, on the days that she believed
him, made her feel marginally better.

She still couldn't get used to the resources available to
successful American designers. Tom employed three people
just to scour the world's best shops and markets for him.
Every so often they would return to Manhattan and spend a
week arranging everything into themed room sets for Tom and
the other team heads to examine. It sounded like the ideal job
for Sissy, Madeleine thought, if a little obsessive.

'Doesn't it get lonely?' she asked.

Anna Trewlit, who had just returned from a trip round

India, Australia and Fiji with trunks of exquisite finds, from scraps of aboriginal textiles and Fijian woodwork and jewellery to the entire collection of an up-and-coming lingerie designer in Sydney, looked at Madeleine in astonishment.

'Why, no. I have my Treasures. And if ever I get a little homesick for my apartment, I just unwrap everything I've bought and arrange it round the hotel room so it looks completely different.'

Sick, thought Madeleine, surveying the beaded Indian lampshades and carved statues that were clearly Anna's surrogate children, but very pretty. The fabrics that Anna had brought back would possibly appear at a later date, Tom explained, in one of the Fitzgerald homeware ranges. They would have to be reworked, of course, because they were a little too ethnic in their current state, but the colours were perfect for next year's rug collection. The jewellery was the perfect complement for the spring mainline clothes, and would probably be used, as it was, for the catwalk show. The exquisite lingerie, Madeleine knew, would be dissected on the cutting table and used as the basis for the TF evening-wear section.

The ethics of all this troubled her. She had always known that plagiarism at this level went on. Once, a well-known model – the 'face' of Paolo Bianco, the hugely successful Italian designer – had bought eighteen of Madeleine's outfits from Harvey Nichols and to her certain knowledge, they too had ended up on Paolo's cutting table. She had even been quite flattered at the time. But to be colluding with it herself was a different story.

'Ah, don't worry about it,' said Kevin Krocket, when she delicately broached the subject with him over a pastrami sandwich in the deli next to their communal building. 'Design these days is in the editing.'

Tom, Madeleine privately conceded, was a brilliant editor.

'But it's not fair on the little designers.'

'Oh puh- leese. Little, schmittle. We're all at it. Don't tell me you've never been into that fabulous Victoria and Albert of yours to do a little "research" into Charles Worth or Molyneux. I know I have. I've even been inspired by some old Tom

Fitzgeralds. It's part of the great circle of life. And incidentally, I might be little by American standards, but I still turn over eighteen million dollars a year.'

He was right. She had sometimes delved into the past for ideas. She'd never gone as far as buying up somebody else's designs so that she could cut them up and crib them, but then she'd never been able to afford to. Perhaps it wasn't that Tom copied more than anyone else, simply that he did it better. The problem was that she needed to stop seeing everything from a British perspective and start looking at life though robust American eyes.

'You're on, Leonardo. But I'm warning you, I'm fanatically tidy. Joan Crawford has nothing on *my* phobia about wire hangers.'

At 3 p.m., Trudy ushered Inspector Reece into Cassie's office. He looked too burly and prosaic for it. His feet, planted parallel on her sisal matting, looked absurdly large. She was needed over at Scotland Yard, for routine enquiries. There's nothing routine about it as far as I'm concerned, thought Cassie grimly. She walked out of the office as calmly as she could, abreast of him, not behind. Thank God detective inspectors were plainclothes – and thank God it had been Reece's sidekick who had interviewed her staff. She sauntered past the two round tables of agent bookers and waved them a casual goodbye, as if she were just nipping out for a haircut. With any luck none of them would realise what was going on. The uniform shape of their eyes, as round as the little mouthpieces on their telephone headsets, unfortunately suggested otherwise.

'I had no idea things were so bad with Cassie. It all seemed to have blown over before I went away,' said Sissy. They were swigging Salty Dogs in the bar of the Grand de Milan. It had been a long day. Five shows, five delays and not a single new idea.

'Well, I don't suppose Tulah's little escapade helped matters.

But I have to say, the whole thing's very fishy. I didn't tell you what happened the night of Seth's party, did I?' She told Sissy about the fax.

'God, it's a bit melodramatic, isn't it? I mean, you can almost hear the cod mafioso accent.'

'Well, if someone is setting her up,' said Janie grimly, 'they're doing it very effectively. The police won't leave her alone. Reece seems intent on interrogating every model who's ever been on her books, which will take for ever, of course, as they're always away, and turn out to be utterly futile. It's so unfair.'

'Is it? Cassie might be innocent, but who knows about all the girls on her books. She can't possibly superintend them all. Some of them might have been smuggling drugs and some of the bookers might have been using their models' accounts to launder money. There's so much sloshing around in that business, and a lot of it cash. Anything could have gone on under Cassie's nose and she might not necessarily have known about it.'

'I'm not sure I like it when you're this objective.'

Janie finally got through to Cassie at Blomfield Road the next day. She sounded drained, as she was entitled to, having spent most of the preceding night at the police station – but more worryingly, she sounded defeated. She was talking about closing Hot Shots regardless of whether or not the police finally got round to charging her.

After her conversation with Cassie, Janie had been in no mood to sit through the pretentious offering from XTC, which was entitled 'Vivre La Mort', nor read the programme which droned on illiterately about 'the religiosity of sheer'. She pounded out five hundred scathing words on the show for Doug Channing.

Donatella and Giovanna Extasia, the two designers behind the hugely successful XTC label, seem to labour under the impression that what women really need in life is a wardrobe of clothes that make them look as though they're suffering from chronic osteoporosis. Sometimes, of course, the avant-garde, when we first see it, looks strange, even ugly. Sometimes it takes years for it to be accepted by the mainstream as beautiful. But if it is truly ground-breaking, it never insults women. What Donatella and Giovanna showed in this new collection did precisely that. It was very ugly, very insulting and, perhaps worst of all, very foolish. Fashion designers shouldn't continue to get away with this kind of dross. Any right-thinking woman would be wise to boycott all their products this season.

'Blimey,' said Doug, 'makes a change from the usual copy, which, if you don't mind my saying, errs on the complimentary side.'

After the day's final show was over at eight, she flung herself on to her bed. It was too late to call the children. They were staying with her mother, and Eleanor, generally exhausted early in the day by their antics, liked to have them in bed by five.

The phone rang. It was Sissy.

'I thought I'd better remind you, before you get too engrossed in the remote control, that the last helicopter leaves in forty minutes.'

'What are you talking about?'

'Oh, Janie, you can't have forgotten. It's only the other party of the year – Paolo Bianco's ActivSport launch. He's helicoptering us all out to St Moritz. Why else do you think he sent out all those ski outfits?'

Janie groaned. She had been looking forward to a night on the phone. First to Seth and then, probably, to Tom. He had taken to calling her with what he called his cultural-exchange updates every week or so. She peered inside her wardrobe. Sissy was right. The padded cream pouf she had mistaken for a spare pillow was indeed a quilted ski jacket, with a crimson PBAS logo which looked like a feeble facsimile of the Nike swoosh spattered across its back. Her heart sank. It would be at least eleven o'clock before they got there, but there would be hell to pay if Phyllida found out she hadn't gone. According to Sissy, Bianco had lured Todd Woodward from the set of his latest £150 million action movie to act as guest of honour, along with half a dozen or so Hollywood luminaries, and Quentin Coady, the Oscar-winning set designer, had been working on the igloo concept for months. It sounded ghastly. She turned the shower on full in the hope that the steam would revive her and flicked on the remote while she waited for the bathroom to mist up.

They were screening the end of the Dolce e Gabbana show. Isabella, pony-stepping through a pool of neon light, was a Valkyrian figure in a silver lamé goddess dress. Just the other side of Isabella, Janie could make out Magnus fanning himself in the second row, pausing only to scribble a brief note, probably facetious, to the exhausted-looking journalist next to him: herself. Whatever you thought about Isabella, she looked amazing, thought Janie. Perhaps the rumour about her having been a teenage stripper was true. If so, it had certainly paid off – she really knew how to work an outfit.

She was about to switch channels when Jo-Jo appeared in the final frock, a chiffon confection with embroidered roses. The entire outfit was barely the size of a petal and made a fine showcase for Jo-Jo's legs. How was it possible to be simultaneously fine-boned and voluptuous? It defied the laws of physics. Jo-Jo had already mastered her particular catwalk turn, a serene, athletic stride and a secretive half-smile. Halfway along, she was joined in her odyssey by Stefano Gabbano and Domenico Dolce themselves, who put their arms around her and kissed her expansively on her forehead. Quite a tribute. Janie tapped the other buttons, wondering if there might be news of Tulah. Instead, on RAT 2, she found live coverage of Paolo Bianco's party.

Limited as Janie's Italian was, it soon became clear that disaster was taking shape on the screen in front of her. Not much was happening, apart from the endless circling of a vortex of helicopters. And that, it transpired, was the problem. A group of animal rights lobbyists had staked themselves across the helipads to protest against Bianco's fur collection, and none of the helicopters could land. Police in riot shields had been called in, and a lengthening queue of forlorn-looking fashion editors shivered on the fringes of the scene. White placard-wavers gathered in the gloom like Ku Klux Clan figures, chanting

'Death to the murderers'. When Sissy called her from the lobby at twenty past eight, she had become so absorbed in the awfulness of the unfolding scene that she hadn't got round to changing. Reluctantly she tore her eyes from the screen and headed for the shower, but not before she had watched two policemen escort Zoffy Villeneuve from the scene for inciting the protesters to violence by taunting them with her pâté de foie gras sandwiches.

There were now four messages from Detective Inspector Reece on Jo-Jo's hotel voicemail requesting her to contact him. She had so far ignored all of them, but every time she walked into her room and saw the telephone's red light winking malevolently at her from the bedside table, she felt as though a squall of anger were about to carry her off. Not again. She'd been through police investigations before, when her father and stepfathers had been on the scene; had watched her mother suffer agonies of shame and humiliation. She simply couldn't let the whole cycle begin again.

'Disaster!' exclaimed Sissy, as she hurtled into the lobby to meet Janie. 'Todd Woodward, the guest of honour, has broken his leg.'

Janie and Sissy finally arrived at the helipads at quarter to nine. The winking neon-blue police lights gave the frosty night air a peculiarly poignant, modern beauty, Sissy thought. It was pretty ironic that staid old Paolo Bianco should be causing the biggest riot the city had witnessed since the Allies arrived in 1944.

The ruction had started when four hundred members of the public turned up to board the helicopters earlier in the evening. Apparently the rumour circulating Milan all that day – or perhaps it was true, another of Paolo's publicity stunts – was that the fifty most beautiful people to get there first would be flown, along with the other five hundred officially invited guests, out to St Moritz. The sight of the obstructing protesters had whipped the crowd into a frenzy. The numbers had swelled dangerously with the addition of a hundred banner-wavers protesting against the inherent body fascism of only inviting conventionally attractive people.

It was with great regret that Hester Carmichael, chief protagonist of the animal rights group, called off the sit-in. Via a loudhailer and an interpreter, she addressed her fellow supporters, promising that she would devote the whole of her column in the *Washington Chronicle* tomorrow to the perfidy of Bianco's company.

And that was it. The protesters, both sets, drifted aimlessly away, and the guests began to board the helicopters. The views, through the glass-bottomed floor, as they pulled away from the sodium-lit streets, were dizzying. Before long they were soaring over treetops and the Alps loomed eerily ahead of them. Sissy hugged her knees excitedly and a hush fell over the passengers. Even Janie felt a frisson of anticipation.

The vista from the cabin window of The Proprietor's Gulfstream VI was pretty spectacular too. Anastasia gazed back wistfully at the darkly shadowed volcanic peaks of St Kitts. It had been a blissful eight days, despite her original misgivings.

It was true that her relationship with The Proprietor had progressed at roughly the same velocity as they were currently flying at in his jet. After Finn's opening they had drunk champagne in the bar of the Dorchester until the small hours. The following day he had sent her an opal-and-pearl bracelet to match, the accompanying note said, her eyes and skin; and after dinner on their second date she found herself accompanying him back to his house in Holland Park where, she fancied, she gave him a night to remember. Even so, Anastasia felt it was a little soon to be going on holiday with him and had fretted that it smacked of desperation on her part. Fortunately, he took it for impulsiveness, part of her exotic mysteriousness.

She sank back into the cream leather upholstery and

stretched out a bronzed foot fetchingly laced into Angel's finest silver lattice sandals. She had to hand it to the Red Door, they gave a good pedicure. The shoe boy was pretty talented too; she hoped the accounts he had promised to submit were as attractive as his shoes. The Proprietor had gone to talk to his pilot. Having demolished *Vogue*, *A La Mode* and *Friends of the RA* (not quite as thoroughly as the first two), she got out a mirror and checked her reflection. The sun had done her good, whatever beauty editors said about it. She felt relaxed, she looked rested and ridiculously youthful. A lock of white-blond hair fell in her eyes. She brushed it back and, as she did so, The Proprietor, emerging from the cockpit, seized her hand and brushed his lips against it.

'You've made me very happy this past week, Anastasia. Thank you.'

She laughed softly, touched. Although shorter than she generally liked, and grey-haired, with bright blue eyes that darted across their sockets like tropical fish in a too-small tank, he radiated power even when he was dressed in casual trousers and a beach shirt. He was clever and immensely well read for a business tycoon; a patron of the arts and, she had discovered while they were away, the owner of a couple of London theatres. A diary of twinkling First Nights beckoned at her invitingly. Anastasia had spent her life attaching herself to men for entirely Machiavellian motives. It seemed too good to be true that one of the world's most influential tycoons, now sitting directly opposite her, should turn out to be quite so irresistibly attractive. Her only cause for uneasiness was his devout churchgoing which, she could only hope, had taught him plenty about the divine importance of forgiving others their sins.

And now they were returning to Europe in time for her to make it to the fashion shows in Paris. While she was away she had been mulling over a new business route into the fashion business. Of course she would probably give Angel a few thousand to help him on his way. It would be amusing to be a backer – and might even give her good returns on her investment. But it would probably be peanuts compared to what she had in mind. It was Janie who had given her the idea when she had mentioned that a number of designers, including Bella Scarletti and Kevin Krocket, were frenetically searching for retail space in London. If Anastasia became their UK agent – and in her view she had all the right credentials and contacts – she would finally have found a respectable and lucrative source of income that would give her the perfect excuse to invest in yet more clothes. All she needed to do was establish herself publicly as someone who really knew about fashion. The interview she had done with Janie was the perfect starting point, except that the silly girl still hadn't run it, and now she must be away at the collections. Still, a little detail like that wasn't going to hinder Anastasia. She rubbed her big toe along the inside of The Proprietor's thigh, crooked her little finger at him and laughed seductively.

Seth mopped his brow for the umpteenth time. The autumn winds scattering leaves across Janie's lawn were chilly, but digging up the baby magnolia tree that Barry had finally succeeded in destroying was proving hot work and far more exhausting than he had envisaged. The sky, viscous and grey, seemed to hover six inches above his head, threatening to thunder before he'd finished. It would be worth it, though, to watch Janie light up when she saw the new one he was planting. He had asked around to find out where to go for a mature evergreen magnolia, and had ended up driving to a specialist nursery in Suffolk, returning to London with a twelve-foot beauty strapped to the roof of his car.

From time to time he caught Gloria eyeing him coldly from one of the upstairs windows, where she was hanging some new blinds. He still couldn't fathom why she disliked him so vehemently. Still, he had to hand it to her, she was nothing if not direct, and had made her disapproval of him clear from the start.

'You might be a very nice man, but Meess Janie ees already married,' she had told him reprovingly, once when they were alone in the kitchen. 'And marriage,' she continued, smashing some boiled potatoes, 'ees sacred.'

Seth knew it wouldn't help his case at all to point out that Matthew didn't appear to feel the same way, and left the kitchen defeated.

Janie said it was because Gloria had always adored Matthew.

'She hates all men but he alone – with the possible exception of Jesus Christ – can do no wrong in her eyes.'

If Gloria hadn't been quite so frosty, Seth would have quite liked to have asked her about Matthew. Janie, from loyalty and a sense of unresolved frustration, rarely discussed him. Seth respected this – indeed he showed a marked reluctance to talk about any of his past love affairs – but he couldn't help feeling curious all the same.

He wondered what would happen to him and Janie. One thing was for sure: he had to get her on her own for a while, and to hell with Gloria. He knew she had a bit of a gap between the Paris shows ending and the New York ones starting, so maybe he'd be able to organise something for then. It did mean he'd have to butter Gloria up, so she would look after the children. But it would be worth it. Otherwise he'd never feel he'd really given their friendship, or whatever it was, a chance to progress into anything else. In the past he had always been happy to let relationships drift along amiably, although things between him and Martha had ended up anything but amicable. Whatever happened, his relationship with Janie should never become acrimonious. For one thing it wasn't fair on the children. And, if he were honest, it didn't seem quite fair on him. He thought of her wearing his old tweed coat, which she had insisted on taking to Milan with her, even though he had said the other fashion editors would probably have it committed for fashion crimes. When she got back he would have to see if he couldn't somehow get her to finalise things with Matthew one way or another.

By unanimous vote, Brigitte was the human sensation of Paolo's party. Jean-Jacques, Enrico's rising protégé, had dyed her hair silver with a new fixing solvent he had discovered in a drug-store in SoHo, and she was wearing a pair of Aeron's silver-laméd bustle trousers to match.

The non-human sensation was the caged polar bear Paolo had had flown in, and the herd of reindeer, which had been dyed yellow, emerald and crimson – the colours of the ActivSport label.

'Good job the animal-righters aren't here. There'd be a war,' remarked Sissy.

'I think it's disgusting,' said Janie, pulling up the collar of Seth's coat. She felt cold despite the monstrous heaters whooshing out hot air.

'One must admit the igloos are impressive – in a surreal sort of way.' Magnus Finnegan, sporting his customary pastel cravat beneath a snow suit, had joined them.

They gazed at the two vast domes that had been fashioned out of imported bricks of ice. One had been laid out as a glacial dining room, with thousands of edelweiss floating in formaldehyde-filled stars that dangled precariously from the ceiling; the other had been cleared for dancing and gaming. Todd Woodward, his leg in plaster, was being spun round it in a wheelchair by Paolo Bianco's head of PR.

'Why doesn't he just give the money to charity?' said Janie disapprovingly.

''Twas ever thus, my dear,' said Magnus. 'Fashion parties have always been hopelessly tasteless. I think it was the inherent vulgarity of the whole business that finally caused Mildred Euphranie to throw herself from the twenty-third floor of Celestial Magazines. And that was back in 1947. She was wearing Balenciaga at the time. Such a waste.'

'Of Mildred or the Balenciaga?' prickled Janie.

'Touché, my dear. Probably the Balenciaga, to be honest. Mildred was past her prime.'

'Talking of bad looks,' said Sissy, 'Lindsey Craven's actually wearing her freebie ski jacket. Typical. By the way, I forgot to say that Doug rang from the office just before we left. He's beside himself with excitement. Some model has faxed the *Gazette* a photocopy of her breast.'

'How remarkably unpleasant,' shuddered Magnus.

'Yes, but the point is photocopied fashion pix are *tout le rage*. Joel Eliot's done an entire campaign using his laser printer. Anyway, apparently this particular bosom had a tiny scorpion tattooed over the nipple so it must be Isabella. I think she was very miffed at not being included in Joel's original oeuvre.'

'He's not running it?' said Janie, more resigned than indignant.

'Across four columns, I'm afraid. He's got some art buff to write a spurious piece about how modern technology is turning portraiture upside down. Portraits my elbow.'

'Wrong again,' sniffed Alice, gliding up in a fuchsia mink she must have stolen from the *A La Mode* fashion cupboard. 'It's a strictly boobs–or–buttocks genre.'

From the echoing recesses of one of the igloos, an electric guitar wailed the mournful opening chords of a familiar tune that had been rereleased with freshly composed lyrics commissioned by Paolo Bianco.

'Crikey, it can't be Scorcher Morehouse,' said Sissy, rushing off to investigate. 'What a prostitute. Any minute now he's going to launch into "Una Paloma Bianco".'

Janie went in search of Jo-Jo, whom she had glimpsed a moment earlier looking forlorn.

Paolo Bianco's people had done a formidable job with the guest list, wooing and blatantly bribing some of the entertainment world's most bankable stars, including four Oscar nominees and two past winners, plus a sprinkling of Euro-royals, into flying over for the evening. It was amazing how even the richest people could be bought for the price of an all-expenses weekend at the Villa d'Este and a new wardrobe of clothes. Of the man of the evening himself, there was no sign. 'Probably gone to hang himself in shame,' sniffed Magnus.

Janie found Jo-Jo kneeling down next to a wheelchair, engaged in polite conversation with Todd Woodward. She looked exquisite in an olive-green fur-lined silk Eskimo outfit that Jean-Paul Gaultier had sent her after he saw the picture of her wearing one of his ball-gowns in *A La Mode*. She extracted herself from Todd's vice-like clasp as soon as she could and led Janie over to the ice bar.

'God, thick or what!' she exclaimed.

'I think he's heavily sedated,' said Janie.

'Heavily made-up, more like. Did you see the mascara?'

They found an unoccupied patch of simulated walrus rug and sipped their frozen vodkas.

'Of course, beaver-trimmed beanbags are what every well-dressed igloo is wearing these days,' said Janie in disgust, leaning back into one.

'I know,' giggled Jo-Jo, 'but it's a laugh, isn't it?'

'Is it? I thought you looked a bit glum earlier. How's it going? Everyone says you're the new star of the shows, by the way.'

'Really?' Jo-Jo's eyes lit up. The truth was that she was experiencing tremendous highs and lows, and sometimes they almost smashed into one another. Apart from Unity, the other models, slightly wary of the hype surrounding her, weren't unkind, but nor were they exactly welcoming. She was tired, living in a permanent state of overexcited nervousness, and lonely. She had hoped Ben might make it to the party and stay for the weekend, but he couldn't get away from the set of *Sons and Lovers*.

Sissy slipped out of the sheepskin Aeron had lent her from his Primitives collection. The heaters, great angry-looking furnaces, had been stoked up to full, and Sissy could already see the ice bars beginning to melt. Rivulets of water were starting to trickle down the inside of the igloos, and the guests were perspiring in their arctic layers. Sissy had a terrible premonition of trouble, but at least now she could get some mileage out of the slinky lace dress she was wearing. She linked arms with Magnus and persuaded him to circulate round the igloos with her.

'You look healthy.' Lindsey Craven's eyes bore into Sissy's cleavage. 'Somebody obviously had a good holiday.'

Sissy ignored her. The response from the other fashion editors, though perhaps more subtle, was similar – an uncomfortable combination of curiosity and envy. For the first time in her career, Sissy was struck by the dearth of men at fashion parties. Maybe that was why all the women set such a premium on what they wore – they were always dressing to impress each other. And women, as Sissy knew only too well, were one another's most vicious critics.

'We are a bunch of terrible bitches, aren't we?' she sighed.

'I know I am,' said Magnus, sidling up to a waiter and returning to Sissy's side with two more tumblers of vodka. 'Never say something nasty to someone's face when you can much more safely say it behind their backs.'

'But it's all so pointless,' said Sissy, gesturing towards the ornate table settings. 'We go to all these lavish parties, all done up to the nines, but there's no real joy in it. God, when I think of the stunts I used to pull to get a freebie frock to wear to one of these things. Once I had to get my friend Violet to fax Colette Dinegan in Sydney on Beeb headed notepaper to tell her I was co-hosting the Lottery, just so she'd lend me one of her dresses. It's not even *fun*. There's no . . . sexiness.'

'Oh, you silly girl. That's what makes it so chic. If there were the remotest chance of any of us getting laid at any of these things, people wouldn't get nearly so het up about what they wore.' He gargled serenely on the contents of his tumbler.

'The thing is' – Jo-Jo chose her words as carefully as she could – 'that there's been a lot of talk about Cassie.'

'Really?' said Janie evenly. She eyed the trim on Jo-Jo's hood disapprovingly. Beaver, if she wasn't mistaken.

'Yeah, and at this dinner at Bella's palazzo last night, somebody, I think it was the woman who writes for the *New Yorker*, said . . . well, she asked me who I'd thought of getting as a new agent.' She looked at Janie, desperate for her approval, a sign that showed Janie thought it was all right for her to go ahead with what she'd been thinking about doing for days.

'Of course, I wasn't even thinking of leaving Cassie,'

continued Jo-Jo hurriedly, 'but I don't really fancy being pulled in for questioning by the police. It happened too many times when my dad was around. I've left all that behind. Between you and me, Janie, what d'you think is going to happen? I mean, if she hands over to Saffron now Hot Shots could still pull through, but otherwise . . .'

'Look,' said Janie firmly, 'I don't know what vile rumours were swirling around at Bella Scarletti's last night' – she made her name sound like a disease – 'but they are just that – rumours. I know Cassie as well as I know myself, and she is one of the most honourable people you could hope to meet.' Janie shifted uncomfortably on her beanbag. 'She is totally innocent of any of these drugs allegations. In fact, you might tell the next person who repeats them to you to brush up on the laws of slander. What Cassie needs is support and loyalty – it's what she has unstintingly given to you, after all.' She knew none of this was Jo-Jo's fault, but she was flushed and angry, despite herself.

'Yes, but . . . well, Janie, you know that at least half the secret of success in this business is to do with reputation and image and—'

'Really,' said Janie coldly. 'I hadn't realised you had such a wealth of experience of "this business". In fact, before Cassie took you under her wing I seem to recall that you wanted nothing to do with "this business". Christ, you girls – all you ever think about is yourselves. As I recall, two years ago, Jo-Jo, the check-out till at Tesco's was about the summit of your aspirations.'

She regretted it as soon as she had said it, of course. But it was too late. Jo-Jo looked at her, genuinely shocked.

'Thanks for the advice, Janie.' She got up. Janie tried to think of something to say to make amends. Jo-Jo's eyes flashed dangerously.

'You're all the same, you lot. You pretend to make friends, you pretend that we're all on a level, but you're just a bunch of bourgeois hypocrites out to exploit us. Well, Mum might fall for it, but I'm not.' And with that she stalked off into the crowd.

Chapter Fifteen

Edward Rushmore was mystified rather than annoyed by his conversation with The Proprietor. He was used to having what he called muscular discussions with his employer about the tone of the *Gazette*'s political editorial, particularly over the previous election. He was not at all accustomed to receiving instructions about its features content. It particularly didn't make sense that The Proprietor should interfere over such a trivial-sounding story. Still, he had an unfailing nose for news. And he paid all their salaries. He dialled through to Phyllida.

'The Proprietor says there's a woman called Anastasia Monticatini who's going to be a big fish in the fashion industry. Apparently she's about to change the landscape of British retailing.'

'Very "hold the front page",' said Phyllida scathingly. 'I'll get the tea lady to look into it.'

'No need. Janie Pember's already done an interview, it seems. All you have to do is get the copy from her. Good piece this morning from her and Sissy Sands about that fashion party. What a débâcle. Can you imagine having to evacuate six hundred people off a freezing mountain because of a flood caused by your own calor gas heaters?' He chuckled.

'Hardly calor gas,' said Phyllida icily.

'No . . . quite. Anyway, it elicited a laugh in the Rushmore household, I must confess. And you'll get this other story together? By tomorrow? The Proprietor's most insistent we do it quickly. He thinks the other papers will be queuing up to interview her once they finally get wind of what she's doing. Clever woman, that Janie.' He sensed a certain froideur at the other end. 'Jolly clever of you too, Phyllida, to have spotted her.'

Tulah had been released but the police were keeping her in suspense as to whether or not they were going to charge her. Once she was more or less free, she almost began to enjoy the notoriety, but she was still livid that it was now too late for her to do any of the Milan shows. It meant she would have to do extra ones in Paris to make up for lost earnings. And because the French didn't pay as well as the Italians, she'd have to put up with being in a lot of humiliating shows.

Cassie, meanwhile, felt she would go mad if Inspector Reece and his sidekick didn't start asking her different questions. She had gone over and over the same ground with them. In fifteen years of explaining gently to young, hopeful girls that they weren't going to make it as a model, she felt she had never had to choose her words so cautiously. Even before her conversation with Jess, Cassie had more or less known that Bellissimo had been using some of its models to smuggle drugs into Europe – the rumours had circulated for years, and they probably weren't the only agency in the world to be abusing their position. Cassie had done her utmost to arm her models with the necessary knowledge to repel suspicious overtures from anyone. But she had never had any real proof about Bellissimo – and the business was a seething cauldron of rumours and slander. Besides, in the early days of Hot Shots' *entente cordiale* with Bellissimo, the agency had been one of the best in Milan. How the mighty tumble, she thought wryly. Yes, she had had frequent dealings with Bellissimo in the past, she told Reece warily, but she had not been in contact with them at all for years. As she explained to Inspector Reece, the amount of prestigious work coming out of Milan had dropped off dramatically since the early nineties. Also, Jim and Sergio had started to quibble about money. The twenty per cent cut which Cassie levered on every girl she 'gave' them they rejected as too high, even though it was the market rate. Cassie hadn't been interested in negotiating. And finally, yes, she had thought there was something vaguely unsavoury about the way they ran their operation.

'What do you mean by that exactly?' Inspector Reece had asked her.

'Simply that I had begun to hear the rumours about them some time back, which is why I more or less stopped working with them five years ago. Not,' she said pointedly, 'that one should always believe rumours.'

'Which is why, presumably,' said Reece, looking at his notes, 'you were perfectly happy for Jess Murray to work with them, oh, what was it, eight months ago?'

'That was Jess's personal decision. They were offering to take far less commission than the agency we normally work with there. It was a one-off job for her. Besides, Jess is a mature twenty-eight-going-on-forty-year-old who has been in the business for ten years and knows the score.' An unfortunate choice of word in the context, thought Cassie, biting her lip.

'This "prestigious" work that Bellissimo supposedly finds your girls. Would it include marketing tinned bolognese sauce?'

'The bolognese ads were extremely lucrative.'

'I see. So you would "advise" your girls to advertise anything if the price was right?'

'Not anything, no. And it would depend entirely on what stage they were at. I can assure you, Inspector, that there have been many, many occasions when I have advised models to turn down lucrative jobs for more artistic work. But there are times when the opposite approach is more appropriate. Jess is coming to the end of her career as a catwalk model. Posing for the cover of *Vogue* is not what makes them millionaires, believe me. It's the downright commercial work that does that. And yes, sometimes it *is* for bolognese sauce. Or for instant tea or potatoes or antifreeze or burglar alarms. They all do it, even the most exclusive supermodels. Only most of the time the public here never knows about it because it would ruin their image. So we make sure that when they sign a five-hundred-thousand-pound contract to advertise Japanese fly-spray, the advertisement only gets shown in Japan. That's our job. It takes a lot of planning, Inspector Reece. And it makes us all a lot of money. There is no spare time – or need – to run a drugs empire on the side.'

'Is there anywhere you wouldn't advise your girls to work?'

'Naturally I wouldn't send them to a war zone. And if I thought they were inexperienced and naïve, I wouldn't suggest that they work in countries where the local population could be . . . troublesome.'

'But you didn't have any qualms about packing Jo-Jo Banderas off to Moscow. She had only been with you, what, five months? Or perhaps you don't consider a flourishing, notoriously violent Mafia and a surging drugs culture to be troublesome?'

'My deputy Saffron was to have accompanied her, but at the last minute she went down with flu and I felt Jo-Jo could probably cope on her own. It was that or miss out on the career opportunity of her life. In any case, she was heavily chaperoned. And she is a remarkably streetwise young woman,' said Cassie evenly.

'More streetwise than you think,' said Inspector Reece quietly. 'We have reason to believe that she returned to London with a good deal more in her suitcase than she set out with. We've a strong suspicion that she made contact with a representative of the Bellissimo agency in Moscow and that they got along like a house on fire.'

'They haven't a shred of evidence,' said Michael Croft round at Cassie's flat later, 'or they would have hauled Jo-Jo in by now. What we have to do is get hold of her before they do.'

'I've already tried,' Cassie said desperately. 'She's checked out of her hotel in Milan. The hotel in Paris says she cancelled her booking there and her mobile's dead. God, how many times do I have to tell them never to switch off their mobiles? I could kill her.'

'I wouldn't advise it,' said Michael dryly. 'At least, not yet.'

★   ★   ★

Jo-Jo cancelled her booking at the Bristol with a heavy heart. She had been thrilled to stay in the hotel in the summer when she had done a shoot for Yves Saint Laurent. She loved its light-filled lobby and quaint swimming pool, and was immensely gratified that Cassie had suggested staying there. But she needed time to think, and that meant finding somewhere Cassie wouldn't track her down. Like a child who believes it's invisible because it has closed its eyes, she convinced herself that if she booked a hotel herself, she would be untraceable. So she went from one landmark hotel to another – and checked in at the Crillon on the Place de la Concorde.

Sissy and Janie boarded the evening Alitalia flight from Linate airport to Charles de Gaulle. In her dark glasses and blond belted coat, Sissy looked like a sixties film star, Janie thought. She was certainly taking her new role as siren of the hack pack seriously.

'I can't believe this schedule. There are a hundred and fifty shows in Paris this time,' groaned Janie, helping herself to two bottles of Chianti from the stewardess's trolley. 'And I suppose Phyllida will be on the phone at the crack of dawn tomorrow demanding blood.'

'You're in luck there,' said Sissy. 'You don't need to file anything until the weekend. They've got hold of another photocopy shoot and they're running your Anastasia piece in the centre of the Saturday supplement.'

Janie stared at her, horrified. 'Could you just trot that past me again?'

'Your Anastasia masterpiece. Phyllida rang me about it at lunch. She wanted to talk to you but you were hobnobbing in Bice with Bella Scarletti – I hope she takes some ads in the paper after that. Anyway, apparently our esteemed leader has taken a personal interest in it. Lord knows why, but he's very keen to run it while the Paris shows are on. It was on

353

the F drive, wasn't it? What's the matter? You've gone terribly pale. Janie?'

'The matter, Sissy, is that the piece was extremely rough. It wasn't finished, it wasn't checked. In fact the only thing it was was rather snide and nasty. I was in a bloody bad mood with Phyllida when I wrote it and I stuck in all sorts of suppositions that I haven't begun to investigate.'

'Snide and nasty? Sounds par for the *Gazette*'s course to me,' said Sissy blithely. 'Cheer up. We'll call them as soon as we land. In any case, I bet the subs will have given it their best shot, toning it down, taking out all the jokes, et cetera.'

'If that's meant to fill me with confidence,' snapped Janie, 'it bloody well doesn't.'

By the time they had telephoned the sub-editors from Charles de Gaulle, it was 11 p.m. The piece had been put to bed. It was now whirring away irretrievably in the system that mysteriously whizzed words off computers and on to newspaper pages. Janie was in tears. 'I don't think you realise how serious this is,' she sobbed.

'Oh, Janie.' Sissy squeezed her hand. 'Don't you think you might be overreacting? You're awfully tired. I'm sure it's not as bad as you think.'

'Every time I remember a bit more of it, it seems a lot, lot worse.'

'Be rational. Try to remember what you wrote.'

'That she was vain, self-obsessed and ruthlessly socially ambitious.'

'All self-evident, I'd say – and not necessarily defects.'

'I also said that she was a brilliant self-invention; that she had the dress sense of a barely reformed, very high–class hooker, and that her plastic breasts were the most realistic thing about her.'

'I see,' said Sissy after a long pause.

They drove into Paris in silence, save for the rhythmic whine of the windscreen wipers. Sissy took off her sunglasses. It somehow seemed appropriate. As they splashed through the Place de la Concorde, she spotted Jo-Jo delicately sidestepping a puddle in Manolo mules as if to the stiletto born. She stopped at the taxi rank outside the Crillon. She must be on her way to a last-minute fitting. Sissy motioned to their driver to pull over.

'Hi, Jo-Jo. This where you're staying? Chic or what?'

Jo-Jo peered through the open window of Sissy's taxi and, seeing Janie, looked sheepish.

'Erm, I'm just off to a fitting at Karl's. Everyone says the clothes for tomorrow's show are gorgeous.'

'They'd better be,' giggled Sissy. 'I've written a huge profile on Chanel's revival for Sunday. Need a lift?'

'Er, no thanks. Better dash.' Jo-Jo slid into her waiting taxi.

'God, she's looking good,' said Sissy, staring after her. 'Isn't it incredible how fast they metamorphose? It seems only yesterday that her eyebrows made Denis Healy's look groomed.'

'Doesn't it just?' said Janie sourly.

'You don't think we should tone this down a little?' Phyllida's deputy had asked her at 9.30 p.m. just as Janie and Sissy had plunged into the second bottle of Alitalia Chianti.

'Whatever for?'

'Well, it's just that it seems a little rough. The copy doesn't feel as though it's been worked as much as usual. And she's left queries all over the place.'

Phyllida was riven by two opposing impulses. On the one hand she had got a considerable amount of mileage at the *Gazette* from taking credit as the person who had discovered Janie. On the other, her highly talented protégée was driving her up the wall in a frenzy of jet-propelled envy.

'Oh, that's probably just the style. It's very stream-of-consciousness. But I like that. Makes it seem immediate. As for those queries, I shouldn't worry too much. Janie is so thorough about checking. She probably forgot to take them out.'

★   ★   ★

Sissy had followed Janie upstairs to make sure that the man-agement of the Montalembert hadn't given them tiny rooms like last time. Phyllida was just going to have to accept that fashion editors needed bigger rooms because they required a larger than normal amount of closet space. It was bound to be tax-deductible.

'Crikey, you have to admit, Janie, that there is nothing like the sight of half a dozen obscenely large bouquets and a couple of new unsolicited chiffon dresses to lift the old heart. These,' she said, reading the card that was attached to a large carrier bag, 'are from Jean Berceau. "The rest of your order to follow. We hope you like it." Janie, you sly thing. I didn't know you'd ordered these.'

'They offered me a very good discount,' said Janie sheep-ishly.

'I bet they did. They'll look great on you,' she said, peering inside and parting the tissue paper. 'Oh my God, there's two suede jackets in here as well. Three shirts . . . a wrapover skirt. And a pair of trousers, and some suede boots. Very Tom Fitzgerald . . . crikey, they are Tom Fitzgerald. I hope for your sake he's offering you an amazing discount.'

But Janie was looking at a first edition of Gertrude Jekyll's *Colour Schemes for the Flower Garden* that Tom had sent over. The phone rang. She answered it, hoping against hope that it was the subs to say they had somehow retrieved her piece. Sissy went to inspect the wardrobe.

It was Tom, thanking her for the list of suggestions for plants for the north end of the terrace at Firefly. She tried to conceal her disappointment.

'I hope this isn't a bad time. It's a little late there, I know, but it's so difficult to catch you guys during the day.'

'It's fine.' Sissy tiptoed out of the room. 'It's nice to hear from you.'

'You sound low, pippin.'

'It's a long story. So do you.'

'Do I?' He seemed disappointed. 'I thought I was coping admirably. You know, laughter through the tears and all that.'

'What's happened?'

'Are you sitting comfortably? Because I'm afraid I'm about to begin.'

Belinda had left him.

'No great surprise there, of course, Janie, my pippin. She had been aching to do it for years.'

'I'm sorry.' Janie didn't know what else to say.

'Oh, I'm not. I just wish she had managed to do it with a bit more style. She was so obsessed with inner cleanliness that our toxic relationship was bound to be junked sooner or later. But running off with your personal trainer – it's so démodé. But that's Belinda. Always one step behind the trends. I dare say I wasn't all sugar and spice myself. Well, that's my news. Your friend Madeleine is a darling, by the way. Very tactful, very controlled – she's got me tiptoeing the line big time, I can tell you. Oh, if you don't like the clothes, blame her, she picked them out . . . you're not insulted, I hope. It's just that Madeleine mentioned you never have time to shop.'

Janie didn't have the heart to tell him that she didn't accept professional gifts. Besides, the jackets did look very beautiful. Perhaps she could find a way to return them after the shows. And she jolly well wanted to keep the book.

'Oh, listen to me bleating about clothes. You said you had a problem.'

Janie explained.

'Anastasia Monticatini, you say? It's funny. That name's awfully familiar.'

'And about to get more so. She's set to be very big in fashion retailing.'

'Is she now? I can almost picture her. I'm sure our paths intersected a few years ago when we were thinking of opening a store in Moscow. She had some shopping mall there.'

'Are you sure? Her line is that she lived in Italy and made a living hand-smocking children's dresses or something equally unlikely.'

'Well, I didn't meet her personally. We were dealing through dozens of intermediaries. But that name . . . once stumbled across, never forgotten. And you know, while I gather her businesses were indeed varied and wide-ranging, children's clothing didn't seem to be among them.'

'I see,' said Cassie icily down the line to Paris. 'It would have been nice if you'd had the courage to tell me to my face.' This wasn't entirely fair – it was Cassie who had personally arranged Jo-Jo's schedules, and they'd left no time for cosy tête-à-têtes with her agent.

'I'm sorry,' said Jo-Jo quietly. 'It's just that I had to make the break as soon as possible. I can't take any more hassle from the police, Cassie. That Inspector Reece came to see me twice when I was in London and it's doing my head in. He practically accused me of bringing drugs back from Moscow in my vanity case. Apparently some creep's crawled out of the woodwork there to finger me. Everyone says it wouldn't have happened if I'd been with a different agency.'

Cassie had often planned her reaction in the event of a major model leaving her, but it had never happened, and now the circumstances were such that she didn't know what to say, other than appeal in her most rational, measured tones to Jo-Jo's better instincts.

'My better instincts are to do what's best for my career so Mum and me can have a future that's less crappy than our past,' Jo-Jo retorted hotly, when Cassie had finished.

'Thanks for the support,' Cassie said sarcastically. 'It's really decent of you.'

Something in Cassie's tone, eerily controlled, reminded Jo-Jo of the scathing way Janie had spoken to her at Paolo Bianco's party. 'You're so fucking superior when you have nothing to be superior about. I don't owe you anything, other than your precious twenty per cent for these shows, which I'm more than happy to have deducted from my final balance sheet with Hot Shots. And after that I'm getting the hell out. . . . You know, if you'd only shown a bit of remorse, I might have reconsidered. As for decency – what's decent is putting

as much distance between me and your sewage of an agency.'
Shaking, she slammed the phone down.

For the first time since she'd left home for good at seventeen,
after one row too many with her mother, Cassie found herself
weeping uncontrollably.

Anastasia, still in her negligee, slid her arms around The Proprietor and began working her way beneath his towel. For a
man of his years, he was in remarkably good shape. He looked
at her adoringly. They were standing by the balcony of their
suite, and in that diaphanous confection of hers she looked
like a naughty little Greek goddess. She was an extraordinary
woman, he mused: strong-minded and keen to please at the
same time. She clearly had a shrewd brain but she wasn't one
of those damned militants he was always coming up against
on his newspapers. On the contrary – he chuckled inwardly,
remembering what she had managed to do to him a few hours
earlier – she was an old-fashioned coquette, the little minx –
cool as a snow queen in public and unbelievably explicit in bed.
He would have to treasure this one. The profile was a good
start. He couldn't wait to see her reaction when she opened
the paper.

At his request, they had conducted their affair to date with
the utmost discretion. He was engaged in what looked set
to be lengthy and world-record-breakingly expensive divorce
proceedings with his third wife, and his lawyers had advised
that a publicised relationship with anyone else could be ruinous.
Besides, he couldn't face another lecture from Father Conlon.

To her own surprise, Anastasia wasn't bothered by this. It
was true that it would do her own social standing no end of good
to be linked publicly with an international billionaire tycoon. In
the past she would have wanted to cash in on the liaison as soon
as possible. But something told her she could be in for the long
haul with The Proprietor. He clearly adored her, even finding
time to accompany her to Paris – on the pretext, of course, of
checking up on one of his French cable stations. And she was

rather fond of him. But she had no illusions. She would have to behave herself. He might have been a kitten with her so far, and pleasingly straightforward for one so famously cunning, but as she knew only too well, ruthless cats always bared their claws sooner or later.

He led her over to a table laden with croissants, brioches and the morning's newspapers. The Georges V did the most marvellous breakfasts, she thought bitterly. She would put on half a stone while they were here if she wasn't careful. He poured two cups of steaming coffee and passed one to Anastasia – black, with a quarter-teaspoon of honey, as she liked it. He was learning fast. Then, with a flourish, he presented her with a beautifully ironed copy of the *Gazette*.

'As promised, the first of many adoring profiles.'

They read the article together. Halfway through the fourth paragraph, Anastasia looked at him sullenly.

'Is this some kind of joke?'

'The tone is a little robust,' he conceded smoothly. 'But there's probably a very amusing punch line.'

By the time they had finished reading, he was almost lost for words. He didn't care what the smartarses at the *Gazette* called this kind of writing, he wasn't having any of it in his paper.

He smiled thinly. 'Nice wry touch.'

'You think so?' said Anastasia woodenly. 'You think "she has the almost-too-perfect taste of someone with an imperfect past" is a nice, wry touch? You think "she must have made several plastic surgeons very happy" is a nice wry touch?'

'You know the British press. If a piece doesn't hurl a few insults at its subject everyone thinks it's a put-up job.'

'This one was meant to be,' Anastasia said stonily.

'Oh, darling, what can I say? Somebody's got their wires horribly crossed. Whoever is responsible for this' – he examined the byline – 'I'll have them hanged, drawn and quartered.'

He looked across at her in horror. She was crying.

'Anastasia, please . . . sweetheart. Look, no one believes anything they read in the papers anyway.'

* * *

Janie and Sissy sat at a table outside the Café Flore. There was nothing more Sissy could think of to say. Personally she thought the tone of Janie's interview was fine. Feisty was good, Phyllida was always telling them. But there were at least six mistakes in the piece. Most were minor. Janie hadn't mentioned Anastasia's new title, she had said Anastasia's house was opposite the Dorchester (a geographical impossibility) when it was across the road from Claridge's, and worst of all that she was forty-five when Anastasia had expressly told her that she was thirty-five – all of which might militate against her if it ever went to court.

'Which, of course, it won't,' said Sissy. 'She'll be thrilled just to be in there – and across three-quarters of a page. No such thing as bad publicity.'

After a second shared bottle of wine, she was feeling less bullish. 'It's my fault too,' she said in a small voice. 'I should have checked with you before I told Phyllida where the piece was. I don't know what came over me. I'll share the responsibility. If you get sacked, I'll resign in protest.'

Janie looked at her aghast. Bad as she felt about the article, it had never occurred to her that it might be a sacking offence. She dimly remembered Sissy telling her once that Eddie-babes was as sweet as pie as editors went, but that the one thing he couldn't abide was inaccuracies. He had once famously thrown the motoring correspondent's borrowed BMW keys through a window of the thirteenth floor because his piece had got the launch date of a new model wrong.

They shuffled miserably to the rest of the day's shows. Janie felt too dispirited to take notes. She watched them with new eyes. The now-certain knowledge that this was the last time she would be covering them gave them a new poignancy. For once she could fully appreciate the passion and dedication that went into them. As she and Sissy sat in an increasingly irascible queue of taxis in a blocked one-way street on the way to Aeron's show in an old tannery late that evening, the thought that she would never again share in these absurd, exciting adventures made her feel bleak. She needed this damn job. They couldn't take it away from her. She had mouths to feed, damp courses to install . . . and, dammit, she liked it.

The phone woke her at 8.30 the next morning. A genteel American accent she couldn't place.

'It's Lee Howard, Janie. I hope I didn't disturb you. Listen, I was wondering whether you might have time to meet me this morning. There are no major shows on and I thought it would be good to have a chat. Eleven, say – at the Georges V? They do a wonderful breakfast.'

She was sitting in a corner working her way through the Sunday papers. She had absent-mindedly twisted her dark brown hair up the back of her head and speared it in place with a pencil. She looked youthful and energetic, and very ostentatiously capable.

'I hope you didn't mind coming up here,' she said, smiling. 'It's a little off our beaten track, which is why it's such a useful meeting place. The fashion crowd never come this far. And I did so want to talk to you in private. Don't look so worried. It's a proposal.'

Lee wanted Janie to become her European contributing editor for *Eden*.

'I want someone who can make sense of fashion for the readers – who'll interpret the pictures for them sometimes. We'll need at least eight features a year. They can be interviews as well as sociological articles. We want quirky angles and your style is just right. You should be able to fit it around your job at the *Gazette*, though of course I understand you'll have to ask their permission.'

Janie didn't tell her that was unlikely to be necessary. The salary was ridiculous – almost as much as what she was paid for working full time at the *Gazette*. It would make a real difference to her and the children's lifestyle. It would be a lot of extra work, but it would mean that she might even be able to get the leaking roof fixed.

'I'd like to start by asking John Galliano to interview Aeron Baxter – everyone says they're the two brightest British talents – and getting you to mediate. What do you think?'

'I can do it all from London?'

'That's the point. You'll be the magazine's European ears and eyes. You might have to travel for some of the profiles, but only to Paris or Italy. What do you think? You could be back home in a day.'

What Janie thought was that this was an answer to her prayers. What she said, as evenly as she could, was that she was most interested and would let Lee know in the morning, after she had spoken to her editor. She was deeply impressed by her own self-restraint.

On the way out, she saw Jo-Jo in earnest conversation with an animated woman who was dressed head to toe in crimson leather. In her current good humour, Janie decided to overlook their disagreement. She waved at Jo-Jo, but Jo-Jo couldn't see her. Or wouldn't.

Jo-Jo was trying very hard to concentrate on what Marie-Elise was saying. It was difficult because Marie-Elise spoke very quickly and tossed all sorts of percentage figures into the conversation as if they were detonated bombs she was anxious to offload.

'The bottom line, Jo-Jo, ees that Roar is ze biggest agency in Paris. If we do sign zat deal with Allure in New York zat I mentioned you, we will be well on the road to being global. *Alors*, what's your problem? You 'ave a very bright future with us, Jo-Jo.'

'But how do you see that future shaping up? What would your strategy for me be?' asked Jo-Jo, trying to sound business-like. Cassie was always talking about strategies, always stressing the importance of taking the long-term view.

'Oh, strategy – *bouf*! Look, the modelling world ees in a state of flux at the moment. You can't guarantee a long career to any girl. It may 'appen, it may not. So my strategy, since you ask, ees to make as much for us all now, while we can.' She smiled, or rather bared nicotine-stained teeth, at Jo-Jo.

'I see,' Jo-Jo said miserably. She felt at sea and was furious with herself because of it. Cassie's mother-hen act had driven her mad, she had thought at the time, but Marie-Elise's coldness wasn't entirely appealing either. Still, Roar was the agency name on all the girls' lips at the moment. She wished there was one adult whose advice she could trust. Adult! Christ, what was she talking about? *She* was an adult. She was so distracted that on the way out she collided with a slender blonde woman in pastel cashmere and sent her flying.

The woman, a little winded, was about to open her mouth when she swivelled on her heels and disappeared into a waiting lift. It was a fleeting encounter, but Jo-Jo could have sworn it was the madame from Moscow. Must be recruiting again, Jo-Jo giggled to herself, temporarily distracted from Marie-Elise's arctic manner.

She would have liked to have called Ben straight away to find out what he thought of her leaving Hot Shots, but he was so wrapped up in Paul Morel, his character in *Sons and Lovers*, that he never took any calls on set. And when she did get through he went off into great rambling tracts of bullshit. He was so lost in his part that sometimes she wondered bitterly if he'd even notice if she stopped ringing him altogether. All that stuff about them moving in together was just waffle – they never even had time any more to look at apartments, let alone move into one.

When he finally rang her mobile she was due on at Aeron's.

'Honey, just remember that to know your own nothingness, to know the tremendous living flood which carries you always, can give you rest within yourself. We're only grains in the tremendous heaven, so why fret about yourself?' he drawled.

'And what the pissy fuck does that mean?' She was getting into a panic. Aeron, who got notoriously nervous before shows, was signalling frantically at her to get in line.

'It's D.H. Lawrence,' he said, sounding a little wounded. 'Roughly translated it means no worries . . . oh, and that loyalty is very valuable. But then, of course, so is your precious career.'

'He gets very involved with what he's doing,' she told Tulah after the show. She felt full of remorse for losing her temper and wanted to be able to justify herself. She, Unity and Tulah had become allies over the past few days. Having missed Milan, Tulah almost felt like a novice again, and was glad to hook up with Jo-Jo. 'He's kind of doing Method.'

'Well, I pity you when he lands the lead in the remake of *The Texas Chainsaw Massacre*,' said Unity, giggling.

Jo-Jo couldn't confide in Tulah or Unity about her decision to leave Hot Shots. Cassie was their agent too. As much as she liked them, she felt their reaction wouldn't be in any way objective. She had made her decision and must abide by it. The best she could hope for was that she didn't cause a mass exodus from Hot Shots.

Harry and Peace followed Seth back on to the terrace. It was early evening and droopy clumps of lavender surged gently in the breeze. Finn's was empty, apart from a group of BBC executives who were savouring the last liquors of a very long lunch. The moon was already loitering palely in a corner of milky grey sky.

'So that's it, really. We could seat a hundred and sixty if they were on long tables. Of course, in the summer we could use the garden.'

'A hundred and sixty's perfect,' said Peace. 'I want the evening to have an exclusive aura. Harry reckons the real charity money is in corporate sponsorship, so I'm only inviting people whose businesses turn over ten million or more.'

Seth suppressed a smile. It always threw him when Peace trundled out her hard-bitten sales act. But he had to hand it to her, she had certainly done her homework. The projected figures for the evening at Finn's were extremely impressive. And what she said made sense. It was pointless expending energy on overblown galas that cost a fortune to produce. Better to target people with sizeable fortunes to give away. She must be doing something right. Since its inception, HOPE had already raised £650,000. It would have been a lot more, Harry confided to Seth, if Peace had had her way. She had wanted to donate most of her own money to it, but Harry had reasoned that if she did that, she would end up having to give up running HOPE and go back to modelling full time to support herself in the manner to which she had unconsciously become accustomed.

'And you're sure it's okay to take Finn's over for one night? It's incredibly kind of you,' said Peace.

'Yuh, we really, you know, appreciate it,' mumbled Harry, 'and if there's anything we can do in return—'

'How about a weekend in the cottage?' said Peace suddenly. 'I bet you and Janie could do with a break. You could stay in the main house except that Harry's let it out to some very rich Americans for the autumn.'

'Yuh, sorry about that, but Peace got them to agree to such a terrific fee we couldn't say no. We prefer the cottage anyway, don't we, Peace?'

Peace nodded.

Seth looked at her fragile, upturned face and thought that even if he hadn't wanted to let her have the night at Finn's for his dead brother's sake, the sight of her beautiful smile would have won him round sooner or later.

Gloria took the train to pick the children up from Eleanor, who was bed-bound with flu she had caught at the weekend, while protesting a proposed local bypass. Eleanor's normally immaculate kitchen was a disaster area. Nell had attempted to give the twins their breakfast, but the only food she could reach was a chocolate cake which Mrs Jessop, Eleanor's daily, had made the day before and which was now smeared all over the walls. Gloria surveyed the chaos unemotionally.

'Is Mum back?' asked Nell brightly.

'Not yet, darling. She arrive day after tomorrow.'

Nell began to cry softly. 'I want her. And I want my father too.'

The twins, faintly recognisable as earthlings beneath the layers of chocolate, joined in.

Gloria inhaled deeply and took off her coat. She could see they wouldn't be making the next train back to London. Or the one after that. Secretly she was relieved that Eleanor was too sick – or more likely booked up to attend some rally or other – to have the children. This definitely scuppered Seth's plans to go away alone with Janie, since Gloria had to go into hospital at the weekend to have a varicose vein removed and wouldn't be able to look after the children for them.

When the kitchen was finally looking spotless, the kettle was on and Nell and the twins were out in the garden taking it in turns to sit in the wheelbarrow, Eleanor miraculously appeared downstairs.

'You are an absolute saint, Gloria. I hope my daughter realises how lucky she is to have you.'

'Oh, she does,' said Gloria coolly. Eleanor didn't look that ill to her.

'Now you must stay for lunch,' said Eleanor, which Gloria knew translated as an invitation to make it. 'And tell me the news.'

Gloria had often suspected Eleanor of cultivating a tendency to idleness, but the two of them were united by their contempt for the male species and, despite her disapproval, Gloria had a soft spot for Eleanor. In turn, Eleanor often ran the theories from her women's consciousness-raising sessions past Gloria and they would inevitably end up setting the world to rights.

'So what's he like, this Seth Weiss?' Eleanor asked while the children bickered over their sausages. 'Janie is being very coy. I must say, after Matthew I would have thought she'd be put off men for good.'

Gloria bridled. 'Mr Matthew is a good, kind man and a wonderful father.'

'Was, Gloria. Was. Useless with money, though. Don't see the point of them myself, if they can't at least take care of the household accounts.'

Normally Gloria would have stayed to endorse the point; the two had whiled away many an enjoyable hour annihilating their husbands. But instead, after clearing away a hastily thrown together lunch, she gathered the children's belongings together as quickly as she could, signed Eleanor's bypass petition and called a taxi. She didn't want to be drawn out on Seth. She couldn't put her finger on what it was about him that made her uneasy. He was extremely polite to her and very attentive to the children. Too attentive perhaps. She had occasionally caught what looked like a flicker of boredom in his eyes when he was playing with them. Mr Matthew never looked bored. He had his faults, Gloria knew. He couldn't iron to save his life. But he loved Janie and his children. Seth might love her too, for all Gloria knew. But it wasn't the same as Matthew's love. In short, Gloria decided, the problem with Seth was that he wasn't Matthew.

Possibly for the first time in her life, Sissy found herself passionately interested in a man who didn't design beautiful clothes. She took to scanning the business pages of the British newspapers every day, in the hope of seeing some mention of Everything She Wants. God knew, she thought grimly, she was never going to see it featured on any of the fashion pages. Waiting for shows to start, she would catch herself reconfiguring Nari's features, trying to conjure up his face, the ways his eyes had crinkled up in hospital when she said something especially provoking, how he had looked at her when he saw her off at the airport (she had never been seen off at an airport before). She amused him, she knew, and the thought gave her pleasure. In Buenos Aires she had begun to hope – suspect, even – that he found her attractive. Why, then, had the stubborn, irritating man failed to contact her in Milan? According to Jean, he was in the Far East again. Well, they had telephones there, didn't they? After two exhausting days of proliferating desperation, Sissy composed a formal letter, informing Nari that she had inherited a small sum of money, and was at a loss to know how best to invest it – did he have any suggestions? If nothing else, Nari's rapacious capitalist instincts would prompt him to get in touch with her directly. Instead, she received a fax from Jean with the name of his accountant.

★   ★   ★

'It's a bloody balls–up, Edward, that's what it is – to be rectified. Immediately,' snarled The Proprietor, slamming down the phone on his editor so hard that he heard the plastic split. He was in a sticky situation. Anastasia, despite her valiant attempts, was unable to laugh the article off as he had originally suggested and was clearly mortified by the whole incident. Not that she ever complained, but every time he looked at her, it seemed her beautiful grey eyes filled with tears. She would start to talk about something cheerful, and her voice would tremble and break off. She was naturally too distraught to attend any of the fashion shows.

On the other hand, sacking Janie was a bit draconian and might draw attention to his and Anastasia's affair.

'Don't be angry on my behalf,' she told him bravely. 'I should have known better than to trust a journalist. She seemed so friendly – but I suppose she hadn't had the proper training.' She dabbed at her eyes with a lace handkerchief.

'What do you mean?'

'Oh, just that she didn't take many notes during our interview. Hardly any, really.'

That was it. He wasn't having sloppy practices on his publications. He called Rushmore back three-quarters of the way through the afternoon conference.

'Get rid of her. She's a liability. This time it's just a defenceless woman trying to make an honest living. Next time it could be a litigious politician.'

'Hardly. She's a fashion journalist,' Edward Rushmore pointed out reasonably. 'The best we've had. Ever. And I have to say that feature was very popular with the readers. We've had dozens of e-mails asking for more of that kind of thing.'

'Sack her.'

'At least,' beseeched Edward, 'think about it. Now I must dash. Got to go to a rock and roll party at Downing Street. I must say, London's frightfully jolly at the moment. I'll speak to you tomorrow.'

A little later that evening, The Proprietor's PA in London

faxed him an advance page proof she had somehow got hold of from *The Python*. Beneath a photograph that had showed him arriving simultaneously with Anastasia at the opening of Finn's ran the article he had been dreading, under the headline 'Who's That Girl?'

When the billionaire owner of PPS, the planet's largest communications network, was recently spotted talking to a mystery woman at the opening of top people's restaurant Finn's, tongues started wagging. The Proprietor, as he is known the world over, has been steering clear of the fairer sex recently, thanks to becoming embroiled in a bitter divorce wrangle (and him a Catholic!).

However, The Python *can reveal that the gorgeous busty blonde at his side is none other than Countess Anastasia Monticatini. Yes, that's right. The same Anastasia who featured in a big profile this weekend in the* Gazette, *The Proprietor's dreary lapdog of a paper. Are these two events, we ask ourselves, in any way related?*

PPS, The Proprietor's third wife and mother of two of his children, famously declared in the July issue of Beau Monde *magazine that she intended to fight for what was rightfully hers in the divorce, whatever it cost emotionally. 'I refuse to be cowed by a ruthless bully,' she was quoted as saying. Oh er, Propriet-er, what's happened to your sense of Propriety? Take some advice from* The Python*'s love line (calls 39p a minute): maybe this is one magnate who ought to stagnate when it comes to his love life . . .*

Seth was waiting at Heathrow with two air tickets dangling from his jacket pocket when Janie's forlorn figure pushed her trolley through the blue channel. She lit up with surprised delight. She hadn't expected to see him. He extracted the tickets.

'Bermuda. Flight leaves in an hour. I know it's a bit of a haul, but I thought you could fly straight from there to New York for the shows — and we'll have somewhere hot and sultry to make hay in while the children are away.' He grinned. 'Don't worry,' he said, seeing her consternation, 'I called Sissy in Paris and she arranged some leave for you with Phyllida.'

Janie felt her life spinning away from her control. She didn't know whether to feel relieved or frightened. 'Oh, Seth,' she grimaced apologetically, 'I didn't tell you, did I? Eleanor went down with flu. The children are back in London with Gloria, but she's due in hospital tomorrow. I don't think there's any way—'

A barely perceptible veil of – what? Irritation, frustration? She couldn't tell – fell across his handsome features momentarily. With a supreme effort of will, he shook off his disappointment and ripped up the tickets.

'Don't worry, they're replaceable . . . So, let's move swiftly on to Plan B,' he said, humour restored.

Jo-Jo had stayed on in Paris after the last show to shoot another cover for Italian *Vogue*. Unity had gone to Northumberland to visit her parents and Tulah was working in Mexico. She was completely on her own. Not that it mattered during the day, when she was working harder than she'd ever thought possible. But the contrast, when she was back in her room at night and there were no stylists or hairdressers to prod and tweak her, couldn't have been starker. She could probably go to any party she wanted, but the team she was working with didn't speak English and the one time they had all gone out together, Jo-Jo had ended up bored and lonely. She might just as well go back to her room, watch some TV and practise poses. She was beginning to understand the processes she could use to transform herself from angel to vixen to child – and it made her feel powerful. She had never felt good at anything before, but, she thought, staring at her reflection in the mirror, she could do this. She sucked in her cheeks. Perhaps Zoffy was right – she could stand to lose a few pounds. As Marie-Elise had said, two things on a woman's body that could never be too prominent were her nipples and her cheekbones.

★ ★ ★

The Orsett estate, all fifteen hundred acres of it, stretched across some of the loveliest countryside in Dorset, although the torrential rain obscured quite a lot of it.

'On a clear day you can see across to Lulworth Cove apparently,' said Seth above the noise of the heater. They swept through some ornate crested black gates, past bedraggled-looking sheep and sodden rhododendron bushes that seemed to meander for miles. The trees had had most of their leaves whipped from them by the fierce winds and their spindly branches swayed like arthritic ballerinas. As they reached the top of a hummock, a vast ornamental lake came into view.

'Water, water.' Daisy clapped her plump little hands.

'Everywhere,' they said simultaneously, and laughed.

'Oh, Seth, it's beautiful,' exclaimed Janie, hugging him. They followed Harry's instructions and drove past the main house – an exceptionally romantic fifteenth-century half-turreted building, with secretive-looking leaded windows – through a copse until they came to the cottage. It was actually rather large for a cottage, more like a Gothic hunting lodge really, brick and cobblestone with ornamental white eaves and latticed windows. A squiggle of smoke from the main chimney eddied into the khaki-coloured skies. Harry had clearly sent someone from the main house to get the place ready for them.

'I suppose you're going to tell me this is where Hansel and Gretel live,' said Nell.

'Well, who would you like to live here?' asked Janie.

'Johnny Depp.'

Janie looked at her daughter, mystified. She was definitely seven going on seventeen. When had Nell turned into a proto-teenager? At this rate she would be discussing pension schemes by the time she was sixteen. They bundled the children inside with a box of toys and videos and unpacked in the rain. Janie saw that Seth had brought his fishing rod.

'Bit optimistic, weren't you?'

'Rather pessimistic, I thought. I'm hoping we have such a

wonderful time I won't get a chance to use it.' He pulled her towards him and kissed her.

Eventually she spoke. 'I'm sorry it hasn't worked out quite as you planned,' she said.

'Don't apologise. It'll be fine. I've always wanted to live out *Five go Mad in Dorset*.'

Fine it was not. Thundery, showery, unseasonably frosty. But not fine. Janie fed the children and was bludgeoned into having a bath with them. At nine she finally settled them into bed and promptly collapsed over a stack of *Country Life*s. Harry had arranged for a huge Fortnum's hamper to be delivered and Seth disappeared into the kitchen. At ten, exhausted, they sat down in the pale blue dining room to eat. Seth had braised some beef in red wine and it smelled delicious, but Janie suddenly felt too nervous about their sleeping arrangements to eat very much. She drank two-thirds of a bottle of wine instead. She wanted so much to be close to Seth, and yet somehow it still felt like a betrayal of Matthew. She needn't have worried. By eleven she had fallen asleep on her place mat. She woke with a start the following morning and peeped gingerly across the bed to see if there was evidence of another occupant. There wasn't. Seth must have carried her up there and gone to sleep in another room. She looked at her watch. It was nine o'clock. She looked at her clothes. They were pyjamas. The process by which she'd been united with them didn't bear thinking about. How? When? Nell? Seth? She couldn't decide which of them would be worse. She got up guiltily and went downstairs.

The children were playing trains in the hallway with a cheerful-looking teenager who had a snake tattooed on her shorn scalp, a lip ring and a geriatric-looking Jack Russell on her lap.

'This is Fidget,' said Nell. 'Oh, and this is Zoe. She brought the railway track over.'

'It used to be Harry's, apparently,' Zoe said in her gentle Dorset burr. 'I work for him in the main house and he said I was to look after you. I'll take the kids to see the horses later, if that's all right. Your husband's in the kitchen garden – taking advantage of a break in the rain. It's never normally like this, by the way.'

'He's not her husband,' Janie heard Nell say as she stepped outside. 'Grandma says he's her lover.' The kitchen garden, when she found it, was back towards the main house, a magnificent display of herbs, vegetables and edible flowers. Seth was lying on a pathway, with a needle and thread.

He turned towards her footsteps.

'Not really my forte, I'm afraid. But I thought I'd better do something before the birds completely demolish what's left of the the fruit. These cages must predate the war. There's something rather comforting about that, don't you think?'

She smiled. There was certainly something comfortable about seeing Seth there, in that setting. 'It's a wonderful garden. I had no idea Harry kept such a spruce ship.'

He stood up. 'Sleep well?'

She nodded. 'Thanks for looking after me.'

'I was thinking,' he said, putting an arm round her, 'that if it stays fine we could pack a picnic and take the boat out on the lake.'

'How did I get into my pyjamas?' she asked, trying to sound casual.

He grinned. 'A little help from your friends. Don't worry, I kept my eyes closed – one of them, anyway.'

They sauntered back to the cottage, but by the time they reached the gate fat drops of rain had begun to fall.

There was no television in the cottage and no telephone either – Harry's immutable rule. Peace had to make do with a crackly mobile when she was there. Normally their absence wouldn't have bothered Janie but she was beginning to worry about what they would do with Nell if the rain persisted. They played Snakes and Ladders most of the afternoon, even though Janie suspected that Nell was only joining in to humour them. And Seth disappeared into the kitchen for two hours to rustle up some pumpkin ravioli which none of the children ate. Apologetically, Janie went into the kitchen to heat up some baked beans and found Jake feeding Seth's ravioli to Fidget.

Watching the children flick beans at one another, Seth said irritably that if parents weren't so ready to pander to their children's whims they wouldn't be so damned finicky, which Janie said was nonsense – just the sort of thing you'd expect from someone who had never watched a child sit obdurately in front of a plate of painstakingly julienned vegetables – and they had their first quarrel. Defeated, she fell into bed early, not long after the children.

She woke in the middle of the night and stared into the dark, feeling foolish. It was so unfair of her to behave like this when Seth had gone to so much trouble. Or maybe she was deliberately trying to goad him, to find a reason not to deal with a relationship that was threatening to run away with her. If so, it was pretty cowardly on her part, especially as he hadn't flinched from taking her on. She sat for an hour or two, wondering what Martha was like. In marked contrast to Matthew, who was open about all his relationships, Seth hated discussing his. Perhaps that's why part of him seemed so unfathomable. The cottage was chilly when the fires went out and her breath was beginning to mist. She tiptoed into the children's room. The cold was making them sleep deeply. She went down to the kitchen and made herself some ginger-and-apple tea. Outside it had stopped raining. A lemon crescent-shaped moon cut a swathe through the scrim of stars like a scythe. She wondered which group was Orion. Matthew knew all the constellations. In the summer he would lie for hours in the garden with Nell inventing inhabitants for all of them. She wondered whether he was watching them now and whether they looked different from Guatemala.

'Oh, go *away*, Matthew,' she said aloud.

Passing Seth's room, she heard him call out to her softly.

'Couldn't you sleep either?' he asked gently.

She shook her head. He held out his arms. She trembled by the door.

'I don't know about you,' he said, 'but Plan B seems to have gone badly wrong.'

She walked round to the side of the bed, untied her bathrobe and shivered as it slithered to the floor. Then she slipped in beside him.

'Doesn't it ever stop raining in Dorset?' asked Nell the next afternoon, looking up from a game of Ludo with Seth.

'How about I show you all how to make proper hamburgers.'

'No thanks. Grandma says meat is murder.'

'How about a swim? We could go into Yeovil. There's a great diving board. I could teach you.'

'Dad's going to teach me to dive.'

'Well, how about the dinosaur museum? Have you—' He stopped, appalled. Nell's face had crumpled up and tears were coursing silently down her cheeks.

'Do you miss him?' he asked softly. She nodded mutely. He went to hug her but she shrugged him off, her small fists pounding against his chest.

It took Janie hours to comfort her. 'I feel so guilty,' she told Seth later. 'I had no idea she felt so deeply. We've never really talked about it – she seemed to be dealing with everything so well, once Matthew stopped interfering.'

'She's bound to miss him.'

'But I stopped Matthew writing to her. I said it was upsetting her. I had no right.' Her voice quivered. 'I had no right. I've been in such a fog.' She looked at Seth, her eyes brimming with tears. 'Oh, Seth, I'm so sorry.' He tried to smile, to tell her that it didn't matter. But he couldn't help thinking that it did. He had felt so elated that morning, as if their relationship were finally going somewhere. But now, if he believed in omens, and he tried not to – they had always been Finn's indulgence – he would have said they weren't good.

Chapter Sixteen

Edward Rushmore poked his head jubilantly round Phyllida's door.

'Janie's up for a Press Society award' – he scanned the letter in his hand – 'for her "witty and irreverent profiles". First time a fashion journalist's ever been nominated. Isn't that marvellous news?'

Phyllida didn't think it was remotely marvellous and she couldn't stand Edward when he was in proselytising mood. She had spent the nine days since the publication of Anastasia's interview assiduously placing copious amounts of clear blue water between herself and her erstwhile protégée. Now she was going to have to doggy-paddle a long way back. Or was she?

'Marvellous,' she said sweetly. 'If you happen to set store by those things. Personally I find the idea of journalists patting themselves on the back rather nauseating. Anyway, Edward, I've been meaning to talk to you about Janie's replacement. I've had a stack of applications – all very discreet, of course.'

'Well now!' He coughed. 'No need to be hasty. That might not be necessary. The Proprietor happens to set a great deal of store by awards. You of all people should know that, Phyllida, after what happened that time you were pipped at the post by . . . oh, who was that girl who ran the features desk at *The Probe* . . . ?' Phyllida glowered.

'Er, anyway, where was I? Ah, yes. What we really ought to do is start running Janie's photograph by her name – build

377

up her profile, rather than damning her without a fair trial. I'm sure The Proprietor will rethink . . . you know this nomination could just be the answer to a maiden's prayer.'

'Oh, for Christ's sake, Edward. You saw that piece in *The Python*, later confirmed in the *Sunday Times*. Janie Pember's finished at PPS.'

He stared at her disapprovingly.

'I don't think one should automatically assume that the *Gazette* exists solely to promote the friends and acquaintances of its owner. There is, Phyllida, such a thing as journalistic integrity.' He glided out of her office, metaphorical halo floating serenely above his silvery white quiff.

Phyllida stared after him contemptuously. Over my dead body, she thought.

'Harder,' snapped Anastasia. '*Harder*. Oh, for heaven's sake, Gunter, doesn't anyone know how to give a proper massage any more?' She swatted his chunky hands off her shoulders and swung her legs impatiently over the side of the bed, ignoring Gunter's petulant pout. As her towel slithered on to the floor, she barely noticed him ogling her tanned, lithe body. She felt like a bottle of champagne that had been left in the deep freeze too long and was about to implode. She knew she was driving everyone mad, including herself. But there was nothing she could do about it. The problem was that having instantly divined that the way to The Proprietor's heart was to play the meek damsel in distress, she was now obliged to continue the role. It had been quite amusing to begin with. But now her *me miserum* act was wearing a bit thin. And with her fashion career on hold for the time being, she was bored – a state of affairs she recognised as dangerous.

Early on in her career, Anastasia had made a tidy sum suing the Moscow newspapers – enough at any rate to buy herself a rather ornate dacha outside the city. But The Proprietor, who was torn between the desire to avenge Anastasia and reluctance to sack an award-winning writer, had conveniently cast her as an all-forgiving saint. In an ironic twist Anastasia understandably could not enjoy, she found herself having to urge The Proprietor, in that breathy voice he loved, not to be too harsh in his treatment of Janie, when what she really wanted to do was skin the bitch. She didn't know how much longer she could keep playing Miss Goody Two Shoes, but she had a nasty inkling that The Proprietor's affection for her was largely predicated on what he took for her piety – that corny old Madonna–whore fixation. She had even found herself attending Mass with him. It wouldn't have been so bad if she could have vented her spleen on the Moscow office. But Irina and Nadjia were running things in an exemplary fashion. Business, she reflected glumly, had never been better. She needed a diversion. The more malicious the better.

She leafed idly through a pile of magazines. Jo-Jo was on the cover of four of them. There was an article about model agencies in the November issue of *Vogue*, with a picture of Cassie beaming away in a steel-grey Jil Sander trouser suit, although what she had to smile about was beyond Anastasia. Some people were shameless. Or maybe it required more than average ingenuity to humiliate them. Orchestrated whispering campaigns and anonymous tip-offs to Scotland Yard clearly weren't enough. Perhaps she should get Vladimir to compose some more explicit Bellissimo faxes for Cassie; making sure this time that the police actually saw them. And it was probably about time, she thought, that the *International Gazette* ran an exposé on Hot Shots. It would have to be carefully, tortuously, planned. She would also enlist the help of a few of the more vicious tabloids too. She smiled lubriciously and dialled the Moscow office.

'What kept you?' Irina asked insolently. 'It's been three hours since your last call. We thought you'd died.'

Anastasia ignored her. 'That bunch of thugs you're employing as security at the salons – arrange for one of them, preferably the one who was caught with his hand in the till, who you insisted on giving a second chance to, to be caught by the police in possession of some drugs. If he could manage to say that he got them from an English model, tell him I'll make it worth his while. Don't sound so put out. At least this way you get to screw him twice.' She giggled nastily. Few things excited her more than a really vicious game of cat and mouse.

Janie sprawled luxuriously across the outsize sofa, mesmerised by the woman daubing a giant purple circle with her feet on a wall in the apartment across the street.

'Performance artist,' giggled Madeleine. 'Sometimes she just stands there, upside down and naked for hours on end. Leonardo went to see her show out of neighbourly solidarity. She talks to her vagina. He said it was very enlightening.'

Janie reached for another spare rib. They were eating Chinese and drinking French to celebrate Madeleine's new apartment. Janie had spent her last few days in London chasing Aeron and Angel for a piece on London's most talented designers. It was her first article for *Eden* and it had been nail-biting trying to reach everyone on the phone. Then, at the last minute, Phyllida had refused point blank to send Sissy to New York on the grounds that it was an unnecessary extravagance. After the ensuing traumas this had caused, Janie found it almost relaxing to be in New York, although she felt a pang every time she thought of Nell and Daisy's tear-stained faces. Jake had gone all stoical on her and refused to look up from Nell's Barbie doll when she left. At least this was probably the last time they would all have to go through that agony, what with her job apparently on the line . . . she didn't want to think about all that tonight. She'd rather hear about the upturn in Madeleine's fortunes. She'd certainly landed on her feet with the apartment. Leonardo seemed charming and was quite clearly besotted with her, even if Madeleine couldn't see it, and she was obviously revelling in her new job. At this rate she wouldn't ever want to come back to London, thought Janie despondently.

'Oh, Janie, cheer up. I met Lee Howard the other night. She'd give you a staff job here tomorrow. So would Tom, for that matter. He thinks you're God's gift to the literate world. Not that you aren't, of course. He'd probably create a new position for you.'

'It's not just the job,' said Janie. 'To be honest I haven't a clue what's happening there. They haven't had the good manners to tell me whether or not I'm actually fired. It's Seth and Matthew and Nell . . .' To her horror she found tears streaming down her face. Madeleine hugged her and passed her some kitchen towel.

'I'm just so tired,' sniffed Janie, 'of living my life in limbo.'

She had pulled herself together by the time she had dinner with Tom the following night. For someone on the eve of their show, he oozed bonhomie and seemed remarkably calm.

'I'm too old and rich to get wound up about a show, pippin,' he told her on the way to his favourite restaurant. 'Besides, I employ enough people to do that for me.' His eyes twinkled like freshly rained-on periwinkles against his tanned skin. Janie couldn't help wondering if he'd had his chambray shirt dyed specially. It matched his eyes so perfectly.

The restaurant, a chic, luxuriously bare palace, with over-head fans and an expensively underdressed clientele, was buzz-ing. Janie noticed numerous sets of eyes swivel in Tom's direction as they walked to their table. Fifty really wasn't that old, she thought, taking the opportunity to examine him as they sat down, especially when the years had been as kind to the body as they had to Tom's. He was popping with good health, with the fragrant good looks of a miniseries leading man and the kind of sleek healthiness that only Americans seem to pull off success-fully. They could wear the most utilitarian clothes and somehow still look expensive because their shoes were immaculate, their skin glowed and their hair shone. There was an article in that.

A waiter who looked like a male model trotted over and recited the list of specials with such bathetic wistfulness that he might have been auditioning for a part in a Steven Sondheim. Listening to the dying fall of crème brûlée with cranberries, Janie wondered how his customers ever stopped giggling long enough to place their orders.

'He did Shakespeare in the Park this summer, bless him,' said Tom apologetically when the waiter finally departed for the wine list. 'Spear-carrier and understudy for Duncan. It's ruined his menu delivery . . . but the food is superb.'

For about an hour they kept to small talk – plants, children, Madeleine, whom Tom generously attributed with already making a huge difference to the team.

'You won't see it tomorrow, of course. A lot of that was prepared before she arrived. But next season will look terrific. There won't be a thing for Belinda to wear.' He raised his glass. 'Chin-chin.'

Janie couldn't help laughing. He was irrepressible. After almost a bottle of Dom Perignon, she was finally beginning to unwind. Madeleine was right. Tom had an amazing ability to use his privilege and cheerfulness to envelop everyone around him with a protective cocoon.

'How come you're always so calm?' she asked. 'I mean, here you are out with a journalist on the eve of an important collection—'

'Not just a journalist. A friend, I hope. One thing I've learned in life is always to mix business with pleasure.'

He watched her relax into her seat. There was a natural sporty elegance about Janie that reminded him of old photographs of English women touring the Continent in the thirties. She was dressed extremely simply – a white shirt, black velvet trousers that emphasised her long legs – her hair loose over her shoulders, the merest slick of make-up. She was a born minimalist, he decided. And he loved the way he could see her breasts. English women were always inadvertently revealing their breasts. For such a nation of Puritans they were extraordinarily lax about underwear. Belinda's would have been bound and gagged in La Perla.

'That's better, pippin,' he said. 'You laughing, I mean.'

'Have I been that glum?' she asked.

'I'll forgive all if you tell me what the problem is.'

Something about his manner – warm and non-judgmental – made her want to tell him everything, even the bits she hadn't confided to Madeleine, who for all her compassion seemed to think that Janie's romantic problems were the kind most women dream of.

'So are you in love with either of them?' Tom asked finally.

'Yes. No. Oh, I don't know. Mostly I think I hate Matthew. Then I find myself longing to see him, if only to close the door on our relationship. It's bloody frustrating, you know, wanting to be absolutely clear in your contempt for someone and then finding yourself fantasising about the first time you slept with them.'

Tom was smiling.

'But then it's okay, because quite soon I find myself hating him again. But then again—'

'He's the father of your children and—'

'Not so you'd notice. To be perfectly honest I think that's the problem. I could forgive him for going all doolally on me, but not on Nell and Daisy and Jake. It's almost a year since he's seen them, for God's sake. So yes, although there's a residue of love, there are layers and layers of recriminations. And the longer he's gone, the less inclined I am to dig through them. In fact I'd rather not deal with them at all.'

'And Seth?'

'That's just it. I don't know. It should be perfect. It *is* perfect – I think. But perfect doesn't somehow feel quite enough . . . at least not for him. He's very *committed* to his work.'

'I know exactly what you mean. Sometimes you do a collection that just seems like the best taste ever and then when you see it all together you think what this really needs is a little injection of something just a bit tacky – you know, just the wrong side of the tracks – to spice it up a bit . . . Oh, sorry. I don't know what came over me. Comparing your troubles with a fashion collection.' He looked sheepish. 'Listen, what you need is a break. From everything. How about if you and the kids came and stayed at Firefly in a few weeks? Personally December's one of my favourite times there, but if the bracing air doesn't appeal, we could always fly you down to Tobago.

The four of you could have the place to yourself if you wanted. Could be just what you need.'

Janie dimly recalled reading an article in *Vanity Fair* that had described Turtle House, Tom's Caribbean beach complex, nestling in the lush curve of Englishman's Bay, and was touched to the core by his kindness. He guarded his privacy there religiously and no journalist had ever been. To her horror she felt an army of tears slipping down her cheeks again. She searched for a handkerchief and made do with the tablecloth, accidentally upsetting a bottle of Château Haute Brion '83. Duncan perked up, as if he'd just been called to arms to slay Macbeth. So did several of his colleagues. There was much dabbing and blotting and flapping of hands. The evening had taken a nosedive. Tom motioned the maître d' for a cab.

'Sorry for being such a misery,' Janie snuffled as they bounced along Madison Avenue. 'Too much wine. Too much whining, come to that. I'll say one thing for my job – it's taught me to pack away vast amounts of alcohol.' It was unforgivable of her to wallow in self-pity, she thought, especially when Tom had problems of his own. She gave into the tears and mascara sloshing down her face. The huge apartment blocks on either side of the avenue were ablaze with light. Some of the trees had been threaded with early Christmas illuminations. Manhattan looked ridiculously pretty and strangely oblivious to her problems. She was even learning to love the noise, the jiggling sound the manholes made every time a car drove over them, the endless echoing of traffic as it bellowed round the skyscraper canyons, and the way the truck horns sounded like ships coming into harbour. She wondered how much it would cost to fly with the children down to Tobago and whether her redundancy package might cover it.

Tom saw her craning her neck.

'My entire first year here I did exactly what you're doing now. Cost me a fortune in osteopathy. But it was worth it. I'd spent the first eighteen years of my life longing to be here. It seemed the most glamorous place on earth. I did every corny tourist routine. Carriage rides through Central Park, cocktails every Friday in the Rainbow Room, moonlight skating at the Rockefeller Center.'

'You can skate there at night?' Janie blew her nose and revived slightly at the vision of Tom pirouetting on ice.

'You can, pippin, and I did. *Every* night. I got pretty good, actually. Came second in the under-nineteens state competition. Could have gone on to do it in the Olympics – except they didn't do it in the Olympics in those days. There, that dates me.'

'You're having me on. And I know how old you are, Tom, I've read it in your press clippings.' She blew her nose again.

'Good Lord, you don't believe a word of those, I hope. Anyway, my precious, you won't have read about the ice skating because the first thing my PR did in 1973 was expunge it from my personal history. She pointed out that it made me sound like a raging queen. My mother said I should fire her. She said I was only ever good at two things and ice skating was by far the more respectable option. She didn't think making women's clothes was a terribly *appropriate* way for a man to make a living, you see. Poor Mother. Robin Cousins hadn't come out then, you see – and frankly I doubt if my mother would have believed him if he had. She thought anything athletic must be *okay*, if you get my drift.'

'Prove it. Prove you were worthy of at least second place.'

'Now, pippin, you don't really mean that.'

'Never been more serious.'

'Only if you do it with me.'

'I am the worst ice skater ever. I'll cramp your style hideously.'

'Prove it.'

The taxi turned into East 61st and headed west before turning back downtown towards the Rockefeller ice rink. It was pretty deserted apart from half a dozen isolated moonlit figures who span round the rink at terrifying speeds, their skates tearing menacingly through the ice, their breath trailing little puffs of smoke in the cold night air. Tom took Janie's hand and led her gently towards the centre because, he explained, if they stayed near the edge she would never let go of the rail. The sudden blast of a freezing November night had rapidly sobered her up, and she was having second thoughts about the whole venture. Gingerly she stepped on to the ice and pushed one foot in front of the other, her blades making feeble little stabs in the surface while she clung with both arms to Tom's left arm. She shivered and Tom produced a lilac cashmere scarf from the recesses of his coat.

'Be prepared, take cashmere spares.'

After a while she began to relax and felt the blades of her skates beginning to propel her across rather than through the ice. Tom was endlessly patient and kept up a stream of increasingly pornographic jokes to take her mind off her fear. He was probably a marvellous dancer, thought Janie, and suddenly found herself mourning the passing of the foxtrot and the waltz – there was something about Tom that belonged firmly to another era, Errol Flynn's perhaps. She wondered whether his PR department could do something with that image.

After an hour or so she felt that at least her bottom was no longer at right angles to the ground. There were only two other skaters now. Janie, still clinging to Tom, but much more stable despite her giggling, began to pick up speed. Exhilarated after several turns, she felt breathless and, on the pretext of needing to rest, persuaded Tom to do a few circuits on his own. He lived up to his claims – he was an athletic, graceful skater who clearly got more of a thrill out of taking calculated risks at very high speed than perfecting fussy flourishes. There was nothing effeminate about his performance on the ice. She was faintly surprised – and surprised to find she was surprised. She hadn't given Tom's sexuality much thought, but had casually assumed, along with many people in the industry, that he was gay or bisexual and that Belinda was, to adopt *Blitzkrieged!!* terminology, his Beard. As Sissy had pointed out, no one who spent as much time posing for such ruthlessly macho publicity shots as Tom did (he was forever being photographed astride horses, dangling from a parachute or ten feet above a mogul) could possibly be straight. But to judge from tonight, they'd all got it wrong. How awful, thought Janie with a pang. Far from being vaguely inconvenienced by Belinda's departure, he was probably heartbroken.

'*Voilà*,' he said, slicing to a dramatic halt in front of her. 'The legacy of a misspent youth. Calvin and Halston had Studio 54. I had ice skates. Edgy, don't you think?'

He didn't look the picture of an inconsolable man, she had to admit. After a couple more turns round the rink together, Tom pointed out that they'd been there for one and a half hours. They headed off to a little all-night bar in the West Village. Three Bloody Marys down the line they were feeling sufficiently ebullient for Tom to repeat his invitation.

'I mean it. A holiday would do you good. It's very private too. The press never get down there. Madeleine could come, if you like. I'm sure we could spare her for a few days.'

The lure of Madeleine was tempting, not just because she would be good company but because if Tom was happy to have Madeleine there he presumably saw Janie in a platonic light. She said she'd think about it, see if she could get some time off work, sound things out with Seth.

'Invite him along too, if you think it would help. It's amazing how a good holiday can repair a relationship. Take it from one who built an entire marriage on good holidays.'

Janie felt that after the Dorset débâcle, her first holiday alone with Seth should be spent, as they'd promised themselves, on their own. But she was deeply touched by the offer all the same.

Seth sounded a little abrupt. Janie's call had arrived at just about the same time as sixty or so orders for main courses and a restaurant critic from the *New Yorker*.

'Whoops,' she giggled, still a little breathless from the skating. 'Not great timing. I can't get to grips with British Summer Time – is it over yet or not?'

'The clocks went forward a week ago,' said Seth a little too sharply. Two of his kitchen staff were sick and Brad Pitt had taken them all by surprise by arriving for an 8.30 booking that had been made in an alias name, trailing nine guests and a dozen paparazzi.

'Whoops again. Anyway, pippin,' slurred Janie, lapsing into Tom-speak, 'I have an indecent proposal for you that couldn't wait.'

'I'm afraid it will have to. We're chocka and the crowd could turn very ugly if my soufflés don't perform as expected.'

'I've never known anything of yours not rise to the occasion—'

Seth grunted.

Janie could feel herself blushing. 'Anyway, I've got us a holiday all planned. No packing required. Well, just a sense of humour.'

'Janie, not now.'

'Day after tomorrow. Meet me in St Louis. Or at least St Kitts. Actually, I'm not quite sure where it is, but by tomorrow a.m., or yesterday p.m. your time, or whatever, I'll have all details. In fact, if you hang on while I wade through some clippings, I may even—'

'Janie,' Seth said through clenched teeth, 'for Pete's sake, not now. You're drunk.'

Yeah, but in the morning I shall be sober and you'll still be a spoilsport, she thought, but didn't say. There didn't seem much point, as Seth had hung up.

Phyllida was in a foul mood. In the absence of Janie she had been asked by Channel 4 News to take part in a studio debate about ageism in the media. Phyllida's opinion – well known amongst the *Gazette*'s NUJ members whom she despised almost as much as she did avant-garde fashion designers – was that there were no *isms* of any kind in the media and that suggestions to the contrary were likely to have come from her favourite hate group – whingeing wimmin. The problem was that having accepted Channel 4's invitation, she now couldn't get an appointment with Antony, her hair colourist, for two weeks. Phyllida had set her heart on a soft Titian red. An article in *The Python* said it was a gentler solution for greying hair than the peroxide highlights she normally had. Red certainly worked for Gayle Hunnicutt. It had been a tense morning for all concerned, with Phyllida screeching at Lorna to tell Antony that if he couldn't find her a slot, she wasn't going on air, because if The Proprietor caught her on TV with grey hair she'd be out of a job faster than you could say shifting demographics. And if she had to cancel Channel 4, Antony might just find himself the subject of a *Gazette* watchdog exposé on rip-off salons. Itching for a fight, Phyllida went walkabout, while Lorna wearily double-checked that there would be a make-up artist on hand in the studio.

Edward Rushmore wasn't in his office, so, with the following day's proposed fashion visuals tucked under her arm, Phyllida marched up to the next floor and across to an enormous bowl of lilac and crimson blooms. It was like showing a red rose to a bull. Phyllida never got flowers. The fashion desk was constantly smothered in them – gifts from grateful clients they'd featured on their pages and further proof in Phyllida's eyes that the world of consumer journalism was a cesspit of corruption.

'Is this ironic or what?' she asked, flinging a photograph on to the light-box, where Sissy was hunched over a line-up of Christian Lacroix transparencies, trying to find a picture that would illustrate her feature on 'The New Mix and Matching'.

It was a striped Yoko Rakabuto angel dress with integral organza wings made from yoghurt cartons from winter 1997 that Sissy had been planning to run down-page to illustrate a short filler she had written on modern classics. She had been dying to get it into the paper for ages, but Janie had never found room.

'Iconic, actually,' said Sissy neutrally.

'Moronic, more like. Oh, but that's fashion all over, isn't it? Do something absolutely ridiculous and degrading and call it di-bloody-rectional or better still *ironic.*' She pounced lasciviously on the last word. 'Christ, I don't suppose most of you can spell ironic, let alone define it. Well, things are going to change around here, let me tell you. You can forget irony. From now on, if it doesn't sell in the Hull branch of Etam, it doesn't go in.'

Sissy watched as Phyllida's angry-looking tomato power suit receded towards the coffee machine like a heat-seeking missile. What was ironic, thought Sissy, returning to Lacroix's leg-o'-mutton wedding dress, was that according to Angel, Aeros was baning his next collection round suburban Eighties style, which meant Phyllida's horrific shoulder-padded jackets would be the height of fashion. It just showed – if you kept anything long enough it became a classic. Sometimes, thought Sissy, it was hard to keep faith with fashion.

Except that it had finally become a lucrative source of income for Sissy. Typical. After half a dozen financially barren years during which she had watched disbelievingly while certain of her peers had made small fortunes moonlighting for anyone who asked them, she suddenly found herself in demand as well. In the three weeks since she had got back from Argentina, she had had four requests from major designers wanting her to style their new advertising campaigns, and Angel had asked her to direct his next show, which he announced was going to be properly funded, despite the fact that Anastasia appeared to have lost interest. No thanks to Sissy, said Angel loftily, he'd managed to find a new backer himself.

Sissy didn't really consider herself to be a stylist at all. She was a journalist, who happened to specialise in fashion. But needs must. And on a newspaper you had to be prepared to turn your hand to anything. Or that was what Louisa had always said. Within a month of starting as Louisa's so-called editorial assistant, Sissy had found herself not just calling in outfits for the shoot and ironing them, but deciding which ones they should photograph. After a couple of months Louisa gave up all pretence of directing the exercise and let Sissy choose the photographers, models, make-up artists and hairdressers herself. It wasn't very long before Louisa, who suffered from the most excruciating migraines every time another slash in the *Gazette*'s budget meant that they would have to shoot on Brownsea

Island instead of going to Mauritius, began not bothering to turn up at the studio at all. As well as having to engage in some spectacularly creative accounting with Louisa's expenses, Sissy found herself marshalling endless teams of people to produce images to illustrate Louisa's increasingly abstruse articles. She never got an on-page credit for any of this, but as Louisa pointed out, it was Invaluable Experience. Invaluable, that was, to Louisa, Sissy thought through gritted teeth as she and a skimpily dressed model froze inside a beach hut while the photographer smeared turquoise gel over his lens and tried to make the coastline round Studland look like Barbados.

And now the goosebumps were finally laying their golden eggs. Alec Marolo was relaunching himself, and had asked Sissy to help him out as a design consultant. Vittorio Chacha wanted her to do a billboard campaign and Boldacci had offered her ridiculous sums of money and club class tickets to Harbour Island to style a fourteen-page catalogue. The timing, given that she no longer strictly needed the money, was perverse, but it was gratifying to be asked all the same.

'So you see,' she had said to Angel that morning, 'I don't know if I'll be able to give your show the attention it deserves. The Boldacci job may well clash because they want Dirk Von Litten to shoot it and he's only got one day free between now and Christmas . . .'

'I see,' said Angel in a voice that suggested he didn't at all. He still hadn't altogether forgiven Sissy for not pulling off the deal with Anastasia.

'Look – I'm not saying no definitely. It's just that I want to do a good job and the Boldacci's going to take a lot of planning.'

'I don't see why,' said Angel testily. 'Just put whatever looks most hideous together and he'll be thrilled.'

Sissy sighed. She felt Angel was being deliberately obtuse. It was very mean-spirited of him, especially after all the times she had helped out on his collections for nothing. However, he had a point about Boldacci, who made some of the most unattractive clothes on the planet which – for reasons Sissy had always found unfathomable – sold to the tune of hundreds of millions of pounds. Boldacci never confined himself to a ruffle where a swag, a bow, a jabot and a sunray pleat could also be incorporated. Minimalism had passed him by. So had any other trend from the last fifteen years. The last time he had been vaguely cutting-edge was in 1971. Aeron, who had worked for Boldacci during his year out from St Martin's, had once told her that the only way his younger design assistants could tune into his taste was to lock themselves into a room together for three days before they started work on each collection and drop acid. Nevertheless, she wanted to do the job. Working with Dirk Von Litten would boost her CV no end. And she was beginning to suspect that her stock might be about to take a nosedive on the *Gazette*.

Sure enough, that afternoon a memo arrived from Phyllida's office stating that henceforth all clothes featured in the *Gazette* must be obtainable from the high street. It was ridiculous, of course. The *Gazette* had the most upmarket readership of all the national broadsheets, but Sissy knew better than to reason with Phyllida in her current mood. Gritting her teeth, she spent the rest of the afternoon on the phone to the PRs from Etam, Littlewood's, Dolcis and (oh, brainwave) Everything She Wants, calling in clothes for Friday's shoot. Then she rang Asprey's and Tiffany's and reserved £500,000 worth of jewellery, including some darling little platinum bands that had rubies and emeralds rattling around on the inside, so no one could see how much they were worth. If Phyllida insisted that the clothes had to be horrid, then Sissy would jolly well make sure they had decent accessories on the page. Out there was a public crying out to be educated in the finer things in life. Once she had realised that this gave her the perfect excuse to call Nari, who still hadn't been in touch since she got back from Argentina, it promised not to be such a bad day after all. Everything She Wants turned out not to have a PR. Company policy, Jean informed Sissy primly, when she finally got through to her. 'Nari doesn't believe in pandering to the press.' How pathetically naïve, thought Sissy.

'How laudable,' was what she said. 'The thing is, Jean, we're changing our policy. We want to be more consumer-friendly. It would be a great pity not to be able to bring your stupendously good-value-for-money product to the attention of our readers.' Having to beg Everything She Wants to send in some of their tat, so that she could have it photographed by an up-and-coming photographer who would make it look as palatable as possible for an estimated two million readers, signalled a low ebb in her career, she thought. Normally retailers and designers were overcome with gratitude and a desire to denude the nearest florist at the mere suggestion that they were about to be featured in the *Gazette*'s esteemed pages.

Jean sounded distinctly unimpressed. 'I don't know—' she began.

'Perhaps I should speak to Nari. I'm sure he would want Everything She Wants to be represented—' This was getting ridiculous. There was not one item in all thirty-five branches of Everything She Wants that could possibly be of interest to the ABC1 readers of the *International Gazette*, but Sissy never could resist the thrill of the chase.

'Nari's not here,' said Jean curtly.

'Well, could you take a message?' said Sissy, sounding urgent. 'And tell him it's a question of reaching four million readers.'

She gave the number of the fashion department's third telephone line – the one they reserved for Angel, Seth and Cassie. Ten minutes later it rang. Nari's voice sounded even more perfectly pitched than she remembered. She tried to sound businesslike.

'It's a new policy – to alert our readers to the existence of the multiple and variety sectors.'

There was an expectant silence on the other end.

'The key individual players in that group, apart from Everything She Wants, of course, being Etam, C&A, BHS, Littlewood's . . .' It was a roll-call of names straight out of Sissy's worst nightmare. And still the silence.

'The thing is that while the *International Gazette*'s readership segments primarily into ABC1s, qualitative research has shown that a sizeable portion – up to one million readers, to be precise, accounting for ten per cent of the total expenditure in this market – shop at least once a fortnight in variety chains.' This was total claptrap, the jargon culled from the yellowing stack of *Retail Week*s in front of Sissy. 'What it boils down to is not so much a demographic shift in our readership as a dramatic shift in their buying patterns. Our researches have identified it as cross-socio spend . . .'

'Sissy . . .' The voice sounded neutral enough, but she was positive she could hear his mouth stretching into a grin. 'Flattered as I think I am by your readers' new buying patterns and cross-socio spend, I'm afraid we simply can't help with your request.'

'What happens when *The Python* calls in for stuff, or magazines like *Chantal*?' said Sissy, trying to keep the petulance out of her voice.

'The same thing, I'm afraid. We're simply not set up to send out clothes for the press to photograph. We barely manage to get enough samples to the factories sometimes.'

It was Sissy's turn to go silent.

'I'm sorry. I suppose it sounds very ungrateful, but our priority must be to ensure there's always stock available for the customers.'

'We don't usually encounter this much resistance when we want to feature something,' Sissy said incredulously, and consequently sounding frostier than she had intended.

'I suppose I might be able to find a spare sample somewhere.' He sounded doubtful. 'Sleek and stretchy, I believe you wanted? Then I could get it biked over.'

'Well . . .' Sissy's brain went into turbocharged mode. 'Colour's important too. I could always come and meet you – or whoever – at the warehouse, to save sending over the wrong thing – our features editor has such unpredictable taste. We could go through them together, then and there, and I could bring it back with me.'

'Fine. It'll probably be whoever, I'm afraid. I've got to be in Leeds by five.'

'Great,' said Sissy as breezily as she could, which was how, at 3.15 that afternoon, she found herself hopelessly lost in a tailback on the Mile End Road, *en route* to some horrific warehouse to collect an even more horrific outfit for a non-existent story.

After an hour and three quarters of driving round increasingly similar-looking converted warehouses and a minicab bill that had already racked up fifty-seven pounds, she reluctantly agreed with the driver and they turned round and came back.

Waking up with a stygian hangover from her night out with Tom Fitzgerald, Janie checked the time. It was seven in the morning and Aeron had finally returned her call from Paris, where he'd been up all night rehearsing for his interview with Gilles de Gaumard. She dovetailed his quotes into her piece as seamlessly as she could and faxed it over to Lee; she couldn't afford to miss her first deadline. Lee, although unfailingly courteous, had a severity about her that suggested she had never allowed small personal mishaps – births, deaths, minor earthquakes, say – to get between her and her professionalism. Pleading delay due to alcohol poisoning didn't seem an option.

Several blocks further south, Jo-Jo was balancing on the bath ledge so that she could see her bottom from three angles in the Royalton's bathroom mirrors. It wasn't the smallest bottom she had seen that day. In fact, it was quite possibly the biggest. She had looked grotesque in the vol-au-vent dresses Molly Dee had put them in the day before. They had all looked grotesque – that was the purpose of doing a Molly Dee show, Unity said philosophically; it kept you relatively humble and stopped you believing all the guff *Supermodel* magazine wrote about you.

Unity had a really cool grip on life. Even when *A La Mode* had shaved off all her eyebrows and they'd taken a whole year to grow back, she hadn't flapped. She unerringly saw the big picture, and when you thought about it, she couldn't help being posh. It was Unity who had impressed upon Jo-Jo the necessity of developing a defining trait that would set her apart from everyone else.

'It's more important for me, of course,' she had said in her tickety-tock Vivien Leigh staccato, squinting at her reflection in Jo-Jo's mirror and emitting a perfect halo of cigarette smoke. 'I *needed* an idiosyncrasy, being more what you'd call a character model. You're just drop-dead beautiful. But even you could use a USP – Unique Selling Point,' she explained, seeing Jo-Jo's baffled expression. 'It's about attitude. I was lucky, with the aristo tag and everything. You could try the Cindy Crawford professional-to-a-fault tactic. Although in another six months you'll be Girl of the Season, without even trying. You're a classic. Still, you're obviously terribly ambitious and tough as old boots – must be to have changed agencies so early on.'

Jo-Jo didn't feel up to either of those tributes, and she certainly didn't want to discuss the way she'd handled her departure from Hot Shots. She steered the conversation round to mortgages, which were beginning to fascinate her, while Unity practised a spectacular pigeon-toed strut which she hoped would take up most of the catwalk and make it impossible for anyone else to walk alongside her.

'And for my next trick, I'm going to lose a stone and a half.'

'But you don't need to, you're slim as a beanpole,' Jo-Jo remonstrated.

'Sweetie, you know quite well that it's not about normal perceptions of beauty. No earthly good being slim, gotta be skinniest. Last season Kristof told Isabella and Grace he couldn't use them for couture any more because they were getting too big. So Grace retires and Isabella loses two stone. Freaky or what? Apparently she's on three packets of cigarettes a day and they're calling her Speedy GonSuarez on account of the amphetamines. If you ask me she's living proof that the Duchess of Windsor was wrong. But the designers and editors have gone nuts about her. It's resurrected her career, for the nineteenth time. The moral is, as I say, that in order to be GoS you've got to get a USP. Here, what I really came round for was to show you this.'

She chucked Jo-Jo a Sotheby's catalogue. 'They're having a sale of Picasso's etchings next month. My accountant tells me they'd be a good investment. Some of them aren't too hideous either. What say we make a night of it?'

Unity's lecture certainly provided Jo-Jo with food for thought, or rather starvation rations. Jo-Jo was doing quite a lot of thinking at the moment. She had thought going on shoots was character-building enough – there was only so much of Zoffy's malevolence one could take – but at least the locations were usually breathtaking and there was always someone like Dodie or Enrico to share the strain. But the shows were different. From about five in the morning onwards she spent the whole day tearing from one to another, sitting in traffic, listening to her driver swearing, having her hair yanked by hairdresser after hairdresser, listening to the designer swearing, hoping her skin wouldn't break out from all the lights and elaborate make-up. Then, as Unity put it, you had to va-va-voom out on to the catwalk in the full glare of one thousand pairs of eyes, without the safety net of a studio or clever lighting. And you walked miles – Unity reckoned at least five a day, including trips to the loo. By 11 p.m., when Jo-Jo got back to her hotel, she was usually too exhausted to socialise, although she forced herself because Unity had told her this was all part of a model's career strategy. But the parties were weird, with gaggles of beautiful women and gay men eyeing one another suspiciously, wondering if there wasn't a better party round the corner. The fashion world's social gatherings were uniquely designed to promote maximum unease amongst the greatest number of people. It was never enough to be invited; you had to be invited to the inner sanctum. Most parties had at least three cordoned-off areas for minor, major and middle-ranking VIPs. There was always the thought that somewhere, someone else was having a better time in a more exclusive corner. Apart from Unity and Tulah, she still hadn't got to know the others very well yet. Ben had had to go straight from the set of *Sons and Lovers* to start work on *Dead Before Sunrise*, a noirish thriller set in Montana. Marie-Elise, who had made a big deal out of looking after Jo-Jo personally rather than assigning her to one of her underlings, wasn't the sort of person you could just ring up for a chat and a bit of long-distance hand-holding. She had made it clear that she only expected to hear from Jo-Jo in an emergency.

The truth was that Jo-Jo felt lonelier than she ever had in her life. Even Gloria's nagging would be preferable to the same old songs that kept coming round on MTV and VH1, but she hadn't called her for a couple of weeks at least, and couldn't face the inevitable tirade. She padded over to the mini-bar and got out a Coke and a packet of pistachios. Then she found herself on the bath rim again, surveying her bottom, which was as firm and taut as a Worcestershire pear. The Verve were playing on the television, followed by Scorcher Morehouse's latest attempt to break into the ragga market with 'Kill me now, bitch'. It was very depressing. She clambered down and tipped the nuts and Coke into the loo. From now on her body was a temple. Unity was right. Why do this job if it wasn't to be Girl of the Season?

Anastasia cooed down the telephone to Lindsey Craven as she had once cooed to Janie.

'I wondered if you might be interested in a little story about a few dozen outfits I'm auctioning at Sotheby's for Peace Grant's charity.'

In her excitement Lindsey almost impaled herself on one of her rock rings. 'Why a tabloid?' she asked suspiciously. She was still sore that Janie had nabbed the first interview with Anastasia.

'Oh, I adore *The Python*, so entertaining. And such a huge circulation. I want the world to know about this sale – so we can raise as much money as possible. Shall we say tea at my place on Thursday?'

Lindsey's capitulation was so rapid and complete that Anastasia was almost disappointed. She had been girding herself for a major putsch and was in danger of scoring a complete putsch-over almost before she started.

Tom Fitzgerald had been in the business long enough to know
when applause was genuine. He had a hit on his hands. There
was a long way to go, of course, as he kept explaining to
the editors clustered around him after the show, but he felt
confident they were on the right path. Making his excuses,
he extricated himself from the pouting maws around him and
made his way over to Janie, who was deep in conversation with
an exhausted-looking Madeleine, and led them both up to his
sanctuary on the thirty-eighth floor.

It was the first time Janie had seen Tom's private suite of
offices. They were an all-white, almost religiously sparse haven,
in the centre of which were three Brancusi sculptures. French
doors ran along two walls and opened on to a terrace with
spine-tingling views towards the Hudson. Tom ambled over
to the juice bar in the corner and poured some banana-and-
seaweed cocktail from the fridge. Janie and Madeleine eyed the
bilious liquid dubiously.

'Come on, girls, it's great for your colons,' he said cheerfully. 'Listen, Madeleine, aside from telling you how much I
appreciate your sparkling contribution to today's small triumph,
I got you here to help me convince your heavenly friend that
she needs a holiday. For some reason she doesn't seem to be
jumping at my offer. What do you think – too proud or too
suspicious?'

Janie blushed and they both shrugged helplessly at Tom.

'How about if you chaperone us?' Tom looked steadily at
Madeleine, whose expression flickered between consternation
and panic. 'Bring a friend, if you like . . . Come on, you might
as well accept. I have absolutely no compunction about pulling
rank, and if all else fails, pippins, I'm going to force-feed you
both seaweed and banana until you agree to come.'

Lee Howard had finally called Janie at her hotel to congratulate
her about the piece on Aeron and the new British designers.

She apologised for not getting back sooner, but since the first issue of *Eden* had hit the news-stands in September to universal acclaim, she'd been inundated.

'You'd think it would get easier, once the magazine was up and running,' she said in her clipped tones. 'But the work keeps proliferating. It's like some terrible disease – except I love it.' Janie was itching to see the offices and was thrilled when Lee asked her if she would pass by to run through some queries and talk the art director through the story.

It was 9.30 in the morning when Janie arrived outside 720 Fifth Avenue. The lift was packed with slender girls in dark trouser suits, all silently eyeing up each other's food parcels – everyone was far too busy to lunch out, reserving special disdain for anyone laden down with too many carbohydrates. The offices of *Eden*, on the twentieth floor, looked like a homage to an Ideal Home Exhibition *circa* 1952; awash with pastel laminated surfaces and furniture with stiletto legs. The editors, also with stiletto legs, sat deep in conversation with their headsets, snacking on translucent shavings of mango and pineapple. Janie wondered if they chose their meals to match the colour scheme. It was extraordinarily ordered; in London, a magazine that had barely been going for six months would have comprised six or eight journalists huddled over two computers and a telephone. But at *Eden*, the solemn-looking cubicles that kept all the staff in solitary confinement gave the impression of having been there for ever. There seemed to be a huge number of people for one magazine, but, as Janie remembered from her days of dealing with the American counterpart of *Beau Monde*, New York-based magazines were run with a largesse that brought tears to the eyes of the harassed staff in London. In London, *Beau Monde* had four fashion editors and two assistants. On the American edition, besides the four general senior editors, there had been three fashion editors who only dealt with bags, shoes and belts. There were two knitwear directors and two lingerie editors. Another editor had specialised in hair accessories and another in swimwear. All of them had at least one assistant. At collection time they all stayed in separate five-star hotels, drove in separate limos and appeared to loathe one another with an intensity that was only rivalled by their passionate desire to out-accessorise each other. *Eden* looked as though it was heading in exactly the same direction.

A secretary appeared and apologised for the delay, but the editor was talking to one of her star photographers. She ushered Janie to an ingeniously uncomfortable seat outside a sandblasted glass door with bubble patterns on it that led to Lee's office. Through one of the clear circles, Janie could just see Lee pacing the floor with a telephone headset clamped over her ears. Whoever she was talking to, the conversation had got pretty heated. 'I don't care if you do think the tiger looks better dead. We're not killing endangered species . . .' Janie heard Lee saying firmly. Mesmerised, she watched while Lee continued to pace in front of a full-length mirror, still talking to the photographer and all the while expertly tying and retying the blond cashmere jumper that was casually flung around her shoulders. There was a palpable sense of paranoia pervading the entire floor, she thought. Her ruminations were cut short by a yelp emanating from the midst of a clique of accessories editors who seemed to be stalking a pair of satin-and-pearl mules that were apparently the wrong shade of duck-egg blue. After a few moments Lee herself wafted over in a haze of blond cashmere.

'Ladies, might I suggest calling Angel for a fresh pair?'

'He's gone to an ashram,' said a girl wearing a sheer pink dress and a giant Philip Treacy hat shaped like a starship.

'I still think we should air-brush the picture afterwards,' said a sixty-year-old-looking skull that appeared to have no body between it and the pair of red satin wedge sandals that anchored it to the ground.

'I think that would be dishonest to our readers,' said Lee with the patient air of a psychiatric nurse.

'We used to do it all the time at *Belle*,' the skull began. 'Once, when the circulations director told us we had to stick to Caucasian cover girls because they sold better, we tinted Naomi Campbell white. They never ran it in the end – it was around the time of the LA race riots. It was such a shame – she looked so beautiful . . .'

'Yes, well, I want *Eden* to be different. I want our readers to feel they can really trust us. If we show a sandal in pale blue, they have to be able to buy it in that exact colour.'

They stared at Lee's retreating figure in dismay.

'She's so . . . populist,' mouthed the one in the Philip Treacy hat disparagingly.

Lee introduced Janie to Jack Villiers, her award-winning art director, who shoehorned a mouth that was already too big for his face into a lupine smile for Janie's benefit, and spent the rest of their meeting pressing his considerable girth up against her, while the three of them fleshed out some ideas for the layout of Janie's piece on the hot designers. Between them Lee and Jack had created an airy yet information-packed magazine that had managed to strike an intelligent balance between elegance and accessibility. Afterwards Lee led Janie back to her office, deep in thought.

'Well handled. Jack loves to test out newcomers by sexually harassing them. It's only high spirits.'

And a towering ego, thought Janie. Instead she told Lee how much she liked the feel of the magazine. 'It looks like a calm oasis in a news-stand of freneticism and it's got an air of authority that makes you think it's been around for years. You've been very clever.'

Lee looked at her pensively. 'You don't have to answer me instantly, but how would you like to come and live in New York? My fashion features director has decided after all to go and join her husband, who's been posted to Damascus. I know you have children and it would mean uprooting them, but we would pay all your relocation expenses. Job-wise, it wouldn't be that dissimilar to what you do in London except that you'd have a team of five working under you . . .'

'. . . and twenty times the budget,' said Sissy on the line from London later that day. 'You have to take it, of course. Phyllida's being vile, by the way – and her hair looks very peculiar. It's gone sort of *Aladdin Sane*. This is your big break, Janie. We're talking major expense account. According to Jo-Jo, Zoffy bought enough rugs, chests and lamps to entirely redecorate her beach house when she was doing that shoot for them in Tanzania last month. They had to shut down the souk afterwards for stocktaking, apparently. And *Eden*'s managing editor didn't bat an eyelid. I really think the Brits could learn a thing or too about the price of creativity. Anyway, I expect the salary's three times what you're earning—'

It was five times, as a matter of fact.

'And thirty times the stress,' commented Janie. 'Sissy, you can't imagine what they're like. They all have glass windows on their doors – presumably so Lee knows when one of them's keeled over. You wouldn't know otherwise – the place doesn't exactly throb with the sound of merry laughter. I was there for two hours and no one *smiled*—'

'You could spend your weekends in the Hamptons.'

'Along with everyone else in the fashion business.'

'It's sizzling with energy.'

'Paranoia was more the noun that came to mind. Have you ever noticed how they all dress identically?'

'But they have the best accessories. Christ, Janie, I've just worked out you could probably afford a real Hermès Kelly – the alligator version.'

Even on her new salary she would not be spending criminal sums of money on endangered species, Janie thought indignantly.

'And it wouldn't matter,' continued Sissy, reading her mind, 'because think what you'd save on manicures – they only cost $6 there. Just think, no more mud under the nails.'

'And I could spend $200 on a blow-dry. The prices here are outrageous.'

'I'm amazed you know what one is. But don't worry, you can charge all grooming outlay to Dexter. Part of the magazine's image budget. Angel says all the girls from *Eden* order his shoes on their company credit cards.'

'There was this little coven of fashion editors having a major *crise* because a pair of shoes were the wrong shade of pale blue. Even Lee spent twenty minutes arranging a jumper that was supposed to look as though she'd just chucked it on. It can't be healthy to be that anal.'

'It doesn't matter. They can put their shrinks on expenses too.'

'The bottom line,' said Sissy, calling Janie back on her way out from the office, 'is that things are getting pretty heavy here. Phyllida's gone berserk. She's sent round the most spiteful memo slashing our expenses to shreds. I've already had one run-in with her about it. I told her we don't do public transport. But she wasn't in the mood to negotiate. Honestly, I doubt if you can even fit a Globetrotter through those turnstile thingies they have on the Underground. I would seriously consider taking that job, Janie. And I would seriously think about offering a junior position to your loyal assistant from England.'

'Please, please try and come out. Even if it's only for a few days,' Janie pleaded with Seth. 'I can quite see that you wouldn't want to stay at Tom's but—'

'Why can you quite see that?' he asked irritably. 'D'you think I'm too parochial for your fashion friends?'

'Not at all,' said Janie reasonably, 'I just thought you might prefer to have some time on your own with me.'

He softened. 'Of course, I'd love to, but it's impossible just now. You must see that. I'm sorry.'

Janie did see that. Finn's had barely been open three months. But she couldn't help being disappointed. She felt she was on the brink of giving up quite a lot for Seth – her marriage, for one thing. And he couldn't spare her a week's holiday. If they couldn't be spontaneous at the start of their relationship . . .

'I promise I'll make it up to you in a few months. Once this place is up and running by itself.'

She tried not to sound reproachful. 'Just don't blame me when you get a postcard from somewhere wonderful.'

'You mean you're still going?' He sounded mildly affronted.

'Why not? Flights are awfully cheap to the Caribbean from here and it won't cost much to fly the children out. We could all do with the break. From the sound of it, things have turned a bit tricky at work.'

'I would have thought,' said Seth, sounding just a little bit sanctimonious, 'that that was every reason to get back to London as quickly as possible.'

Sissy turned off the Baron's Court Road and trudged wearily towards the shabby mansion block where she still lived with Diana. As usual, the hideously pollarded trees in their street had shed their leaves before any others. A council rubbish bin squatted forlornly on the pavement where it had been left by one of the dustmen. At a pinch, the street could have hired itself out for depressing backdrops along the lines of those used in *Bladerunner* or *The Full Monty*. Almost slipping on a soggy crisp packet, Sissy marvelled at how she could have lived for four years in the same road and feel absolutely no affection for it.

And yet, since her windfall, which she'd kept secret from everyone apart from Nari and her accountant, she had been uncharacteristically tardy about organising herself into actually spending her money. She was happy enough to read about spending it. In fact she was becoming addicted to the business pages – a fantasist investor – and knew the precise state of the world's stock markets at any given moment. But spending – that was the oddest thing. She wondered whether it was the same as with sex – once you had permanent access to it you went off it. Before her first appointment with Nari's accountant she had imagined that her life was about to change beyond recognition. But after David Stevens had gently pointed out that £150,000, tax-free, although a tidy sum, was not, these days, the stuff that retirements were made of, she found herself becoming uncharacteristically cautious. She was even seriously considering his suggestion that she use £30,000 or so of it to secure a mortgage on a small flat in a sensible part of London, as opposed to buying a broom cupboard in one of the giddily fashionable areas she had always dreamt of colonising. (She drew the line at Finsbury Park.) Meanwhile she was busy watching David get on with investing the remaining sum on a mixed portfolio of blue-chip stocks, Peps and some Norwich Union shares, the dividends of which, he said, should afford her some nice summer holidays. It wasn't quite the thrill she'd imagined from riding the surge of the Dow Jones and the Han Seng, but it was better than nothing, she supposed. The point was, as David repeatedly told her, that Anastasia's money would ease her life, rather than transform it.

Still, small comforts were better than big discomforts, particularly if she were about to join the ranks of the unemployed. If that really were the case, she had better not commit herself to too extravagant a lifestyle. For the first time in years she found herself using the Tube – Phyllida had meant what she said about the fashion department having to take public transport. The *Gazette*'s petty cash officer had categorically refused Sissy any more advances and she wasn't about to start spending her own money on fares to and from the office.

The refuse collectors hadn't done a very good job. The street was littered with carrier bags. Nari would be pleased, she thought, as she got closer to them – someone had been very busy buying up Everything She Wants, which was bloody incredible, considering Nari's imperial march south had only got as far as Birmingham. The bags seemed to be forming a trail. By the time she reached her entrance, she had passed about five of them. There were another six in front of her, one for each step, only these were full. She peeked inside the first one. Inside was a fuchsia ruffled shirt and mustard maxi skirt in the kind of synthetic fabrics Sissy thought people only wore inside spaceships on low-budget BBC sci-fi productions. The next bag contained three hideously cheap-looking crocheted cardigans in shades of teal and orange. The bag at the top of the stairs had a note pinned to it.

Your wish is my command. Nari. Sissy's heart leapt. Inside was a bunch of flowers in colours carefully selected to match the clothes. She almost thought they looked ravishing. Gently kicking the warped front door, she heard the phone ringing in the flat. She raced upstairs.

Him!

'For a putative investigative journalist you're not very observant, are you?'

'Where are you?'

'Outside, in my car.'

She ran to the window and saw his Aston Martin parked across the road between a skip and a caravan.

'You never made it to the warehouse,' he said accusingly. 'But in the spirit of forgiveness and because I know it's a little hard to find, I picked some out myself and decided to deliver them myself. Personally I think it was all a ruse to get at my body.'

'I hope,' said Sissy sternly, 'that you're not going to turn out to be an arrogant bastard.'

'I'm right, though, aren't I?'

'Well, I'm certainly not after you for your colour sense.'

The brochure that Janie picked up – purely for research purposes and because, by chance, she found herself standing practically outside the Trinidad and Tobago tourist office on the way to Kevin Krocket's studio – looked very tempting. So she kept her attention glued to its limpid seas throughout Kevin's show – anything rather than catch Jo-Jo's eye. Her shoulders were sandwiched between Suzy Menkes's sausage-roll hairdo and Vincent Diego, whose basilisk eyes flicked back and forth across the catwalk. Madeleine, who had sneaked off from Tom's to give Kevin some moral support, sat discreetly behind Janie. It was one of those intimate Manhattan presentations where the models practically paddled across the fashion editors' laps. Kevin's studio, smaller than most and reached by a Heath Robinsonesque industrial elevator, was hopelessly inadequate for the task of staging any kind of show, but because he was a poppet and because they were grateful for any opportunity that made them look self-sacrificing, press and buyers risked life and limb every season to see his show. One year Hester Carmichael had fallen through a plasterboard partition wall in the crush to get in. Far from suing, she'd sent Kevin a whopping bouquet the following day to thank him for helping her locate an ancient discontinued Helena Rubinstein lipstick that she'd found at the bottom of her handbag in the topple.

The models had to change in Kevin's personal bathroom, and every millimetre of space was corralled into seating area. Unity accidentally turned the microwave on with her fox stole when she practised a new wiggle in the kitchen area, and the atmosphere, already tropical, became so electrically charged that Alice's new apricot-coloured hair extensions started to levitate. The place was clearly a complete fire hazard, but New York's A list adored Kevin as much as the press and behaved themselves in the front row as serenely as if they were geisha girls, which in a way, thought Janie, they were. The collection went down a storm and, skipping the crush of congratulations afterwards, Janie made a beeline for the elevator, which was jammed somewhere in the vicinity of the seventh floor, and took the opportunity of studying the list of flight prices.

'Boy, did Unity work that kitchenette,' giggled Kevin to Madeleine from the depths of a broom cupboard. He was smothered in YSL's pink lipstick from all the kisses – and with his head-to-toe outfit (even his cropped white hair looked like a matching dusting of cashmere) he looked like nothing so much as a windswept cyclamen. 'I thought Luella Lopez was finally going to explode – though not, please God, before she placed a massive order.'

Madeleine caught up with Janie at the head of the queue for the elevator, which had finally juddered its way up to Kevin's floor.

'Tempted, then?' she asked, signalling to the brochure clamped to Janie's breast.

'It does look gorgeous,' said Janie sheepishly as the elevator's accordion doors clanged behind them. 'But it doesn't seem right accepting Tom's hospitality.'

'Oh, Janie, scrupulous as ever. You're his friend. Tom's very generous to his friends.'

'I've only known him a couple of months. Weeks really.' The lift chuntered noisily and then stopped a foot above the seventh floor again.

'That's practically for ever in the fashion world.' The elevator was overpopulated and very hot. Petronella Fishburn, glassy-eyed and sweating, had let her mink cloak slither round her scrawny shoulders and began frantically fanning herself with one of the roses they had all been presented with at Oscar de la Renta's show that morning. The wilting petals scattered like confetti. Magnus tussled with his cravat and Luella passed round some Rescue Remedy. People were starting to close their eyes or focus on the floor, anything rather than confront each other's increasingly hysterical expressions.

'Listen, I'm game if you are. And at least you know that with Tom the strings would be strictly unattached,' continued Madeleine.

'I'm not so sure,' said Janie thoughtfully, casting her mind back to his macho performance at the Rockefeller ice rink.

'Oh, come on, Janie. Tom's the most famous closet gay since Rock Hudson.' The conversation around them, already slowing thanks to the tension caused by the delay between the eighth and seventh floors, squeaked to a halt.

'Does a gay man get an erection by being in close proximity to a woman?' Several sets of eyes around her snapped open. Jet-lag and the noxious vestiges of her hangover had made Janie reckless. Oblivious, she continued. 'All I'm saying, Madeleine, is that until the ice experience I would have said the same as you. But the other night, after dinner, he was extremely affectionate, if you get my drift. The perfect gentleman. But give that man a set of blades and . . . well, put it this way, either he was very pleased to see me or he had an extra-large cashmere scarf stuffed in his trouser pocket.'

It took a while to get back uptown. After Luella had accidentally

409

pressed the elevator's alarm button, the fire department had evacuated the entire building and insisted on taking a head count to account for everyone on Kevin Krocket's guest list. By the time Janie could call London, she felt a little awkward. She hadn't got round to speaking to Cassie for days, and she thought it might seem callous now, especially as the main purpose of the call was to ask her advice about taking up Tom's offer. Still, she had to start somewhere if the imagined rift wasn't to become real. But the telephone rang and Cassie's answer machine did the talking.

Eleanor was out too, probably breaching the peace somewhere or other in the name of people power. Her answer machine gave a garbled account of her recent movements, while a tinny version of 'Sisters Are Doing It For Themselves' blasted away in the background. Janie was too dispirited to leave a message. As a last ditch, she tried Sissy's mobile and caught her *en* ebullient *route* for dinner with Nari at Kensington Place.

'You absolutely mustn't think of doing anything else other than going to Tobago,' said Sissy, juggling with a purple contact lens in the back of a cab. 'It's vile at the office. Apparently The Proprietor's in a stink about something. Probably been mugged by a corporate raider. Phyllida's clamped down on everyone and the entire features floor is up in arms. Doug Channing got plastered at the Groucho last night, stole two books of their receipts and has been auctioning them off to the highest bidders today. Everyone's determined to fiddle as much as they can in protest at Phyllida's swingeing cuts. Even Gina's agreed to finally put in some expenses.'

'The problem is I haven't officially applied for any leave.'

'Oh, don't worry about that, you could well be sacked by tomorrow, the mood everyone's in. Have you thought any more about the job at *Eden*? I'll sort out the holiday thing, by the way. Lorna's so miffed with Phyllida that she'll pretend you sent in your holiday memo yonks ago. Have a marvellous time. You probably won't be able to charge your flights, after all this, but I suppose it's still worth a go.'

Janie had thought some more about Lee's offer, as it happened, but Sissy's mobile cut out before she could offload her apprehensions. The truth was she didn't really want to uproot herself from London. There was too much at stake there, even if her job at the *Gazette* was coming to an end. Lee had called her the day before to ask her to give her an answer in the next two weeks. There was no doubt, the offer was tempting: Lee had told her she would entrust Janie with the task of ensuring that *Eden*'s fashion reporting never fell into the dumbing-down trap that ensnared so much other coverage. She dialled the mobile again but Sissy had switched it off. That was it, then, she thought disconsolately; no one, apart from Lee Howard, who was practically a stranger, gave a damn what she did. Janie was left feeling forlorn, unaccountably peeved and, however inappropriately, demob happy. It was a risky state of affairs.

By ten o' clock the next morning she had organised flights for Nell, Jake, Daisy and Gloria to JFK for the coming Friday, and onward flights for all of them and Madeleine to Tobago the following Sunday.

'No need, pippin,' chirped Tom euphorically when she told him. 'What do you think Learjets are for?'

Thus it was that at 2 p.m. on Sunday Tom's nippy little plane skimmed over the lambent coastline of Tobago, finally disgorging its nine passengers on to the tiny runway that lay like a melting ribbon of liquorice between the shimmering white sands of Crown Point.

As she felt the first rays of sun seeping under her skin, any doubts Janie had about the wisdom of her latest decision evaporated. It had been pouring in London, freezing in New York. This had to be what they all needed. She had two weeks in which to think about nothing.

As they jolted along the twisty road in the two customised Jeeps that had come to meet them (sisal matting on the floor, muslin blinds and Tom Fitzgerald crests on the steering wheels and hub-caps), lush plantations on one side, dazzling sandy beaches on the other, the heavens opened, the roofs went up and they were treated to a tropical thunderstorm of epic proportions. The children were entranced.

'Doesn't anything scare 'em?' asked Tom, impressed, as the skies cracked open.

'Not any more,' shouted Janie, surprised to find it was more or less true. It was she who felt frightened. By the time they rounded the last hill before Englishman's Bay stretched out voluptuously before them like a warm, inviting courtesan, the storm had cleared and the skies were crystal blue again. But the storm seemed like an omen to Janie. She might have two weeks to think about nothing, but at the end of them she was going to have to reach a decision that would change their lives.

Chapter Seventeen

Standing in the doorway of Turtle House, Tom waved across the turquoise pool which stretched out in front of him like a sleeping scarab to the silvery curve of sand where Nell appeared to be giving the twins a yoga lesson. The warmth from the sun-wizened wooden deck lapping the house shot up his feet and through his entire body. Twenty feet out at sea, Janie was keeping her eye on them all from a transparent lilo bobbing aloft peaks of foam. Gloria was out gathering armfuls of orange-blossom cuttings from the immortelle trees that fringed the hinterland of the bay. Madeleine and Leonardo had gone scuba diving.

Their quotidian activities had soon assumed a comforting routine. He smiled contentedly. The house and its idyllic beach were as he had always hoped they would be, but had never until now achieved, peacefully invaded by people having a good time. He and Belinda had woefully underused Turtle House, in spite of the fuss they had both made about restoring it to its original colonial spendour after Hurricane Flora had almost annihilated it in the 1960s – and despite keeping a permanent staff of five running the place under the watchful eye of Cyril, an ancient native Tobagoan whom Tom had installed at Turtle House in anticipation of the frequent holidays he had planned to take there. Tobago was too isolated for Belinda's taste. She preferred the pungent social mix of Barbados and only ever graced Turtle House when she was recovering from one of her cosmetic operations or one of her dermabrasions went wrong. And somehow Tom never had the heart to go there alone.

He had envisioned Turtle House as a soothing retreat, a laughter-filled home from home for the children he hoped he and Belinda might someday have. But a home from which home? There indeed had been the rub. He was so busy running the empire and all his other houses that he never had time to retreat there. Cyril and his under-staff tended to the restful, elegant beach complex faultlessly. The engine of hospitality was kept permanently ticking over – Alan, the Michelin-starred chef, kept half of Tobago in soufflés. But the whole set-up was a niggling stain on Tom's conscience; he was, deep down, anti-profligacy, the legacy of his Southern Baptist upbringing. His mother would have loved this place, but she had gone before they'd finished it. He flinched at her memory, and the sad and disbelieving cloud that had engulfed her when Petronella Fishburn's vitriolic attack on her beloved son's creative integrity had been splashed across the *New York Oracle* all that time ago. She had died a year later, in 1984, pain and indignation etched across her tired features. He still couldn't forgive Petronella for that.

It was years before he had allowed any journalists back into his shows, let alone permitted any of them to interview him or visit his homes.

He tore himself back to the present and the indolent nest of shade that cocooned the house. Further away, a low-level sandcastle, homage to Frank Lloyd Wright (Leonardo had half trained as an architect before throwing it all in to design frocks), was under siege from the sea. Jake was laughing uproariously as the waves smashed through its ramparts.

He had had reservations about Leonardo joining them, wary that it would lead to accusations of favouritism back at HQ, but they were all getting along so famously and had sworn so solemnly the previous night over the dregs of some vintage port to keep the entire escapade top secret, that he decided not to give the miseries in the office a second thought. He'd institute a new bonus scheme on his return – each senior Tom Fitzgerald employee would henceforth be entitled to a week at Turtle House for every four years' loyal service.

Those kids were really something, he thought, observing Daisy and Jake, three-quarters obliterated by outsize sunhats, finally escape the tyranny of Nell's yoga lesson by burying one another in the remains of Nell's sandcastle, while she attempted to demonstrate what looked to Tom, from his observations of Belinda's yogic meditations, to be the Cat asana. Gorgeous-looking too, which didn't hurt. The mother wasn't bad either, he thought, gazing admiringly at Janie's limber body, sheathed in an elegant halter-neck one-piece as she waved back, before tipping off the lilo and wading towards the shore to rescue Daisy from Nell's considerable wrath.

Really, thought Tom beatifically, it was like something from an Eternity ad . . .

After a couple of storms the first two days, the weather had behaved perfectly. The past few days had been terrific fun — astonishingly so, considering all the unknown constituents of the group. He, for instance, had instantly been attracted to Janie's wry manner the moment he caught her expression when he'd shown her the Degas hanging in Belinda's gym at Firefly, but he'd had no inkling she could be so . . . raucous. When they had played Truth or Dare the other night she had had no qualms about shimmying up a coconut tree when Leonardo had challenged her, nor about performing a tap-dance in flippers on the jetty. It was English humour, he guessed, but he liked it.

And he liked the fact that she was intensely private beneath the exuberance. That suited him. Perhaps Belinda was right when she accused him of being repressed, in denial, afraid of closure, a commitment phobic (phobic about committing to what? He'd married her, hadn't he? Her wardrobe? Her French lessons?).

Maybe love was too emotive a word for the controlled appreciation he had felt for Belinda's attributes. But he had admired her. She was educated and glamorous, strong of will and sharp of mind, and in those days she'd worked for a living — in the modern art department at Christie's. Maybe she was right and he was incapable of harbouring passion for anything but his work. Perhaps if he left his body to science they'd open him up and find a style almanac where his heart should be.

He wondered whether Janie might not be equally muted in her passion, or perhaps she was simply reserved. Certainly he hadn't quite got the measure of her elusiveness. Her relationships with Matthew and Seth both seemed inconclusive. He knew that she had called Seth once or twice from Turtle House, but Tom, lurking on some pretext or other to half listen in, had noticed that their conversations were brief, unflamboyant. Janie could never get the timings right so Seth was always in the middle of wood-roasting something at Finn's. Emotionally it was as if she were semi-detached from both Seth and Matthew – but she never really talked about it. It was fine by him. He had always found Belinda's obsessive self-analysis distasteful, and far preferred to josh himself and others out of a bout of depression.

Temporarily deprived of the Medici shenanigans of Seventh Avenue, he had thrown himself into plotting elaborate entertainments for everyone. Halfway through the holiday, when Nell's eighth birthday arrived and neither of the paternal figures in her life was with her to celebrate (Tom found this hard to understand, but, ever tolerant, he refrained from judging, assuming they must both have their reasons), he organised a spectacular day. It commenced with a breakfast birthday cake made out of mangoes, pineapple and ice cream. This was swiftly followed by the arrival of a large glass-bottomed boat which Tom had hired so that they could all go turtle-spotting. To Nell's ecstasy, they discovered a whole family of leather-back turtles basking near one of the coral reefs.

'First time ever,' laughed Tom gleefully. 'Turtle House? Huh! Shoulda sued the last owners for breaching the Trades Description Act.'

The day culminated in a mini-fireworks display on the beach which attracted all the locals and should have finished by lighting up the sky with Nell's name, but instead daubed the legend 'Hapy Brithday Hell' across the bay.

'Zack must have found a new job as a pyromaniac,' giggled Madeleine.

Nell was almost as impressed by the day's events as she had been by the trip Tom had taken her and Gloria on the second day they'd been there to see *Gone with the Wind* at a ratchety old cinema in Scarborough. As the palm trees creaked all around the Roxy and the rain lashed the promenade, Nell became one with Scarlett and her troubles, while Gloria, who'd never managed to see the epic the whole way through, was completely won over by Tom, whom she thought the most charming man she'd ever met. He was also a fashion designer and must therefore be gay – which meant he posed no threat.

Janie was enjoying herself as much as the children. She had even managed to stop agonising about Lee's job offer, Seth and the problems at the *Gazette*, deciding, with uncharacteristic fatalism, that things would sort themselves out. If – and only if – she got fired, she would take the job in New York. As for Seth – if things were meant to be, they would end up together. There. It was amazing how tractable life's problems turned out to be when you spent all day on a beach.

'You are a very kind man,' she said softly one night, after the children had finally collapsed into bed and Madeleine and Leonardo had slipped off skinny-dipping. She couldn't help concluding that Tom's behaviour on Nell's birthday had thrown Matthew's shortcomings into starker relief than ever.

Tom shrugged. He couldn't think of anything to say about the pleasures of sharing his good fortune that didn't sound toe-curlingly smug.

'And you certainly know how to show a girl a good time,' said Janie, thinking of Nell's tumultuous excitement when they'd seen the turtles.

'That's me, all stylist over content,' he cracked. It was true, he reflected. The superficialities of life consumed him. Even here, in this ecological paradise, surrounded by this marvellous family, his initial thoughts had all been concerned with how decorative they were.

'Don't do yourself down,' said Janie, looking straight at him

417

with a serious expression. They were sipping beer by the floodlit pool. Madeleine had told her that besides underwriting his arts foundation, Tom anonymously donated millions to children's charities. 'Wasn't it Noël Coward who said that some talents are so delicate they crumble in the face of too rigorous an examination? The point being that they're no less important for that.'

'It was Wilde, as a matter of fact, pippin. D'you think he was right?'

'I think you shouldn't underestimate your considerable gifts, foremost amongst which is your ability to make people feel better about themselves just by being around you.'

Shortly after this outburst Janie drifted off on one of the hammocks. Then Madeleine and Leonardo tipped up and threw her in the pool where she performed a surprisingly elegant front crawl and then proceeded to drag Madeleine in, after which they both serenaded one another with snatches of *Cosi Fan Tutti* and Alanis Morissette. The British, observed Tom, bless them, were a most peculiar race. It must be their primitive plumbing system – made 'em thrilled to see water whatever the time of day. Belinda and practically every other woman he knew would have had to have had counselling to help them recover from the trauma of getting their hair unexpectedly wet. Janie didn't give a hoot. Yes, she had certainly given him plenty to think about.

Things were going swimmingly for Zack. Aurora Snow turned out to have been exactly his kind of woman, and he slipped into her hot seat effortlessly. As fate would have it, his gratifyingly hefty salary from the paper coincided with a trend in smart circles for dabbling in the occult. Zack was becoming quite a fashion accessory, and over the autumn had read the palm of every aspiring It girl in London. He'd even had a call recently from the Contessa Monticatini – although, as Seth had pointed out, she was not so much an It chick as an apparatchick. Zack wasn't complaining. Anastasia paid in cash and kept inviting him back. And she amused him. She was such a drama queen

– and so grateful for his little nuggets of gossip about the fashion world, even if she seemed to take a mawkish interest in its seamier side.

If he could just sort things out with Cassie life would be perfect. But the chances of that were decreasing exponentially. She was more and more waspish every time he saw her. Reasonable as ever, Zack blamed Inspector Reece. He hung around Cassie like one of Petronella's vampirish cloaks. It could only end badly now, Anastasia had observed darkly. It was merely a matter of time.

The pale lilac taffeta ribbon binding Jo-Jo to a mango tree had lodged itself under her ribcage. They'd had to wait two days for that fucking ribbon, and a further three for Zoffy to round up what she referred to as 'leetle peasants' to add local colour to the shoot. She'd have to forget the Picasso sale.

Jo-Jo felt lousy. There were rivulets of sweat coursing down her body, Aeron's corseted ballgown was lacerating her back, and she kept blacking out. Blimey, she thought, there had to be easier ways of seeing the world. Not that she'd seen much of Vietnam since they had arrived. If it's Sunday it must be the south-eastern hemisphere, Dodie had remarked cheerfully. But Jo-Jo had an ululating humdinger of a headache. For three days they had camped in the jungle and she had hardly been able to open her eyes.

She had lost almost sixteen pounds in three weeks. Her ribcage stood out like the strings on a grand piano and her stomach felt as though it were permanently stapled to her spine. Her cheeks were more starkly contoured than the Cairngorms and her eyes were like satellite dishes. Ben didn't like her being so scrawny but Ben wasn't here, and the last time they'd been together he'd acted strangely. *Weltschmerz*, he called it. She wished he'd give up on Method. His new role as a jaded detective in *Dead Before Sunrise* was having an unsalutary effect on him – and, now that Reece was on the prowl, her.

Marie-Elise liked her new look. 'Let's face eet. Theen ees

edgy,' she had rasped when she'd last seen Jo-Jo shortly before the Vietnam trip.

Zoffy said much the same thing. 'You look *deee-vine*,' she pronounced on seeing her at the airport, her cockroach eyebrow pulsating in pleasure. 'Such a clothes 'orse.' Dirk grunted. He preferred more amazonian girls. One of the reasons he was initially drawn to Jo-Jo was her loose, athletic grace. Whatever the rest of the world said about his pictures, essentially they portrayed strong women.

Despite Zoffy's disdainful attitude towards Jo-Jo, she was constantly badgering Marie-Elise to put first options on her, which meant they were working together constantly. They were becoming quite the team. Jo-Jo had to concede that whatever Zoffy's failings as a human being, she was a brilliant stylist. The last two sets of pictures they had done with Dirk had been ecstatically greeted, and as a reward Zoffy had honoured Jo-Jo with the revelation that she ''ad a feeling for twinsets'. As predicted by Cassie, Dirk's career was firmly in the ascendant again, following a fallow creative period in which he had trod water. *Vanity Fair*, in a profile on Dirk's revitalised genius, called his portraits of Jo-Jo 'sublimely disturbing, their morbid undercurrents brilliantly cutting through the froth of contemporary fashion to reflect the glittering underbelly of popular culture', and went on to make various gushy comments about her influence on Dirk's latest body of work. Jess, who had once been one of Dirk's muses, had even written Jo-Jo a note.

Darling J-Junior

Hope you don't mind my writing to you like this but I feel I know you because of the bond we share through collaborating with the world's biggest living shit. I trust it will do for your career what it did for mine. Okay, so the pictures aren't very politically correct (to this day I've never shown them to my mum) but technically he's brilliant. Just don't let him decapitate you.

Give my love to the old pervert.

Love,

J-Senior

★　　★　　★

Jo-Jo snapped awake to hear Dirk yelling at her to concentrate. The pain from the ribbon seemed to have ebbed away and so, apparently, had the peasants. Probably bored out of their minds. She looked down and saw a trickle of blood seeping through the pink silk corset. *Vanity Fair* would probably call it art. Bleeding art . . . bleeding heart. She was feeling woozy again. Never mind. The point was, as Jo-Jo now realised, that in this business it wasn't enough to be thin, you had to *feel* thin. And Jo-Jo only felt thin enough these days when she felt light-headed. She hadn't eaten for two days. Three was the magical boundary, she had discovered. After that, you simply didn't feel hungry. Tulah had recommended her some soya-based wafers that, when ingested with a Diet Coke, made you feel so nauseous you either threw up instantly or couldn't eat for the rest of the day. She had taken up smoking as well. And *voilà*. It was so easy she couldn't fathom why anyone bothered with Weight Watchers. Genevieve Fairfax had complained that she looked drawn in her last test shots. Well, fuck 'em. She'd rather do cutting-edge work anyday than grin inanely in front of some naff liposome.

'Und zo how is Marie-Elise?' Dirk enquired that night in a rare outburst of warmth.

'Oh, you know, pretty genius, I s'pose.' Jo-Jo shrugged. 'Keeping wolves from the door.'

'Does that include takink every job that comes your vay?' He'd heard Marie-Elise had booked Jo-Jo to film a Japanese TV commercial for mopeds straight after Vietnam. It was hardly in keeping with the ultra-sophisticated image she was rapidly acquiring.

Jo-Jo shrugged her shoulders limply again. 'Whatever.'

Exasperated, Dirk frowned at her. To his astonishment he saw tears welling in her eyes. She looked so pathetic slumped there, so different from the feisty, obstreperous, vibrant girl of a few months ago. And Dirk, who was so used to making models weep with frustration and discomfort, who was so inured to the suffering of others, came the closest he had ever been to feeling compassion for a fellow human being.

Sissy skeetered along the Brompton Road, dodging puddles and hooting taxis with the insouciance of an SAS commando. She had spent her first night at Nari's in Egerton Crescent (great house, shame about the repro furniture). She was as elated to discover that she still remembered the basic manoeuvres of a successful heterosexual date as she was alarmed at being late for a meeting with Alice, who had promised to take her prop-scouting in Harrods. But Alice had ditched her mobile for a pager – much edgier, she said; she'd written a piece on them for *Shag* and got a freebie as a present – but it was hopelessly unreliable so no one could ever get hold of her anymore and she was for ever being stood up.

True to character, Alice was smoking furiously and scowling malignantly from the staff entrance on Hans Crescent. Sissy peered at her through her translucent umbrella. Alice was very beautiful, she conceded generously, but there was no doubt that when she scraped back her hair, which was now dyed a pale shade of buff, into a chignon, she looked like a boiled egg.

'Why didn't you go in?' she asked sheepishly.

'In case you hadn't noticed, the doors are locked. It's only five past nine.' Sissy had forgotten that Alice had made an appointment for them both to visit the store before opening time. 'You get much better attention that way and they'll show you old stuff from the stockroom if you ask them nicely.' Alice buzzed the intercom and they scuttled in from the sleet.

Harrods' school uniform department, situated on the fourth floor, had latterly become a much-frequented haunt for London's growing band of cutting-edge stylists. The reason was obvious, Alice had explained bossily. Now that the world's most famous celebrities and royals were turning up in public in increasingly advanced states of nudity, and *Blitzkrieged!!* had done a fashion shoot in which the most prominent accessories had been a used condom and a sanitary towel, the next big thing had to be prudery. The St Trinian's look had everything, as Alice saw it: it was prim *and* kinky at the same time. Alice had already sold its charms to Giovanna and Donatella Ecstasia, who were about to launch Be Happy, a diffusion XTC range, and had hired Alice at obscene expense to style a thirty-page catalogue trumpeting its arrival.

'Happiness is the next big thing. I'm so over that cheesy misery-guts look, aren't you? So Clinton can put that in his pipe and not inhale it. Anyway, the catalogue's going to be laid out like a comic. Everyone's going to be smiling. You know, teeth, the lot,' crowed Alice. 'Cool, *non*? Perhaps we should call it a cata-comic.'

'Catatonic, more like. I don't see how I can use the school uniform theme if you've already flogged it to the Ecstasias,' Sissy said grumpily. She couldn't help feeling a prickle of envy at Alice's good fortune in working for the chic XTC sisters. Of all the rich designers in the world, she had to end up working for Boldacci.

'That's exactly the point, neophyte. If we all do it then it's bound to be big. Zoffy's doing it for Kristof too. Anyway, mine's got a stalker in it, as well as twelve-year-old models – modern, don't you think, and *very* bad taste. It's bound to be picked up by all the tabloids.' She plopped a boater on the back of her chignon. 'Don't worry. Boldacci'll be gagging for it. I take it he is a pervert like the rest of them.'

Sissy felt uncharacteristically naïve. As Dirk had been too busy shooting arty pictures for his forthcoming exhibition, she was now doing the shoot with Joel Eliot, the scarily hip London photographer whose meteor was sizzling as brightly as Jo-Jo's, and as luck would have it, her fashion radar, normally highly sophisticated, appeared to be malfunctioning. Thank God Alice was bailing her out. 'Can I help you?' A disapproving-looking assistant glided up.

Alice swivelled round, lobbing her cigarette at Sissy, and beamed angelically. 'I'm afraid my twin sisters and mother have all gone down with a bug so I'm here on their behalf – Mummy was so worried about things running out before term starts.'

'How unfortunate,' intoned the assistant astringently. In theory the department strongly disapproved of these louche fashion creatures coming in brandishing their foreign company credit cards and hijacking a term's worth of school goods. And to what end, Mrs Lilliath, the department head, wanted to know? Paedophilia and sluttishness, that was what. But it was too exhausting to argue, and Mrs Lilliath was on her day off.

'Which school was it?' the assistant asked, eyeing Sissy's cigarette suspiciously.

'Schools, actually. Well, it's a bit complicated . . .'

Forty-five minutes later they emerged with a mountain of burgundy, brown and navy serge, plus some recherché pieces from the bowels of the stockroom that belonged to a school which had been closed down by the authorities fifteen years earlier. Alice was ecstatic.

'No one will have those striped sou-westers. With a bit of adaptation I bet they could make genius boob-tubes.'

On the escalators down they passed a surly-looking Angel, who was on his way up to do some research into Start-Rite's Mary-Janes, which had come to him in a dream as being ripe for reinvention as a wedge. He had fallen out very badly with his mystery backer and in Sissy's absence, he had made little progress with Anastasia, who seemed to Angel to be woefully distracted by other business, and he was still mortally offended over what he saw as Sissy's treason. As they swept past one another looking in opposite directions, he jangled his metal briefcase noisily so that she would notice he was ignoring her.

Sissy felt uncharacteristically glum. After years of consoling herself for her lack of commercial success with the knowledge that she was twice as talented as everyone around her, she was petrified she might not be able to pull the Boldacci job off. Alice, who thought all designers were congenitally feeble-minded, remonstrated.

'Look, he's bound to love whatever you do: a) you're young . . . *ish*, so he'll think anything you say is bound to be hip, and b) he actually believes all that Cool Britannia crap and c) he's moronically unsound of judgment. As he's entitled to be. That's what they pay us for – to be groovy, talented and witty. I hope you stipulated a gorgeous location.'

Sissy had indeed explained in her brief to Boldacci that the only way of making the concept for her amusing boarding-school story work was by switching it from Harbour Island, which after her fortnight in BA sounded dull, to Japan, which she'd always wanted to see. Alice approved because she said all Japanese men fantasised about having sex with schoolgirls, so it was very appropriate, and Sissy could make the pictures very witty, which was what Boldacci was crying out for. But Sissy was starting to wonder whether it was such a good idea. She had no objection to being paid by a humourless Roman to lodge his tongue firmly in his cheek. But why did it have to happen when things were finally zipping along so satisfactorily with Nari? Right now, she didn't feel like being in a different postcode from him, let alone half a dozen latitudes and longitudes away.

If I die now, thought Madeleine, it could have been worse: nine-tenths of her body swayed gently in a hammock, a dangling foot was being lightly fondled by Leonardo, who was sitting on the deck beneath. Nell was attempting to read aloud from a ravaged house copy of *Gone with the Wind* for the benefit of her new invisible friend, an adopted daughter called Scarlett.

'Just my luck,' Janie had groaned the first day Scarlett made her presence felt. 'We get rid of Stanley and I inherit a grand-daughter. Nell keeps lecturing me about child-rearing now.'

'Couldn't you teach her the principles of sending people to Coventry?' Madeleine asked. She felt Janie was in danger of taking Nell's eclectic band of companions too seriously. Nell seemed happy enough. Madeleine peeled a grape and placed it between Leonardo's lips. If anyone a year ago had predicted that she would voluntarily find herself holidaying on a Caribbean island with other fashion colleagues, she would have pleaded for mercy. But somehow she seemed to have washed up with three of the nicest people in the business.

She flicked through the latest issue of *Beau Monde* and stopped short at the portrait of Kristof, whose hooded eyes peered blankly from his puffy, aesthete's features. He had been photographed especially for the issue in his library in Venice by Helmut Newton; his face preternaturally pale from the skin whitener he used by the crate; his eyes ringed with kohl. He was leaning thoughtfully on one pudgy hand; one of his signature linen kerchiefs billowed from the other; his not quite subtly enough lipsticked mouth had aimed at a smile but settled for a rictus of petulance. He looked as though he had myxomatosis. 'Kristof the Thinker', read the caption. Sitting for Newton was certainly an accolade. But achieving that kind of status in the fashion world seemed to require complete insanity. Kristof, Boldacci, Bella Scarletti, Giovanna and Donatella were all, to varying degrees, narcissistic lunatics. Aeron was well on his way too. It started with an idiosyncrasy, decided Madeleine – everyone in the business had to have one: strange dress codes, unhealthy jewellery fetishes, weird food allergies – and ran rampant from there. It was because their endeavours, when dragged on to a bigger world stage, were so Lilliputian. Adopting the mannerisms of eccentricity was just another ploy for self-advancement. She squinted at Tom, taking a call on the mobile in the pool. Almost sane, but only because his particular idiosyncrasy has been an obsessive reserve with the press – and that had almost certainly lost him a small fortune in publicity.

Cyril padded noiselessly across the deck and deposited a wad of newspapers by the silver tea tray. Madeleine prodded Leonardo with her big toe and he darted off to fetch them. They were generally at least a day late and Janie was boycotting them. But ever since the start of their stay, when they had read about Gilles de Gaumard hiring Aeron to be Design Director at the House of Lara at a reported salary of one million pounds a year, the other three had been hooked. Each afternoon at around 4.30 they marked the papers' arrival with Earl Grey and an hour of quiet absorption in the gossip pages, while Janie interred herself in Tom's extensive collection of botanical first editions. It had become another one of their pleasant holiday rituals. Leonardo turned to the arts pages of the *New York Times* to see if his neighbour's genitalia had made it into the review section. Madeleine leafed through the business sections of the broadsheets. It was some minutes before she saw the front page of *The Python*.

'Jesus Christ,' she exclaimed, ramming the paper under Leonardo's nose. Beneath a photograph of a grim-faced Cassie driving off in a taxi was the screamer headline 'GONE TO POT'.

> *Yesterday the glamorous world of Cassie Grange, high-flying boss of Hot Shots model agency, was looking distinctly frayed around the edges. The 36-year-old blonde was arrested trying to flee Britain at London's Heathrow airport. Grange, who had been earlier cautioned by Scotland Yard not to leave the country and who looked tired and haggard, insisted she was there to meet a friend, but had luggage with her and was clearly under stress.*
>
> *Grange, who catapulted a dazzling roll-call of young models on the road to fame and riches, including Peace Grant, Jess Murray, Tulah Delaney and new contender Jo-Jo Banderas, has been fighting rumours of sleazy goings-on at her agency for months. Recently she had gone to ground at her home in West London where she has been helping police with their inquiries into her alleged involvement in drugs deals.*
>
> *Ever since her protégée, the 22-year-old millionairess Peace Grant, went public about her heroin addiction last March, Grange cont. on pages 4 and 5.*

Even Leonardo, who didn't know Cassie and could therefore take a more stoical view, was hard pressed to put a positive spin on the story, which, Madeleine noticed, carried Lindsey Craven's byline. Janie naturally wanted to fly back to London immediately. The Lear could be ready in a couple of hours, Tom said. She felt bad about dragging the children away – perhaps they could stay? – but her oldest friend's already besmirched reputation lay smouldering in ruins. She started to tremble. Madeleine took her arm and stroked it soothingly.

'The last thing you need worry about is the children. They've had a wonderful time and they're due back tomorrow anyway.'

Janie looked at Madeleine in astonishment. She'd been so relaxed and contented she'd lost track of the days.

The journey back home was plagued from the start. Fog-bound on the runway at Crown Point, the jet had to land again for the night in Jamaica because of a violent storm. By the time they reached the coastline of Ireland, they'd been in transit for twenty-two hours. Talk about reality check, thought Janie as the Lear circled the private runway at Luton, rocked gently by bracts of coal-coloured cloud. She hadn't been able to sleep during the flight – there was too much to think about: decisions about the divorce, about Seth, about the job offer she'd annexed at the back of her mind for the past fortnight – her inability to commit to one party line appalled her. And of course there was Cassie. However much she tried to reconfigure that particular situation, it still came out disastrously. Even Gloria had begun to speak sympathetically of Cassie. And in the past tense.

There'd been an IRA scare and London was at a standstill. There wasn't a taxi within shouting distance of Luton. They struggled on the train to King's Cross and caught the Tube to Michaelmas Road, by which time they were all practically weeping with fatigue. Even two weeks without Gloria had left its mark on the house. The floors looked dusty. There were no tempting smells from the kitchen, only a back-log on the answer machine, including a businesslike message from some dusty-sounding official at the British embassy in Guatemala City.

Now that she was home, Janie realised she didn't have a clue how to track Cassie down. What did one do in these situations? Call Scotland Yard and leave a message?

The phone rang. It was Seth, from a call-box.

'What are you doing there?' he said gruffly.

'Where are you?'

'At Heathrow. I was supposed to be meeting you, remember?'

She hadn't. 'We've just arrived,' she began sheepishly. 'I tried to come back early when I heard about Cassie.'

'Very heroic,' said Seth acerbically.

There was a pause.

'I don't suppose you know where she—' began Janie.

'At home. They've released her without bail. I could run you there if you like.'

'It might be better if I go on my own,' said Janie softly. 'Nell sends her love, by the way.'

'Give her a hug—' The pips went.

'Needless to say, you look fantastic.' Cassie kissed Janie stiffly and slumped back into the window seat from where she'd hardly strayed since being released.

Janie wished she could return the compliment but *The Python* had been right about one thing. Cassie did look haggard and, unheard of for her, unkempt; so did the flat. Several half-empty cans of Slim Fast were clustered round the base of a Tom Dixon lamp. Barney would be suicidal if he could see the fruits of his labours. Still, it was hardly surprising, given the little knot of photographers she'd seen lurking across the road from Cassie's flat. She wished too that they had been able to talk to one another more openly the past month, and that there wasn't this skyscraper of stilted emotions and stifled opinions between them. She considered telling Cassie her own problems, anything to revive their old sense of camaraderie, but her predicament was trivial compared with Cassie's. Listening to her lifeless rendition of events, she understood that what pained Cassie most was the humiliation. Agencies lived or died by their reputations, and hers was in tatters.

The real story behind *The Python*'s hysterical headlines naturally turned out to be far more prosaic and, as anything involving Zack was bound to be, verging on farce. Having been summoned to Paris to read some tarot cards at a dinner party Anastasia was hosting for The Proprietor, Zack had turned up at Heathrow without his passport, a small overnight bag and his 'lucky' pack of tarot cards. 'He missed about three planes, but he had his vitamin B complex with him, so that was all right,' said Cassie, not quite smiling. 'Since I'm the keeper of Zack's spare key, he rang me to ask if I would send some things over to the airport. I hadn't been very nice to him lately, so I thought I'd run them over in person. Bad move.'

'But how did the police know you were there?'

'God knows, but Reece has been on my back for months. For all I know he could have impregnated me with a listening device. Anyway, eventually I managed to convince them that I wasn't trying to do a runner. But not before *The Python* splashed the whole misbegotten venture across their front page. That's one for Mummy's scrapbook.'

Michael Croft had told Cassie that strictly speaking she could sue *The Python* for printing unfounded allegations, but since the essential facts of Lindsey's story were true, he didn't rate her chances of winning a court case.

'But what about your good name?' expostulated Janie.

'No such thing as bad publicity,' said Cassie bitterly. 'At least, that seems to be everybody else's view.' And chillingly, they were right, up to a point. In the past twenty-four hours Cassie's phones hadn't stopped ringing with chat-show requests, memoires deals and at least a hundred enquiries from fourteen-year-olds desperate to know how to get on to the catwalk. Max Clifford had even called to invite her out to lunch.

'So onwards and forwards?'

'Oh, I don't know. Notoriety doesn't get you very far in the end. It'll all implode sooner or later – probably sooner. Anyway, I seem to be losing my taste for telling twelve-year-old girls to wait a couple of years before they consider breast implants. I'm sick of dealing with oleaginous creeps like Diego. And he's one of the goodish guys. And I might not be under arrest any more for being in possession, but I could still face charges for running an international drugs syndicate.' She stood up bleakly. 'Now, if you don't mind, I'm going to bed. I feel as though I haven't slept for years.'

Janie was desolate. She had never seen Cassie so passive. It was as if someone had taken a pair of pliers to her emotional tripwires.

From her window seat, Cassie, also feeling bleak, watched Janie trudge down the road. She knew she had been unfairly harsh, especially when Janie had made so much effort to see her. But she still felt somehow let down. Ever since Janie had gone back to work, what with the shows, Seth and the children, Cassie had somehow felt squeezed out. Even when they did meet up, Janie always seemed frazzled. Cassie was annoyed with herself for minding. She knew she was behaving like a teenager but she couldn't help it. As a child she had liked relationships to slot tidily into her life, like so many bits of doll's house furniture. Nothing, really, had changed. Only Janie had gone and messed it all up. Much as she liked Seth, Cassie was starting to feel that nothing would go right until Matthew finally took it into his head to come home.

Phyllida had finally achieved her personal nirvana. In her hands lay the answer to the Janie conundrum. Giovanna and Donatella Ecstasia's director of PR had faxed the *Gazette*'s advertising director to inform him that they would henceforth cease to advertise any of their products in the *Gazette* following Janie's 'hostile and wholly unwarranted attack on their show last month'.

'Not what you want to hear, I suppose,' soothed Lorna, reading the offending communication out to Phyllida. Barely suppressing an earring-to-earring smirk, Phyllida was in Edward Rushmore's office before Lorna had reached yours faithfully. Oh, there'd be a battle, of course, thought Phyllida. Or more of a skirmish perhaps. Edward would drool on about journalistic integrity, not being bought by the advertisers and so on — but without much conviction. Edward prided himself on the sterling standard of advertising in his paper, almost as much as on its editorial. Phyllida had often thought that his idea of a cracking time would be a weekend spent comparing and contrasting the *Gazette*'s stylish spreads for Armani sunglasses and

Calvin Klein khakis with the *Telegraph*'s endless ads for chairlifts. The defection by XTC was the beginning of the end.

It was even better than she'd anticipated.

'It's far, far worse than you know,' he sighed. 'I've just spoken to The Proprietor and these Ecstasia women have threatened to withdraw all their advertising from the whole of PPS. I must say I think it's a bit extreme. I mean, fair comment and all that. But apparently their business is worth about five million pounds a year overall. The Proprietor is baying for blood.' He shook his head sorrowfully, and Phyllida tried to marshal her features into a template of grief.

'She'll have to go,' they said simultaneously.

> Bliss was it that dawn to be alive,
> But to be young was very heaven!

The words floated unbidden through Phyllida's internal sound-track. Good God, she realised with a jolt, Wordsworth. It must be twenty years since the last time she'd felt moved to spout that crap.

No one at the *Gazette* actually got round to biking over the letter informing Janie of this decision. Lorna decided to leave it on file so that at least Janie would get paid as long as possible, what with Christmas coming up and everything, and she certainly wouldn't be e-mailing Phyllida's memo about Janie's rotten replacement. In fact, owing to a peculiar configuration of events, combined with Lorna's machinations, it was another ten days before Janie discovered that she'd been sacked. She spent a not unpleasant first day back from Tobago unpacking and settling the children. At five she got hold of Seth at Finn's. He sounded much more like his old self.

'If I get to you about eleven with some bruschetta and some salami it should be just about right for high tea, Caribbean time.'

'Mmm . . . on second thoughts, sod the salami and just get

here as fast as you can. God, I've missed you.' She skipped upstairs and unpacked an ancient copy of *Finnegans Wake* that she had found lurking incongruously at the back of a cookery book stall in the market at Speyside in Tobago, and placed it under the pillow on Seth's side. Later, when the children were in bed and even Gloria had retired exhausted, she ran herself a bath. She was about to climb in when she heard someone grappling with the front door. Expecting Seth, she ran down to the hall.

'Oh, it's you,' she said coolly. 'Frankly I didn't think you'd feel it was appropriate to stay here any more—'

She paused. Jo-Jo looked terrible: gaunt and vacant-eyed. She dropped her suitcase in the middle of Janie's hall and let out a dry sob.

'I know I've been a total bitch and a complete pillock. But right now, I just really, really want my mum.'

Chapter Eighteen

It could have gone either way, but in the event Gloria was brilliant, as Jo-Jo had instinctively known she would be. She didn't wail in horror over her daughter's poor, stick-insect limbs. Not a word of reproach passed her lips when Jo-Jo toyed listlessly with the tuna sandwich Gloria insisted on making for her. Even when Jo-Jo lit up a Marlboro, Gloria remained heroically polite. She listened quietly, made soothing noises at appropriate times and, while Jo-Jo took an inordinately long shower, she prepared a bed so that when her daughter finally showed signs of needing sleep, at around 2 a.m., she could tuck her up, and limp with jet-lag though she was, sat with her until she fell asleep, just as she had when Jo-Jo was a small child.

Janie, immensely impressed by Gloria's self-control, made mental notes for her future negotiations with Nell and Daisy and then tactfully withdrew upstairs with a left over bottle of Slobby's Croatian wine. Whatever misdemeanours Jo-Jo had committed in the past few months – and her betrayal of Cassie was just one of them; she had taken Gloria for granted abominably – she deserved a second chance.

By the time Seth arrived she had almost nodded off. Taking in the tense atmosphere downstairs, he made a wry face at Janie, drinking in everything that had changed about her, from her sunbleached hair to her sand-buffed toes, and announced that he wanted to inspect her tan. He swept her back upstairs, which was precisely where he wanted to be with her anyway. He smelt wonderful, a musky mixture of skin and wood. Afterwards, when they were devouring the bruschetta, she leant over and kissed the tip of his nose and told him she'd missed him.

'Really?' He sounded surprised.

'Really.'

'You don't have to say that, you know. I'd sort of come round to the idea that we might be—'

'Might be what?'

'On hold. Until you sort things out in your mind about Matthew,' he said casually, slicing her some lemon tart.

'Sorted,' said Janie. And suddenly they were. The fact that there hadn't even been a birthday card from Matthew waiting for Nell when they got back had clarified things in Janie's mind. 'Matthew and I have no future together.' The words tasted sour on her tongue.

They were silent while they both digested this. Seth spoke first.

'Do you think Daisy could learn to tolerate my cooking?'

'Do you think you could tolerate mine?'

He licked a crumb off her lips. 'No need, my darling. You have unique talents. Why not stick to them? I'll keep to the kitchen . . . it could be the makings of a perfect partnership.'

'What about the job at *Eden*?' he asked her later still.

'I called Lee today to thank her for her very generous offer and to tell her that I'd prefer to remain a freelance contributor.'

Seth shook his head, puzzled. 'I can't believe you passed that one up. You could have been very grand – my sister tells me magazine editors are treated like minor celebrities in New York these days. And it would have sorted all your financial worries out.'

'Precisely the reasons I didn't go.' She looked at his baffled expression and giggled. 'Oh, Seth, can you imagine me working in a place that employs a *panty-hose* editor? They take themselves so seriously on *Eden*. I mean, Lee's very intelligent and informed but even she's slightly manic. I know Phyllida is too, but at least we all have a laugh about her – it's all so humourless in the *Eden* offices. And the more established the magazine gets, the worse it will become. Besides, after all these years, I don't think I could get my head round being financially solvent – and, well, things aren't so bad here. I don't even want to think about it any more. I'm far more interested in whether you might finally be going to spend a whole night here.' She began singing. 'We Can Work It Out' spectacularly out of tune until Seth could stand the torture no longer and silenced her with another mouthful of tart.

Gloria paced the kitchen. As far as she could make out, Jo-Jo was going to be fine. She was ridiculously thin and desperately disappointed that Genevieve Fairfax had decided not to sign up a face at all, but blacking out in Japan would probably turn out to be a blessing in disguise. She had spent five very uncomfortable days in a Tokyo hospital with so many drips and wires plugged into her that she had felt like an adapter. She had almost been sued by the moped client and the whole experience had clearly given her a serious fright. And all the monstrous Marie-Elise had apparently been worried about was whether the injections had left visible track marks up her arms. 'She couldn't stand to think she might be losing out on her twenty-five per cent,' said Jo-Jo bitterly. She was exhausted. Marie-Elise had made her grovel to the moped client and finish the job, despite the increasingly frequent blackouts. Then, when Jo-Jo was in the depths of her delirium in hospital, she'd faxed her an itinerary of her engagements for the next month which included trips to Tel Aviv, Hong Kong, Helsinki, Zagreb, Sydney and Vladivostock to promote Bella Scarletti's new line of tableware.

'Honestly, Mum, my flight chart had so many criss-crossing routes on it, it looked just like the surface of one of Bella's poxy cut-glass finger bowls. When Genevieve Fairfax decided they were going to stick with nameless models, all she could do was scream at me down the phone. And me at death's door. I thought Cassie was a fuss-pot but Marie-Elise is just a callous bitch.'

Later, propped up in bed, with Gloria stroking her hair, she apologised for not keeping in touch.

'I've been a complete brat. And worse, a clichéd brat. Selfish, self-obsessed and stupid.'

There was hope for her yet, thought Gloria, and she finally dozed off.

Jo-Jo's self-obsession didn't exactly evaporate overnight. Over a very late breakfast the following morning, she filled Seth and an unexpectedly mellow Janie in on every minute detail that had led to her Damascene conversion. Not that she was going to give up modelling, she said. There was too much money in it and she was determined to earn enough to set Gloria up for the rest of her life. But she was going to do it with integrity. She was going to behave with decency and respect for all her colleagues and show teenagers that it could be a worthwhile career. Also, she would not be posing in any more pictures that portrayed women in a negative or degrading light; there would be no fur (this was a sop to Janie), and she would henceforth be pacing her career with its longevity in mind.

'And the first thing I'm going to do is go and beg Cassie's forgiveness and ask if she'll take me back.'

The others looked at her in silence.

Finally Seth spoke. 'Hot Shots might be closing. Things came to a head this week and, well, Cassie got arrested and—'

'Fucking hell,' blurted Jo-Jo who had, until now, firmly subscribed to the belief that middle-class people never got hassled by the police. 'Sorry, Mum.' Then, never slow to seize on a grand gesture, she said, 'All the more reason to go back to Cassie and show her some moral support. I'll get on to it today.' She sipped some of the Complan Gloria had bought and worked out her strategy. Who'd have thought it? Cassie arrested. Coolsville.

It was Saturday, but she felt there was no time to lose and corralled Janie into helping her pen a press release for the newspapers. The first paragraph outlined the bare bones: owing to differences of opinion on how her career should be handled, Jo-Jo would henceforth be leaving Marie-Elise and returning to her first agency, Hot Shots, with whom she had previously enjoyed the most cordial relations. As of immediately. Janie thought they should leave it at that. But Jo-Jo was determined to write some kind of personal mission statement.

My decision to leave Hot Shots two months ago was, with hindsight, entirely misconceived. In this business it is vital to have an agent who nurtures you and who has your long-term interests at heart. Unfortunately my subsequent agent turned out only to be interested in using me for quick-term gain. I now have the experience to recognise that Cassie Grange is someone I can trust completely. She is a person of the utmost integrity and I am convinced that these current aspersions on her character are malicious and entirely without grounds.

She agonised for hours over its composition and was just mulling over the first lines of her Models' Manifesto when Janie pointed out that brevity was the soul of news and she would miss the deadlines for the Sunday editions altogether if she didn't get on with faxing the release. *The Probe* had removed Matthew's fax line so they had to send it from the local newsagent's, which spoilt the drama a bit for Jo-Jo, until she had the bright idea of offering Janie an exclusive interview with herself in which she promised to wax lyrical about Cassie's shining virtues.

'I'll also talk about the love-nest Ben and I are buying, or might be buying, in New York, if you like,' she offered nobly. 'That is the sort of thing you guys like to write about, isn't it?'

Janie, who'd been going through some bills and still didn't know she'd been fired, was secretly so relieved at being handed a way of redeeming herself with Phyllida that she wrote the piece immediately and went back to the newsagent's to fax it at five. The features desk would be thrilled – they'd probably clear space for it in tomorrow's pages, which would mean more brownie points with Edward. Maybe she could ask for a raise, or at least a company car. She was almost looking forward to going in on Monday.

Sissy absolutely did not want to see another twist of unidentifiable pickled vegetable ever again. Tokyo was turning into a
nightmare. Not only had the waterfall gardens outside her hotel
bedroom given her cystitis from all the consequent trips to the
loo, but on the flight over, Brigitte had read a guidebook that
said Japanese businessmen spent all weekend getting drunk and
throwing up in the streets and was refusing to shoot outside until
someone located a pair of waders for her. It was never going to
happen. Brigitte was six feet in her crotchless stockinged feet.
To lure her out, Sissy showed her the clothes, whereupon
Brigitte promptly went down with food poisoning. Since she
only ever ate tofu and Twiglets and everyone knew Japan was
a world Mecca for tofu, Sissy suspected the food poisoning was
a ploy to get out of wearing Boldacci's horrible clothes. And
they were truly horrible – lumpy felt amoeba-type shapes that
were so stiff Sissy could never tell whether or not she'd left the
hangers in. It was very difficult to incorporate the navy school
hats and dinky purse-bands she'd brought out. Fortunately Joel
was astonishingly laid back, but this carried its own penalties, and
Sissy began to fret that they might really come back without any
pictures at all. Finally he suggested they ditch Boldacci's clothes
altogether and just use the uniforms.

'It's not about specific products,' he drawled thoughtfully,
sucking on an enormous spliff, 'it's about branding; creating a
seductive image, right?'

Er, not exactly, thought Sissy, but felt too panicked to
protest. With any luck Joel's pictures would be so blurry no
one would see anything anyway.

'Anyway, if we shoot all this uniform stuff, Boldacci might
put it into production,' he said optimistically.

Having surfed spectacularly successfully to the top of the
profession on the crest of his fashionable London charm, Joel felt
he was doing his clients a favour of Live Aid proportions simply
by agreeing to accept their million-dollar fees. Sissy, envious of
his sublime arrogance, sighed and considered faking a stroke.

And to think that during all those years of trudging along to Lipstick Studios in EC1 to shoot pictures for the *Gazette* she'd kept herself going by believing everything would be so much easier once she'd graduated to A-list models and locations.

Brigitte, on the other hand, perked up immeasurably when she saw the mini maroon kilt and tie that Joel had picked out for her.

'Very Weimar, *ja*,' she growled knowledgeably, which worried Sissy no end but seemed to be exactly what Joel wanted to hear. Cheered up, Joel and Brigitte agreed to shoot the next set on location in Shinjuko, in front of a garish cliff-face of neon-lit department stores, where Brigitte was even more encouraged to see gargantuan billboards of Jo-Jo wearing bunches and blue eyeshadow astride a pink moped.

'Poor Jo-Jo,' cooed Brigitte. 'Such tacky pictures, *ja*?' Her alarmingly wide red mouth stretched into such an enormous grin that she looked as though a piece of raw steak had been clamped across her face. The shoot was starting to inhabit a parallel universe with the storyboards Sissy had so painstakingly dummied up for Boldacci. The school theme was still there, but instead of the youthful, cheeky, urchin appeal Sissy had envisioned, Joel's Polaroids looked dark and seditious. Brigitte vamped up the Weimar theme shamelessly, producing a suspender belt from somewhere and sending Joel's assistant into a department store to buy some more fishnet stockings. Any minute now, thought Sissy, she would burst into 'Life Is A Cabaret'. A crowd of business suits had clustered round Brigitte.

''Sright, give it edge, girl,' drawled Joel, handing her a lacrosse stick. Sissy popped another painkiller and tried to astrally project herself back to Egerton Crescent. Alice had at least been right about one thing – the Japanese men surrounding Brigitte seemed very taken with her prefect's badge.

It was 6.53 in the morning when the shrillness finally woke Janie. It seemed to have been clanging inside her head for ages. The telephone was on Seth's side and she had to wriggle out from under his arm and clamber over him to reach it. It was Piers, Matthew's father, sounding breathless and even more crackly than usual – and for him, distinctly alarmed.

'Darling Janie, hope I haven't disturbed you. Not too sure what the time is here, let alone in London.'

She felt herself blushing. She and Seth hadn't got to sleep until four. Thank God he hadn't picked up the phone.

'Piers, how lovely to hear from you. Where are you?'

'Prompram – Ghana,' he added helpfully. 'Marvellous trip. We're on the brink of resurrecting a species the world thought was extinct – if only the buggers would let us get on with things. Anyway, never mind that, how are you, my darling, and those gorgeous grandchildren of mine?'

'We're fine,' said Janie, puzzled. Endearing as Piers was, he wasn't calling, she knew, to make small talk about the children.

'What is it, Piers?' she asked anxiously.

'Oh, my darling. Nothing, nothing at all. Just thinking about you, what with Christmas coming and everything.'

This was even less convincing. Piers didn't know one end of the Gregorian calendar from another.

'Matthew okay?'

'I'm not sure I've heard from him that recently,' she said guardedly.

'I see. Only I wrote him a letter about the breakthrough we've made here – to get his advice about approaching the press, really. Gave him a poste restante address and everything. Haven't heard a dicky – it's not like Matthew not to respond at all. Still, I'm sure it's nothing to worry about. Just one of my hunches, that's all. Used to be so reliable, but like the old flirting techniques, they're not what they were.'

Janie felt alarm rising from the pit of her stomach like bile, and tried to suppress it for Piers's sake. 'I'm sure he's fine,' she said, as much to reassure herself as him. 'He's been moving about a lot. Perhaps he never got your letter.'

She didn't know why Piers's phone call rattled her so

much. Between Guatemala and Ghana the future of letter-writing was probably pretty bleak. But Piers had sounded distinctly anxious. And that wasn't like him at all. She called the Guatemalan embassy later that day, and after what seemed an inordinate time during which they passed her from department to department and every voice sounded identical, turned up absolutely no trace of Matthew whatsoever, which, she supposed, must be a good sign.

Finally she was handed back to the first identical voice (oh my God, what if the whole embassy is manned by one person, she panicked) which politely suggested she contact the British embassy. She then tried to get hold of David Carter at the *Probe*'s tiny bureau in Moscow, only to be informed that he had gone to cover a story in Georgia, by which time it was half past ten and she was late for work.

Janie spent most of her first week back in London away from the office, out on appointments with PRs and designers. Phyllida had been out of the office too, on a freebie at a very serious health farm where the primary healer had taken one look at her stress count and banned her from seeing any newspapers. It was halfway through the second week before the two of them coincided in the office. Huffing up the stairs into her cube, it took all of five seconds for Phyllida's eyes to alight on Janie's piece about Jo-Jo, which Lorna had helpfully marked SCOOP and stapled to the top of a pile of clippings for her to peruse.

'Which fuckwit printed this?' she screeched, turning puce.

'How was I to know you'd been stupid enough to fire Janie?' Doug Channing asked irritably when she finally tracked down the culprit. Now he'd never score with Janie. 'It was a great piece and you know it.'

'All right, keep your toupee on, and don't be surprised if we get sued for inaccuracy as per usual with one of her pieces,' hissed Phyllida. 'As of next week we'll have a proper journalist *in situ*. Lindsey Craven is a real pro – did you see her scoop on Cassie Grange?'

Doug looked at her pityingly. It was tragic the way some middle-aged women couldn't cope with younger competition.

Mindful of her toxin levels, Phyllida made Lorna break the news to Janie in person. Lorna felt dreadful. Janie went very quiet – probably in shock, and what about those poor little 'uns? – and began clearing her desk. Then she thanked Lorna for all her support and hugged her. That was bloody it. Lorna felt damp-eyed for the rest of the afternoon. No bloody way was she informing Personnel about Janie's dismissal. Not before Christmas anyway. It would be months before anyone in accounts noticed they were paying two fashion editors. Phyllida could stuff that in her swingeing cutbacks and lump it.

To everyone's surprise – everyone, that was, apart from Jo-Jo – the interview she concocted with Janie really did seem to signal a ceasefire in the press, which had had an absurd proportion of its artillery aimed at Cassie in the past weeks. And it lifted Cassie's spirits so much that she allowed Saffron to bully her back into going to the office. The staff all stood up to applaud her when she walked in and it was all she could do not to turn on her heels and flee in a sob-storm of emotion.

'The prodigal daughter returns.' Cassie smiled weakly and hugged Jo-Jo. They were having a quiet drink in Finn's, to bond and discuss the next steps in Jo-Jo's career. Cassie had already been through Jo-Jo's contracts with a fine-tooth comb. Jo-Jo decided to come clean about everything, even the moped ads and the Genevieve Fairfax fiasco.

'The first thing you do,' said Cassie firmly, 'is take a month off and put some weight on. Then we'll see about you doing the couture in Paris after Christmas. But only Chanel and Aeron's. You silly girl, you were perfect. In any case,' she continued mock-chidingly, 'heroin chic is officially démodé. Now, the pictures you've been doing with Dirk are great – I knew it was going to be his time again. But you should work with one of the new English lot as well. Diversify but keep it very select . . . I liked those early pictures you did for *A La Mode* with Joel and he's come on an awful lot since then.' Warming to her speciality, she outlined her ideas for the coming year. 'Oh, and don't worry about the moped ads. I think I can sort it so they never get seen outside Tokyo.'

Jo-Jo, who had thought she alone knew what was really going on in fashion, looked at her admiringly. 'You don't know how good it feels to work with someone with integrity and taste.'

'Oh, Hot Shots has that all right,' said Cassie dryly. 'We may be a sinking ship but we'll go down tastefully.'

'Forgive me for disagreeing,' said Jo-Jo. 'I swear it will only be this once. But the first thing I'm going to do is visit Inspector Reece. He can inspect all he likes. There's nothing in my bloodstream but Mum's Complan, and possibly the very last traces of some disgusting soya-based wafers.'

Janie couldn't remember how she got home. She went straight outside and began digging and hacking and clipping and mow-ing. She was out there for hours. Somehow imposing order on her garden made her feel more in control of her life. She didn't even notice it had started to snow. Eventually, Gloria, just back with the twins from playgroup, came and escorted her in.

Only when she began thawing out over a mug of tea did it hit her. It was a catastrophe, of course. Even worse than before, because over the past year, while her star had been rising at the *Gazette*, she'd stepped up their outgoings considerably. What with Gloria coming full time and Slobby's departure the books only just balanced (patchy as Slobby's financial input had been, he'd made her feel she was doing something by occupying one of her rooms). She'd even made provision to start paying Will back for Nell's school fees. *And* she'd probably blotted her copybook with Lee by turning down the job. So no hope even of freelancing. Great timing. Story of her life. David Carter had finally returned her call, but hadn't heard from Matthew recently either. He sounded as depressed as she felt; he had to come back to London in a few weeks to sign some custody papers. She heard herself inviting him to spend Christmas at Michaelmas Road and, through a clamped stiff upper lip, she heard a muzzled but grateful-sounding yes. Talking to David reminded her of the message from the British embassy. Guiltily dialling the number to Guatemala, she was put on hold for ages until the line failed. She tried three more times and then gave up. She was still feeling desperate when Seth turned up with a magnum of champagne and some Beluga caviar.

Bleakly she told him what had happened at the *Gazette*.

'Great,' he said, smothering her muddy hand with kisses, 'because I've just had some incredible news. I didn't want to tell you before in case it all went belly up. Harry wants to back a branch of Finn's in New York. He's spent the last six weeks getting all the funding together and finding a location and today it all fell into place. We've found an amazing site in SoHo and if all goes to plan we'll open in early spring and . . . well, how do you fancy living with me in New York for a year or two?'

Janie had never seen Seth so animated. The words tumbled out in a heap. They could get a place near Central Park, or maybe something more rural upstate would be better for the children. He'd have to come back regularly to London, of course, to keep an eye on the original, but now that Deirdre had finally walked out of Le Château without any encouragement from Seth, he would be able to take her on without feeling guilty about Sebbie and she would run Finn's brilliantly. And Janie could take the job at *Eden* after all. He had it all worked out.

New York.

Why not? Everyone else in the fashion business was moving there.

Exactly.

While Janie frantically renegotiated her overdraft and racked her brains for anything she'd been good at at school which might help her find long-term employment, something unprecedented was happening to Tom. All his life he had craved peace and serenity. Now suddenly he found the silent orderliness of his Manhattan apartment strangely enervating. In the middle of important summits to discuss the looming perfume launch, which was turning out to be one of the most ambitious since the launch of ck one, he found himself missing Jake and Daisy. Once, mid-pitch to a posse from Wall Street who had convened to argue through the flotation of Tom Fitzgerald on the stock exchange, he started to giggle at a knock-knock joke Nell had told him. Wandering through the design studios, it took all his self-control not to fax some of the sketches for the next collections over to London to see what Janie thought of them — she was so clearly the ideal Tom Fitzgerald woman. He began to think the unthinkable and then, slowly at first, to plot it. By 23 December, he had consulted with his lawyers, his accountants and his soul and drawn up a proposal to Janie which, because of its serious nature, could not be faxed, e-mailed or telephoned to her but was instead entrusted to Madeleine, who was flying back to London to lend Janie some festive support.

'Oh my God,' exclaimed Janie, reading the letter twice through before attempting to rally her thoughts.

Dearest Pippin,

Knowing what an honourable person you are, I fear you may find what I'm about to suggest strange and alien, but I urge you to read and reread this letter and to lay your preconceptions aside until you have thoroughly considered all its ramifications.

In the past weeks, since returning from Turtle House, I find my thoughts endlessly turning to you and your delightful brood (how is Scarlett, by the way?). Inevitably this got me thinking about my life and the chain of events which led me, with so much and no one to share it with, to be sitting here, attending numerous brainstorming sessions on the forthcoming launch of my new scent, which the marketing gurus, with exquisite irony, have decreed shall be called En Famille. And you, with so much in other ways, and no one to take care of it all. So to distract myself from the rigor mortis brought on by all the other business propositions I've been engaging in recently, I came up with one that is far dearer to my heart.

In short, Janie, I'm suggesting that we marry — yes, you and I — and that in return for you and the children coming to live with me for an initial period of, say, seven years, I would make you all financially secure for the rest of your lives. When I say live with, obviously this could be open to our interpretation. All I know is that I would benefit enormously from your company and flatter myself that I could be of some emotional support to all of you. Also, to be completely frank, you and the children would considerably add to the lustre of Tom Fitzgerald the myth, particularly in view of the nature of the new perfume (from which you would obviously receive substantial royalties).

This might not be the most conventional or romantic proposal of marriage you've ever had, but after much reflection, I feel we have both been through too much pain not to be completely honest. And after all, there are worse reasons for marrying than friendship. What do you think? (If this seems hasty, I can only quote that other immortal, Marvell — But at my back I always hear/Time's wingèd chariot hurrying near,/ And yonder all before us lie/Deserts of vast eternity.

Please think long and hard and cast aside any initial preconceptions. I think we could be a marvellous partnership.

Yours ever, T

PS: Don't think I'm taking advantage of what happened with the Gazette. This has been brewing in my subconscious ever since I saw you looking like Deborah Kerr on that lilo . . .

'And to think I thought he was sane,' whistled Madeleine when Janie showed her the letter.

'Oh, I don't know,' said Janie pensively. 'Perhaps he has a point.'

'You can't mean that. What about Matthew? What about Seth? What about love? Principles? You can't marry Tom. You'd be a walking billboard for a perfume.'

'There are worse things,' said Janie defensively.

'Like what?'

'Like being another Worrying Government Statistic,' Janie blurted, before rushing out of the room.

Tom hadn't stipulated any time limit for Janie's decision, though obviously he must want things sorted out before *En Famille* launched in the spring. Janie, throwing herself into last-minute preparations for Christmas, let the proposal swish around her brain and her conscience, and found herself ricocheting between extreme reactions: on the one hand she was appalled by its amorality and on the other more attracted than she cared to admit by its sound, if callously reasoned, sense.

On good days she was proud of what she had achieved with Michaelmas Road. On bad days she felt one step from destitution. The Wednesday before Christmas, a syndication cheque arrived from the *Botswana Chronicle* which had bought one of Matthew's articles for £5.95. Exasperated, she found herself inviting round an estate agent. She was still reeling from his estimate later that evening. What with the booming economy and the house's marvellously airy aspect, the estate agent thought she and Matthew would easily triple their initial investment. That would be a first, she thought grimly. How bloody typical that the place should look so homely just when its future had never been so uncertain.

At least it would be full of life this Christmas. What with Madeleine and Jo-Jo, they were going to be quite a houseful. Eleanor, inevitably, was keeping her options open until the last minute. But Cassie had meekly agreed to spend the day with them and Ben had already called Jo-Jo from Montana to say he was on his way. Gloria had worked her usual magic on the house, placing huge glass vases of holly and white roses on every highly polished surface. Even the fire in the dining room had stopped smoking. Seth had volunteered to do the cooking to Janie's initial relief, until she saw the lavish menus he was planning and remembered that most of the guests were so depressed or debilitated that nothing might get eaten. The only bright spot was that David Carter, due to touch down at Heathrow at any moment, was as notorious for his ferocious appetite as for the bloodiness of his recent divorce. His arrival, late in the afternoon on Christmas Eve, reminded her that she'd never succeeded in getting through to the British embassy. Well, it would have to wait until after Christmas now, she thought guiltily.

If all that weren't nerve-racking enough, Ben and Jo-Jo had invited everyone out for pre-Christmas sashimi at Nobu on Park Lane. Everyone, that is, apart from Seth, who to Janie's crushing disappointment had to work.

Deciding to take advantage of her newly leisured state, Janie ran herself an early bath. Soothed by the blissful cocktail of puffy clean towels and essential oil of geranium, she had almost succeeded in ascending to a transcendental state when the doorbell jangled hyperactively.

It was Sissy, just back from Japan and in a frenzy. She had gone into the office to find Lindsey ensconced at Janie's old desk. Pausing only to clear her things, book a removal van for the sofa and fireplace, dial the senior fashion editor at Australian *Vogue* and leave the phone off the hook, she had then swept out of the office and headed straight for Janie's.

'The worst was that Lindsey looked so smug,' she wailed, and poured herself another whisky. The implications of what she had done were at last sinking in. She loved her job at the *Gazette* and now she'd jettisoned it, even as Lindsey had been extending the nicotine-stained hand of friendship. She'd tried calling Janie from the office, but the line at Michaelmas Road was constantly busy. She rang Nari, but Jean said he was probably about to enter Libyan airspace at the moment on his way back from Singapore. In desperation she called Alice, who couldn't talk for long because Caro was on the warpath about a lost suitcase, but she said comfortingly that Sissy was doing the right thing because principles were obviously about to become very chic.

'And to cap it all, Lindsey's bound to get the exclusive on Anastasia's wedding trousseau,' wailed Sissy.

'What do you mean?' asked Janie wearily.

'Well, I don't suppose The Proprietor would take kindly to his fiancée giving interviews about the wedding to the competition . . .' She broke off. 'Oh, Janie, don't tell me you don't know? It was even on CNN in Tokyo. It's Anastasia and The Proprietor. They're getting married. Maybe that's why he's been in such a filthy mood – he can see the alimony payments already. Either that or he's been had up for stripping assets or whatever it is tycoons do. Anyway, this marriage obviously explains why your piece about her went down so badly. And if I hadn't flogged her my titles he probably wouldn't have so much as looked at her. He's a terrific snob, you know.'

'*What?*' said Janie, reaching for the whisky. 'Forgive me, but you lost me about two miles back there.'

'Don't look so shocked. How d'you think I knew so much about Isabella's latest surgery? We were there together in Buenos Aires – well you didn't think I'd entrust my boobs to anyone in London, did you? And where did you think the money for them came from in the first place? Sissy gesticulated at her breasts with more braggadocio than she felt. 'Dr Mendez is simply the best. An artist in fact. I'd recommend him without a qualm, if you ever get the urge . . .' Janie looked particularly school-marmish.

'What did you think I was doing in Argentina – catching up on my holiday reading? I was zooming these babes from thirty-two A to thirty-six C – and don't let anyone ever tell you that size doesn't matter. I had to drag myself from my deathbed to do those collections with you. You're s'posed to rest for a month. Anyway, Isabella and I found ourselves recovering on adjacent loungers. And when you've got nothing else to do but recuperate, you do a lot of talking. God, she's screwy. I wasn't supposed to tell any of this, incidentally. Part of the contract with Anastasia was that I would keep my mouth shut in perpetuity.'

'I won't tell her if you won't,' said Janie dryly.

It took a couple of hours and three-quarters of the bottle of Scotch before Janie felt she'd unravelled everything. Even then there were all sorts of missing strands.

'. . . so you see it's all my fault. In retrospect Anastasia probably planned everything from the moment I mentioned my stupid family that night at Finn's. I'll bet she did her research on The Proprietor with her customary thoroughness. She certainly made a beeline for him the moment he arrived back in town. And now the blushing bride-to-be is holding court in London.'

'I knew there was something phoney about her,' proclaimed Janie triumphantly later over the sashimi.

'You mean apart from her hair, teeth, bosoms, cheekbones and knees?' said David Carter. 'Well, all that stuff about being brought up by Carmelite nuns in Florence is total crap for a start.'

The table was agog. David was normally so mild-mannered – and such an unlikely source of information about someone like Anastasia. Third and Second World microeconomics were more his usual line of interest. Caught like a rabbit in the glare of their curiosity, he continued, gingerly at first. 'Not that I've made a serious study of her, you understand. But Anastasia, as she calls herself these days, is quite well known in Moscow – in which city, incidentally, she has spent most of her life. In fact she's become quite a role model for a certain kind of working girl in Russia – and men, for that matter. Get to know any important entrepreneur out there and sooner or later he'll give you a card for one of her establishments. It's quite a big scam, actually. I might even have to write it up for *The Probe* as a sort of deep-throat story. All rogues lead to Anastasia, as it were. And good luck to her. It's not everyone who gets to found as flourishing a chain of brothels as Anastasia, née Olga Norduv. Naturally there have been other businesses along the way – property speculation, a shoe factory, assaults on the fashion world – and very successful they have been too. But the core is those brothels. Anastasia is Russia's most inventive madame.'

It wasn't an easy act to follow, but Jo-Jo managed.

'Fuck me, I was right,' she giggled. It was her turn to be the focus of everyone's scrutiny. 'Ages ago – it seems like years – when I did that first shoot with Sven in Russia, I bumped into Anastasia and she tried to sign me up as one of her girls. I didn't realise it was her at the time, but somehow she knew who I was because she went frigging purple when Sven's assistant turned up.'

'How on earth did she think she could get away with it?' said Ben. 'I assume The Proprietor doesn't know this little detail about his beloved's background?'

'She's been trying to offload them for ages,' said David, unexpectedly warming to the spotlight. 'Every time she goes back to Moscow she puts them on the market, but the siren call of all that loot they've been making gets the better of her; she might find things a bit trickier now, though. Apparently, the Countess Montecatini has pulled off one too many less than kosher deals out there. She managed to palm off a particularly unprofitable scrap metal business for far more than it was worth by cooking the books spectacularly. To be fair, that sort of thing happens all the time out there now. It's all part of the game. Unfortunately for Anastasia, the man she sold it to isn't a very good sport.'

While the others degenerated into raucous speculation, Janie fell quiet. Some distant memory, half forgotten, was niggling at her, and through the fug of whisky and shock she couldn't quite recall it. Just after midnight she remembered; the time Anastasia had called her at the *Gazette*, ostensibly to talk about some fashion shows, but in reality to spread some malicious rumours about Cassie and Jo-Jo. Rumours, Janie now realised, that she could only have invented herself.

Chapter Nineteen

Janie kept her hand on the intercom. Little flurries of snow were starting to settle on the railings and she was rapidly sobering up, but determined not to lose her nerve. David Carter had volunteered to come with her but she felt it was better to go alone. It must be past two in the morning – Christmas Day, she realised with a jolt. What better time to catch a socialite at home?

Anastasia, punctilious even in the wee hours, was seated at her dressing table fastidiously administering pre-measured drops of Fruition to the fine lines gathered like sentinels round her mouth when she heard the buzzer. A sixth sense, finely honed, brought on an eerie premonition, confirmed when she saw Janie's belligerent expression on the security screen.

'This had better be good,' she said evenly, opening the door. She led the way down the beige hall to the drawing room, her satin pyjamas flapping almost comically in the silence.

'I was about to say the same,' said Janie tersely, 'about your explanation – for all the havoc you've wrought, I mean.'

Anastasia walked over to her grand piano where she kept a small silver tray of drinks and poured them both a shot of vodka.

'Pass,' she said silkily, her manicured hand betraying only the slightest tremor – and an engagement ring featuring a diamond the size of Corsica. 'I'm afraid I don't know what you're getting at.'

'Oh, please, Anastasia – you do still prefer that name, don't you? – let's both behave like intelligent human beings. I'll tell you what I know. You can give me your version and, who knows, we may even be able to come to a deal. You like those, don't you?'

Anastasia looked at her scornfully but said nothing. Janie was well rehearsed. Over several coffees David had filled her in with all he knew about Anastasia, some of it proven fact, some well-informed speculation, all of it tailor-made for lurid headlines.

'Right, then, I'll begin. Olga Norduv was born in Moscow about forty-one years ago. As far as I know there are no aristocratic connections, but then presumably that's why you were so generous to Sissy. But I'm running ahead of myself. Olga's life was uncomfortable and dull. So she did what many girls like her only dreamed of – she got out of the Soviet Union and eventually found herself in West Germany where she met Dieter Mannheim, a handsome racing driver. They married and life took a turn for the better. For the first time in her life Olga – or had she changed her name now? – had money to spend on clothes, jewellery, parties . . . and boy, did she spend. Oh, she lived a high old life, hardly the discreet, tasteful paragon she later became – and not everyone approved. Some of Dieter's friends were repelled by her coolness in the face of Dieter's increasingly frantic risk-taking both on and off the racetrack, and blamed her rapacious extravagance for pressurising him to do it. But Anastasia was happy. Moscow seemed a long, long way away. Then, rather inconveniently, Dieter got himself killed and Olga, through an unfortunate series of events, found herself back in the USSR, penniless.' Janie's voice had become less vibrato and had acquired a lilting, almost mocking tone. 'Back in Moscow one thing sustained her. She met a photographer called Vladimir Miscov, who promised to launch her as a fashion model. For a short time, it almost looked as though he'd succeed. She was only twenty after all and very pretty. She was photographed for a couple of teenage magazines and she and Vladimir became exceptionally close. But ultimately it became clear that nothing very serious would come of it and Vladimir, not knowing how to break it to Olga and possessed of monumental ambition for himself, simply disappeared one night. Olga was devastated at first, but ever the pragmatist, she took whatever mundane job fell in her path, worked her way up to being a secretary for various members of the Politburo, and with glasnost and perestroika, eventually found the means to set up her own business.

'In retrospect Olga would have preferred her business to be something a little more blue-chip than brothel-keeping, but you have to hand it to her, she excelled at being a madame. Besides, what's a girl with little formal education to do? She diversified – into property and retail. She dabbled in antiques, draped herself in mink, slept her way through the Politburo in a strictly upwardly mobile position – but nothing satisfied her. She yearned to return to the sophistication of the West. Somewhere along the line – you'll have to forgive me, Anastasia, some of the details have been very efficiently buried – she settled briefly in Florence and married, so the Italian connection isn't entirely bogus. But still it wasn't enough. She craved respectability, which was turning out to be harder to acquire than money. She left her Florentine and eventually found herself in London—'

Janie took a gulp of vodka. Anastasia sat still. The last ember of the fire had gone out and the room suddenly seemed cold. She tried not to shiver.

'Oh, don't stop, this is fascinating.'

'Having accomplished her first mission, which was to make herself rich, Olga set about achieving her second goal, to become a cultured member of international society. So she hired tennis coaches, booked French lessons, enrolled in classical music appreciation classes and learned to play the piano. She took an art course at the Uffizi and an interior decorating course at the Inchbold. Her charity commitments alone cost her a fortune. She was discreet and low-key – she'd learned her lesson in Monaco, where even the racing set had started to distance itself from her ostentatious ways. Elocution teachers and etiquette seminars helped her kick over the traces of her years in Moscow. A traditionalist at heart, she bade her time patiently, until perfect husband material number three – or is it four? We're not entirely clear on whether she ever married Vladimir, I'm afraid – came along. Then she laid her not unattractive bait ... You look pale, Anastasia. I hope I'm not boring you. Or does the script simply sound too familiar?'

Anastasia smiled coldly. 'How terribly old-fashioned of you, Janie, to hold someone's background against them.'

'Oh, don't get me wrong, Anastasia. I don't sit in judgment on your distant past – any of it. It's what you've been up to recently that I object to.'

Anastasia looked at her expectantly, a defiant half-smile on her lips. Janie's heart began to pound. She was on far shakier ground now, having pieced together the rest of the story herself on the way from the restaurant. She still didn't have the final details straight. But if she played her hand carefully, Anastasia might reveal the truth.

'At last, Olga's story looked like having a happy ending. A grand society wedding was announced and suddenly she was the talk of London. But Olga had made one small mistake. On one of her business trips to Moscow she had accidentally approached a girl from London to work for her, which was odd, because she was normally so cautious. Unfortunately for Olga, this girl became famous – and so fast. Terrified that she might spill the beans, Olga set about destroying her credibility and wrecking her agent's reputation for good measure. It turned out to be remarkably easy. She began to drop little hints about Jo-Jo and Cassie to her friends in high places. The press had gone berserk over Peace Grant, and Olga found that if she just took the time to get to know the gossip hacks, most of them were charmingly suggestive.

'But spreading innuendo among the great and the good wasn't working fast enough. So Olga took the law into her own hands – she'd had plenty of experience, after all – and applied a little gentle pressure on her victims. And this is where luck really was on her side. When she had been in Milan, early in the year, trying to ingratiate herself with the fashion community, she had made the most extraordinary and, at the time, shocking discovery. Coming out of one of the shows, she had bumped into Vladimir Miscov, whom she hadn't seen for more than twenty years and almost didn't recognise. He, of course, instantly remembered Olga, who was every bit as fragrant as she had been all those years ago. After exchanging awkward pleasantries, Vladimir, a little remorseful perhaps, and certainly in need of all the support in high places that he could muster, begged Olga's forgiveness and insisted on taking her for a drink so that she could hear his side of the story. This turned out to be so tortuous and bathetic that she almost missed her plane back to London. However, in her quest to behave in a ladylike fashion, she decided that the quality of mercy was not strained – indeed, could be very useful – and forgave Vladimir everything. After that, it wasn't difficult to persuade Vladimir to help her trash Cassie and to arrange for a few incriminating faxes to be sent to Cassie's office from Milan. And if that wasn't neat enough, Olga's new friend, The Proprietor, turned out to be the most powerful media mogul in the world. Through him she rapidly learned what little she didn't already know about manipulating journalists. Placing front-page stories was child's play . . . I assume it was Zack who inadvertently let you know that Cassie would be at the airport that day?'

She stopped. Anastasia walked silently back to the piano, opened a filigree case of cigarettes and lit one.

'Very clever, Janie. But what is your point? It's your word against mine and, let's face it, your word isn't deemed very reliable these days, is it?'

'Oh, don't worry about me, Anastasia, I've got plenty of back-up. To my certain knowledge, at least one broadsheet newspaper has been investigating your Russian businesses for months.' Janie, out on a limb now, decided to risk David Carter's theory. 'They're particularly interested in that scrap-metal business you bought for fifteen thousand roubles and sold a year later to Andrei Zubetsky for nine hundred thousand. You see, they believe you weren't entirely frank about its accounts when you made your sales pitch. And for some reason they seem to think that Zubetsky, already distinctly out of sorts over the deal, would be, let me see, stark raving mad were the words they used, I think, when he discovered quite the extent to which you'd cooked the books.'

For the first time Anastasia visibly paled. How in God's name had this got out? She'd been so careful. She'd only done it to teach Zubetsky a lesson. He was an unprincipled thug. Unfortunately he'd gone on to be a hugely successful, notoriously brutal thug, with connections the length and breadth of Moscow's Mafia. If he ever found out she'd be finished. Not even The Proprietor's billions would save her.

She marched over to her bureau and took out her cheque book.

'How much do you want?'

'I don't want your money, Anastasia. That's one self-improving lesson you still haven't learned, isn't it? I don't want my old job either, in case you were thinking of whispering some sweet nothings to The Proprietor. The only thing you can give me is my friend's reputation and sanity back.'

'I'm not sure I can do that, as a matter of fact. A speeding train isn't so easy to turn around,' she said sulkily.

'I dare say a few phone calls to your friends on the gossip pages, a little pillow talk to The Proprietor and some glowing editorial on Cassie would help enormously. And I'm sure between us we could come up with a story about those faxes that would satisfy Scotland Yard without getting you implicated too much.'

Anastasia didn't respond.

'If you don't co-operate, I can promise you that the journalist leading the investigation into your past will have no compunction in publishing. As a matter of fact, his editor's just itching to get hold of a watertight story that would drop your beloved fiancé in the soup. His devotion to his religion annoys some of them, you see – and you know what a vicious business newspapers are, and the depths to which some people will stoop. In any case, I hardly think a born-again Catholic would relish the irony of being married to the world's most successful brothel-keeper.'

'And if it turns out that I can help?'

'He'll drop it. He owes me a big favour.'

Anastasia thought for a few moments. 'Very well. I'll do everything in my power. I didn't enjoy it anyway.'

Janie shot her a pulverising stare.

'You don't know the half of it,' said Anastasia quietly. 'You stand there accusing me from the comfort of your moral little universe – and you just don't have a clue, do you? Uncomfortable? Life in Moscow in those days was unbearable. We lived in a two-room flat – my parents, two brothers and a sister – that stank of cabbage and sweat. When we weren't squabbling we bored each other to tears. It was a daily struggle just to get food – and when you cooked it you wondered why you'd bothered. No privacy, no hope, no dignity – do you know that some months you couldn't even get sanitary protection? Can you imagine what those sort of conditions do to a self-conscious teenager? It wasn't just dull – it was deathly.'

She lit another cigarette. 'Now let me tell you a story. This girl Olga you seem to know so much about had one trump card. She was a beauty. At least, that's what everyone in her neighbourhood told her. Men were always chatting her up with a view, they said, to photographing her. Believe me, Vladimir Miscov wasn't the first, or last. But he was by far the most compelling. Hard as it is to believe now, he was sweet, innocent-looking and sincere. I adored him – probably more than I've ever loved anyone else. There was something vulnerable about him and I trusted him with my life, not just my career. I was devastated when I woke up to find he'd just left. I think perhaps a little of me did die that morning . . .' She brushed away a tear impatiently, and Janie, feeling herself momentarily soften, turned away.

'I won't bore you with the excuses I invented for him. Suffice to say I convinced myself that he had gone to the West to forge a path for both of us and that I made up my mind to find him. I was sure he must have gone to London, which was *the* place for aspiring photographers and models at that time. It took me two years to get there, and by the time I did I was really too old to be starting out, but of course I didn't know very much about it in those days – and even if I had, I would probably have carried on anyway. Needless to say, Vladimir, if he'd ever been in London, had long since disappeared. Once more, I had to fend for myself. I looked up the most successful agency in town, which at that time was a set-up called Flick, where your friend Cassie Grange was working.

'And I'll tell you something about Cassie – she wasn't quite in Mother Teresa's league in those days. You see, I didn't just pick on her all these years later for the hell of it. In those days Cassie was still working in her university holidays – Hot Shots was barely a twinkle in her eye. But everyone said she was going to be the one. So when I walked into the Flick offices, I walked past all the other bookers in the room and marched straight up to her desk. She was perfectly polite, but she made a fatal mistake. Instead of telling me to forget modelling then and there, she told me to come back when I'd lost weight. So I lost weight. Then she said my hair was wrong. I cut it short. Then it was my nose. I changed it. Curves were in. I saved up and got some. Finally I'd transformed myself, exactly as Cassie suggested. I plucked up courage and went back for what I knew would be my last shot. She was busy but graciously spared a moment to look me up and down. That's when she finally had the guts to come out with it. "You know what?" she said, as casually as if she were about to tell me what was on television that night. "Your look is over. There's nothing you can do. Go home, forget about modelling and do something interesting." It was the most humiliating moment of my life. So don't be so quick to seize the high ground – you do that a lot, you know, Janie. You have no idea how you would have turned out in my shoes.'

'I hope I would never want to deliberately destroy other human beings,' said Janie, in a quiet voice that surprised even her with its self-control; at that moment she loathed Anastasia with a violence that shocked her. 'You can't possibly imagine that anything that's happened to you exonerates your behaviour—' She stopped herself, as the futility of trying to seek full retribution dawned on her. She might be able to frighten Anastasia into backing off Cassie, but she would never really carry out her blackmail threats and Anastasia was bound to end up as a glamorous pillar of the Establishment.

By the time Janie had satisfied herself that Anastasia would keep her word, there was movement in the staff quarters. She stepped out into the snow and hailed a cab. The lights on the Christmas tree in Park Lane were twinkling, reminding her of the houseful waiting back at home. Only Seth wouldn't be there. He'd been working at Finn's until two, and to avoid being woken by the children opening their stockings at 5.30 in the morning, they'd arranged that he should spend the night at his flat and come over later in the day.

It was almost six when she pulled up outside Michaelmas Road. Another cab had drawn up ahead of them. Maybe one of her house guests had been called away suddenly. David? But it wasn't David. A gaunt figure in a baggy coat lifted a canvas bag out of the taxi and swung round towards the gate. It was Matthew.

Chapter Twenty

'It's probably for the best,' said Cassie gently. 'You need to get used to one another again.'

'I know,' said Matthew sadly. 'I see that now. The funny thing is that even up to the moment the taxi pulled up outside Michaelmas Road, it had never occurred to me that things might have changed so radically between us. I really thought, all those months I was away, that time would have just stopped for everyone else. The sublime arrogance of ego, I s'pose.'

'You're being very hard on yourself. I expect it was your optimism that saved your life. "My nature is/That I incline to hope rather than fear/And gladly banish squint suspicion,"' murmured Cassie, a long-ago-remembered snatch of Milton inexplicably surfacing for the occasion. She couldn't think of anything else to say. They had been over it all so many times, she and Matthew, the past few weeks. Now that he'd moved out of Michaelmas Road to Will's flat in Islington, he'd taken to dropping in on her for an early evening drink and a confessional. He was probably lonely, Will being a workaholic who never left the office before nine.

It had been quite an entrance, a tumultuous start to the festivities, she'd give Matthew that. After her initial shock Janie seemed to fall into a kind of trance, a state of normality so heightened that it was almost surreal. Madeleine, woken by Nell's hysterical caterwauling, had immediately grasped the situation and discreetly telephoned Seth to tell him to stay

465

at home. The rest of them had carried on with the day as best they could, for the sake of the children, although Daisy and Jake, having failed to recognise Matthew, were the only genuinely upbeat participants at lunch.

Over the next few days the other guests had tactfully melted away. Ben had whisked Jo-Jo off to try some skiing in Aspen; Gloria had gone to stay with the Scotts; David had to go back to Moscow, though he had promised Janie he would bury the Anastasia story; and Madeleine moved in temporarily with Cassie before flying back to New York. Matthew, still surfacing from the euphoria of being home, at last tried to make sense to Janie of everything that had happened to him in the last year.

'Basically he's been bloody well "finding himself",' said Janie bitterly one day. 'While I was trying to hold the family together and get on with life, Matthew was peering into the "abyss of his soul".'

'It's not that self-indulgent, be fair,' said Cassie, surprised to hear herself defending Matthew. But Janie was being harsh. There was no denying that Matthew had been weak initially to stay away, and that he'd probably used the orphanage as an excuse to escape his own problems at home. But until the last few days, Cassie hadn't appreciated how deep-rooted those problems had been. She knew that Janie and Matthew bickered sometimes, but no more than other couples – certainly far less than most.

'Why didn't you tell me you and Matthew had discussed divorce?' she asked Janie one day, sounding hurt.

'Matthew told you that?' said Janie warily.

'He also said things got bad even before the twins were born. God, what are friends for, Janie, if not to confide in?'

'I don't think we could even acknowledge it ourselves, to begin with,' said Janie quietly. 'It's quite a strain, you know, being the Perfect Couple. Anyway, when the Rio trip first came up it seemed like an ideal excuse to take a holiday alone together, but . . . well, by the time it came round we could barely speak to one another without fighting, and suddenly it turned into an excuse for a trial separation.'

466

'So you'd decided that before Matthew even left?' asked Cassie in astonishment, her old hostilities towards Matthew suddenly starting to fray. She had always assumed Matthew had instigated the separation once he'd got to Guatemala.

'I know what you're thinking,' said Janie. 'I haven't been exactly straight about all of this with anyone, least of all myself. All I knew was that to get through the first few months without Matthew I had to hate him – and the longer he stayed away the easier it became. I still can't understand how he could bear not to be in touch with the children all that time.'

'It was you who stopped him writing to Nell—'

'He could have disobeyed.' Janie's expression was savage.

'Jesus,' said Cassie, 'you only have to look at him to see he's been through a rough time.' This was true. Bearded and sun-scorched, Matthew had a haunted look in his eyes and for the first time in his life looked gaunt.

'Yes, well, only Matthew could make working in an orphanage a treasonable offence,' retorted Janie, her indignation only partly compensating her for the guilt she felt for not doing enough when Matthew's father had called her before Christmas to tell her he was worried about his son. 'There's you, hounded by Scotland Yard for six months, exploited by drug-runners and the Mafia, finally arrested, and still you manage to turn things around so brilliantly that Hot Shots is not only a household name but a respected one. While Matthew only has to be in a country for five minutes before he nearly gets blown up by a bomb and then thrown in jail – just for being in the wrong village, apparently. But then he always did have a lousy sense of direction.'

Janie stopped. Strange snorting sounds were coming from Cassie, who had her hand pressed firmly against her mouth. A second later they had both subsided into peals of laughter. Janie knew she was being outrageously unfair, and it felt supremely satisfying.

Matthew was starting to acknowledge that it would take a long time to come to terms with everything that had happened in the last fourteen months. He'd experienced such a welter of emotions – from despair to euphoria – since arriving on Christmas Day, during the course of which the realisation that Janie might just have fallen in love with someone else began to dawn on him only very slowly. Talk about bad timing. He'd felt about as welcome as Banquo's ghost when he'd arrived home that first morning. For a while he'd had nightmares – terrifying apocalyptic images in which the bombs exploded continuously about him while he languished in a military jail. That would teach him to look after his passport, he thought ruefully. His emotions were a mush. Back in London, he even felt guilty about leaving Mungo short-handed at the orphanage, even though, once the British ambassador had finally got them out of jail, Matthew had been in no fit state to help anyone.

It was funny how Mungo hadn't seemed nearly so affected by their experiences. Perhaps he was more robust than Matthew, or more inured – he was always getting tangled up with unpleasant officials and had been chucked in prison more than once. But for Matthew it had all been traumatic. Mungo had warned him that the official powers in Guatemala might not take kindly to the orphanage, which had been set up specifically for native Indian children whose parents had been murdered by the military. But in the end their mishaps had nothing to do with their work. The explosions had been an army exercise that went wrong, and even their arrest, a month later, had been a mistake. He and Mungo had been enjoying a weekend's break camping on the outskirts of a tiny village on the edge of the jungle when they were ambushed by a bunch of anarchic soldiers who insisted on believing they were American spies. Eventually they'd been released ten days before Christmas. It had taken them another week to get back to the relative civilisation of Guatemala City. If Matthew hadn't left their passports back in the orphanage in Momostenango, he'd have saved a lot of anguish all round. No wonder Janie was exasperated with him.

He still couldn't bring himself even to contemplate her relationship with Seth, and in any case Janie absolutely refused to discuss it. When he'd moved in with Will, Janie had agreed to his visiting the children every day, on condition that he didn't ask her about Seth. Although initially he'd quizzed Cassie about him, he'd found her obvious affection for Seth too painful to pursue.

'All I can say is that in a funny way you'd approve of him,' she said one evening, in an attempt to describe Seth accurately to Matthew in such a way that he'd let the matter rest. Not surprisingly this did nothing to alleviate his bleakness. After the initial rush of coming home, he had sunk into an uncharacteristic lethargy.

'Perhaps it's time you went back to work,' suggested Will helpfully one day. 'I take it you are still employed by *The Probe*?'

His confidence at a low ebb, Matthew went to see his editor. Hugh St Clair, smarting from a leaked report by the Press Complaints Commission which had criticised the paucity of several of the broadsheets' news coverage from Third World countries, greeted his return more enthusiastically than Matthew could ever have anticipated.

'Tell you what,' said Hugh jocularly, 'before you hurl yourself into the rough-and-tumble of Westminster, why don't you pen a few essays about your time in South America? You could write them at home. Make them personal, readers love all that, and we'll run 'em big. Could be therapeutic. And I dare say there's plenty to write – don't suppose you ran into any Nazis while you were down there?'

Matthew permitted himself a jaundiced smile. For a year he'd found it almost impossible to get any article longer than two hundred words into *The Probe*. Now all of a sudden he was being asked to come up with two thousand. Still, it was a diversion of sorts.

Seth consoled himself the way he knew best – by immersing himself in work. It wasn't difficult. The press reaction in New York to news that a branch of Finn's was opening there had been ecstatic, and Vanessa had already lined up half a dozen interviews with him. He still saw Janie every day, but the little heap of possessions that had gradually accumulated at Michaelmas Road started to find its way back to his flat in Clerkenwell. While Matthew had been five thousand miles away he had seemed a vague, shadowy blur. Now he was back, he had taken on a corporeal relevance. Seth half expected to run into him round every corner. It was hard sleeping with another man's wife. If anything he adored Janie more, but even so, it was a relief when he had to go to New York for a couple of weeks to hire some staff.

His flight just about bisected Tom's, who had decided to pay a visit to Janie in person, on the pretext of checking out a site for a new three-storey flagship shop on Bond Street. Bowled over by the quaint, red-brick charm of Michaelmas Road, he barely noticed that his chauffeur-driven stretch Mercedes had practically brought it to a standstill. Gloria was out with the twins. It was Cassie, fulfilling her new weekly godmotherly duties with Nell, who let him in. He found Janie in the kitchen slaving over her computer. *The Spectator* had commissioned her to review Grace's book, which Vickers and Snood, who'd performed a remarkable rescue operation on it, mainly by getting it ghosted, had successfully marketed as a feminist kiss 'n' tell on the fashion business through the ages. She was also racing to finish an article for Lee, who, to Janie's eternal gratitude, far from bearing her any grudge for not accepting the job at *Eden*, was inundating her with freelance commissions.

'Still keeping the wolves from the door, then, pippin?' She gave a whelp of surprise. His suntanned good looks seemed somehow ostentatiously perfect standing in the doorway of her shabby kitchen.

'I take it from your silence that the answer to my offer was a vehement no?' He looked at her guilty expression. 'Don't worry, I know you've had your hands full one way or another. Madeleine told me it was an interesting Christmas.'

'I'm so sorry,' she said meekly. 'You must think me very rude and ungrateful.'

'I may just find a way to forgive you if you could see your

way to giving me a cutting from that delicious-looking vine growing up the front of your house.'

She smiled and got up to hug him.

'I've shown you my garden, now it's your turn.' She led him outside, past the tubs of clipped box and pleached fruit trees, down to the winter-flowering roses and beyond, to the reclaimed tennis court where her ornamental vegetable patch was finally responding to the constant nurturing that she and Gloria had lavished on it over the last few months. February wasn't the best time to show off a garden, but Tom was enchanted by its variety and size, much greater than the front of the house led visitors to expect. He watched her absent-mindedly plucking some weeds from between the box shoots.

'From rags to ditches,' he said thoughtfully. 'It suits you.'

'You are a talented thing,' he exclaimed, when they were back in the house. 'People would pay you a fortune if you could incorporate some of these ideas in their gardens and roof terraces in New York.'

'Gloria helped too – I couldn't have done it without her,' garbled Janie effusively, relieved that their friendship was back on course. 'And I've got no formal training.'

'You've read more books than most. Besides, you have a real gift.'

'If it's any consolation,' she said later over dinner at the Ritz, 'I was very tempted at one point.'

'A moment of panic?' She didn't answer. 'Don't worry. I admire you all the more. It probably wouldn't have worked anyway. I'm a hopeless insomniac whereas you, pippin, can fall asleep anywhere.' Janie looked at him searchingly. Surely he hadn't imagined they would share a bedroom . . .

'So what are you going to do, pippin? Seth or Matthew?'

Janie rolled her eyes.

'Militant lesbianism?'

'I could always try being on my own,' she said primly. They both looked unconvinced. Janie wasn't the solitary type. She didn't know what she was going to do. She started to miss Seth even before his plane left the tarmac, but at least his absence made her feel less jittery when Matthew came round to see the children.

She tried to leave them all alone together whenever possible, as much out of awkwardness as altruism. Matthew had become withdrawn and intense, unwilling to discuss the past twelve months and incapable of focusing on the future. What with the beard and the wasted physique and the long anguished silences, it was like being visited by a holy man doing penances. He was distant and unapproachable. It was painful too, watching him try to re-establish relationships with the children – the twins were at best indifferent and Nell was often hostile. Janie spent more and more time working in the study when Matthew was in the house. Sometimes she found herself toying with outlines for her ideal gardening book, just as an excuse to stay at the computer. Gloria was at her wits' end; she simply couldn't believe that Janie and Matthew, now there was no ocean between them, seemed intent on throwing their marriage away, apparently without making any effort to save it.

'Ees reediculous and eereesponsible,' she wailed to Cassie, to whom, in her despair and frustration, she had begun confiding. 'They were born for one another.'

'I know what you mean,' said Cassie sadly. She was surprised by their inertia as well. They hardly even seemed to talk. God, whatever else they'd lacked in the past, conversation had never been scarce. 'Maybe they've just grown apart. Maybe being "made for one another" isn't enough. You have to want to be together and perhaps Janie and Matthew don't any more.'

'Well, they should.'

The turnaround in Cassie's fortunes was dizzying. The press, having hounded her for months, suddenly canonised her. Barely a week went past without someone or other from Hot Shots being quoted in *The Python* and even the *Gazette* on every subject from their favourite restaurants to government policies on women's issues. Jo-Jo won VH1's Model of the Season award and made a charming speech at the ceremony in New York in which she acknowledged Cassie, Gloria and Ben, at which point the powers at Genevieve Fairfax, deciding she was a product with considerable media presence after all, changed their minds yet again and signed her up as their face in a multi-million-dollar deal. What with Jo-Jo's increasingly glamorous profile and Peace's increasingly respected one, Hot Shots seemed to have the feel-good factor taped. It reminded Cassie of the early days when she had first set up the agency. Only this time, she thought a little wistfully, she didn't know whether she wanted success desperately enough any more to maintain the necessary momentum. She needed a challenge. It was Zack who signposted it one night when he came round for a quiet supper. Cassie strongly suspected that secretly he still nurtured a small hope that they would get back together, and she knew also that it was never going to happen and that she should stop seeing him altogether. It got worse after a few drinks, when he always turned maudlin, so she spiked his tequila with mineral water and distracted him by requesting he read her tarot cards, even though prophesies of any kind gave her the creeps. Hunched over his lucky pack, he saw all sorts of things – Cassie finding great happiness, Cassie laying to rest her internal demons, Cassie finally getting the hang of Food Combining . . .

'Only teasing about the last bit,' he said chirpily. Cassie scowled.

'I see a man,' said Zack, perking up.

'Never mind all that,' said Cassie nervously. 'What about work?'

'Hot Shots will go from strength to strength – expansion of a very interesting kind. I'm seeing another continent very clearly. It's going to be very important. Your new home, perhaps.'

'Not Asia or Africa,' said Cassie anxiously. 'Please don't let me spend my twilight years in the Third World, God.'

'No, but it does begin with A or—'

Zack struggled for a few more moments until Cassie silenced

him with a hug. He'd given her an idea so obvious she couldn't believe she hadn't thought of it herself.

A little nervously, Jo-Jo had decided to settle in New York for a while. She'd fallen in love with Ben's life and his friends in Malibu, and had wanted to spend time there, but Cassie told her she needed to be in New York at this point in her career and had explained that since so many shoots took place in New York studios, it could mean less travelling in the long run and might even give her some time for a personal life. Ben, laid-back as ever, was quietly thrilled. After six months of scouring Manhattan, they had finally found a duplex on the Upper West Side with amazing views across Central Park, just as Ben had been called away to reshoot some scenes on *Dead Before Sunrise*. In his absence, Jo-Jo, happy but tired and, as always, impatient, had ended up signing the lease on the wrong apartment, a downtown loft in the one street where Ben had categorically not wanted to live. It didn't seem to matter. They were idyllically happy, if both working too hard. And wrong street or not, the loft was rapidly becoming a magnet for visiting friends. Even Cassie, on a business trip to New York, combined with a little light shopping, had deigned to stay with them instead of at the Pierre, which was normally her first choice.

'I love – no, let's get this right – I *adore* you.' He had just watched her dance a jig on opening his birthday card to her – a Picasso sketch he'd bought at the Sotheby's auction.

'Mmm, I know,' said Jo-Jo, feigning indifference. Ben pulled her back on the bed and gazed up at her. She was extraordinary – healthy and glowing from the inside out. He didn't think he would ever tire of looking at her. 'Y'know, some people would love you for your sheer, unadulterated physical gorgeousness or your Genevieve Fairfax contract. But I adore your soul.'

'And my apartment?'

'Even that. We can shack up with your mom for all I care. As long as we're together.'

Jo-Jo wiggled her be-diamonded toes for Ben's benefit and giggled. 'No greater love hath man – blimey, is that Shakespeare?'

'You look fantastic,' exclaimed Tom, surveying Cassie's gleaming hair and skin. He was taking her to lunch at his favourite eatery to thank her for whisking him off on a tour of London's premier retail sites when he had been over in February. 'Careful, or I might lasso you for one of my ads.'

'Launching an outsize range, then?' asked Cassie wryly.

He studied her unabashedly, taking in the way her coolly arched eyebrows seemed to frame everything she said in ironic quotation marks.

'Why do you do that?'

'What?'

'Put yourself down all the time.'

'It's something we Granges excel at. In some it would be called modesty but my mother taught me how to take it a step further and turn it into state-of-the-art self-abasement.'

'Well, you're a very attractive woman. Repeat that to yourself on the hour. Orders of Dr Tom.'

'You're being Masterful-of-the-universe. I take it the meeting went well?'

'You could say that. They seem to think the flotation will be oversubscribed five or six times. How about you? Diego been wining and dining you?'

'Yes, as a matter of fact – and he sent me this rather nice bracelet.' She stretched out her wrist which sparkled with tourmalines and rubies. 'Vulgar, but sweet, don't you think? He's whistling in the wind, but I haven't told him that yet, of course. I want to see him vault through a few more hoops – as well as a few more Tiffany catalogues. I've decided to open up a branch here on my own.' She paused. Somewhere, a subliminal flicker of satisfaction registered as she noticed Tom's expression.

'I've always loved this city and I'd like to live here for a couple of years. Saffron can head the London branch. To be honest, if I don't promote her soon she'll run off and set up her own agency. Diego will go mad probably, and by all accounts he's pretty spectacular when he does, but I'm relishing the show, which I intend to watch from my apartment somewhere up on the ninetieth floor.'

'I hope you don't think I'm a ball-breaker,' she shouted at him a couple of days later over the roar of a helicopter. Tom was taking her on an aerial tour of the island to point out apartments that he knew for a certain fact were discreetly on the market.

'So long as you're kind to animals, whatever you do to Diego's balls is fine by me. He's slept with so many of his models, he probably hasn't got any left anyway.' Cassie was dismayed but hardly shocked by this. Whatever else her agency in New York did or didn't do, it would go out of its way to nurture and respect every single girl it signed on. Maybe she should think about leasing a house for the younger ones to share, like the Ford agency did. It could be fun and informal, but safe and homely – and, she thought, a gleam in her eye, she knew just the person to run it.

Janie seemed to retreat further and further into her study. Encouraged by Tom, she had begun contributing to a couple of gardening magazines and even started to think she might be able to get a column in one of the Sunday papers. Matthew continued to visit the children daily, although no articles had so far appeared in *The Probe*. Writer's block, she supposed sympathetically. Seth was having to spend far too much time in New York but called her faithfully every day. Life took on a reassuring if slightly forlorn routine. And then the call from Dexter Ravensburg came.

'Mr Dexter F. Ravensburg's on the line for you now,' barked his secretary, leaving a moment's pause as if giving Janie time to genuflect. He got straight to the point.

'Nice pieces you've been doing for *Eden*,' he said. 'I'm calling to find if you're ready to take on something bigger. We're launching a glossy monthly aimed specifically at the urban gardener. The market research on it looks most promising – could be huge. Anyway, I thought of you. As editor. If you're interested we should talk in more detail.' Tom, bless him, must have said something about her green fingers to Dexter. She stared out of the window to where Matthew and the children were attempting to move a nest of baby thrushes out of Barry the cat's malevolent reach, and heard herself agreeing to meet Dexter in New York.

'Don't take this the wrong way, but maybe it's time to think laterally.'

'Bored of my Kama Sutra repertoire already?'

'I meant the collection.'

'*Collection*. That's a new one. We've always called them clothes until now.' Sissy knew she had to tread gingerly. Nari was desperately anxious not to be bamboozled by Sissy into taking Everything She Wants so far upmarket that it alienated its existing customers, and he hardly let her near any of the sketches and swatches. Admittedly she hadn't helped her reputation as a visual genius when she accidentally let slip that she'd thought his Chippendale in Egerton Gardens had come from Peter Jones. But she couldn't help herself. She was convinced that with a little tweaking Everything She Wants could appeal across the board.

'Look, at the moment you're selling to people who can't afford to go anywhere else. But if you paid just a little attention to what was going on in fashion you could get everyone – teenagers, hip women in their forties and fifties – coming in at least once a season.' She turned to an article she had earmarked in *Beau Monde* and began to read it aloud. '"The high street has been transformed in the past eight years. The twin propellers of recession and increased product awareness have meant that high-street design has become immeasurably

477

more sophisticated. And as a reward, retailers have seen a huge sea change amongst customers. Shopping on the high street is no longer a necessity; it's cool." And there's this.' She handed him a double-page feature in the *Daily Telegraph* showing celebrities in high-street clothes. 'This couldn't have happened a few years ago, but chain-store clothes are so good now that people are happy to be seen wearing them. If you don't shape up, you get left behind.' She had amassed some figures from Gina about a national chain that had increased its turnover by twenty-five per cent by collaborating with designers, and had also collated some data about demographic shifts. 'I know that the average spend on clothes in the UK is approximately seven per cent of its total household income, which means that the typical woman has about five hundred and ten pounds a year to spend on herself, but at the moment, even allowing for its geographical limitations, Everything She Wants is only accessing nought point two per cent of that money—'

Nari looked at her, impressed. 'So what do you suggest?'

'As I said, some fashion input – good design doesn't cost any more than bad and the average customer is far more fashion-literate than a decade ago. We could try producing shorter runs targeted at key sites; we could launch a petite range – nearly half of all British women are under five feet three – a poster campaign on buses; more sympathetic lighting inside the stores, different signage—' She stopped for breath. The room had gone very quiet. Even Jean had stopped typing.

'In the final analysis it's about respecting the customer. Judging from some of the stuff you sell, Nari, anyone would think you despised them.'

'Anything else?' His eyes were flashing.

Sissy, observing the sparks, said a silent prayer. 'Yes, actually. About the name—'

'There she is. There she is,' exclaimed Cassie, spotting Jo-Jo and Ben hand in hand outside the Dorothy Chandler Pavilion and nearly upturning a jumbo box of Cheerios all over

Madeleine's bed in her excitement. From the speakers Joan Rivers' commentary drooled on breathlessly about the stunning performance in *Sons and Lovers* that had snagged Ben an Oscar nomination.

'Great dress,' whistled Janie admiringly. 'I don't think I've ever seen Jo-Jo look so radiant.'

Madeleine looked at the television and beamed proudly. 'You can't imagine the trouble she put us to. Change this, lengthen that. And until this minute I wasn't sure she'd actually wear it.'

'She did have everyone from Valentino to Aeron Baxter begging her to wear their gowns,' said Cassie smugly. She scrutinised her protégée. After daily exposure to the world's most talented make-up artists, stylists, designers and photographers, Jo-Jo had become fluent in the mystifying language of fashion. And she had added something else – her own innate good taste and elegance. To judge from the number of articles dedicated to her off-duty wardrobe she was rapidly becoming a style icon.

'Ohmigod, Kim Basinger's wearing her sofa again.'

'They do look fabulous together,' remarked Madeleine as the camera panned to Jo-Jo and Ben sitting in the audience. 'Do you think it will last?'

'Not if they're lucky,' said Janie morosely. 'They're far too young to spend the rest of their lives together.'

The other two looked at her indignantly and began pelting her with popcorn. 'Misery!' they said in unison.

Janie was extremely tempted by Dexter's offer. The prospect of bringing beauty and nature to the lives of thousands of urban Americans appealed to her evangelical streak. It would be hard work to begin with, but she'd be able to afford lots of help with the children, and she and Seth had been to see an adorable white clapboard house with a huge garden that was only an hour's drive from New York.

At the end of April Finn's opened in SoHo to all-round ecstasy. The launch party was an encore of the London one, except with an American cast – and if anything more glamorous. Janie lost count of the famous faces there. She knew the place was a hit when she saw Tina Brown, the famously hard-working editor of the *New Yorker*, still there after midnight. Seth, eyes shining with disbelief and a flicker of something else, Janie noticed – that old, detached aloofness, as if he disapproved of the hullabaloo, and of himself for secretly enjoying it – told her he loved her. Unfortunately the runaway success of the restaurant meant that he wasn't going to get back to London as early as he thought, so the break they'd planned on the west coast of Ireland had to be postponed and Janie went home without him.

Back in London she slowly began to introduce the idea to Nell and to prepare herself to break the news to Matthew. While she'd been away his first article had finally appeared in *The Probe*. He seemed happier and less withdrawn. With the children, at least, he was almost back to his old self and, Janie noted with a pang, frequently reduced Nell to peals of laughter. 'Cracking good piece,' said Eleanor, calling to see if Janie had read it. She didn't even add the caveat of 'for Matthew'.

'No, Mother, I have not read Matthew's confessional. I've been in New York trying to find a job,' she said tartly. She'd had quite enough of Matthew's saintly Guatemalan exploits without having to read about them across a double-page spread. But over the next few days she heard so many people talking about it that she felt compelled to unearth a copy. Then she wished she hadn't. Introducing the villagers who had helped build the orphanage in the first place, it was so beautifully written, so lucid and compassionate and unsentimental, that Janie was sobbing by the end, as much for the glimpses of the old Matthew as for the children he was writing about. Over the next few weeks, Matthew's articles on Latin America became required reading for anyone with a claim to being a well-informed humanitarian. While demonstrating his gentle humour and acute observation, he raised important human rights issues, some of which were subsequently debated in the House of Commons. Hugh St Clair began to make noises about Matthew coming back to the paper full time. He shaved off his beard, which as Cassie pointed out made him look less sepulchral and more like Matthew, which was probably a good thing. He was less fragile-looking than before, but still thin.

It was balmy for so early in May – she was struggling to concentrate on an article for *Eden*. Hearing whoops of delight coming from the garden, she wandered out on to the terrace. Matthew had been teaching the children to do reef knots and they had tied him to a tree and were now performing a war dance round him. She heard him plea-bargaining with them.

'Tell you what, I'll tell you jokes and the first one who laughs has to untie me.'

Daisy cackled immediately; Nell held out for four jokes then began laughing uproariously as she reluctantly untied him – and just as suddenly burst into tears.

'I don't know why you're bothering to be so nice,' she snapped. 'We're buggering off to New York any minute and probably won't see you ever again.'

'Pathetic,' said Matthew. 'The essence of a good joke, Nell, is that it has to make you laugh.'

'It's not a joke,' snapped Nell, catching sight of Janie. 'And if you don't believe me, ask *her*.'

He followed Nell's gaze to where Janie stood horrified. She had never seen so much hurt in anyone's eyes before. Damn. The last thing she'd wanted was for Matthew to hear like this, but somehow she'd never found the right time to broach the subject with him. For months he'd been fragile and distant and she had been genuinely frightened that any more upset would result in him having a nervous breakdown. Well, she'd just have to grasp the nettle. In any case, the last few weeks he'd seemed much more robust. Even so, she could see days of soul-searching and self-justification ahead. Unable to bear the sight of their anguished faces, she turned on her heels and fled into her study.

Before she had time to close the door, he was upon her, his face suddenly harsh with anger. He caught hold of her wrist and pulled her round to look at him.

'What gives you the right to go on treating me like this?'

'Like what, exactly?' She was shocked and breathless at his physical roughness, and her voice echoed inside her head, sulky and obstreperous, like a child's.

'Like some emotional leper who doesn't even have the right to be consulted about the welfare of his children.'

She shook her arm free of his grasp, as if he were of no more consequence than some wayward brambles that had momentarily detained her. 'As I recall, you were the one who abandoned all parental rights when you buggered off for a year, severing all contact with your children. You're bloody lucky I let you see them at all.'

'Aren't you forgetting that it was you who forbade me from even writing to them? If I hadn't been feeling so guilty and confused, I would never have agreed to such emotional fascism.'

'Aren't you forgetting you were the one who ran off? Who couldn't cope? Who needed to fucking find himself?' She was yelling now. 'Well, Matthew, I hope it was worthwhile, because you managed to lose everyone else in the process.'

'If you have anything to do with it, obviously.'

'At least I wasn't planning to do it without telling you – which is a hell of a lot more than you are apparently capable of.'

'More distortion of the facts. . . . I'd love to see some of your journalism, Janie. I didn't, as you well know, go to Rio with the intention of breaking all contact with you and the children. It probably won't interest you to know, because it might startle your moral high horse, that until I got lost in the bureaucracy of a Latin American hospital, I'd always been kept up to date on the children by Will. Only Will didn't dare tell you that he was sending photographs and scraps of Nell's drawings to their own father in case it upset you. And while we're on the subject of inaccuracies, it was Nell who told me about your latest plans, not you.'

'I was working round to it.'

'How incredibly magnanimous of you. And when were you going to let me know?'

'When your precious internal equilibrium was slightly less fucked up. Heaven forfend I should disturb your karma.'

He looked at her coldly. 'You really are an insufferable self-righteous bitch sometimes. It's not surprising you were the last person Cassie felt she could talk to.'

Janie blushed, feeling betrayed. Had Cassie really felt like that? And since when had she confided in Matthew?

'At least I was here,' she shouted. 'Dealing with everything. Now that you've had your nice little break from reality, at least do us all the favour of not acting as though you really think you can solve the world's problems.'

His voice was raised too now. 'Dealing with everything – and don't we know it? Haven't you made everyone aware for the past two or three years just how hard your life's been? Well, I'm very glad, Janie, that you've been dealing with everything. Because now you know how it feels.'

His eyes were flashing. Somewhere, in the back of Janie's mind, she registered the fact that he was furious and that his anger was a good sign, but before she'd acknowledged this thought she had slapped him, stormed past him and out of the room, slamming the door behind her, only to stumble across Nell, sobbing in the hall.

In July she began packing up their possessions. She only needed to take the bare minimum because Matthew had decided to move back into Michaelmas Road. In theory it should have been easy, but every time she began rooting through the piles of clothes and toys she unearthed another memory – Nell's first finger painting; the photographs of a holiday in Cornwall when Matthew had taught Nell to swim; baby blond wisps from the twins' first haircuts; the letters Matthew had first written to her – and they all made her unbearably sad.

'It'll all be worth it, darling,' Seth told her. He loved New York even more than he'd expected. Its vitality and restlessness acted like a balm on his natural tendency towards melancholy.

'You'll be quite the power couple,' said Cassie, who was back in New York to sign the lease on her new apartment. 'Seth is the hottest date in town at the moment. Oh, I don't mean like that. It's just that the society mavens out here can't invite him round often enough. Luella Lopez has practically adopted him. She's crazy about him, which means, of course, that everyone else is too. God knows when you'll ever see one another, or the children. Seth's working like a demon. Still, I dare say you'll get some weekends off. And you know, I've never seen him look happier.'

Janie kept telling herself it was wonderful that Seth was finding such fulfilment at last. But the more animated he became about life at ninety miles an hour, the more uneasy she felt.

Sissy had never worked so hard in her life. Initially she had only wanted to prove to Nari that she wasn't a complete airhead. But the more she immersed herself in shopping forecasts, trends and analysis, the more fascinating she found it. Retail was like a crash course in sociology. Why had no one ever told her? When Boldacci approached her to style another campaign for him, she humbly thanked him but declined. To Alice's disgust, she stopped going out. Something told her she needed to devote herself 150 per cent to Project Nari if she was going to win him over.

Jean, who, beneath her flinty Edinburgher exterior had developed quite a soft spot for Sissy, turned out to be a staunch ally, ferreting out all sorts of data and useful addresses for her. Worn down by the pair of them, Nari had grudgingly agreed to implement a few of Sissy's ideas and to consult Barney Frick, now that he'd finally finished all the details on Finn's and Cassie's flat, on designs for the new branches. She worked night and day to improve the ranges while becoming obsessed with overheads and keeping costs down. 'Remember,' she told the first in-house fashion designer ever to be employed at Everything She Wants Ltd, 'ten pounds on a jacket is ten thousand fewer customers.' Her first small triumph was to convince Nari of the importance of keeping the press up to date with their plans.

'If the product's good, then they will be interested,' she told him, when he grumbled that they only ever liked to feature expensive designer clothes. And gradually, they started to prove her right. The prototype shop Barney designed for London was unrecognisable from the others – a concatenation of fizzing pinks and oranges that seemed to suck customers in off the street. After he'd examined the sales figures from the first six weeks, Nari gave the go-ahead for ten more.

'About that name—' he said wryly to Sissy one day. 'Maybe Everything She Wants isn't right any more.'

She didn't sleep for days, ransacking her brain. She wanted something that sounded exotic and reflected the company's colourful, stylish approach to fashion, but also suggested to the customer that there were plenty of bargains to be had. She took Alice and Angel out for expensive dinners, got them drunk and forced them to play word association games in an attempt to come up with something catchy. Finally, it came to her in a dream. Heart in mouth, she put it to Nari.

'I've got it and it's perfect. Succinct, cheerful and very market-friendly.'

'I don't like any of those,' teased Nari.

'Don't mock.'

'Tell me what it is, then.'

Sissy looked nervously across at Jean. She had invested so much in this name, which in the days she'd been churning it over in her mind had turned into a grand project, spawning slogans, a whole new concept in carrier bags and thoughtful details in the changing rooms. She didn't think she could bear it if Nari made a joke out of it.

'All right,' she said, her voice shaking. 'It's Bazaar.'

There was a silence. Nari's face was inscrutable.

'I suppose,' he sighed, 'I'd better put you on the pay-roll.'

'How about if we had special lockers in the changing rooms so that customers could keep their bags safe? Then they'd feel relaxed and try on more clothes.'

'It's a chain store, Sissy, not Harvey Nichols,' said Nari, making a note to do a costing on it – and marvelling, for the millionth time, at her enviable ability to slither joyously through life's obstacles.

'We should do a weekend range. No one ever knows what to wear off duty.'

One day Alice came in personally to the press office to collect a dress she wanted to feature in *A La Mode*'s Bargain of the Month column. 'Keep your hair on. The main reason I've come in is because it's the only way I'll get to see you,' she said waspishly. But Sissy knew it wasn't true. The dress Alice had selected was one of her favourites – a real triumph for the price. She felt a rush of exhilaration. There was a long way to go but they were on their way.

The intensity of the row had shocked them both out of their apathy. Janie, struggling to suppress her anger since Matthew's return and retain what she had perceived as the moral upper hand, finally allowed all her animus towards him to bubble to the surface until they could barely sustain a civilised conversation with one another. And still she didn't feel she was getting through to him.

'Don't recount your resentments to me, tell them to Matthew,' said Cassie wearily one day.

'You're right. But he's gone all long-suffering on me. I feel completely wrong-footed every time I see him.'

'A timely role reversal, I'd say.'

'Cassie . . . did you really feel you couldn't talk to me?'

'I couldn't talk to many people. As much my failing as theirs but . . . oh, nothing.'

'Please tell me.'

'It's just that you're gorgeous and vulnerable and warm and perfect and I love you dearly – but sometimes you're simply not accessible.'

'Accessible?'

'You never suffer from major, soul-searching, life-threatening self-doubts.'

'I see,' said Janie, refusing to acknowledge this insufferable character portrayal Cassie had presented her with, even while she immediately recognised it.

'I hate myself,' she wailed.

'That's the sweetest thing you've ever said.'

She called Matthew at *The Probe*.

'I'm declaring a unilateral truce. I'm going to make a list of everything you've ever done that irritates me and I suggest you do the same. We'll discuss them over dinner – somewhere very smart and discreet so we can't end up yelling.' As truces went, it lacked charm, but at least it got them talking.

'You're not coming, are you?' Seth asked her one night when he was back in London. They were sitting on the terrace in the dark. The moon was casting strange shadows on his face. His voice sounded very quiet.

'What do you mean?' Until now the thought had never crossed her mind, at least not consciously.

'Just that the more excited I get, the more distracted you look. When I talk about Finn's and New York, and everything that's going on there, sometimes I can just hear you slipping away. Oh, I know you think you want to come and you want to be with me – and I think I want it too.' He took her hand and squeezed it. 'I've pictured our life there together down to the last detail – I even know where the herb garden will go.' He tried to smile. 'It's just that hard as I try, I can't actually see you in the frame. I can see the open fires and the hammock on the veranda, but when I look for your face, it's just a shadow.'

'You're just tired,' she said pragmatically. 'Look a bit harder.' She wanted so much to share his passion. It was unthinkable that she shouldn't.

'Shall I just retire to a desert island and let you get on with running my company?' Nari asked her when she produced the dozen prototypes she'd sourced from new factories abroad.

She kissed him ecstatically on the bit of his head she loved best, just where the hair was most in retreat from his forehead. 'I know that means you approve.'

'Hmmm,' he said non-committally.

'Oh, come on, darling, you know I couldn't do this without you. I'm hopeless with numbers.'

This wasn't entirely true. But crazily, they did make a very good team. Yin and yang, Nari supposed, feeling quite ridiculously happy.

He kept waiting for the pain to kick in, for it to lacerate his heart so that he couldn't bear it any more and had to fly home to beg her to reconsider. But there was just a dull numbness. He missed her terribly, yet there was never time to grieve. Luella Lopez had tried to adopt him and threw a huge party in his honour. After that, the telephone in his apartment never stopped ringing with invitations. Madeleine told him it was the social coup of the year. The Lopezes ruled New York society as if they were royalty; Luella's blessing gave everyone else the green light to follow suit – and, as Madeleine pointed out, she had some startlingly attractive granddaughters. Seth was too distracted even to notice the bait. He worked round the clock, dutifully squeezed in Luella's friends' parties when he could, and generally made sure he never had time to think. He had decided that if it really didn't work out with Janie, he would give up on women altogether. He simply didn't have the emotional stamina. He couldn't have made himself more attractive to the female population of New York if he'd hung a placard with the new Finn's weekly profits round his neck.

'You did *what*?' she shrieked above the roar of traffic. It was the start of a stifling New York day and she was standing on her roof terrace watching the yellow stream of taxis snake up

Columbus. God, she loved this city. Even the traffic jams came in Technicolor. She hadn't found her ninetieth-floor apartment. But the twenty-third would do. Behind the parapet she felt cocooned from the chaos beyond. Up here she felt as though even the fumes couldn't get to her. But Janie's chaotic relationships could.

'And after all you said,' she began, a smile tugging at her lips.

'I know, I know, but . . . oh, Cassie, don't lecture. I'm not the first woman in the world to have spent the night with her husband.'

'Yes, but only you could make conjugal rights sound like a one-night stand.'

'If you're implying I'm self-righteous and sanctimonious, spare me,' said Janie tartly. 'Matthew's already taken me through that one, very thoroughly. Even Anastasia said something about it in her big *mea non culpa* speech – and she was right. In fact I'm thinking of raiding your library for some help. Anyway, it's been several nights, actually.'

'Does Seth know?'

'I sort of think he does,' said Janie, thinking of their last forlorn encounter.

Cassie tried another approach. 'Janie, you do know that sex is always best just when you're breaking up – see just about any book in my library for evidence.'

'Oh, Cassie, Matthew and I went through all that two years ago. No, that's just it, it doesn't feel like breaking up. There's none of that wistful stuff. It feels . . . well, it feels more like a beginning.'

'In which case,' Cassie said, marvelling at the mysteriously slow way in which her not-so-perfect friend's mind worked, 'I give up.'

Epilogue

Janie coaxed the hot tap on with her big toe, sank back into the lime-grass-scented bath and gazed up at the ceiling. Endless attempts by the local builder could not make the damp patch disappear. She smiled beatifically at the stack of plump white towels – as long as she had those she didn't mind the rest. In fact she'd grown rather fond of the damp patch. Like Gorbachev's resolutely un-airbrushed birthmark, it had a sort of honesty about it.

At least the house was no longer falling apart. Even after Gloria left for New York to steward Cassie's boarding school, it hadn't lapsed back into its old shabby chaos. Ivy, Gloria's gin rummy partner and replacement at Michaelmas Road, was, if anything, even bossier than her predecessor and had revolutionised Matthew's filing system. In any case, now that they'd promoted him to deputy editor, he was at the office much more. With Matthew happy at work, she felt better about pursuing her own freelance work, which had continued to trickle in steadily. One of the biggest surprises about her new life, other than how blissful it felt to be back with Matthew, was how much she needed to work.

Matthew poked his head round the door. 'Just checking you hadn't drowned – Nell's having a hair crisis. She looks gorgeous but, you know—' He shrugged. 'Women.'

'Send her in,' said Janie, hoisting herself out of the water.

Nell entered, half buttoned into a diaphanous cloud of palest blue, her feet encased in a pair of trainers. What with the heat outside, and the steam in the bathroom, her ringlets, entwined with ivy and small white roses, had gone on the rampage and were frizzing round her temples. The expression on her face was savage. She looked like a borstal-educated Pre-Raphaelite angel.

'You look gorgeous.'

Nell scowled. 'Don't humour me. It looks like an ecological disaster and that Mac red nail varnish I put on looks like I burst a blood vessel.'

'You're too young for nail varnish anyway,' Janie heard herself saying. She sighed. When had Nell got so neurotic about her looks? She was nervous, Janie supposed. It was the first time she'd ever been a bridesmaid, let alone a chief bridesmaid. Well, she was nervous too. She'd never been a matron of honour either. She repaired the damage to Nell's hair and nails, slipped into the antique sprigged dress she'd paid far too much for on the King's Road, and rounded up the twins, who looked adorable in their matching pale blue organdie. She just hoped they'd all behave during the service.

The grounds of Tom's seventeenth-century lodge, on a small hill outside Richmond, looked enchanting. A vast white marquee, its sides looped up with garlands of flowers, flanked the river, and an army of waiters bearing aloft silver trays laden with every drink imaginable had lined up to greet the guests. With the sublime capriciousness of the very rich, they had decided to hold the wedding in London, even though it meant that more than half those attending had to fly in from America. But the house was special to Tom. It was one of the first beauty spots his bride-to-be had shown him in London. He'd fallen in love with it – and Cassie – almost simultaneously.

By the time the bridal entourage had made its way past the mass of photographers swarming outside the register office, the lawns surrounding Filigree Lodge were teeming with fashionably dressed, gently simmering guests. Cassie, who had never looked so beautiful or serene, floated among them all in a halo of happiness and impeccably draped silk, even drawing admiring glances from Alice, who'd gatecrashed the reception and promptly had a row about it with Sissy, who told her that her fashion–show training was turning her into a social Rottweiler. 'You didn't mind when I crashed Anastasia Wotsit's wedding, and that wasn't nearly as grand.'

'That was different. You were there as a spy. Though some attempt you made to blend in, in your Union Jack sari and orange Wonderbra.'

'I wouldn't have bothered at all if I'd known how dreary it was going to be. Just a bunch of sweaty hacks, born–agains and poxy politicians. And it pissed with rain. At least Cassie's got good weather . . . Christ, it's hot.' She fanned herself with a gauntlet.

'They could use some punka wallahs,' said Sissy, silently comparing Alice's chain–mail skirt unfavourably with her own floaty layers. She had recently returned from a visit to India and had fallen in love with a colonialesque way of life out there – as well as with Nari's parents, who, in turn, had been pleasantly amazed by her, especially when they discovered her noble lineage (she didn't feel it was necessary to go into details about why, technically, she was no longer a contessa). Ostensibly it had been a business trip. But half-way round a beading workshop, Nari, finding himself delighting in his native country for the first time in his memory, had prevailed upon her to leave her order books at the bottom of her case for a few days and whisked her off on a romantic tour of Rajasthan and Uttar Pradesh, where she had taught him how to catwalk in front of the Taj Mahal and he had found himself surprising her with half a dozen pashmina shawls. By the time they got back, she had reread *A Passage to India* twice and called Angel from Delhi airport, demanding imperiously that he call his next collection Memsahib. Now that she'd finally convinced Nari to back his business, she felt entitled to boss Angel around for a change.

'I could use some pukka vodka,' said Jess. She was starring at the King's Head in a fringe production of *The Tempest* where the set, sponsored by Stick–u–Like, was constructed entirely from Sellotape. The director had envisaged Miranda as an alcoholic. It was a smash hit and Jess, who felt obliged to at least *look* the part, off–stage as well as on, was half wearing one of Aeron's Renaissance dresses from his last Ruff collection and doing her utmost to look drunk and disorderly.

'Evil dress,' said Alice.

'Thanks,' burbled Jess. 'I think. Aeron says elongating the neck is very modern. Personally I think it's a shamelessly commercial attempt to appeal to all those scraggy fashion fossils.'

'Talking of whom,' said Alice smoothly, as a sprightly blonde spider scampered into view, 'allow me to introduce you to Luella Lopez, Jess.'

'Delighted. I'm such a fan of the Bard,' trilled Luella. 'How thrilling, my dear, that you've made the transition to acting. Do you think I could still get tickets?' Dressed in Pucci and half a bottle of Joy and circulating like a whirling dervish, she looked like a flapping ensign. 'By the way, where is Islington?'

'I'm sure Aeron could accompany you there,' purred Grace mischievously. 'He simply adores Shakespeare too.' She gazed down at Aeron sweetly from her six-inch spike heels. Since graciously making a guest appearance in his triumphant debut couture collection for Lara in the grounds of Versailles, she and Aeron had kissed and ecstatically made up, which, as far as Grace was concerned, only gave her complete licence to tease him about his new society friendships.

'Erm, I'm a bit tied up, Lu, what wiv all the trunk shows and everyfink,' said Aeron weakly.

'Now, you darling boy, you know I can't understand a word you're saying when you put on that accent, so I'll simply take that as a yes. Shall we say tomorrow, downstairs at the Lanesborough at seven?' She laid a spindly hand on his Jolly Roger. 'Don't let me down, now.'

'So tell me about the skiing trip,' said Angel to Alice, who, inspired by all that Sissy had told her about Anastasia, had gone skiing in Gstaad in search of a rich husband.

'It was a nightmare,' moaned Alice. 'I discovered I get vertigo halfway up a chairlift. I don't think I ever made it above sea level after that. I spent the rest of the trip going up and down the drag lift listening to hypnotherapy tapes. Anyway, I'm too young to get married.'

'Hear, hear,' said Jo-Jo. 'That's what I keep telling Ben.'

'We had a bet. If I won an Oscar, you said you'd marry me.'

'I didn't say which Oscar.'

'Well, I'm not too young,' said Madeleine, brandishing the bridal bouquet in one hand and Leonardo in the other. 'And the omens are looking good.'

Down on one of the barges, a jazz band struck up. Janie's heart lurched when she spotted Seth talking to Tom. What to say? She so hoped that he was happy, but to ask him outright might sound patronising. And not to ask would seem evasive. But she had to talk to him. They hadn't spoken for over a year, and she had followed his meteoric progress through magazines and Cassie, who said he was fine. Forlorn, perhaps, but not short of female admirers. He seemed another life away, thought Janie, her eyes automatically seeking out Matthew. He had seen her looking at Seth. He raised an eyebrow. She smiled and he blew her a kiss.

'You look gorgeous,' said Peace, hugging Jo-Jo, for whom she still felt a vague moral responsibility.

'You look pretty wonderful too,' Jo-Jo replied, gesturing at her faintly swelling abdomen. Peace was expecting Harry's baby early in the new year. 'Where is he, by the way?'

'Ensconced somewhere quiet with Sid Skidster. He's a consultant on Sid's new film.'

'What's it about?' asked Saffron. 'I heard he was thinking of filming James Joyce.'

'Oh, he's ditched that,' said Peace matter-of-factly. 'He's working on something completely new. The working title's *Alleluia Hallucination*. Harry's the on-set narcotics expert. How's that for maturity?'

'I suppose seeing the worst nightmares from your past plastered across the screen is one way of breaking with it,' said Saffron doubtfully.

'Oh, it is, Saffie, believe me. Harry says it reminds him why he'll never do drugs again. He says Sid's script makes *Trainspotting* seem like *Brief Encounter*.'

'Ooh, how modern,' trilled Luella.

They were sitting side by side on the jetty. 'You look wonderful,' said Matthew, searching carefully for the right words. Nell had been very unpredictable in the run-up to the

495

wedding. Unpredictable altogether. Janie said it was because teenage started at nine these days, but Matthew couldn't help thinking they were still suffering the emotional reverberations of a year ago, and in their new spirit of always speaking their minds had said as much.

'It is quite pretty, isn't it?' Nell said, smoothing the translucent skirts.

'Very Scarlett O'Hara.'

'You don't think it sticks out too much?' she said, suddenly alarmed.

'I meant in spirit,' he said quickly. 'It's a picture of elegant simplicity.' It had been the most discussed, redesigned outfit in the entire wedding entourage, and Nell had had to fly to New York for three fittings, until Madeleine began to think designing a hundred Oscar nightgowns for Jo-Jo would be a doddle compared with the torture of coming up with a bridesmaid's dress for Nell that pleased everyone.

'I'd like to get married one day,' she said. 'When you were living in Guatemala I thought I wanted to be just like Gloria and Mum and all the other mothers at school but, you know, I think it's better this way.' She leant over and kissed his forehead – and suddenly the burden of guilt he hadn't quite managed to offload ever since he had got back began to slide away.

Over dinner, Janie, sick with nerves about her speech, found herself seated next to Caleb Bron, the producer Cassie had tried to fix her up with the night she'd turned up at dinner with Matthew, all those years ago. The bride's little joke, Janie supposed. Time had done nothing to conquer Caleb's ego. If anything it had bolstered it. He was now the supremely successful head of a digital lifestyle channel. Fortunately he'd also acquired his first garden, attached to a stately he'd just bought in Berkshire, so there was no shortage of conversation. By the time the main course arrived, she'd sketched a prototype formal garden on the back of a placement card, complete with topiary, ornamental vegetables and Elizabethan knot garden. He was amazed. It had never occurred to him that gardeners could look like Janie. He knew that home-improvement programmes equalled ratings nirvana, but whenever he thought of horticulture, somehow 3D sculptures of manure and Alan Titchmarsh wafted before his eyes and his heart sank – which was why, he supposed, his Friday night schedules were still a mess. This girl, however, was a guaranteed smash. By the time she returned from the podium, flushed and slightly teary-eyed, he'd rough-drafted a contract.

'Look, I don't usually do this, but frankly we're getting hammered by Delia Smith on the other side. You're a natural for television and you obviously know your stuff – I think you'd do it rather well.'

Janie was rather inclined to agree. It seemed such a logical thing for her to do – now that the speech had gone down well she was starting to think she was a natural orator – and she just knew, finally, that it would all come right for her on the work front. Outside, it was getting dark; the jazz musicians had been followed by a calypso band and thousands of fairy lights danced along in the trees. 'I feel a fireworks display coming on,' said Madeleine, nuzzling against Leonardo's neck.

'Great speech,' said Seth, finding Janie walking by the river.

'Great food,' she said. 'And thank you.'

'What for?'

'Being so decent.'

'I think, in a funny way, we both found our callings. He looks decent too, your Matthew. And I never could quite hack the idea of baked beans in my kitchen.' He kissed her lightly on the cheek and stalked off, ostensibly to see if Deirdre was all right supervising the chefs.

After Cassie and Tom took their emotional leave of the guests, Matthew rounded up his family. They were going on a belated summer holiday to Italy. Matthew had organised the entire thing, give or take a few details. Janie looked in her bag to make sure she hadn't forgotten them in her nerves and smiled indulgently. She loved her husband dearly, but he never could manage to remember his passport.

Jacket credits:

photographs: Robin Derrick
make-up: Emma Kotch
clothes: Elspeth Gibson, Matthew Williamson,
                 Alexander McQueen, Joseph
shoes: Christian Louboutin, Jimmy Choo